SLEEPOVER

MICHAEL REGINA

RAZORBILL

DEDICATED TO RUBY WARD

RAZORBILL

An imprint of Penguin Random House LLC, New York

First published in the United States of America by Razorbill,
an imprint of Penguin Random House LLC, 2021

Copyright © 2021 by Michael Regina

Visit us online at penguinrandomhouse.com.

Library of Congress Cataloging-in-Publication Data
Names: Regina, Michael, author, illustrator.
Title: The sleepover / Michael Regina.
Description: New York: Razorbill, 2021. | Audience: Ages 8–12. | Summary: Matt's friends plan a fun sleepover to try and cheer him up after he falls into a deep grief over the death of his nanny, but the sleepover quickly takes a turn when they realize the family's new nanny may be an actual monster.
Identifiers: LCCN 2021008380 | ISBN 9780593117347 (hardcover) | ISBN 9780593117361 (trade paperback) | ISBN 9780593117354 (ebook) | ISBN 9780593352908 (ebook) | ISBN 9780593352915 (ebook) Subjects: LCSH: Graphic novels. | CYAC: Graphic novels. | Friendship—Fiction. | Monsters—Ficiton. | Grief—FIction. | Sleepovers—Fiction. | Nannies—Fiction. | Horror stories. Classification: LCC PZ7.7.R4456 Sl 2021 | DDC 741.5/973—dc23
LC record available at https://lccn.loc.gov/2021008380

ISBN 9780593117347 (hardcover) | ISBN 9780593117361 (paperback)

Manufactured in China

The artwork for this book was created digitally.

1 3 5 7 9 10 8 6 4 2

TPLF

Design by Michael Regina | Text set in Milk Mustache

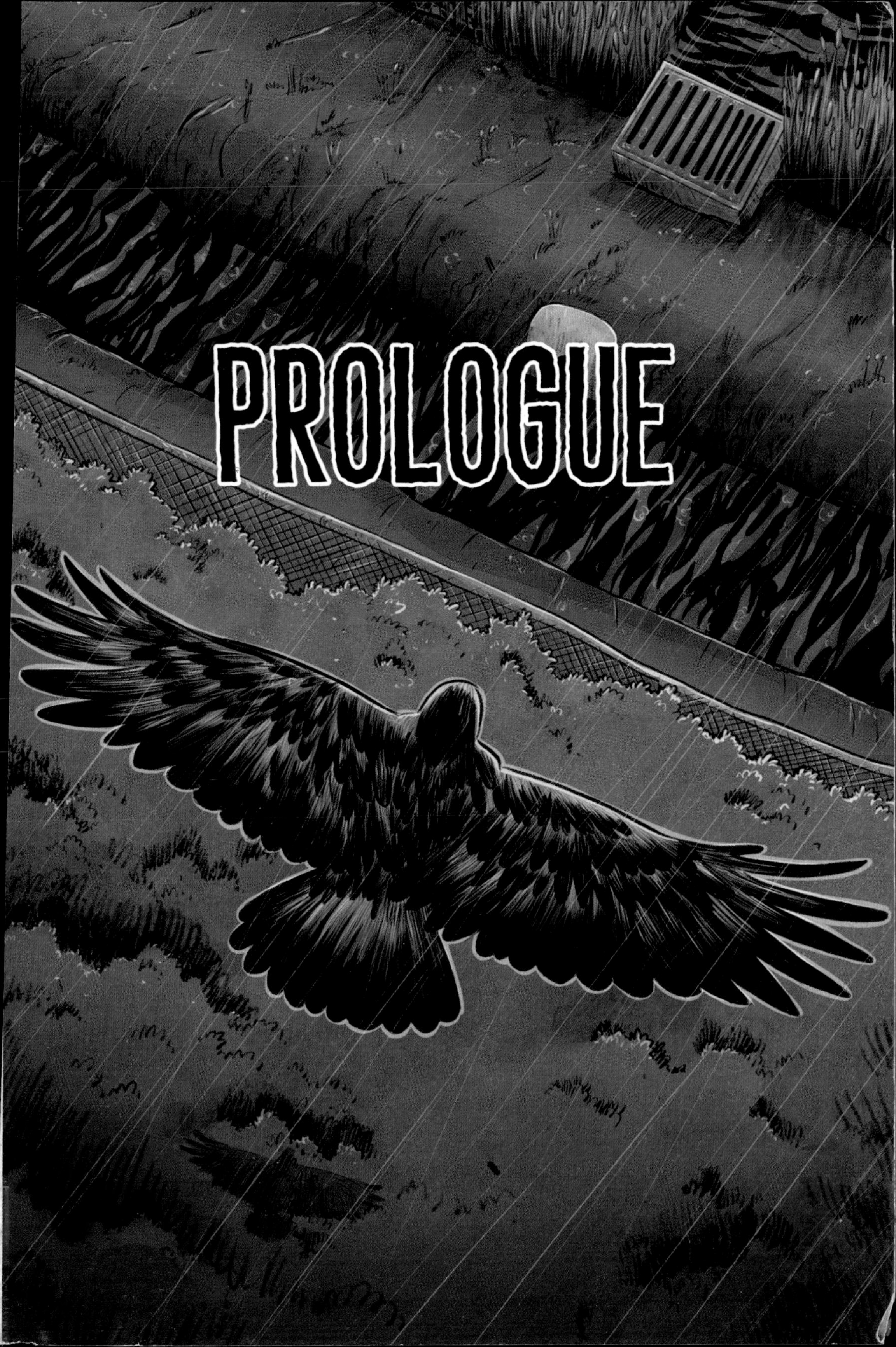
PROLOGUE

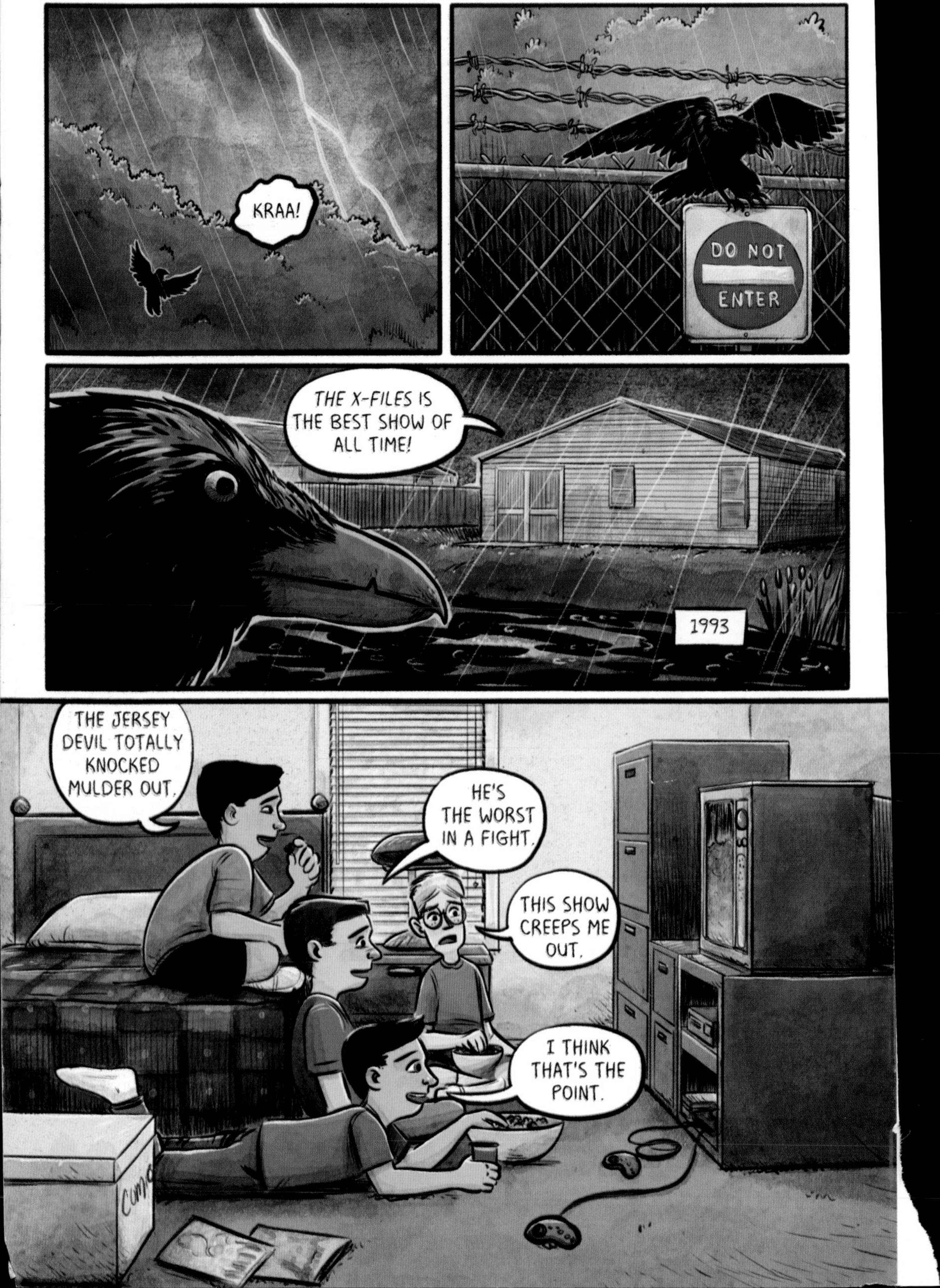
KRAA!
DO NOT ENTER
THE X-FILES IS THE BEST SHOW OF ALL TIME!
1993
THE JERSEY DEVIL TOTALLY KNOCKED MULDER OUT.
HE'S THE WORST IN A FIGHT.
THIS SHOW CREEPS ME OUT.
I THINK THAT'S THE POINT.

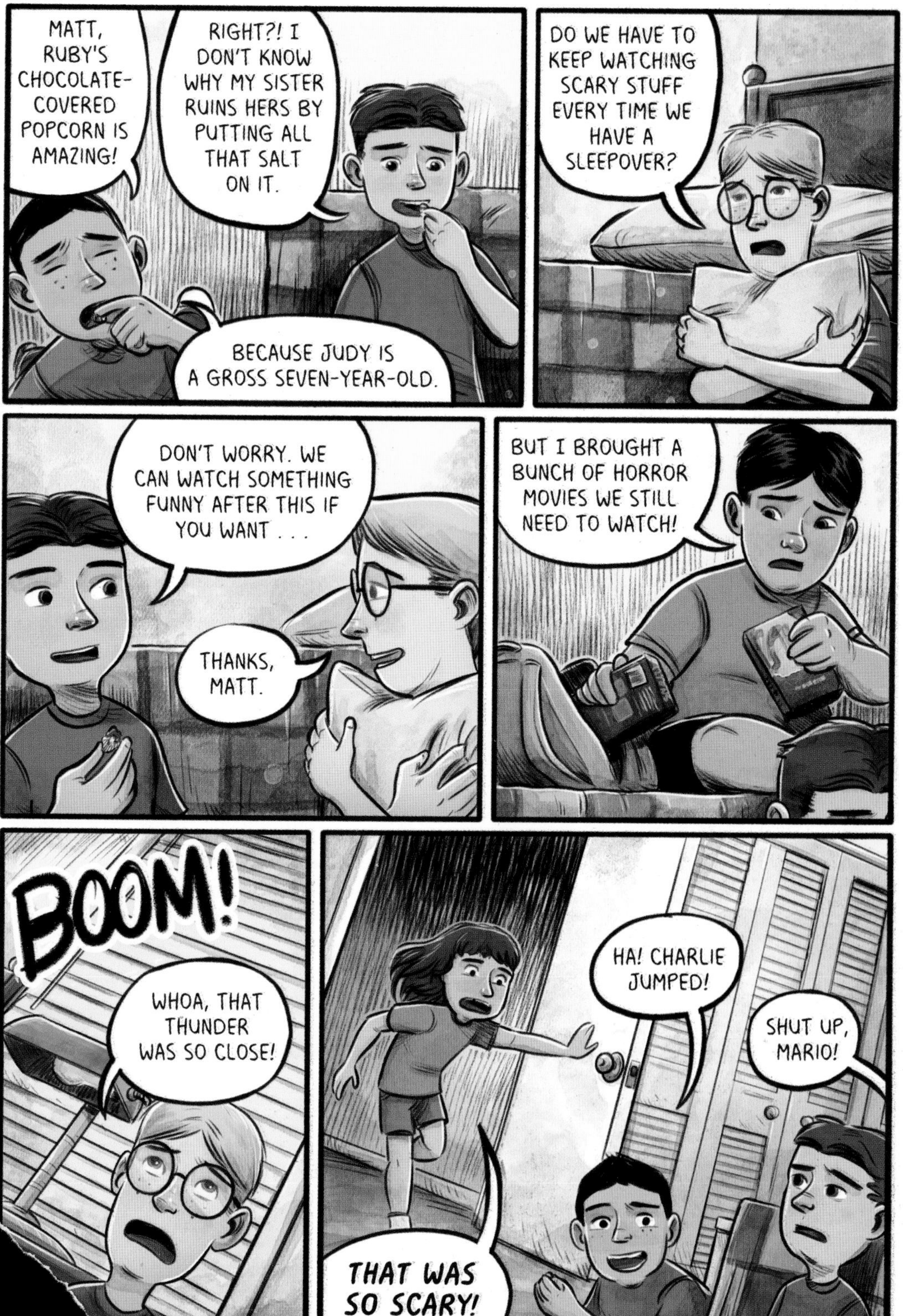
MATT, RUBY'S CHOCOLATE-COVERED POPCORN IS AMAZING!
RIGHT?! I DON'T KNOW WHY MY SISTER RUINS HERS BY PUTTING ALL THAT SALT ON IT.
BECAUSE JUDY IS A GROSS SEVEN-YEAR-OLD.
DO WE HAVE TO KEEP WATCHING SCARY STUFF EVERY TIME WE HAVE A SLEEPOVER?
DON'T WORRY. WE CAN WATCH SOMETHING FUNNY AFTER THIS IF YOU WANT . . .
THANKS, MATT.
BUT I BROUGHT A BUNCH OF HORROR MOVIES WE STILL NEED TO WATCH!
BOOM!
WHOA, THAT THUNDER WAS SO CLOSE!
THAT WAS SO SCARY!
HA! CHARLIE JUMPED!
SHUT UP, MARIO!

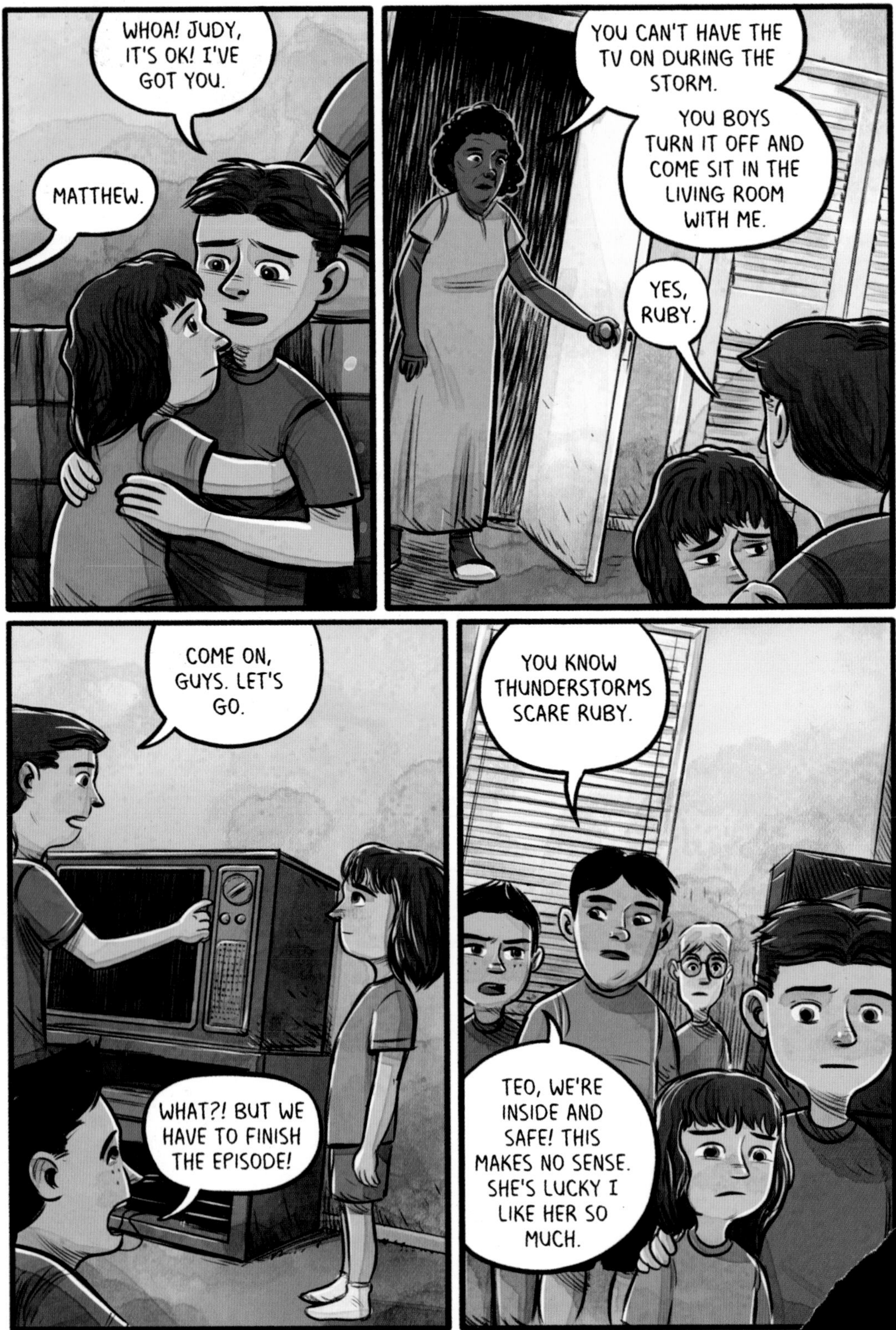

WHOA! JUDY, IT'S OK! I'VE GOT YOU.
MATTHEW.
YOU CAN'T HAVE THE TV ON DURING THE STORM.
YOU BOYS TURN IT OFF AND COME SIT IN THE LIVING ROOM WITH ME.
YES, RUBY.
COME ON, GUYS. LET'S GO.
WHAT?! BUT WE HAVE TO FINISH THE EPISODE!
YOU KNOW THUNDERSTORMS SCARE RUBY.
TEO, WE'RE INSIDE AND SAFE! THIS MAKES NO SENSE. SHE'S LUCKY I LIKE HER SO MUCH.

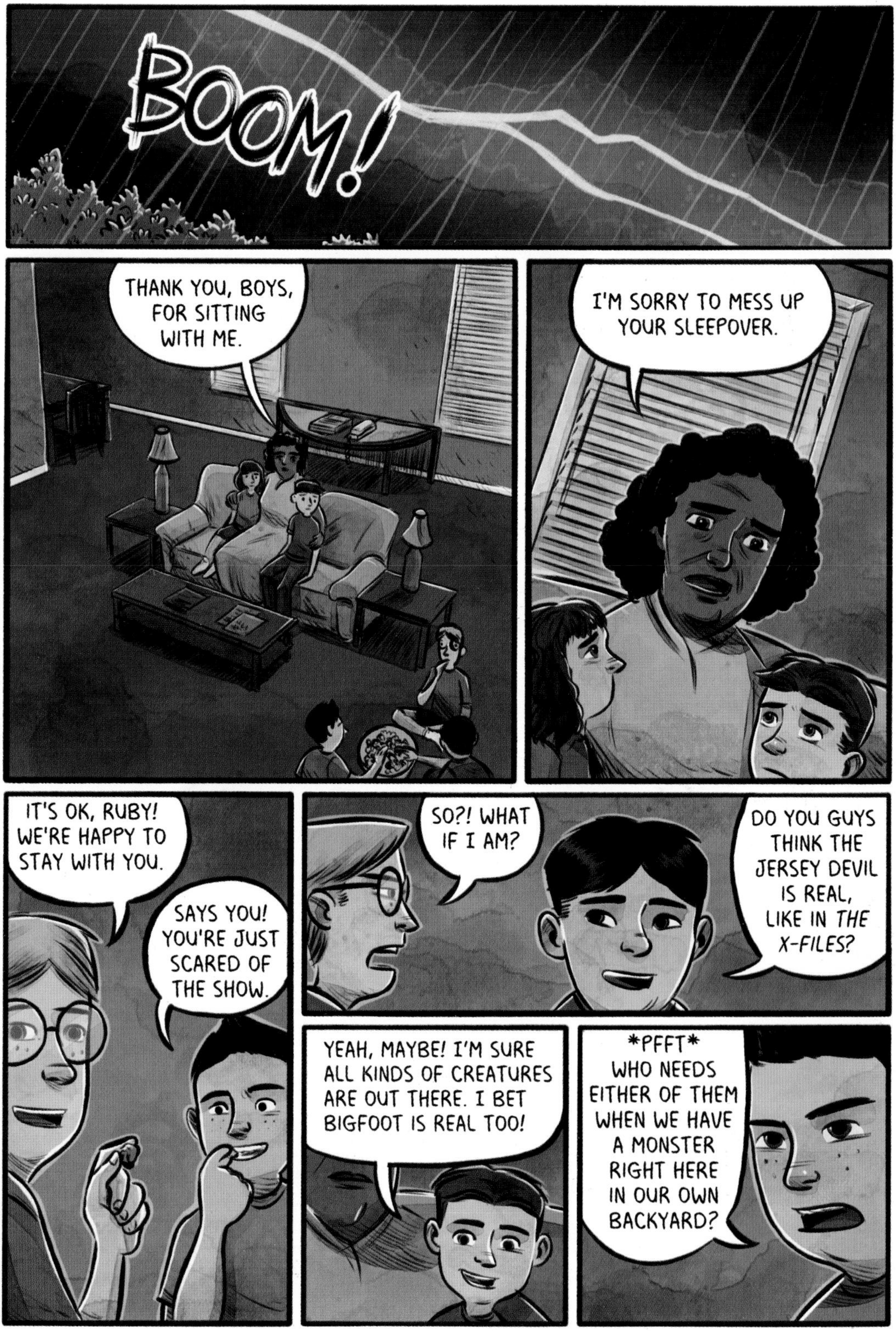
BOOM!
THANK YOU, BOYS, FOR SITTING WITH ME.
I'M SORRY TO MESS UP YOUR SLEEPOVER.
IT'S OK, RUBY! WE'RE HAPPY TO STAY WITH YOU.
SAYS YOU! YOU'RE JUST SCARED OF THE SHOW.
SO?! WHAT IF I AM?
DO YOU GUYS THINK THE JERSEY DEVIL IS REAL, LIKE IN *THE X-FILES*?
YEAH, MAYBE! I'M SURE ALL KINDS OF CREATURES ARE OUT THERE. I BET BIGFOOT IS REAL TOO!
PFFT WHO NEEDS EITHER OF THEM WHEN WE HAVE A MONSTER RIGHT HERE IN OUR OWN BACKYARD?

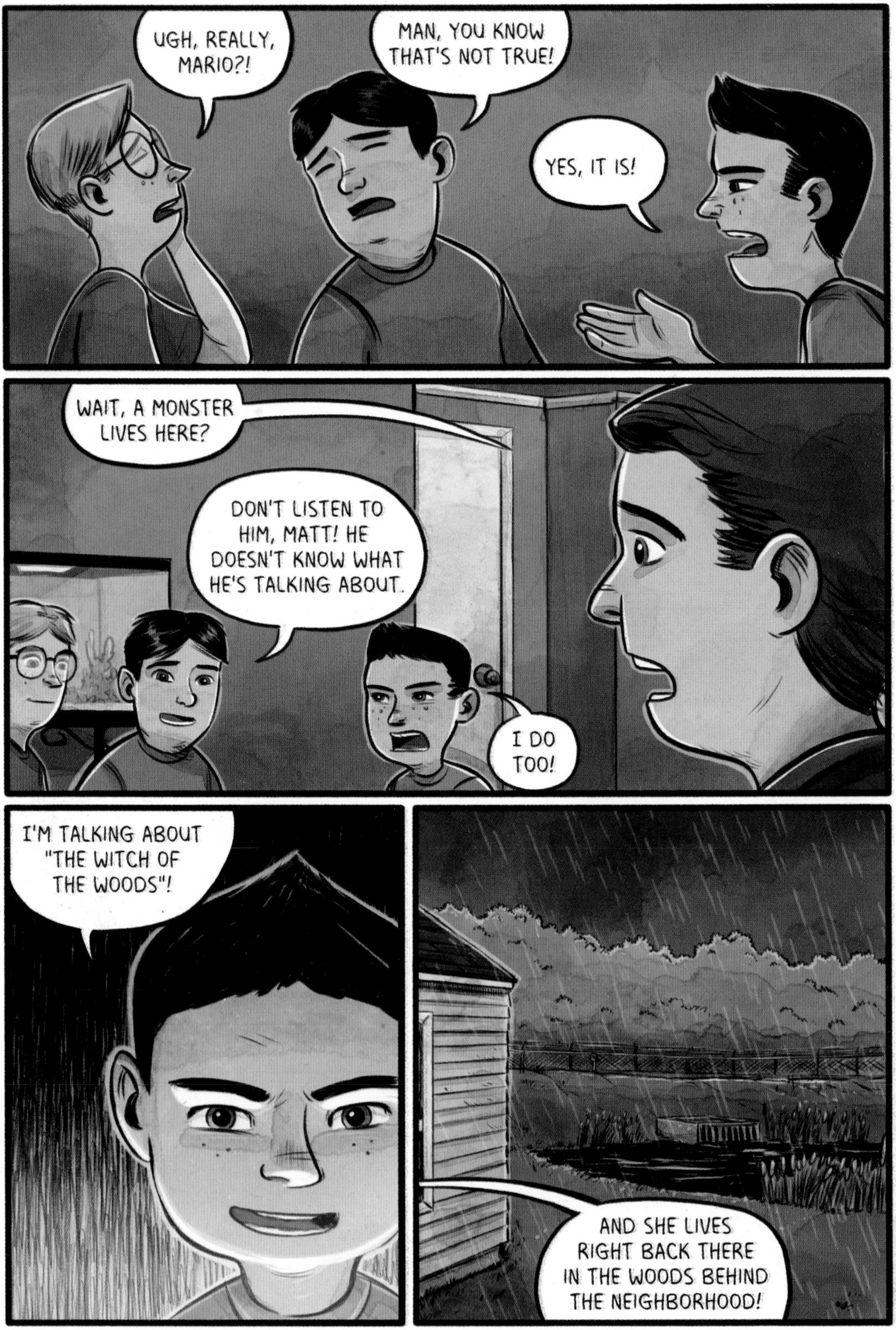
UGH, REALLY, MARIO?!
MAN, YOU KNOW THAT'S NOT TRUE!
YES, IT IS!
WAIT, A MONSTER LIVES HERE?
DON'T LISTEN TO HIM, MATT! HE DOESN'T KNOW WHAT HE'S TALKING ABOUT.
I DO TOO!
I'M TALKING ABOUT "THE WITCH OF THE WOODS"!
AND SHE LIVES RIGHT BACK THERE IN THE WOODS BEHIND THE NEIGHBORHOOD!

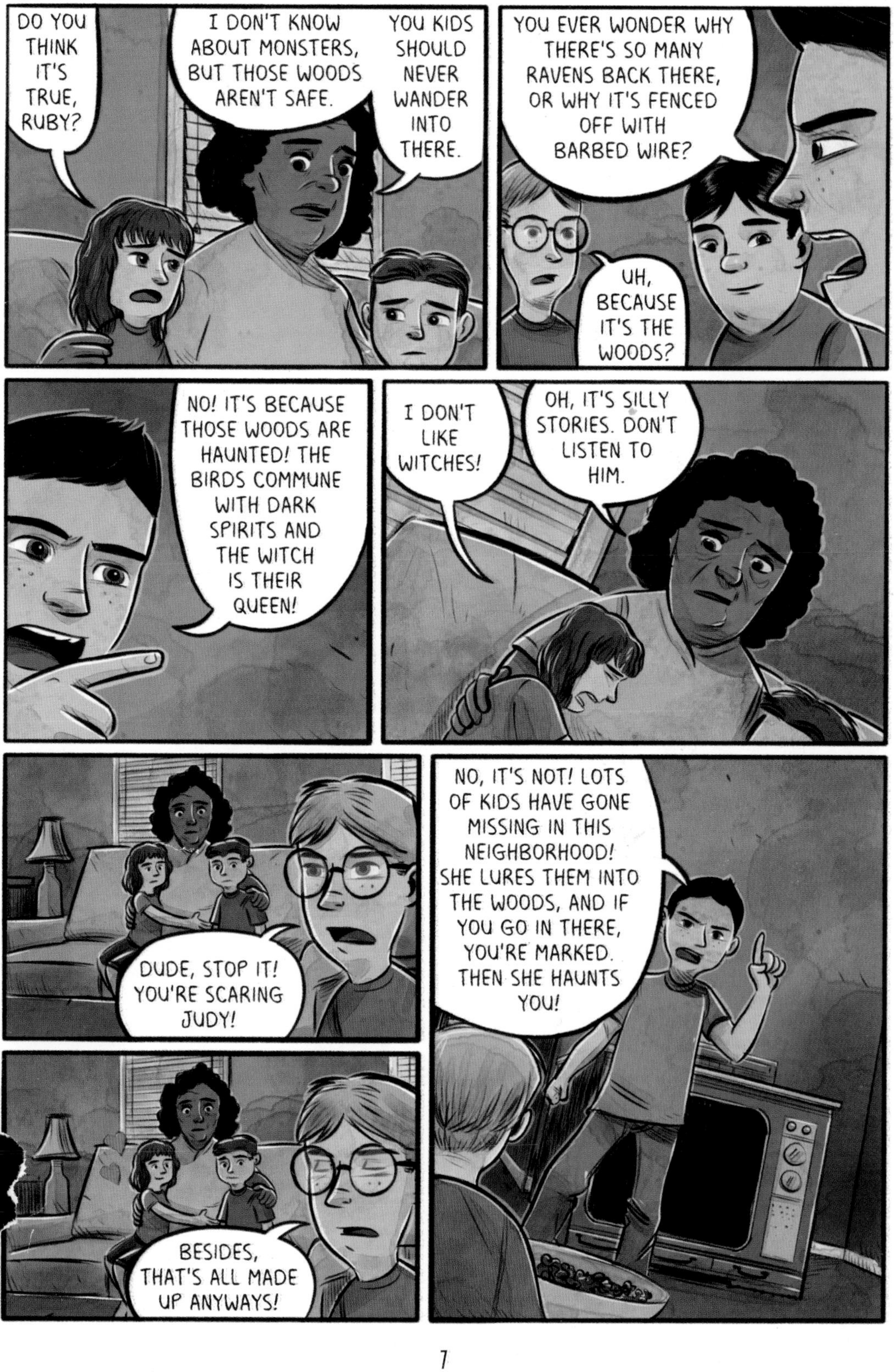
DO YOU THINK IT'S TRUE, RUBY?
I DON'T KNOW ABOUT MONSTERS, BUT THOSE WOODS AREN'T SAFE.
YOU KIDS SHOULD NEVER WANDER INTO THERE.
YOU EVER WONDER WHY THERE'S SO MANY RAVENS BACK THERE, OR WHY IT'S FENCED OFF WITH BARBED WIRE?
UH, BECAUSE IT'S THE WOODS?
NO! IT'S BECAUSE THOSE WOODS ARE HAUNTED! THE BIRDS COMMUNE WITH DARK SPIRITS AND THE WITCH IS THEIR QUEEN!
I DON'T LIKE WITCHES!
OH, IT'S SILLY STORIES. DON'T LISTEN TO HIM.
DUDE, STOP IT! YOU'RE SCARING JUDY!
BESIDES, THAT'S ALL MADE UP ANYWAYS!
NO, IT'S NOT! LOTS OF KIDS HAVE GONE MISSING IN THIS NEIGHBORHOOD! SHE LURES THEM INTO THE WOODS, AND IF YOU GO IN THERE, YOU'RE MARKED. THEN SHE HAUNTS YOU!

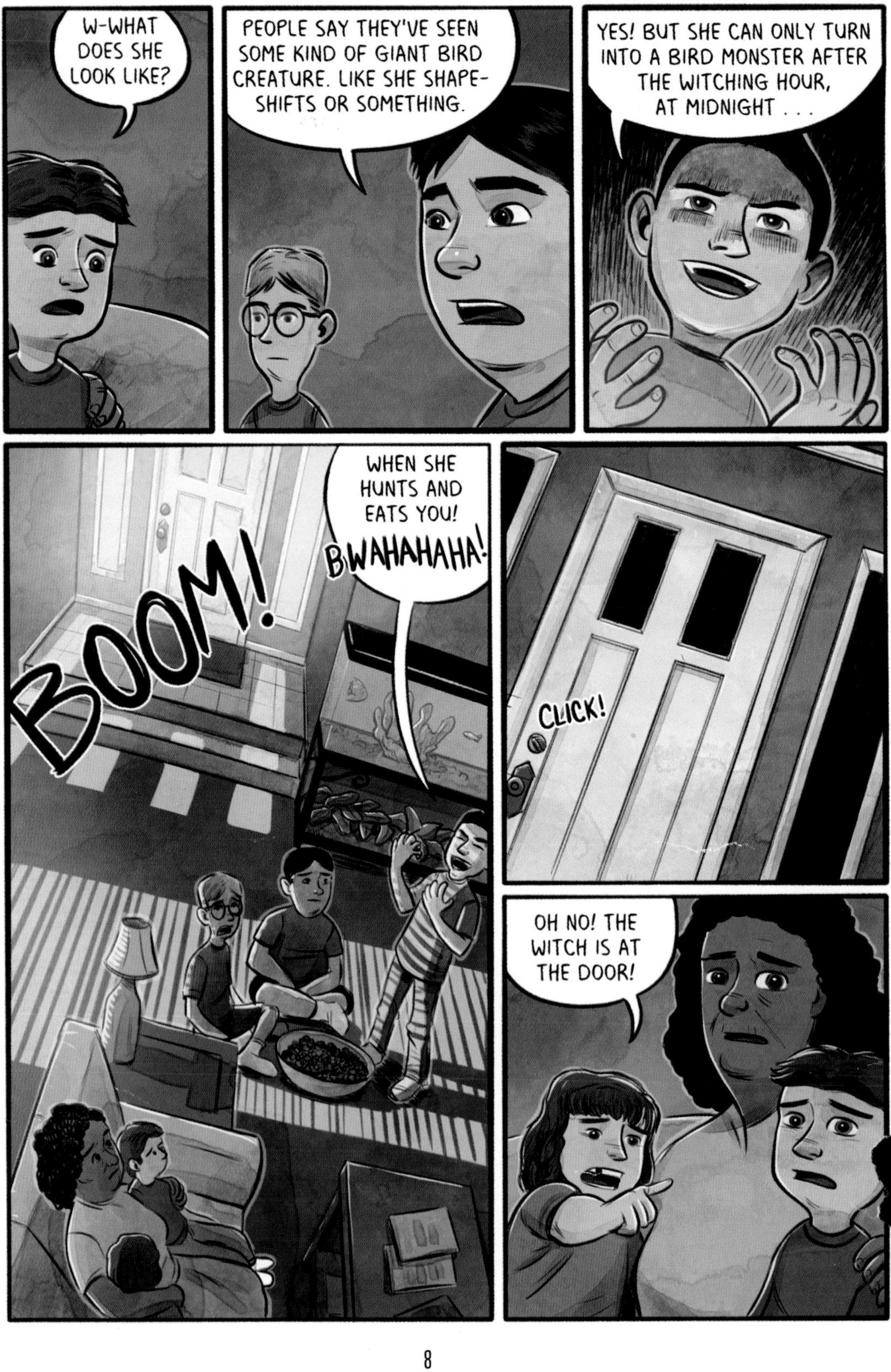

W-WHAT DOES SHE LOOK LIKE?
PEOPLE SAY THEY'VE SEEN SOME KIND OF GIANT BIRD CREATURE. LIKE SHE SHAPE-SHIFTS OR SOMETHING.
YES! BUT SHE CAN ONLY TURN INTO A BIRD MONSTER AFTER THE WITCHING HOUR, AT MIDNIGHT . . .
WHEN SHE HUNTS AND EATS YOU!
BWAHAHAHA!
BOOM!
CLICK!
OH NO! THE WITCH IS AT THE DOOR!

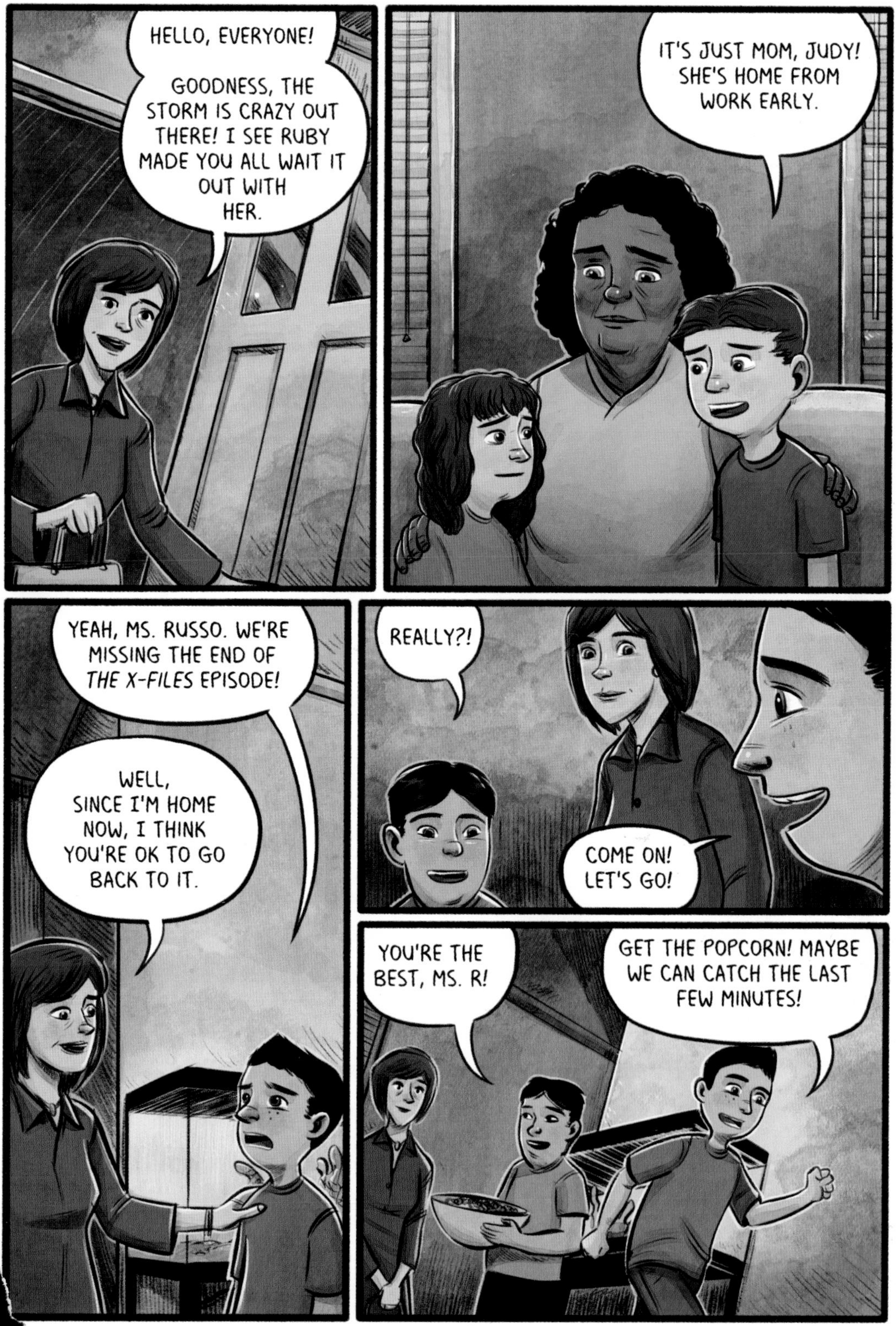
HELLO, EVERYONE!
GOODNESS, THE STORM IS CRAZY OUT THERE! I SEE RUBY MADE YOU ALL WAIT IT OUT WITH HER.
IT'S JUST MOM, JUDY! SHE'S HOME FROM WORK EARLY.
YEAH, MS. RUSSO. WE'RE MISSING THE END OF *THE X-FILES* EPISODE!
WELL, SINCE I'M HOME NOW, I THINK YOU'RE OK TO GO BACK TO IT.
REALLY?!
COME ON! LET'S GO!
YOU'RE THE BEST, MS. R!
GET THE POPCORN! MAYBE WE CAN CATCH THE LAST FEW MINUTES!

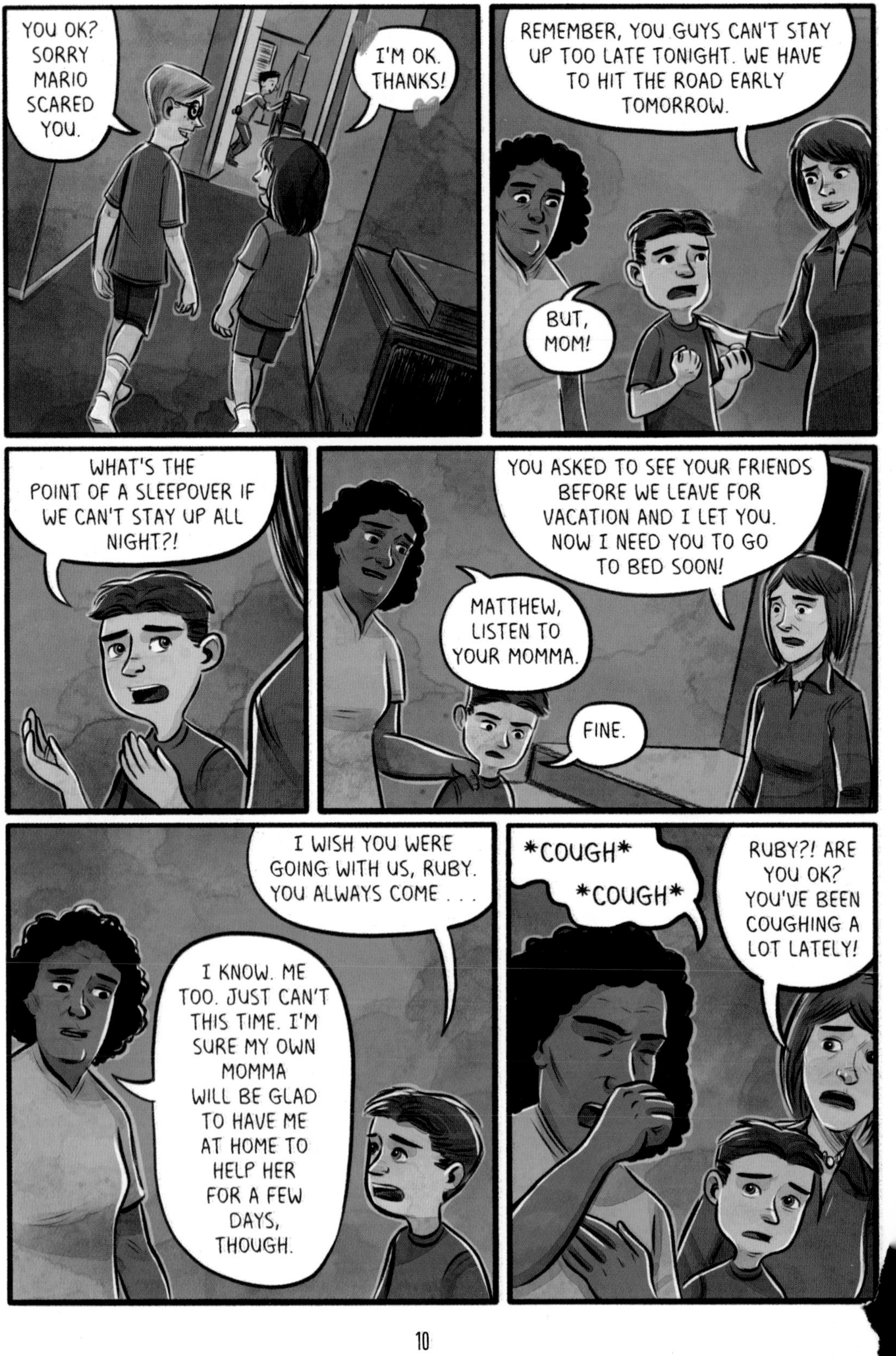

YOU OK? SORRY MARIO SCARED YOU.
I'M OK. THANKS!
REMEMBER, YOU GUYS CAN'T STAY UP TOO LATE TONIGHT. WE HAVE TO HIT THE ROAD EARLY TOMORROW.
BUT, MOM!
WHAT'S THE POINT OF A SLEEPOVER IF WE CAN'T STAY UP ALL NIGHT?!
YOU ASKED TO SEE YOUR FRIENDS BEFORE WE LEAVE FOR VACATION AND I LET YOU. NOW I NEED YOU TO GO TO BED SOON!
MATTHEW, LISTEN TO YOUR MOMMA.
FINE.
I WISH YOU WERE GOING WITH US, RUBY. YOU ALWAYS COME . . .
I KNOW. ME TOO. JUST CAN'T THIS TIME. I'M SURE MY OWN MOMMA WILL BE GLAD TO HAVE ME AT HOME TO HELP HER FOR A FEW DAYS, THOUGH.
COUGH
COUGH
RUBY?! ARE YOU OK? YOU'VE BEEN COUGHING A LOT LATELY!

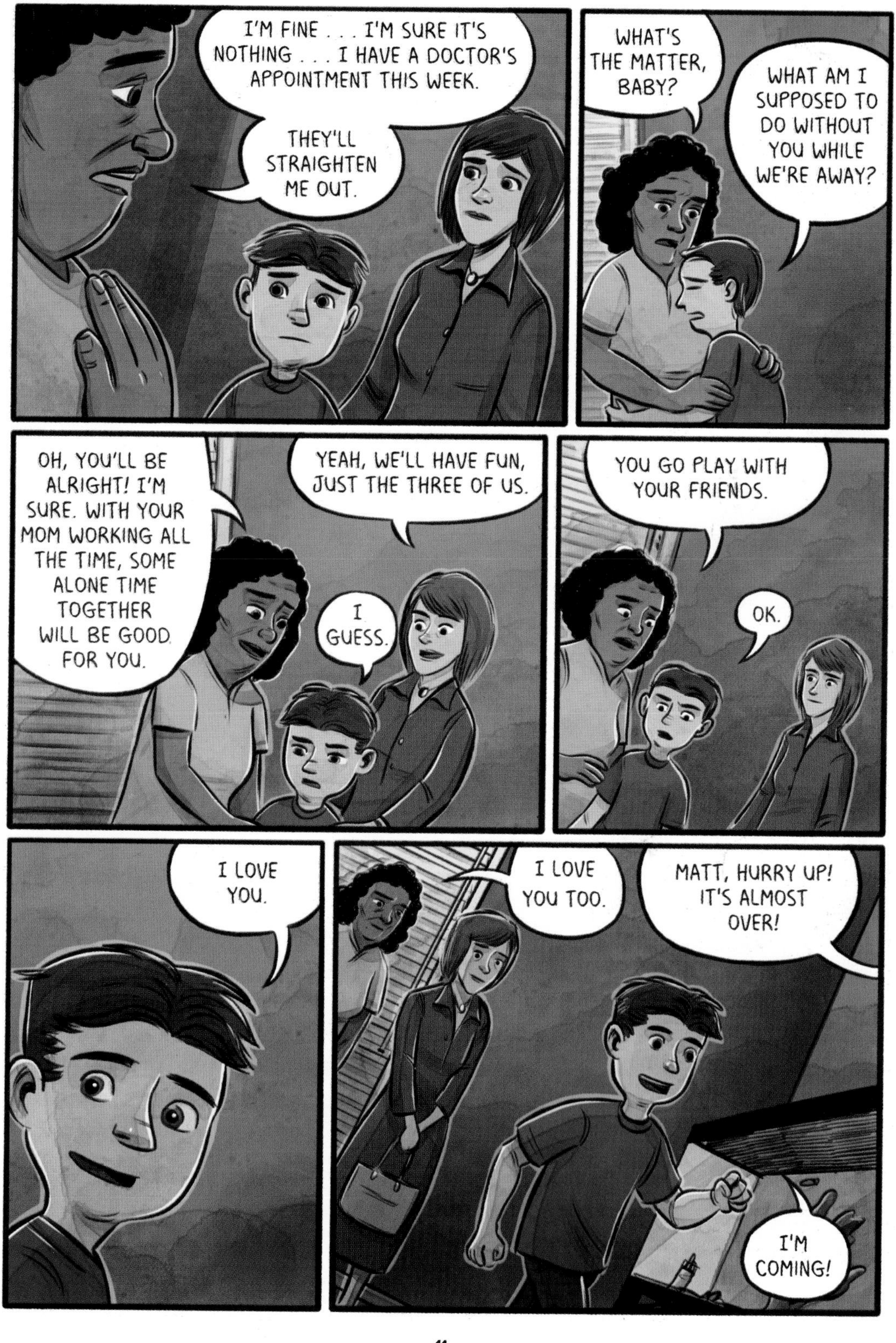
I'M FINE . . . I'M SURE IT'S NOTHING . . . I HAVE A DOCTOR'S APPOINTMENT THIS WEEK.
THEY'LL STRAIGHTEN ME OUT.
WHAT'S THE MATTER, BABY?
WHAT AM I SUPPOSED TO DO WITHOUT YOU WHILE WE'RE AWAY?
OH, YOU'LL BE ALRIGHT! I'M SURE. WITH YOUR MOM WORKING ALL THE TIME, SOME ALONE TIME TOGETHER WILL BE GOOD FOR YOU.
YEAH, WE'LL HAVE FUN, JUST THE THREE OF US.
I GUESS.
YOU GO PLAY WITH YOUR FRIENDS.
OK.
I LOVE YOU.
I LOVE YOU TOO.
MATT, HURRY UP! IT'S ALMOST OVER!
I'M COMING!

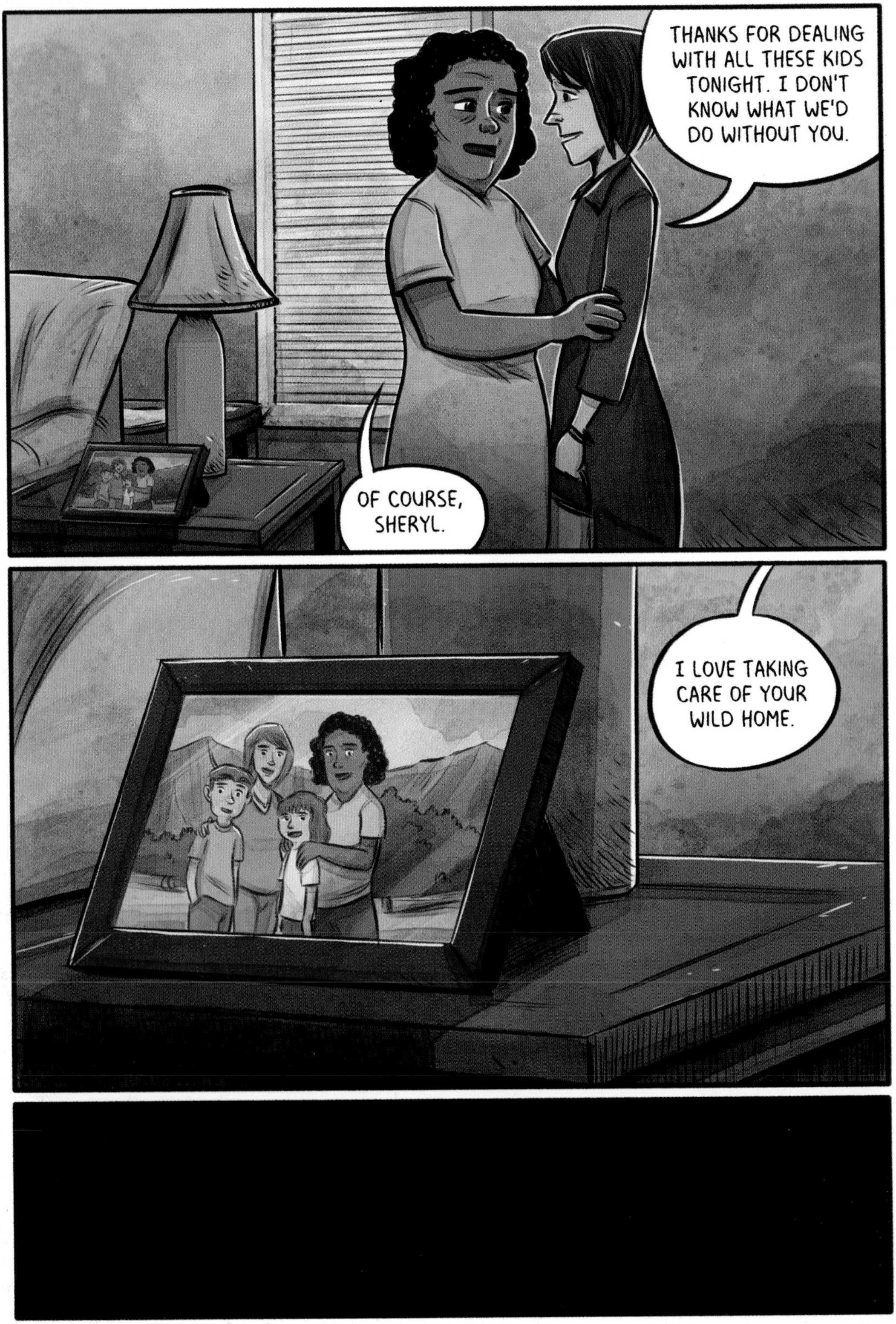
THANKS FOR DEALING WITH ALL THESE KIDS TONIGHT. I DON'T KNOW WHAT WE'D DO WITHOUT YOU.
OF COURSE, SHERYL.
I LOVE TAKING CARE OF YOUR WILD HOME.

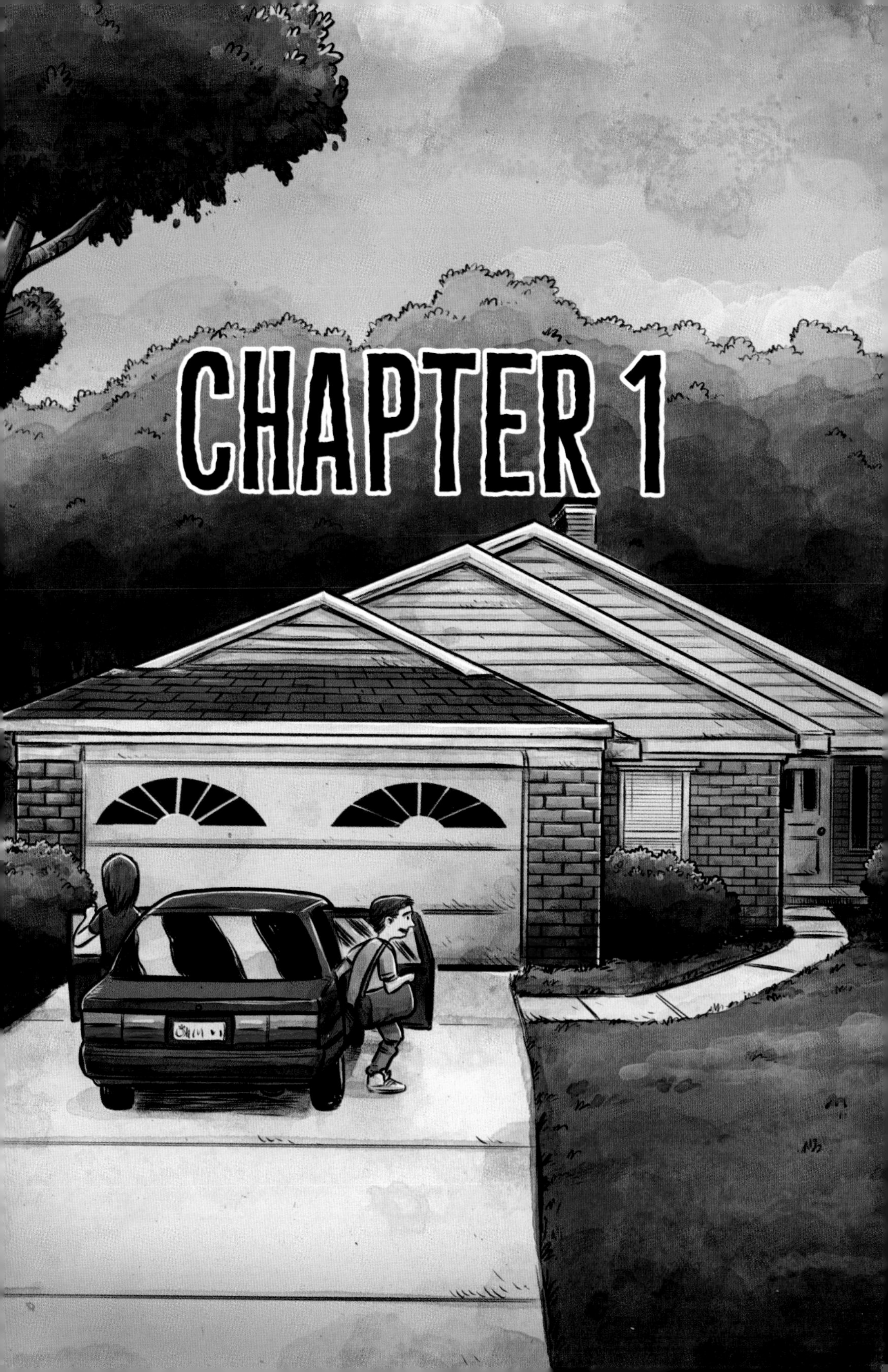
CHAPTER 1

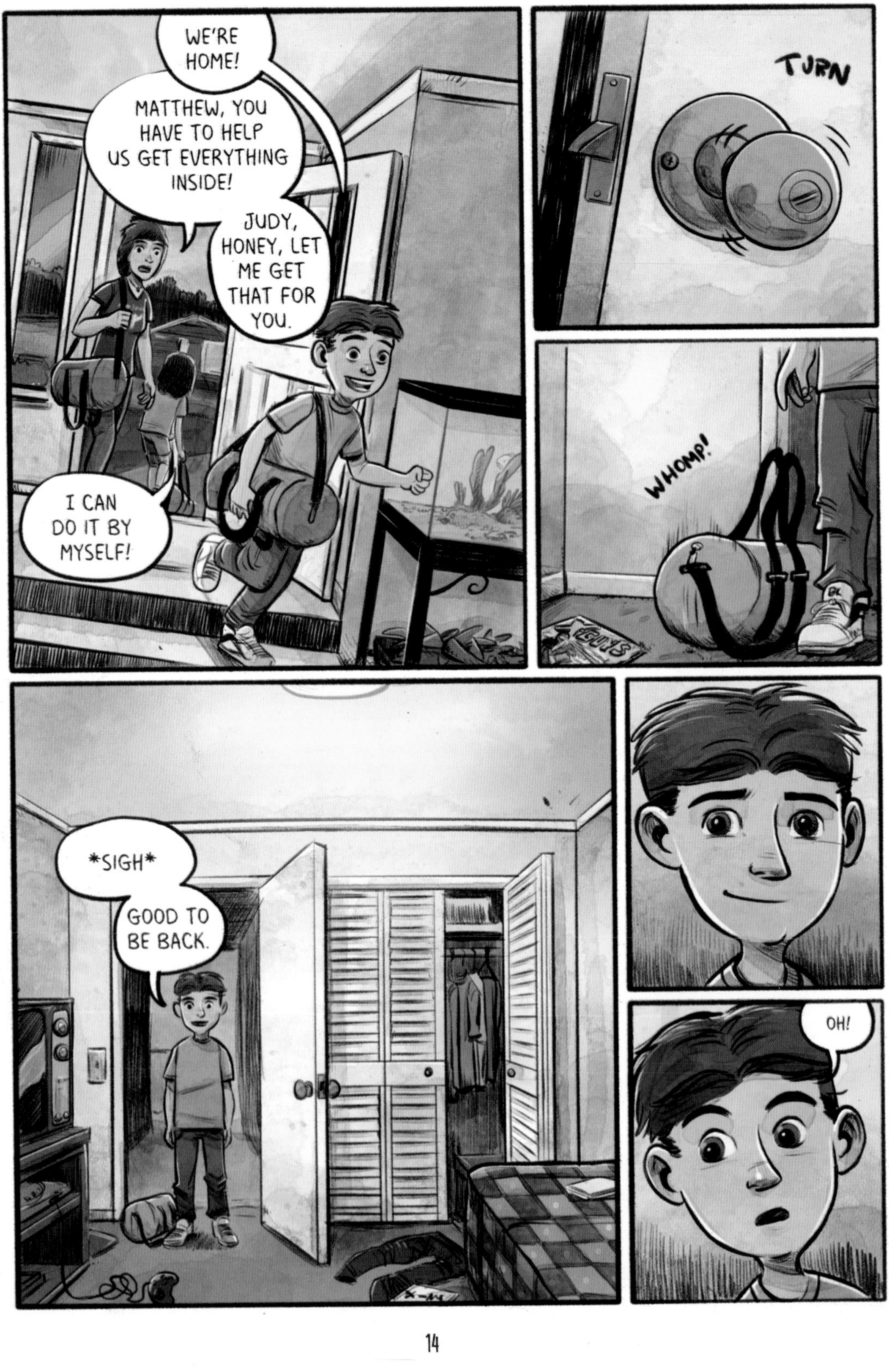
WE'RE HOME!
MATTHEW, YOU HAVE TO HELP US GET EVERYTHING INSIDE!
JUDY, HONEY, LET ME GET THAT FOR YOU.
I CAN DO IT BY MYSELF!
TURN
WHOMP!
SIGH
GOOD TO BE BACK.
OH!

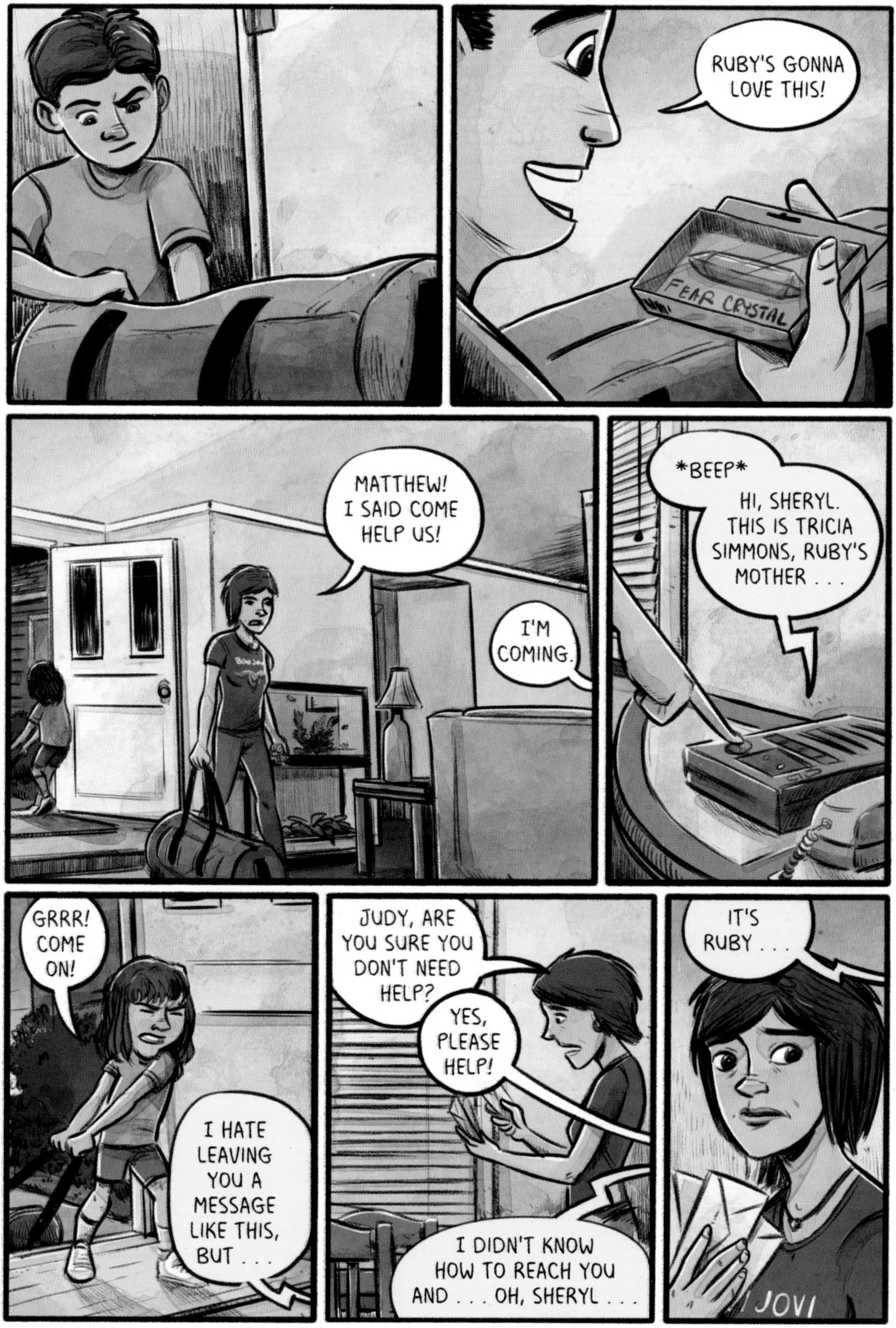
RUBY'S GONNA LOVE THIS!
FEAR CRYSTAL
MATTHEW! I SAID COME HELP US!
I'M COMING.
BEEP
HI, SHERYL. THIS IS TRICIA SIMMONS, RUBY'S MOTHER . . .
GRRR! COME ON!
I HATE LEAVING YOU A MESSAGE LIKE THIS, BUT . . .
JUDY, ARE YOU SURE YOU DON'T NEED HELP?
YES, PLEASE HELP!
I DIDN'T KNOW HOW TO REACH YOU AND . . . OH, SHERYL . . .
IT'S RUBY . . .
JOVI

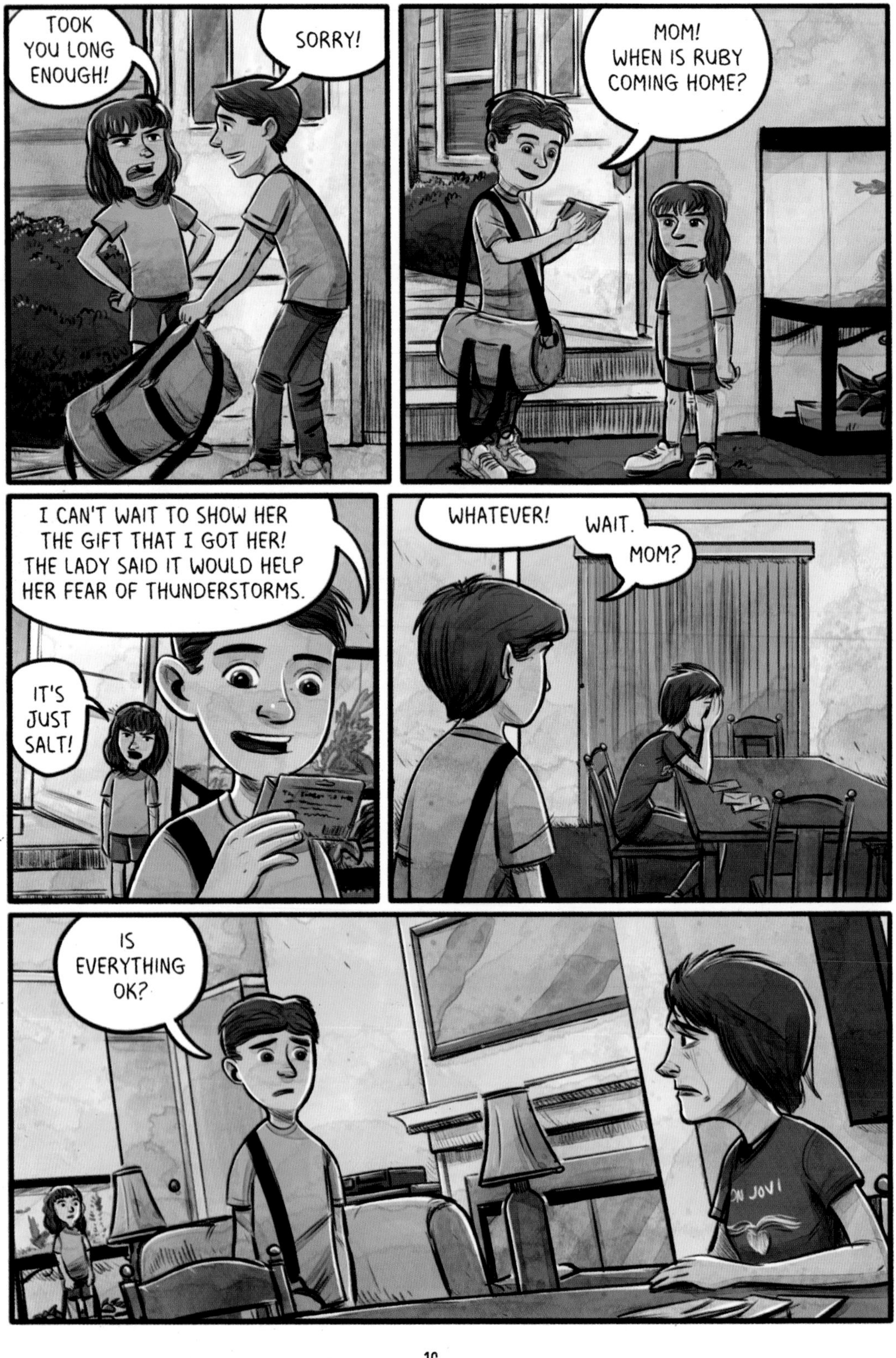
TOOK YOU LONG ENOUGH!
SORRY!
MOM! WHEN IS RUBY COMING HOME?
I CAN'T WAIT TO SHOW HER THE GIFT THAT I GOT HER! THE LADY SAID IT WOULD HELP HER FEAR OF THUNDERSTORMS.
IT'S JUST SALT!
WHATEVER!
WAIT.
MOM?
IS EVERYTHING OK?

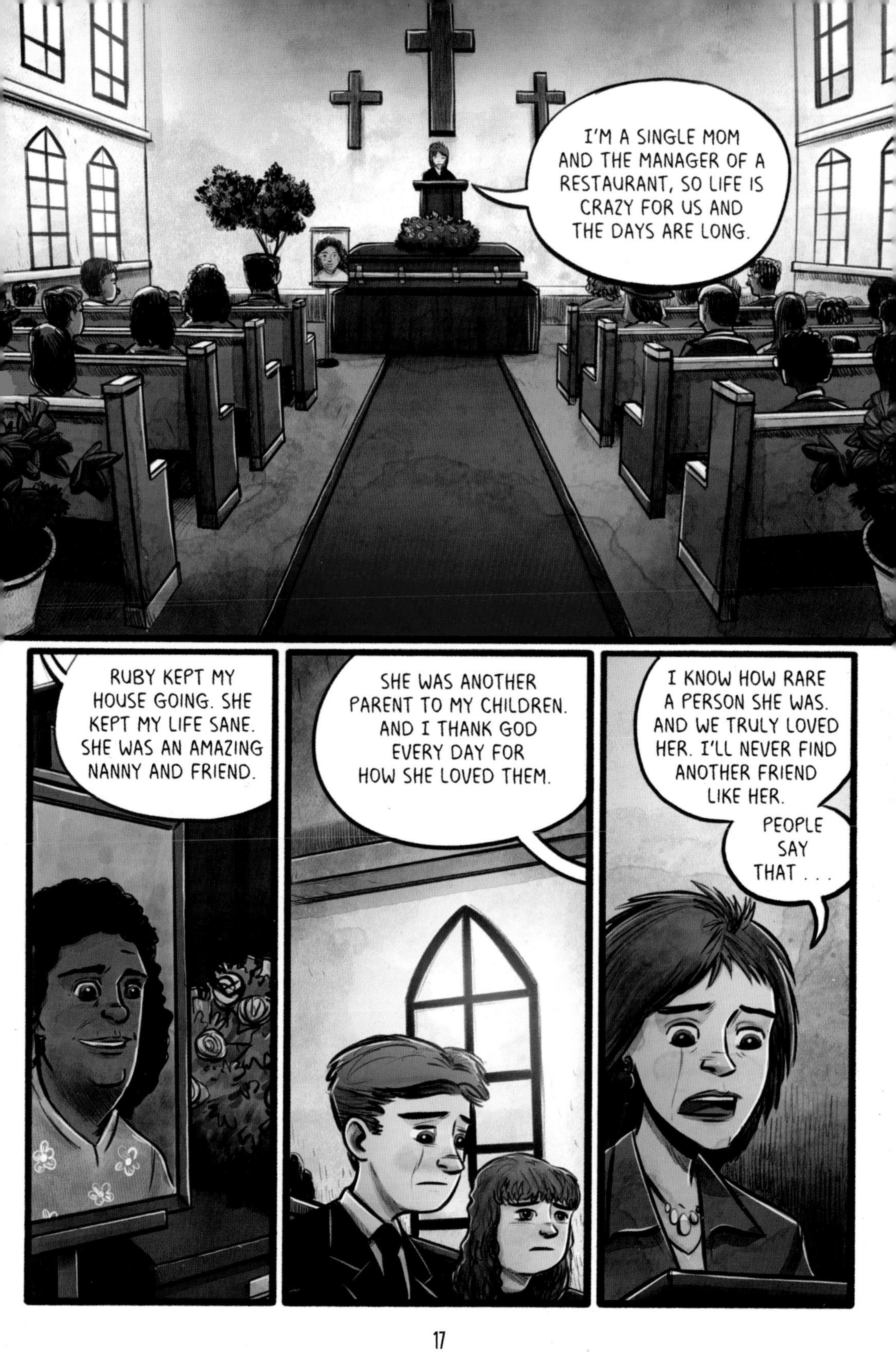
I'M A SINGLE MOM AND THE MANAGER OF A RESTAURANT, SO LIFE IS CRAZY FOR US AND THE DAYS ARE LONG.
RUBY KEPT MY HOUSE GOING. SHE KEPT MY LIFE SANE. SHE WAS AN AMAZING NANNY AND FRIEND.
SHE WAS ANOTHER PARENT TO MY CHILDREN. AND I THANK GOD EVERY DAY FOR HOW SHE LOVED THEM.
I KNOW HOW RARE A PERSON SHE WAS. AND WE TRULY LOVED HER. I'LL NEVER FIND ANOTHER FRIEND LIKE HER.
PEOPLE SAY THAT . . .

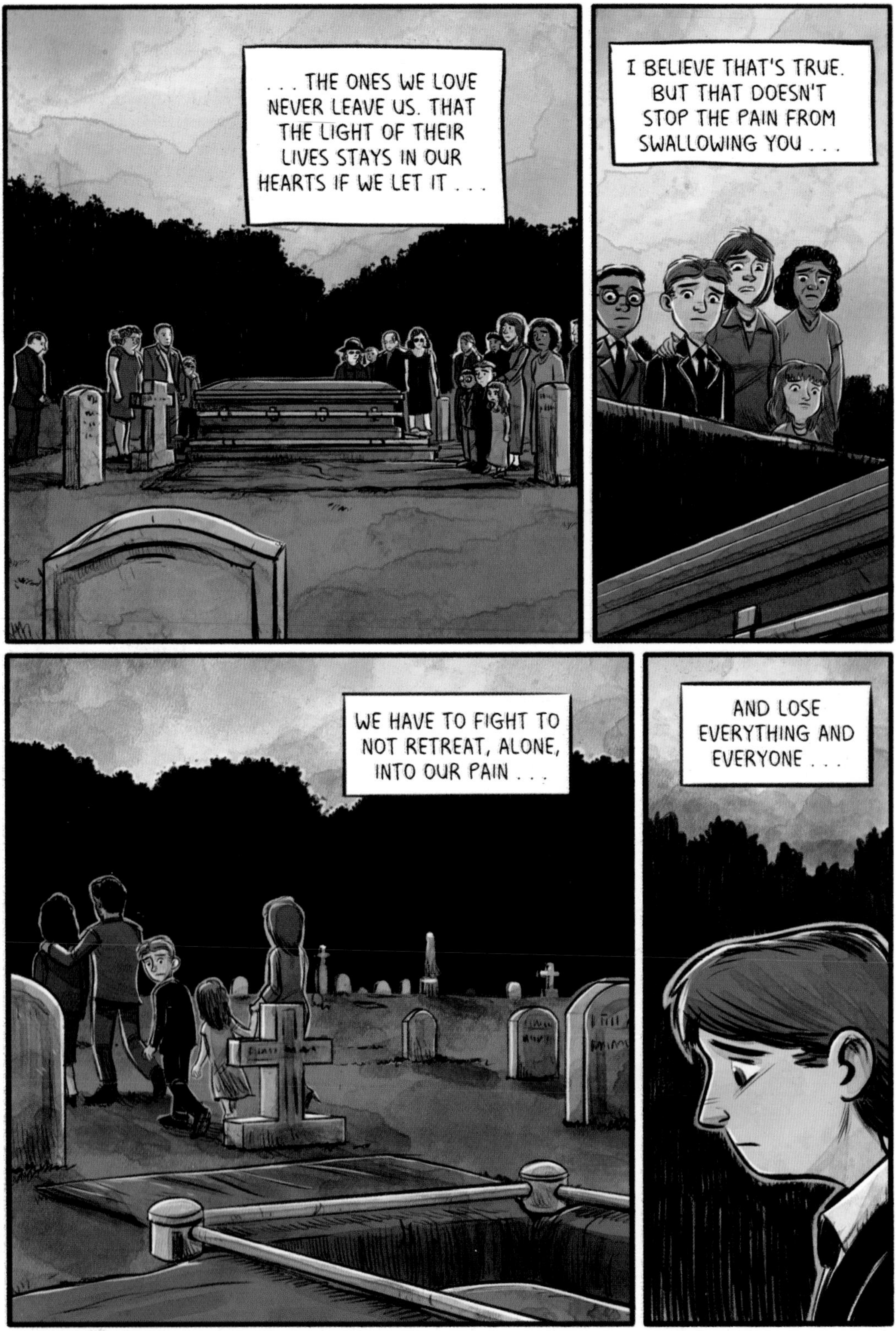
. . . THE ONES WE LOVE NEVER LEAVE US. THAT THE LIGHT OF THEIR LIVES STAYS IN OUR HEARTS IF WE LET IT . . .
I BELIEVE THAT'S TRUE. BUT THAT DOESN'T STOP THE PAIN FROM SWALLOWING YOU . . .
WE HAVE TO FIGHT TO NOT RETREAT, ALONE, INTO OUR PAIN . . .
AND LOSE EVERYTHING AND EVERYONE . . .

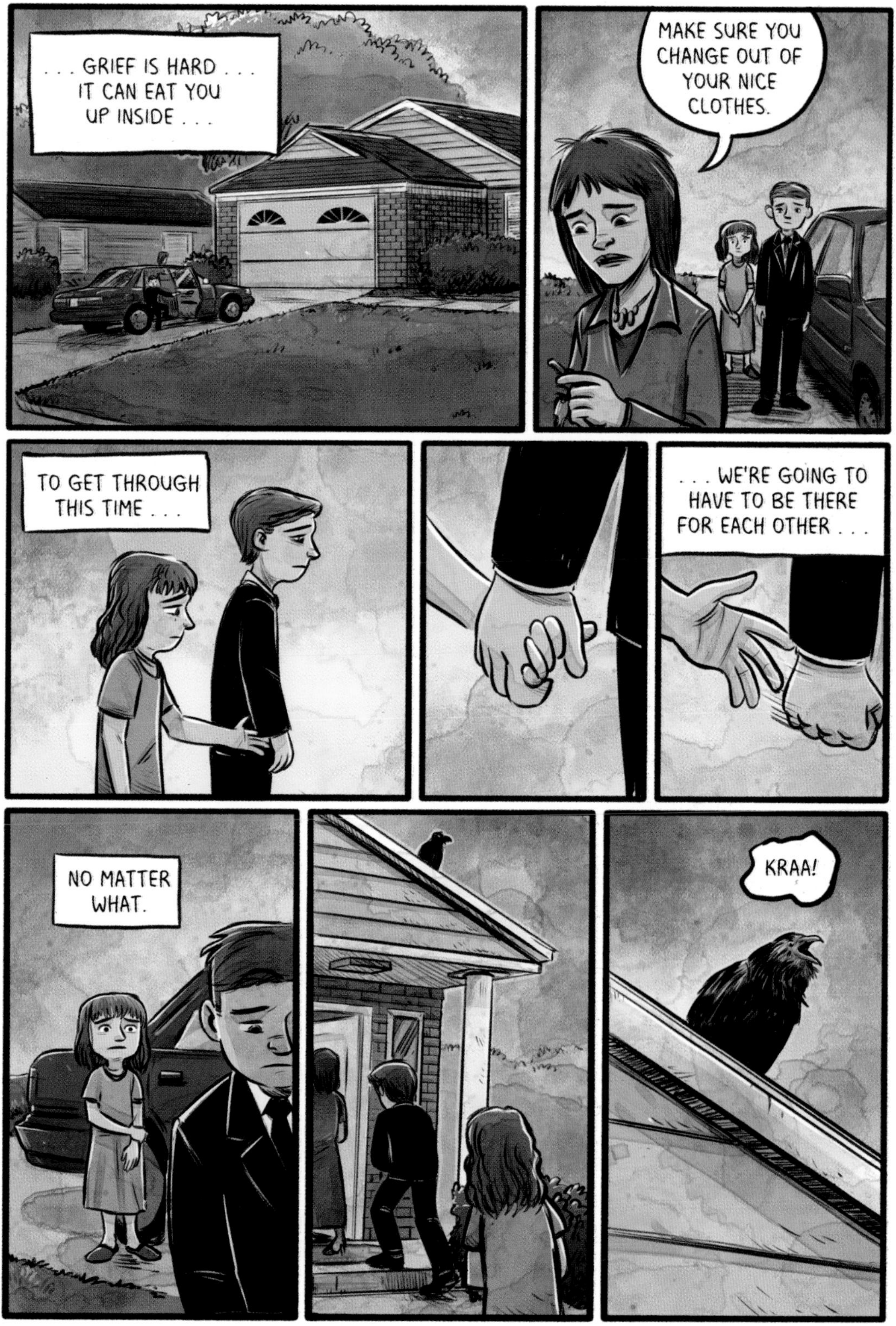
. . . GRIEF IS HARD . . . IT CAN EAT YOU UP INSIDE . . .
MAKE SURE YOU CHANGE OUT OF YOUR NICE CLOTHES.
TO GET THROUGH THIS TIME . . .
. . . WE'RE GOING TO HAVE TO BE THERE FOR EACH OTHER . . .
NO MATTER WHAT.
KRAA!

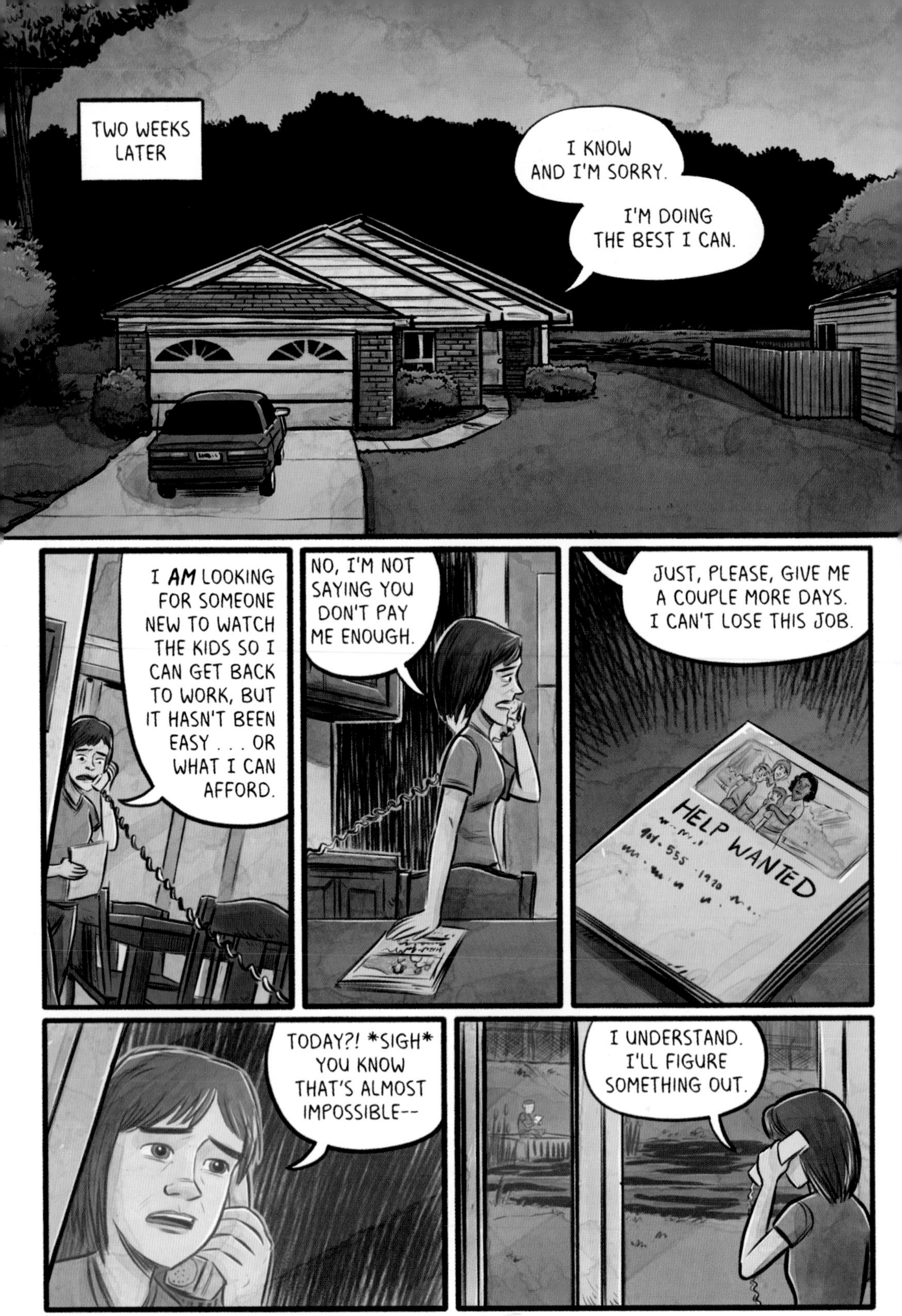
TWO WEEKS LATER
I KNOW AND I'M SORRY.
I'M DOING THE BEST I CAN.
I **AM** LOOKING FOR SOMEONE NEW TO WATCH THE KIDS SO I CAN GET BACK TO WORK, BUT IT HASN'T BEEN EASY . . . OR WHAT I CAN AFFORD.
NO, I'M NOT SAYING YOU DON'T PAY ME ENOUGH.
JUST, PLEASE, GIVE ME A COUPLE MORE DAYS. I CAN'T LOSE THIS JOB.
HELP WANTED
TODAY?! *SIGH* YOU KNOW THAT'S ALMOST IMPOSSIBLE--
I UNDERSTAND. I'LL FIGURE SOMETHING OUT.

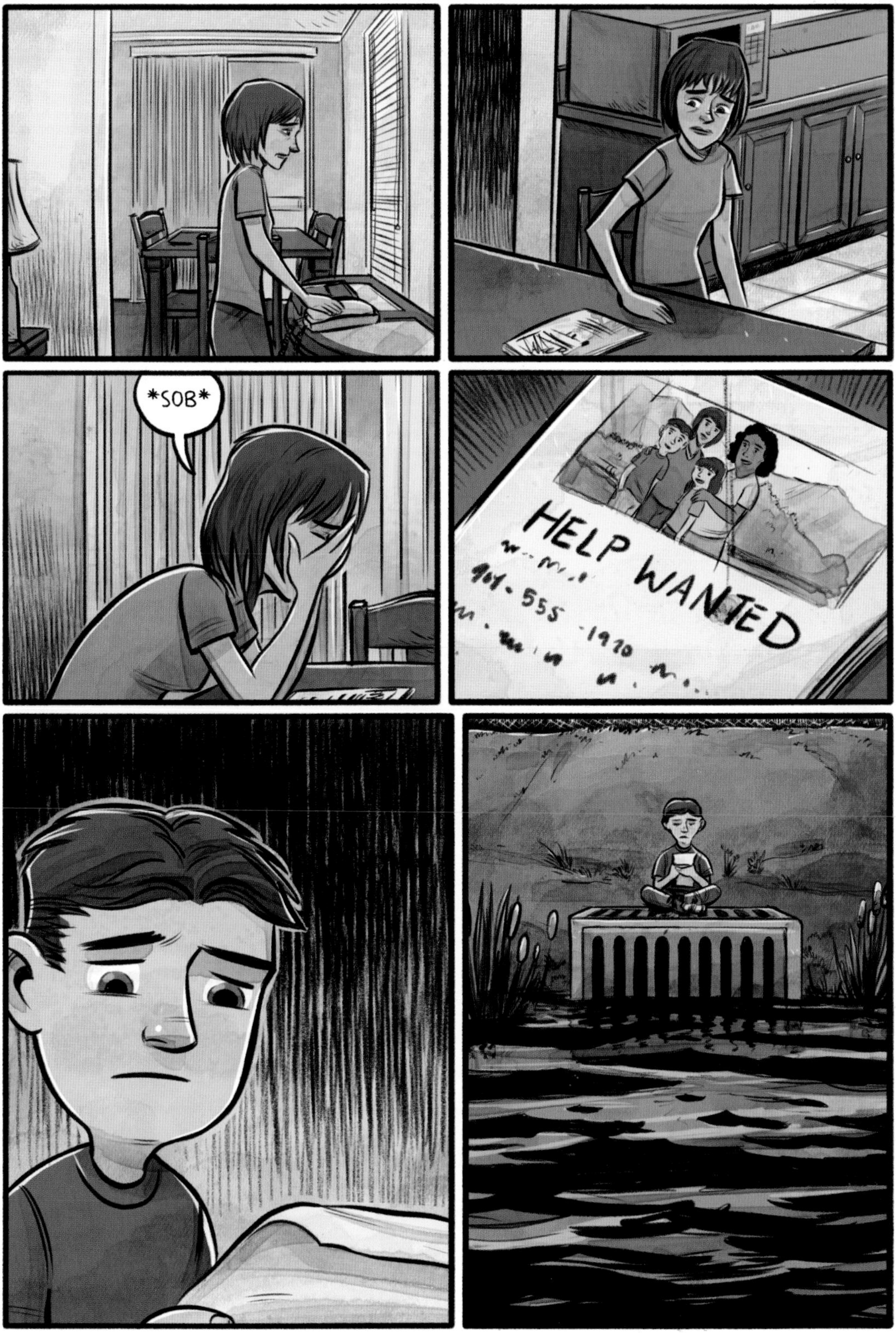
SOB
HELP WANTED

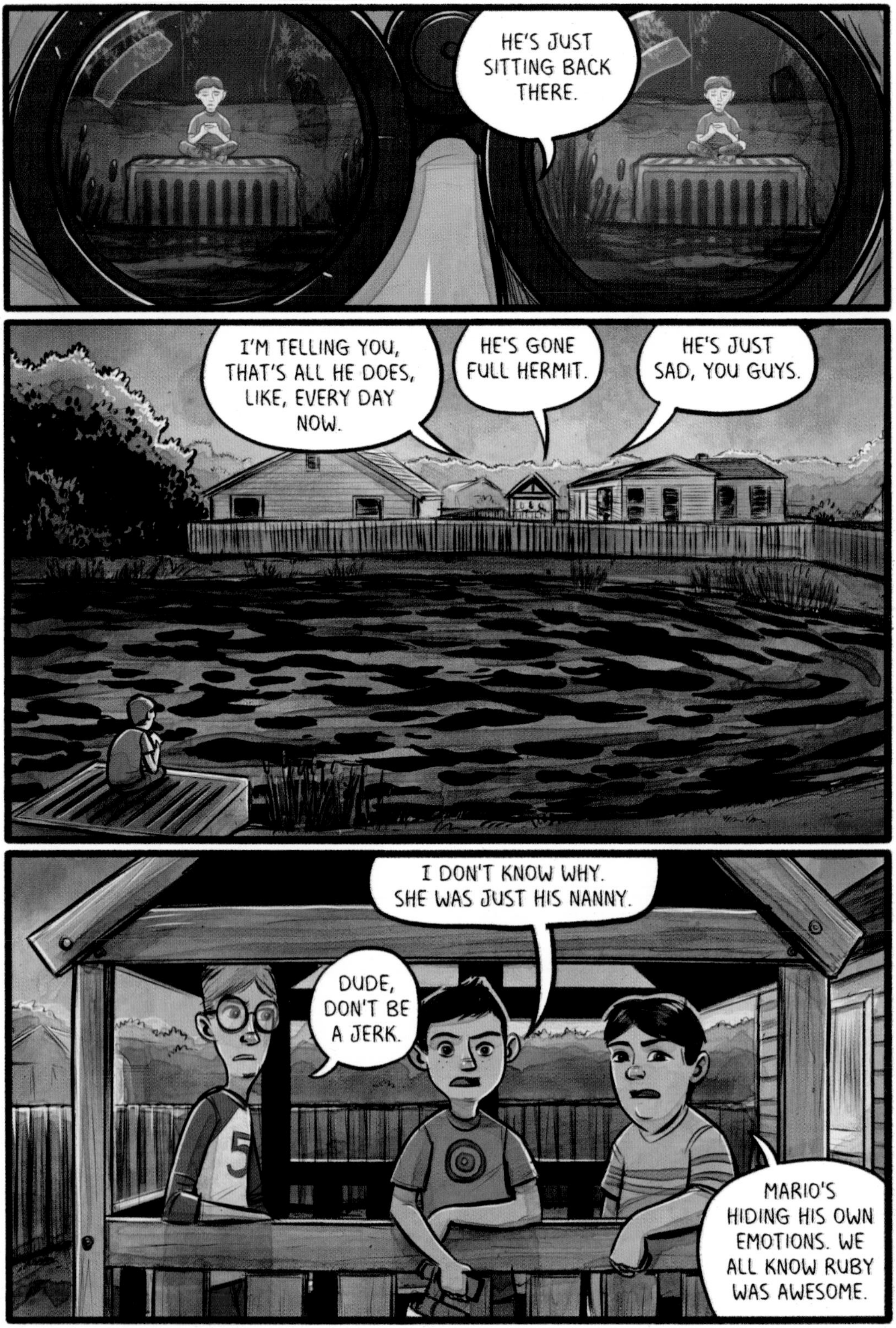
HE'S JUST SITTING BACK THERE.
I'M TELLING YOU, THAT'S ALL HE DOES, LIKE, EVERY DAY NOW.
HE'S GONE FULL HERMIT.
HE'S JUST SAD, YOU GUYS.
I DON'T KNOW WHY. SHE WAS JUST HIS NANNY.
DUDE, DON'T BE A JERK.
MARIO'S HIDING HIS OWN EMOTIONS. WE ALL KNOW RUBY WAS AWESOME.

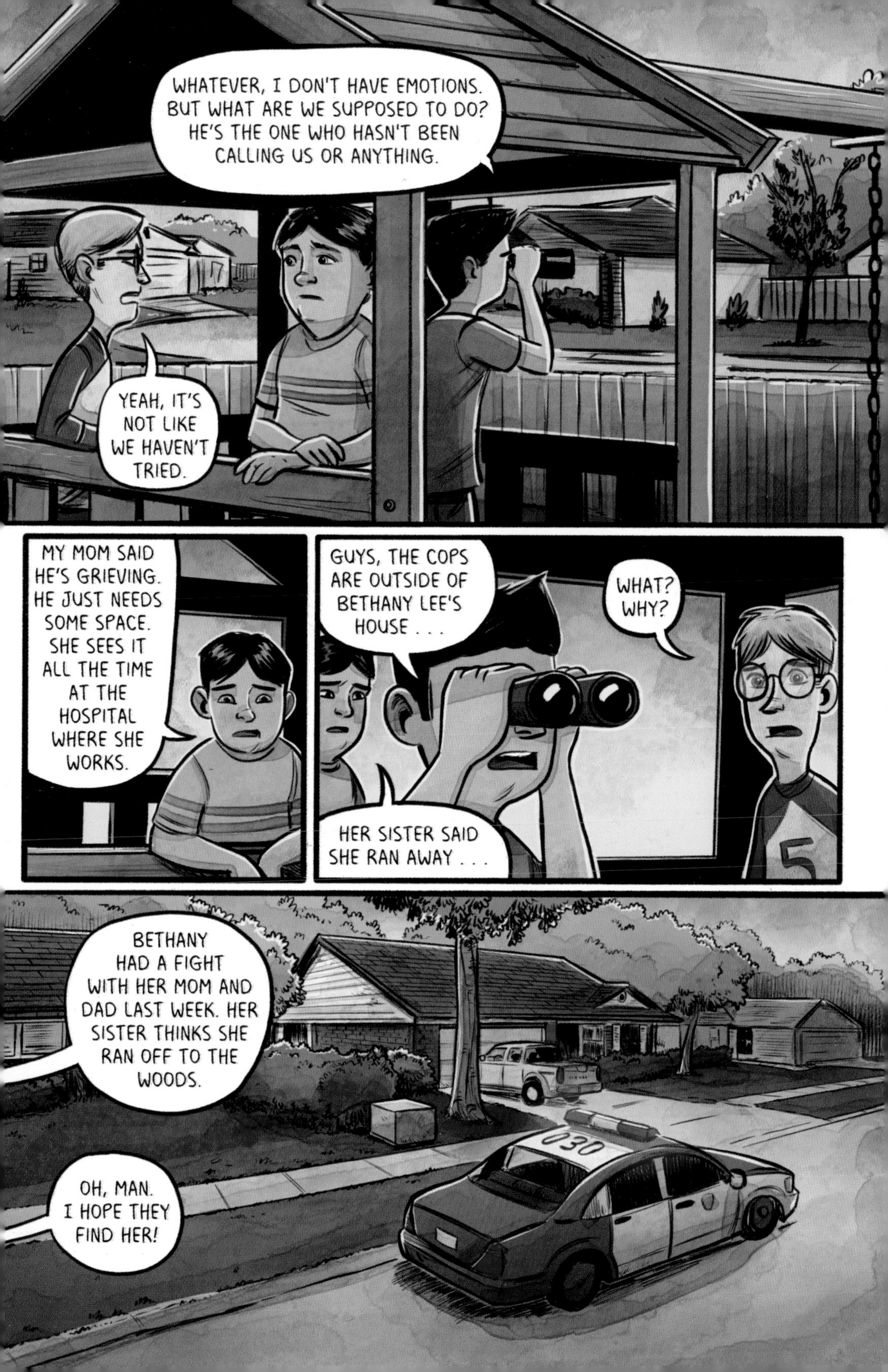
WHATEVER, I DON'T HAVE EMOTIONS. BUT WHAT ARE WE SUPPOSED TO DO? HE'S THE ONE WHO HASN'T BEEN CALLING US OR ANYTHING.
YEAH, IT'S NOT LIKE WE HAVEN'T TRIED.
MY MOM SAID HE'S GRIEVING. HE JUST NEEDS SOME SPACE. SHE SEES IT ALL THE TIME AT THE HOSPITAL WHERE SHE WORKS.
GUYS, THE COPS ARE OUTSIDE OF BETHANY LEE'S HOUSE . . .
WHAT? WHY?
HER SISTER SAID SHE RAN AWAY . . .
BETHANY HAD A FIGHT WITH HER MOM AND DAD LAST WEEK. HER SISTER THINKS SHE RAN OFF TO THE WOODS.
OH, MAN. I HOPE THEY FIND HER!
030

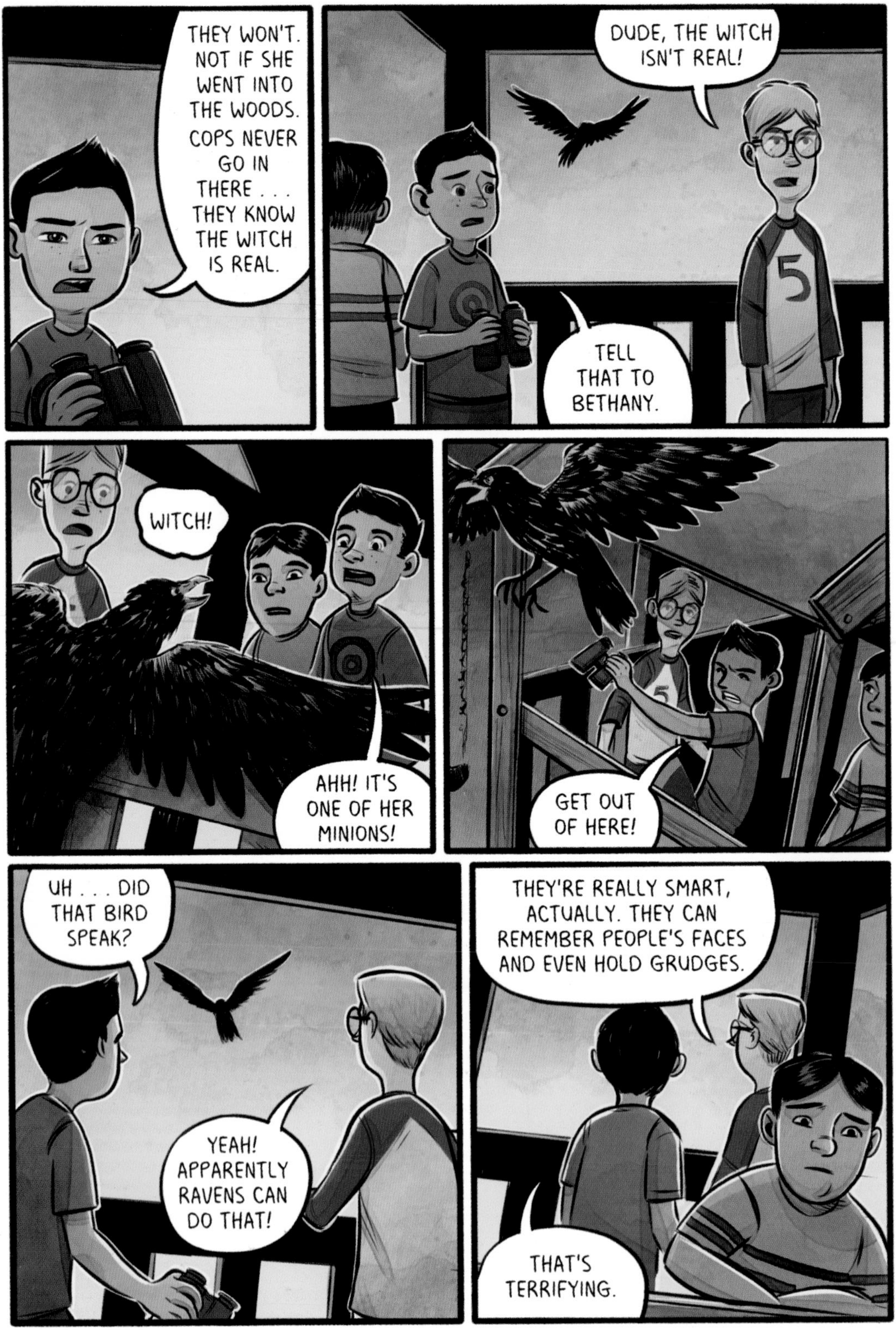
THEY WON'T. NOT IF SHE WENT INTO THE WOODS. COPS NEVER GO IN THERE . . . THEY KNOW THE WITCH IS REAL.
DUDE, THE WITCH ISN'T REAL!
TELL THAT TO BETHANY.
WITCH!
AHH! IT'S ONE OF HER MINIONS!
GET OUT OF HERE!
UH . . . DID THAT BIRD SPEAK?
YEAH! APPARENTLY RAVENS CAN DO THAT!
THEY'RE REALLY SMART, ACTUALLY. THEY CAN REMEMBER PEOPLE'S FACES AND EVEN HOLD GRUDGES.
THAT'S TERRIFYING.

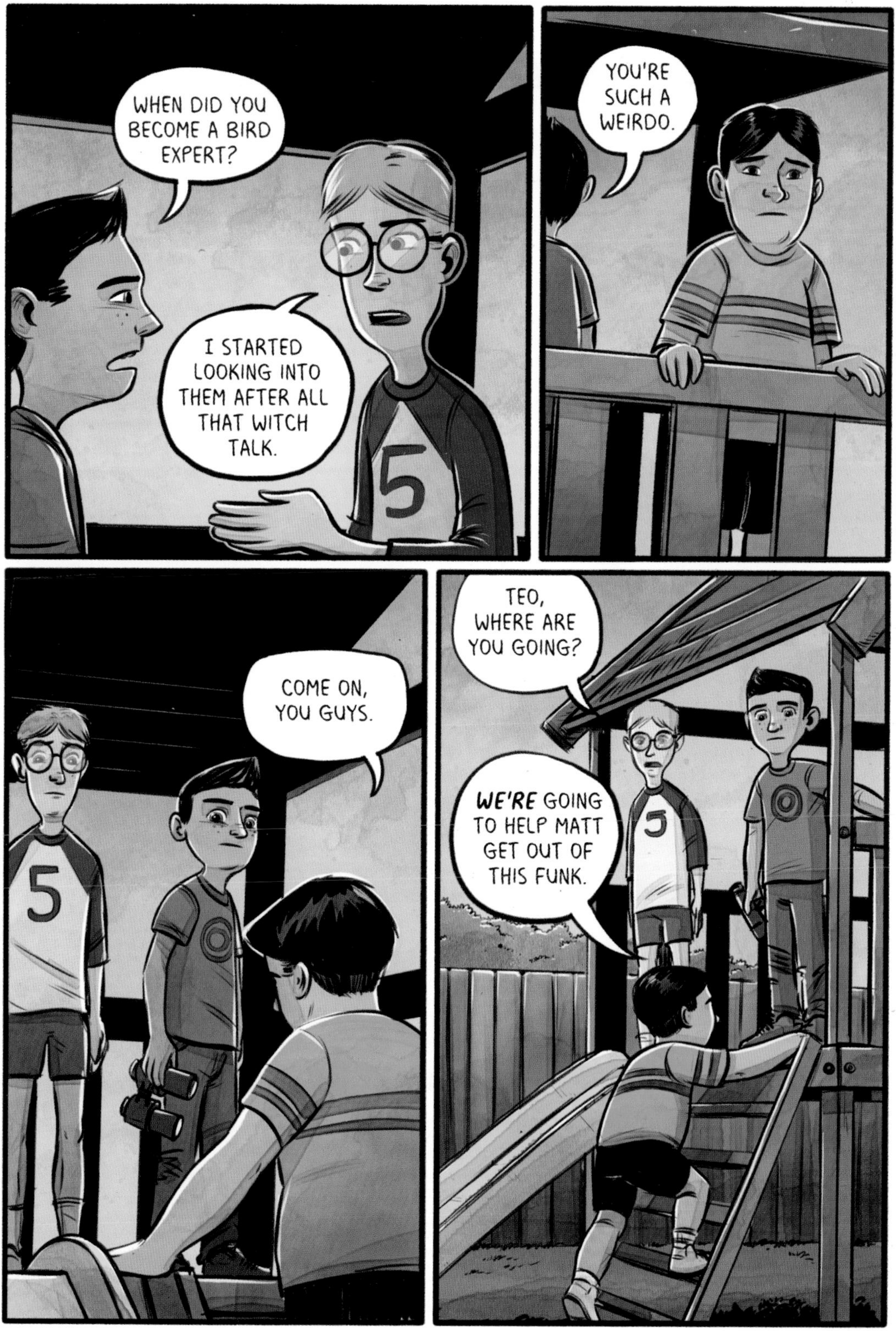
WHEN DID YOU BECOME A BIRD EXPERT?
I STARTED LOOKING INTO THEM AFTER ALL THAT WITCH TALK.
YOU'RE SUCH A WEIRDO.
COME ON, YOU GUYS.
TEO, WHERE ARE YOU GOING?
WE'RE GOING TO HELP MATT GET OUT OF THIS FUNK.

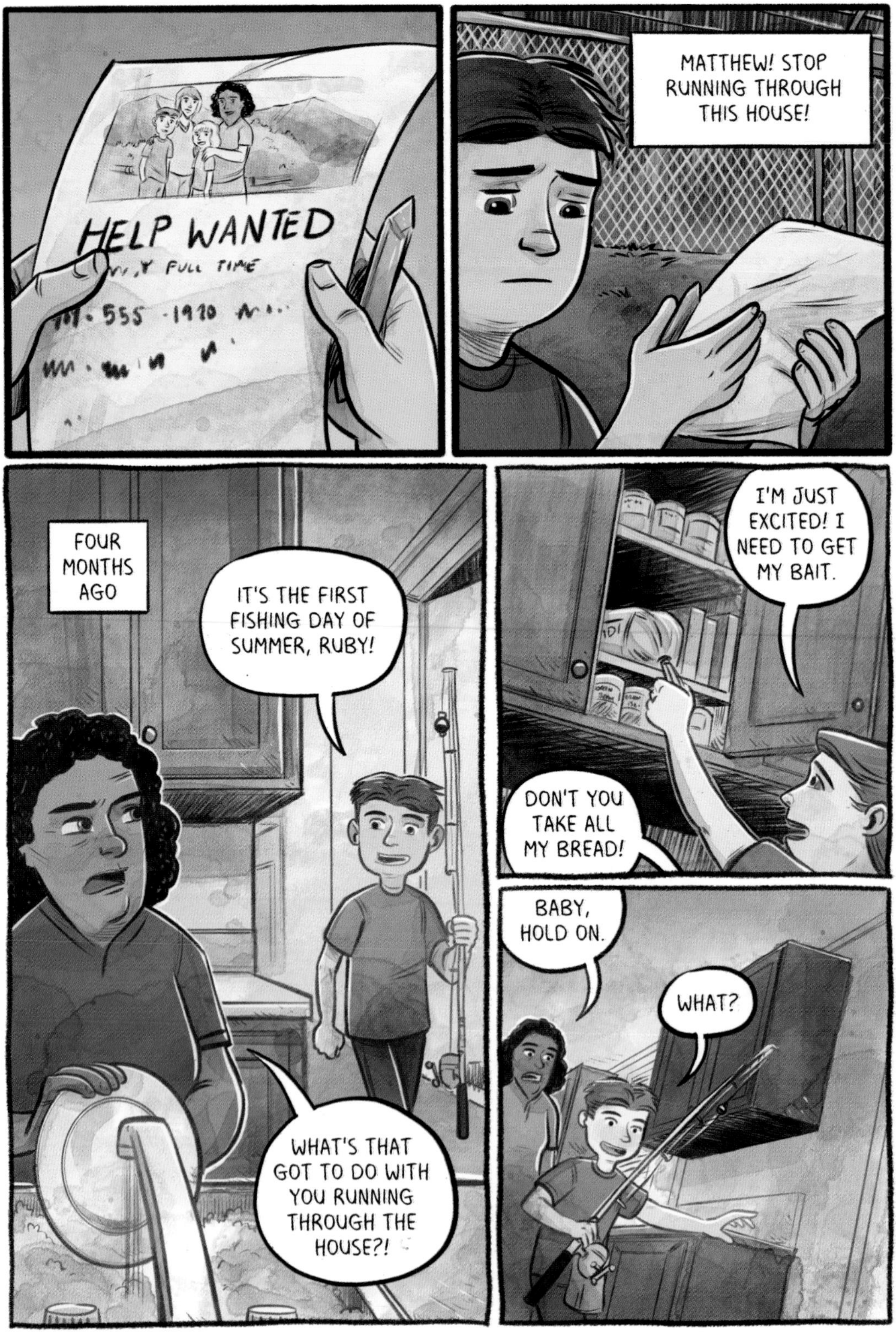
HELP WANTED
FULL TIME
MATTHEW! STOP RUNNING THROUGH THIS HOUSE!
FOUR MONTHS AGO
IT'S THE FIRST FISHING DAY OF SUMMER, RUBY!
WHAT'S THAT GOT TO DO WITH YOU RUNNING THROUGH THE HOUSE?!
I'M JUST EXCITED! I NEED TO GET MY BAIT.
DON'T YOU TAKE ALL MY BREAD!
BABY, HOLD ON.
WHAT?

JUST BE CAREFUL.

I WILL.

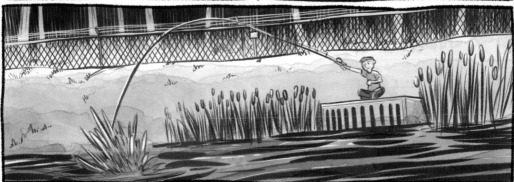

OH! HI, DUCKS!

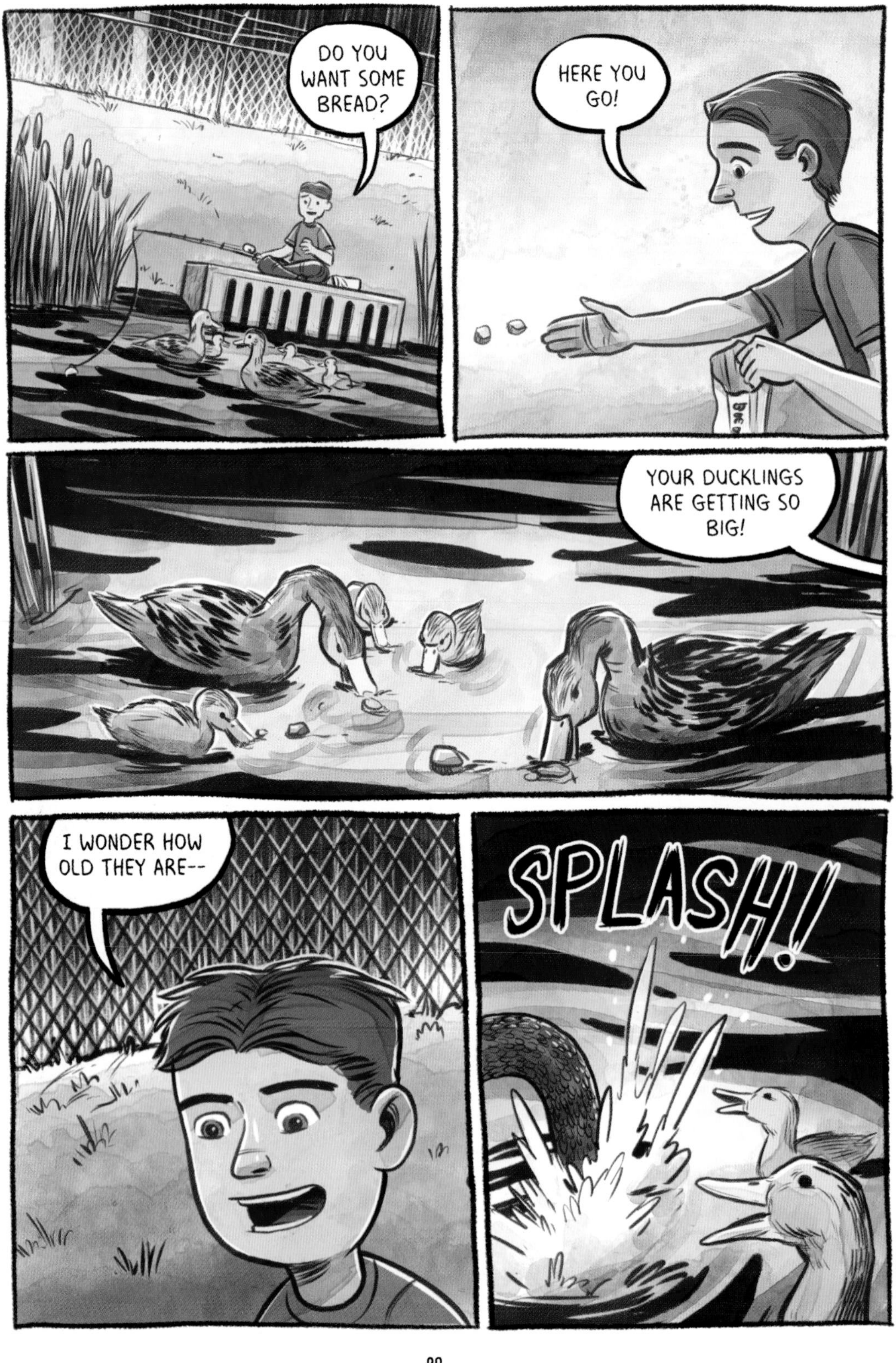
DO YOU WANT SOME BREAD?
HERE YOU GO!
YOUR DUCKLINGS ARE GETTING SO BIG!
I WONDER HOW OLD THEY ARE--
SPLASH!

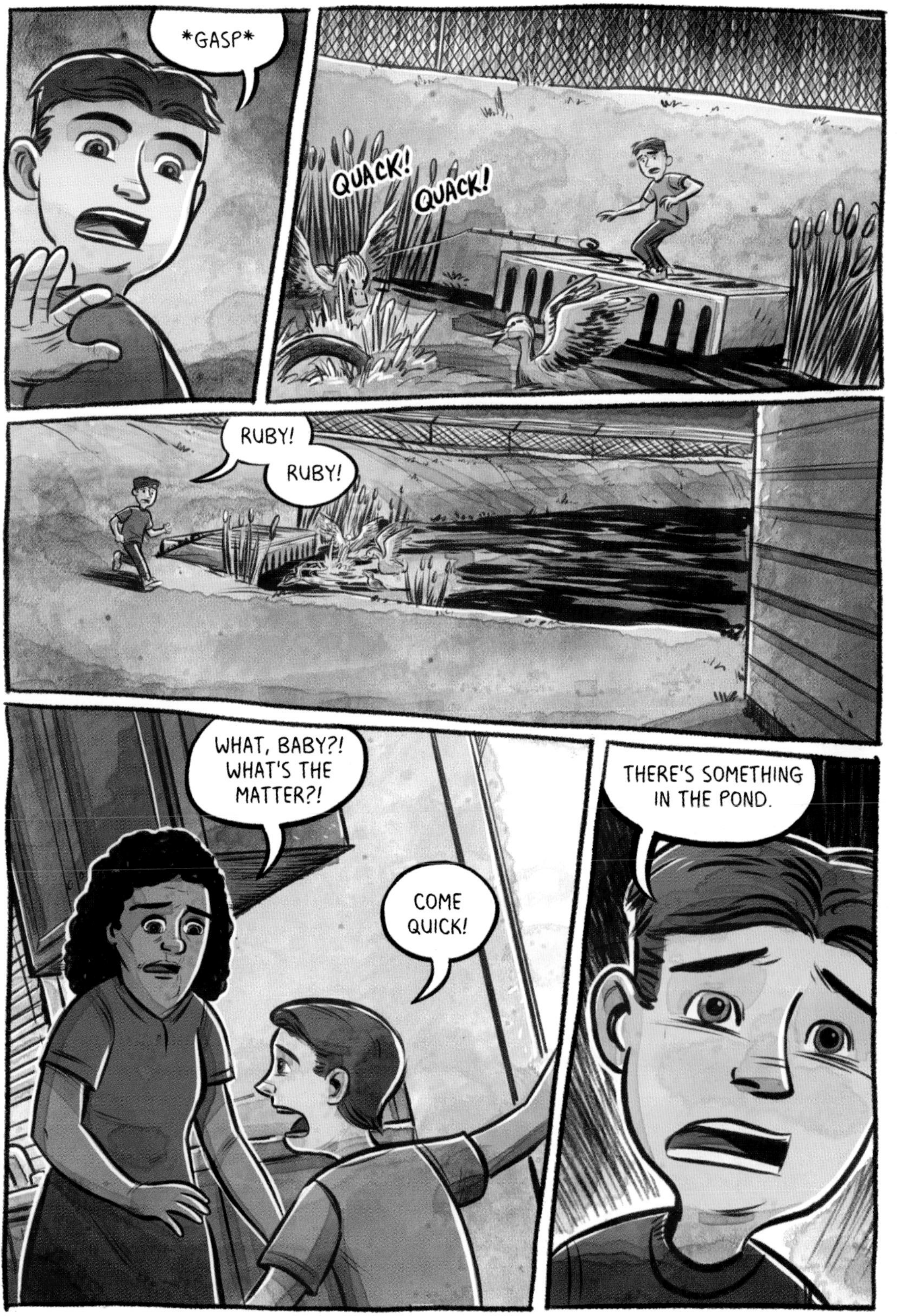
GASP
QUACK!
QUACK!
RUBY!
RUBY!
WHAT, BABY?! WHAT'S THE MATTER?!
COME QUICK!
THERE'S SOMETHING IN THE POND.

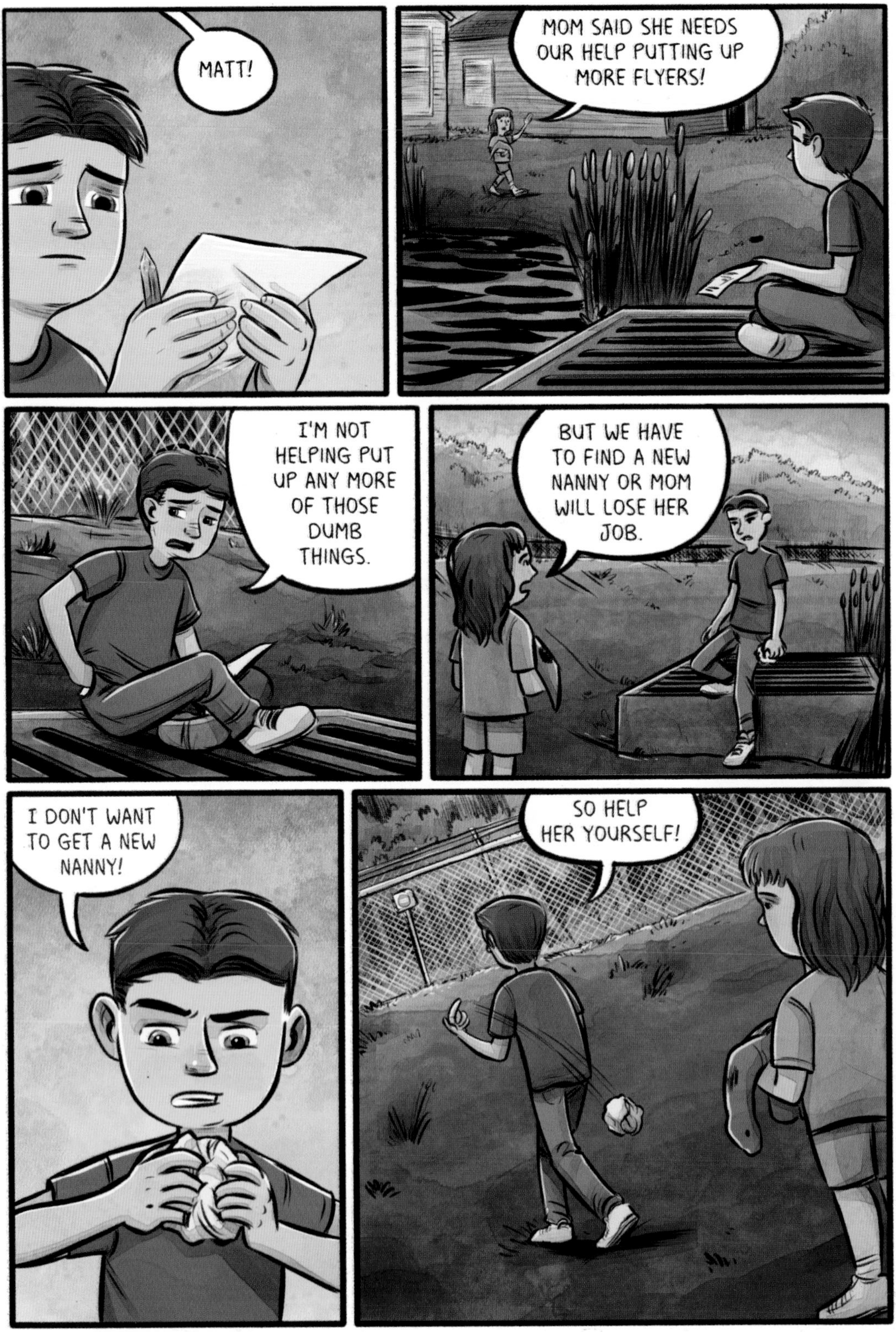
MATT!
MOM SAID SHE NEEDS OUR HELP PUTTING UP MORE FLYERS!
I'M NOT HELPING PUT UP ANY MORE OF THOSE DUMB THINGS.
BUT WE HAVE TO FIND A NEW NANNY OR MOM WILL LOSE HER JOB.
I DON'T WANT TO GET A NEW NANNY!
SO HELP HER YOURSELF!

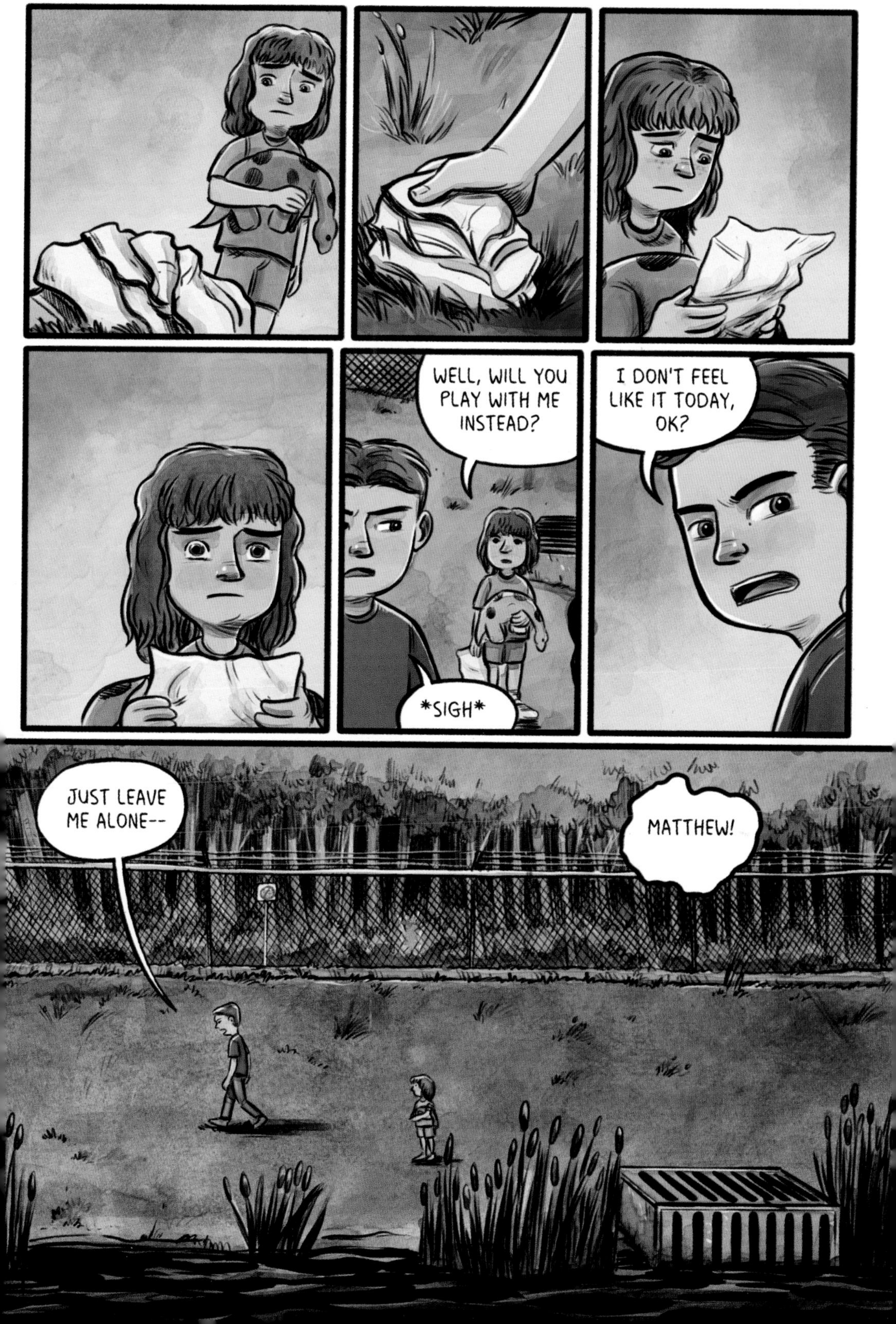
WELL, WILL YOU PLAY WITH ME INSTEAD?
SIGH
I DON'T FEEL LIKE IT TODAY, OK?
JUST LEAVE ME ALONE--
MATTHEW!

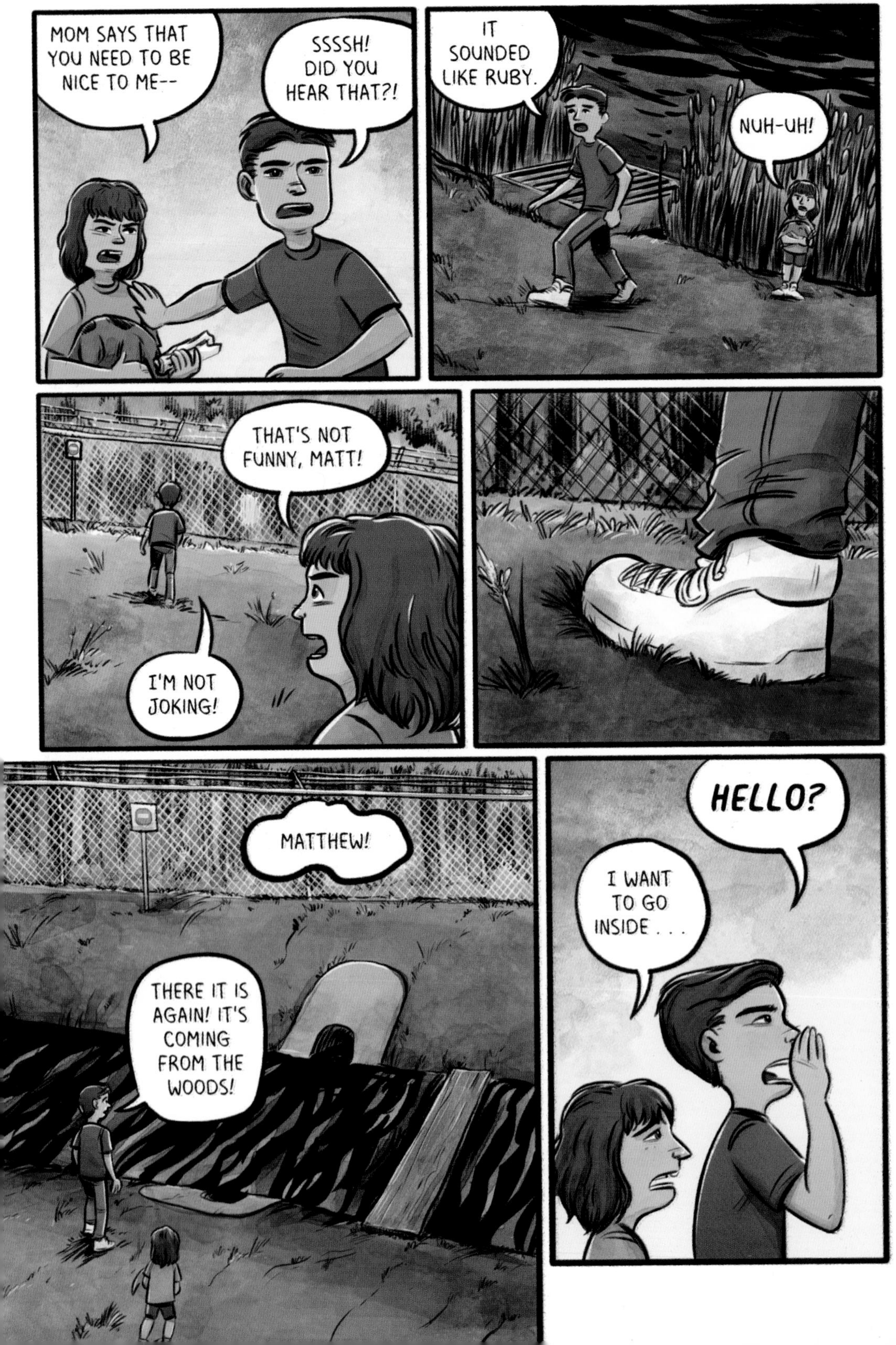
MOM SAYS THAT YOU NEED TO BE NICE TO ME--
SSSSH! DID YOU HEAR THAT?!
IT SOUNDED LIKE RUBY.
NUH-UH!
THAT'S NOT FUNNY, MATT!
I'M NOT JOKING!
MATTHEW!
THERE IT IS AGAIN! IT'S COMING FROM THE WOODS!
HELLO?
I WANT TO GO INSIDE . . .

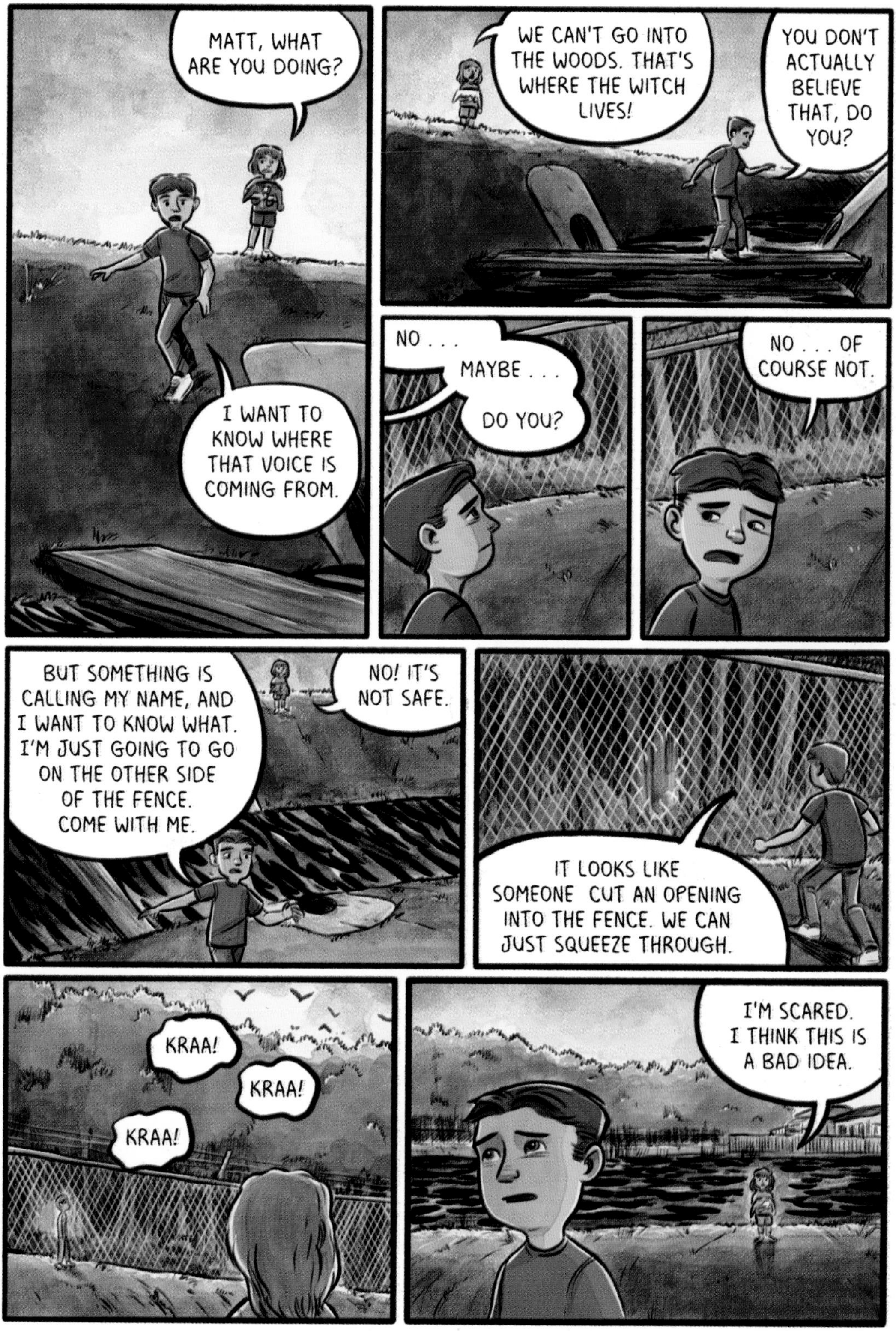
MATT, WHAT ARE YOU DOING?
I WANT TO KNOW WHERE THAT VOICE IS COMING FROM.
WE CAN'T GO INTO THE WOODS. THAT'S WHERE THE WITCH LIVES!
YOU DON'T ACTUALLY BELIEVE THAT, DO YOU?
NO . . .
MAYBE . . .
DO YOU?
NO . . . OF COURSE NOT.
BUT SOMETHING IS CALLING MY NAME, AND I WANT TO KNOW WHAT. I'M JUST GOING TO GO ON THE OTHER SIDE OF THE FENCE. COME WITH ME.
NO! IT'S NOT SAFE.
IT LOOKS LIKE SOMEONE CUT AN OPENING INTO THE FENCE. WE CAN JUST SQUEEZE THROUGH.
KRAA!
KRAA!
KRAA!
I'M SCARED. I THINK THIS IS A BAD IDEA.

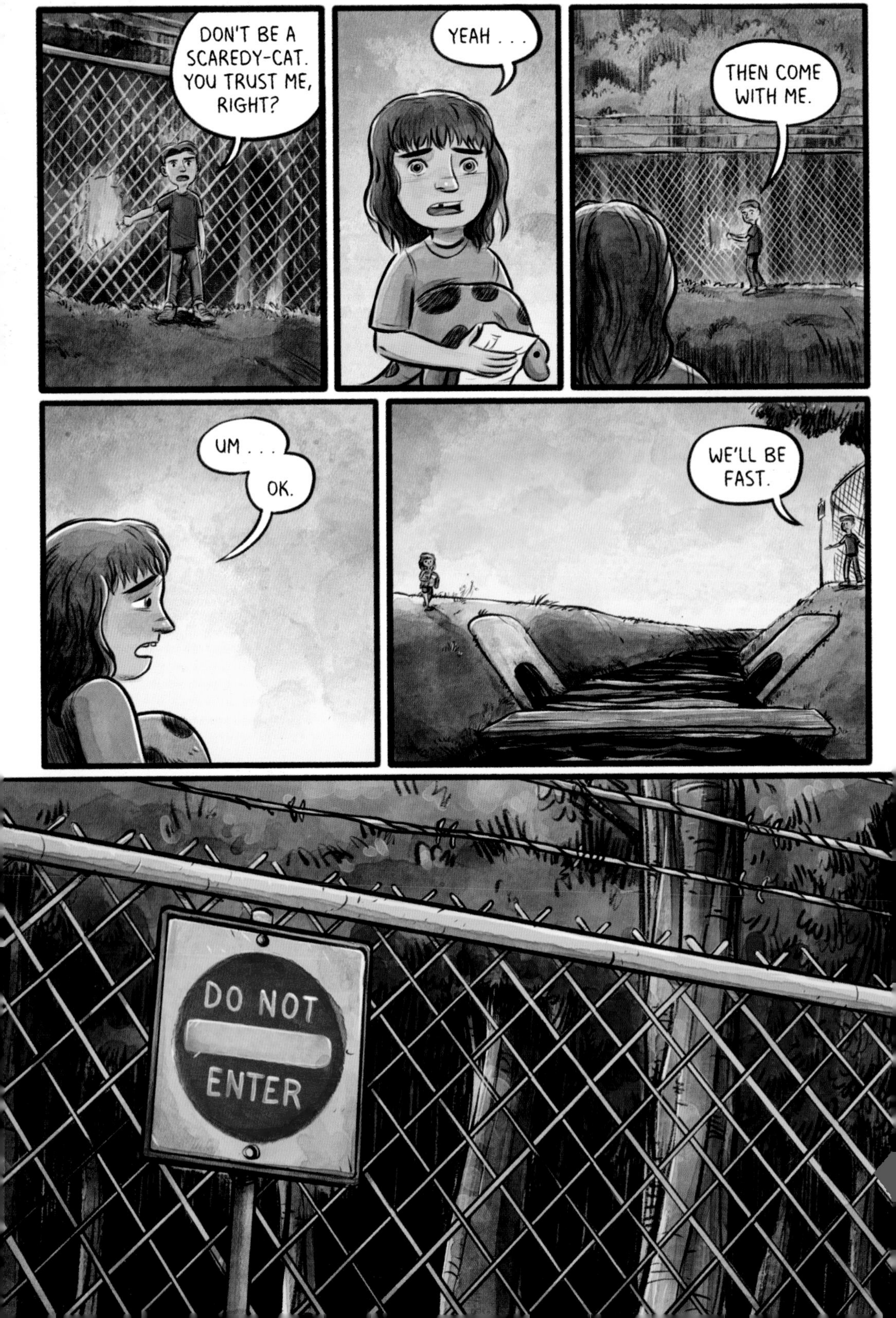
DON'T BE A SCAREDY-CAT. YOU TRUST ME, RIGHT?
YEAH . . .
THEN COME WITH ME.
UM . . .
OK.
WE'LL BE FAST.
DO NOT ENTER

DO YOU THINK IT'S RUBY'S GHOST?

NO. GHOSTS AREN'T REAL!

THEN WHAT IS IT?

CRUNCH!

WHOA!

WHAT IS THAT?!

IT'S A SNAKE'S SKELETON. I THINK IT'S THE SAME ONE--

MATTHEW!

THERE IT IS AGAIN!

I WANT TO GO HOME!

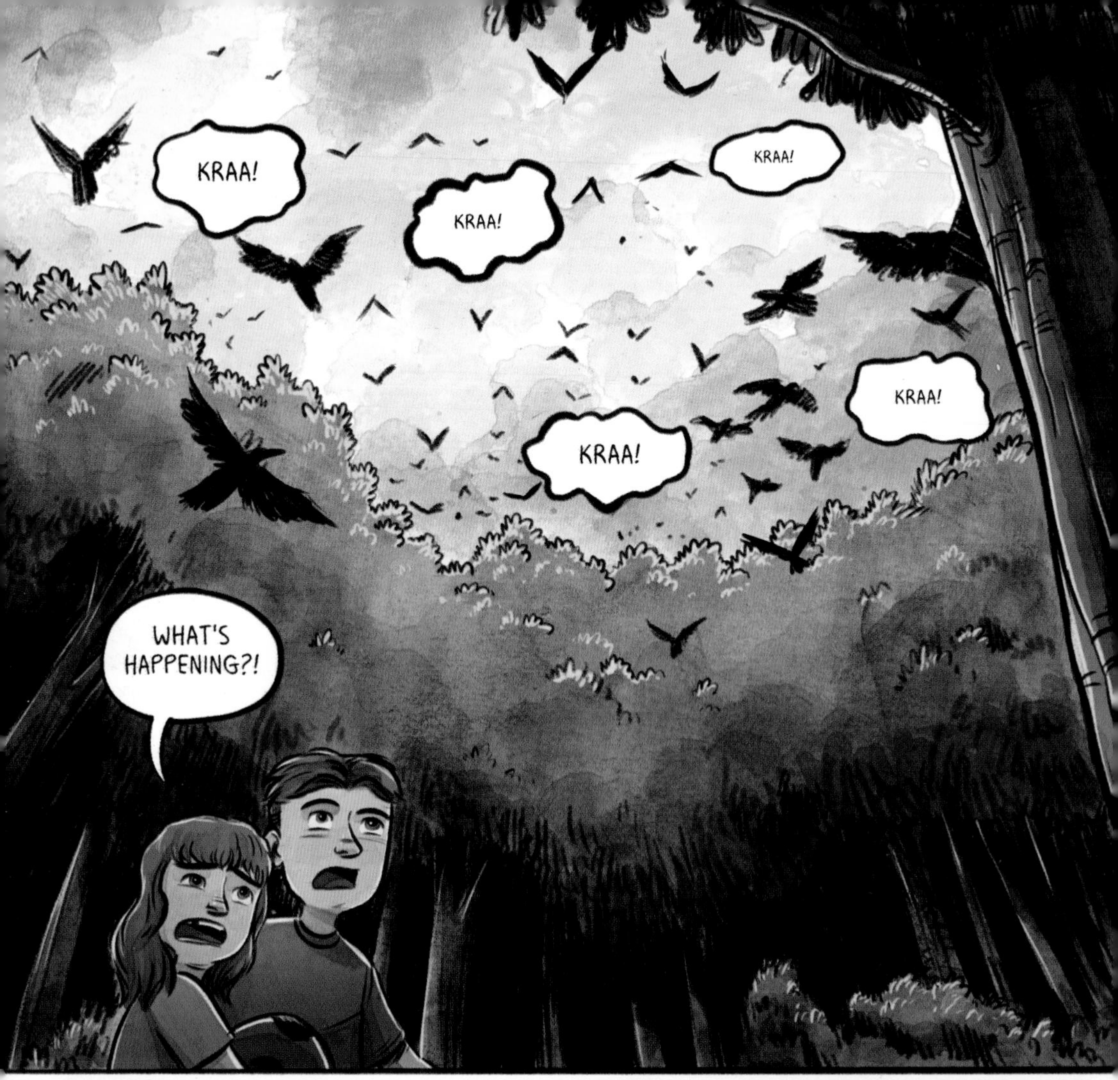
KRAA!
KRAA!
KRAA!
KRAA!
KRAA!
WHAT'S HAPPENING?!

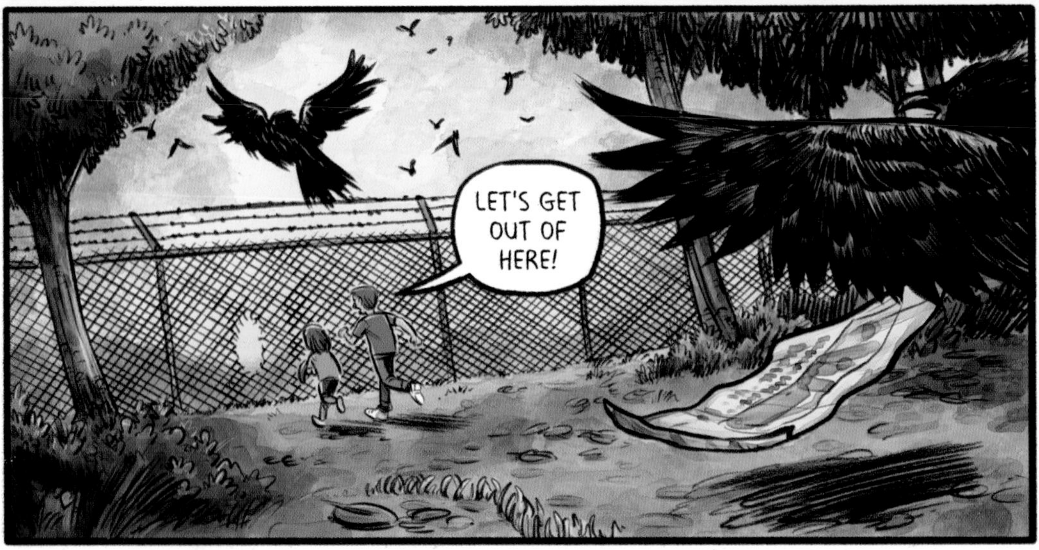
LET'S GET OUT OF HERE!

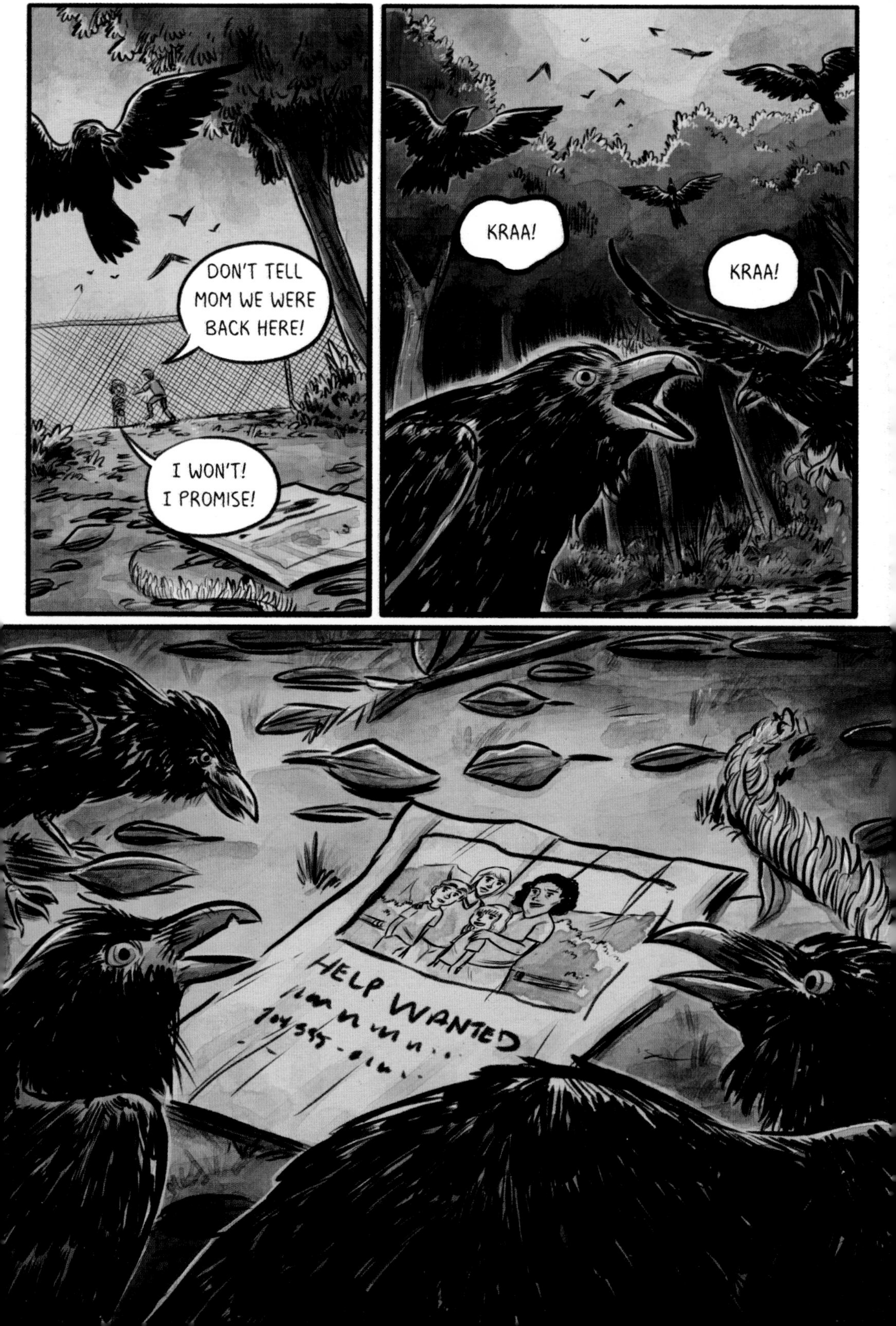
DON'T TELL MOM WE WERE BACK HERE!
I WON'T! I PROMISE!
KRAA!
KRAA!
HELP WANTED

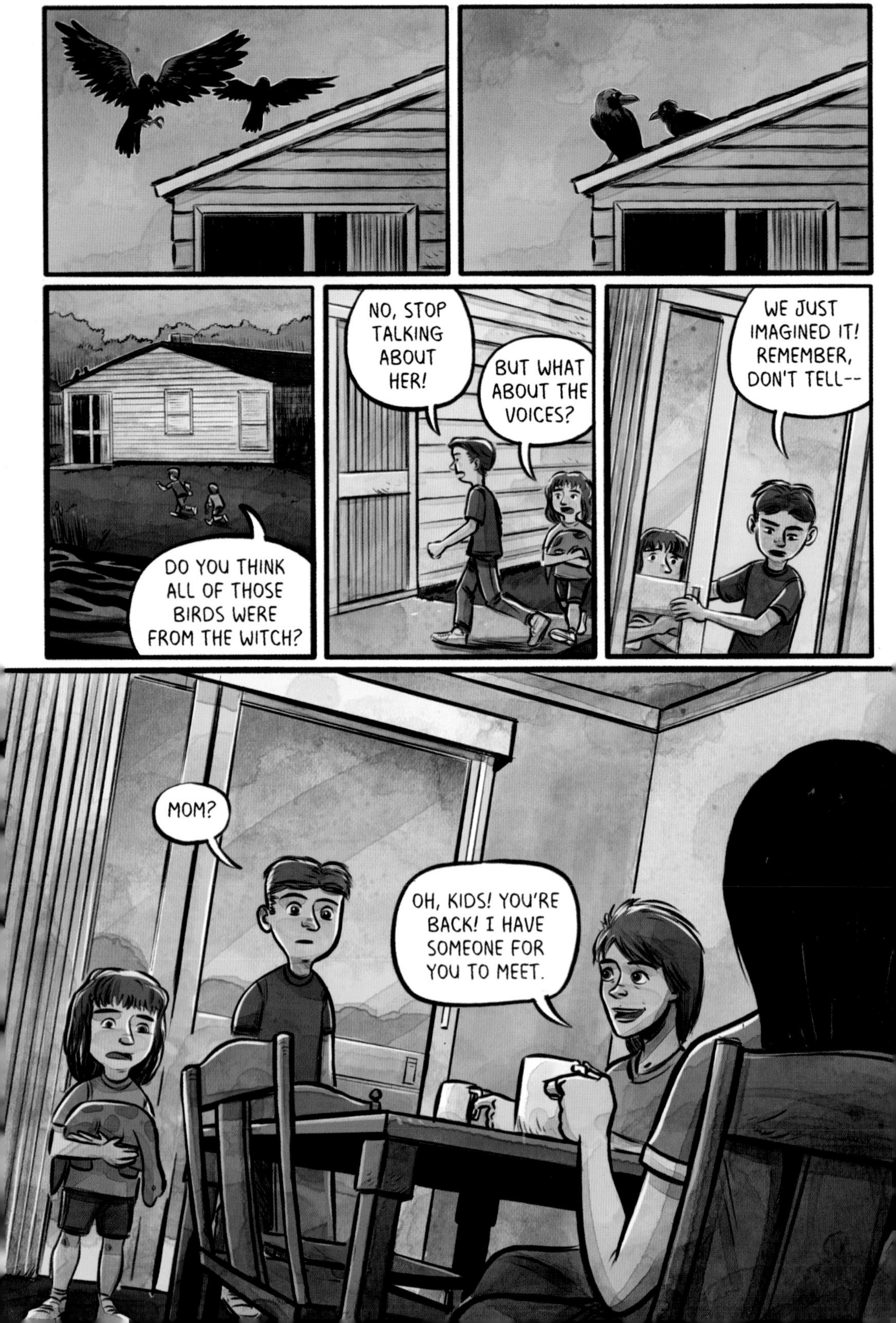
DO YOU THINK ALL OF THOSE BIRDS WERE FROM THE WITCH?
NO, STOP TALKING ABOUT HER!
BUT WHAT ABOUT THE VOICES?
WE JUST IMAGINED IT! REMEMBER, DON'T TELL--
MOM?
OH, KIDS! YOU'RE BACK! I HAVE SOMEONE FOR YOU TO MEET.

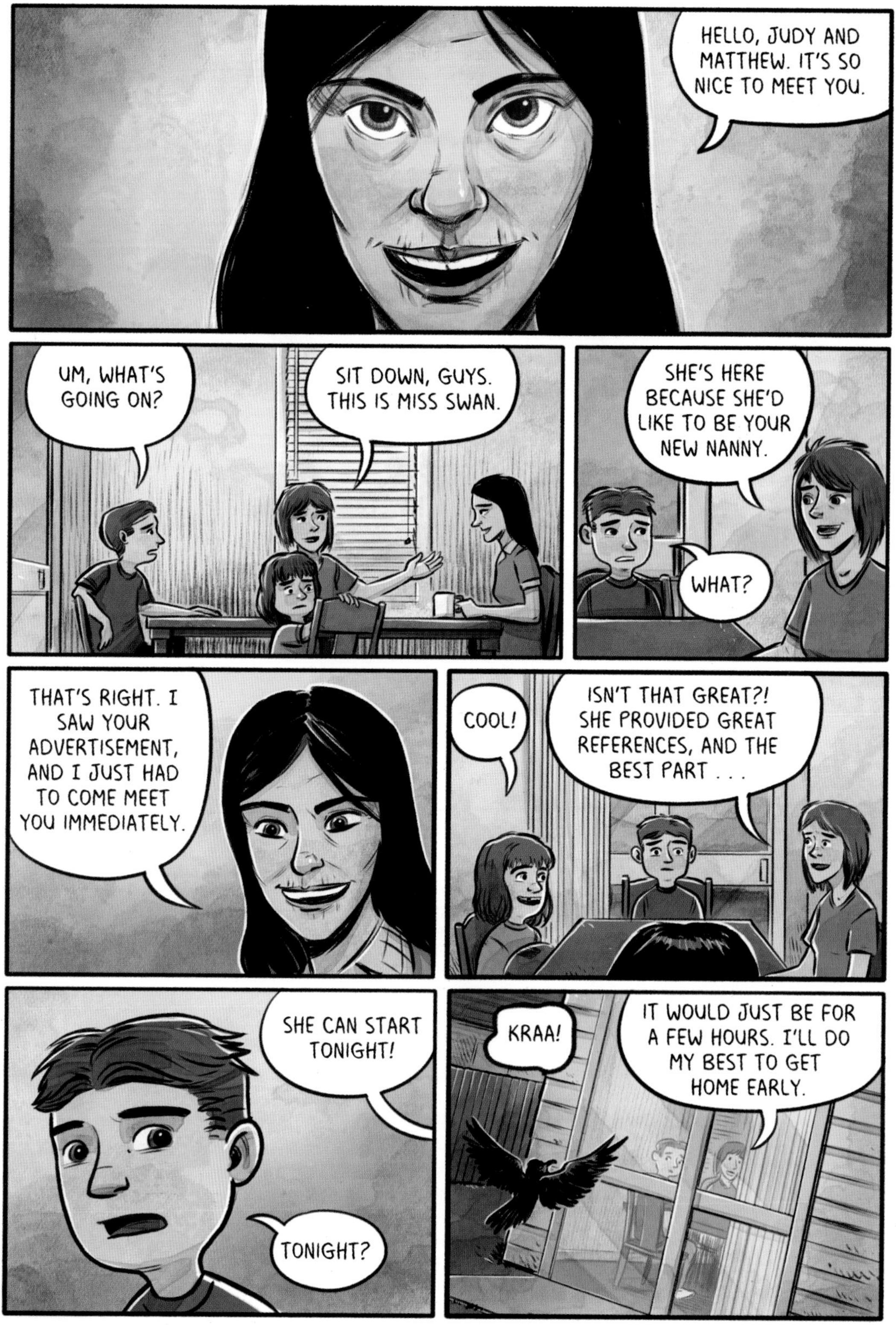
HELLO, JUDY AND MATTHEW. IT'S SO NICE TO MEET YOU.
UM, WHAT'S GOING ON?
SIT DOWN, GUYS. THIS IS MISS SWAN.
SHE'S HERE BECAUSE SHE'D LIKE TO BE YOUR NEW NANNY.
WHAT?
THAT'S RIGHT. I SAW YOUR ADVERTISEMENT, AND I JUST HAD TO COME MEET YOU IMMEDIATELY.
COOL!
ISN'T THAT GREAT?! SHE PROVIDED GREAT REFERENCES, AND THE BEST PART . . .
SHE CAN START TONIGHT!
TONIGHT?
KRAA!
IT WOULD JUST BE FOR A FEW HOURS. I'LL DO MY BEST TO GET HOME EARLY.

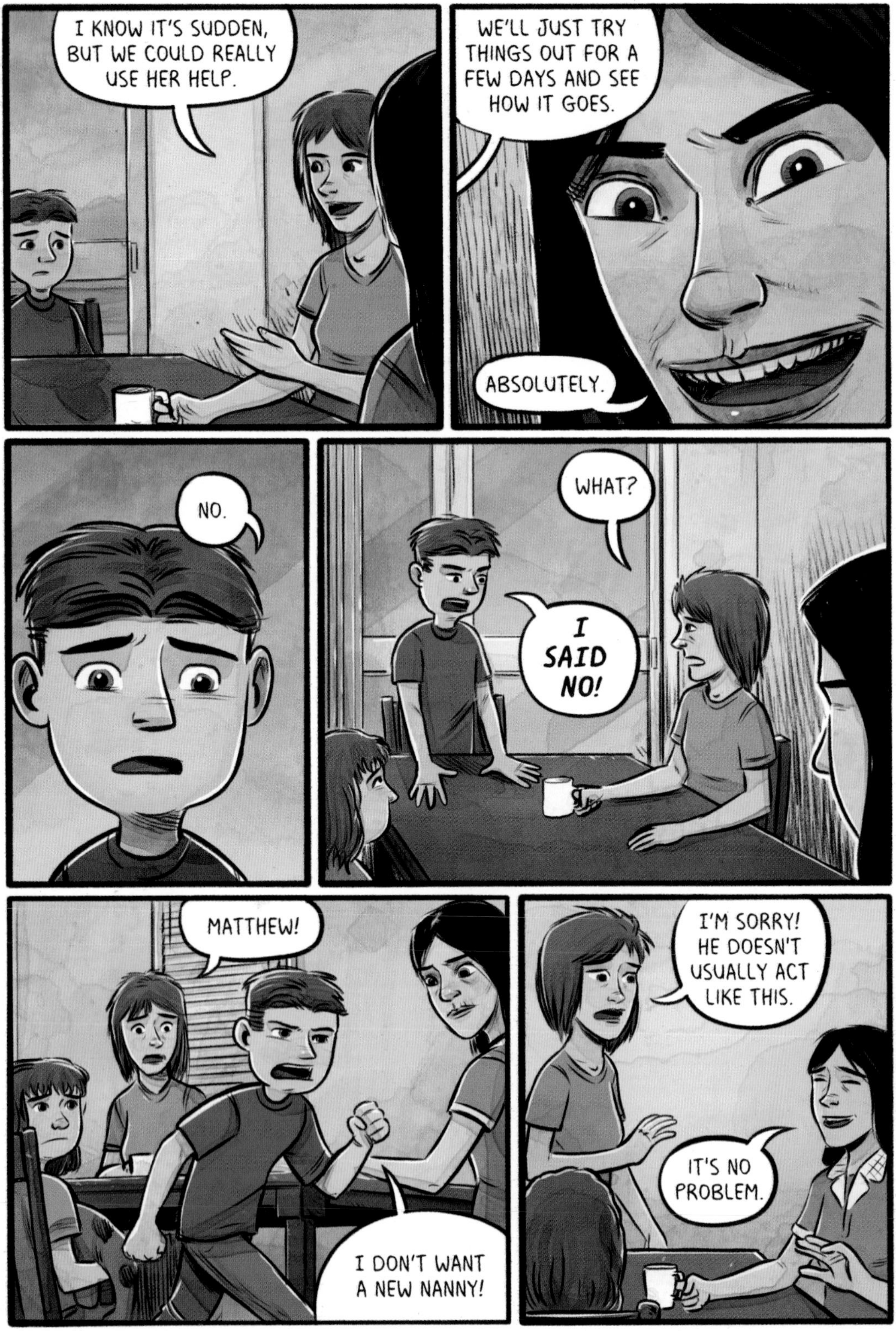
I KNOW IT'S SUDDEN, BUT WE COULD REALLY USE HER HELP.
WE'LL JUST TRY THINGS OUT FOR A FEW DAYS AND SEE HOW IT GOES.
ABSOLUTELY.
NO.
WHAT?
I SAID NO!
MATTHEW!
I DON'T WANT A NEW NANNY!
I'M SORRY! HE DOESN'T USUALLY ACT LIKE THIS.
IT'S NO PROBLEM.

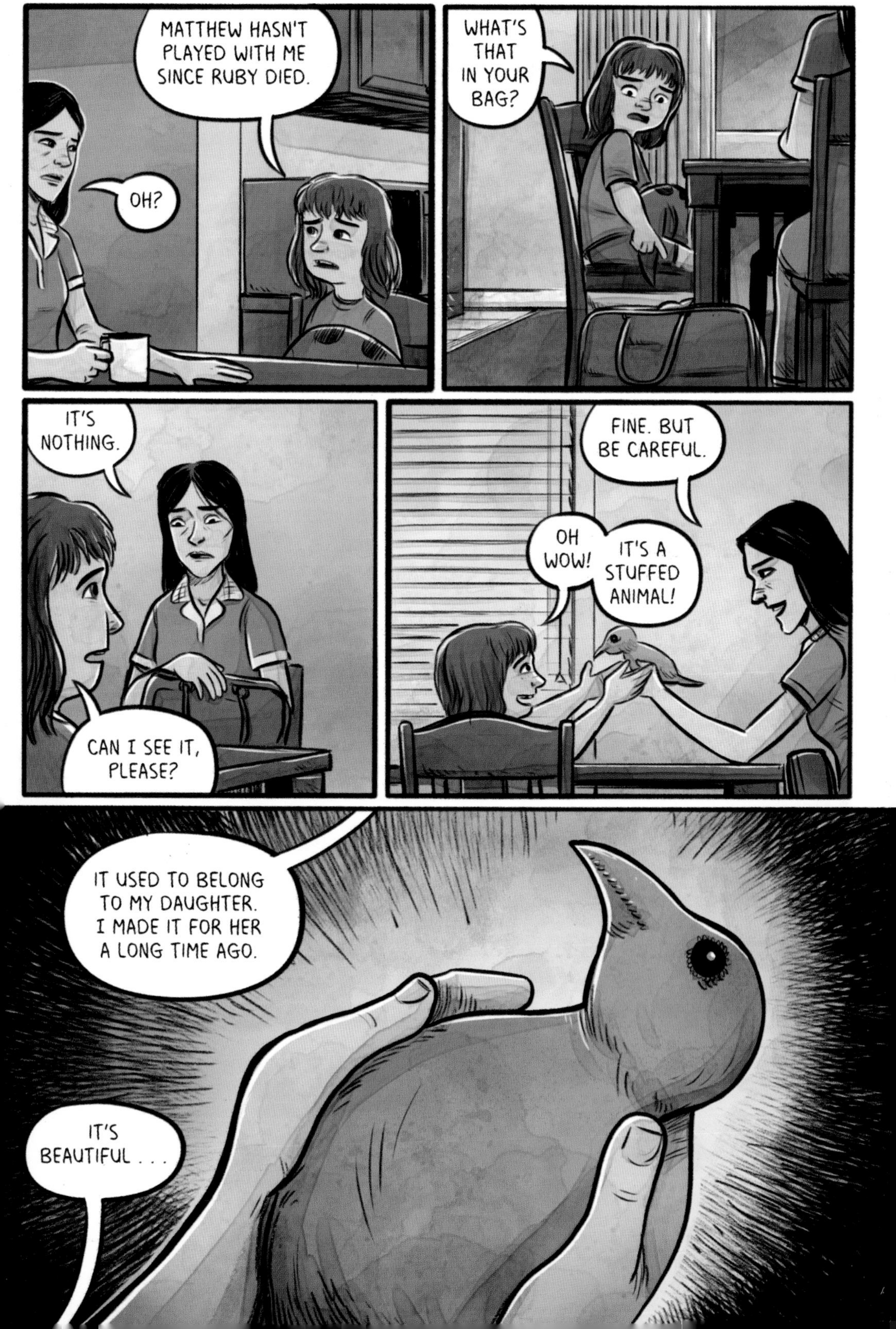
MATTHEW HASN'T PLAYED WITH ME SINCE RUBY DIED.
OH?
WHAT'S THAT IN YOUR BAG?
IT'S NOTHING.
CAN I SEE IT, PLEASE?
FINE. BUT BE CAREFUL.
OH WOW!
IT'S A STUFFED ANIMAL!
IT USED TO BELONG TO MY DAUGHTER. I MADE IT FOR HER A LONG TIME AGO.
IT'S BEAUTIFUL . . .

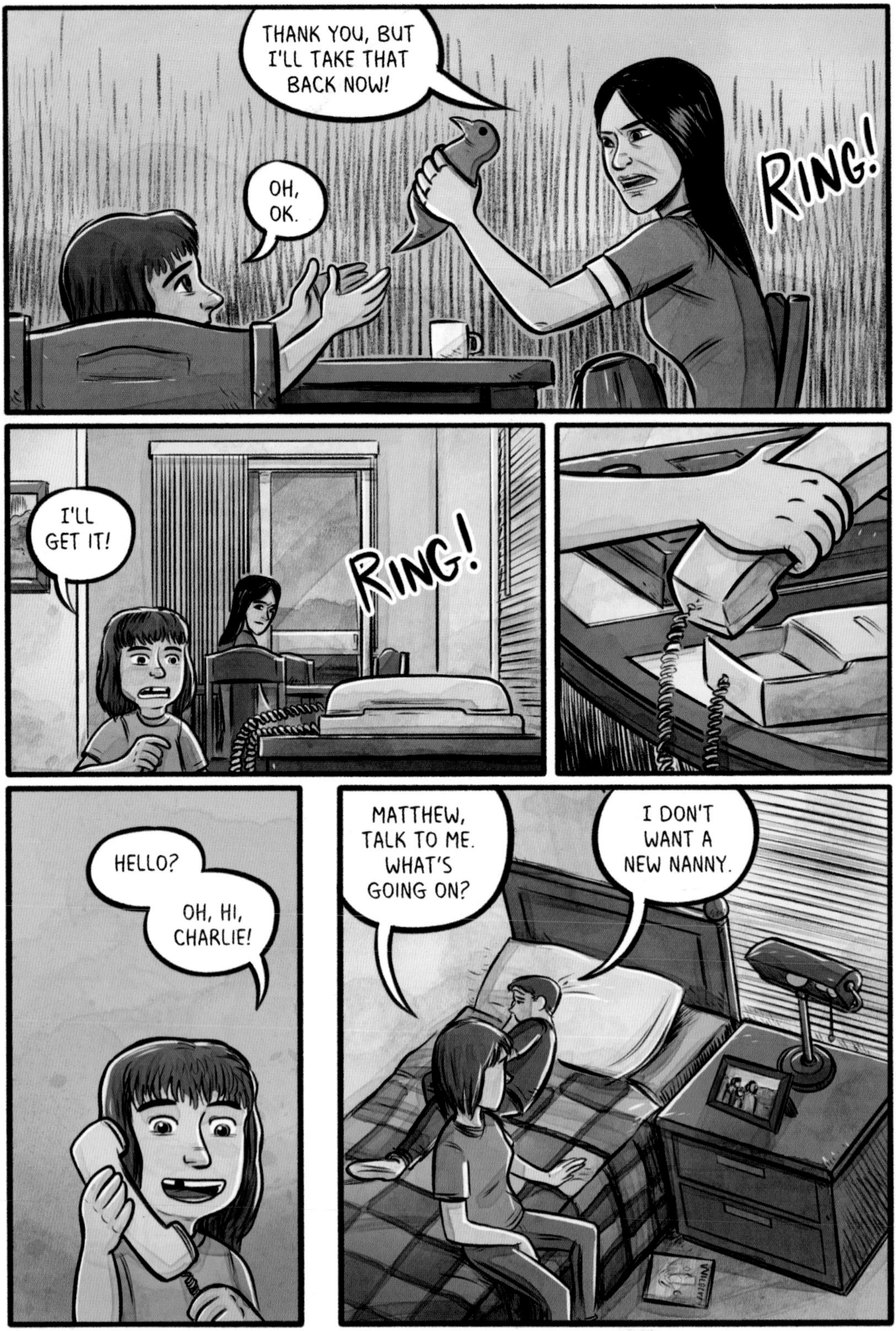
THANK YOU, BUT I'LL TAKE THAT BACK NOW!
OH, OK.
RING!
I'LL GET IT!
RING!
HELLO?
OH, HI, CHARLIE!
MATTHEW, TALK TO ME. WHAT'S GOING ON?
I DON'T WANT A NEW NANNY.

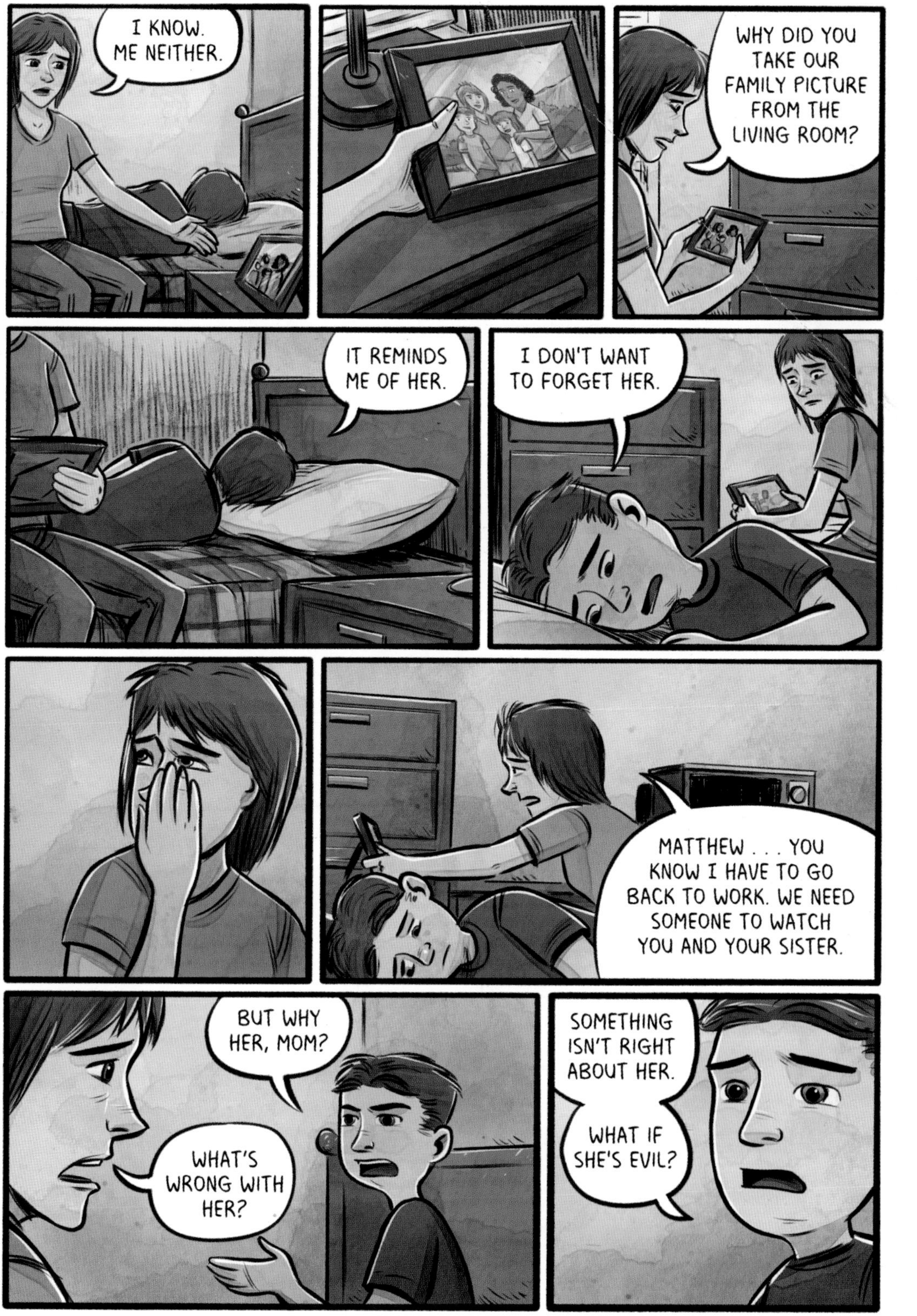
I KNOW. ME NEITHER.
WHY DID YOU TAKE OUR FAMILY PICTURE FROM THE LIVING ROOM?
IT REMINDS ME OF HER.
I DON'T WANT TO FORGET HER.
MATTHEW . . . YOU KNOW I HAVE TO GO BACK TO WORK. WE NEED SOMEONE TO WATCH YOU AND YOUR SISTER.
BUT WHY HER, MOM?
WHAT'S WRONG WITH HER?
SOMETHING ISN'T RIGHT ABOUT HER.
WHAT IF SHE'S EVIL?

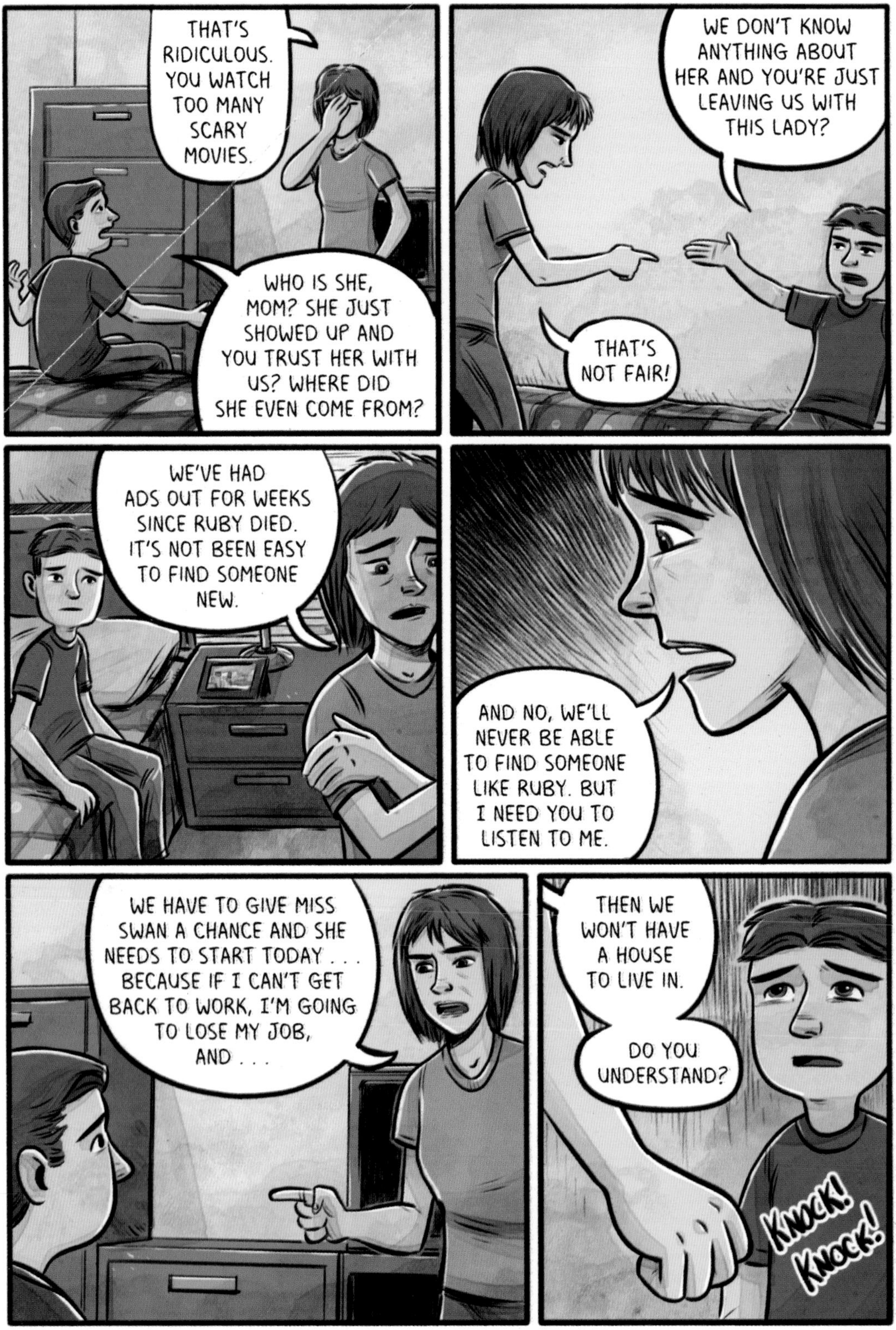
THAT'S RIDICULOUS. YOU WATCH TOO MANY SCARY MOVIES.
WHO IS SHE, MOM? SHE JUST SHOWED UP AND YOU TRUST HER WITH US? WHERE DID SHE EVEN COME FROM?
WE DON'T KNOW ANYTHING ABOUT HER AND YOU'RE JUST LEAVING US WITH THIS LADY?
THAT'S NOT FAIR!
WE'VE HAD ADS OUT FOR WEEKS SINCE RUBY DIED. IT'S NOT BEEN EASY TO FIND SOMEONE NEW.
AND NO, WE'LL NEVER BE ABLE TO FIND SOMEONE LIKE RUBY. BUT I NEED YOU TO LISTEN TO ME.
WE HAVE TO GIVE MISS SWAN A CHANCE AND SHE NEEDS TO START TODAY . . . BECAUSE IF I CAN'T GET BACK TO WORK, I'M GOING TO LOSE MY JOB, AND . . .
THEN WE WON'T HAVE A HOUSE TO LIVE IN.
DO YOU UNDERSTAND?
KNOCK! KNOCK!

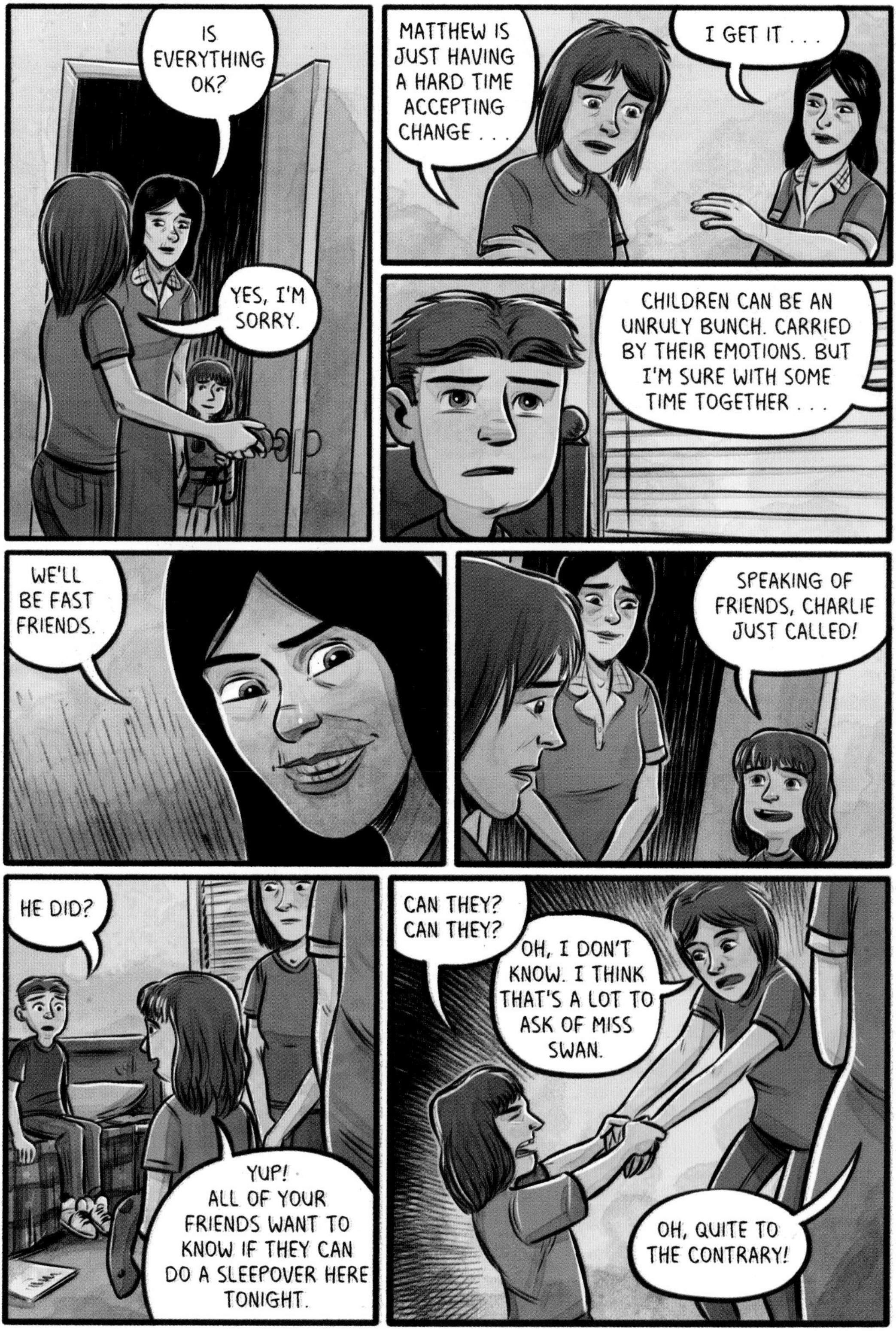
IS EVERYTHING OK?
YES, I'M SORRY.
MATTHEW IS JUST HAVING A HARD TIME ACCEPTING CHANGE . . .
I GET IT . . .
CHILDREN CAN BE AN UNRULY BUNCH. CARRIED BY THEIR EMOTIONS. BUT I'M SURE WITH SOME TIME TOGETHER . . .
WE'LL BE FAST FRIENDS.
SPEAKING OF FRIENDS, CHARLIE JUST CALLED!
HE DID?
YUP! ALL OF YOUR FRIENDS WANT TO KNOW IF THEY CAN DO A SLEEPOVER HERE TONIGHT.
CAN THEY? CAN THEY?
OH, I DON'T KNOW. I THINK THAT'S A LOT TO ASK OF MISS SWAN.
OH, QUITE TO THE CONTRARY!

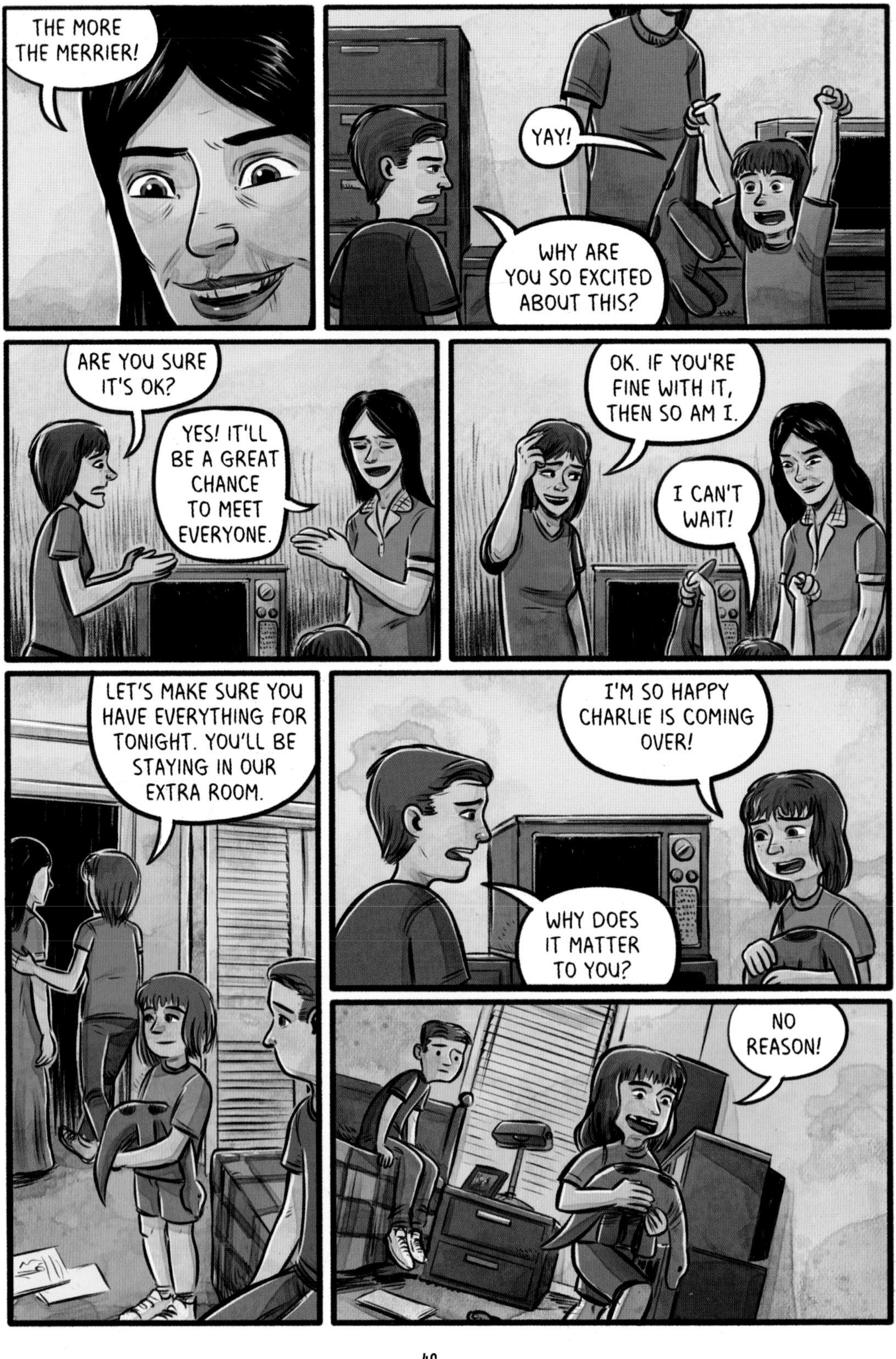
THE MORE THE MERRIER!
YAY!
WHY ARE YOU SO EXCITED ABOUT THIS?
ARE YOU SURE IT'S OK?
YES! IT'LL BE A GREAT CHANCE TO MEET EVERYONE.
OK. IF YOU'RE FINE WITH IT, THEN SO AM I.
I CAN'T WAIT!
LET'S MAKE SURE YOU HAVE EVERYTHING FOR TONIGHT. YOU'LL BE STAYING IN OUR EXTRA ROOM.
I'M SO HAPPY CHARLIE IS COMING OVER!
WHY DOES IT MATTER TO YOU?
NO REASON!

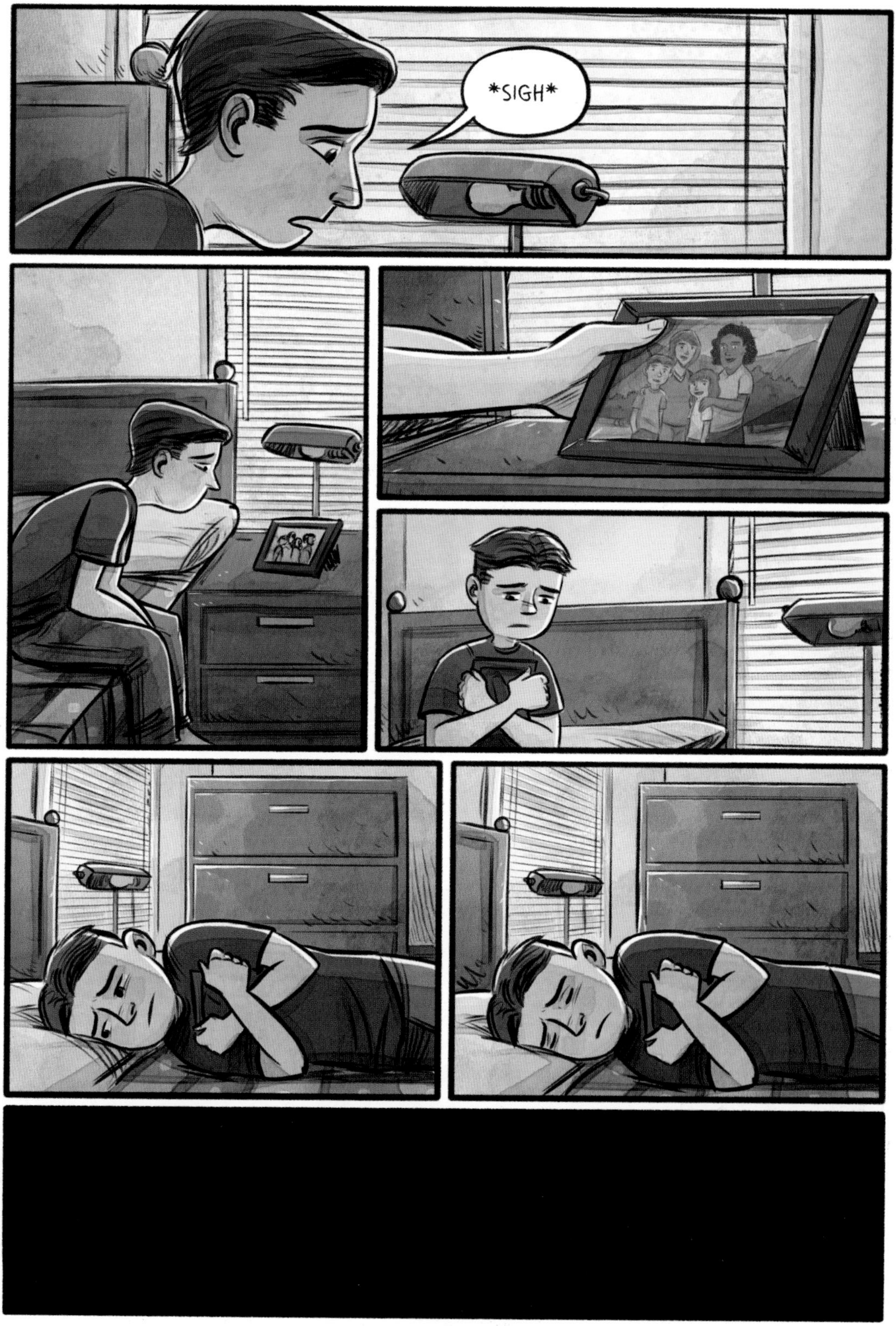
SIGH

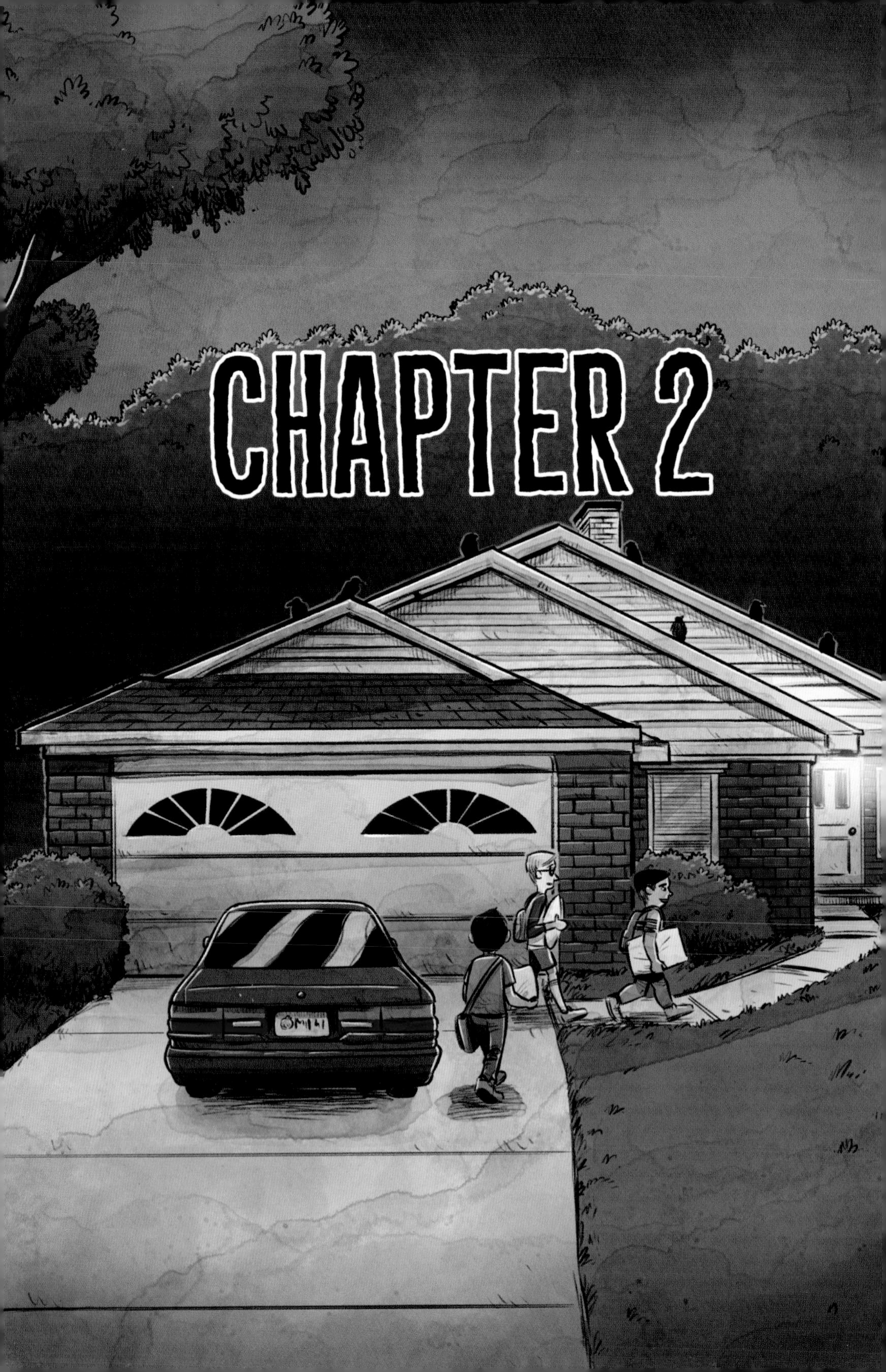
CHAPTER 2

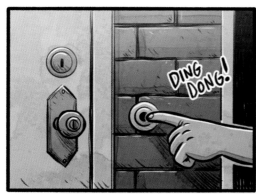

DING DONG!

HELLO, THERE . . .

H-HI. WHO ARE YOU?

CREAK

I'M THE NEW NANNY. YOU CAN CALL ME MISS SWAN.

AND YOU ALL MUST BE MATTHEW'S FRIENDS! PLEASE COME INSIDE.

UM . . .

WEL CO

I'M NOT SUPPOSED TO BE WITH STRANGERS. I'M NOT SURE IF I CAN STAY.

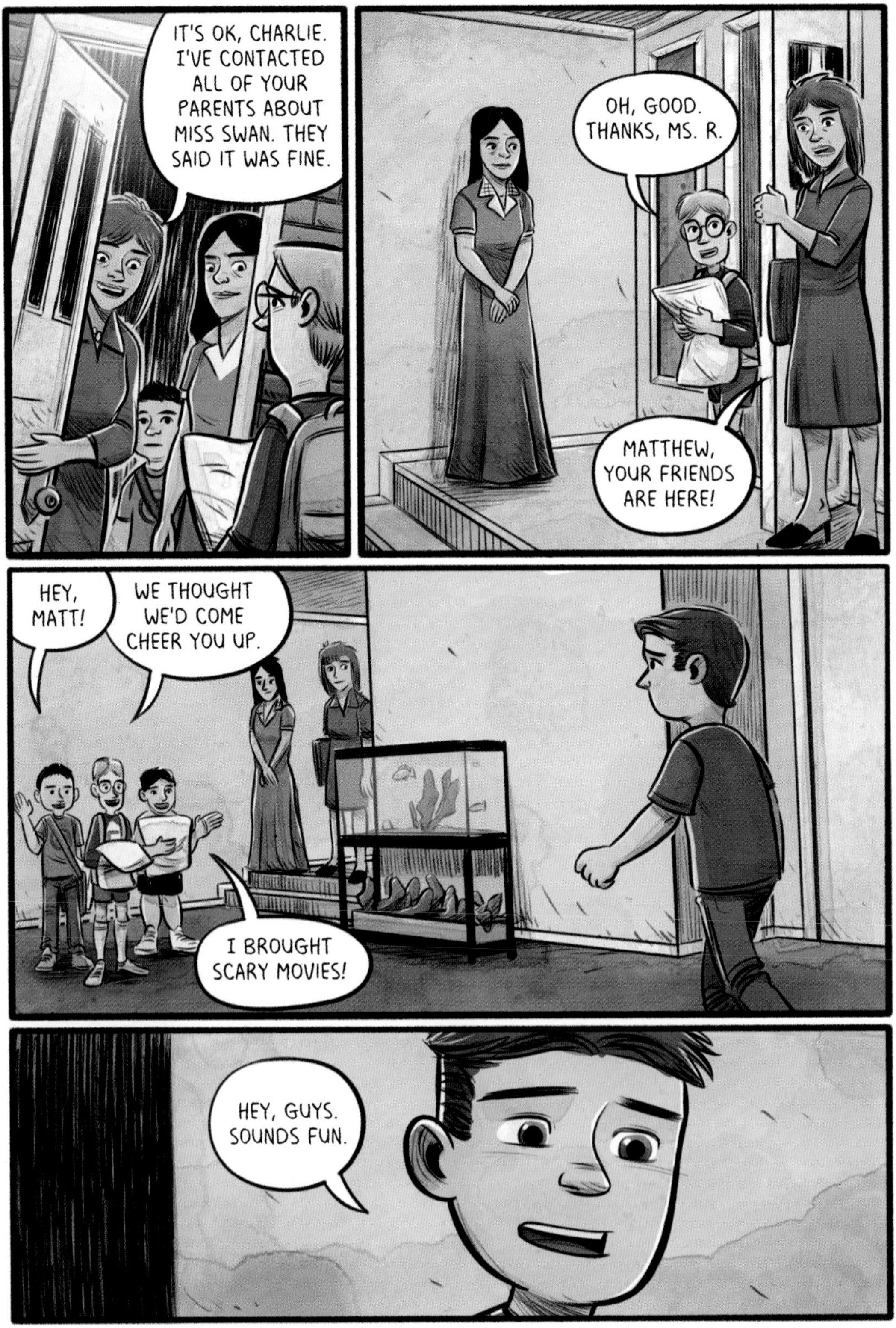
IT'S OK, CHARLIE. I'VE CONTACTED ALL OF YOUR PARENTS ABOUT MISS SWAN. THEY SAID IT WAS FINE.
OH, GOOD. THANKS, MS. R.
MATTHEW, YOUR FRIENDS ARE HERE!
HEY, MATT!
WE THOUGHT WE'D COME CHEER YOU UP.
I BROUGHT SCARY MOVIES!
HEY, GUYS. SOUNDS FUN.

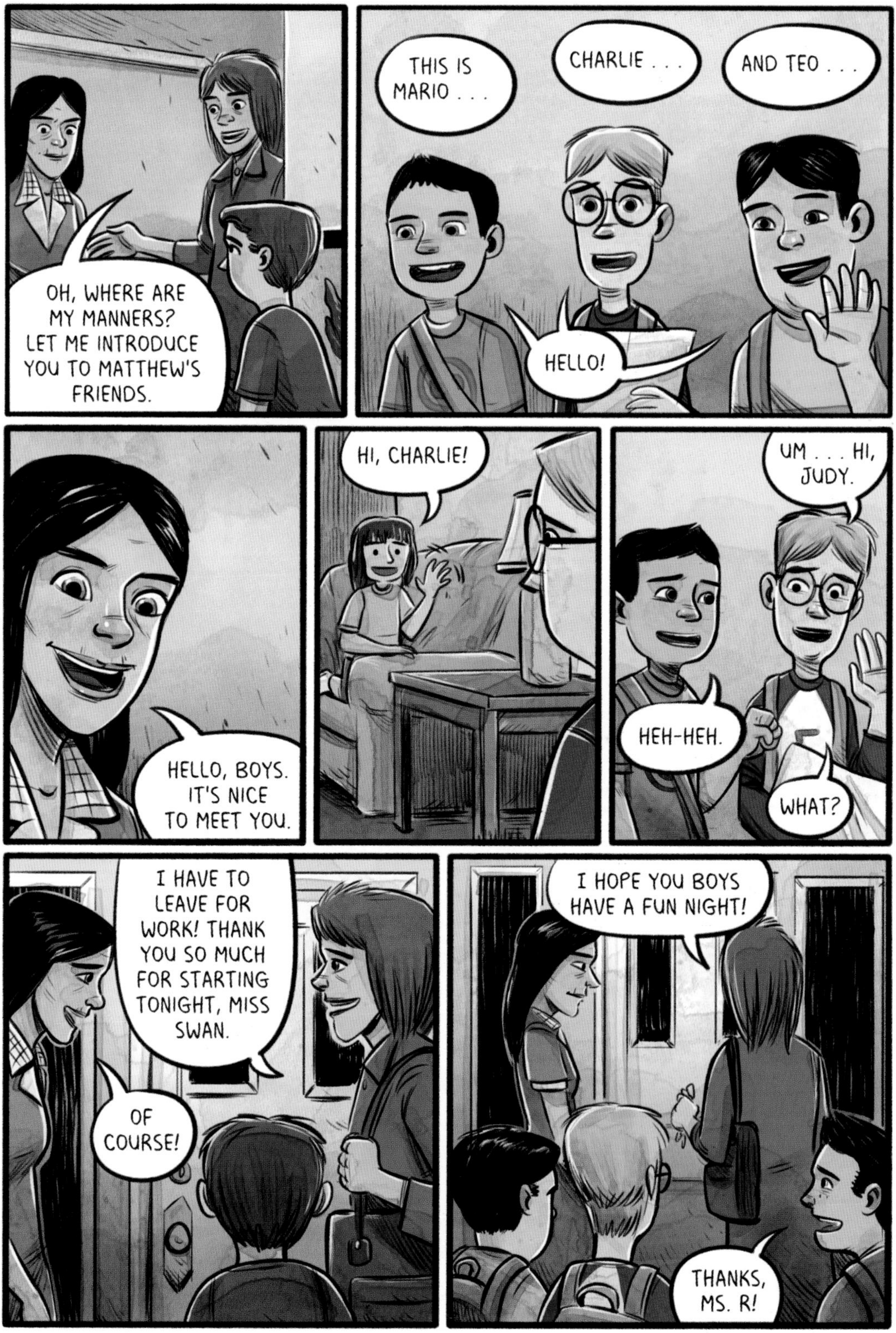
OH, WHERE ARE MY MANNERS? LET ME INTRODUCE YOU TO MATTHEW'S FRIENDS.
THIS IS MARIO . . .
CHARLIE . . .
AND TEO . . .
HELLO!
HELLO, BOYS. IT'S NICE TO MEET YOU.
HI, CHARLIE!
UM . . . HI, JUDY.
HEH-HEH.
WHAT?
I HAVE TO LEAVE FOR WORK! THANK YOU SO MUCH FOR STARTING TONIGHT, MISS SWAN.
OF COURSE!
I HOPE YOU BOYS HAVE A FUN NIGHT!
THANKS, MS. R!

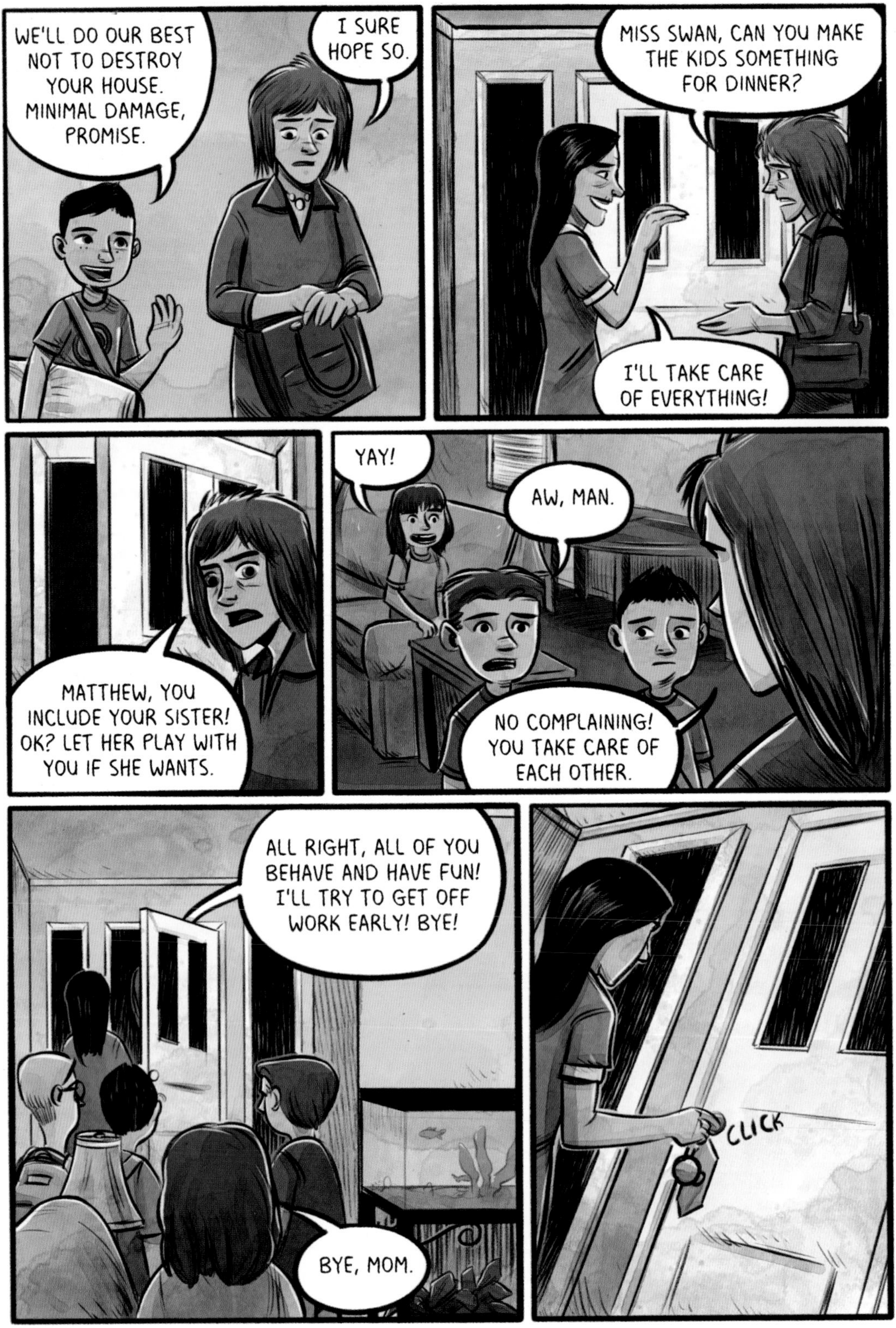
WE'LL DO OUR BEST NOT TO DESTROY YOUR HOUSE. MINIMAL DAMAGE, PROMISE.
I SURE HOPE SO.
MISS SWAN, CAN YOU MAKE THE KIDS SOMETHING FOR DINNER?
I'LL TAKE CARE OF EVERYTHING!
MATTHEW, YOU INCLUDE YOUR SISTER! OK? LET HER PLAY WITH YOU IF SHE WANTS.
YAY!
AW, MAN.
NO COMPLAINING! YOU TAKE CARE OF EACH OTHER.
ALL RIGHT, ALL OF YOU BEHAVE AND HAVE FUN! I'LL TRY TO GET OFF WORK EARLY! BYE!
BYE, MOM.
CLICK

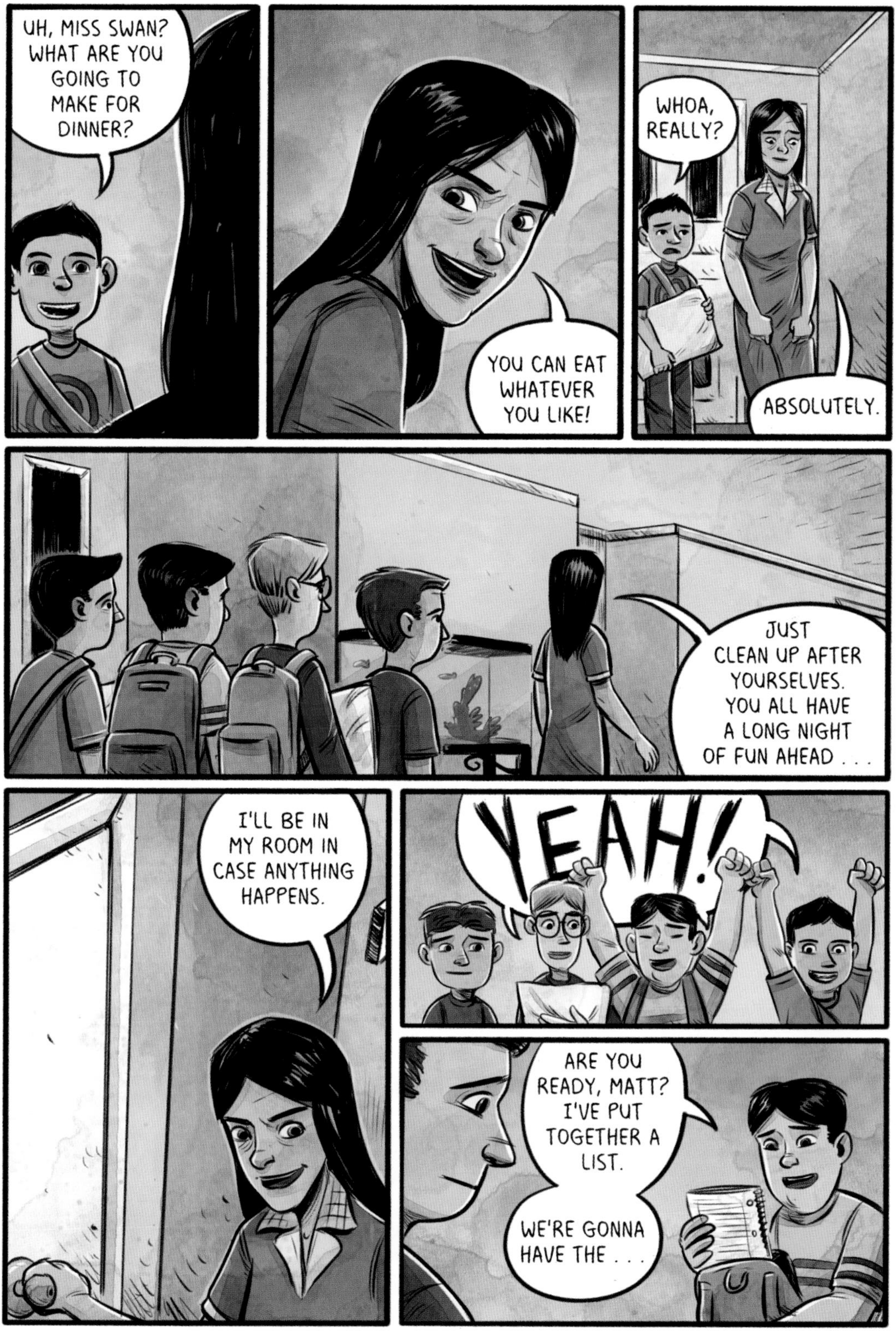
UH, MISS SWAN? WHAT ARE YOU GOING TO MAKE FOR DINNER?
YOU CAN EAT WHATEVER YOU LIKE!
WHOA, REALLY?
ABSOLUTELY.
JUST CLEAN UP AFTER YOURSELVES. YOU ALL HAVE A LONG NIGHT OF FUN AHEAD . . .
I'LL BE IN MY ROOM IN CASE ANYTHING HAPPENS.
YEAH!
ARE YOU READY, MATT? I'VE PUT TOGETHER A LIST.
WE'RE GONNA HAVE THE . . .

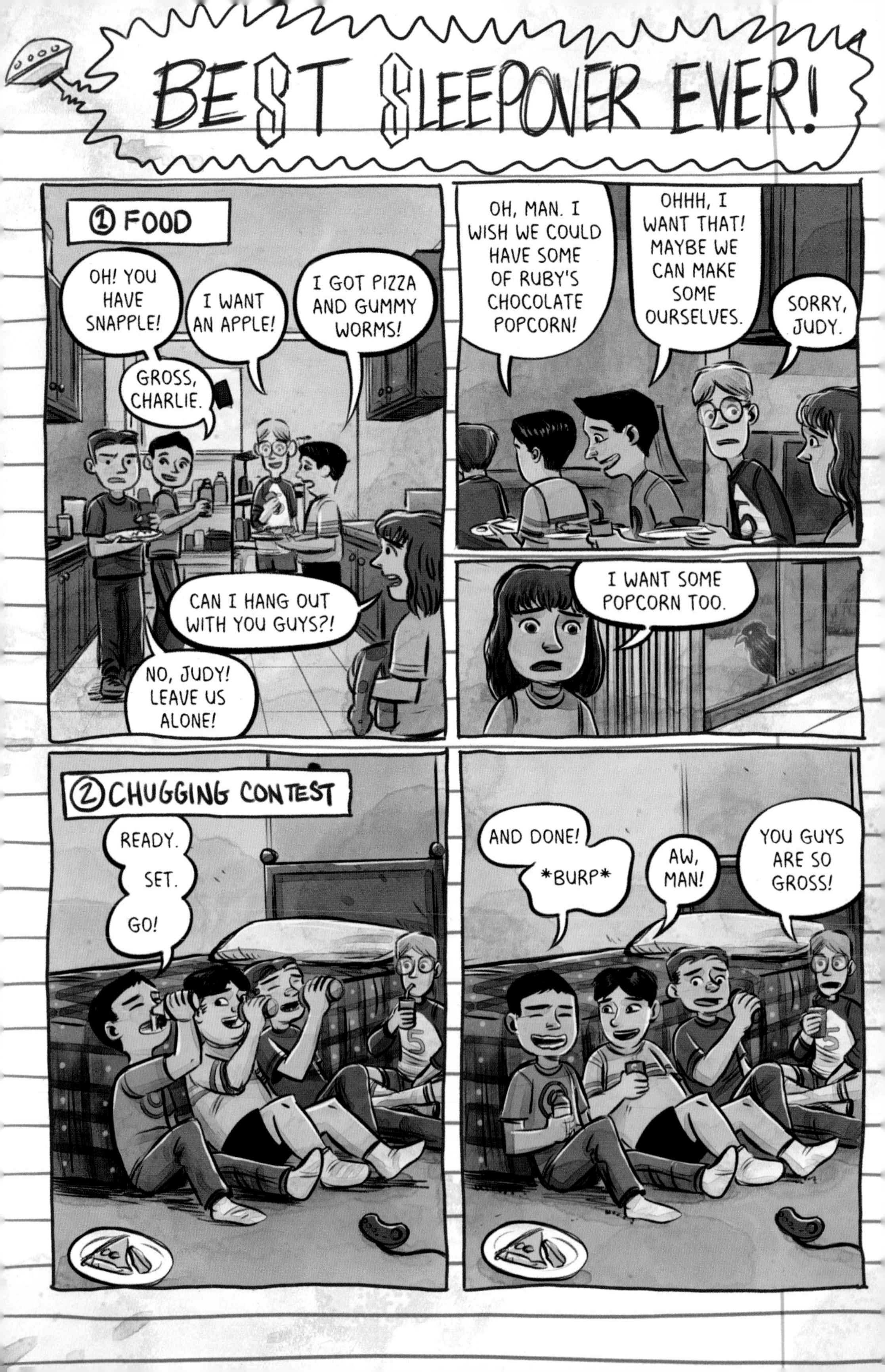
BEST SLEEPOVER EVER!
1 FOOD
OH! YOU HAVE SNAPPLE!
I WANT AN APPLE!
I GOT PIZZA AND GUMMY WORMS!
GROSS, CHARLIE.
CAN I HANG OUT WITH YOU GUYS?!
NO, JUDY! LEAVE US ALONE!
OH, MAN. I WISH WE COULD HAVE SOME OF RUBY'S CHOCOLATE POPCORN!
OHHH, I WANT THAT! MAYBE WE CAN MAKE SOME OURSELVES.
SORRY, JUDY.
I WANT SOME POPCORN TOO.
2 CHUGGING CONTEST
READY.
SET.
GO!
AND DONE!
BURP
AW, MAN!
YOU GUYS ARE SO GROSS!

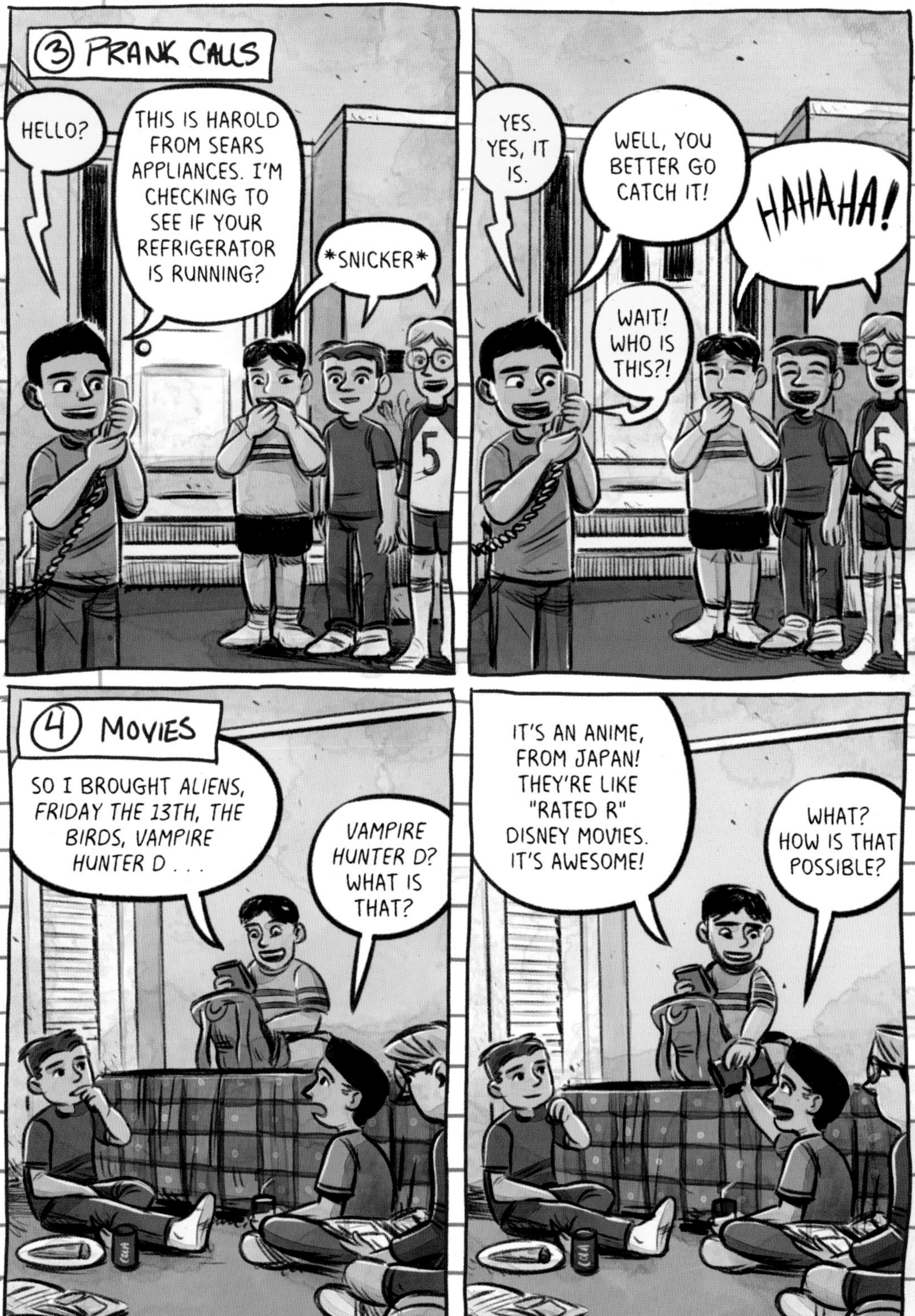
③ PRANK CALLS
HELLO?
THIS IS HAROLD FROM SEARS APPLIANCES. I'M CHECKING TO SEE IF YOUR REFRIGERATOR IS RUNNING?
SNICKER
YES. YES, IT IS.
WELL, YOU BETTER GO CATCH IT!
HAHAHA!
WAIT! WHO IS THIS?!
④ MOVIES
SO I BROUGHT ALIENS, FRIDAY THE 13TH, THE BIRDS, VAMPIRE HUNTER D . . .
VAMPIRE HUNTER D? WHAT IS THAT?
IT'S AN ANIME, FROM JAPAN! THEY'RE LIKE "RATED R" DISNEY MOVIES. IT'S AWESOME!
WHAT? HOW IS THAT POSSIBLE?

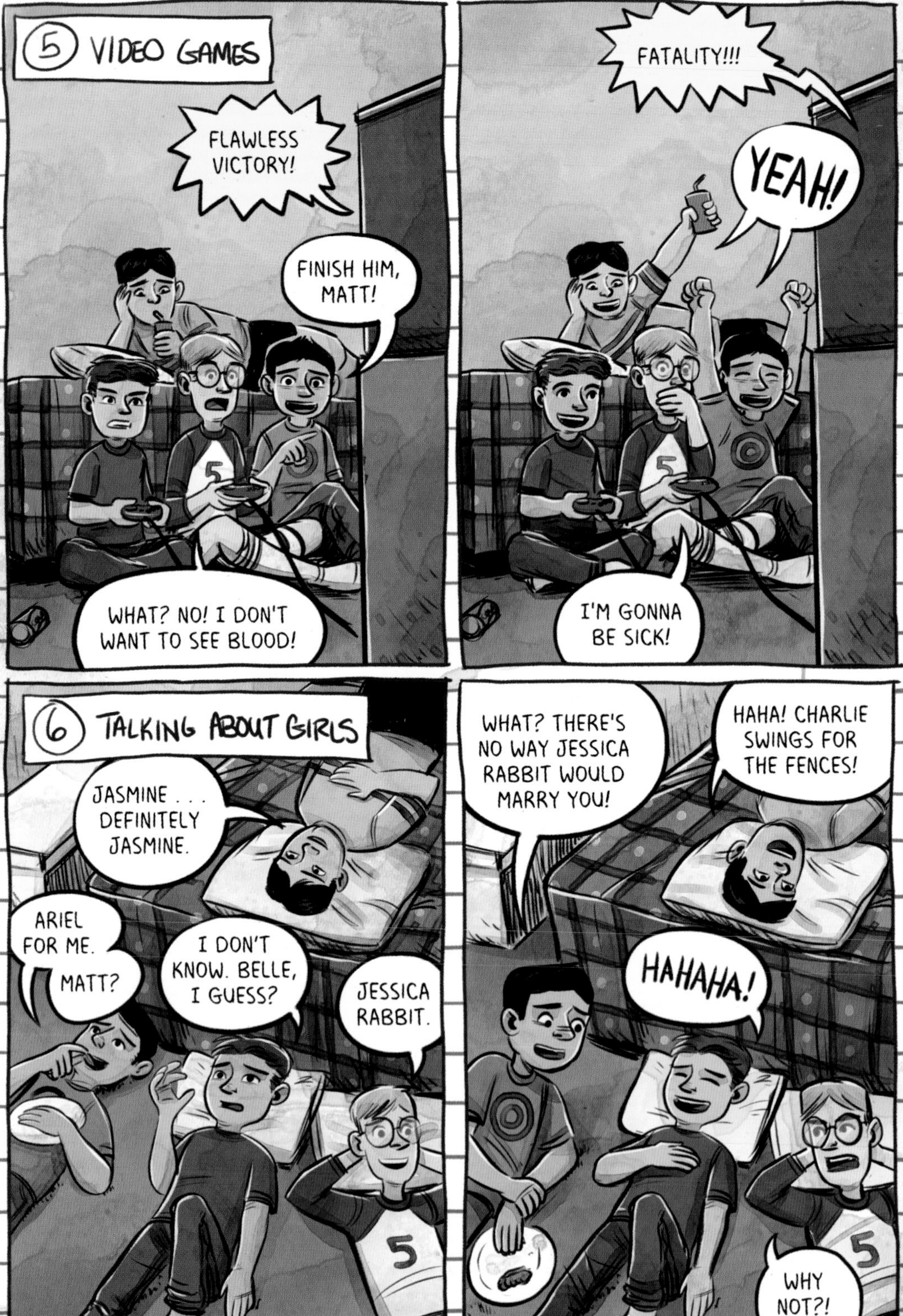
5 VIDEO GAMES
FLAWLESS VICTORY!
FINISH HIM, MATT!
WHAT? NO! I DON'T WANT TO SEE BLOOD!
FATALITY!!!
YEAH!
I'M GONNA BE SICK!
6 TALKING ABOUT GIRLS
JASMINE . . . DEFINITELY JASMINE.
ARIEL FOR ME.
MATT?
I DON'T KNOW. BELLE, I GUESS?
JESSICA RABBIT.
WHAT? THERE'S NO WAY JESSICA RABBIT WOULD MARRY YOU!
HAHA! CHARLIE SWINGS FOR THE FENCES!
HAHAHA!
WHY NOT?!

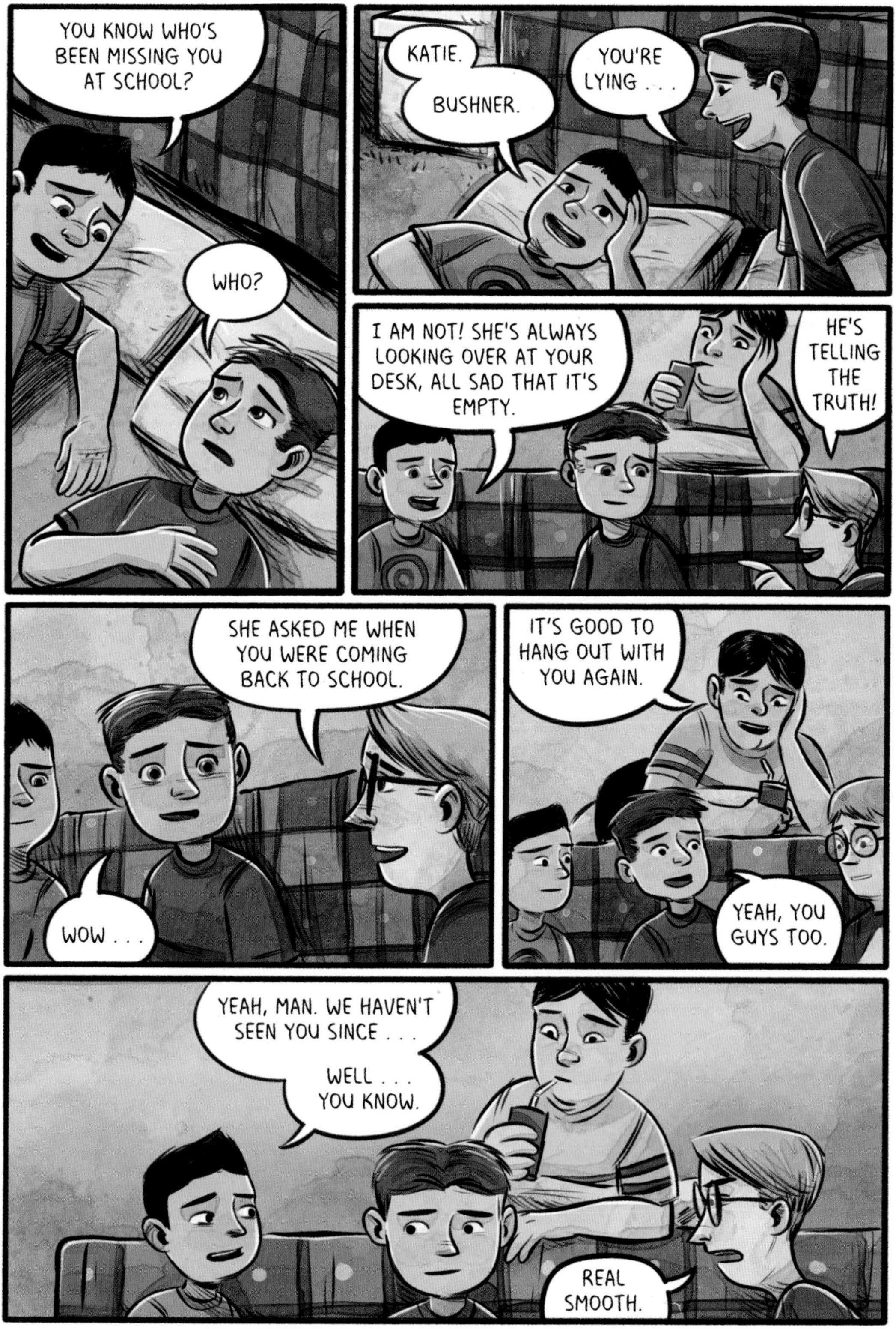
YOU KNOW WHO'S BEEN MISSING YOU AT SCHOOL?
WHO?
KATIE.
BUSHNER.
YOU'RE LYING . . .
I AM NOT! SHE'S ALWAYS LOOKING OVER AT YOUR DESK, ALL SAD THAT IT'S EMPTY.
HE'S TELLING THE TRUTH!
SHE ASKED ME WHEN YOU WERE COMING BACK TO SCHOOL.
WOW . . .
IT'S GOOD TO HANG OUT WITH YOU AGAIN.
YEAH, YOU GUYS TOO.
YEAH, MAN. WE HAVEN'T SEEN YOU SINCE . . .
WELL . . . YOU KNOW.
REAL SMOOTH.

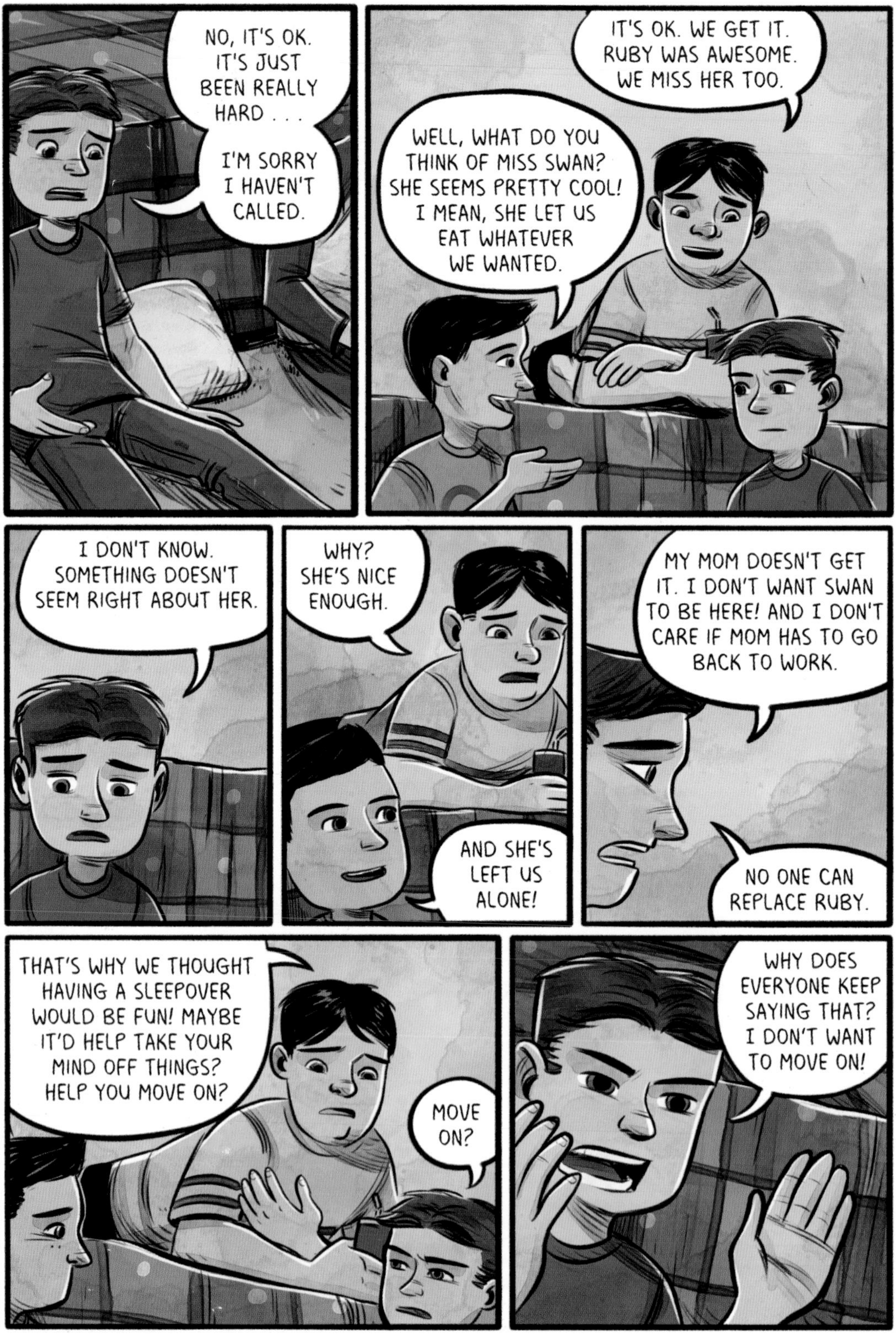
NO, IT'S OK. IT'S JUST BEEN REALLY HARD . . .
I'M SORRY I HAVEN'T CALLED.
IT'S OK. WE GET IT. RUBY WAS AWESOME. WE MISS HER TOO.
WELL, WHAT DO YOU THINK OF MISS SWAN? SHE SEEMS PRETTY COOL! I MEAN, SHE LET US EAT WHATEVER WE WANTED.
I DON'T KNOW. SOMETHING DOESN'T SEEM RIGHT ABOUT HER.
WHY? SHE'S NICE ENOUGH.
AND SHE'S LEFT US ALONE!
MY MOM DOESN'T GET IT. I DON'T WANT SWAN TO BE HERE! AND I DON'T CARE IF MOM HAS TO GO BACK TO WORK.
NO ONE CAN REPLACE RUBY.
THAT'S WHY WE THOUGHT HAVING A SLEEPOVER WOULD BE FUN! MAYBE IT'D HELP TAKE YOUR MIND OFF THINGS? HELP YOU MOVE ON?
MOVE ON?
WHY DOES EVERYONE KEEP SAYING THAT? I DON'T WANT TO MOVE ON!

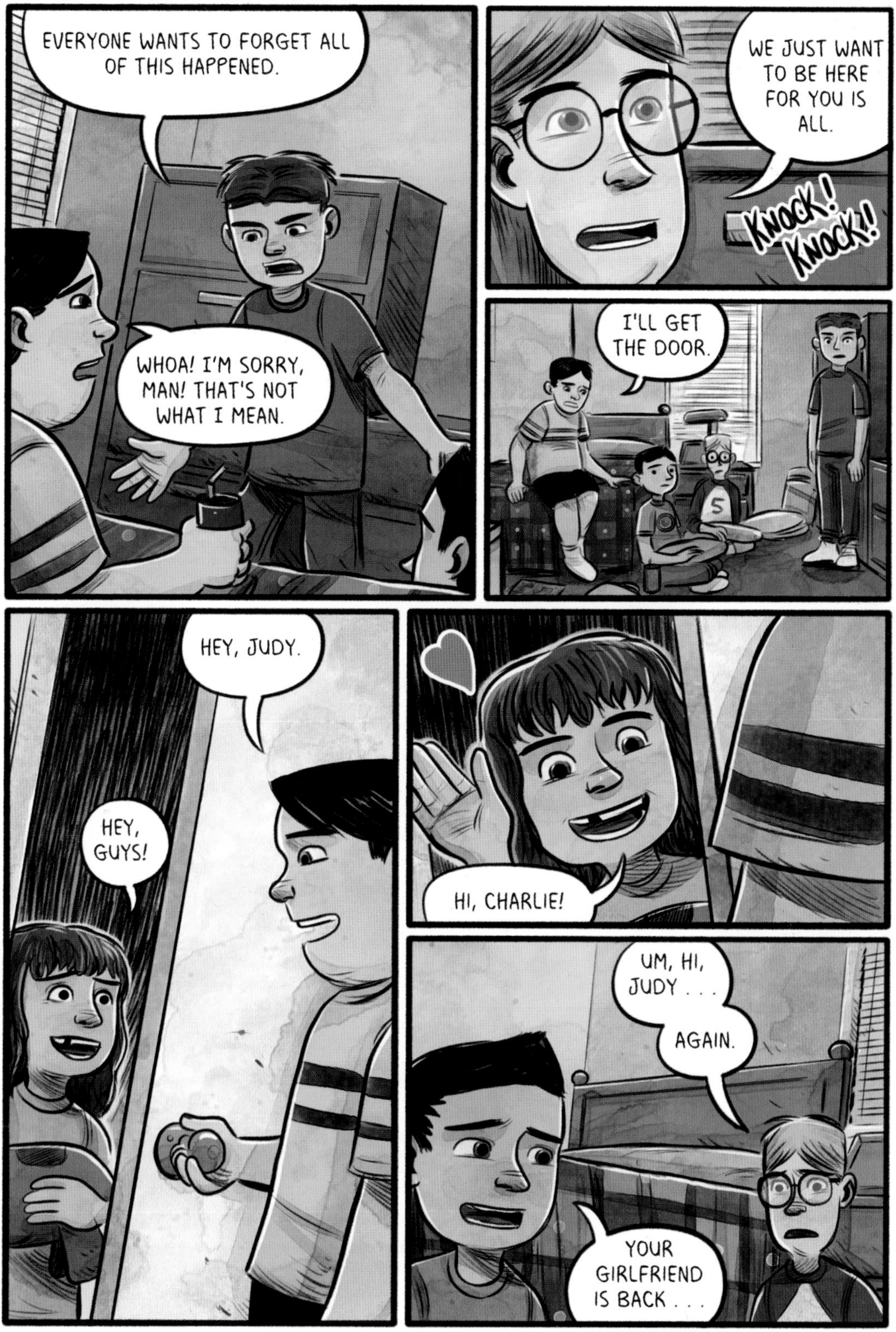
EVERYONE WANTS TO FORGET ALL OF THIS HAPPENED.
WHOA! I'M SORRY, MAN! THAT'S NOT WHAT I MEAN.
WE JUST WANT TO BE HERE FOR YOU IS ALL.
KNOCK! KNOCK!
I'LL GET THE DOOR.
HEY, JUDY.
HEY, GUYS!
HI, CHARLIE!
UM, HI, JUDY . . .
AGAIN.
YOUR GIRLFRIEND IS BACK . . .

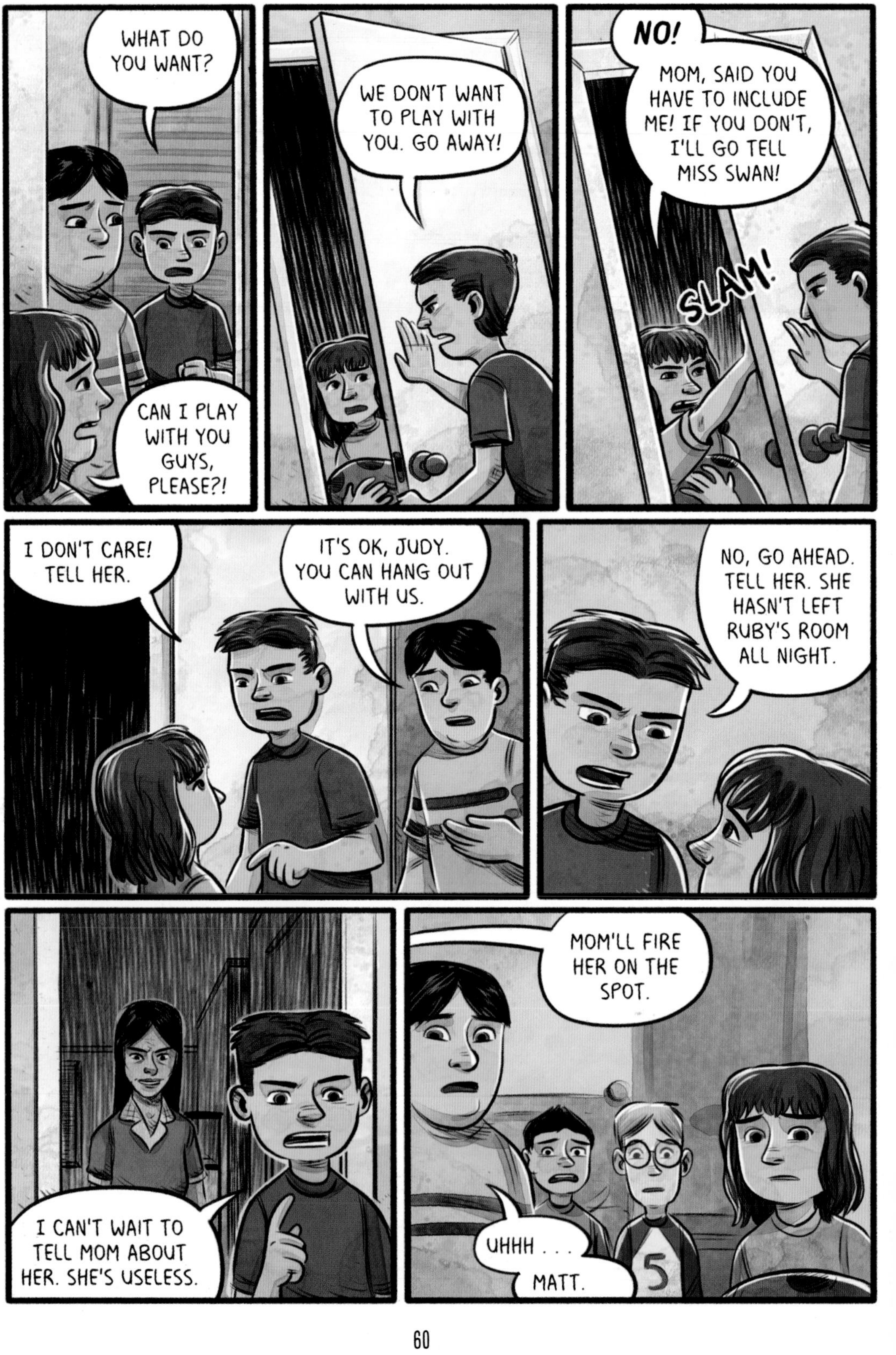
WHAT DO YOU WANT?
CAN I PLAY WITH YOU GUYS, PLEASE?!
WE DON'T WANT TO PLAY WITH YOU. GO AWAY!
NO!
MOM, SAID YOU HAVE TO INCLUDE ME! IF YOU DON'T, I'LL GO TELL MISS SWAN!
SLAM!
I DON'T CARE! TELL HER.
IT'S OK, JUDY. YOU CAN HANG OUT WITH US.
NO, GO AHEAD. TELL HER. SHE HASN'T LEFT RUBY'S ROOM ALL NIGHT.
I CAN'T WAIT TO TELL MOM ABOUT HER. SHE'S USELESS.
MOM'LL FIRE HER ON THE SPOT.
UHHH . . .
MATT.

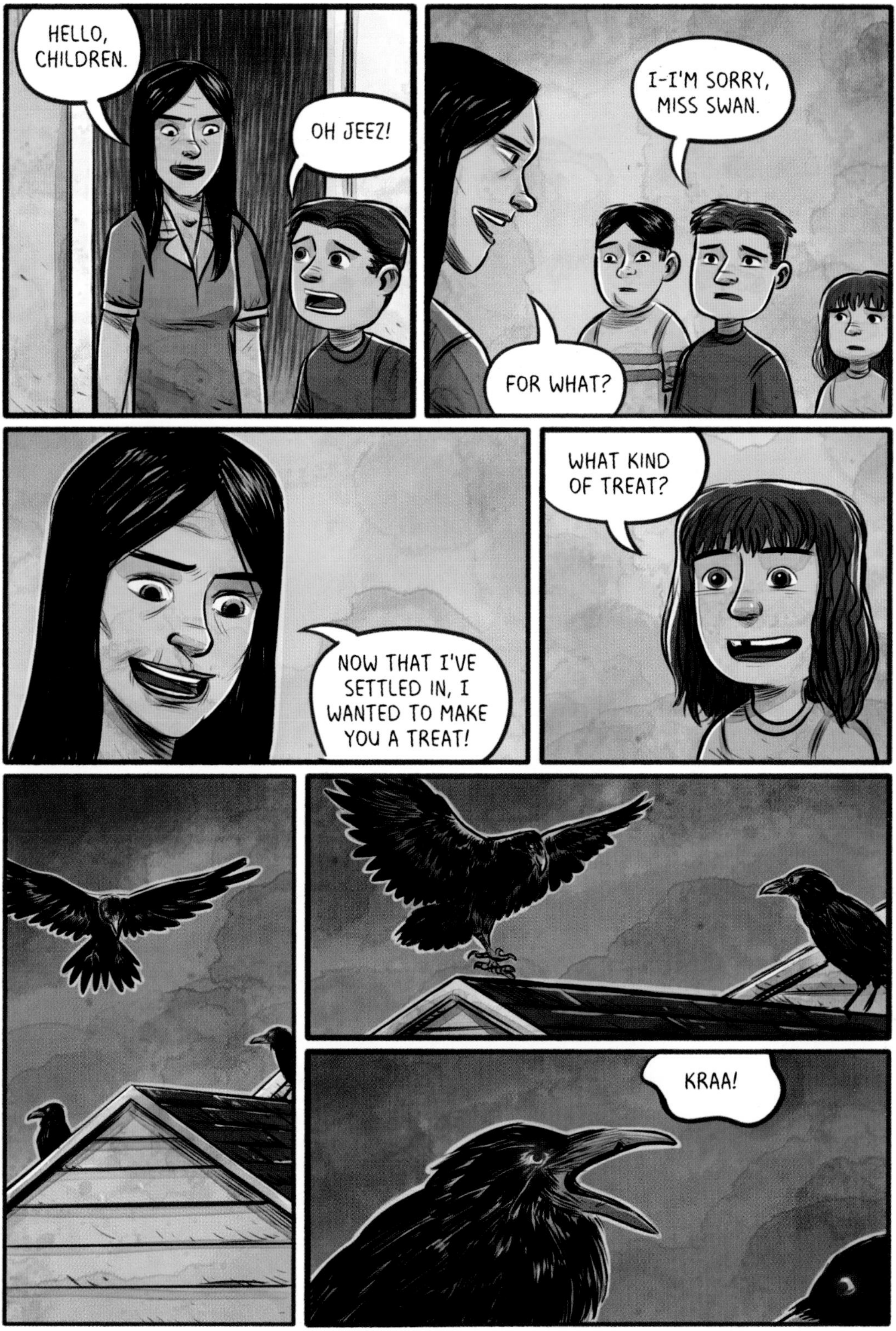
HELLO, CHILDREN.
OH JEEZ!
I-I'M SORRY, MISS SWAN.
FOR WHAT?
NOW THAT I'VE SETTLED IN, I WANTED TO MAKE YOU A TREAT!
WHAT KIND OF TREAT?
KRAA!

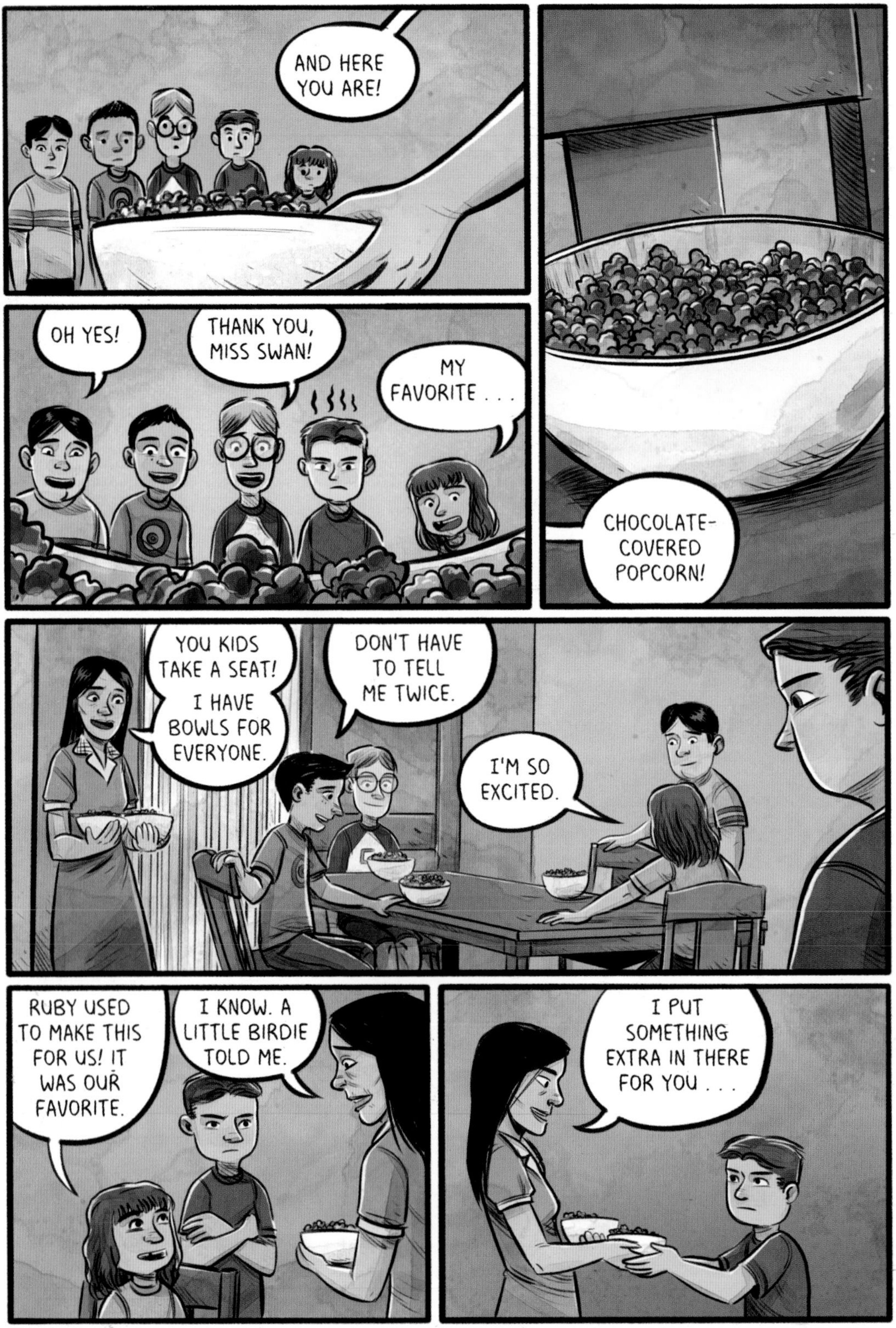
AND HERE YOU ARE!
OH YES!
THANK YOU, MISS SWAN!
MY FAVORITE . . .
CHOCOLATE-COVERED POPCORN!
YOU KIDS TAKE A SEAT!
I HAVE BOWLS FOR EVERYONE.
DON'T HAVE TO TELL ME TWICE.
I'M SO EXCITED.
RUBY USED TO MAKE THIS FOR US! IT WAS OUR FAVORITE.
I KNOW. A LITTLE BIRDIE TOLD ME.
I PUT SOMETHING EXTRA IN THERE FOR YOU . . .

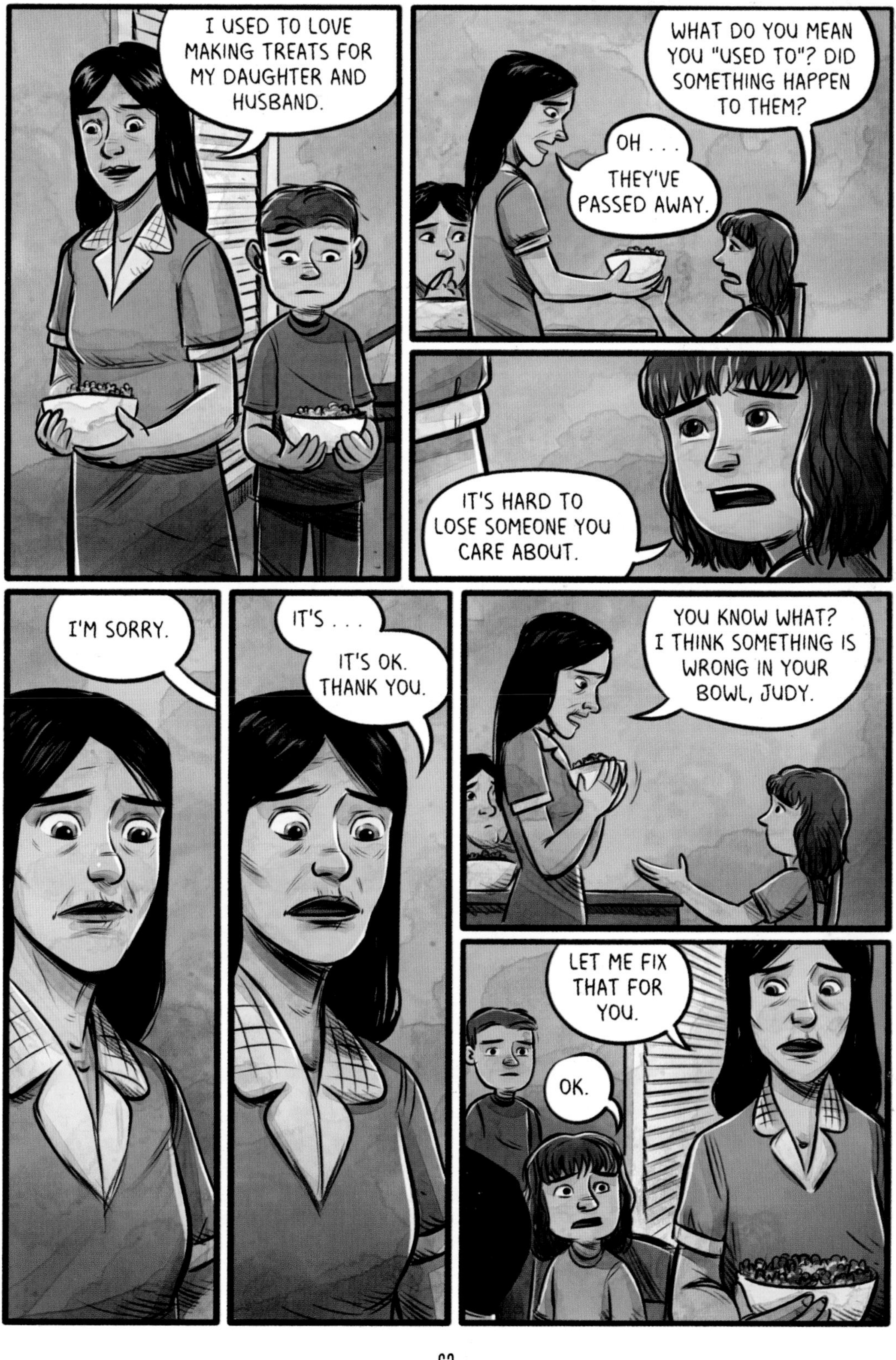
I USED TO LOVE MAKING TREATS FOR MY DAUGHTER AND HUSBAND.
WHAT DO YOU MEAN YOU "USED TO"? DID SOMETHING HAPPEN TO THEM?
OH . . .
THEY'VE PASSED AWAY.
IT'S HARD TO LOSE SOMEONE YOU CARE ABOUT.
I'M SORRY.
IT'S . . .
IT'S OK. THANK YOU.
YOU KNOW WHAT? I THINK SOMETHING IS WRONG IN YOUR BOWL, JUDY.
LET ME FIX THAT FOR YOU.
OK.

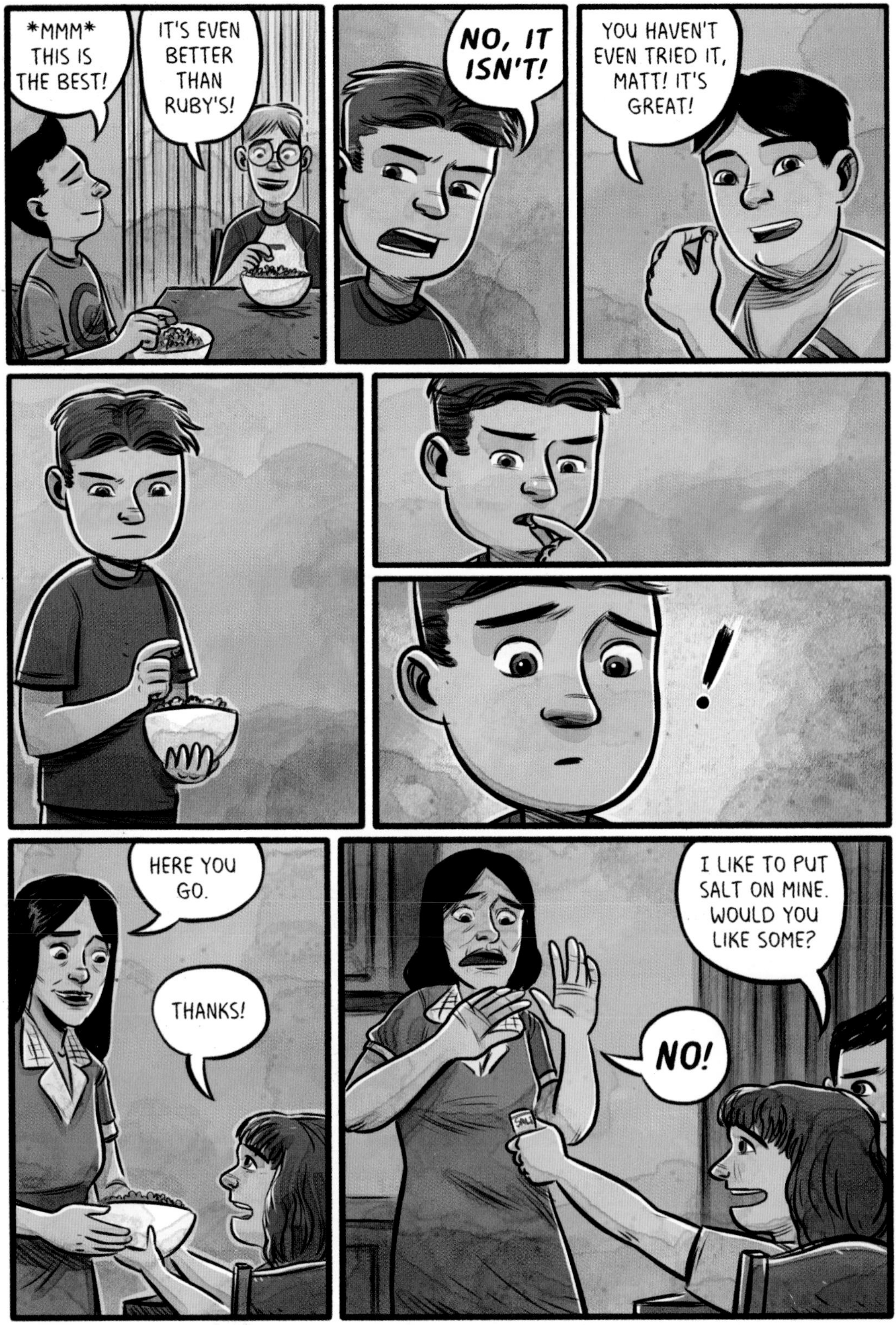
MMM
THIS IS
THE BEST!
IT'S EVEN
BETTER
THAN
RUBY'S!
NO, IT
ISN'T!
YOU HAVEN'T
EVEN TRIED IT,
MATT! IT'S
GREAT!
HERE YOU
GO.
THANKS!
I LIKE TO PUT
SALT ON MINE.
WOULD YOU
LIKE SOME?
NO!

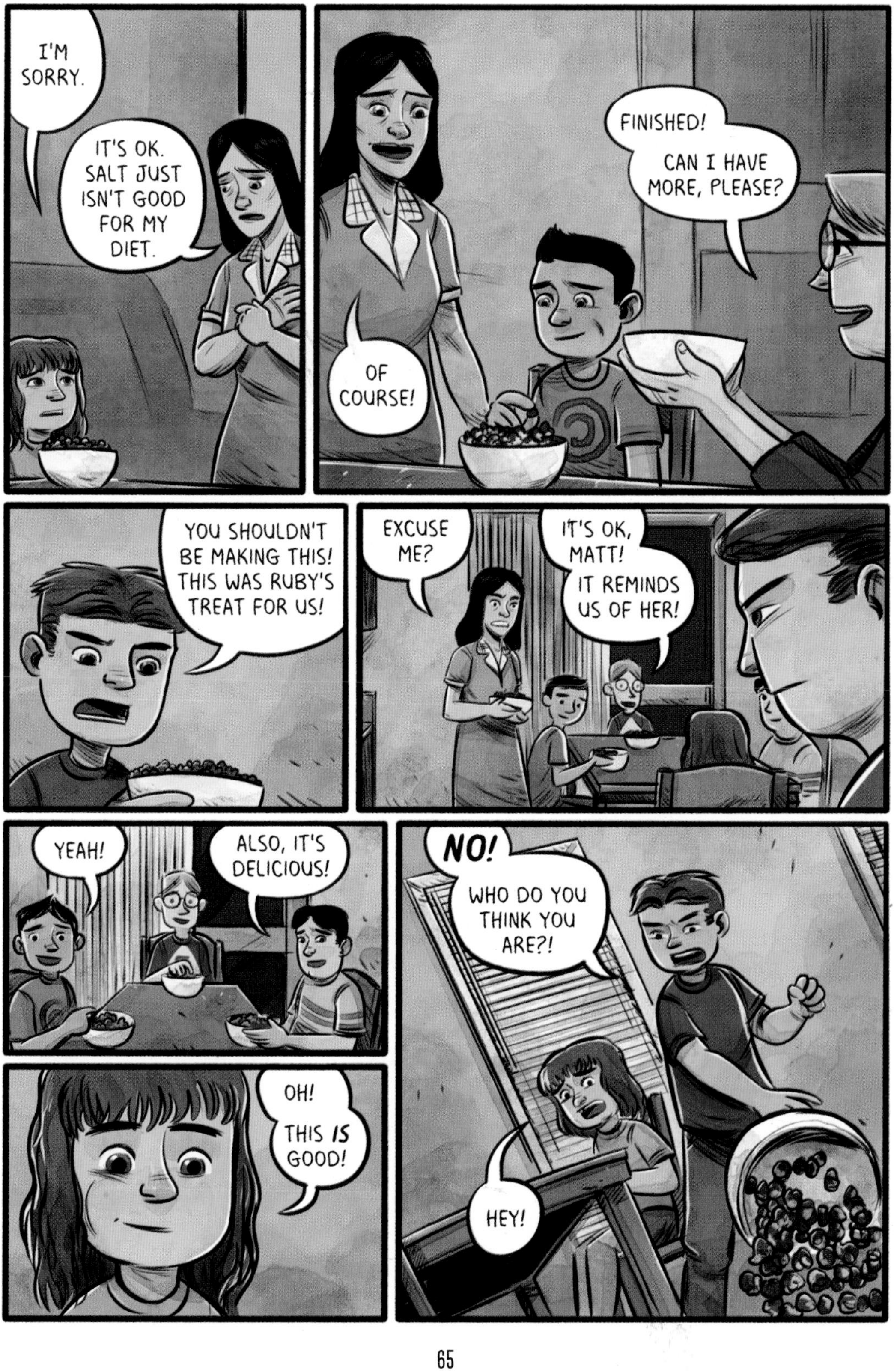
I'M SORRY.
IT'S OK. SALT JUST ISN'T GOOD FOR MY DIET.
FINISHED!
CAN I HAVE MORE, PLEASE?
OF COURSE!
YOU SHOULDN'T BE MAKING THIS! THIS WAS RUBY'S TREAT FOR US!
EXCUSE ME?
IT'S OK, MATT!
IT REMINDS US OF HER!
YEAH!
ALSO, IT'S DELICIOUS!
OH!
THIS *IS* GOOD!
NO!
WHO DO YOU THINK YOU ARE?!
HEY!

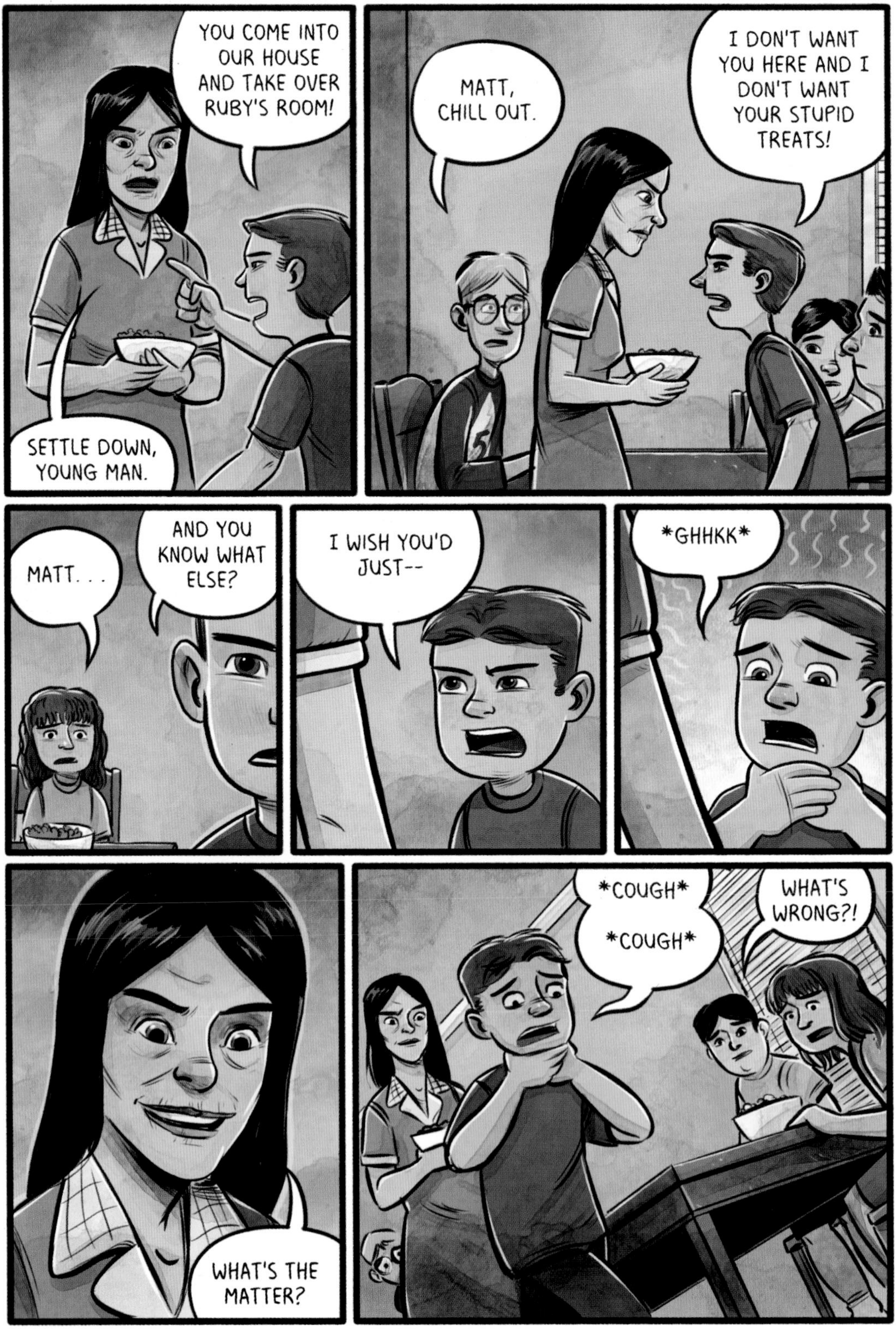
YOU COME INTO OUR HOUSE AND TAKE OVER RUBY'S ROOM!
SETTLE DOWN, YOUNG MAN.
MATT, CHILL OUT.
I DON'T WANT YOU HERE AND I DON'T WANT YOUR STUPID TREATS!
MATT. . .
AND YOU KNOW WHAT ELSE?
I WISH YOU'D JUST--
GHHKK
WHAT'S THE MATTER?
COUGH
COUGH
WHAT'S WRONG?!

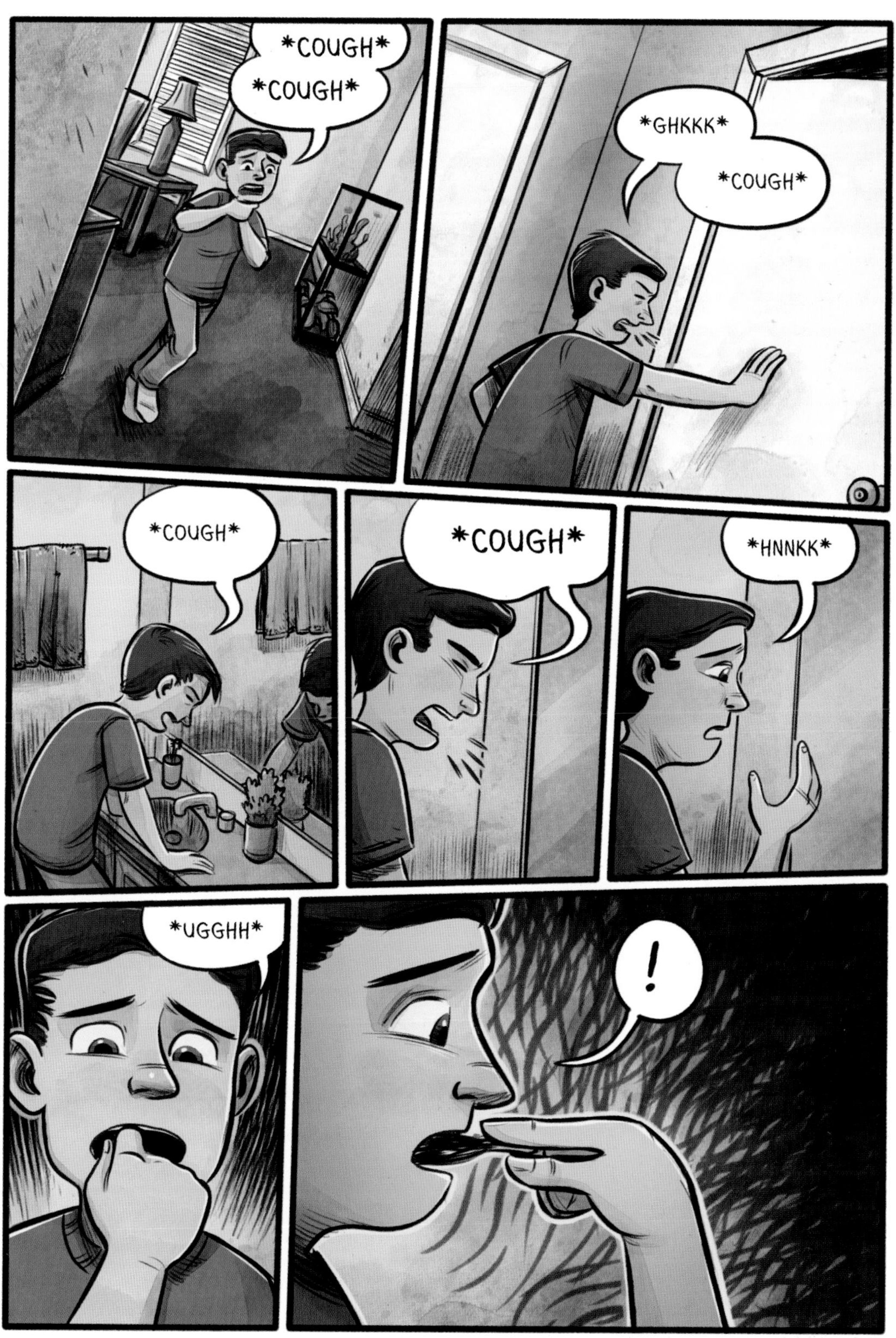
COUGH
COUGH
GHKKK
COUGH
COUGH
COUGH
HNNKK
UGGHH
!

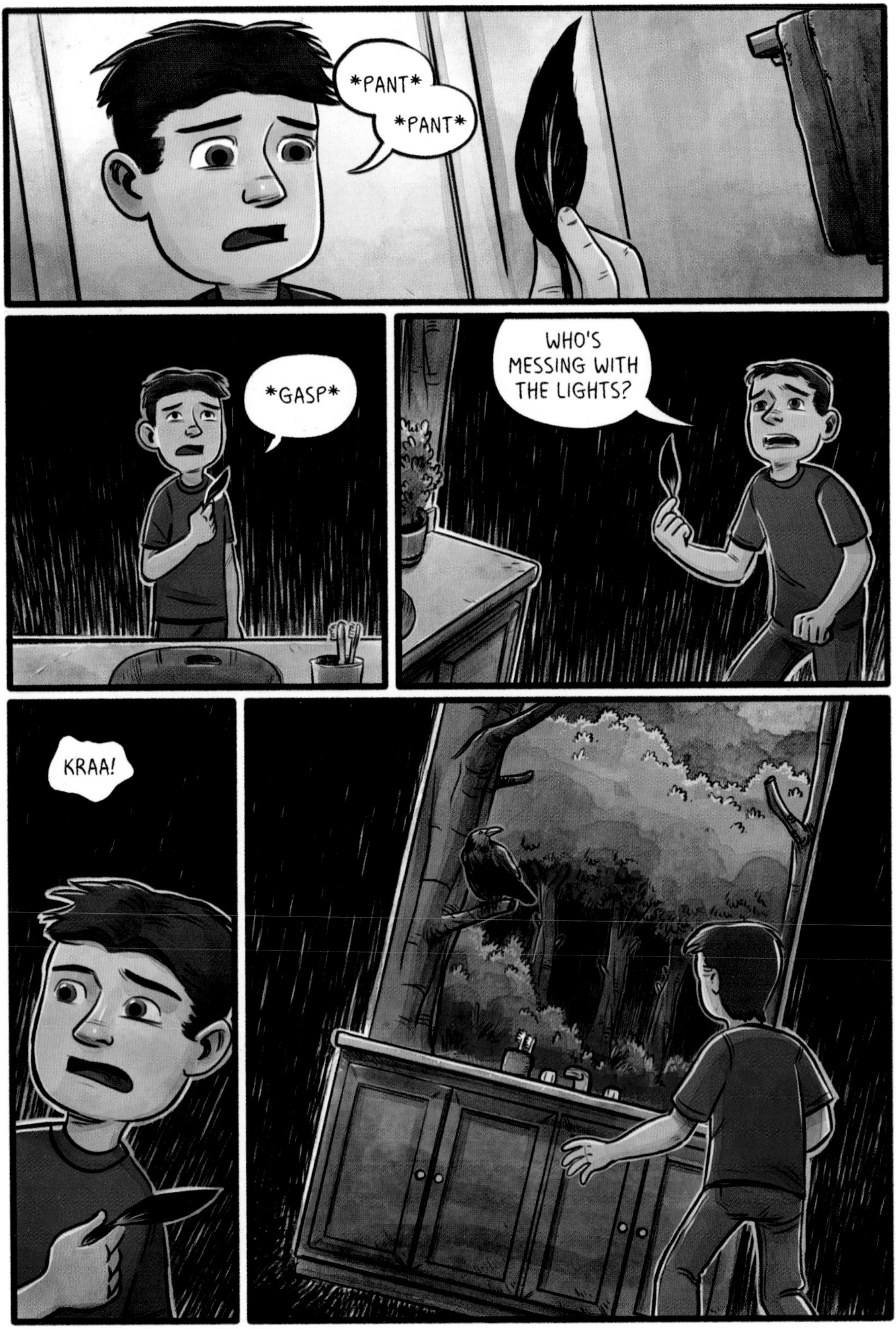
PANT
PANT
GASP
WHO'S MESSING WITH THE LIGHTS?
KRAA!

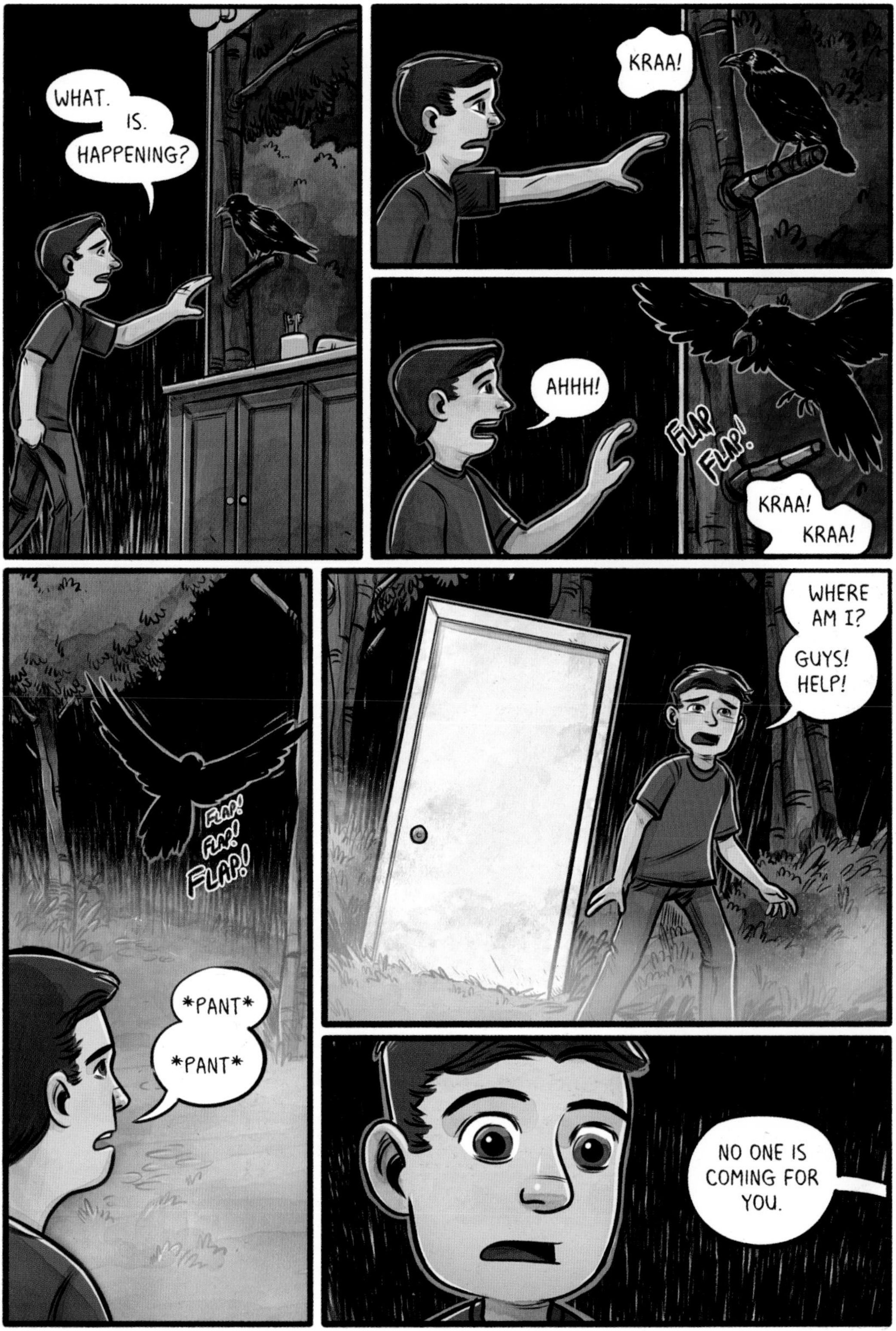
WHAT.
IS.
HAPPENING?
KRAA!
AHHH!
FLAP
FLAP!
KRAA!
KRAA!
FLAP!
FLAP!
FLAP!
PANT
PANT
WHERE AM I?
GUYS! HELP!
NO ONE IS COMING FOR YOU.

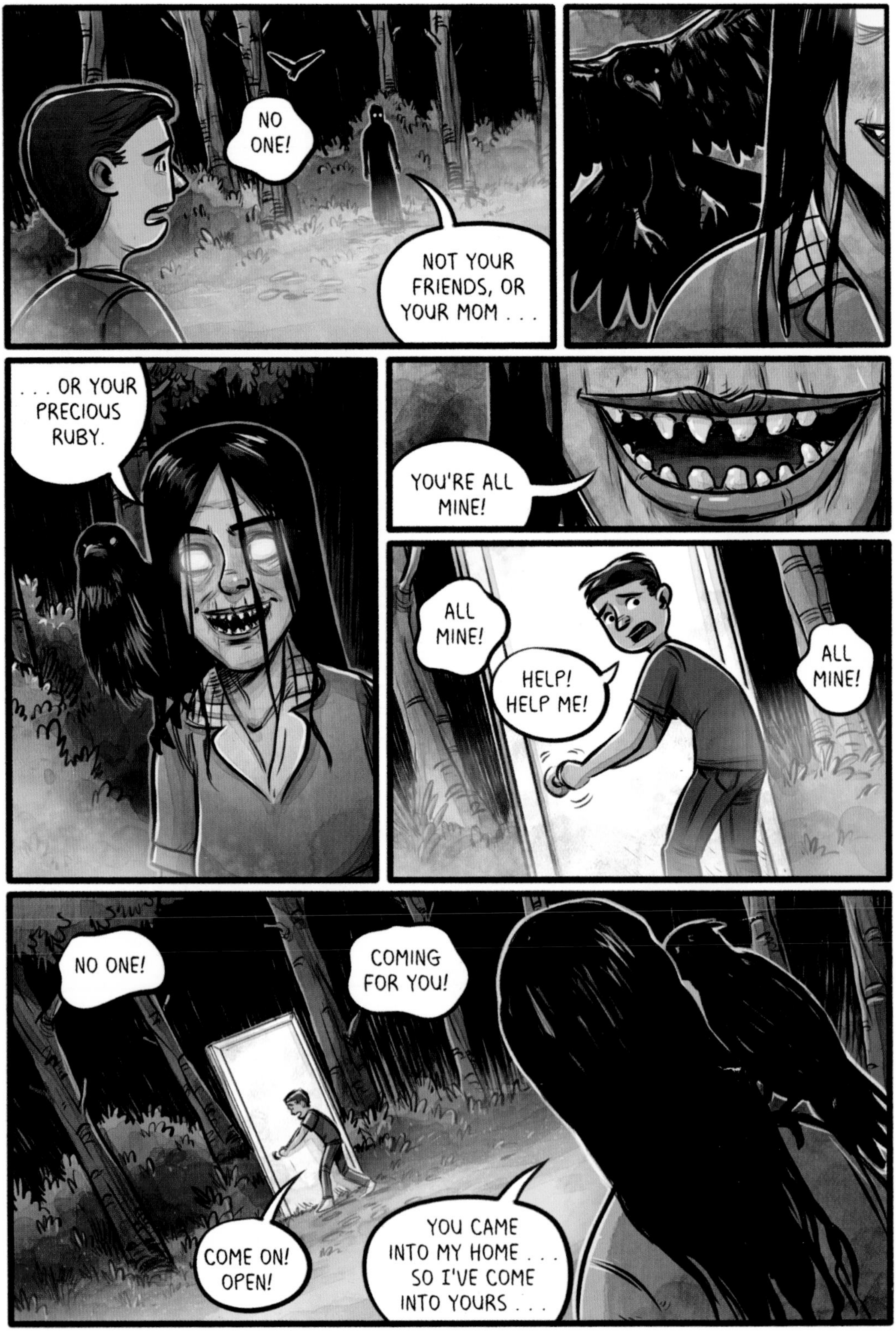
NO ONE!
NOT YOUR FRIENDS, OR YOUR MOM . . .
. . . OR YOUR PRECIOUS RUBY.
YOU'RE ALL MINE!
ALL MINE!
HELP! HELP ME!
ALL MINE!
NO ONE!
COMING FOR YOU!
COME ON! OPEN!
YOU CAME INTO MY HOME . . . SO I'VE COME INTO YOURS . . .

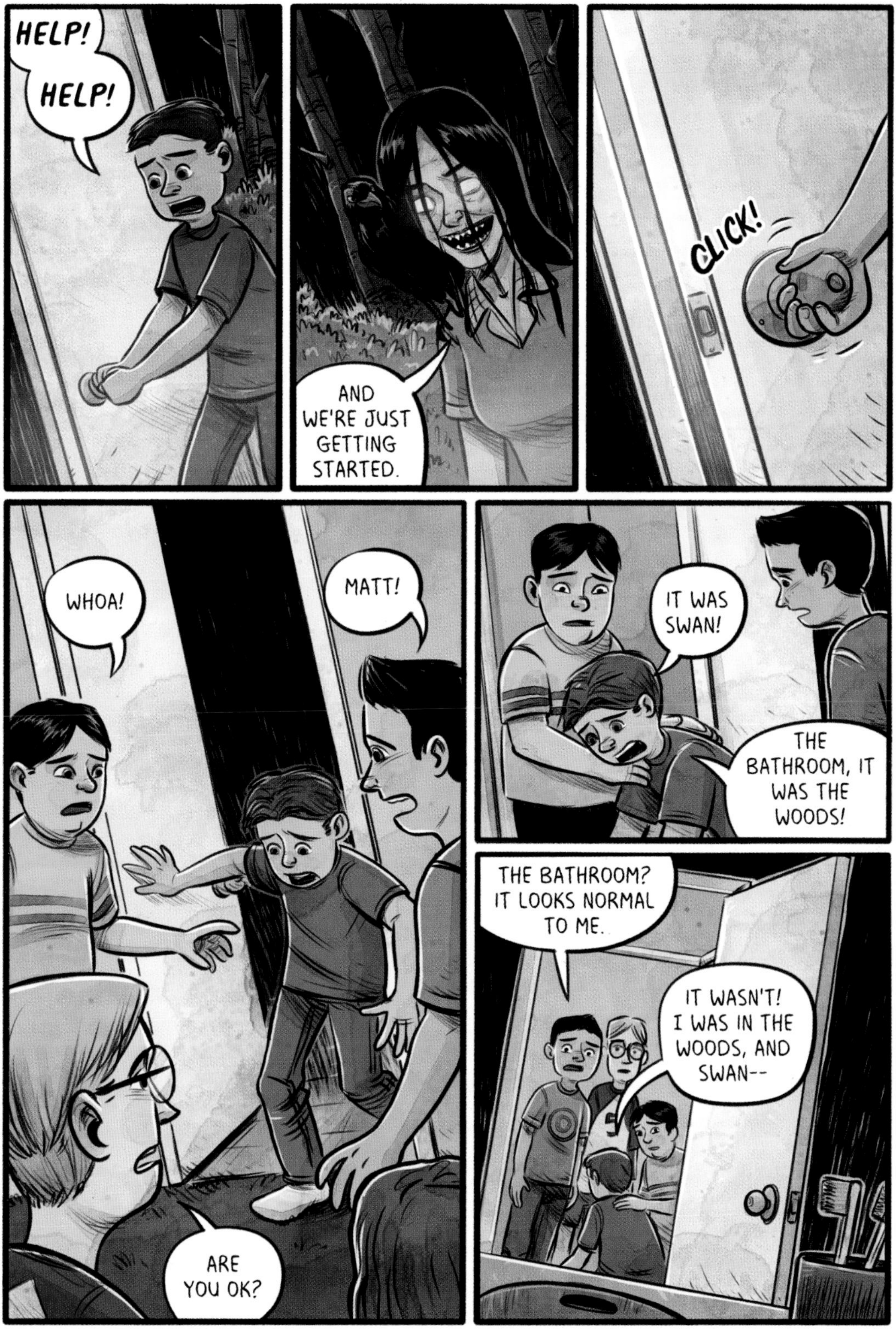
HELP!
HELP!
AND WE'RE JUST GETTING STARTED.
CLICK!
WHOA!
MATT!
ARE YOU OK?
IT WAS SWAN!
THE BATHROOM, IT WAS THE WOODS!
THE BATHROOM? IT LOOKS NORMAL TO ME.
IT WASN'T! I WAS IN THE WOODS, AND SWAN--

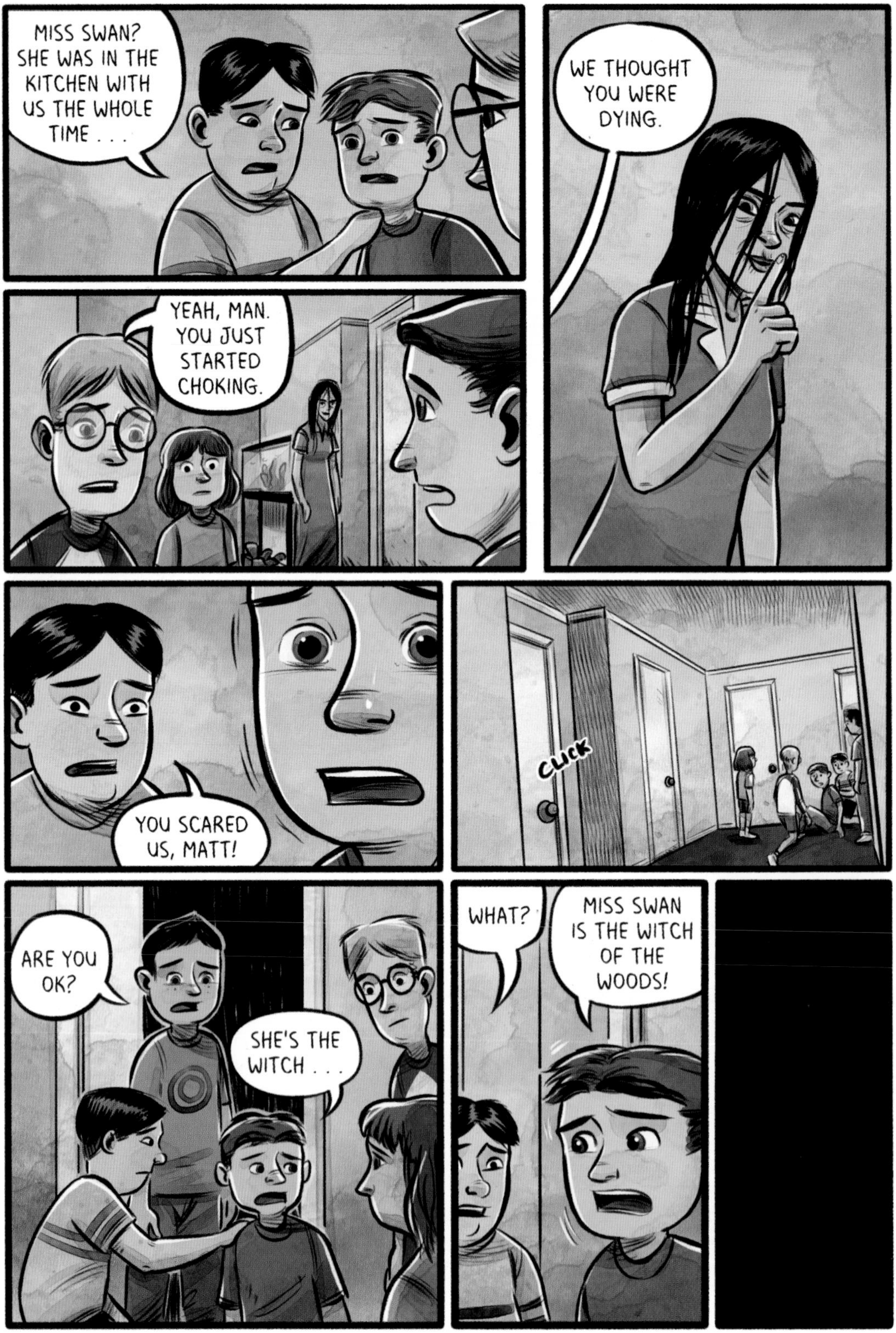
MISS SWAN? SHE WAS IN THE KITCHEN WITH US THE WHOLE TIME . . .
WE THOUGHT YOU WERE DYING.
YEAH, MAN. YOU JUST STARTED CHOKING.
YOU SCARED US, MATT!
CLICK
ARE YOU OK?
SHE'S THE WITCH . . .
WHAT?
MISS SWAN IS THE WITCH OF THE WOODS!

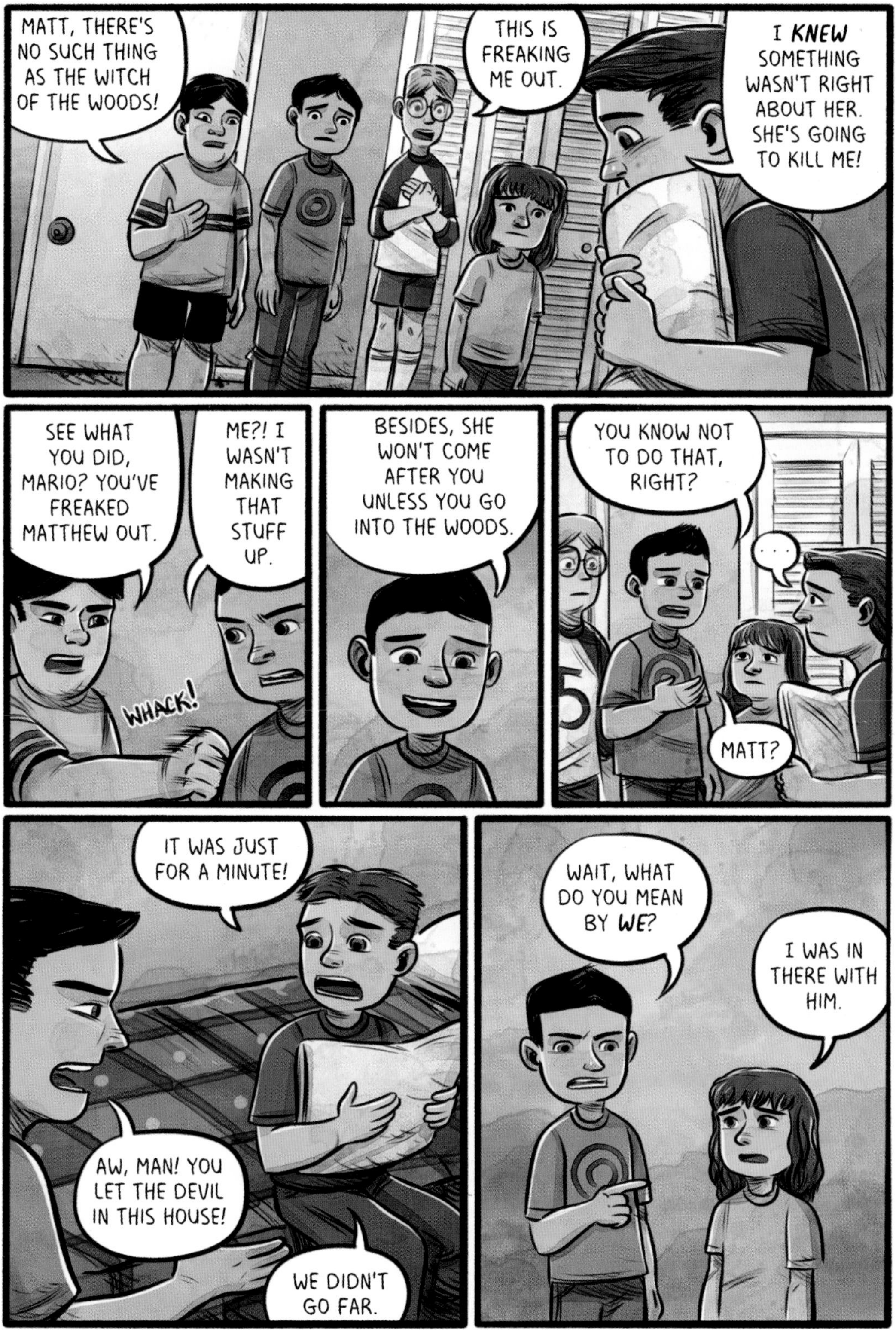
MATT, THERE'S NO SUCH THING AS THE WITCH OF THE WOODS!
THIS IS FREAKING ME OUT.
I KNEW SOMETHING WASN'T RIGHT ABOUT HER. SHE'S GOING TO KILL ME!
SEE WHAT YOU DID, MARIO? YOU'VE FREAKED MATTHEW OUT.
ME?! I WASN'T MAKING THAT STUFF UP.
WHACK!
BESIDES, SHE WON'T COME AFTER YOU UNLESS YOU GO INTO THE WOODS.
YOU KNOW NOT TO DO THAT, RIGHT?
. . .
MATT?
IT WAS JUST FOR A MINUTE!
AW, MAN! YOU LET THE DEVIL IN THIS HOUSE!
WE DIDN'T GO FAR.
WAIT, WHAT DO YOU MEAN BY WE?
I WAS IN THERE WITH HIM.

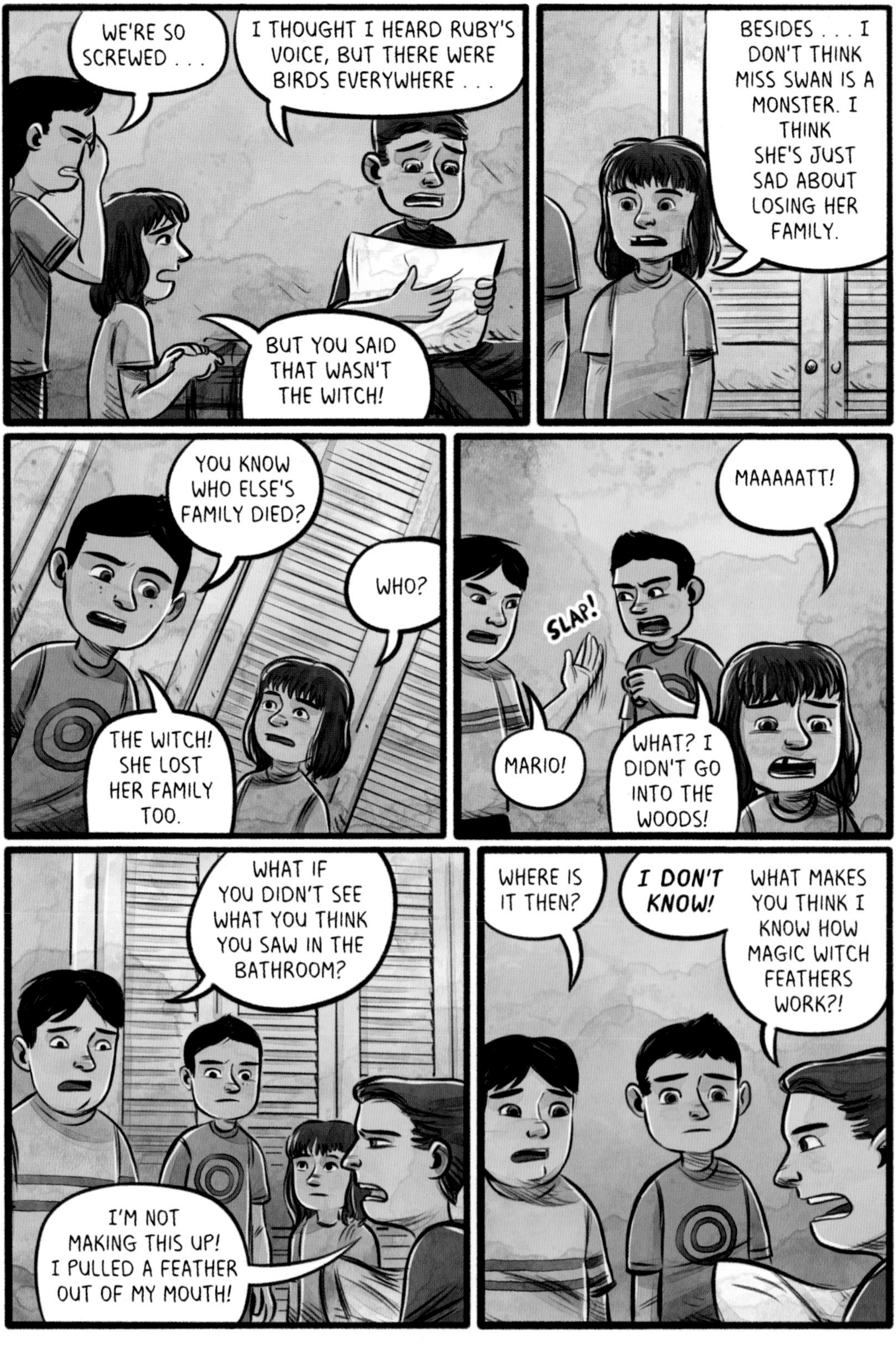
WE'RE SO SCREWED . . .
I THOUGHT I HEARD RUBY'S VOICE, BUT THERE WERE BIRDS EVERYWHERE . . .
BUT YOU SAID THAT WASN'T THE WITCH!
BESIDES . . . I DON'T THINK MISS SWAN IS A MONSTER. I THINK SHE'S JUST SAD ABOUT LOSING HER FAMILY.
YOU KNOW WHO ELSE'S FAMILY DIED?
WHO?
THE WITCH! SHE LOST HER FAMILY TOO.
MAAAAATT!
SLAP!
MARIO!
WHAT? I DIDN'T GO INTO THE WOODS!
WHAT IF YOU DIDN'T SEE WHAT YOU THINK YOU SAW IN THE BATHROOM?
I'M NOT MAKING THIS UP! I PULLED A FEATHER OUT OF MY MOUTH!
WHERE IS IT THEN?
I DON'T KNOW!
WHAT MAKES YOU THINK I KNOW HOW MAGIC WITCH FEATHERS WORK?!

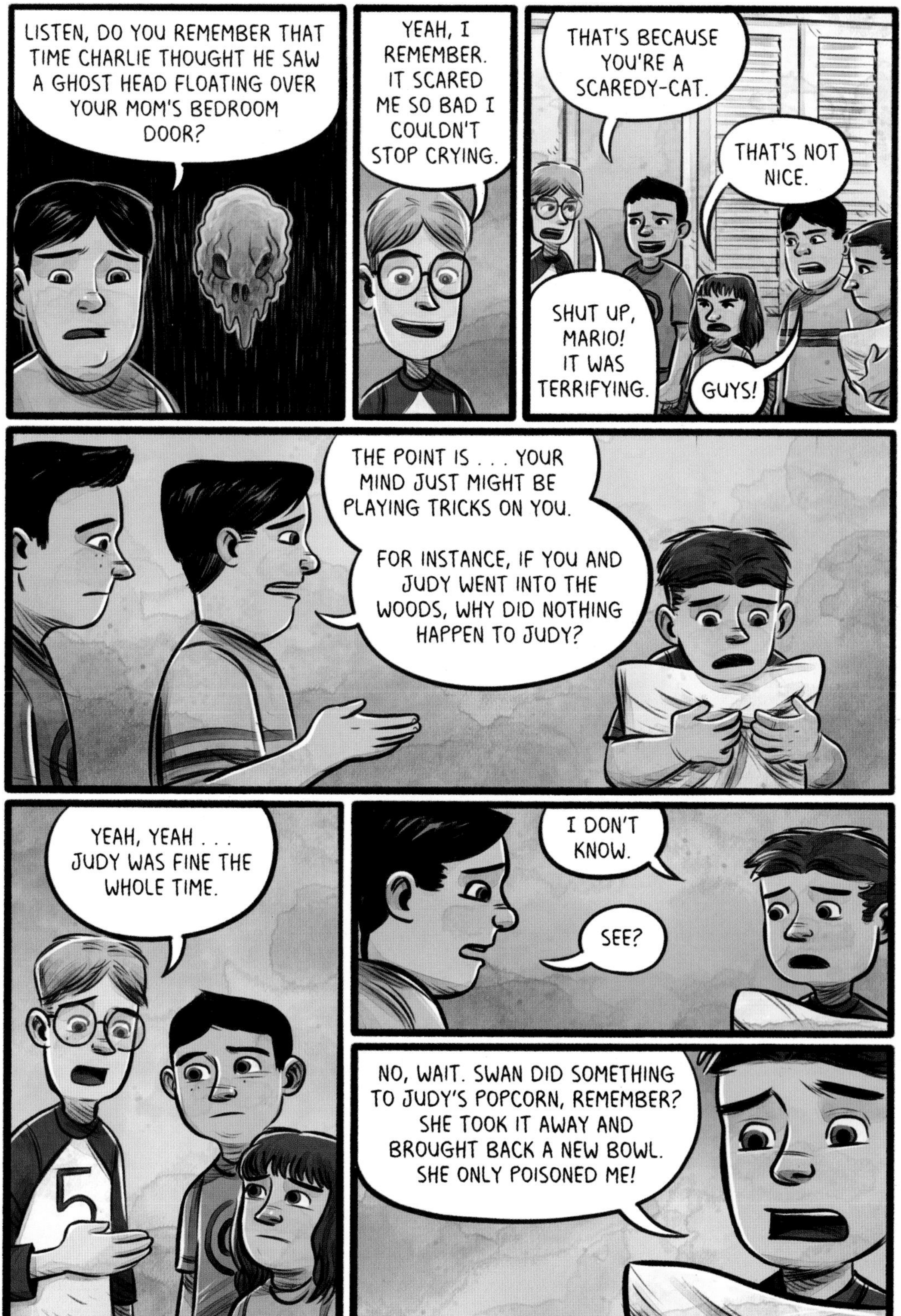
LISTEN, DO YOU REMEMBER THAT TIME CHARLIE THOUGHT HE SAW A GHOST HEAD FLOATING OVER YOUR MOM'S BEDROOM DOOR?
YEAH, I REMEMBER. IT SCARED ME SO BAD I COULDN'T STOP CRYING.
THAT'S BECAUSE YOU'RE A SCAREDY-CAT.
THAT'S NOT NICE.
SHUT UP, MARIO! IT WAS TERRIFYING.
GUYS!
THE POINT IS . . . YOUR MIND JUST MIGHT BE PLAYING TRICKS ON YOU.
FOR INSTANCE, IF YOU AND JUDY WENT INTO THE WOODS, WHY DID NOTHING HAPPEN TO JUDY?
YEAH, YEAH . . . JUDY WAS FINE THE WHOLE TIME.
I DON'T KNOW.
SEE?
NO, WAIT. SWAN DID SOMETHING TO JUDY'S POPCORN, REMEMBER? SHE TOOK IT AWAY AND BROUGHT BACK A NEW BOWL. SHE ONLY POISONED ME!

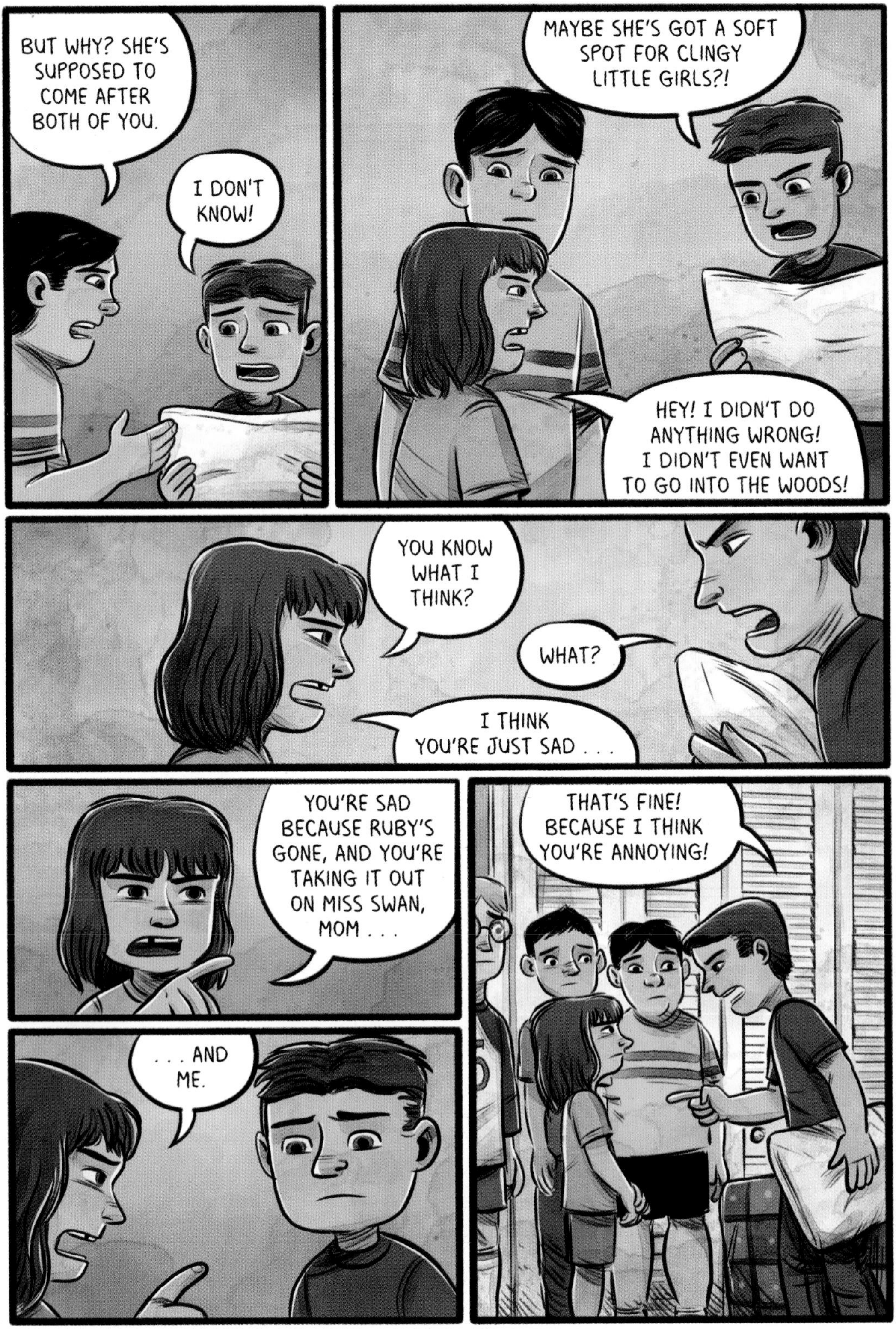
BUT WHY? SHE'S SUPPOSED TO COME AFTER BOTH OF YOU.
I DON'T KNOW!
MAYBE SHE'S GOT A SOFT SPOT FOR CLINGY LITTLE GIRLS?!
HEY! I DIDN'T DO ANYTHING WRONG! I DIDN'T EVEN WANT TO GO INTO THE WOODS!
YOU KNOW WHAT I THINK?
WHAT?
I THINK YOU'RE JUST SAD . . .
YOU'RE SAD BECAUSE RUBY'S GONE, AND YOU'RE TAKING IT OUT ON MISS SWAN, MOM . . .
. . . AND ME.
THAT'S FINE! BECAUSE I THINK YOU'RE ANNOYING!

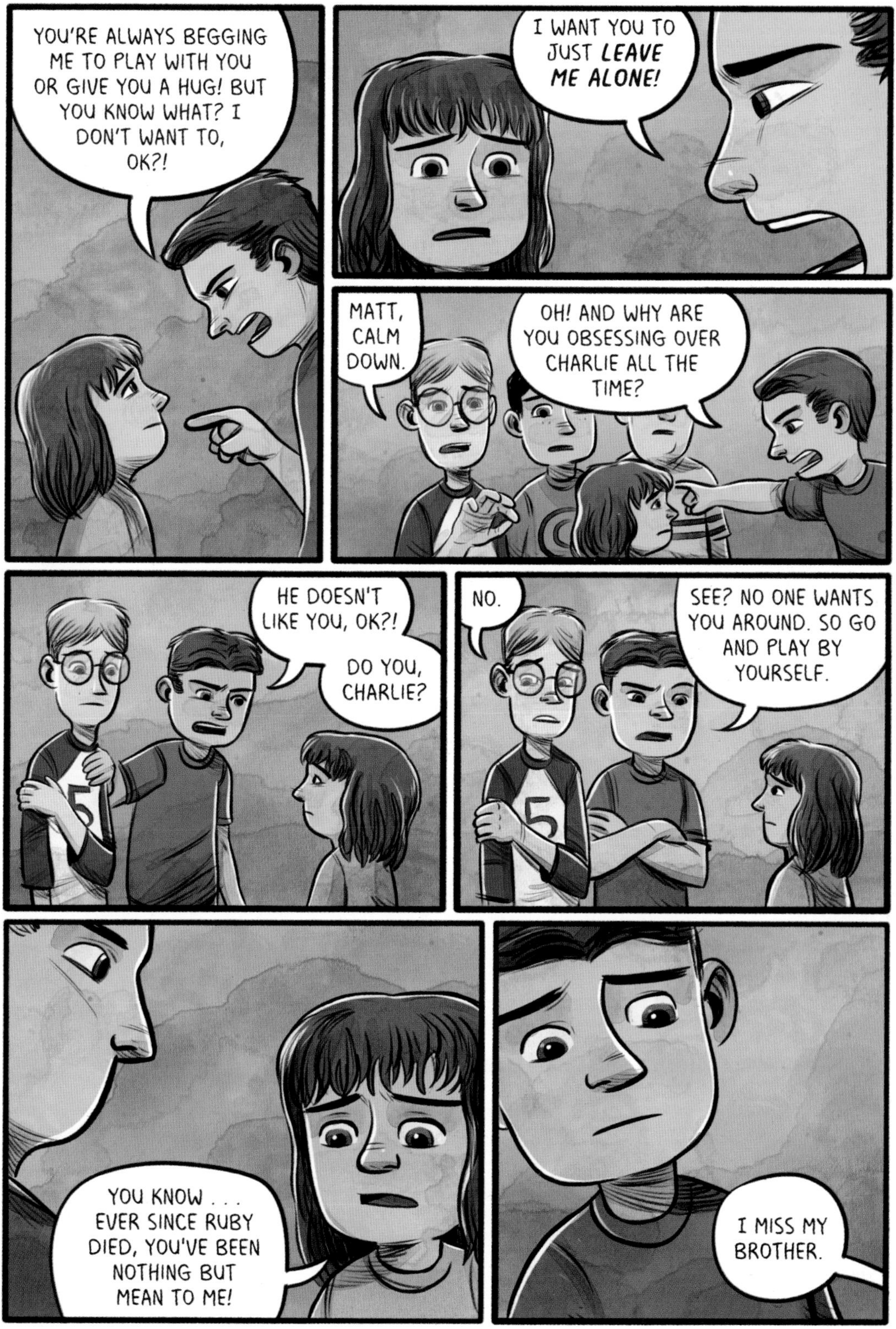
YOU'RE ALWAYS BEGGING ME TO PLAY WITH YOU OR GIVE YOU A HUG! BUT YOU KNOW WHAT? I DON'T WANT TO, OK?!
I WANT YOU TO JUST **LEAVE ME ALONE!**
MATT, CALM DOWN.
OH! AND WHY ARE YOU OBSESSING OVER CHARLIE ALL THE TIME?
HE DOESN'T LIKE YOU, OK?!
DO YOU, CHARLIE?
NO.
SEE? NO ONE WANTS YOU AROUND. SO GO AND PLAY BY YOURSELF.
YOU KNOW . . . EVER SINCE RUBY DIED, YOU'VE BEEN NOTHING BUT MEAN TO ME!
I MISS MY BROTHER.

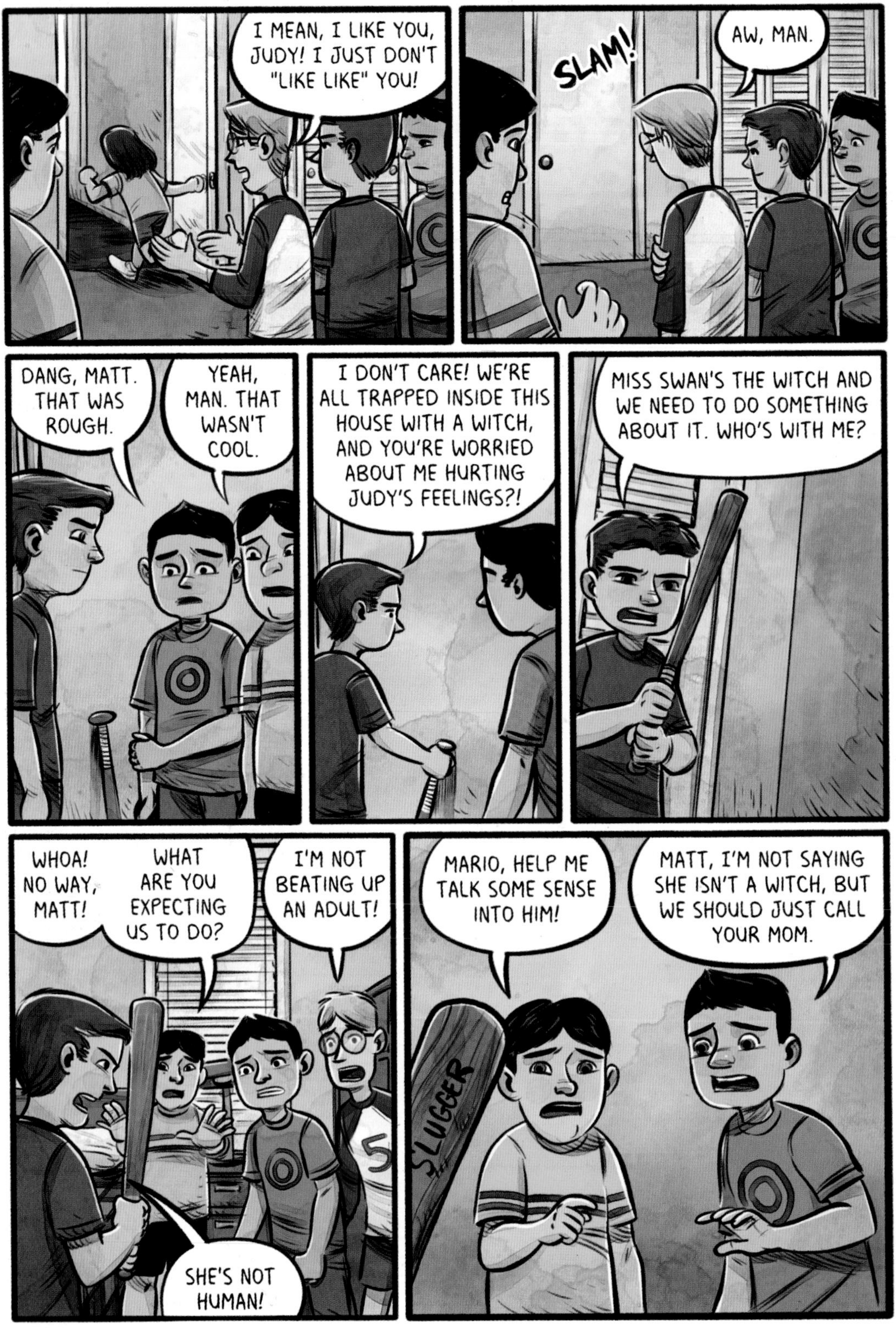
I MEAN, I LIKE YOU, JUDY! I JUST DON'T "LIKE LIKE" YOU!
SLAM!
AW, MAN.
DANG, MATT. THAT WAS ROUGH.
YEAH, MAN. THAT WASN'T COOL.
I DON'T CARE! WE'RE ALL TRAPPED INSIDE THIS HOUSE WITH A WITCH, AND YOU'RE WORRIED ABOUT ME HURTING JUDY'S FEELINGS?!
MISS SWAN'S THE WITCH AND WE NEED TO DO SOMETHING ABOUT IT. WHO'S WITH ME?
WHOA! NO WAY, MATT!
WHAT ARE YOU EXPECTING US TO DO?
I'M NOT BEATING UP AN ADULT!
SHE'S NOT HUMAN!
MARIO, HELP ME TALK SOME SENSE INTO HIM!
MATT, I'M NOT SAYING SHE ISN'T A WITCH, BUT WE SHOULD JUST CALL YOUR MOM.
SLUGGER

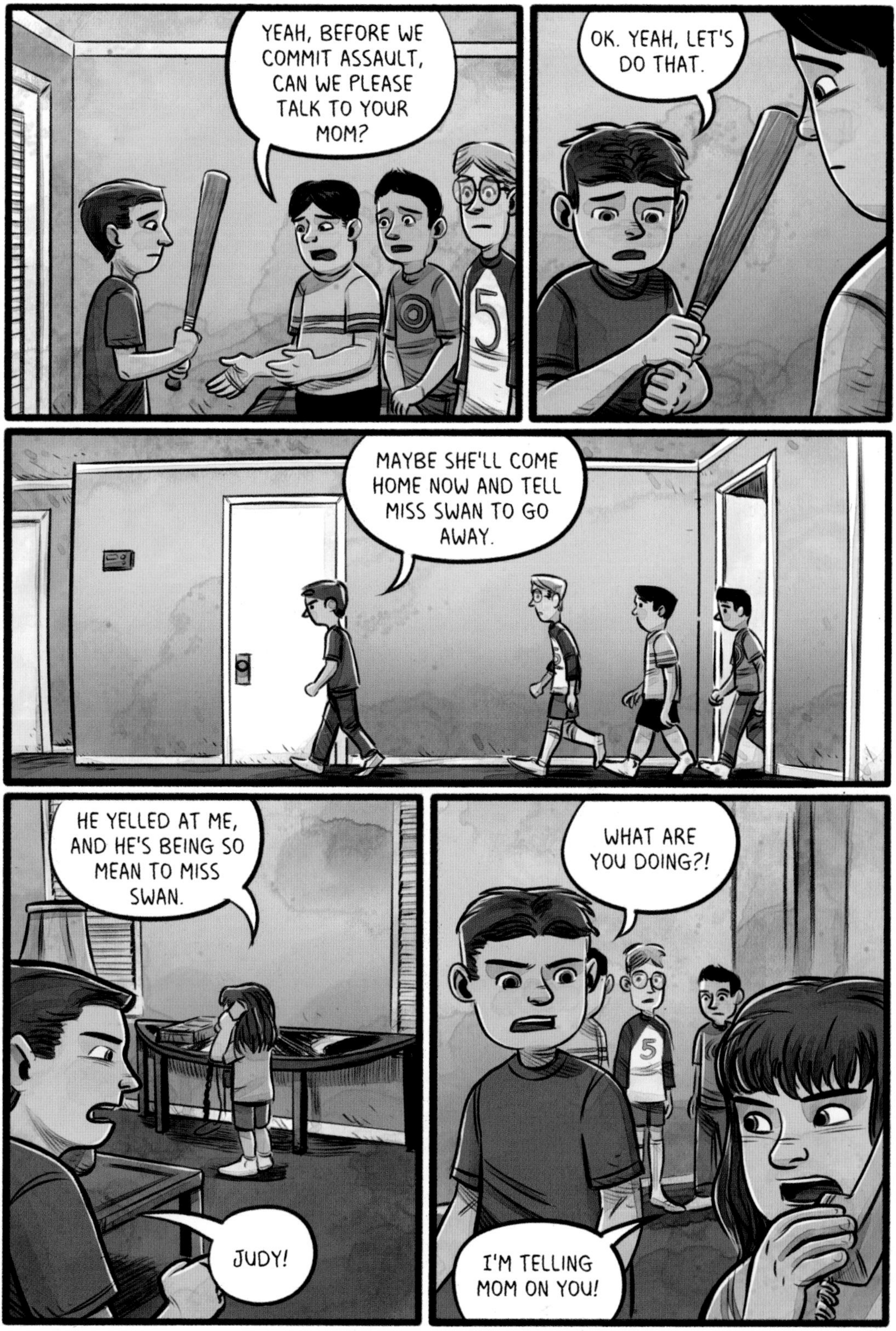
YEAH, BEFORE WE COMMIT ASSAULT, CAN WE PLEASE TALK TO YOUR MOM?
OK. YEAH, LET'S DO THAT.
MAYBE SHE'LL COME HOME NOW AND TELL MISS SWAN TO GO AWAY.
HE YELLED AT ME, AND HE'S BEING SO MEAN TO MISS SWAN.
JUDY!
WHAT ARE YOU DOING?!
I'M TELLING MOM ON YOU!

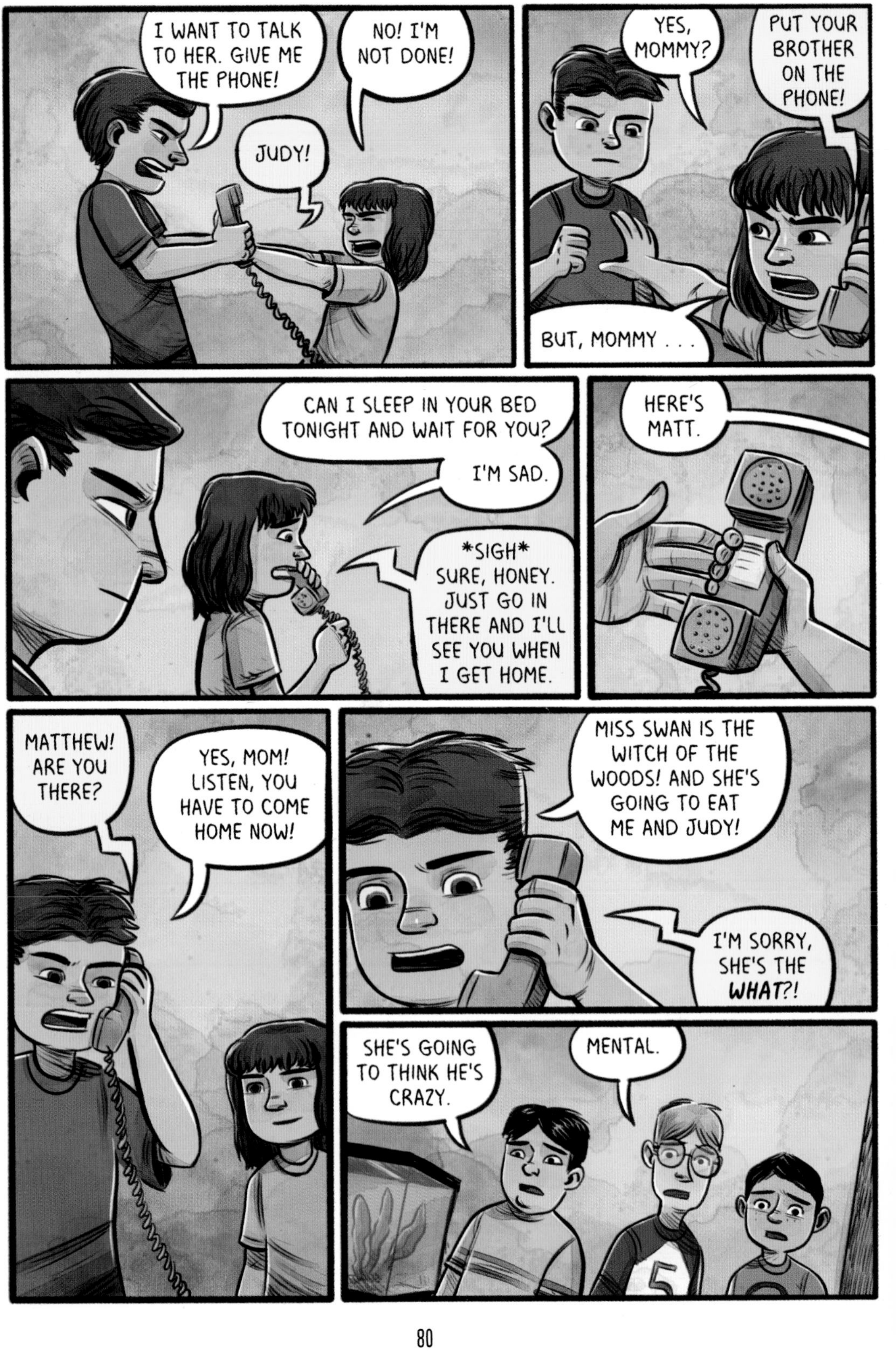
I WANT TO TALK TO HER. GIVE ME THE PHONE!
NO! I'M NOT DONE!
JUDY!
YES, MOMMY?
PUT YOUR BROTHER ON THE PHONE!
BUT, MOMMY . . .
CAN I SLEEP IN YOUR BED TONIGHT AND WAIT FOR YOU?
I'M SAD.
SIGH SURE, HONEY. JUST GO IN THERE AND I'LL SEE YOU WHEN I GET HOME.
HERE'S MATT.
MATTHEW! ARE YOU THERE?
YES, MOM! LISTEN, YOU HAVE TO COME HOME NOW!
MISS SWAN IS THE WITCH OF THE WOODS! AND SHE'S GOING TO EAT ME AND JUDY!
I'M SORRY, SHE'S THE ***WHAT***?!
SHE'S GOING TO THINK HE'S CRAZY.
MENTAL.

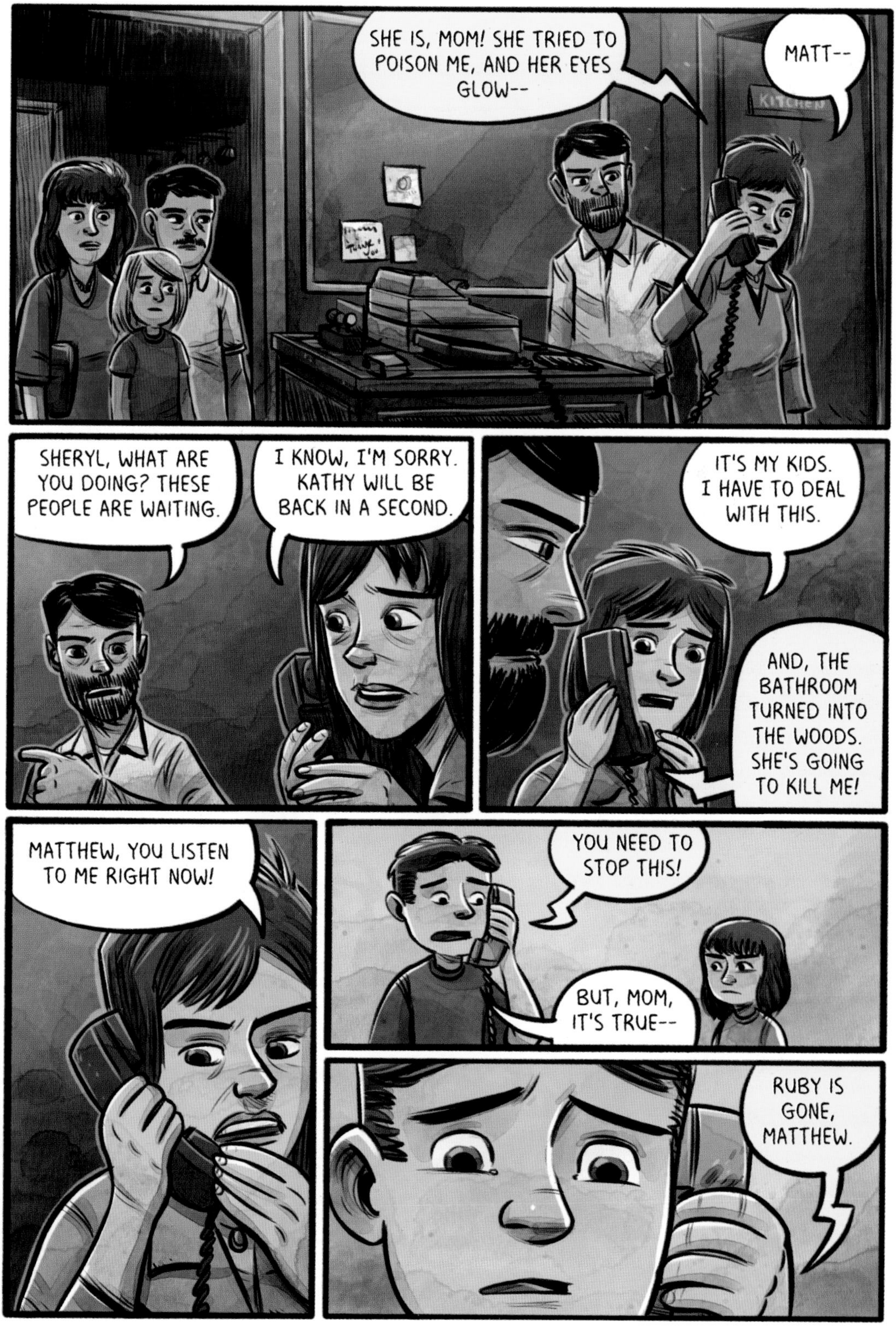

SHE IS, MOM! SHE TRIED TO POISON ME, AND HER EYES GLOW--
MATT--
SHERYL, WHAT ARE YOU DOING? THESE PEOPLE ARE WAITING.
I KNOW, I'M SORRY. KATHY WILL BE BACK IN A SECOND.
IT'S MY KIDS. I HAVE TO DEAL WITH THIS.
AND, THE BATHROOM TURNED INTO THE WOODS. SHE'S GOING TO KILL ME!
MATTHEW, YOU LISTEN TO ME RIGHT NOW!
YOU NEED TO STOP THIS!
BUT, MOM, IT'S TRUE--
RUBY IS GONE, MATTHEW.

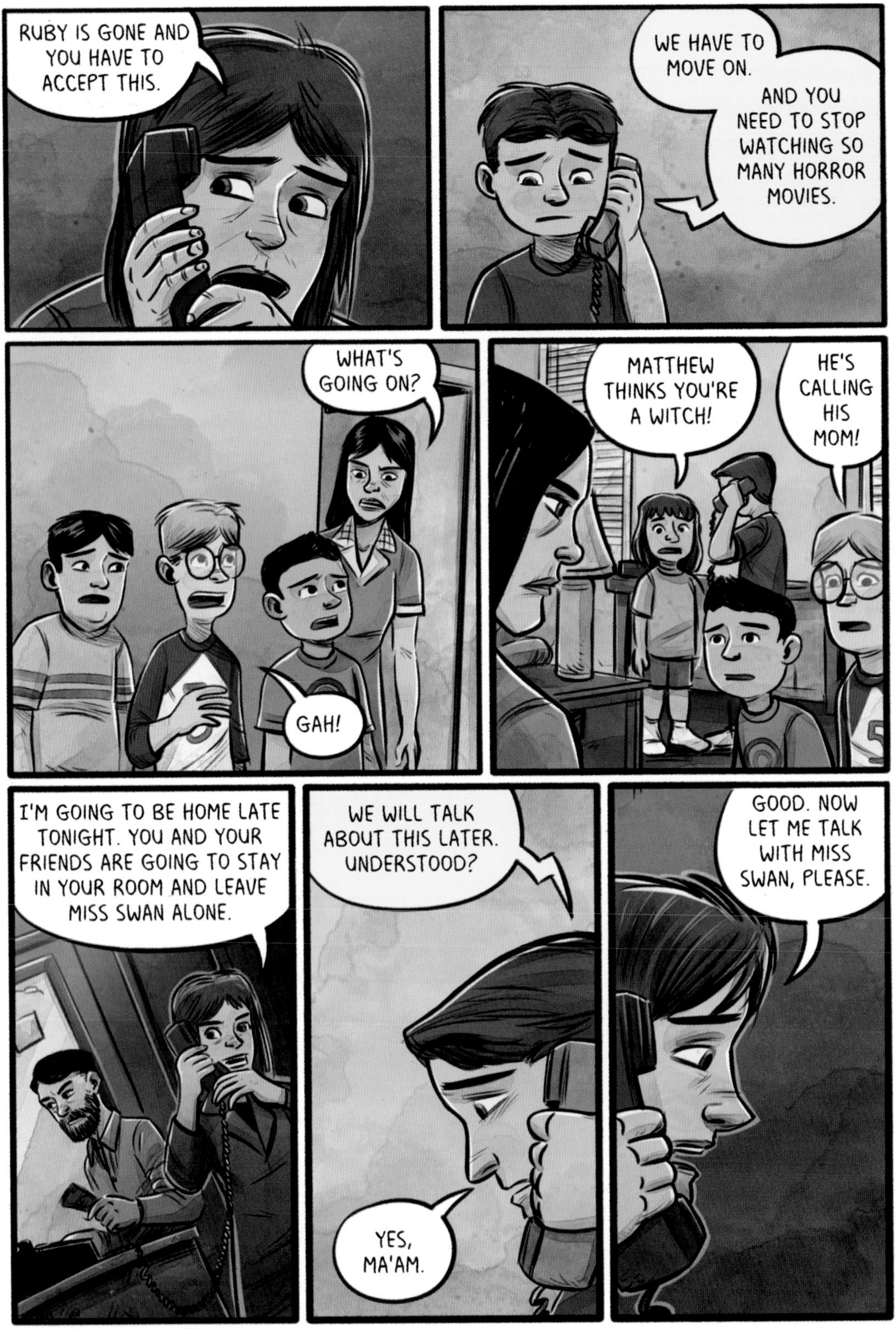
RUBY IS GONE AND YOU HAVE TO ACCEPT THIS.
WE HAVE TO MOVE ON.
AND YOU NEED TO STOP WATCHING SO MANY HORROR MOVIES.
WHAT'S GOING ON?
GAH!
MATTHEW THINKS YOU'RE A WITCH!
HE'S CALLING HIS MOM!
I'M GOING TO BE HOME LATE TONIGHT. YOU AND YOUR FRIENDS ARE GOING TO STAY IN YOUR ROOM AND LEAVE MISS SWAN ALONE.
WE WILL TALK ABOUT THIS LATER. UNDERSTOOD?
YES, MA'AM.
GOOD. NOW LET ME TALK WITH MISS SWAN, PLEASE.

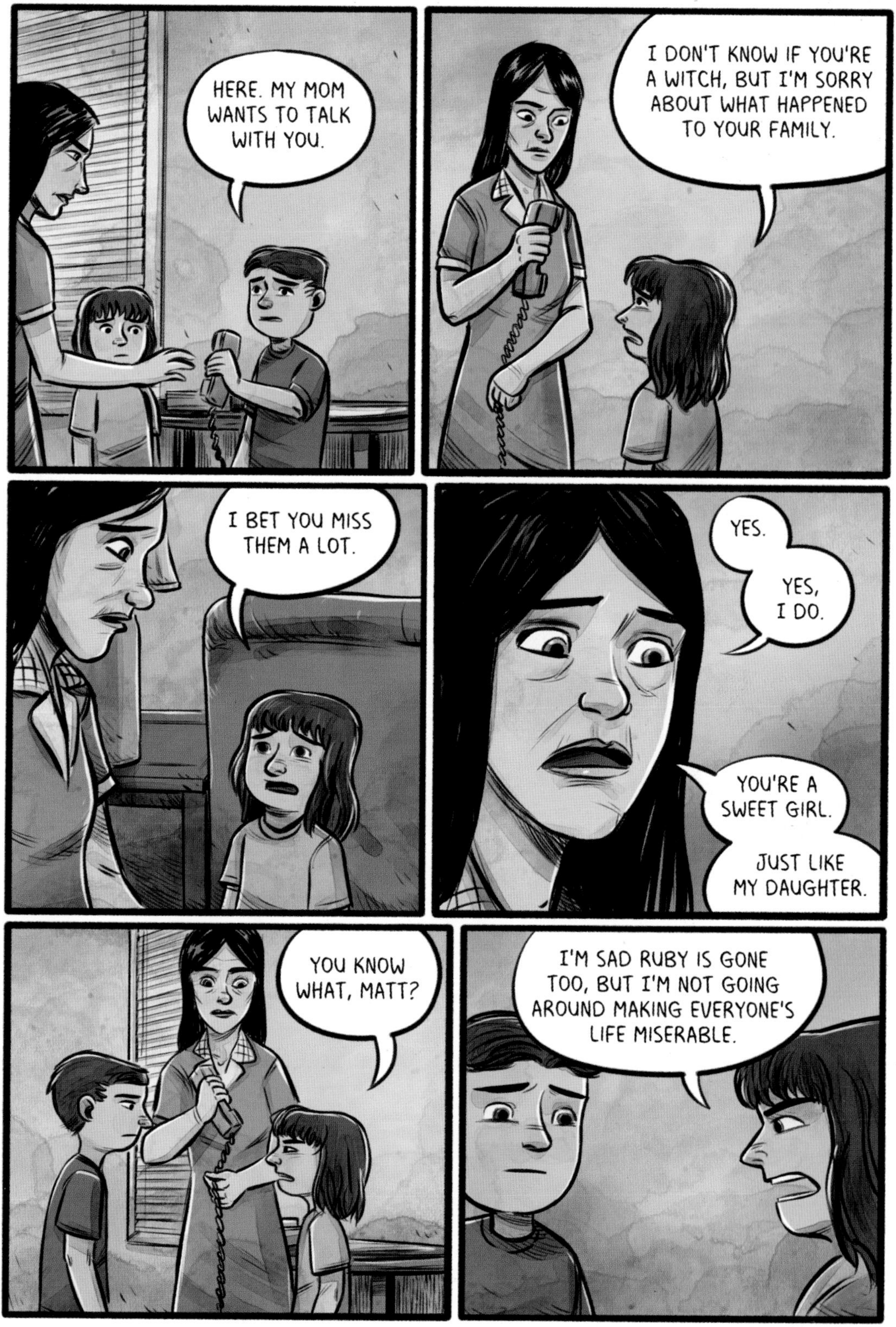
HERE. MY MOM WANTS TO TALK WITH YOU.
I DON'T KNOW IF YOU'RE A WITCH, BUT I'M SORRY ABOUT WHAT HAPPENED TO YOUR FAMILY.
I BET YOU MISS THEM A LOT.
YES.
YES, I DO.
YOU'RE A SWEET GIRL.
JUST LIKE MY DAUGHTER.
YOU KNOW WHAT, MATT?
I'M SAD RUBY IS GONE TOO, BUT I'M NOT GOING AROUND MAKING EVERYONE'S LIFE MISERABLE.

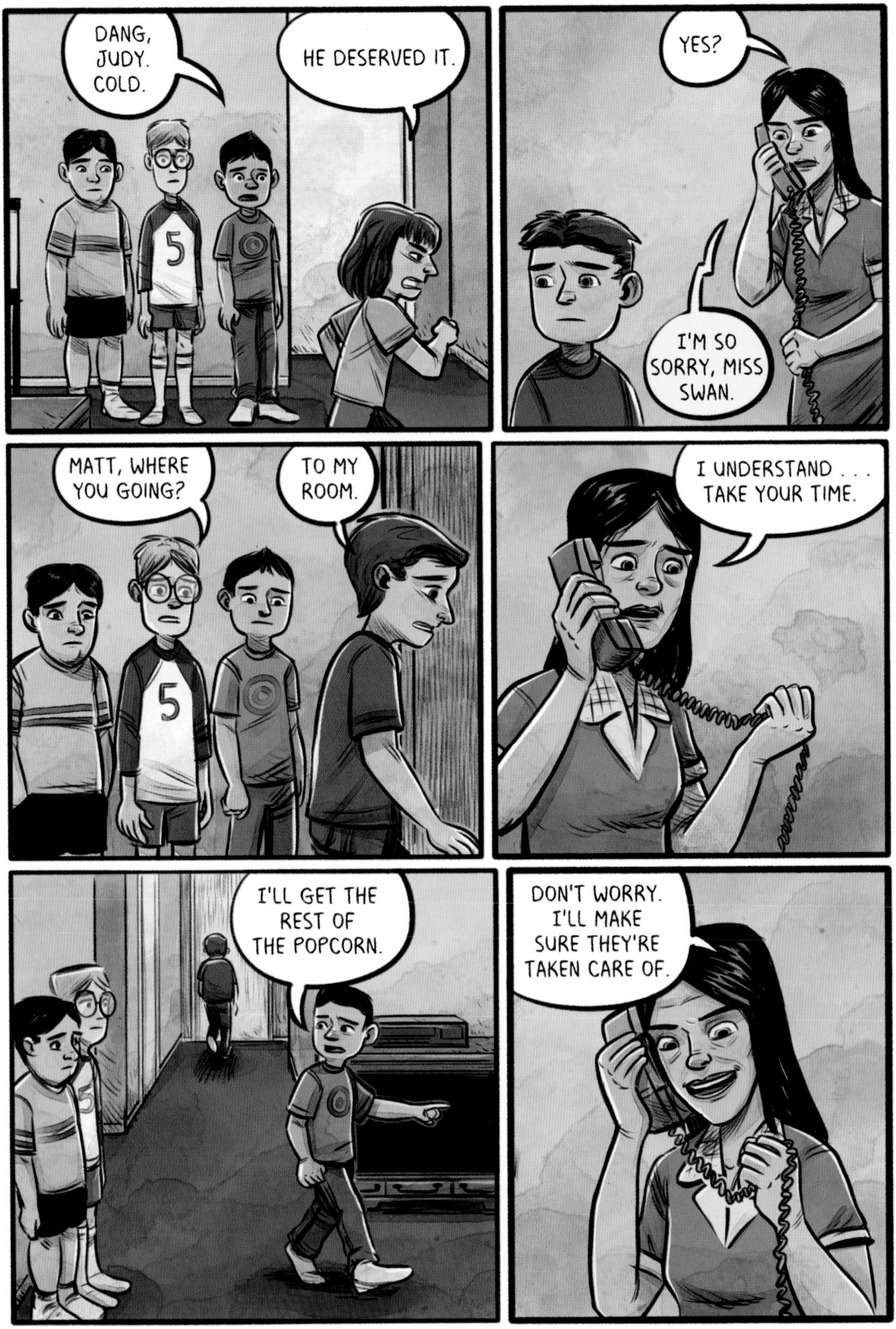
DANG, JUDY. COLD.
HE DESERVED IT.
YES?
I'M SO SORRY, MISS SWAN.
MATT, WHERE YOU GOING?
TO MY ROOM.
I UNDERSTAND . . . TAKE YOUR TIME.
I'LL GET THE REST OF THE POPCORN.
DON'T WORRY. I'LL MAKE SURE THEY'RE TAKEN CARE OF.

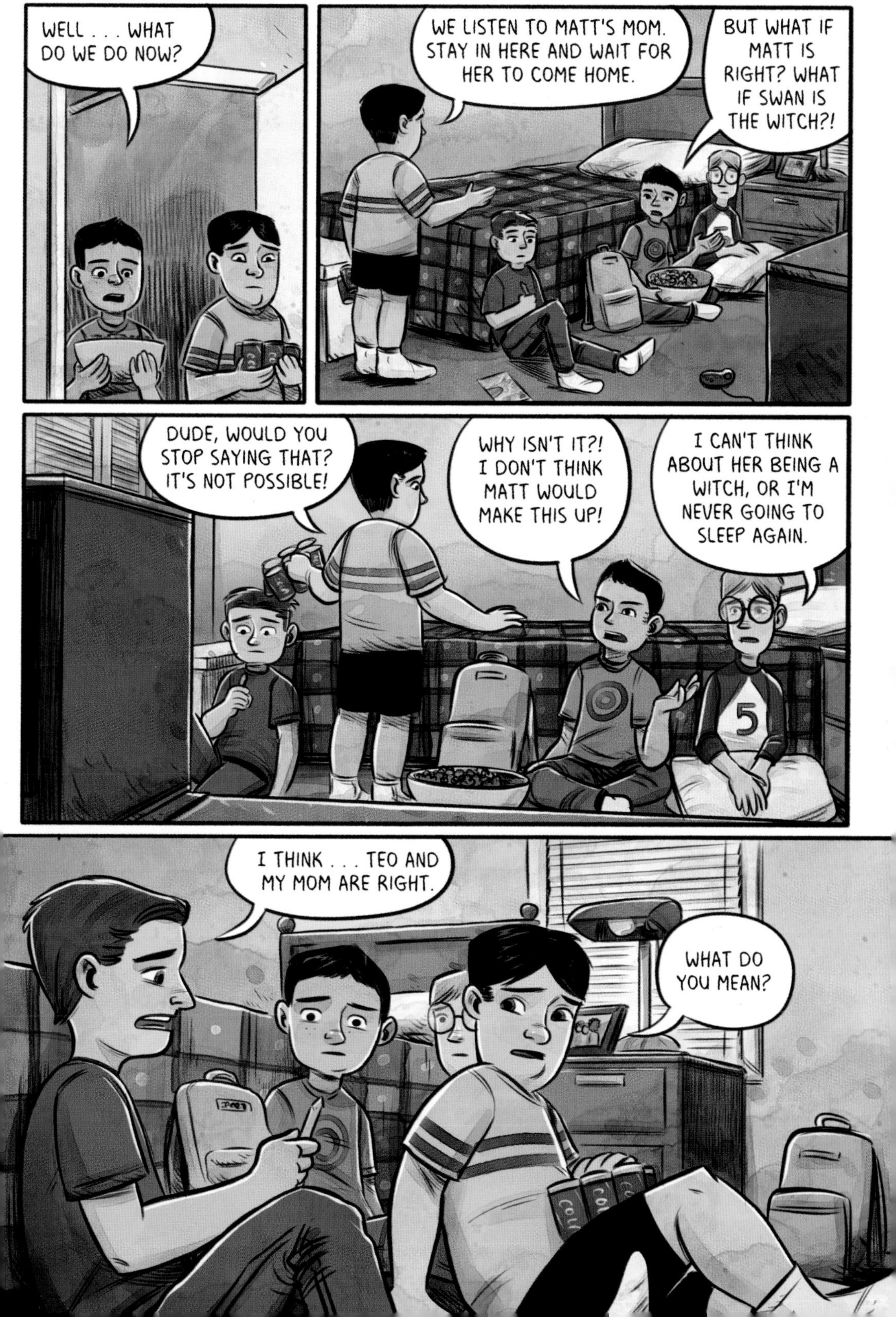
WELL . . . WHAT DO WE DO NOW?
WE LISTEN TO MATT'S MOM. STAY IN HERE AND WAIT FOR HER TO COME HOME.
BUT WHAT IF MATT IS RIGHT? WHAT IF SWAN IS THE WITCH?!
DUDE, WOULD YOU STOP SAYING THAT? IT'S NOT POSSIBLE!
WHY ISN'T IT?! I DON'T THINK MATT WOULD MAKE THIS UP!
I CAN'T THINK ABOUT HER BEING A WITCH, OR I'M NEVER GOING TO SLEEP AGAIN.
I THINK . . . TEO AND MY MOM ARE RIGHT.
WHAT DO YOU MEAN?

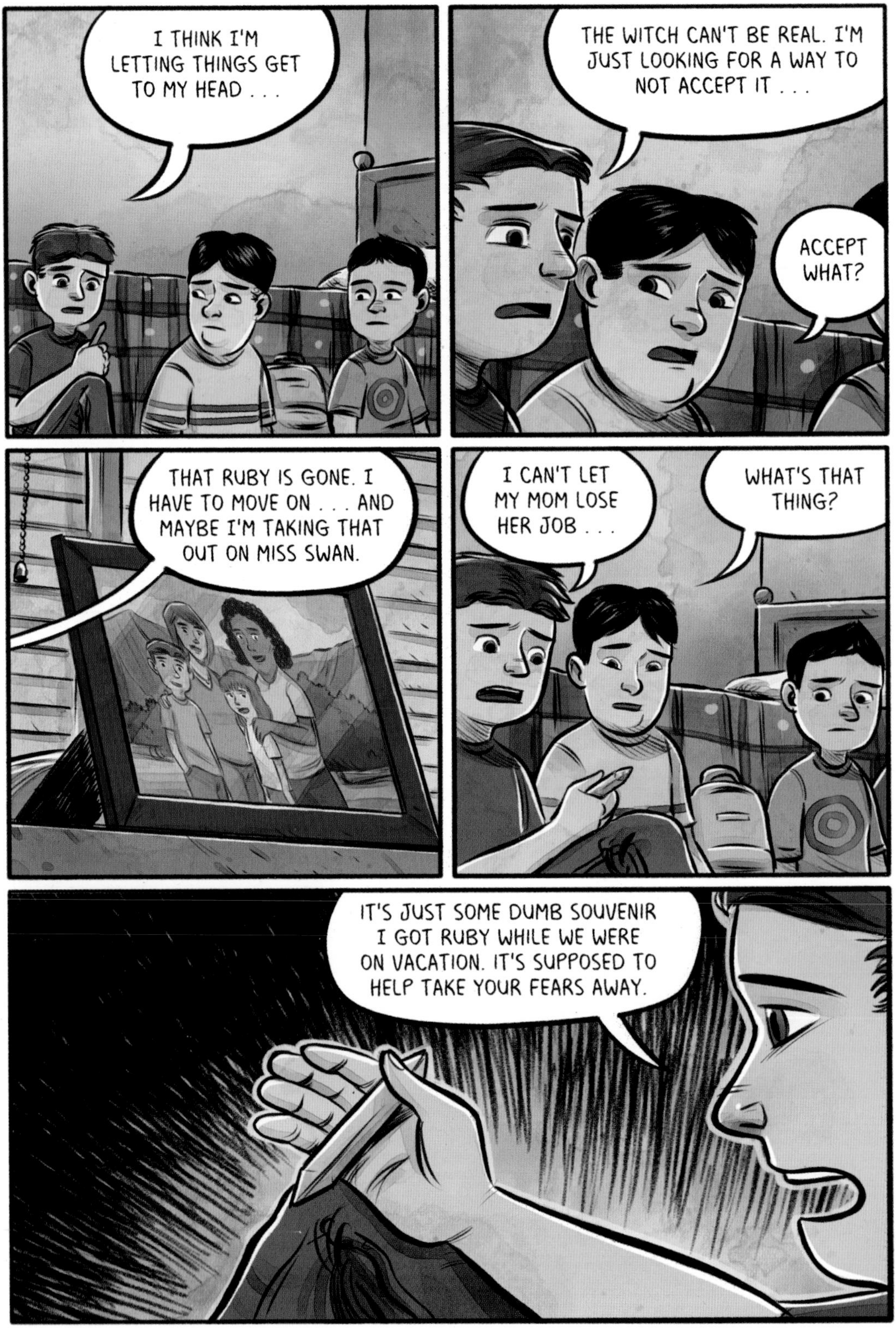
I THINK I'M LETTING THINGS GET TO MY HEAD . . .
THE WITCH CAN'T BE REAL. I'M JUST LOOKING FOR A WAY TO NOT ACCEPT IT . . .
ACCEPT WHAT?
THAT RUBY IS GONE. I HAVE TO MOVE ON . . . AND MAYBE I'M TAKING THAT OUT ON MISS SWAN.
I CAN'T LET MY MOM LOSE HER JOB . . .
WHAT'S THAT THING?
IT'S JUST SOME DUMB SOUVENIR I GOT RUBY WHILE WE WERE ON VACATION. IT'S SUPPOSED TO HELP TAKE YOUR FEARS AWAY.

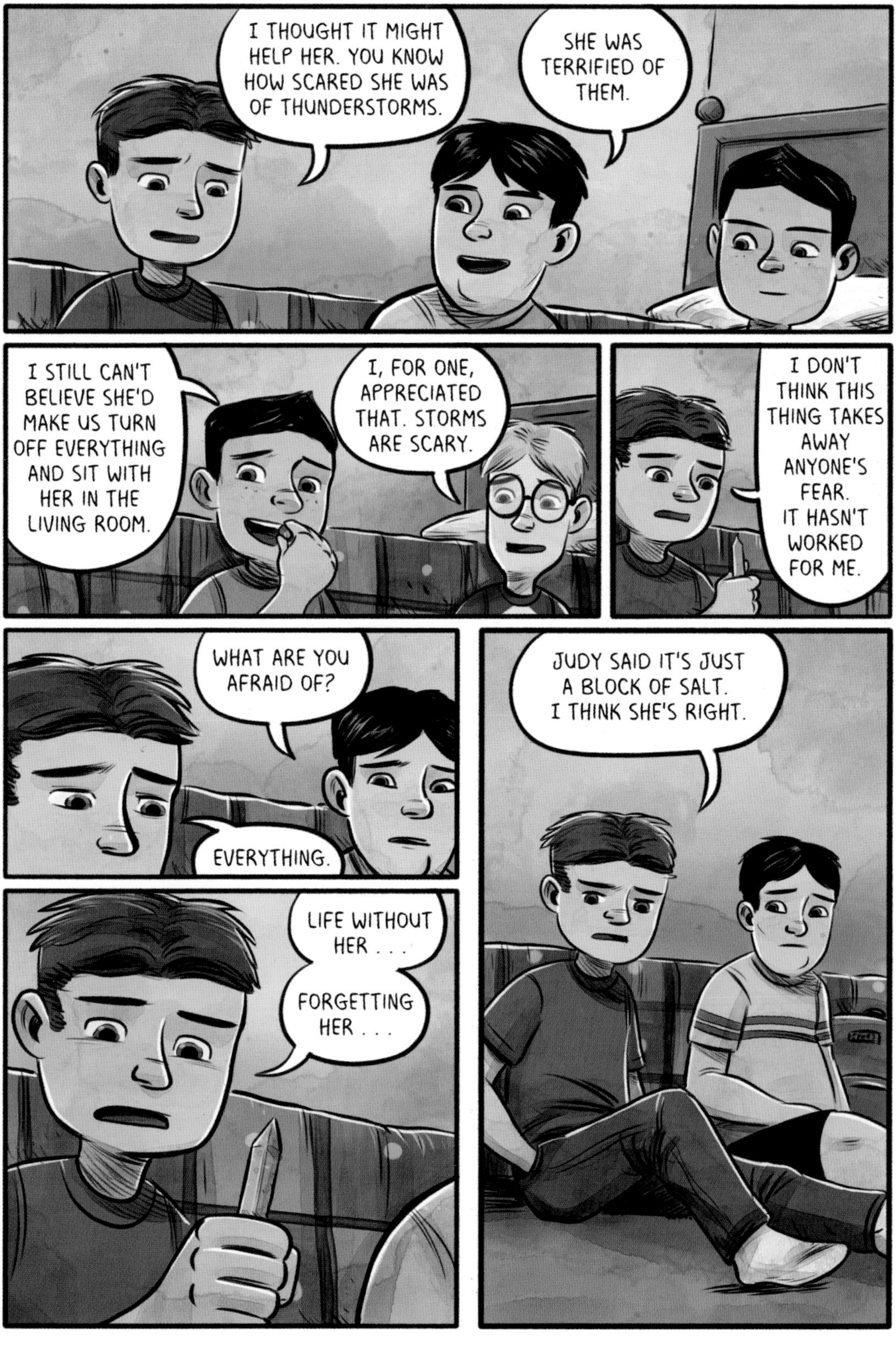

I THOUGHT IT MIGHT HELP HER. YOU KNOW HOW SCARED SHE WAS OF THUNDERSTORMS.
SHE WAS TERRIFIED OF THEM.
I STILL CAN'T BELIEVE SHE'D MAKE US TURN OFF EVERYTHING AND SIT WITH HER IN THE LIVING ROOM.
I, FOR ONE, APPRECIATED THAT. STORMS ARE SCARY.
I DON'T THINK THIS THING TAKES AWAY ANYONE'S FEAR. IT HASN'T WORKED FOR ME.
WHAT ARE YOU AFRAID OF?
EVERYTHING.
LIFE WITHOUT HER . . .
FORGETTING HER . . .
JUDY SAID IT'S JUST A BLOCK OF SALT. I THINK SHE'S RIGHT.

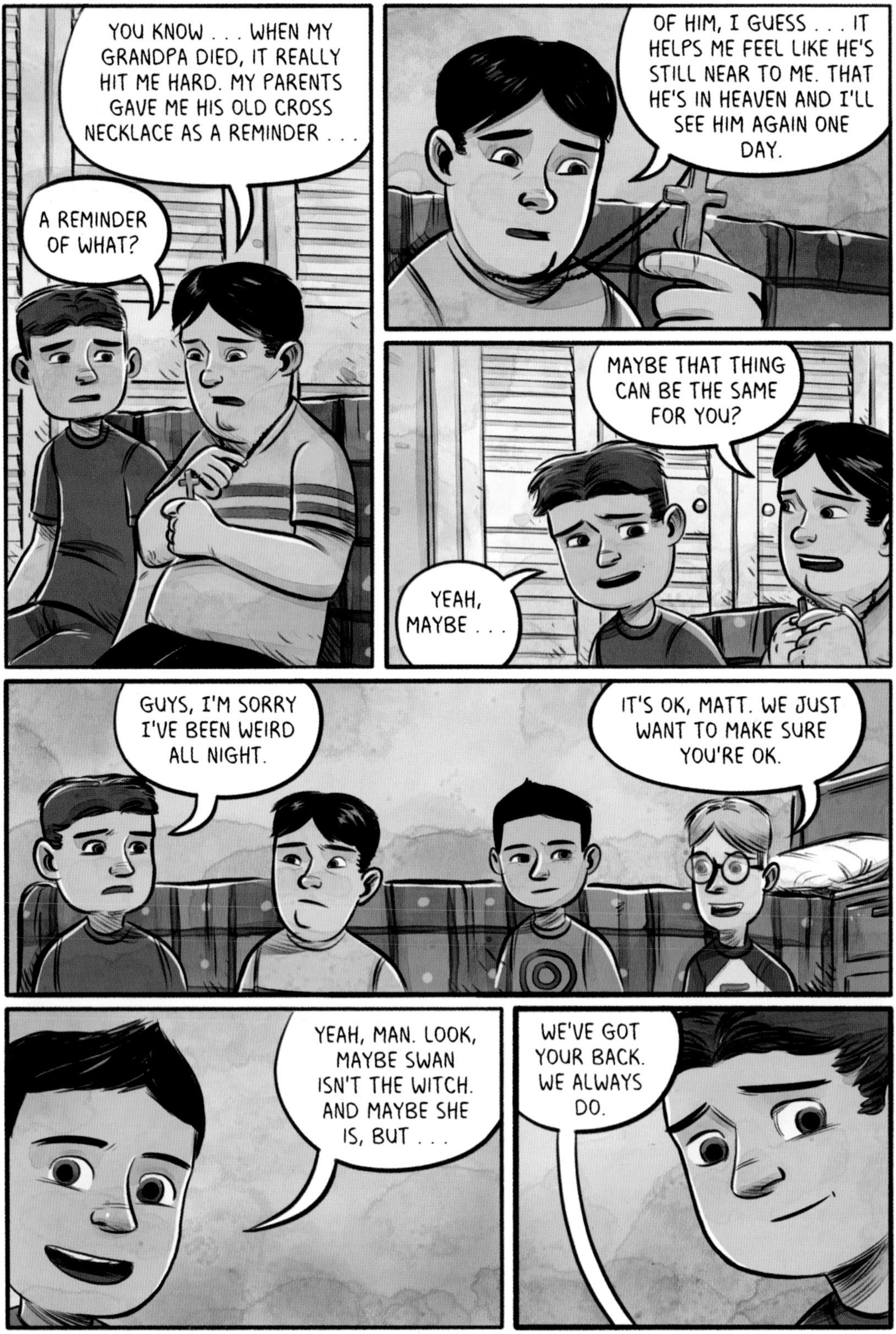
YOU KNOW . . . WHEN MY GRANDPA DIED, IT REALLY HIT ME HARD. MY PARENTS GAVE ME HIS OLD CROSS NECKLACE AS A REMINDER . . .
A REMINDER OF WHAT?
OF HIM, I GUESS . . . IT HELPS ME FEEL LIKE HE'S STILL NEAR TO ME. THAT HE'S IN HEAVEN AND I'LL SEE HIM AGAIN ONE DAY.
MAYBE THAT THING CAN BE THE SAME FOR YOU?
YEAH, MAYBE . . .
GUYS, I'M SORRY I'VE BEEN WEIRD ALL NIGHT.
IT'S OK, MATT. WE JUST WANT TO MAKE SURE YOU'RE OK.
YEAH, MAN. LOOK, MAYBE SWAN ISN'T THE WITCH. AND MAYBE SHE IS, BUT . . .
WE'VE GOT YOUR BACK. WE ALWAYS DO.

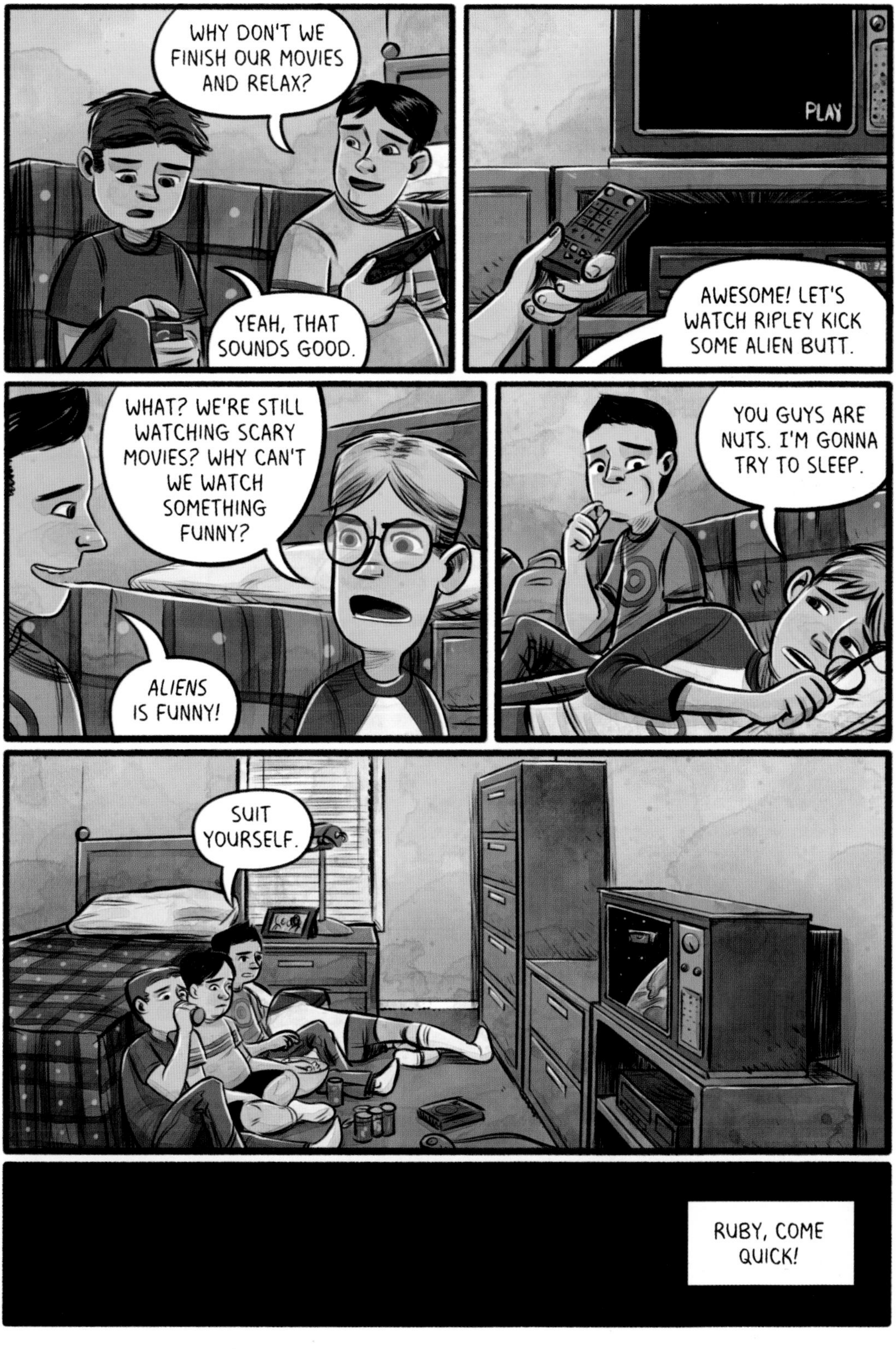
WHY DON'T WE FINISH OUR MOVIES AND RELAX?
YEAH, THAT SOUNDS GOOD.
PLAY
AWESOME! LET'S WATCH RIPLEY KICK SOME ALIEN BUTT.
WHAT? WE'RE STILL WATCHING SCARY MOVIES? WHY CAN'T WE WATCH SOMETHING FUNNY?
ALIENS IS FUNNY!
YOU GUYS ARE NUTS. I'M GONNA TRY TO SLEEP.
SUIT YOURSELF.
RUBY, COME QUICK!

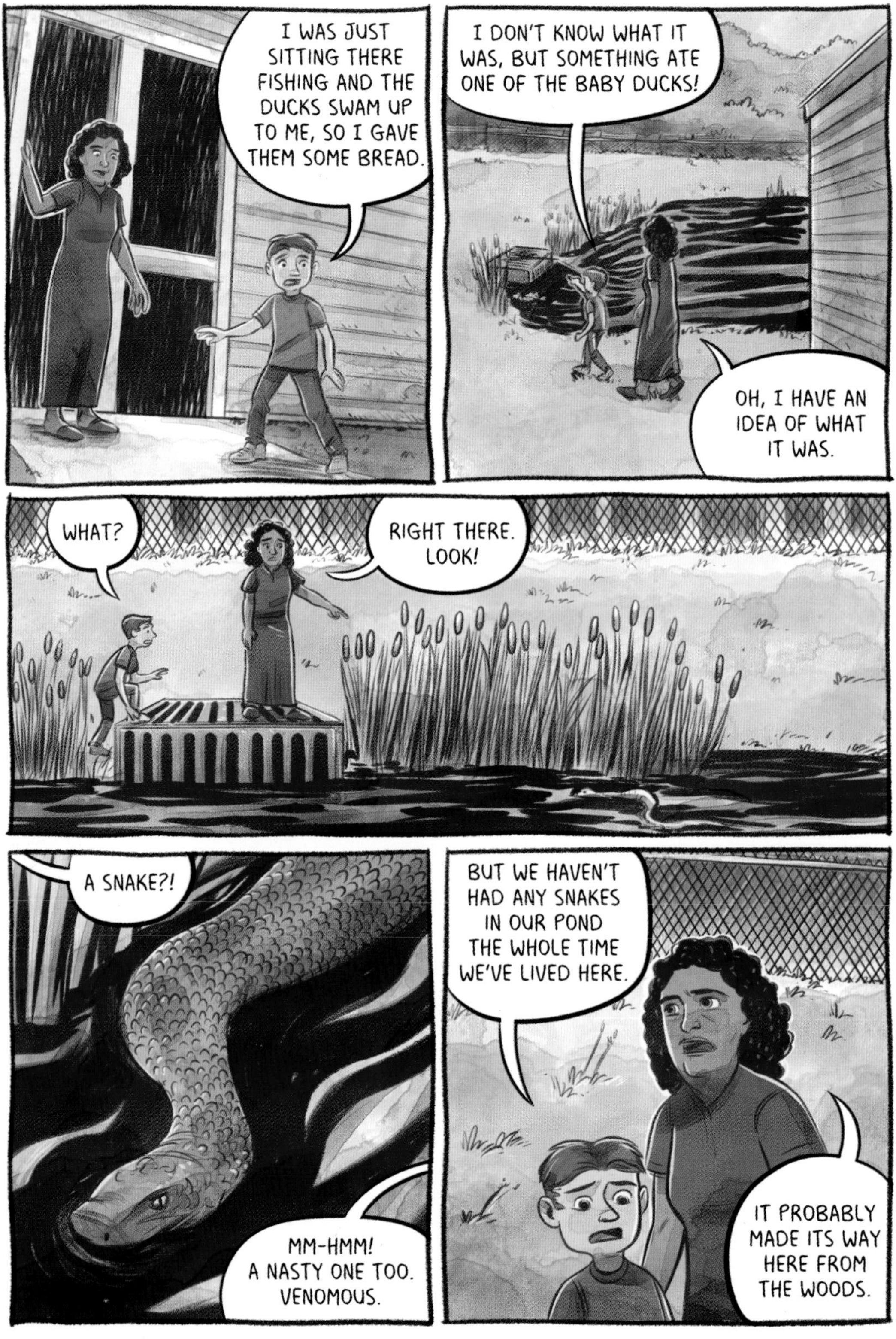
I WAS JUST SITTING THERE FISHING AND THE DUCKS SWAM UP TO ME, SO I GAVE THEM SOME BREAD.
I DON'T KNOW WHAT IT WAS, BUT SOMETHING ATE ONE OF THE BABY DUCKS!
OH, I HAVE AN IDEA OF WHAT IT WAS.
WHAT?
RIGHT THERE. LOOK!
A SNAKE?!
MM-HMM! A NASTY ONE TOO. VENOMOUS.
BUT WE HAVEN'T HAD ANY SNAKES IN OUR POND THE WHOLE TIME WE'VE LIVED HERE.
IT PROBABLY MADE ITS WAY HERE FROM THE WOODS.

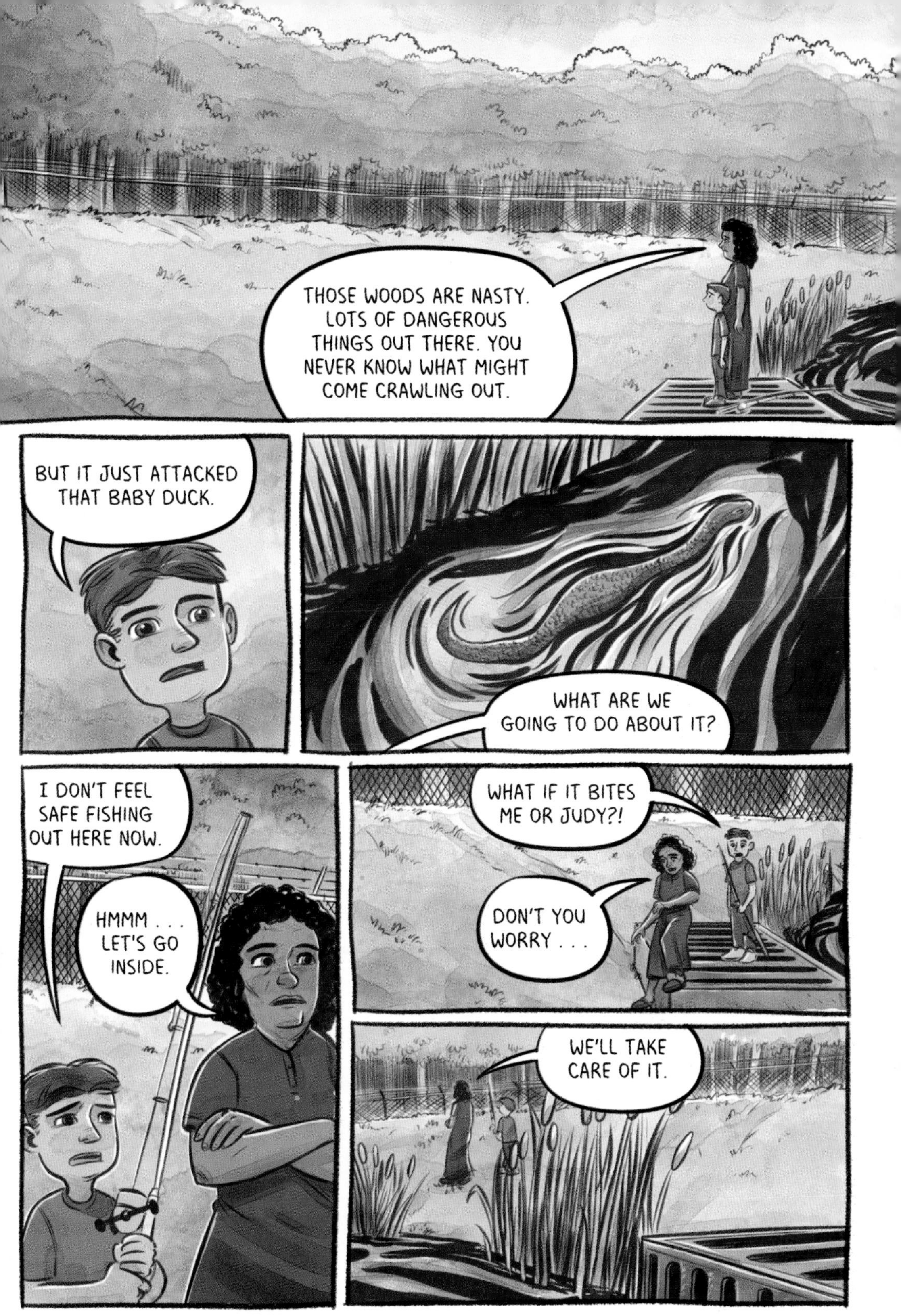

THOSE WOODS ARE NASTY. LOTS OF DANGEROUS THINGS OUT THERE. YOU NEVER KNOW WHAT MIGHT COME CRAWLING OUT.
BUT IT JUST ATTACKED THAT BABY DUCK.
WHAT ARE WE GOING TO DO ABOUT IT?
I DON'T FEEL SAFE FISHING OUT HERE NOW.
HMMM . . . LET'S GO INSIDE.
WHAT IF IT BITES ME OR JUDY?!
DON'T YOU WORRY . . .
WE'LL TAKE CARE OF IT.

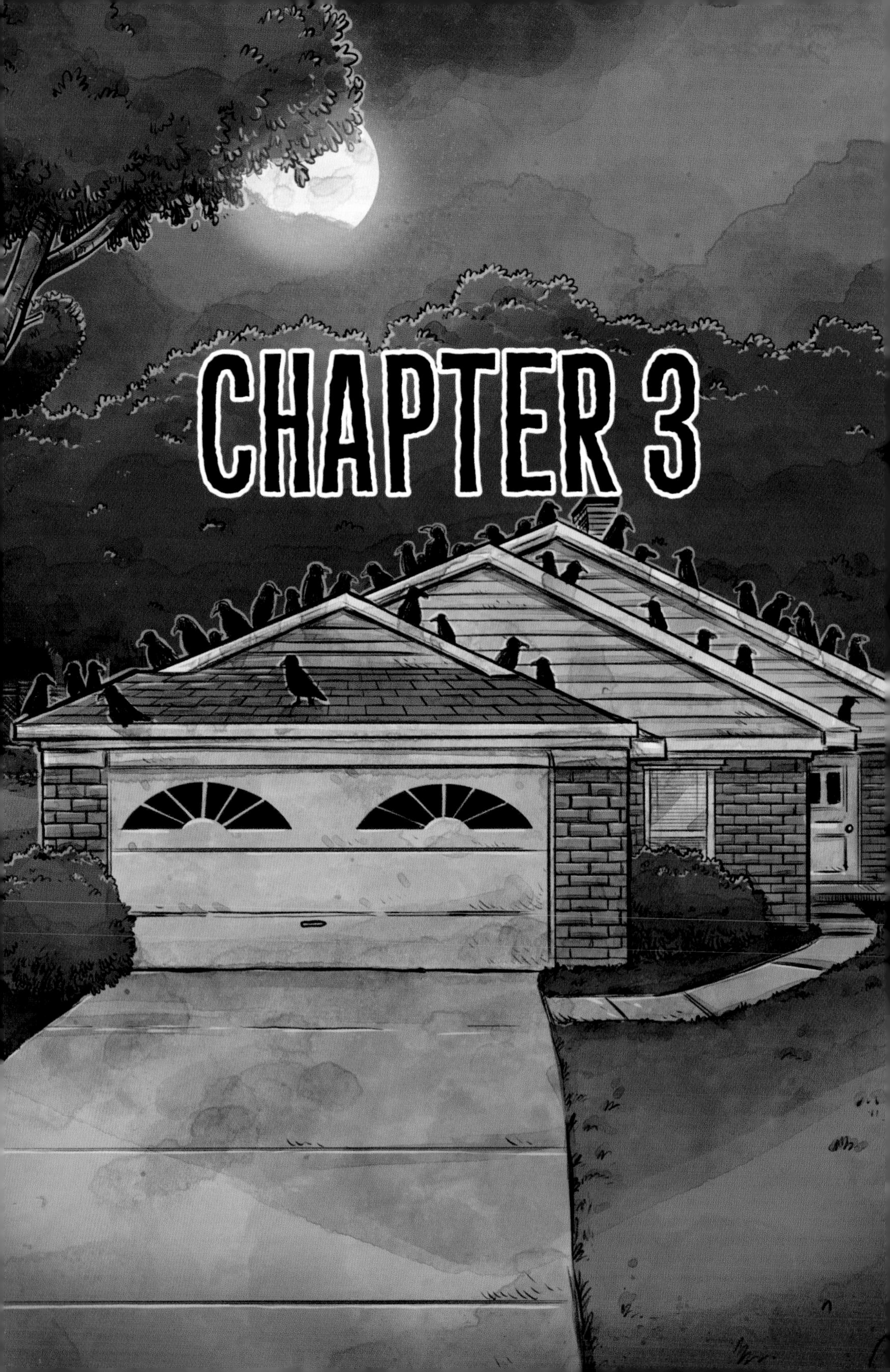
CHAPTER 3

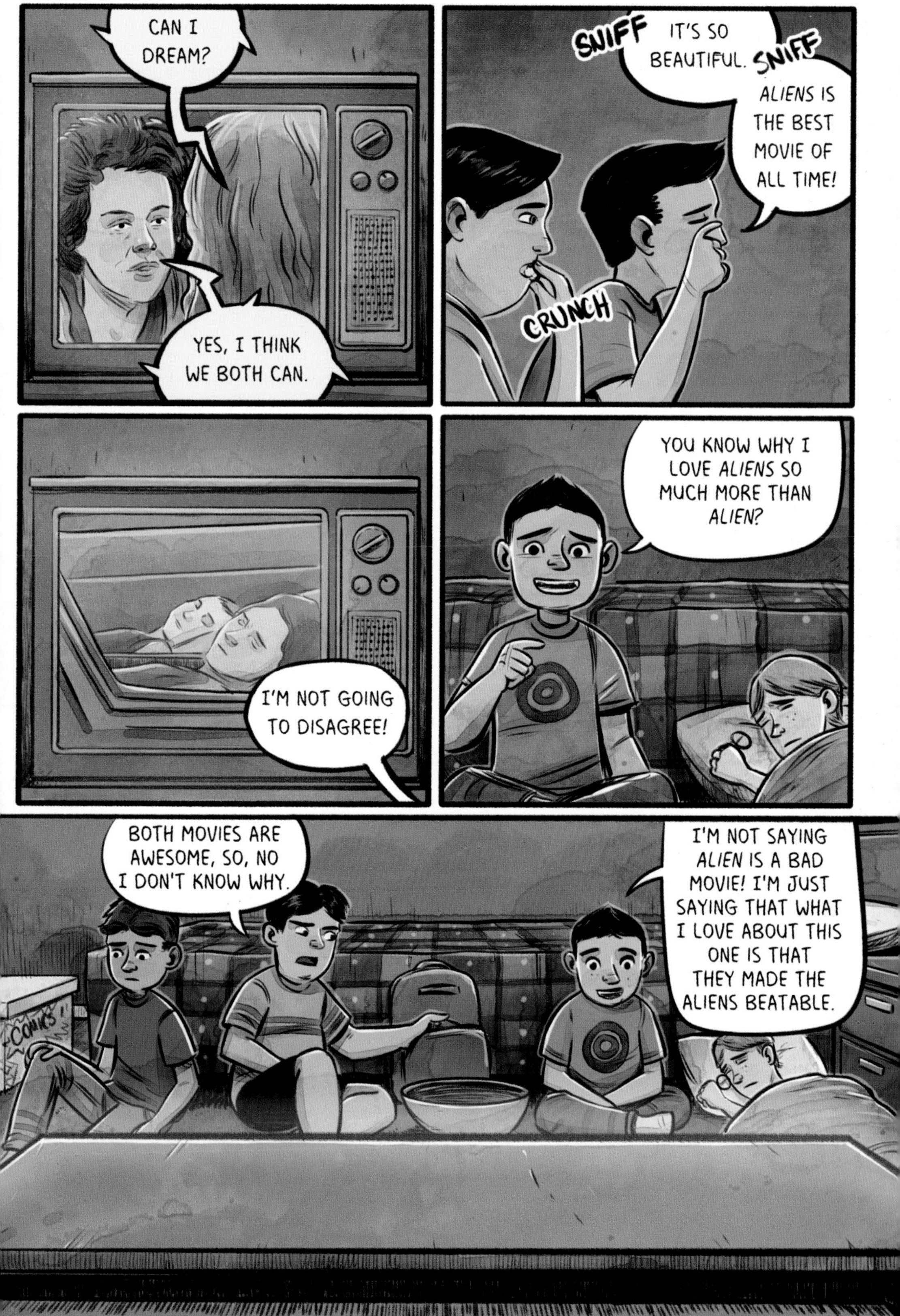
CAN I DREAM?
YES, I THINK WE BOTH CAN.
SNIFF
IT'S SO BEAUTIFUL.
SNIFF
ALIENS IS THE BEST MOVIE OF ALL TIME!
CRUNCH
I'M NOT GOING TO DISAGREE!
YOU KNOW WHY I LOVE ALIENS SO MUCH MORE THAN ALIEN?
BOTH MOVIES ARE AWESOME, SO, NO I DON'T KNOW WHY.
I'M NOT SAYING ALIEN IS A BAD MOVIE! I'M JUST SAYING THAT WHAT I LOVE ABOUT THIS ONE IS THAT THEY MADE THE ALIENS BEATABLE.
COMICS

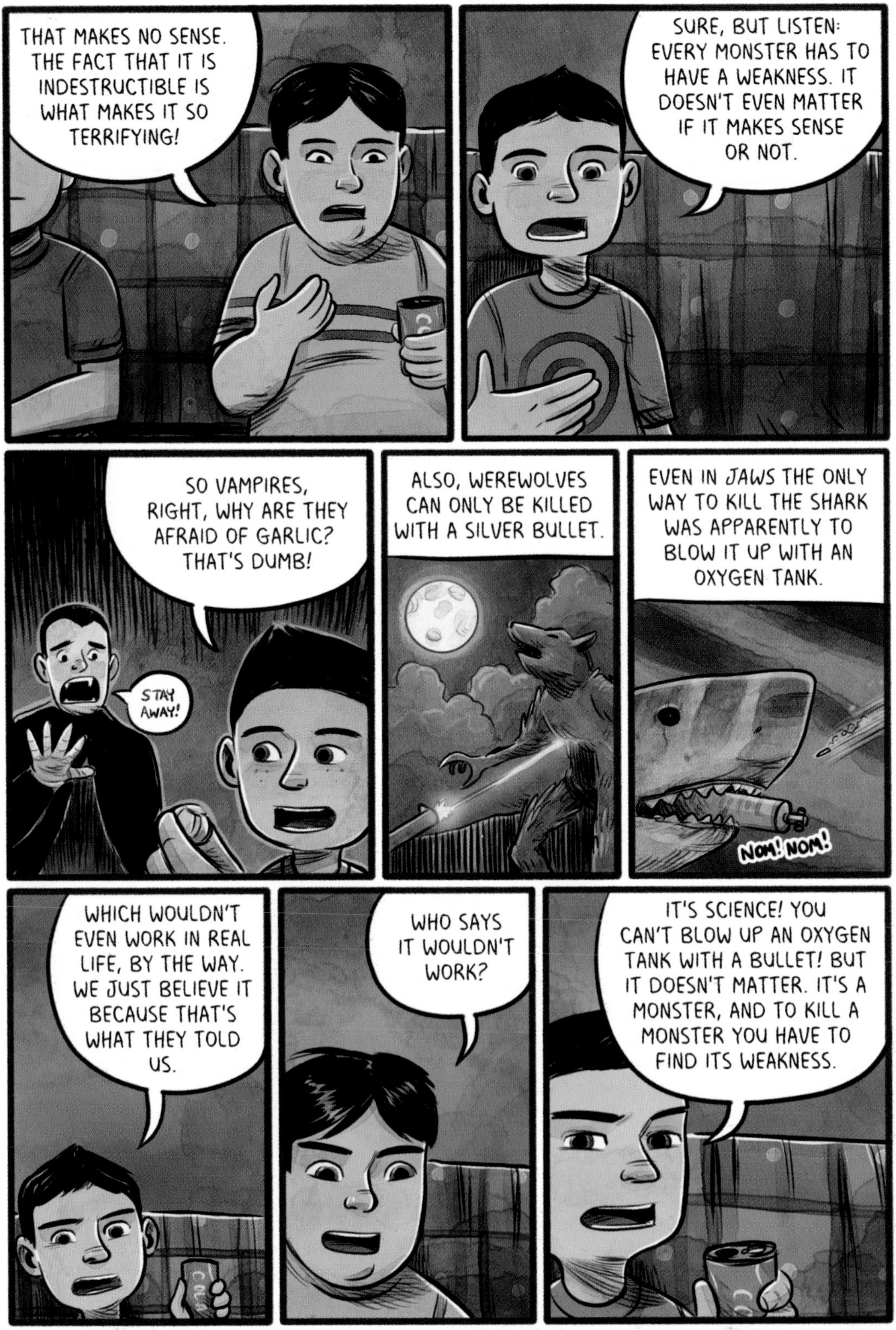
THAT MAKES NO SENSE. THE FACT THAT IT IS INDESTRUCTIBLE IS WHAT MAKES IT SO TERRIFYING!
SURE, BUT LISTEN: EVERY MONSTER HAS TO HAVE A WEAKNESS. IT DOESN'T EVEN MATTER IF IT MAKES SENSE OR NOT.
SO VAMPIRES, RIGHT, WHY ARE THEY AFRAID OF GARLIC? THAT'S DUMB!
STAY AWAY!
ALSO, WEREWOLVES CAN ONLY BE KILLED WITH A SILVER BULLET.
EVEN IN *JAWS* THE ONLY WAY TO KILL THE SHARK WAS APPARENTLY TO BLOW IT UP WITH AN OXYGEN TANK.
NOM! NOM!
WHICH WOULDN'T EVEN WORK IN REAL LIFE, BY THE WAY. WE JUST BELIEVE IT BECAUSE THAT'S WHAT THEY TOLD US.
WHO SAYS IT WOULDN'T WORK?
IT'S SCIENCE! YOU CAN'T BLOW UP AN OXYGEN TANK WITH A BULLET! BUT IT DOESN'T MATTER. IT'S A MONSTER, AND TO KILL A MONSTER YOU HAVE TO FIND ITS WEAKNESS.

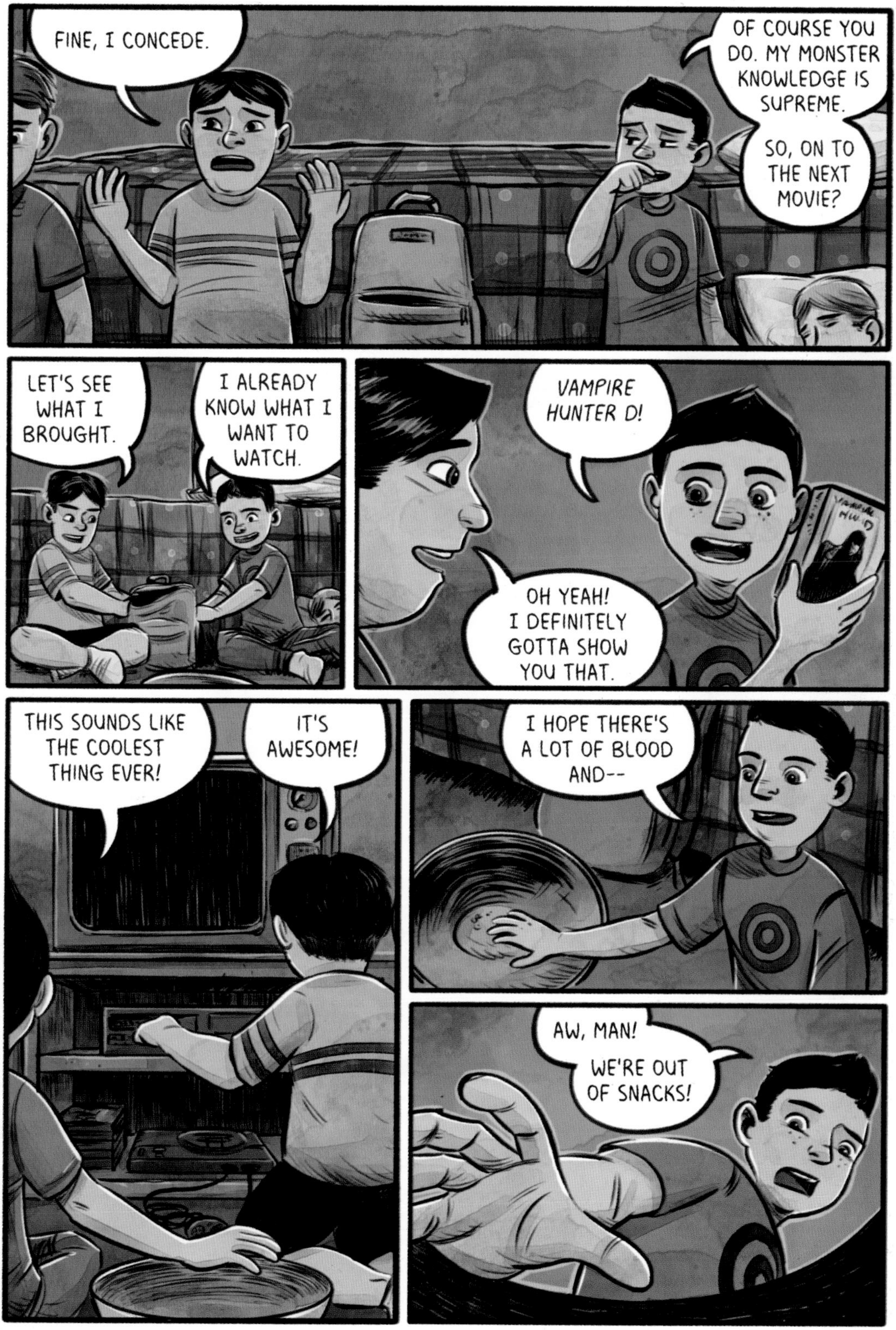
FINE, I CONCEDE.
OF COURSE YOU DO. MY MONSTER KNOWLEDGE IS SUPREME.
SO, ON TO THE NEXT MOVIE?
LET'S SEE WHAT I BROUGHT.
I ALREADY KNOW WHAT I WANT TO WATCH.
VAMPIRE HUNTER D!
OH YEAH! I DEFINITELY GOTTA SHOW YOU THAT.
THIS SOUNDS LIKE THE COOLEST THING EVER!
IT'S AWESOME!
I HOPE THERE'S A LOT OF BLOOD AND--
AW, MAN!
WE'RE OUT OF SNACKS!

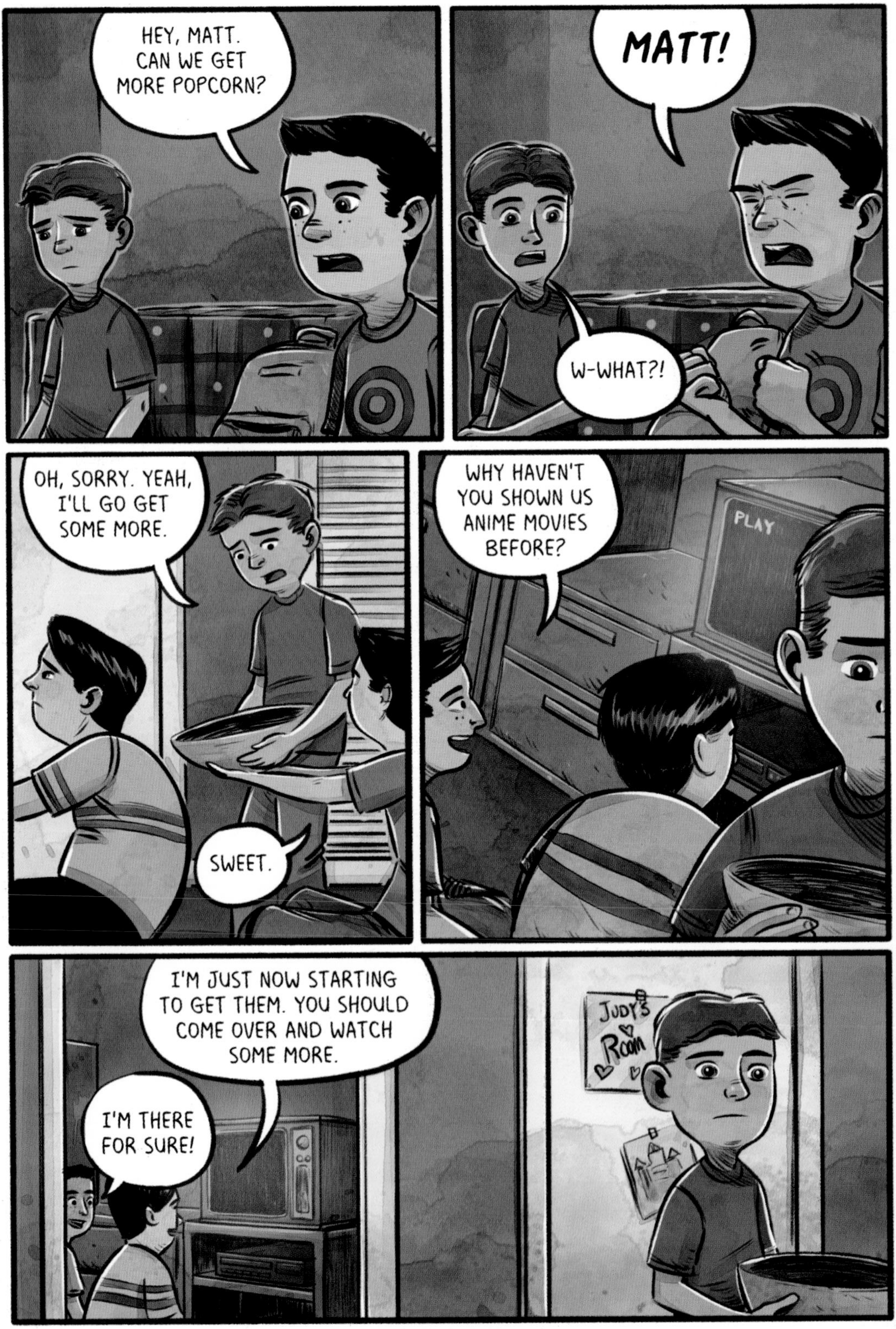
HEY, MATT. CAN WE GET MORE POPCORN?
MATT!
W-WHAT?!
OH, SORRY. YEAH, I'LL GO GET SOME MORE.
SWEET.
WHY HAVEN'T YOU SHOWN US ANIME MOVIES BEFORE?
PLAY
I'M JUST NOW STARTING TO GET THEM. YOU SHOULD COME OVER AND WATCH SOME MORE.
I'M THERE FOR SURE!
JUDY'S ROOM

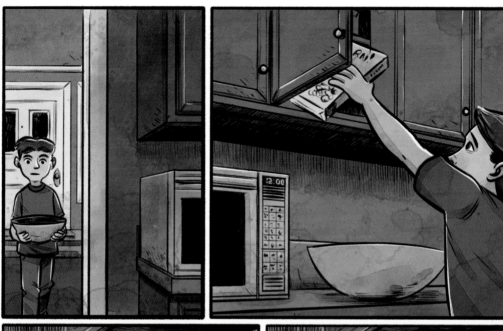

BEEP

VRRRRR

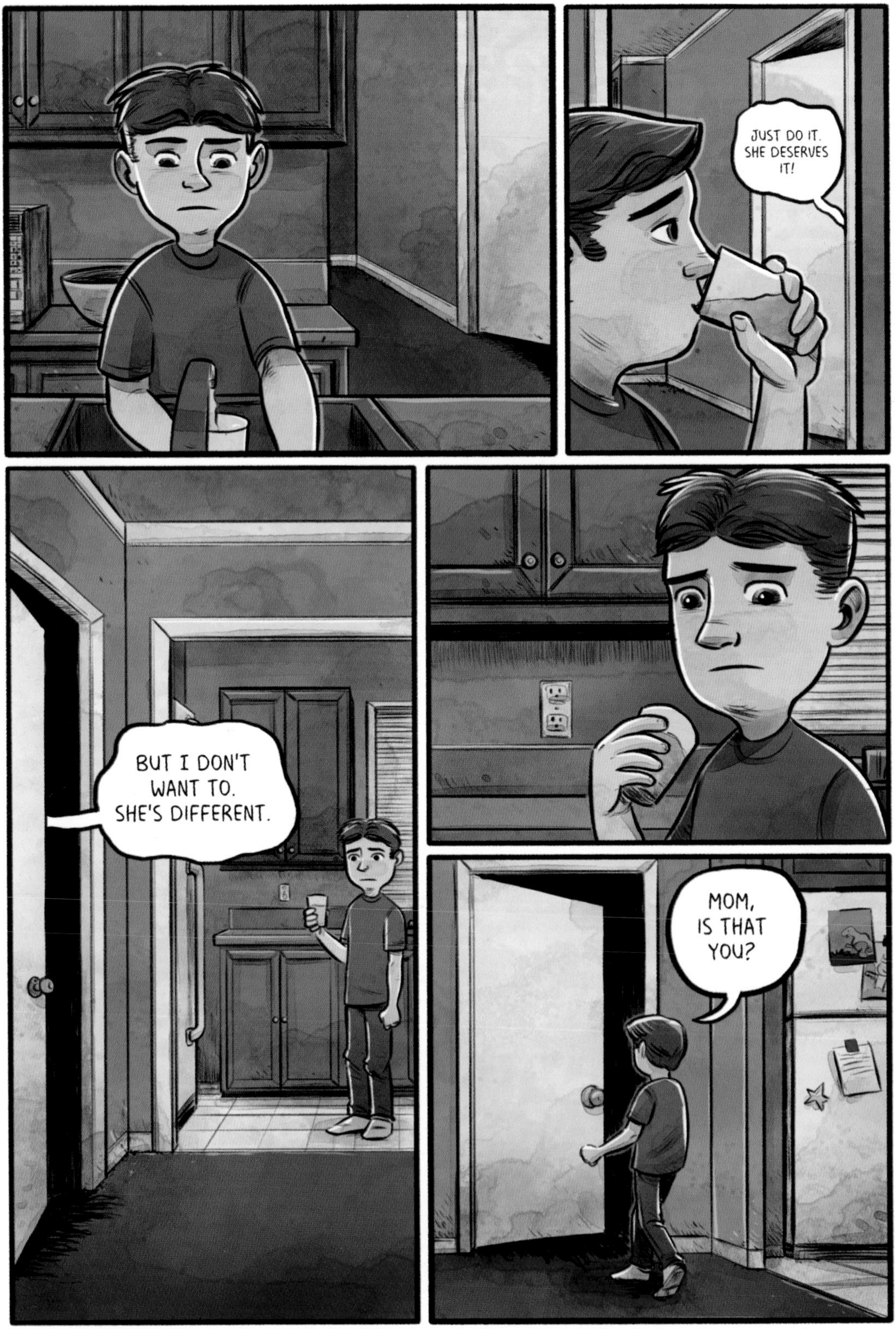
JUST DO IT. SHE DESERVES IT!
BUT I DON'T WANT TO. SHE'S DIFFERENT.
MOM, IS THAT YOU?

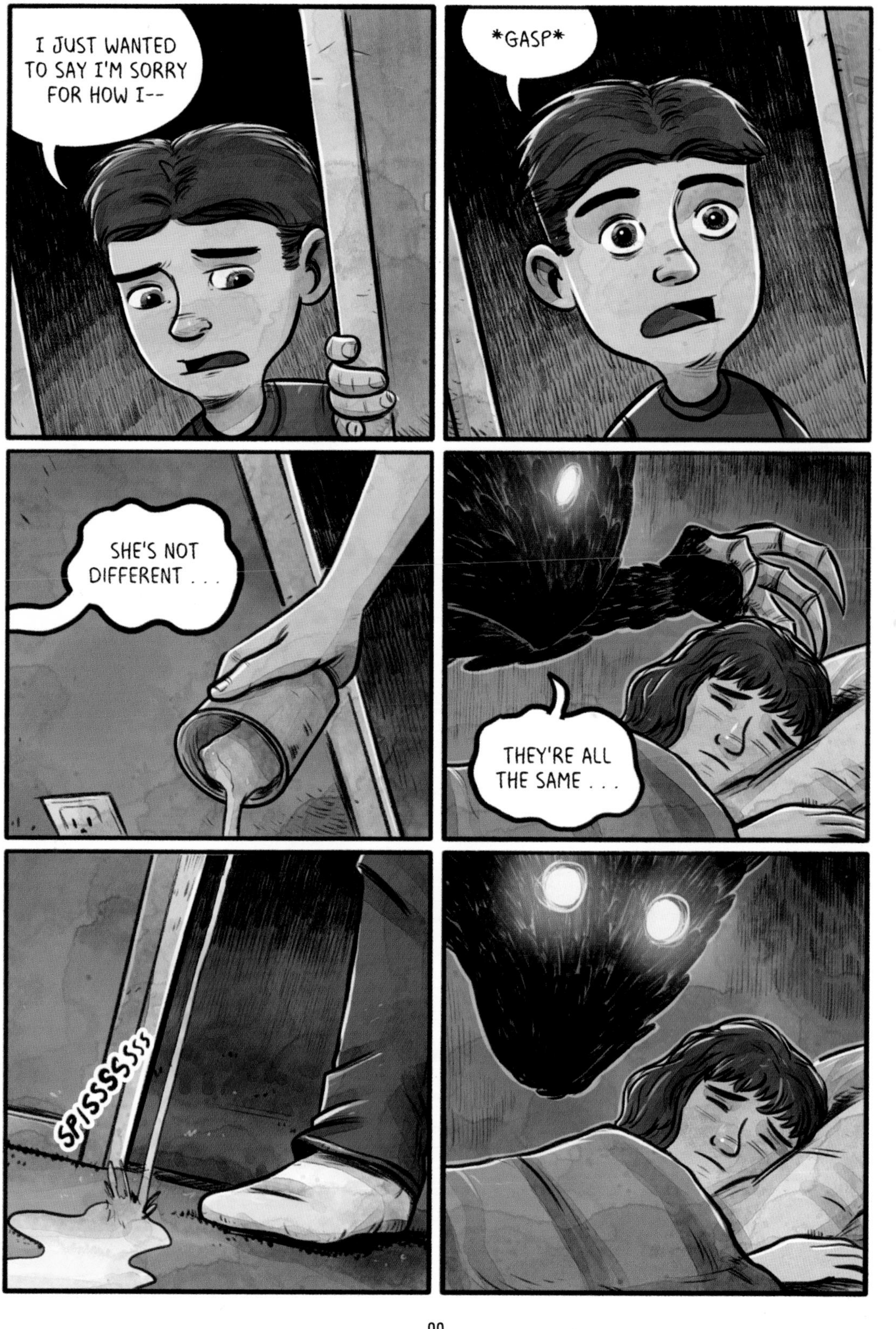
I JUST WANTED TO SAY I'M SORRY FOR HOW I--
GASP
SHE'S NOT DIFFERENT . . .
THEY'RE ALL THE SAME . . .
SPISSSSSSS

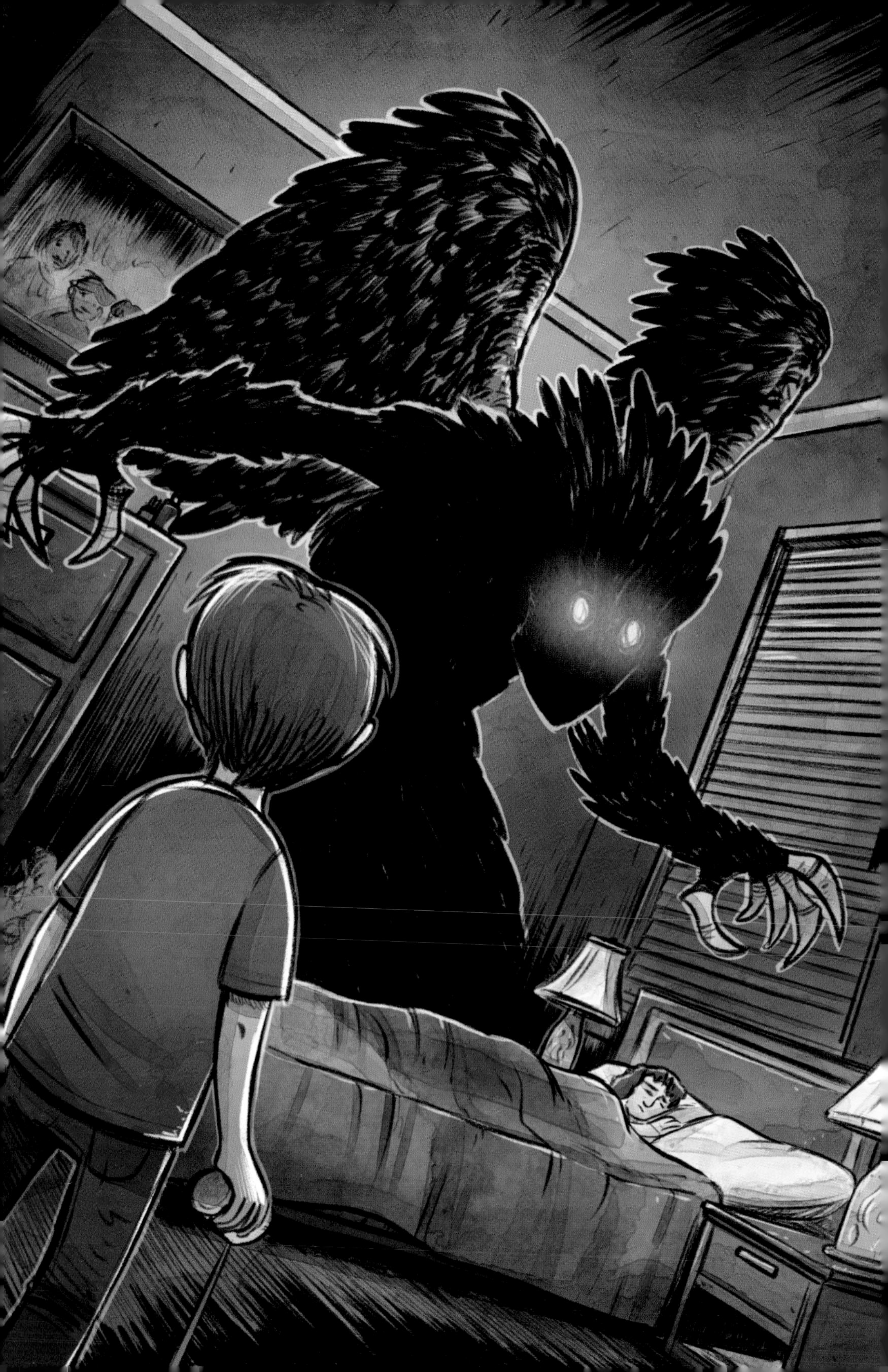

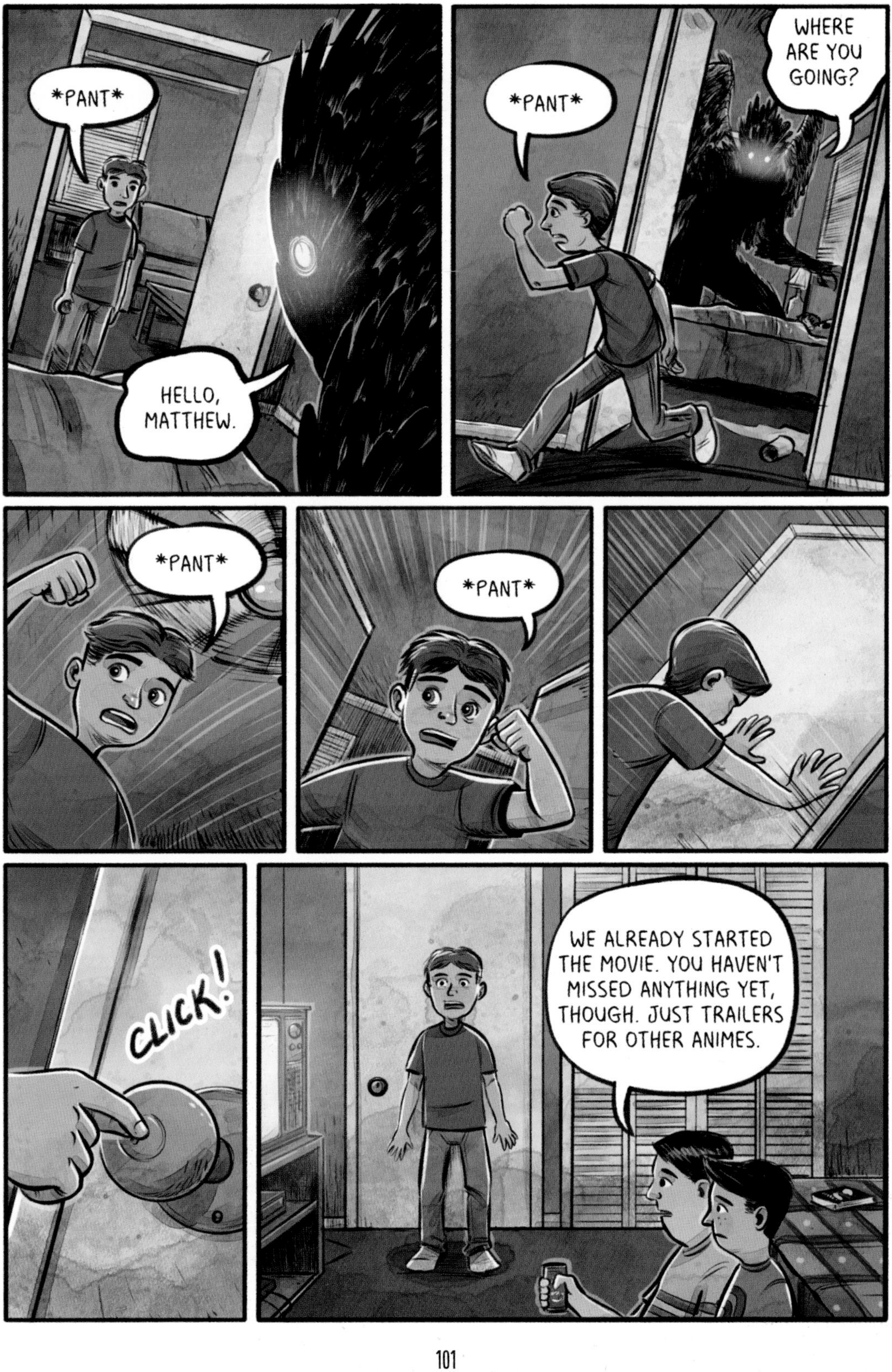
PANT
HELLO, MATTHEW.
PANT
WHERE ARE YOU GOING?
PANT
PANT
CLICK!
WE ALREADY STARTED THE MOVIE. YOU HAVEN'T MISSED ANYTHING YET, THOUGH. JUST TRAILERS FOR OTHER ANIMES.

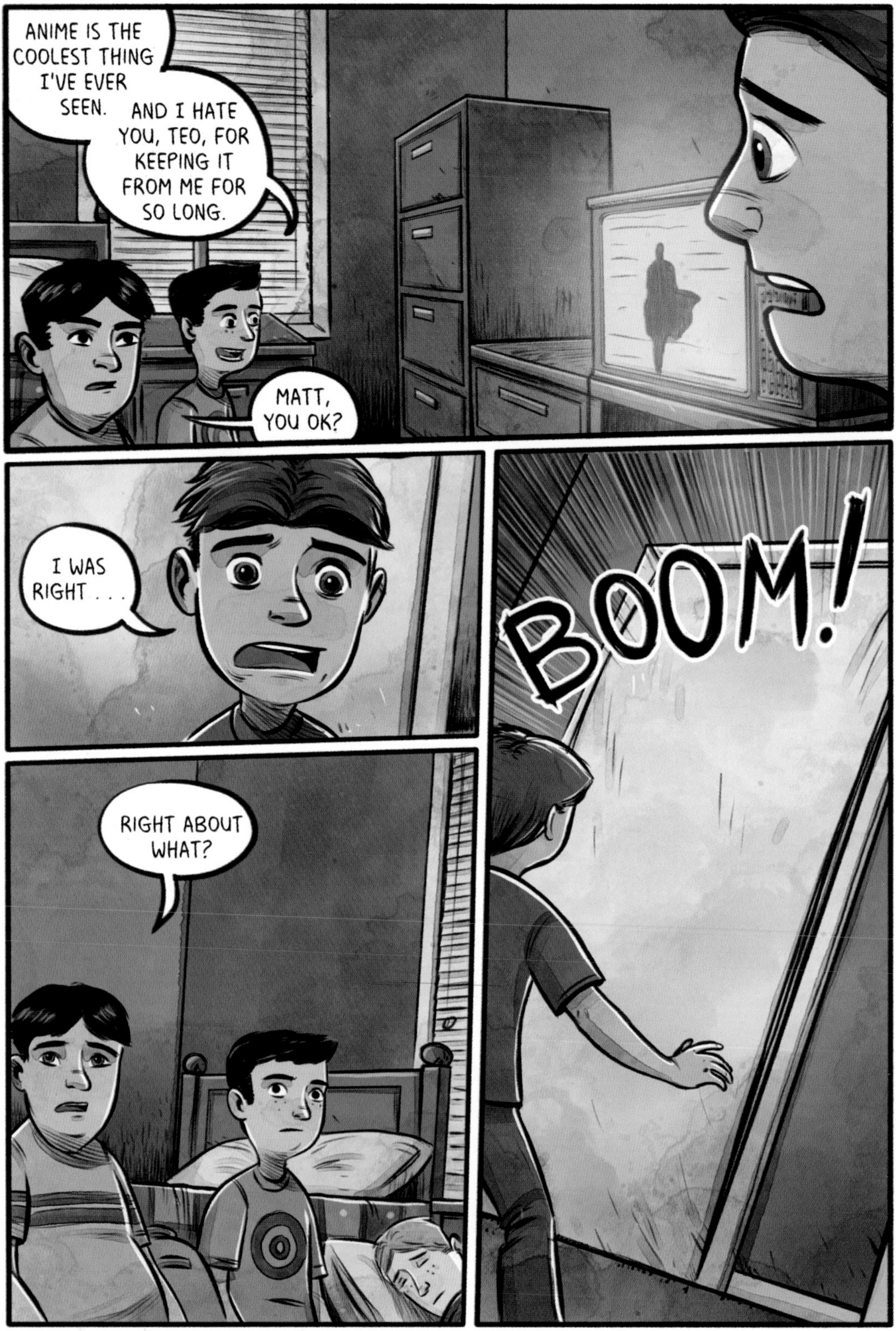
ANIME IS THE COOLEST THING I'VE EVER SEEN.
AND I HATE YOU, TEO, FOR KEEPING IT FROM ME FOR SO LONG.
MATT, YOU OK?
I WAS RIGHT . . .
RIGHT ABOUT WHAT?
BOOM!

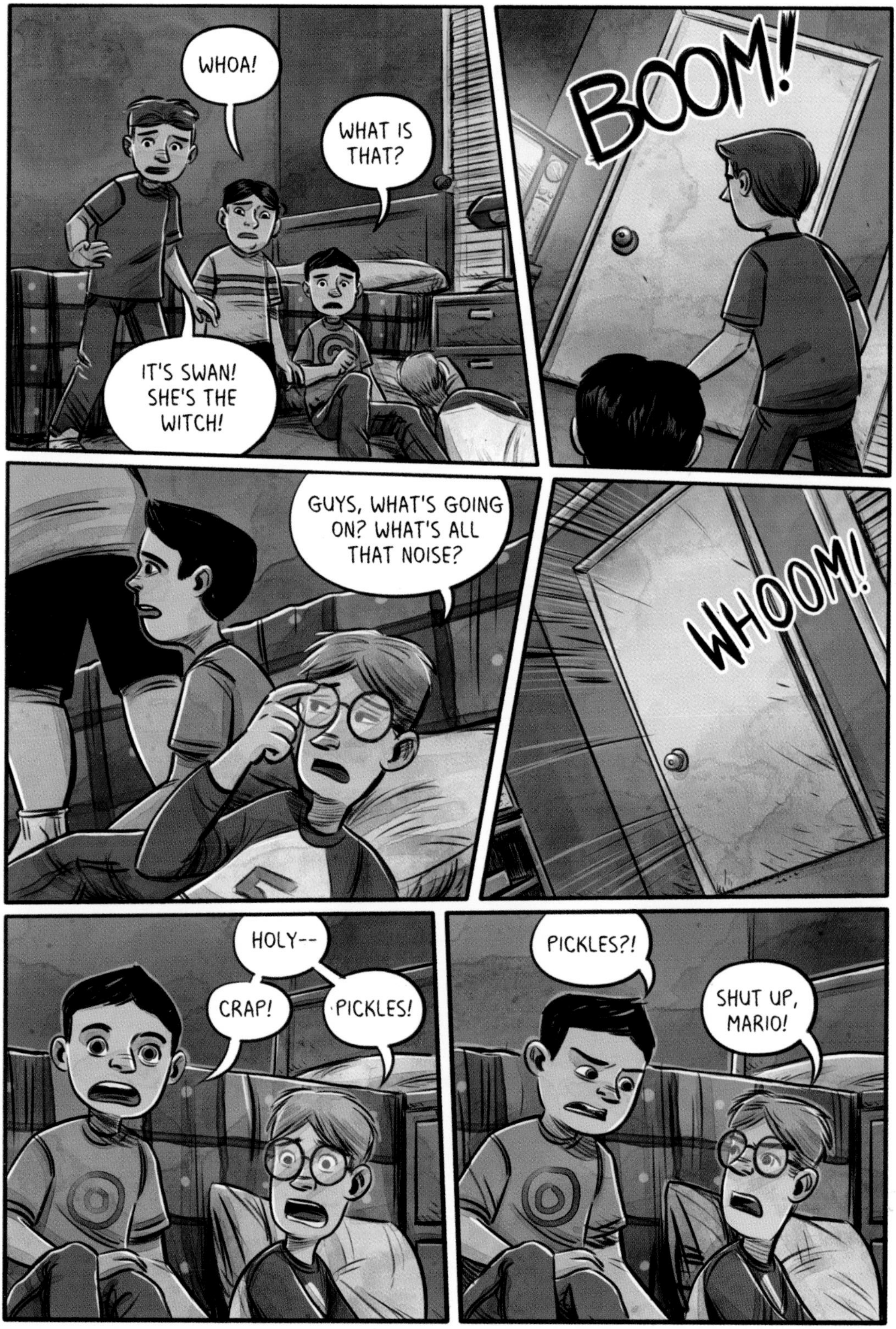
WHOA!
WHAT IS THAT?
IT'S SWAN! SHE'S THE WITCH!
BOOM!
GUYS, WHAT'S GOING ON? WHAT'S ALL THAT NOISE?
WHOOM!
HOLY--
CRAP!
PICKLES!
PICKLES?!
SHUT UP, MARIO!

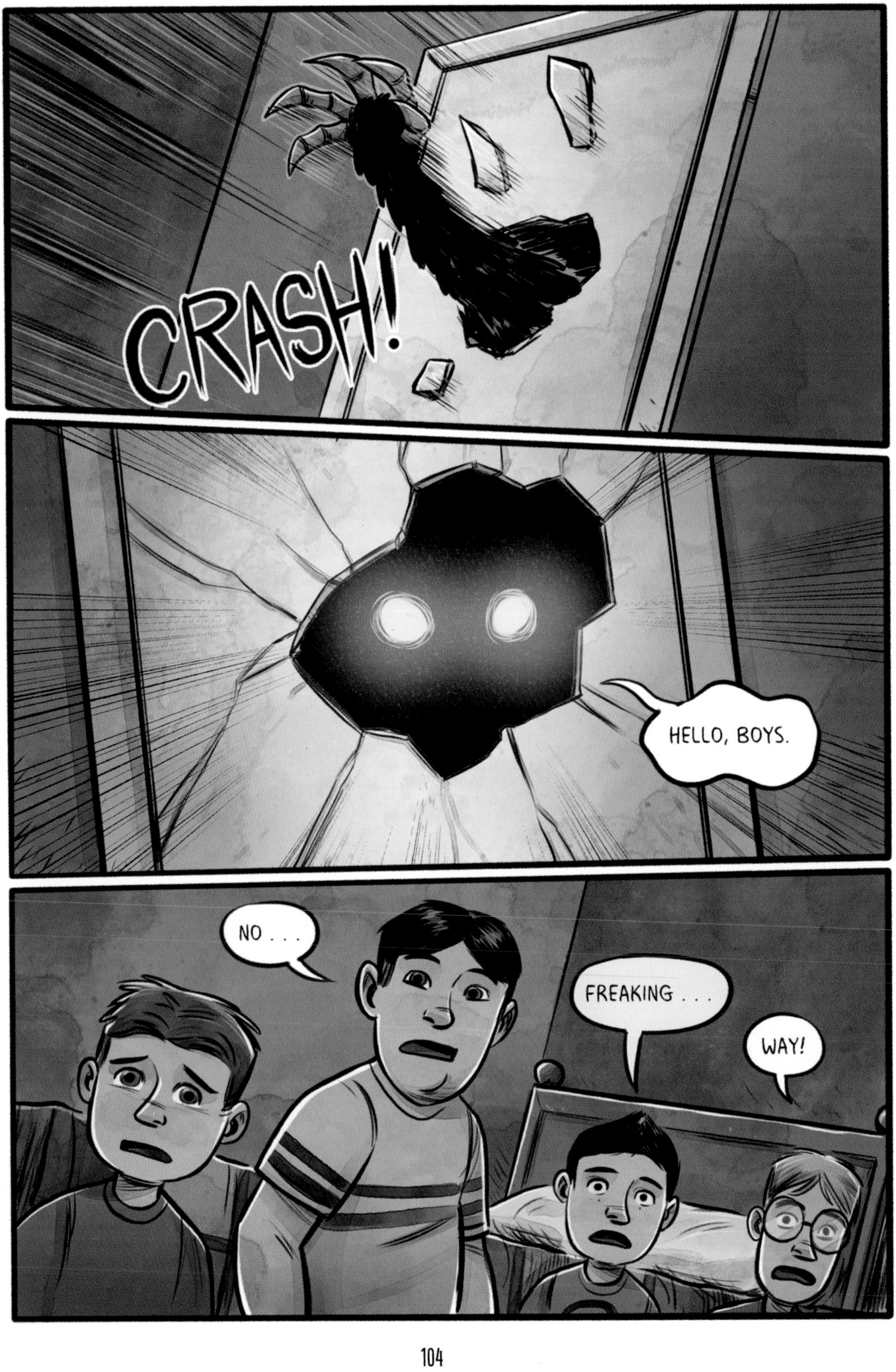
CRASH!
HELLO, BOYS.
NO . . .
FREAKING . . .
WAY!

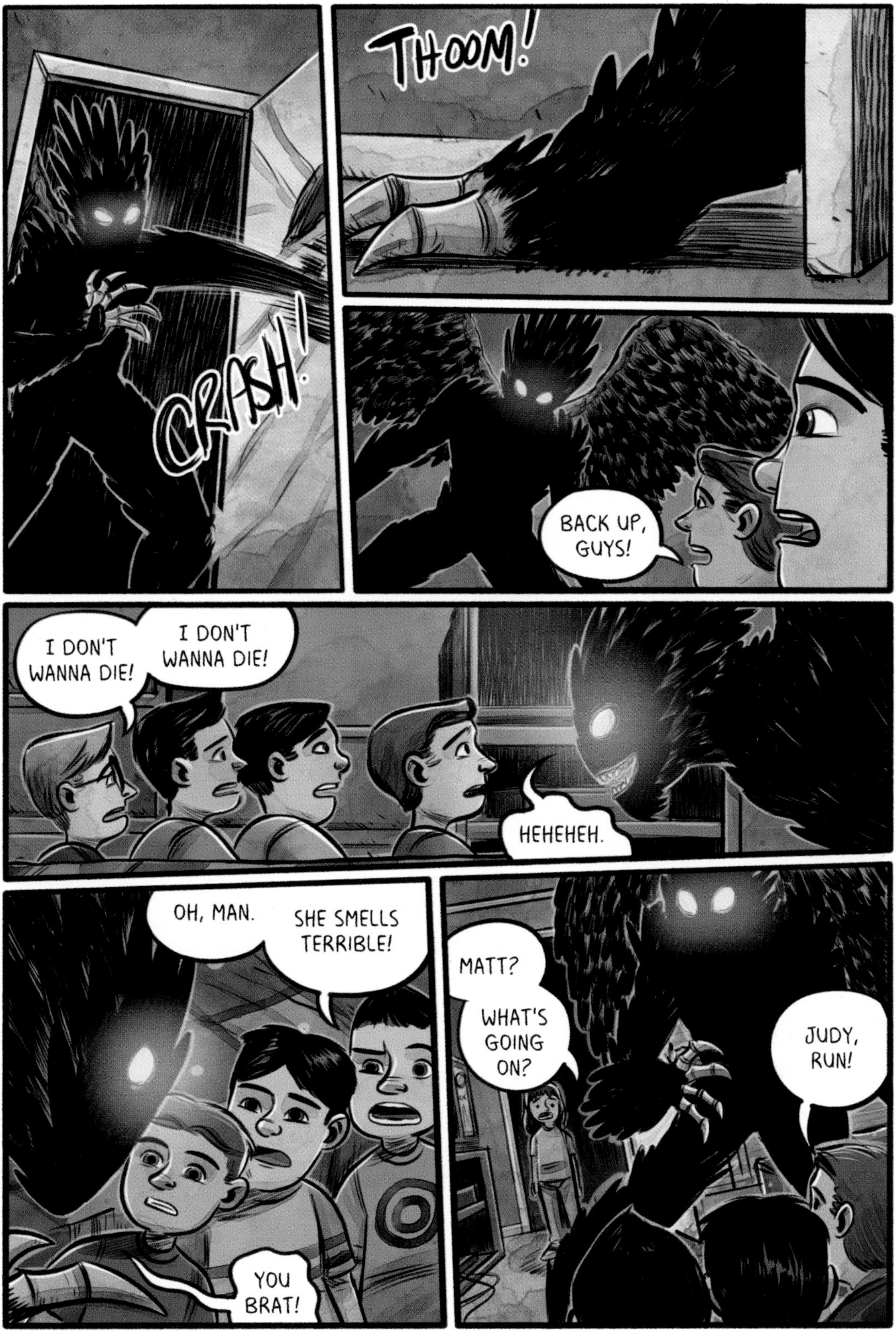
THOOM!
CRASH!
BACK UP, GUYS!
I DON'T WANNA DIE!
I DON'T WANNA DIE!
HEHEHEH.
OH, MAN.
SHE SMELLS TERRIBLE!
YOU BRAT!
MATT?
WHAT'S GOING ON?
JUDY, RUN!

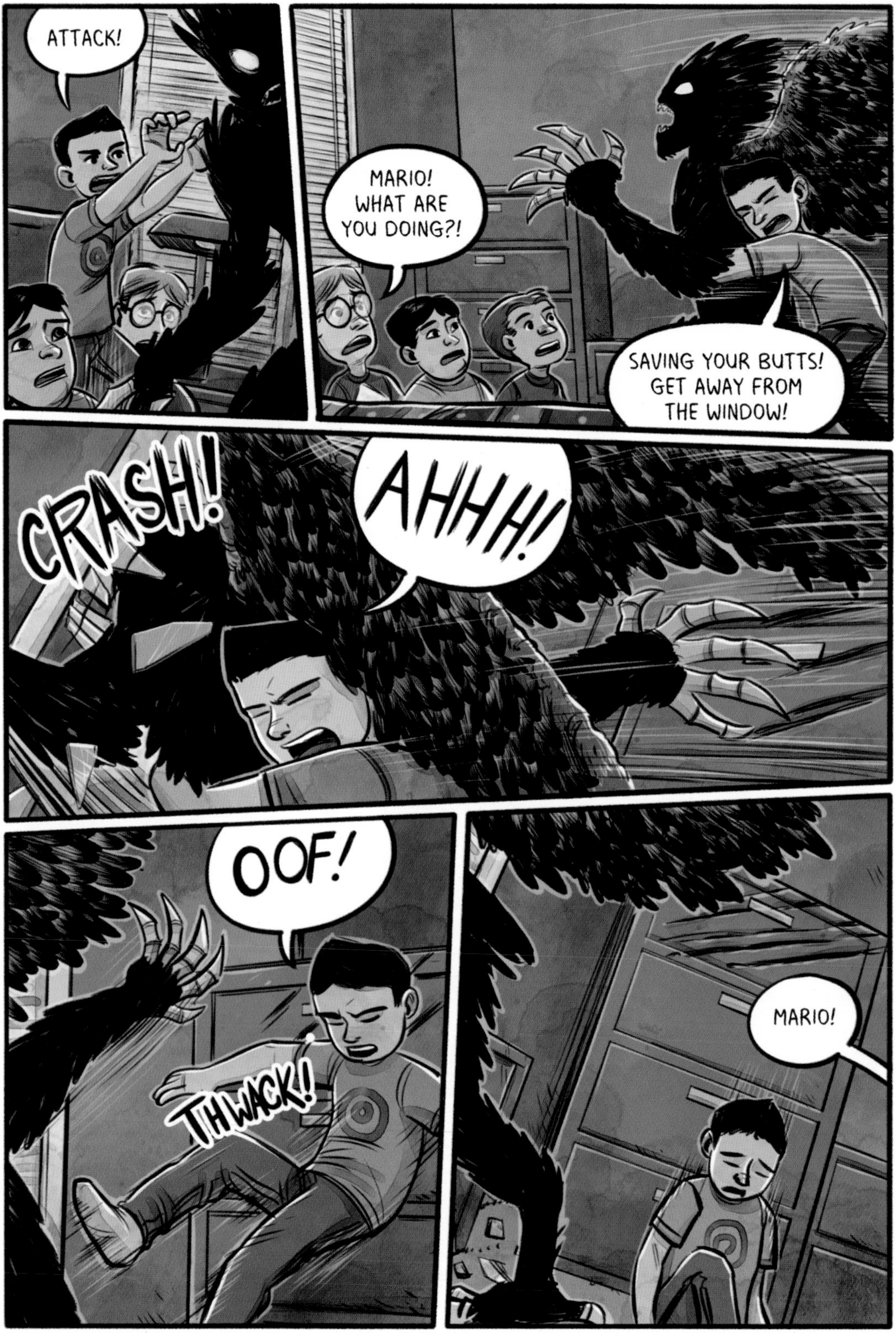
ATTACK!
MARIO! WHAT ARE YOU DOING?!
SAVING YOUR BUTTS! GET AWAY FROM THE WINDOW!
CRASH!
AHHH!
OOF!
THWACK!
MARIO!

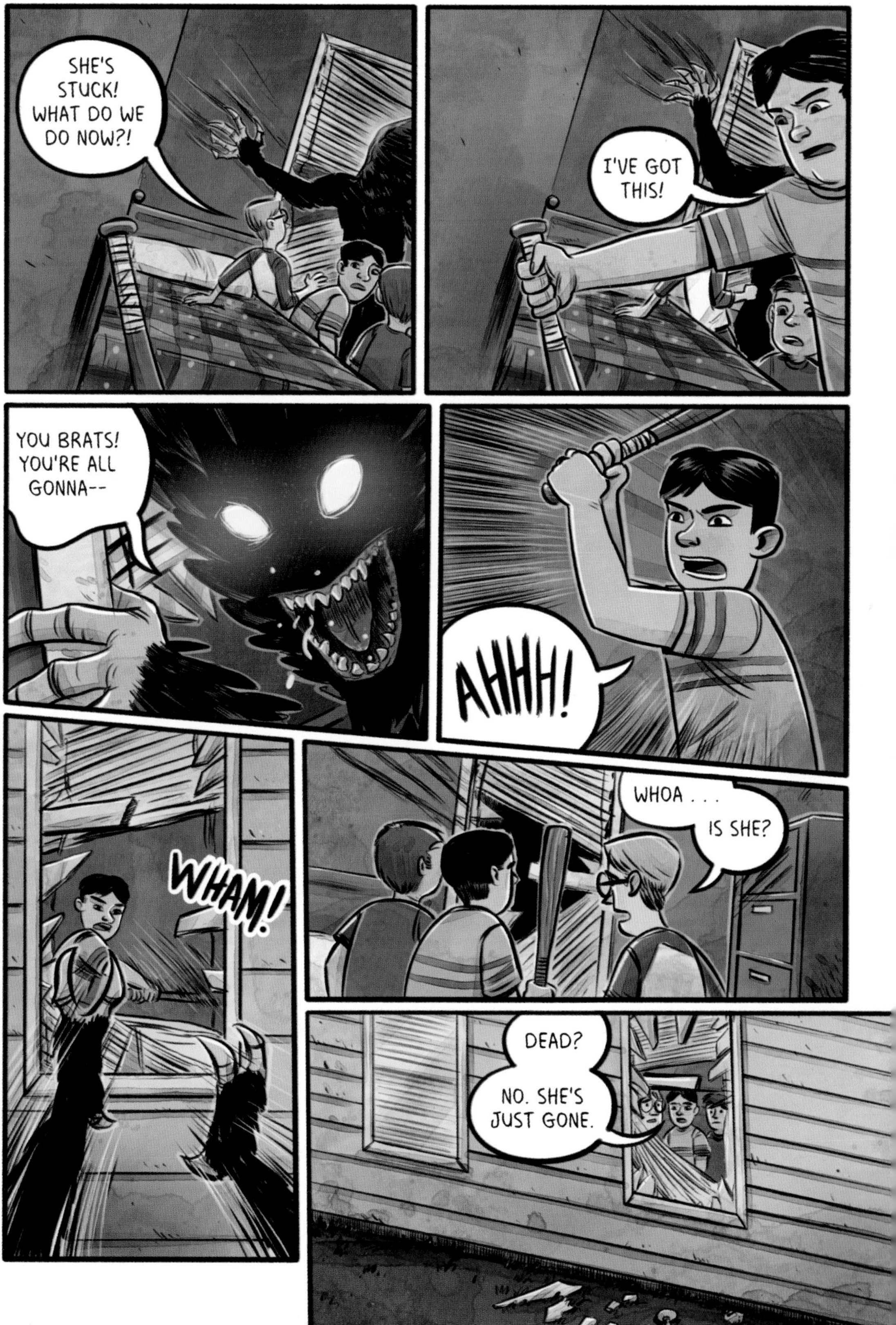
SHE'S STUCK! WHAT DO WE DO NOW?!
I'VE GOT THIS!
YOU BRATS! YOU'RE ALL GONNA--
AHHH!
WHAM!
WHOA . . .
IS SHE?
DEAD?
NO. SHE'S JUST GONE.

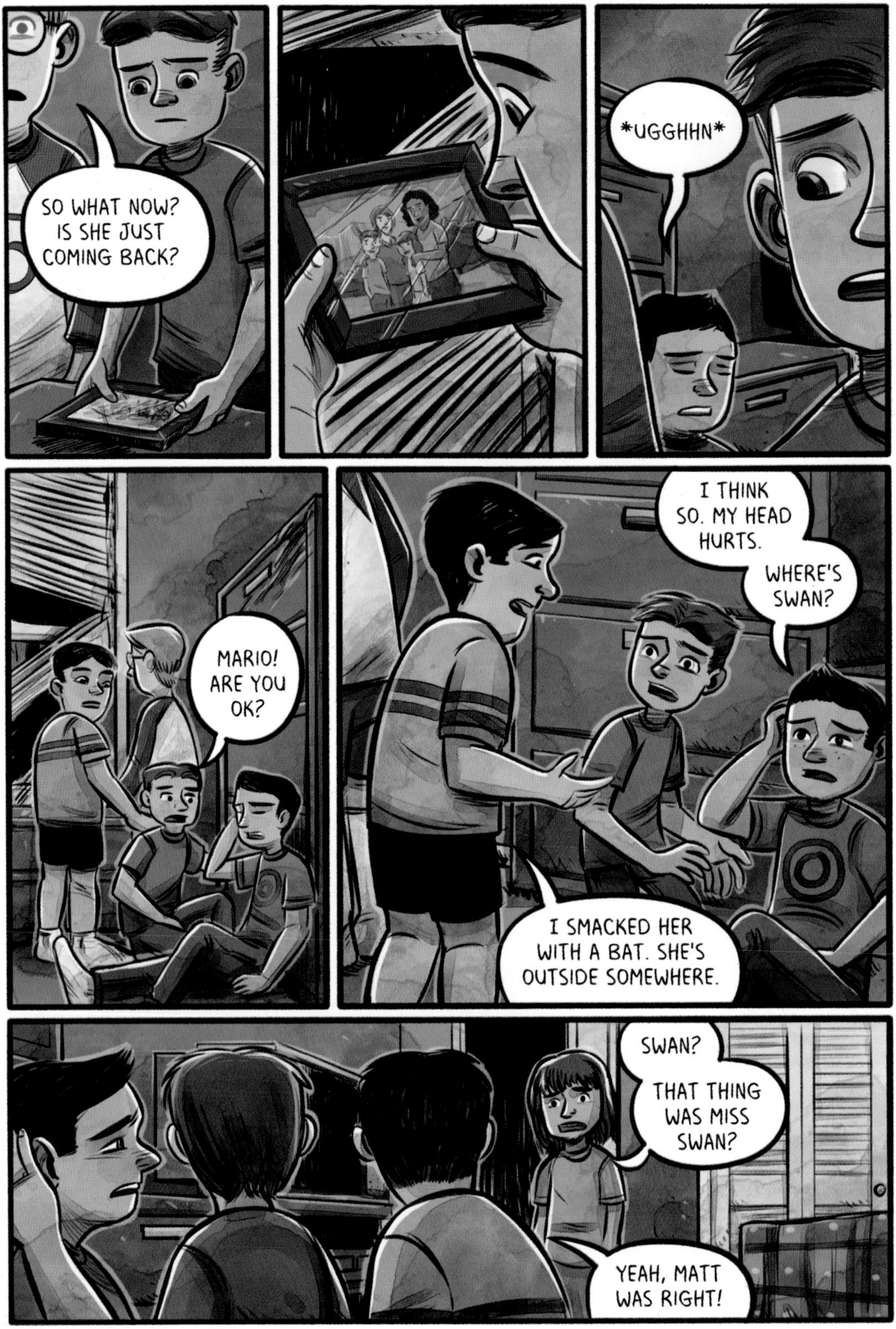
SO WHAT NOW? IS SHE JUST COMING BACK?
UGGHHN
MARIO! ARE YOU OK?
I THINK SO. MY HEAD HURTS.
WHERE'S SWAN?
I SMACKED HER WITH A BAT. SHE'S OUTSIDE SOMEWHERE.
SWAN?
THAT THING WAS MISS SWAN?
YEAH, MATT WAS RIGHT!

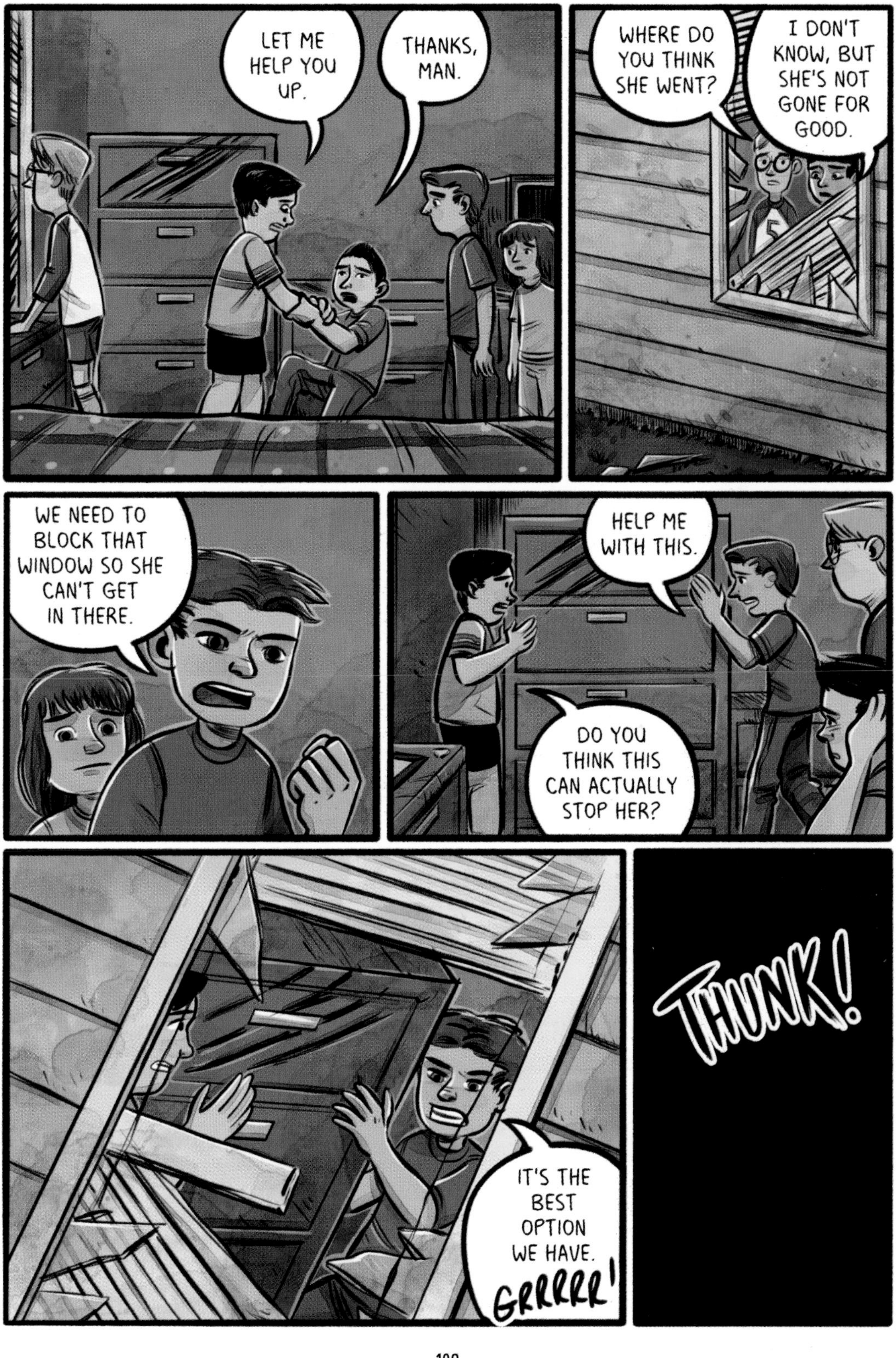
LET ME HELP YOU UP.
THANKS, MAN.
WHERE DO YOU THINK SHE WENT?
I DON'T KNOW, BUT SHE'S NOT GONE FOR GOOD.
WE NEED TO BLOCK THAT WINDOW SO SHE CAN'T GET IN THERE.
HELP ME WITH THIS.
DO YOU THINK THIS CAN ACTUALLY STOP HER?
IT'S THE BEST OPTION WE HAVE.
GRRRR!
THUNK!

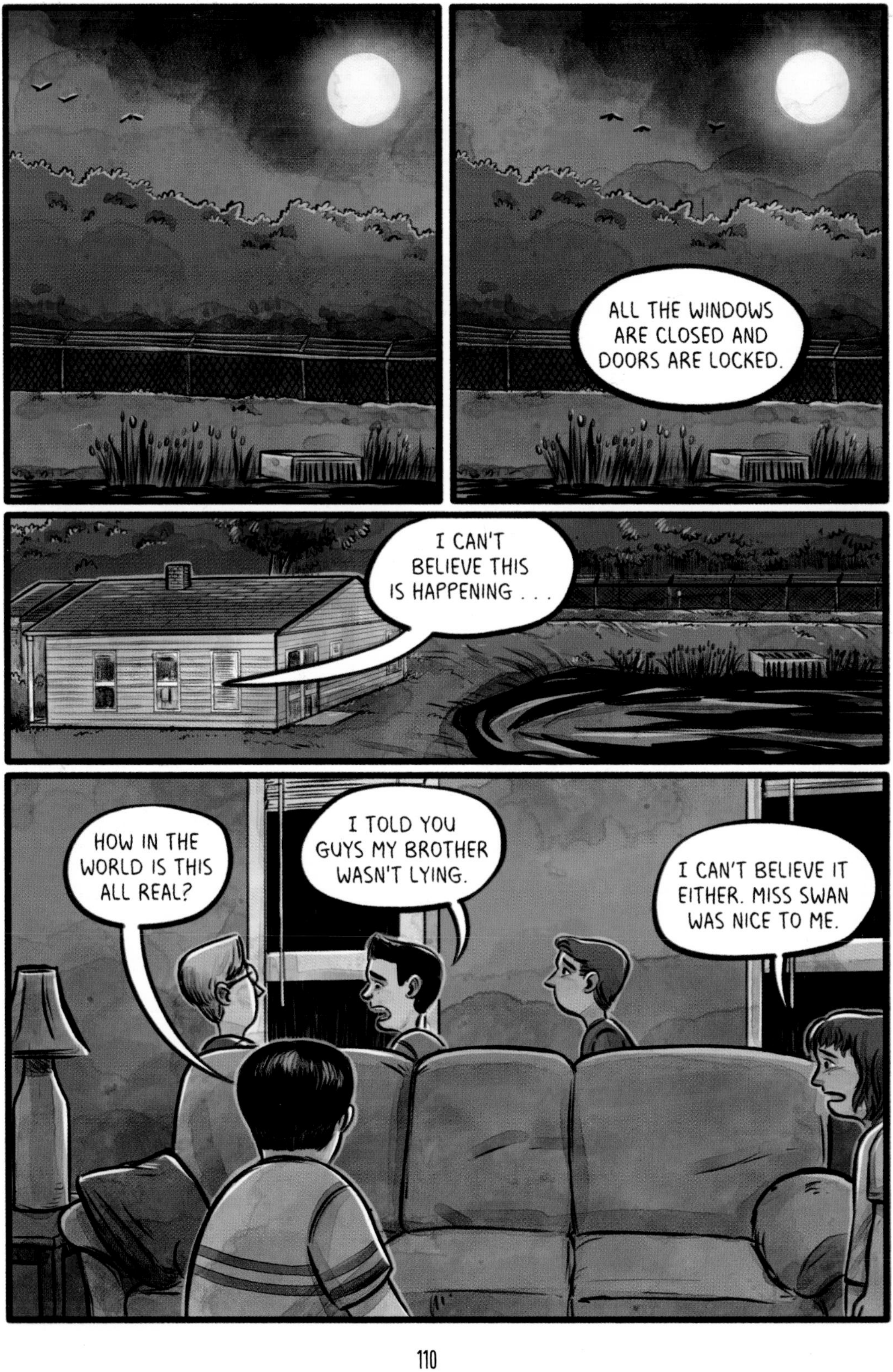
ALL THE WINDOWS ARE CLOSED AND DOORS ARE LOCKED.
I CAN'T BELIEVE THIS IS HAPPENING . . .
HOW IN THE WORLD IS THIS ALL REAL?
I TOLD YOU GUYS MY BROTHER WASN'T LYING.
I CAN'T BELIEVE IT EITHER. MISS SWAN WAS NICE TO ME.

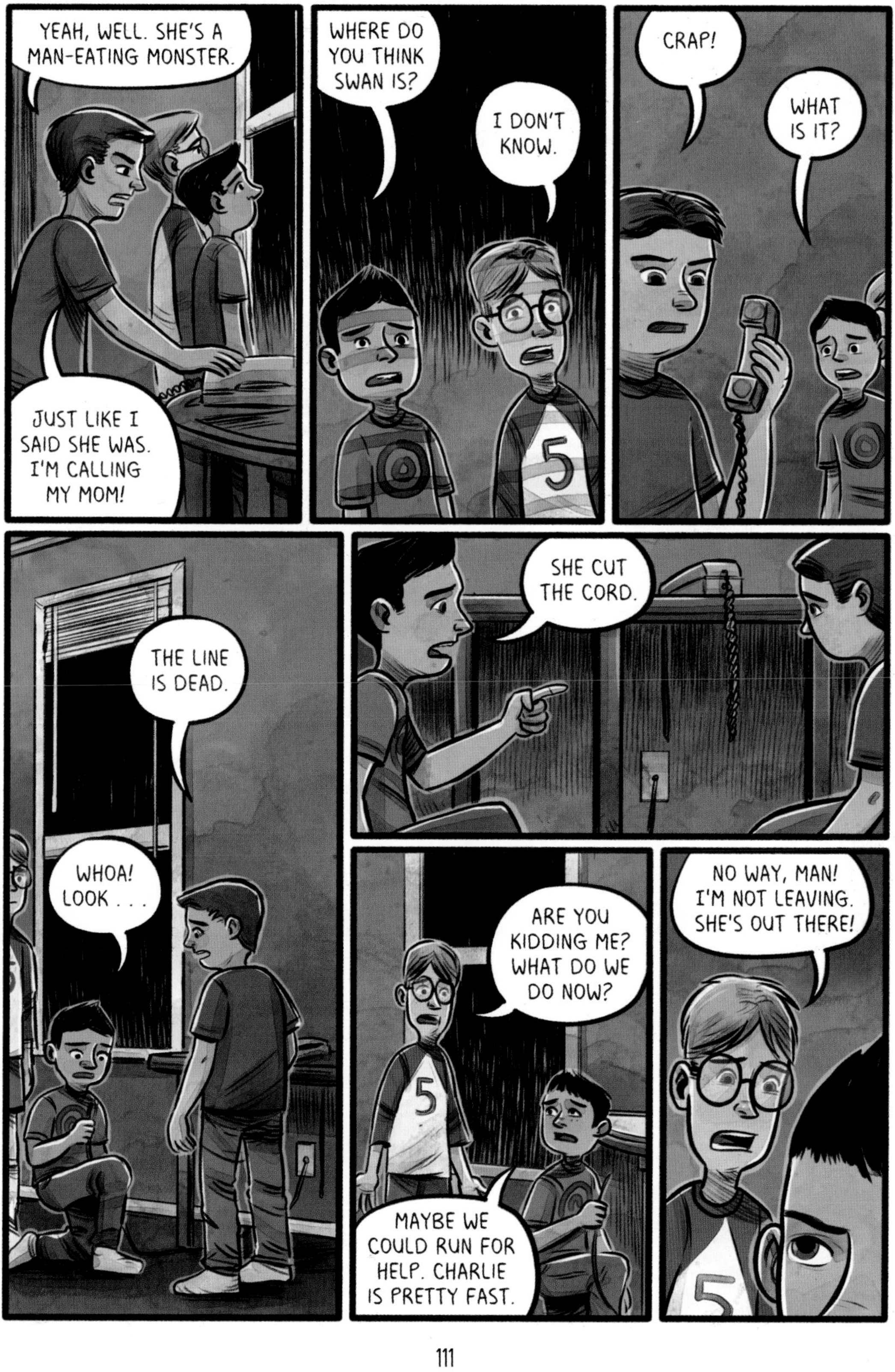
YEAH, WELL. SHE'S A MAN-EATING MONSTER.
JUST LIKE I SAID SHE WAS. I'M CALLING MY MOM!
WHERE DO YOU THINK SWAN IS?
I DON'T KNOW.
CRAP!
WHAT IS IT?
THE LINE IS DEAD.
WHOA! LOOK . . .
SHE CUT THE CORD.
ARE YOU KIDDING ME? WHAT DO WE DO NOW?
MAYBE WE COULD RUN FOR HELP. CHARLIE IS PRETTY FAST.
NO WAY, MAN! I'M NOT LEAVING. SHE'S OUT THERE!

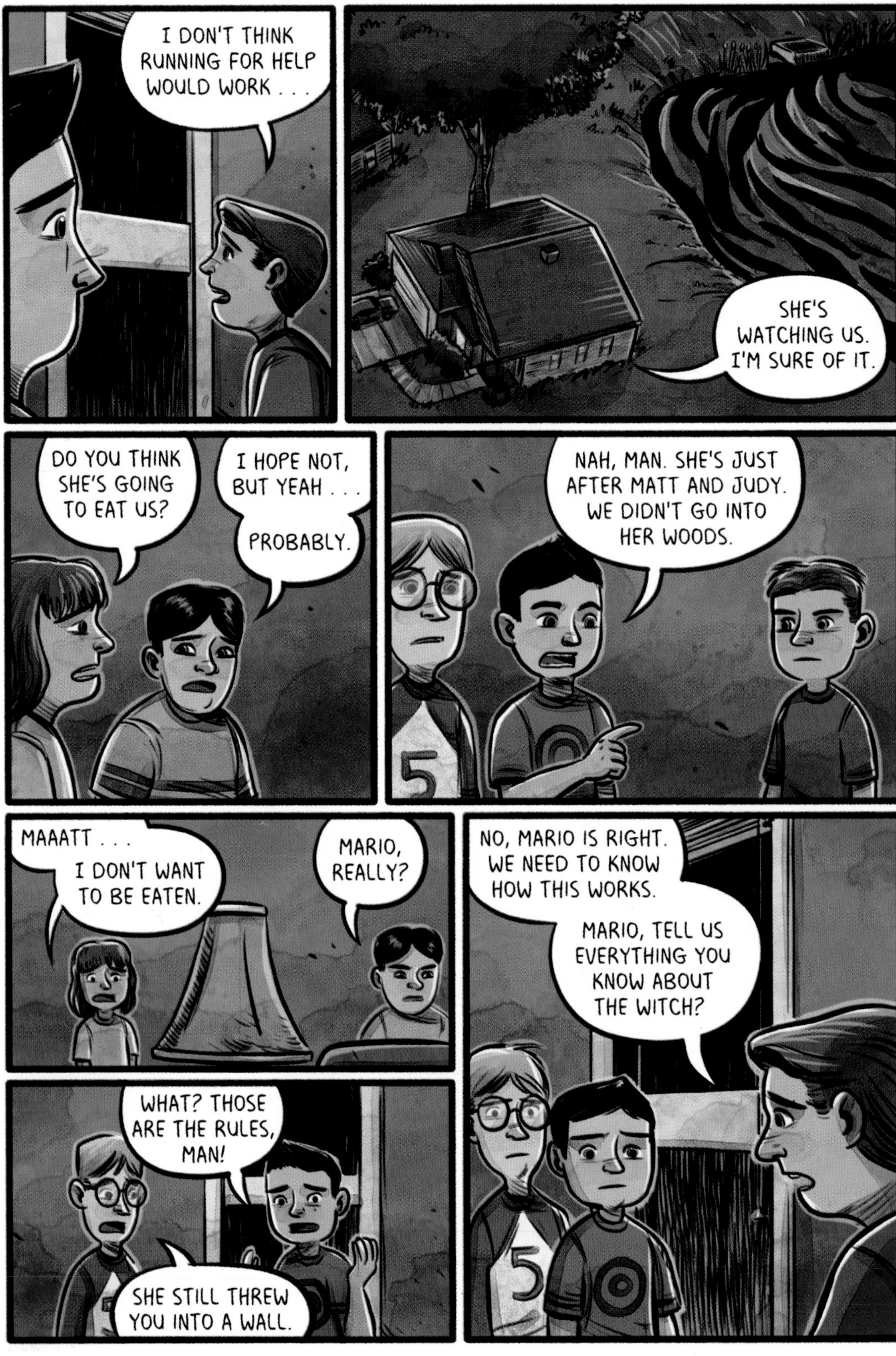
I DON'T THINK RUNNING FOR HELP WOULD WORK . . .
SHE'S WATCHING US. I'M SURE OF IT.
DO YOU THINK SHE'S GOING TO EAT US?
I HOPE NOT, BUT YEAH . . .
PROBABLY.
NAH, MAN. SHE'S JUST AFTER MATT AND JUDY. WE DIDN'T GO INTO HER WOODS.
MAAATT . . .
I DON'T WANT TO BE EATEN.
MARIO, REALLY?
WHAT? THOSE ARE THE RULES, MAN!
SHE STILL THREW YOU INTO A WALL.
NO, MARIO IS RIGHT. WE NEED TO KNOW HOW THIS WORKS.
MARIO, TELL US EVERYTHING YOU KNOW ABOUT THE WITCH?

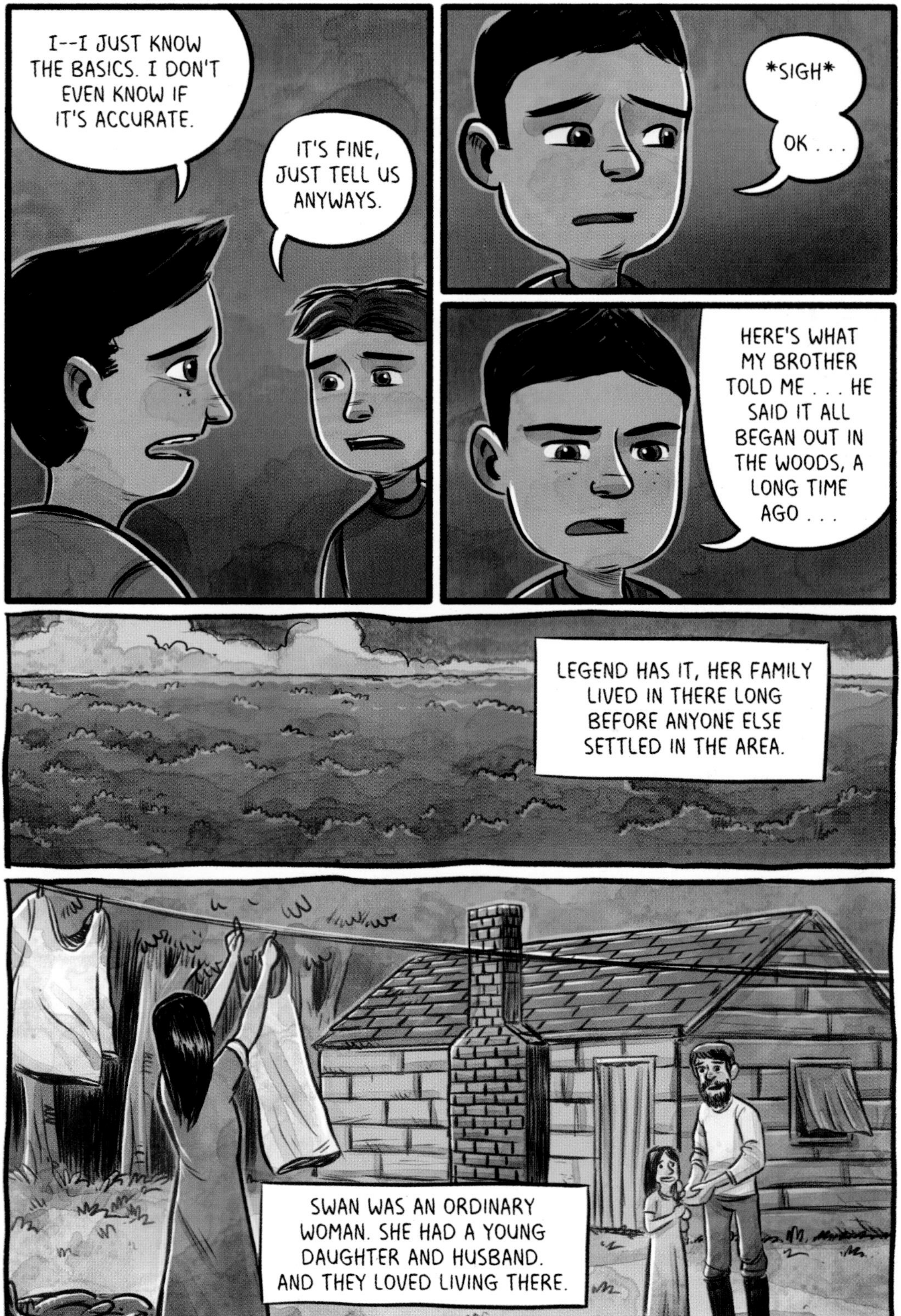
I--I JUST KNOW THE BASICS. I DON'T EVEN KNOW IF IT'S ACCURATE.
IT'S FINE, JUST TELL US ANYWAYS.
SIGH
OK . . .
HERE'S WHAT MY BROTHER TOLD ME . . . HE SAID IT ALL BEGAN OUT IN THE WOODS, A LONG TIME AGO . . .
LEGEND HAS IT, HER FAMILY LIVED IN THERE LONG BEFORE ANYONE ELSE SETTLED IN THE AREA.
SWAN WAS AN ORDINARY WOMAN. SHE HAD A YOUNG DAUGHTER AND HUSBAND. AND THEY LOVED LIVING THERE.

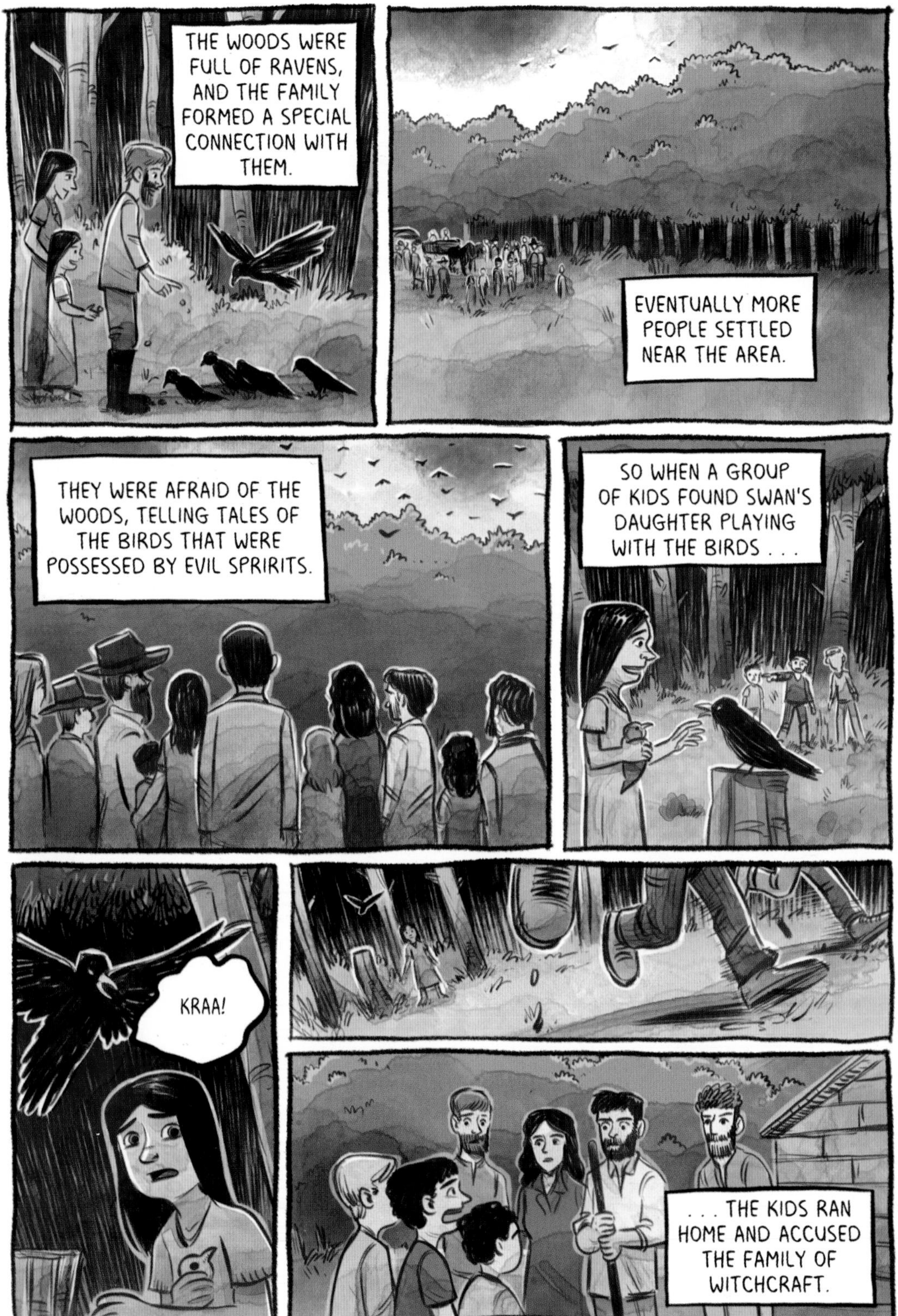
THE WOODS WERE FULL OF RAVENS, AND THE FAMILY FORMED A SPECIAL CONNECTION WITH THEM.
EVENTUALLY MORE PEOPLE SETTLED NEAR THE AREA.
THEY WERE AFRAID OF THE WOODS, TELLING TALES OF THE BIRDS THAT WERE POSSESSED BY EVIL SPRIRITS.
SO WHEN A GROUP OF KIDS FOUND SWAN'S DAUGHTER PLAYING WITH THE BIRDS . . .
KRAA!
. . . THE KIDS RAN HOME AND ACCUSED THE FAMILY OF WITCHCRAFT.

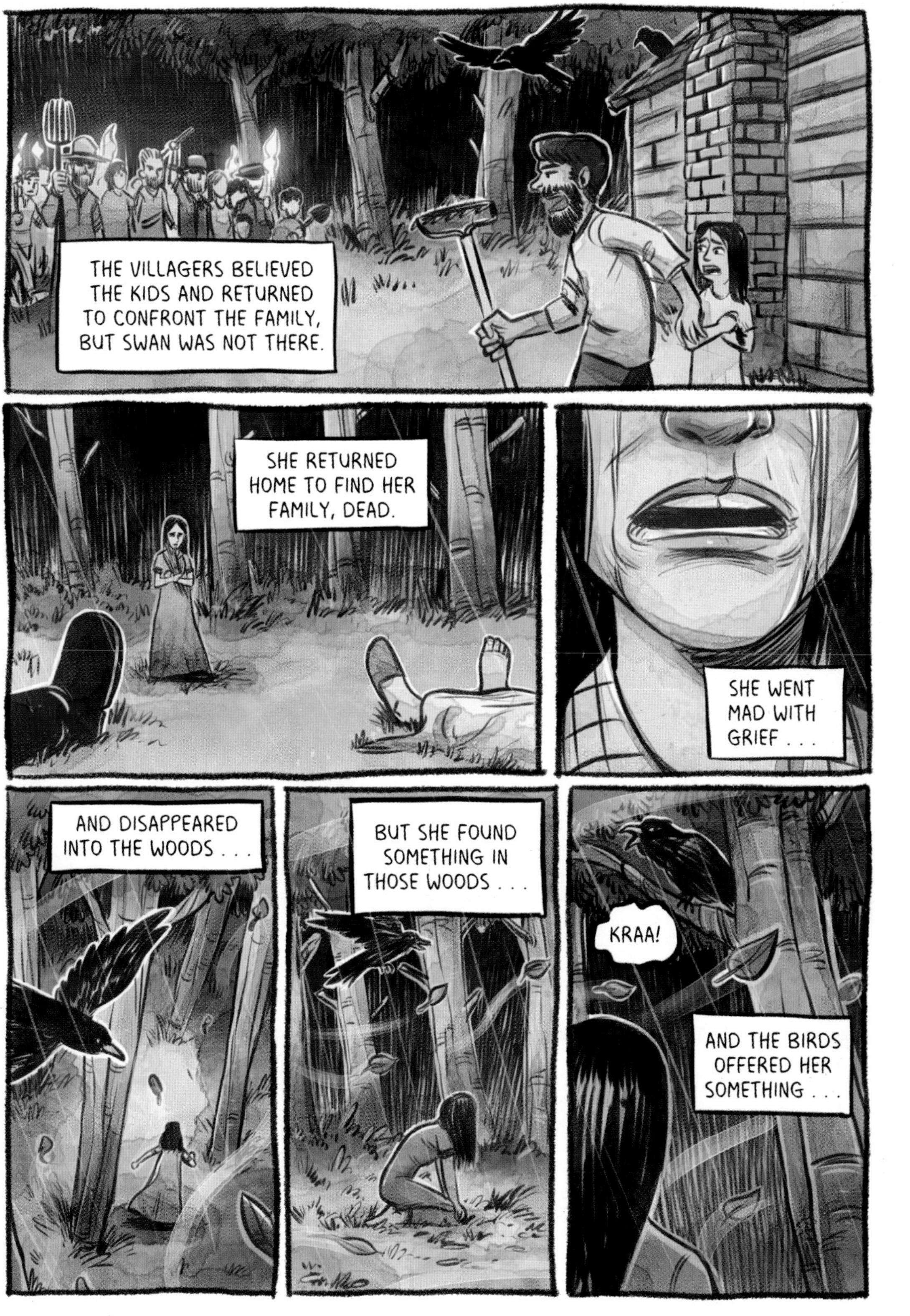
THE VILLAGERS BELIEVED THE KIDS AND RETURNED TO CONFRONT THE FAMILY, BUT SWAN WAS NOT THERE.
SHE RETURNED HOME TO FIND HER FAMILY, DEAD.
SHE WENT MAD WITH GRIEF . . .
AND DISAPPEARED INTO THE WOODS . . .
BUT SHE FOUND SOMETHING IN THOSE WOODS . . .
KRAA!
AND THE BIRDS OFFERED HER SOMETHING . . .

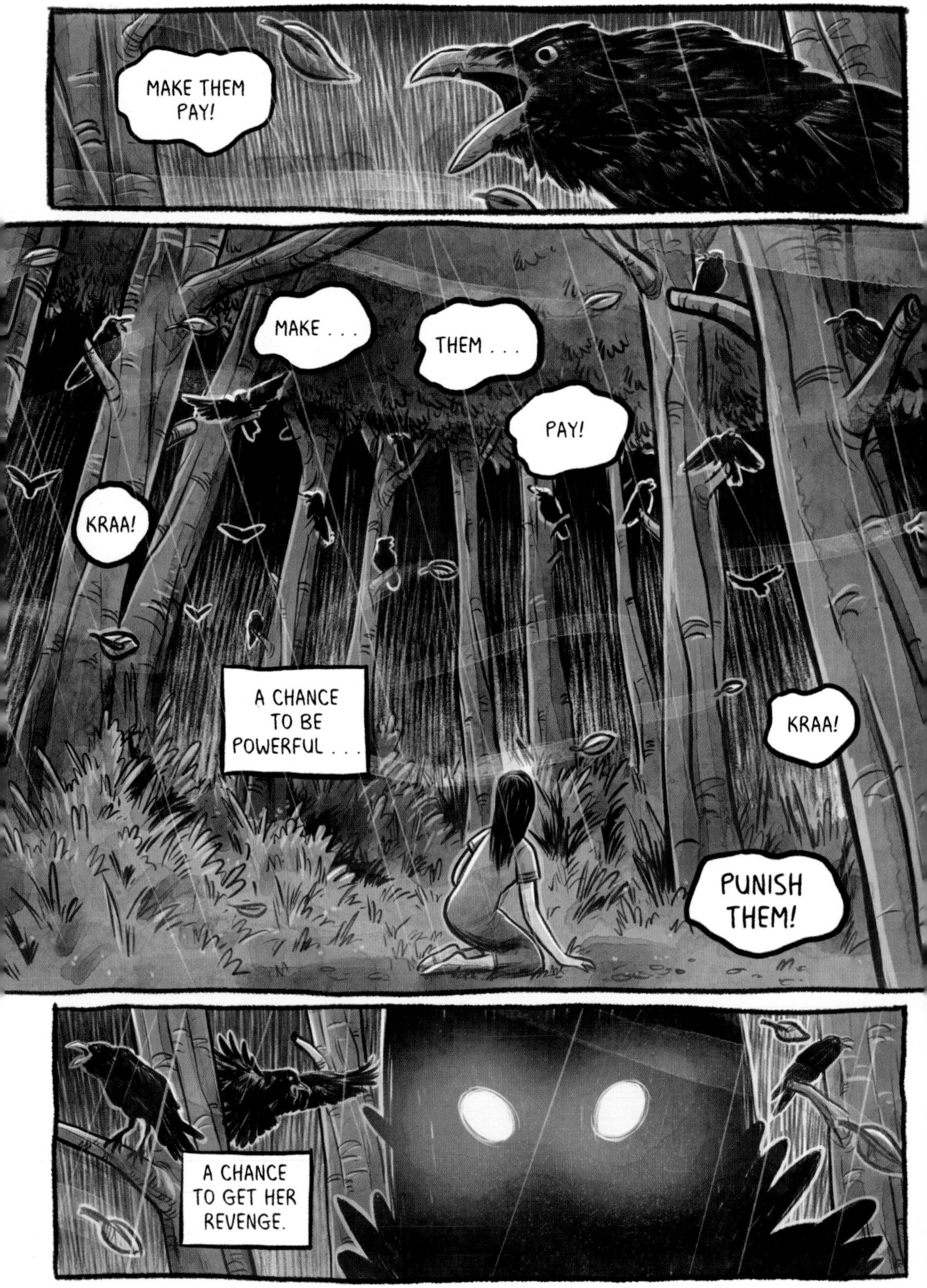
MAKE THEM PAY!
MAKE . . .
THEM . . .
PAY!
KRAA!
A CHANCE TO BE POWERFUL . . .
KRAA!
PUNISH THEM!
A CHANCE TO GET HER REVENGE.

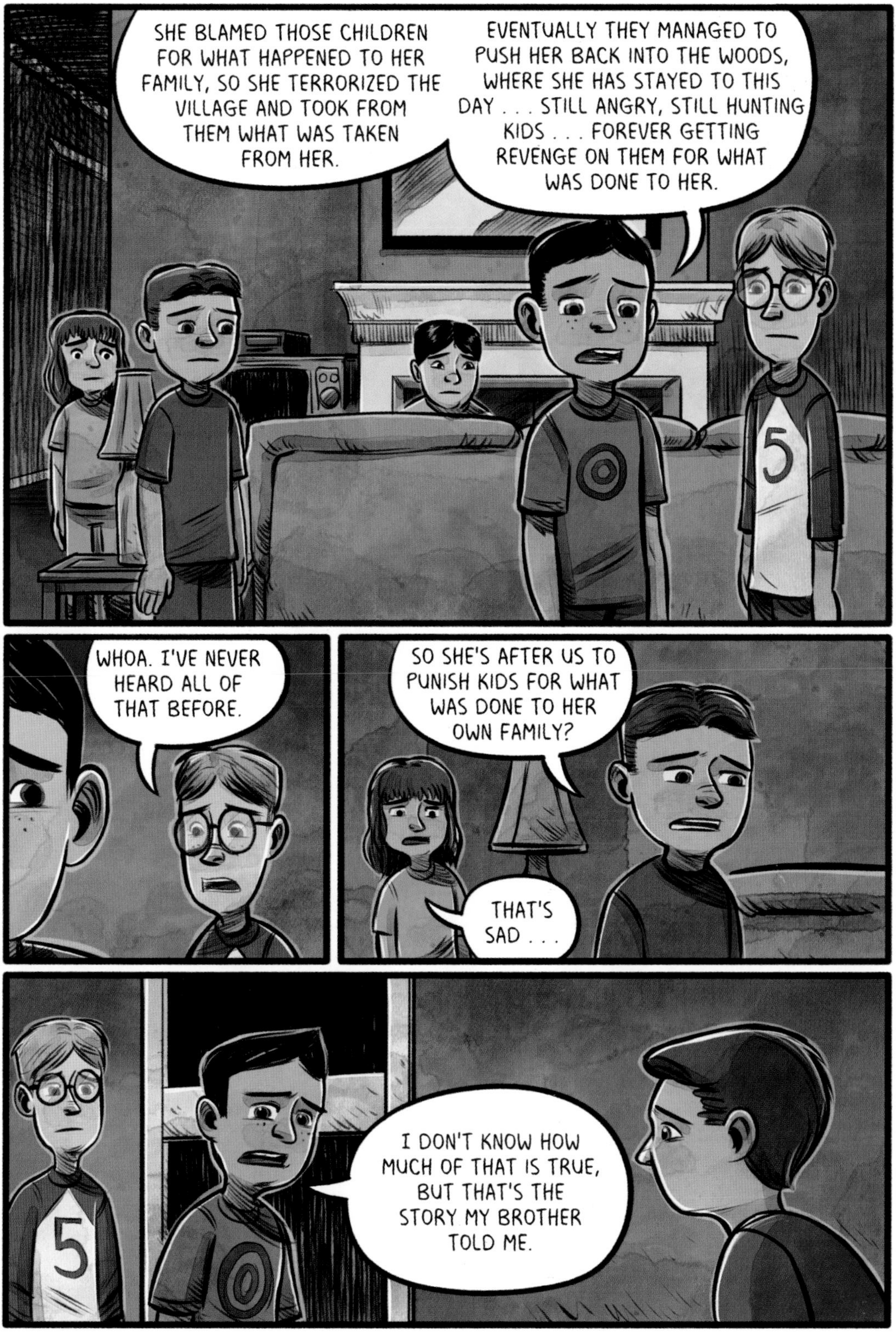
SHE BLAMED THOSE CHILDREN FOR WHAT HAPPENED TO HER FAMILY, SO SHE TERRORIZED THE VILLAGE AND TOOK FROM THEM WHAT WAS TAKEN FROM HER.
EVENTUALLY THEY MANAGED TO PUSH HER BACK INTO THE WOODS, WHERE SHE HAS STAYED TO THIS DAY . . . STILL ANGRY, STILL HUNTING KIDS . . . FOREVER GETTING REVENGE ON THEM FOR WHAT WAS DONE TO HER.
WHOA. I'VE NEVER HEARD ALL OF THAT BEFORE.
SO SHE'S AFTER US TO PUNISH KIDS FOR WHAT WAS DONE TO HER OWN FAMILY?
THAT'S SAD . . .
I DON'T KNOW HOW MUCH OF THAT IS TRUE, BUT THAT'S THE STORY MY BROTHER TOLD ME.
5
5

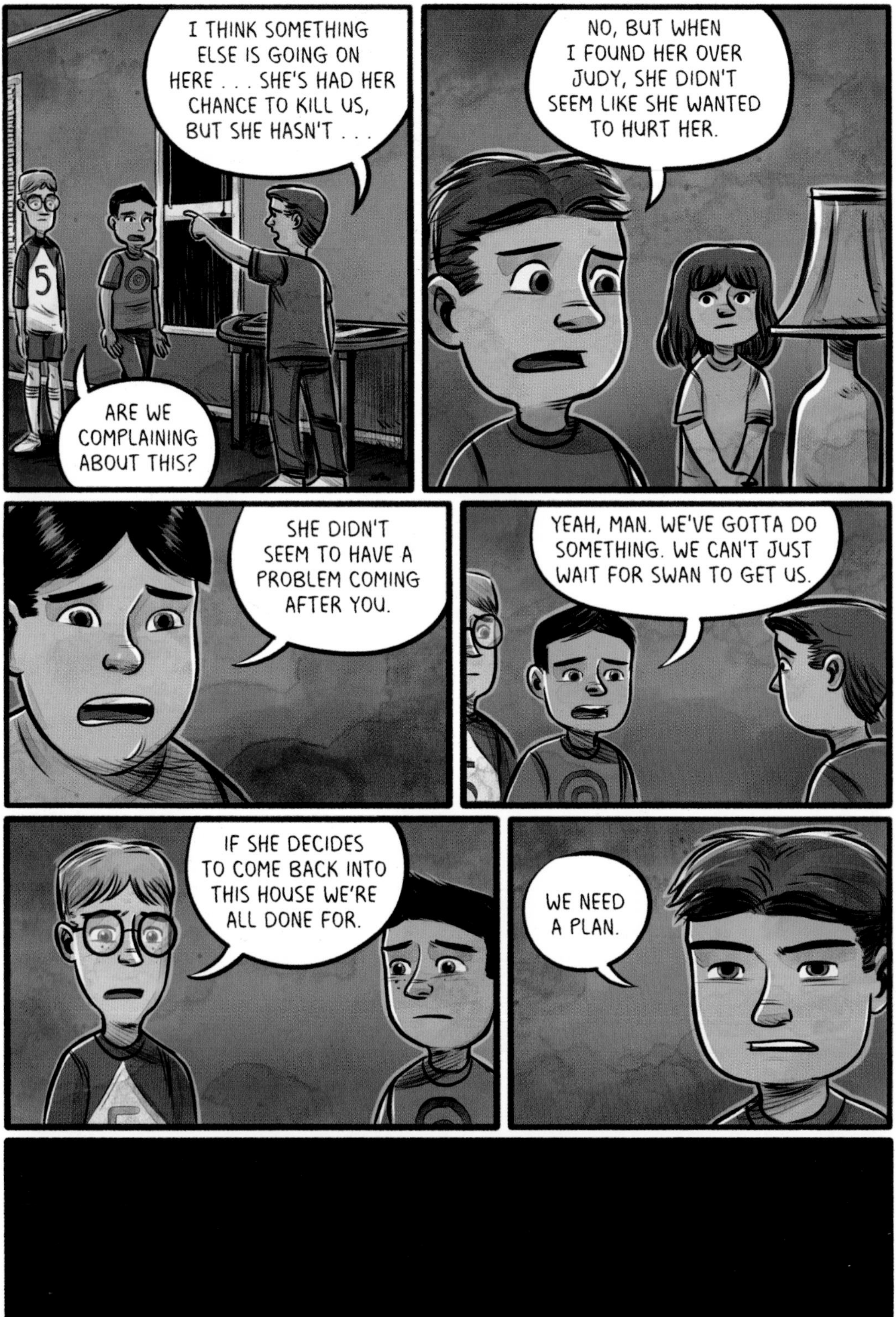
I THINK SOMETHING ELSE IS GOING ON HERE . . . SHE'S HAD HER CHANCE TO KILL US, BUT SHE HASN'T . . .
ARE WE COMPLAINING ABOUT THIS?
NO, BUT WHEN I FOUND HER OVER JUDY, SHE DIDN'T SEEM LIKE SHE WANTED TO HURT HER.
SHE DIDN'T SEEM TO HAVE A PROBLEM COMING AFTER YOU.
YEAH, MAN. WE'VE GOTTA DO SOMETHING. WE CAN'T JUST WAIT FOR SWAN TO GET US.
IF SHE DECIDES TO COME BACK INTO THIS HOUSE WE'RE ALL DONE FOR.
WE NEED A PLAN.

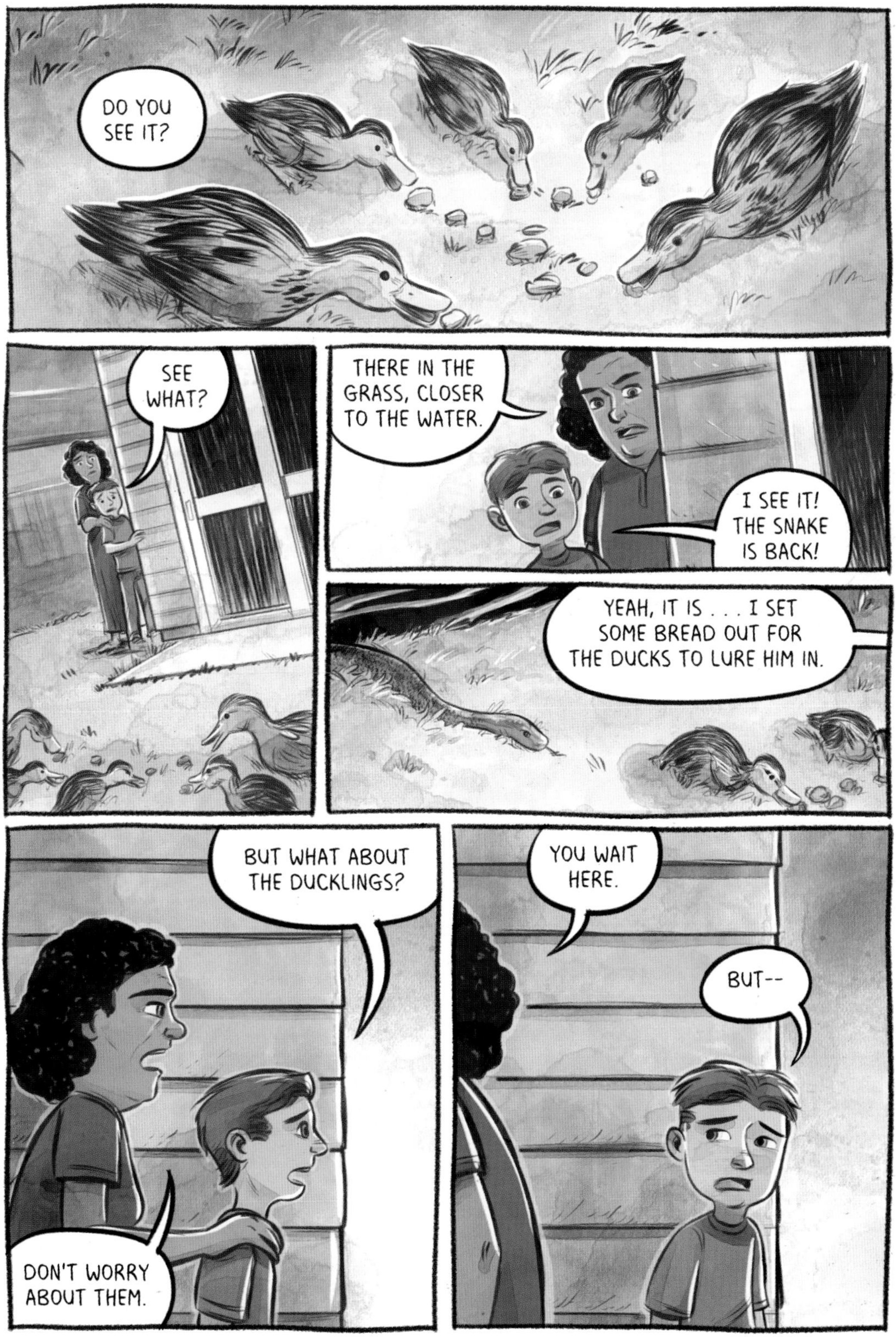
DO YOU SEE IT?
SEE WHAT?
THERE IN THE GRASS, CLOSER TO THE WATER.
I SEE IT! THE SNAKE IS BACK!
YEAH, IT IS . . . I SET SOME BREAD OUT FOR THE DUCKS TO LURE HIM IN.
BUT WHAT ABOUT THE DUCKLINGS?
DON'T WORRY ABOUT THEM.
YOU WAIT HERE.
BUT--

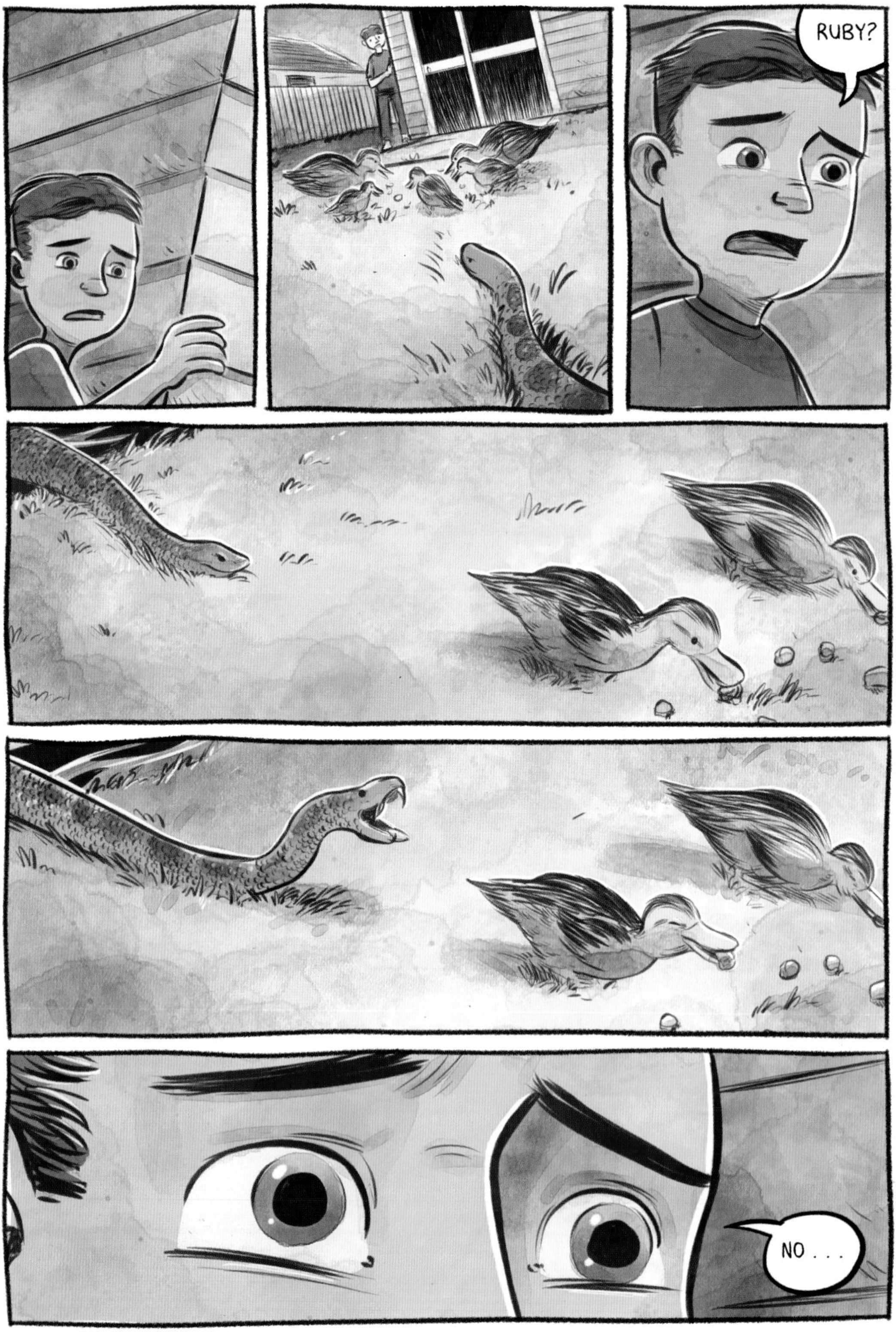
RUBY?
NO . . .

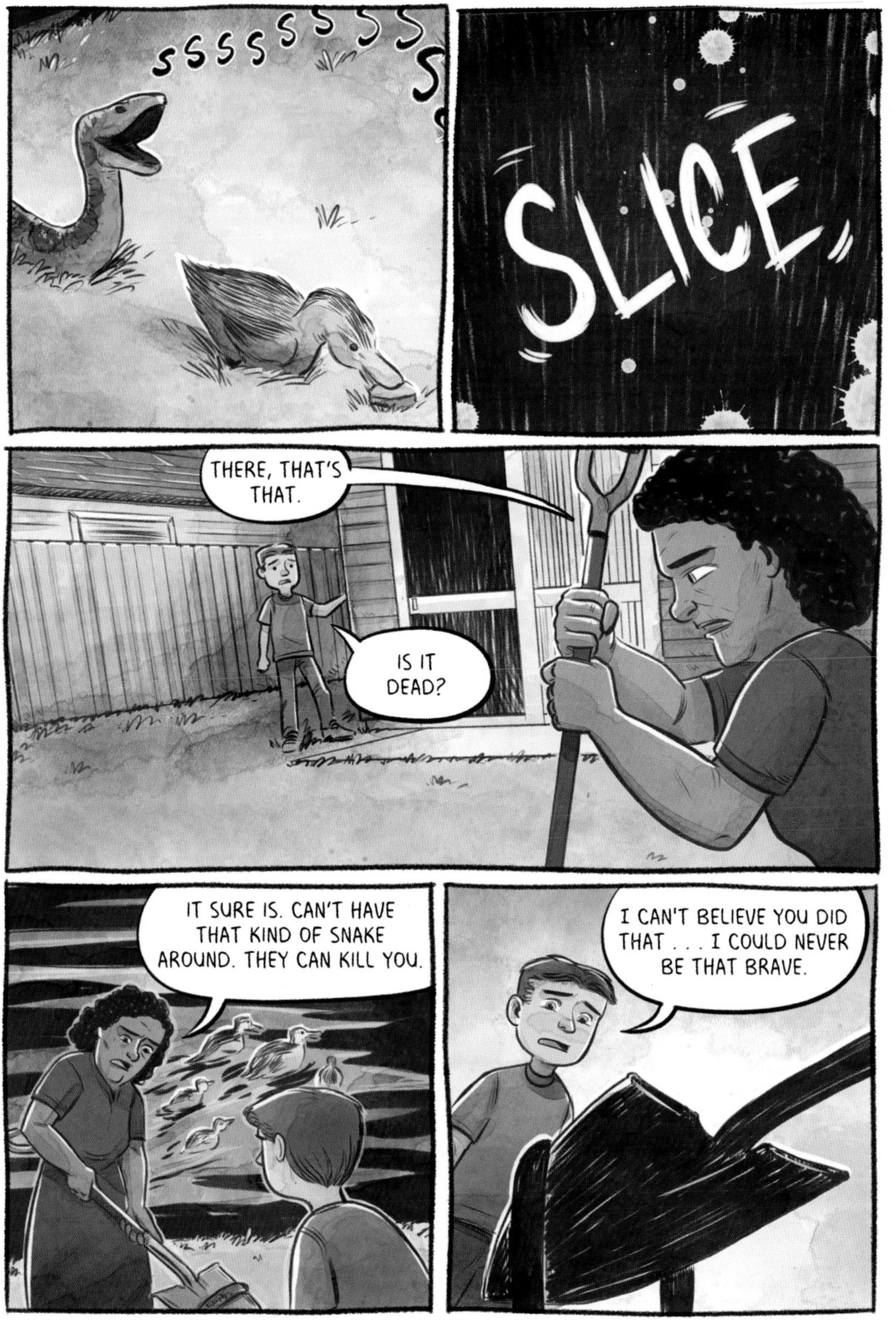
SSSSSSSSSS
SLICE
THERE, THAT'S THAT.
IS IT DEAD?
IT SURE IS. CAN'T HAVE THAT KIND OF SNAKE AROUND. THEY CAN KILL YOU.
I CAN'T BELIEVE YOU DID THAT . . . I COULD NEVER BE THAT BRAVE.

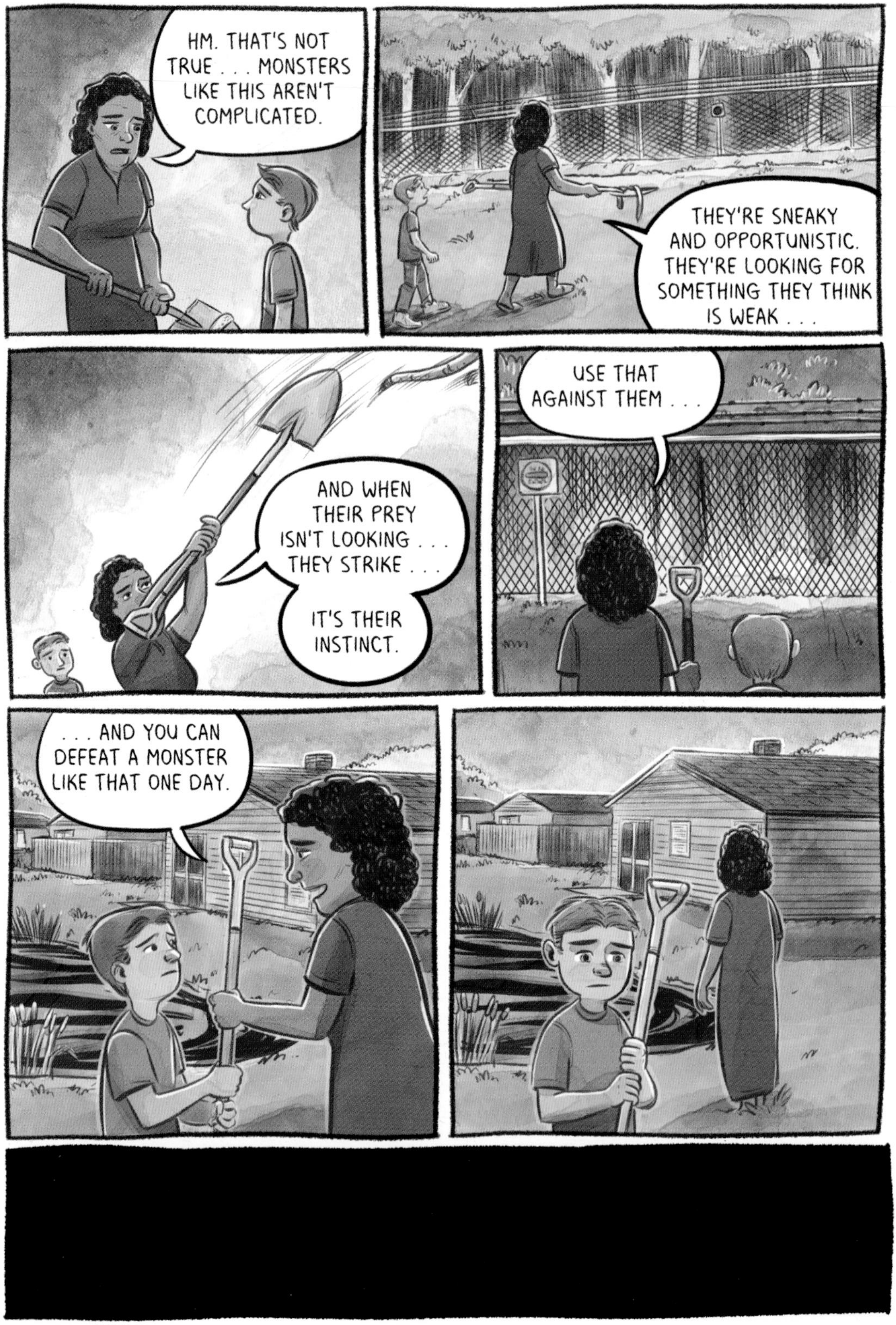
HM. THAT'S NOT TRUE . . . MONSTERS LIKE THIS AREN'T COMPLICATED.
THEY'RE SNEAKY AND OPPORTUNISTIC. THEY'RE LOOKING FOR SOMETHING THEY THINK IS WEAK . . .
AND WHEN THEIR PREY ISN'T LOOKING . . . THEY STRIKE . . .
IT'S THEIR INSTINCT.
USE THAT AGAINST THEM . . .
. . . AND YOU CAN DEFEAT A MONSTER LIKE THAT ONE DAY.

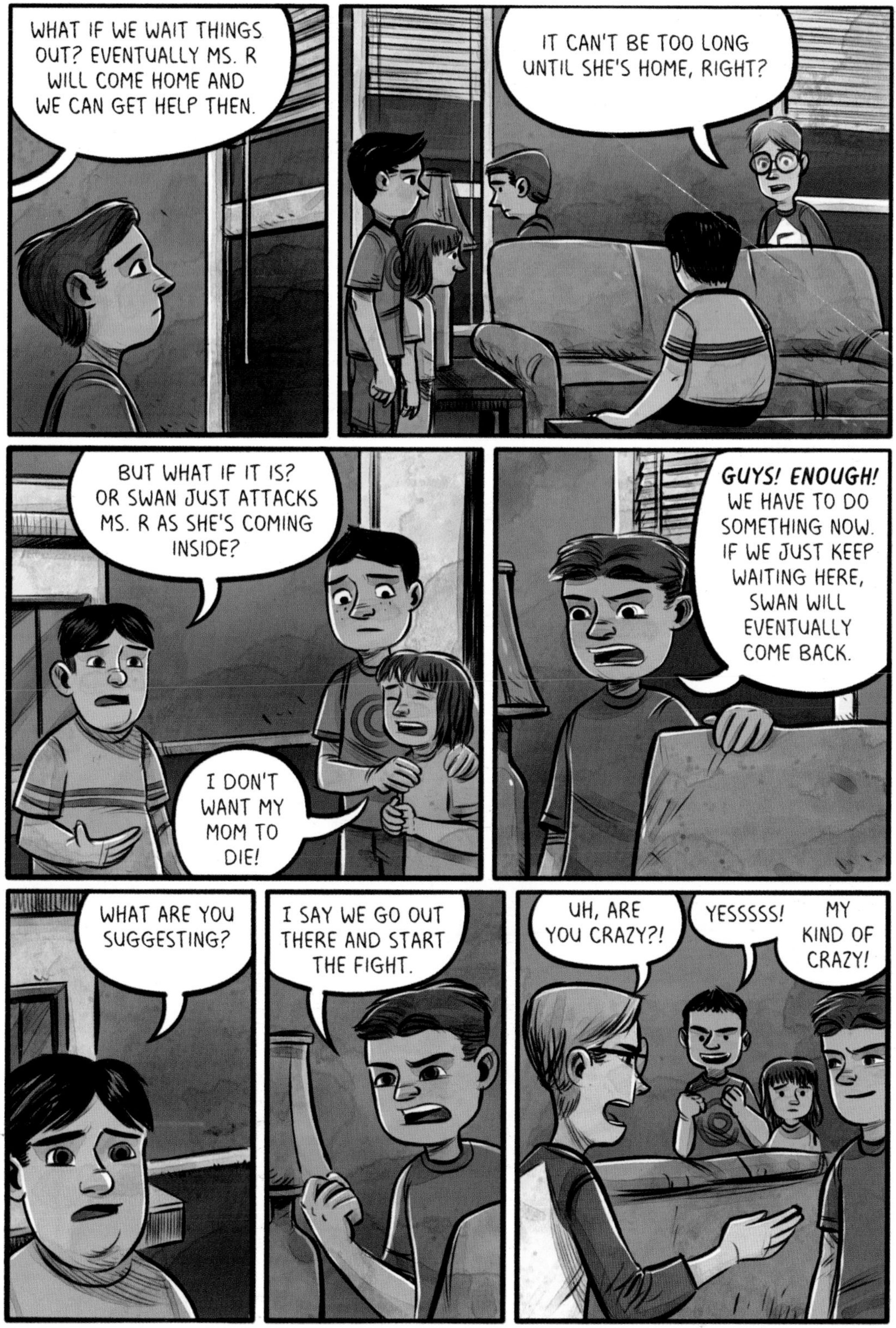
WHAT IF WE WAIT THINGS OUT? EVENTUALLY MS. R WILL COME HOME AND WE CAN GET HELP THEN.
IT CAN'T BE TOO LONG UNTIL SHE'S HOME, RIGHT?
BUT WHAT IF IT IS? OR SWAN JUST ATTACKS MS. R AS SHE'S COMING INSIDE?
I DON'T WANT MY MOM TO DIE!
GUYS! ENOUGH! WE HAVE TO DO SOMETHING NOW. IF WE JUST KEEP WAITING HERE, SWAN WILL EVENTUALLY COME BACK.
WHAT ARE YOU SUGGESTING?
I SAY WE GO OUT THERE AND START THE FIGHT.
UH, ARE YOU CRAZY?!
YESSSSS!
MY KIND OF CRAZY!

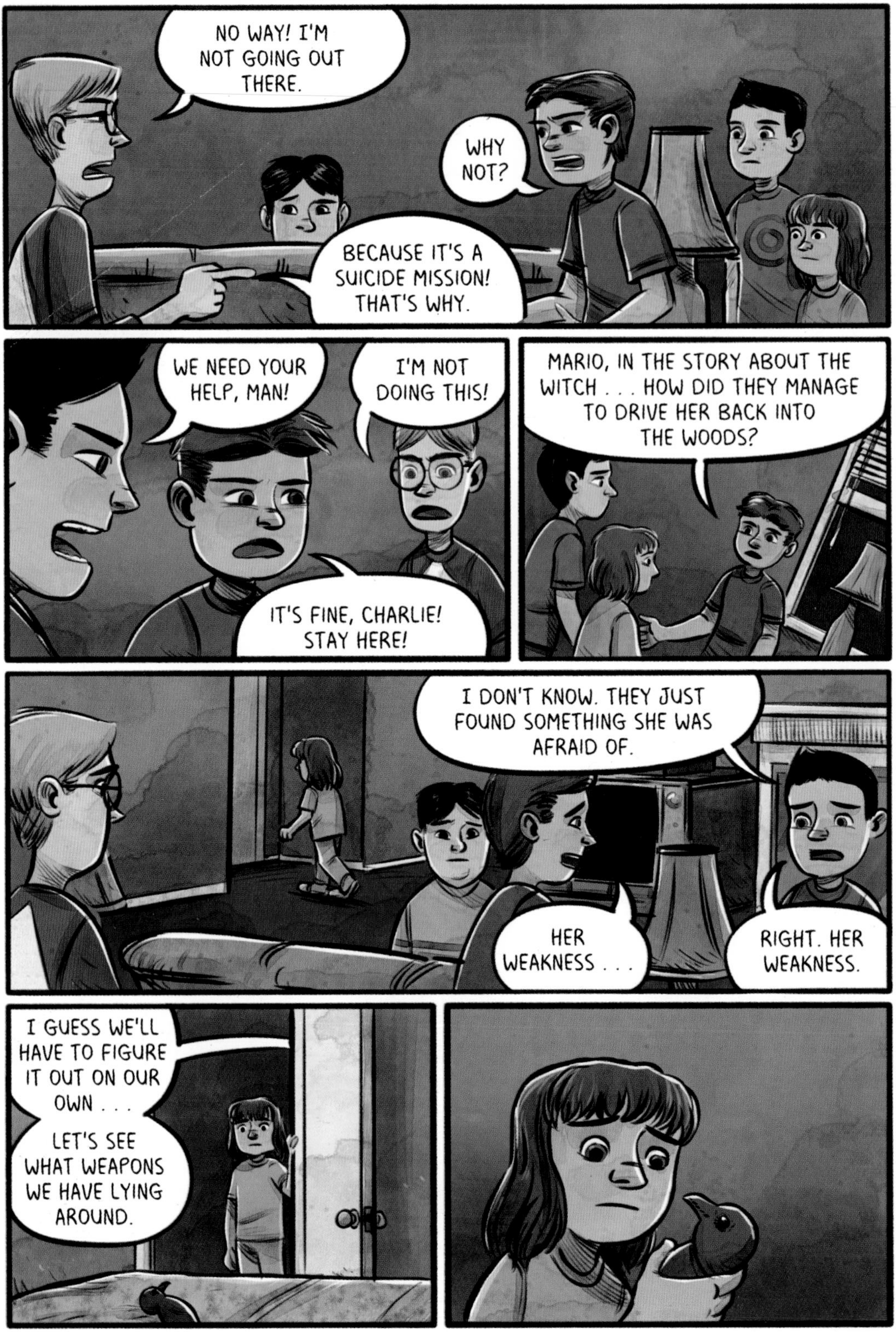
NO WAY! I'M NOT GOING OUT THERE.
WHY NOT?
BECAUSE IT'S A SUICIDE MISSION! THAT'S WHY.
WE NEED YOUR HELP, MAN!
I'M NOT DOING THIS!
IT'S FINE, CHARLIE! STAY HERE!
MARIO, IN THE STORY ABOUT THE WITCH . . . HOW DID THEY MANAGE TO DRIVE HER BACK INTO THE WOODS?
I DON'T KNOW. THEY JUST FOUND SOMETHING SHE WAS AFRAID OF.
HER WEAKNESS . . .
RIGHT. HER WEAKNESS.
I GUESS WE'LL HAVE TO FIGURE IT OUT ON OUR OWN . . .
LET'S SEE WHAT WEAPONS WE HAVE LYING AROUND.

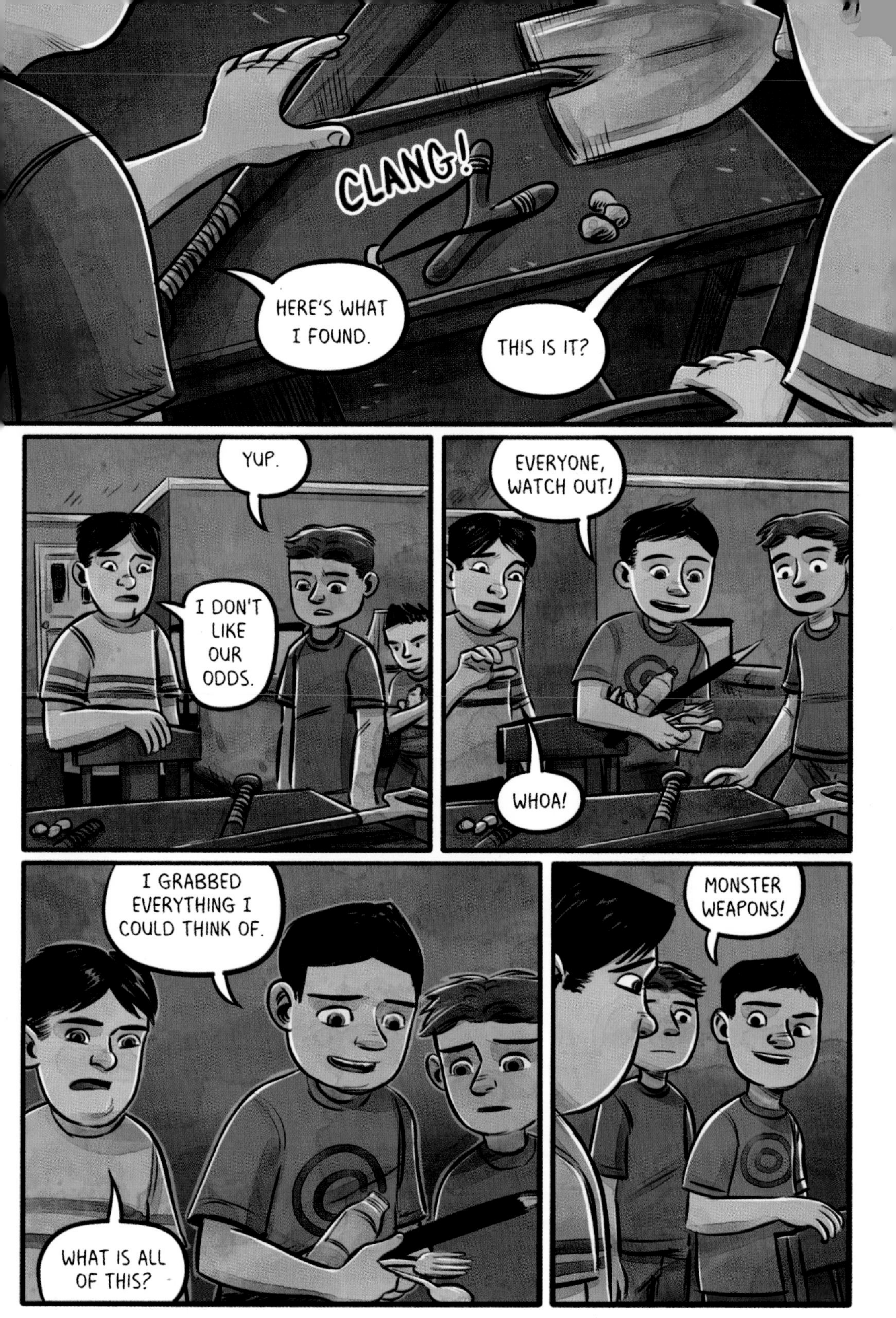
CLANG!
HERE'S WHAT I FOUND.
THIS IS IT?
YUP.
I DON'T LIKE OUR ODDS.
EVERYONE, WATCH OUT!
WHOA!
I GRABBED EVERYTHING I COULD THINK OF.
WHAT IS ALL OF THIS?
MONSTER WEAPONS!

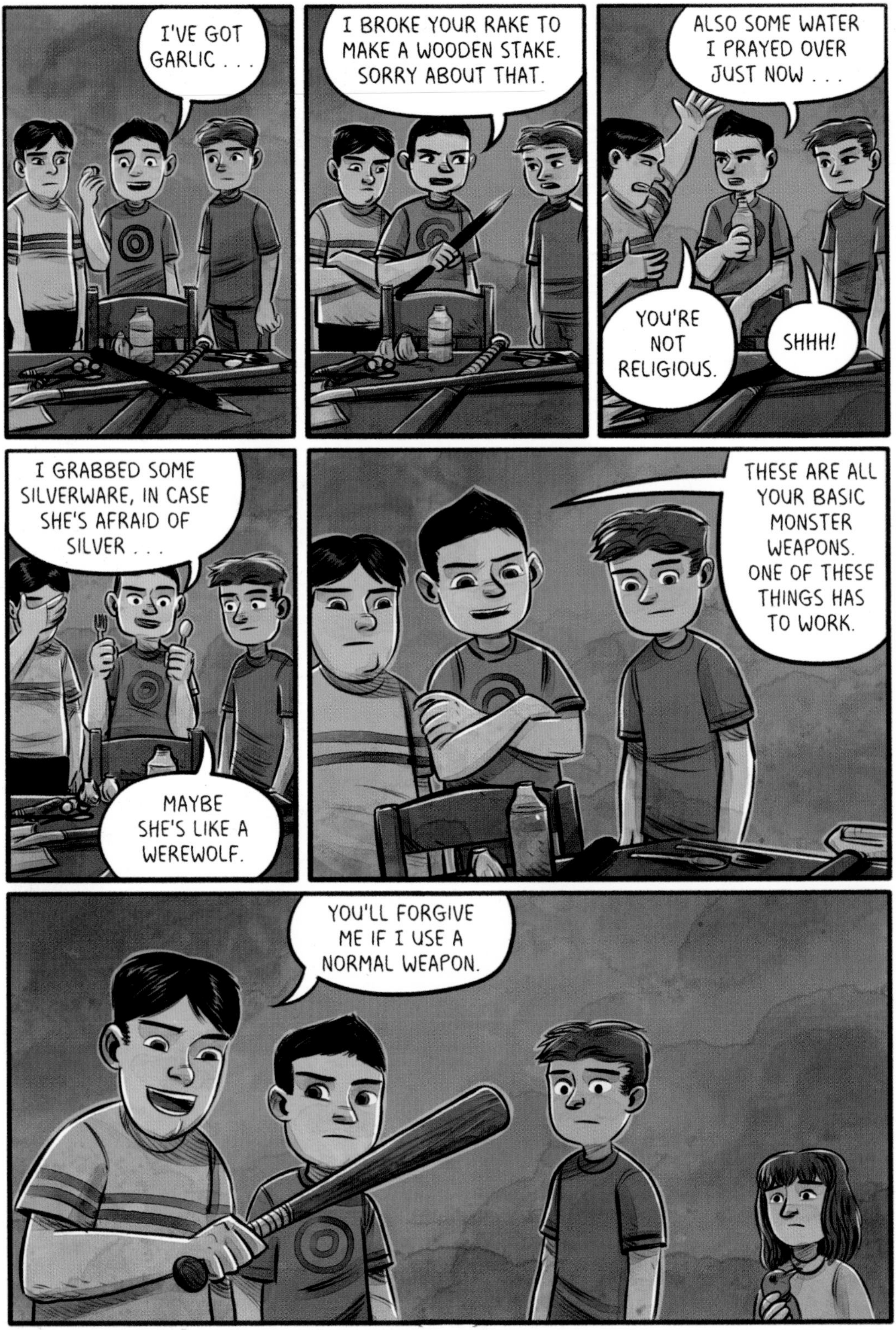
I'VE GOT GARLIC . . .
I BROKE YOUR RAKE TO MAKE A WOODEN STAKE. SORRY ABOUT THAT.
ALSO SOME WATER I PRAYED OVER JUST NOW . . .
YOU'RE NOT RELIGIOUS.
SHHH!
I GRABBED SOME SILVERWARE, IN CASE SHE'S AFRAID OF SILVER . . .
MAYBE SHE'S LIKE A WEREWOLF.
THESE ARE ALL YOUR BASIC MONSTER WEAPONS. ONE OF THESE THINGS HAS TO WORK.
YOU'LL FORGIVE ME IF I USE A NORMAL WEAPON.

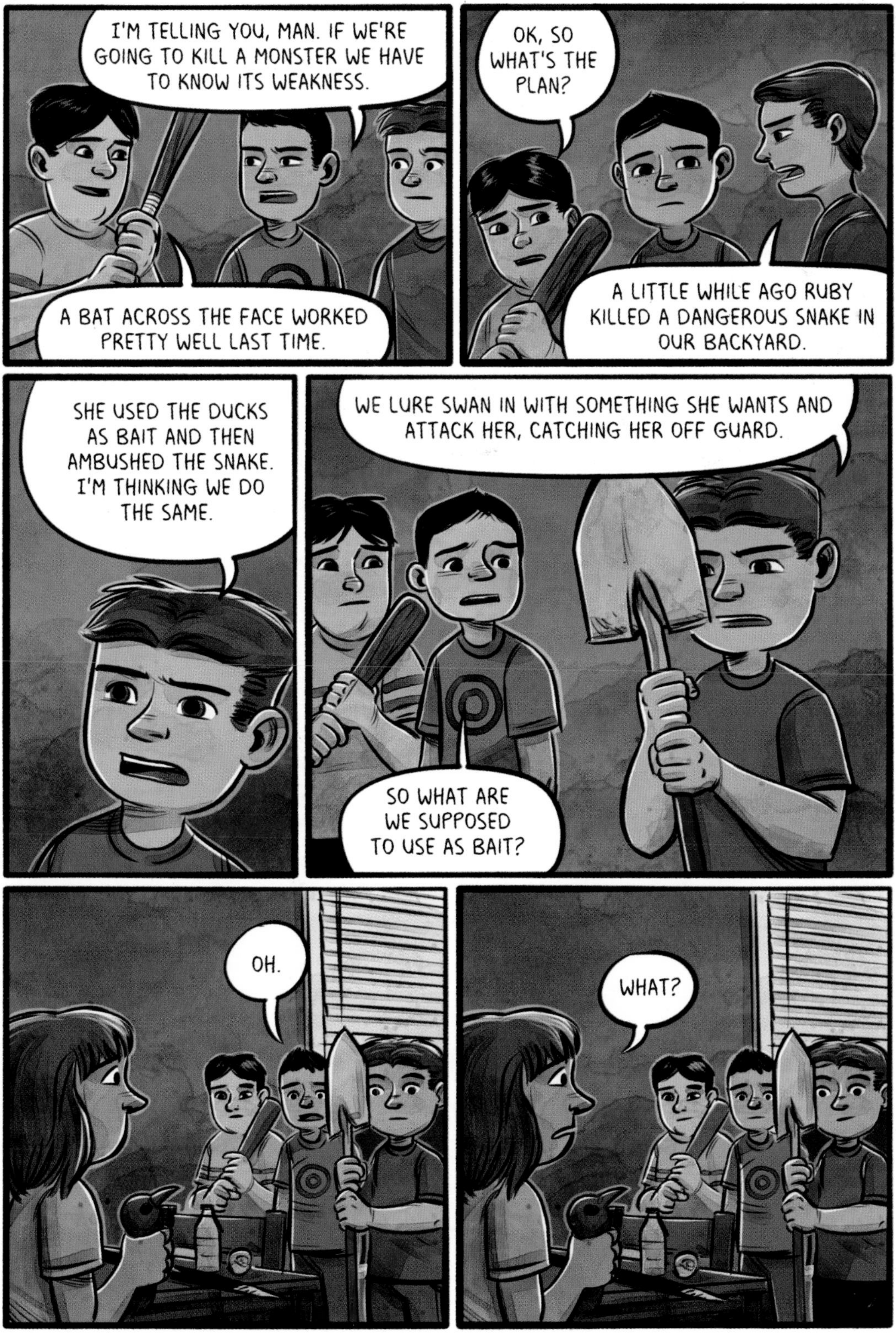
I'M TELLING YOU, MAN. IF WE'RE GOING TO KILL A MONSTER WE HAVE TO KNOW ITS WEAKNESS.
A BAT ACROSS THE FACE WORKED PRETTY WELL LAST TIME.
OK, SO WHAT'S THE PLAN?
A LITTLE WHILE AGO RUBY KILLED A DANGEROUS SNAKE IN OUR BACKYARD.
SHE USED THE DUCKS AS BAIT AND THEN AMBUSHED THE SNAKE. I'M THINKING WE DO THE SAME.
WE LURE SWAN IN WITH SOMETHING SHE WANTS AND ATTACK HER, CATCHING HER OFF GUARD.
SO WHAT ARE WE SUPPOSED TO USE AS BAIT?
OH.
WHAT?

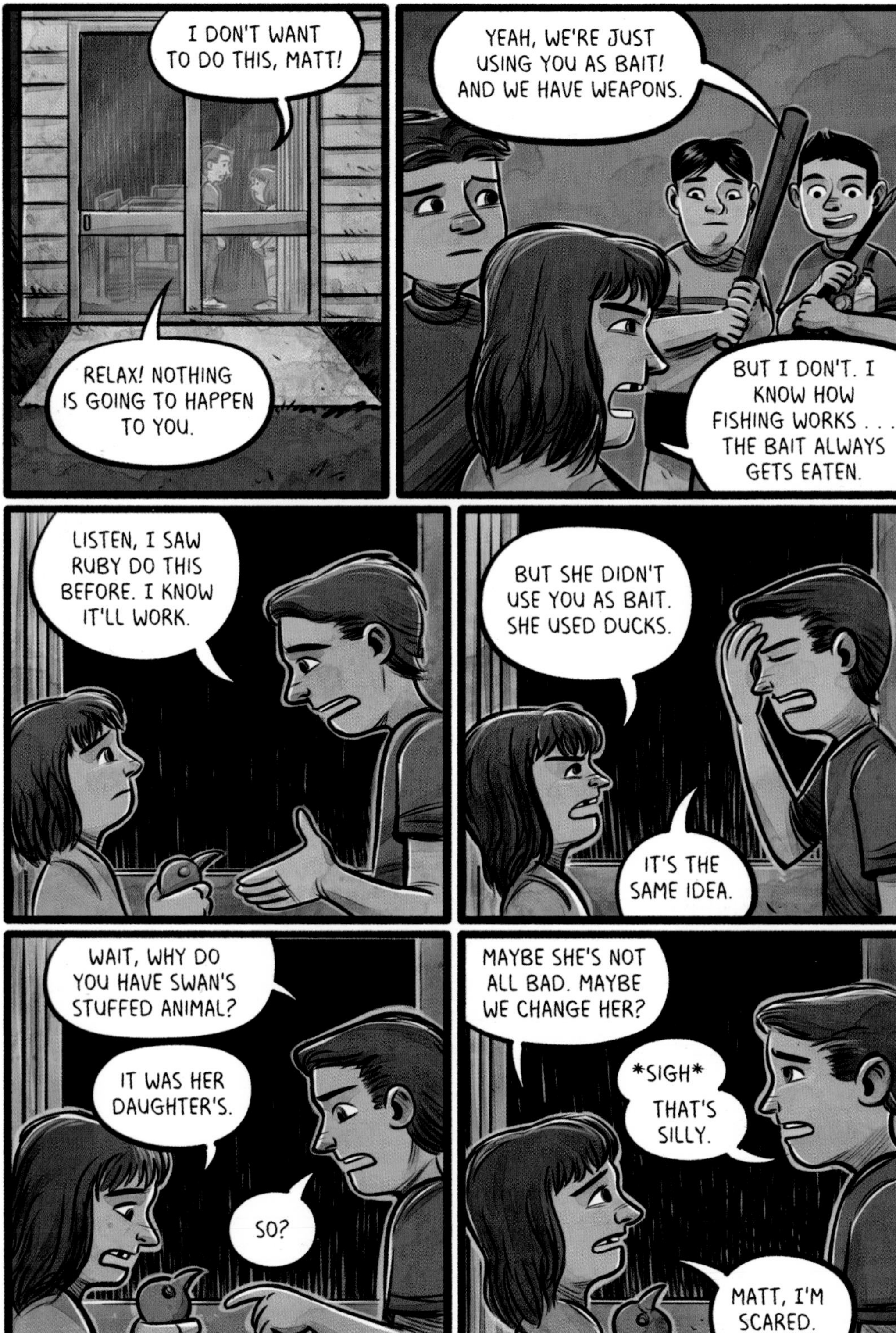
I DON'T WANT TO DO THIS, MATT!
RELAX! NOTHING IS GOING TO HAPPEN TO YOU.
YEAH, WE'RE JUST USING YOU AS BAIT! AND WE HAVE WEAPONS.
BUT I DON'T. I KNOW HOW FISHING WORKS . . . THE BAIT ALWAYS GETS EATEN.
LISTEN, I SAW RUBY DO THIS BEFORE. I KNOW IT'LL WORK.
BUT SHE DIDN'T USE YOU AS BAIT. SHE USED DUCKS.
IT'S THE SAME IDEA.
WAIT, WHY DO YOU HAVE SWAN'S STUFFED ANIMAL?
IT WAS HER DAUGHTER'S.
SO?
MAYBE SHE'S NOT ALL BAD. MAYBE WE CHANGE HER?
SIGH
THAT'S SILLY.
MATT, I'M SCARED.

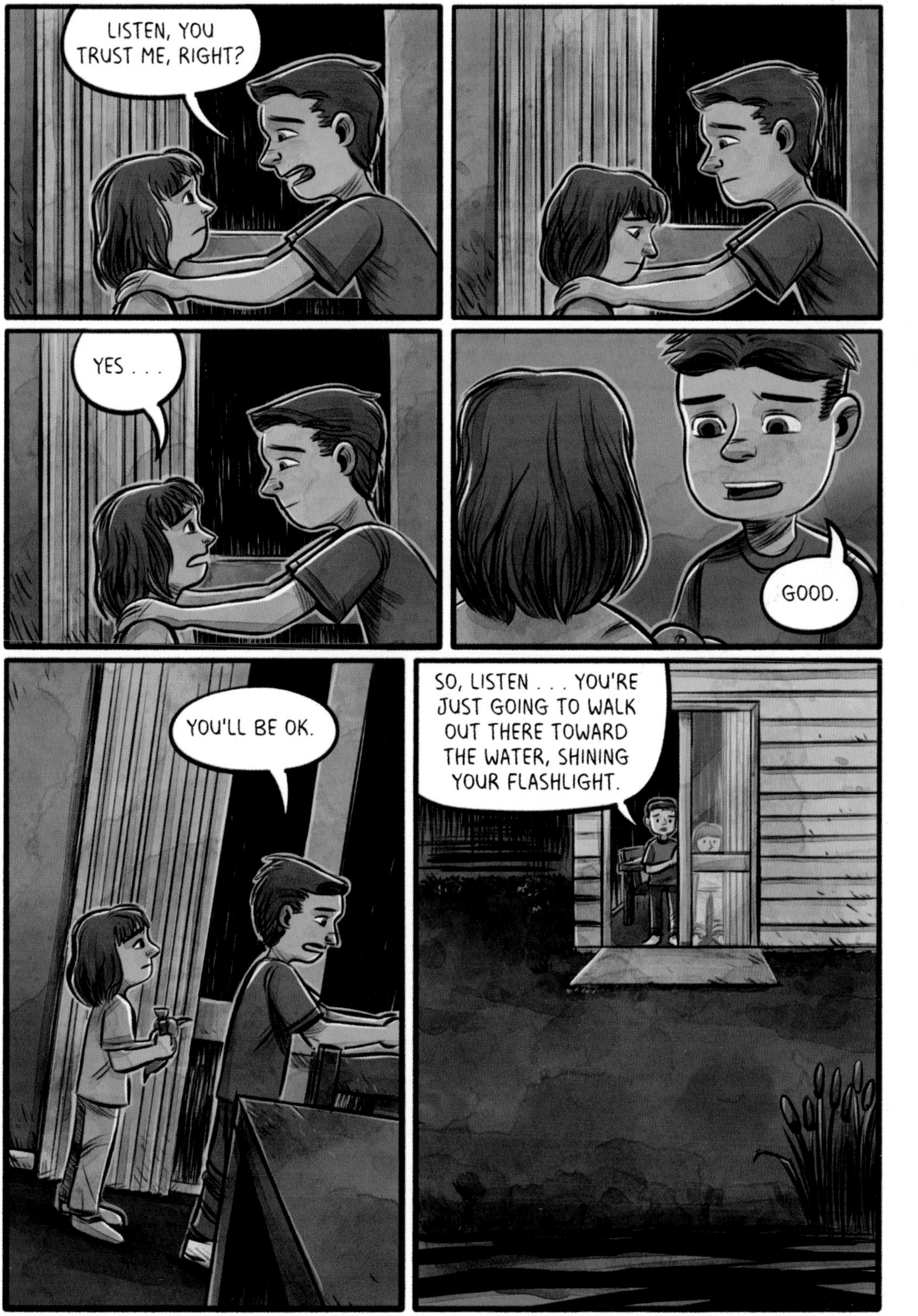
LISTEN, YOU TRUST ME, RIGHT?
YES . . .
GOOD.
YOU'LL BE OK.
SO, LISTEN . . . YOU'RE JUST GOING TO WALK OUT THERE TOWARD THE WATER, SHINING YOUR FLASHLIGHT.

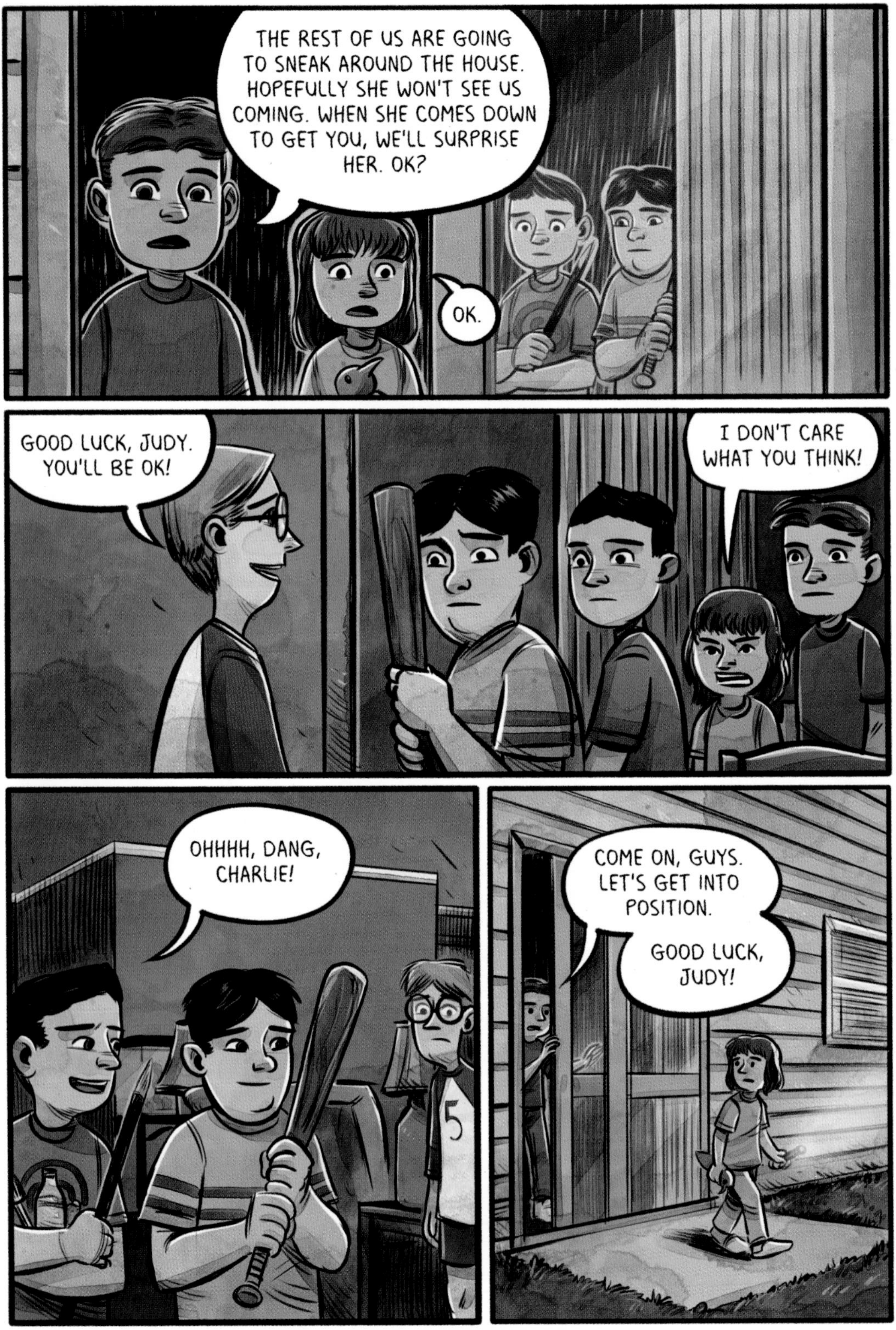
THE REST OF US ARE GOING TO SNEAK AROUND THE HOUSE. HOPEFULLY SHE WON'T SEE US COMING. WHEN SHE COMES DOWN TO GET YOU, WE'LL SURPRISE HER. OK?
OK.
GOOD LUCK, JUDY. YOU'LL BE OK!
I DON'T CARE WHAT YOU THINK!
OHHHH, DANG, CHARLIE!
5
COME ON, GUYS. LET'S GET INTO POSITION.
GOOD LUCK, JUDY!

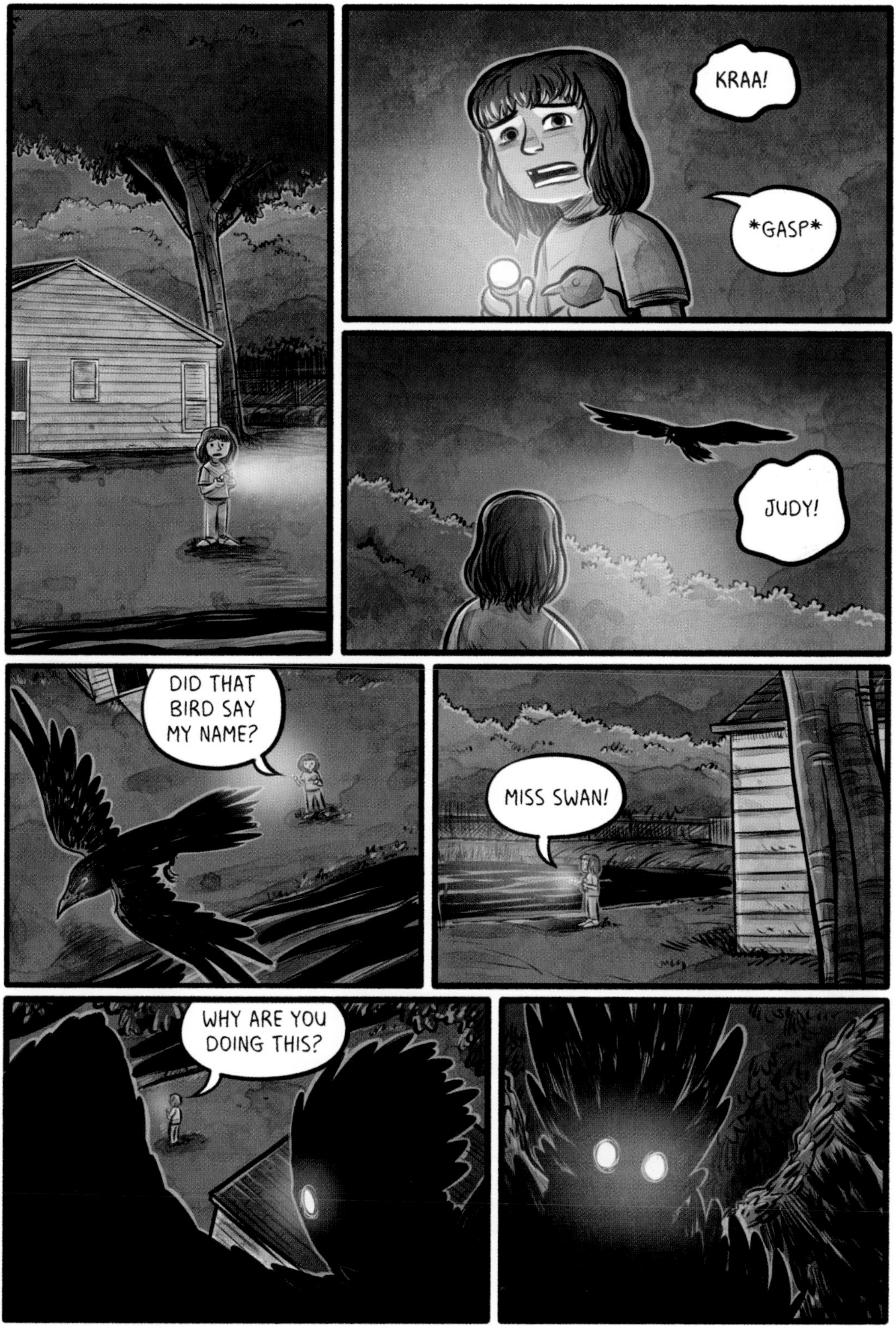
KRAA!
GASP
JUDY!
DID THAT BIRD SAY MY NAME?
MISS SWAN!
WHY ARE YOU DOING THIS?

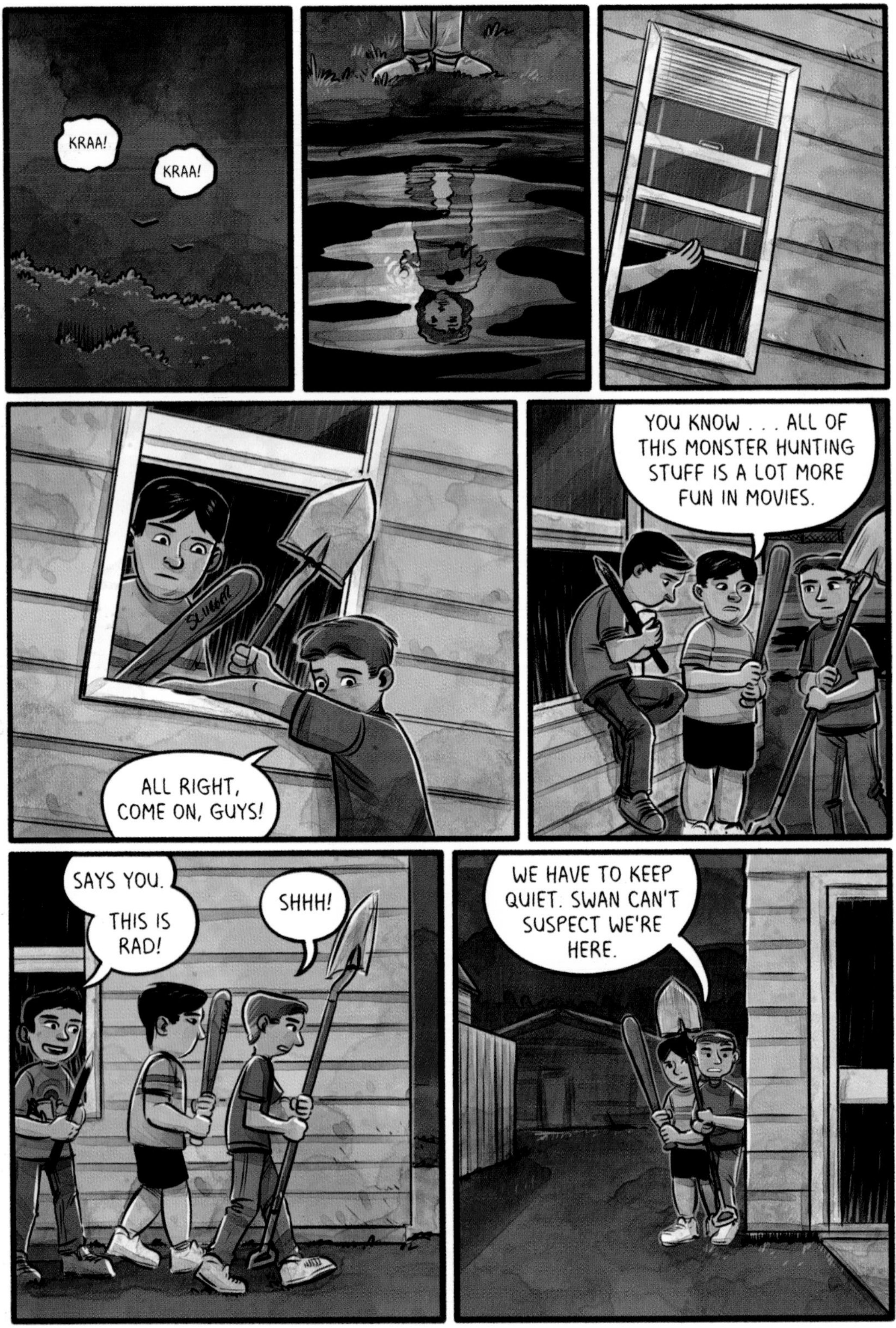
KRAA!
KRAA!
ALL RIGHT, COME ON, GUYS!
YOU KNOW . . . ALL OF THIS MONSTER HUNTING STUFF IS A LOT MORE FUN IN MOVIES.
SAYS YOU.
THIS IS RAD!
SHHH!
WE HAVE TO KEEP QUIET. SWAN CAN'T SUSPECT WE'RE HERE.

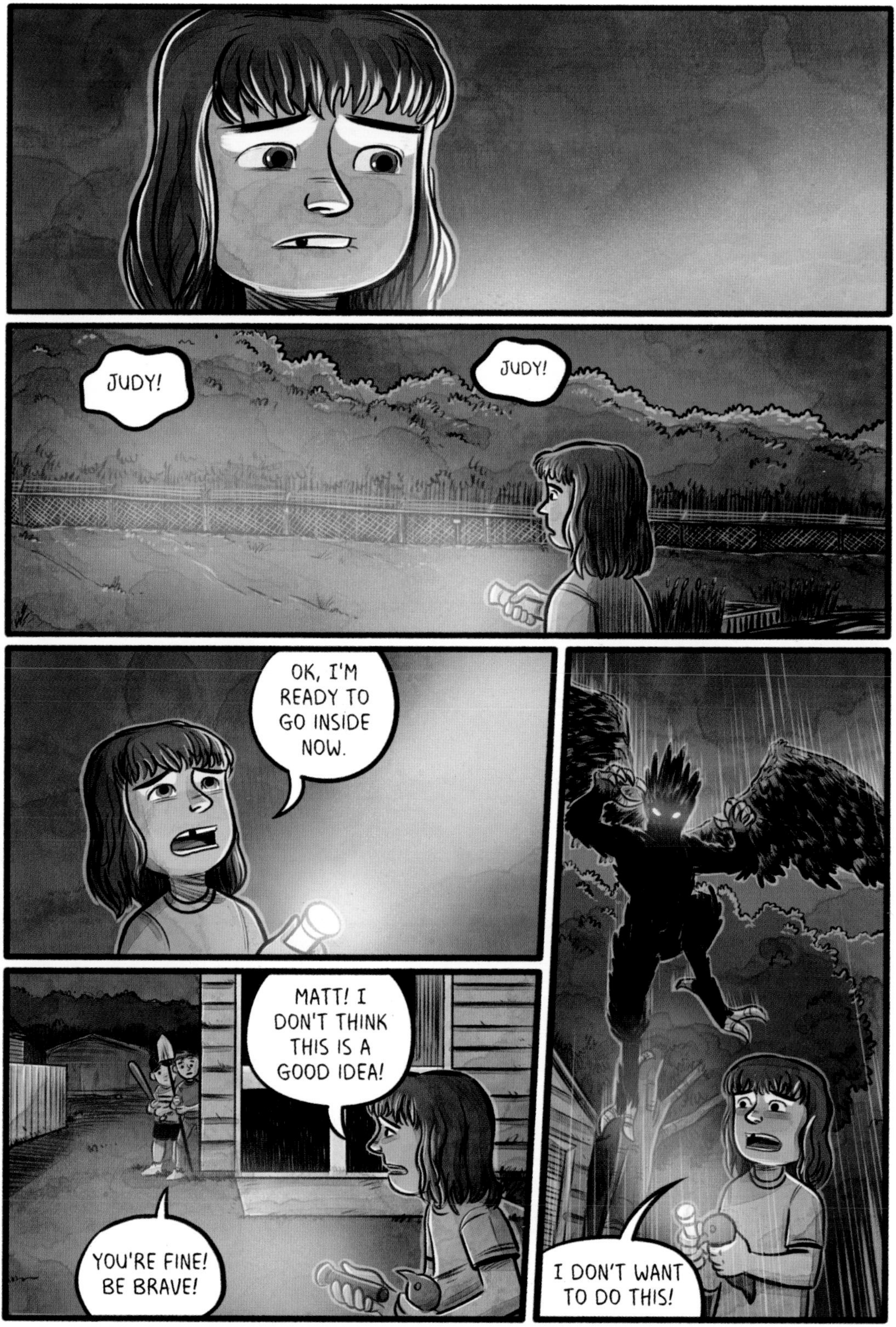
JUDY!
JUDY!
OK, I'M READY TO GO INSIDE NOW.
MATT! I DON'T THINK THIS IS A GOOD IDEA!
YOU'RE FINE! BE BRAVE!
I DON'T WANT TO DO THIS!

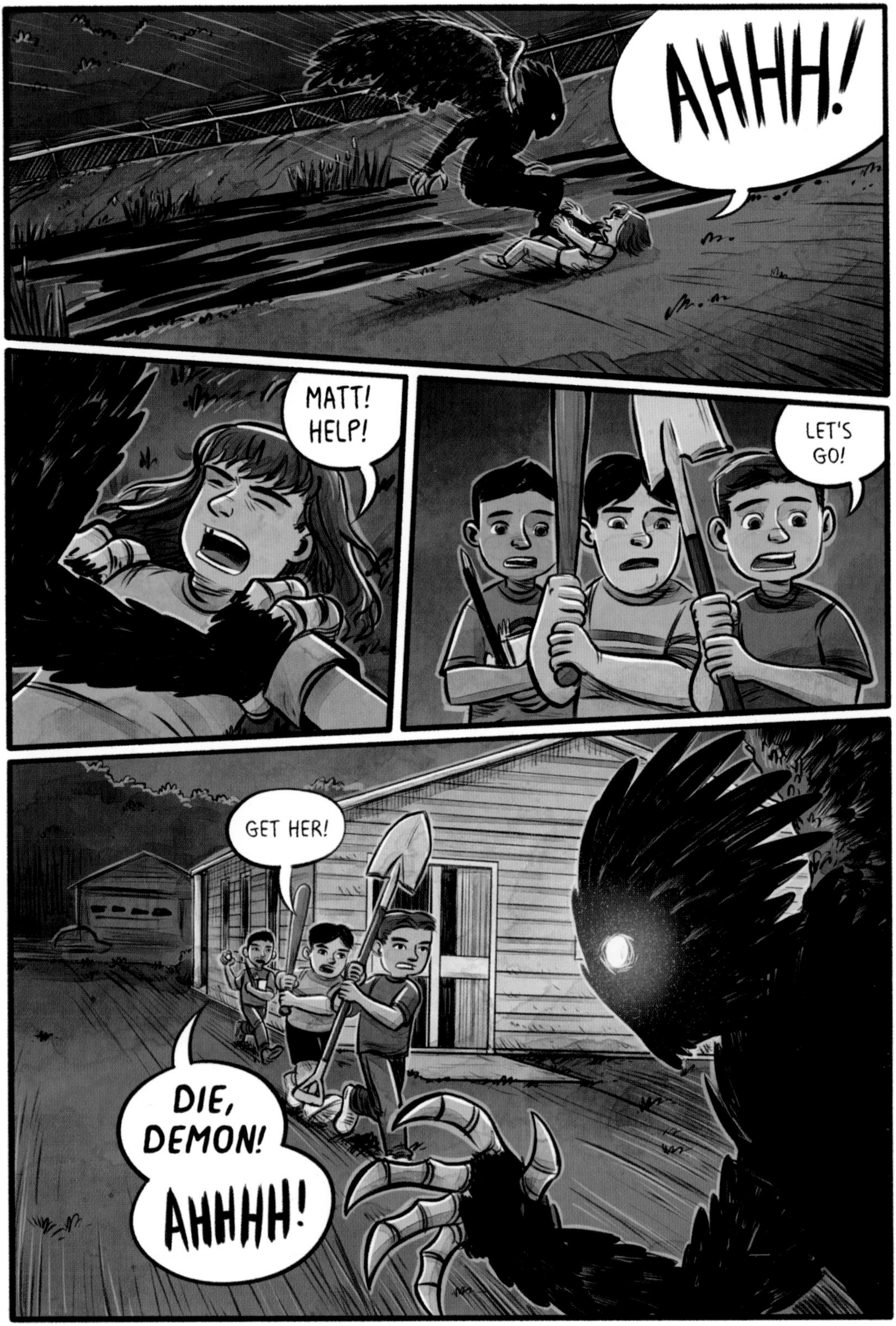
AHHH!
MATT! HELP!
LET'S GO!
GET HER!
DIE, DEMON!
AHHHH!

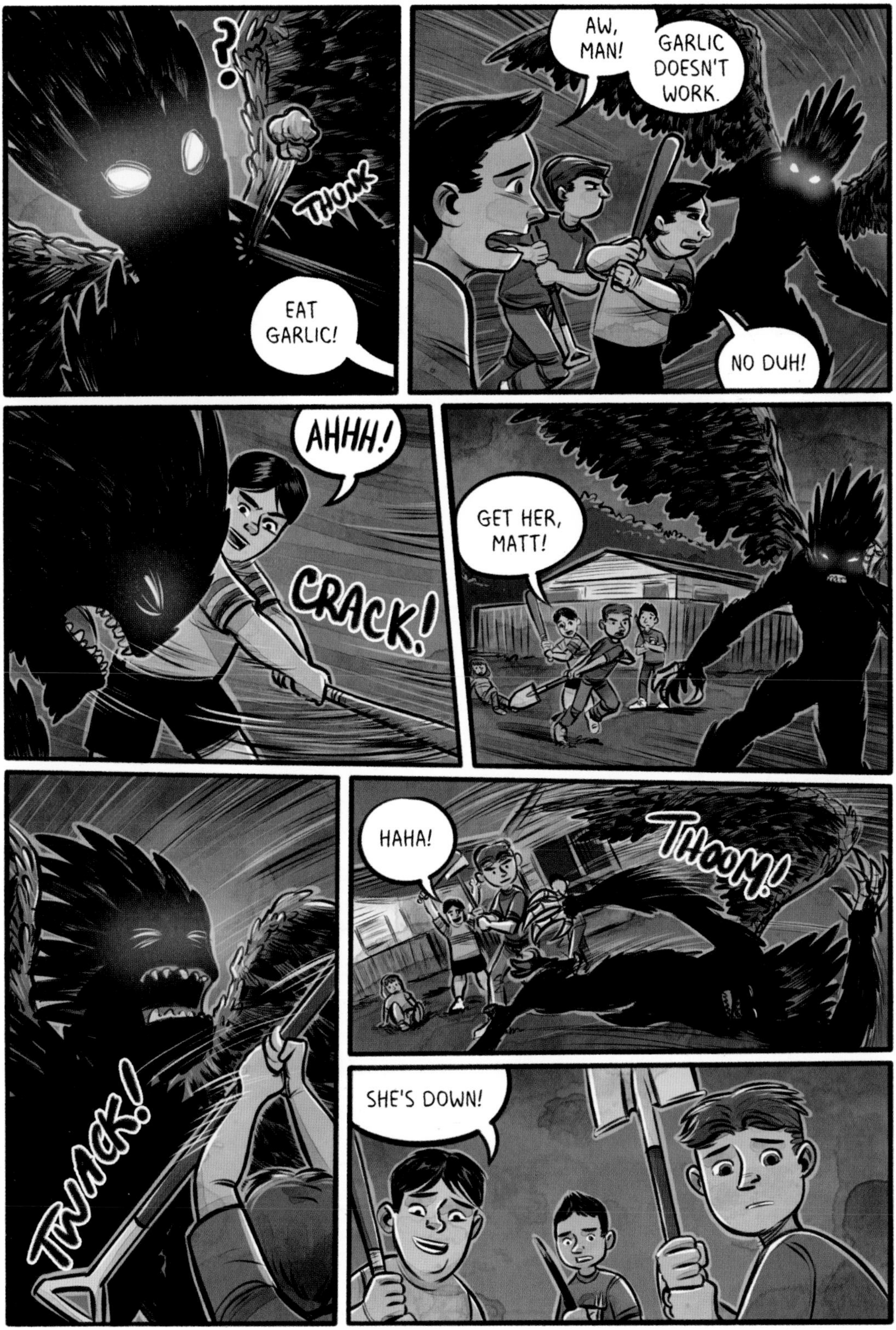
?
THUNK
EAT GARLIC!
AW, MAN!
GARLIC DOESN'T WORK.
NO DUH!
AHHH!
CRACK!
GET HER, MATT!
TWACK!
HAHA!
THOOM!
SHE'S DOWN!

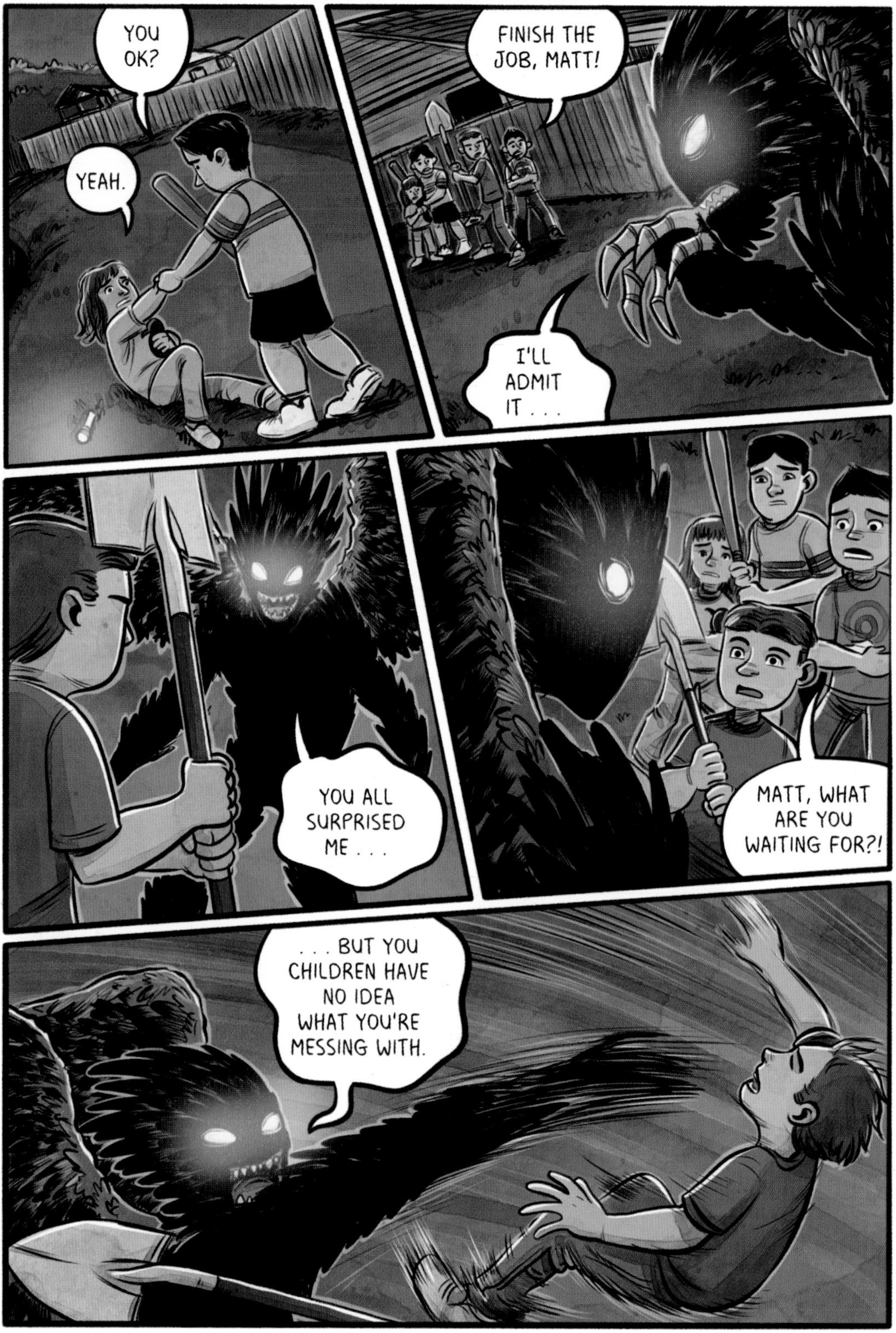
YOU OK?
YEAH.
FINISH THE JOB, MATT!
I'LL ADMIT IT . . .
YOU ALL SURPRISED ME . . .
MATT, WHAT ARE YOU WAITING FOR?!
. . . BUT YOU CHILDREN HAVE NO IDEA WHAT YOU'RE MESSING WITH.

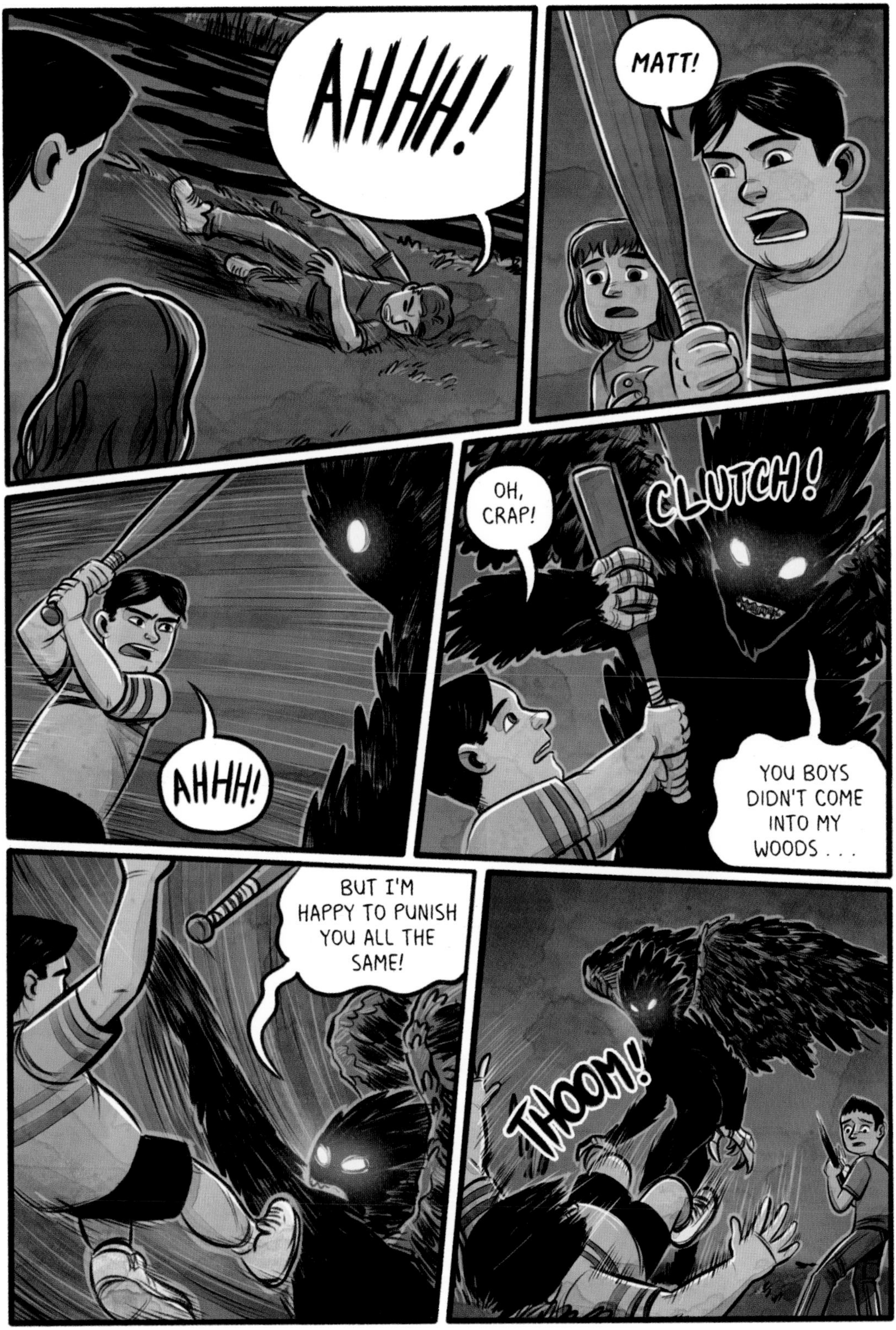
AHHH!
MATT!
AHHH!
OH, CRAP!
CLUTCH!
YOU BOYS DIDN'T COME INTO MY WOODS . . .
BUT I'M HAPPY TO PUNISH YOU ALL THE SAME!
THOOM!

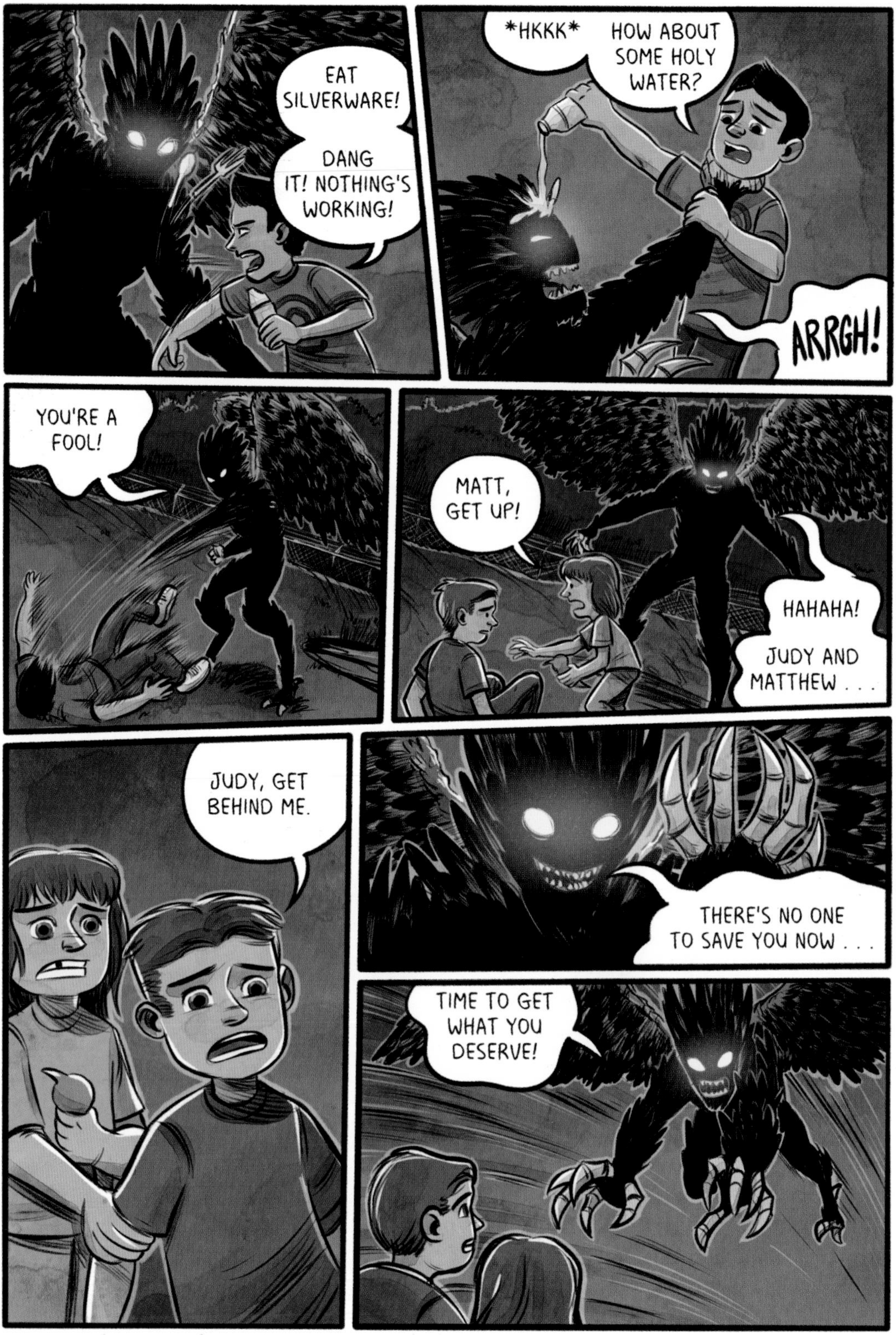
EAT SILVERWARE!
DANG IT! NOTHING'S WORKING!
HKKK
HOW ABOUT SOME HOLY WATER?
ARRGH!
YOU'RE A FOOL!
MATT, GET UP!
HAHAHA!
JUDY AND MATTHEW . . .
JUDY, GET BEHIND ME.
THERE'S NO ONE TO SAVE YOU NOW . . .
TIME TO GET WHAT YOU DESERVE!

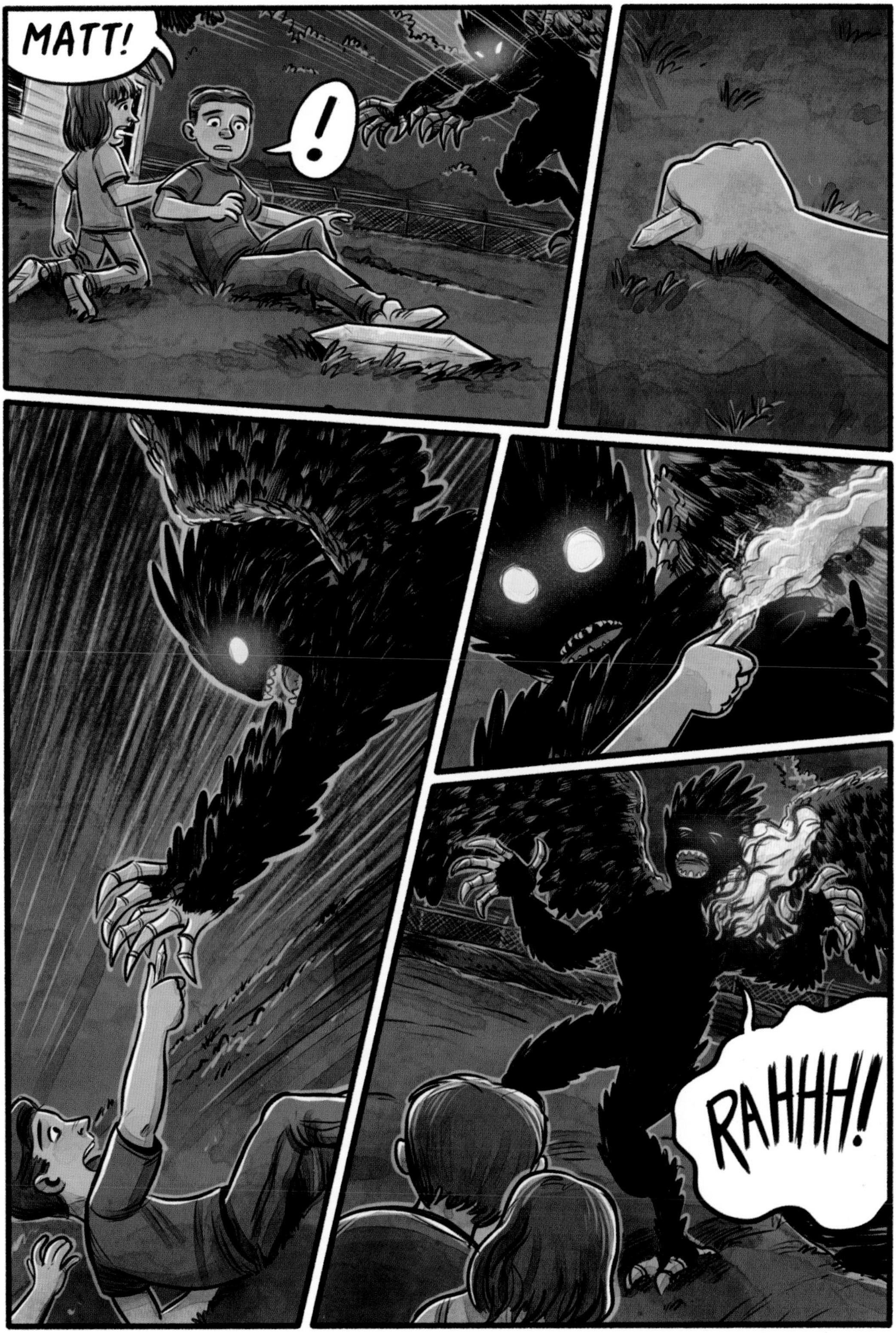
MATT!
!
RAHHH!

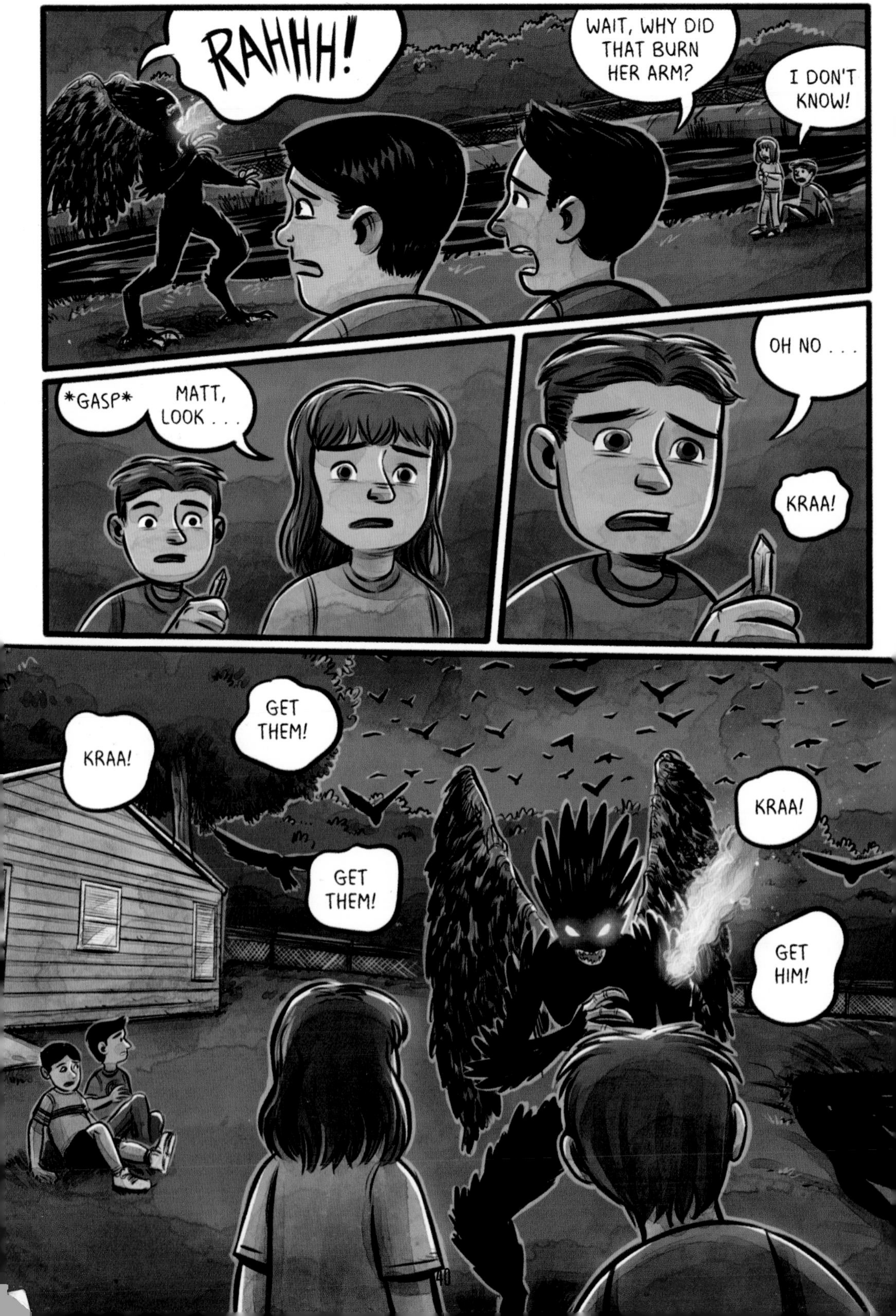
RAHHH!
WAIT, WHY DID THAT BURN HER ARM?
I DON'T KNOW!
GASP MATT, LOOK . . .
OH NO . . .
KRAA!
KRAA!
GET THEM!
GET THEM!
KRAA!
GET HIM!

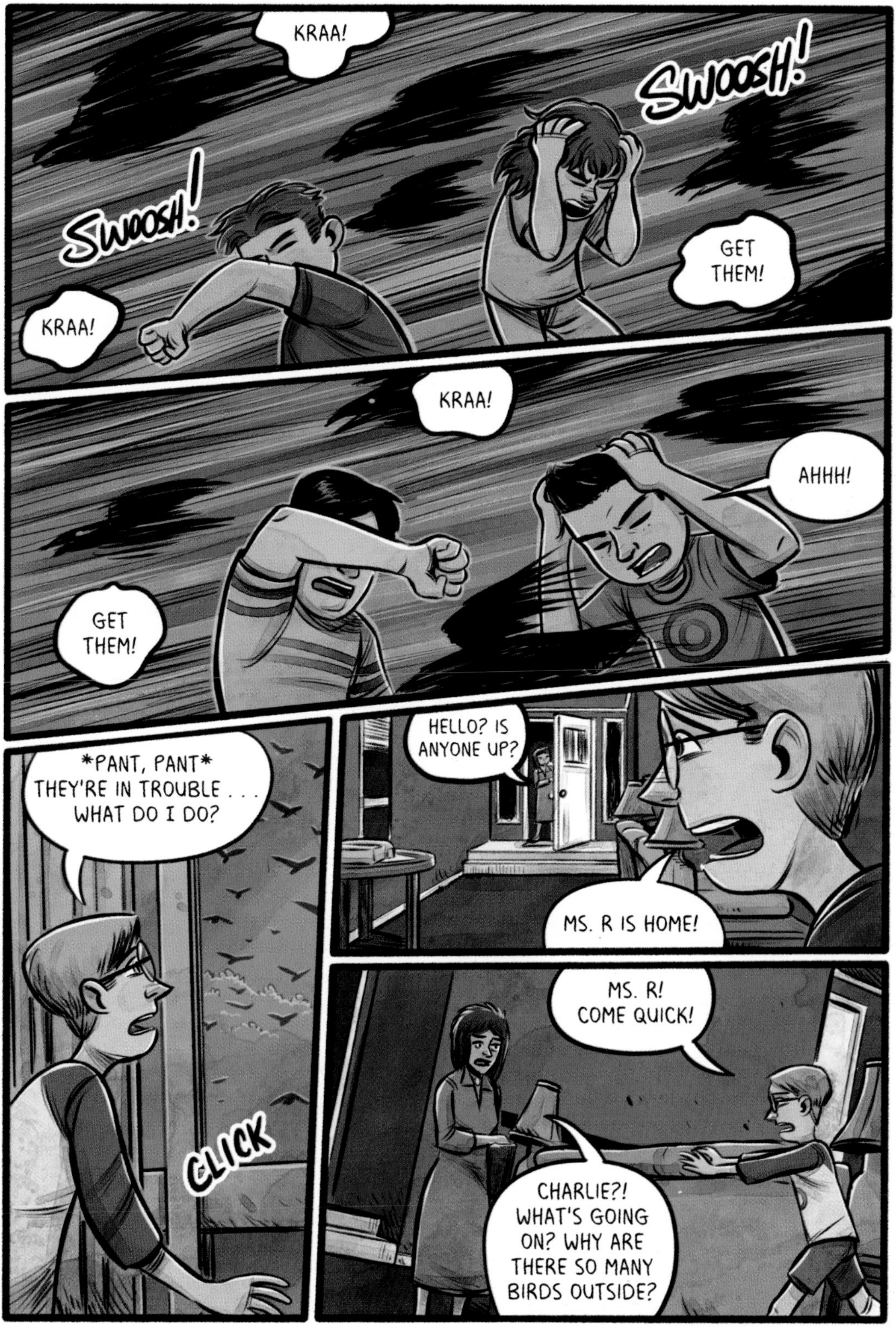
KRAA!
SWOOSH!
SWOOSH!
GET THEM!
KRAA!
KRAA!
AHHH!
GET THEM!
PANT, PANT THEY'RE IN TROUBLE . . . WHAT DO I DO?
CLICK
HELLO? IS ANYONE UP?
MS. R IS HOME!
MS. R! COME QUICK!
CHARLIE?! WHAT'S GOING ON? WHY ARE THERE SO MANY BIRDS OUTSIDE?

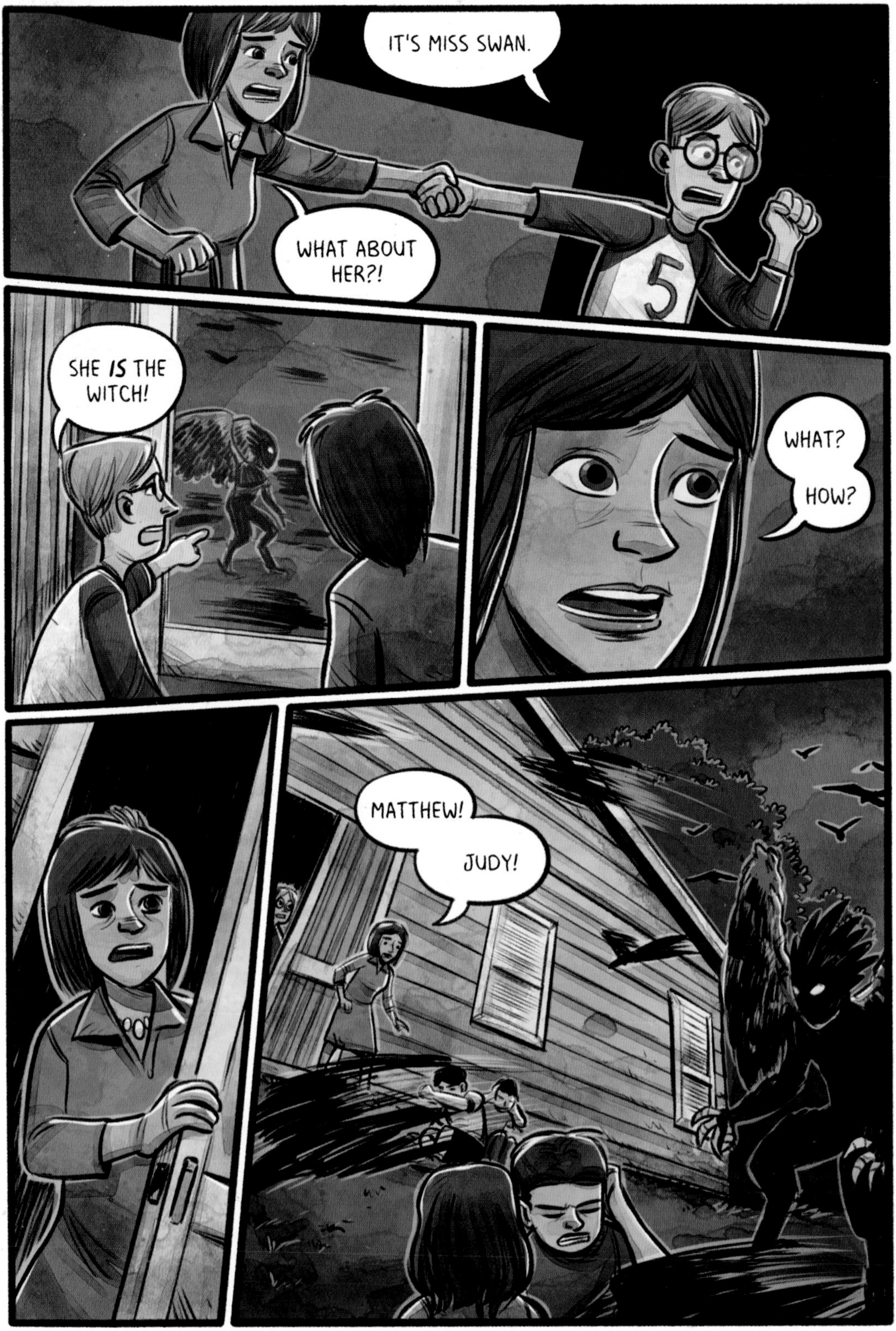
IT'S MISS SWAN.
WHAT ABOUT HER?!
SHE IS THE WITCH!
WHAT?
HOW?
MATTHEW!
JUDY!

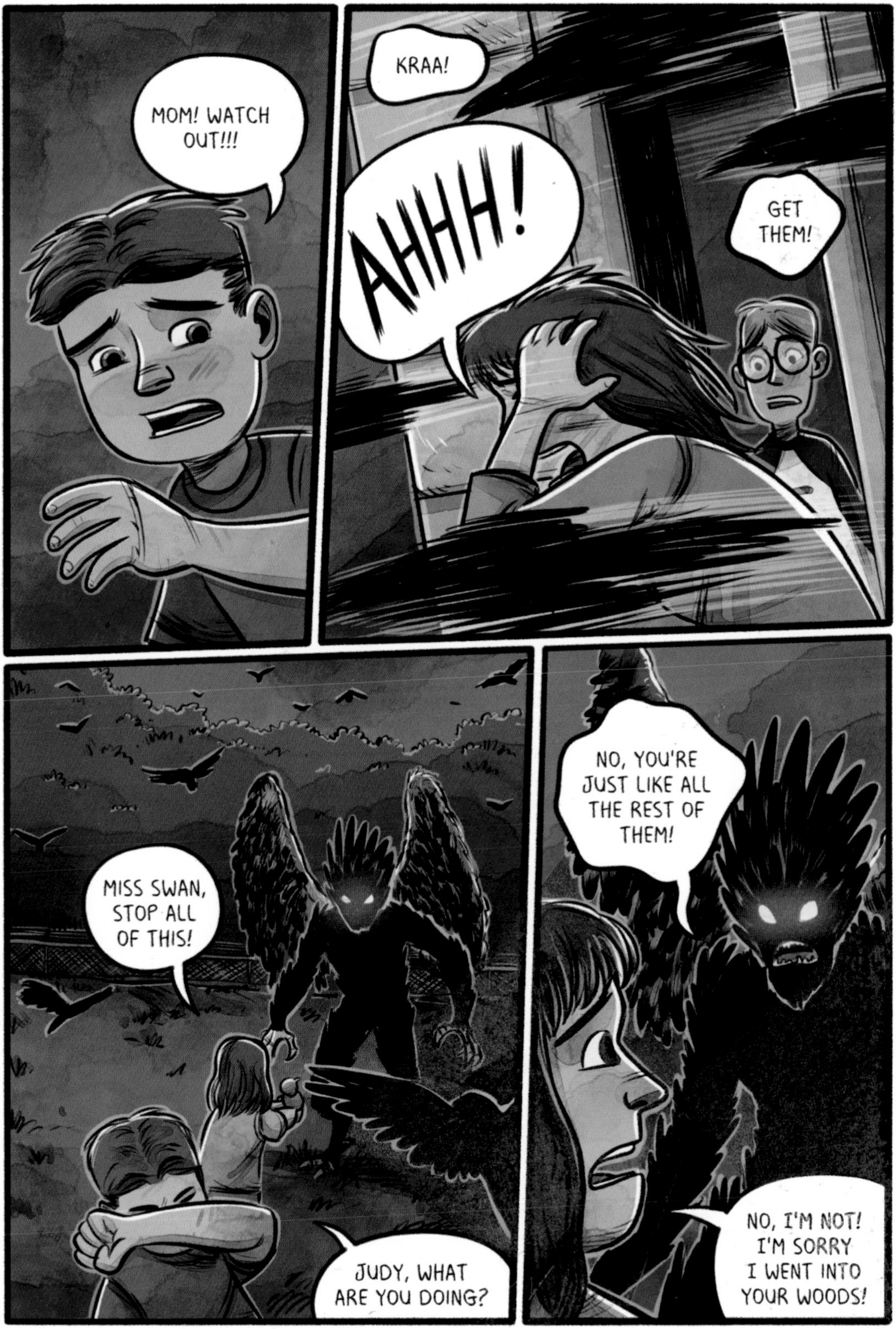
MOM! WATCH OUT!!!
KRAA!
AHHH!
GET THEM!
MISS SWAN, STOP ALL OF THIS!
JUDY, WHAT ARE YOU DOING?
NO, YOU'RE JUST LIKE ALL THE REST OF THEM!
NO, I'M NOT! I'M SORRY I WENT INTO YOUR WOODS!

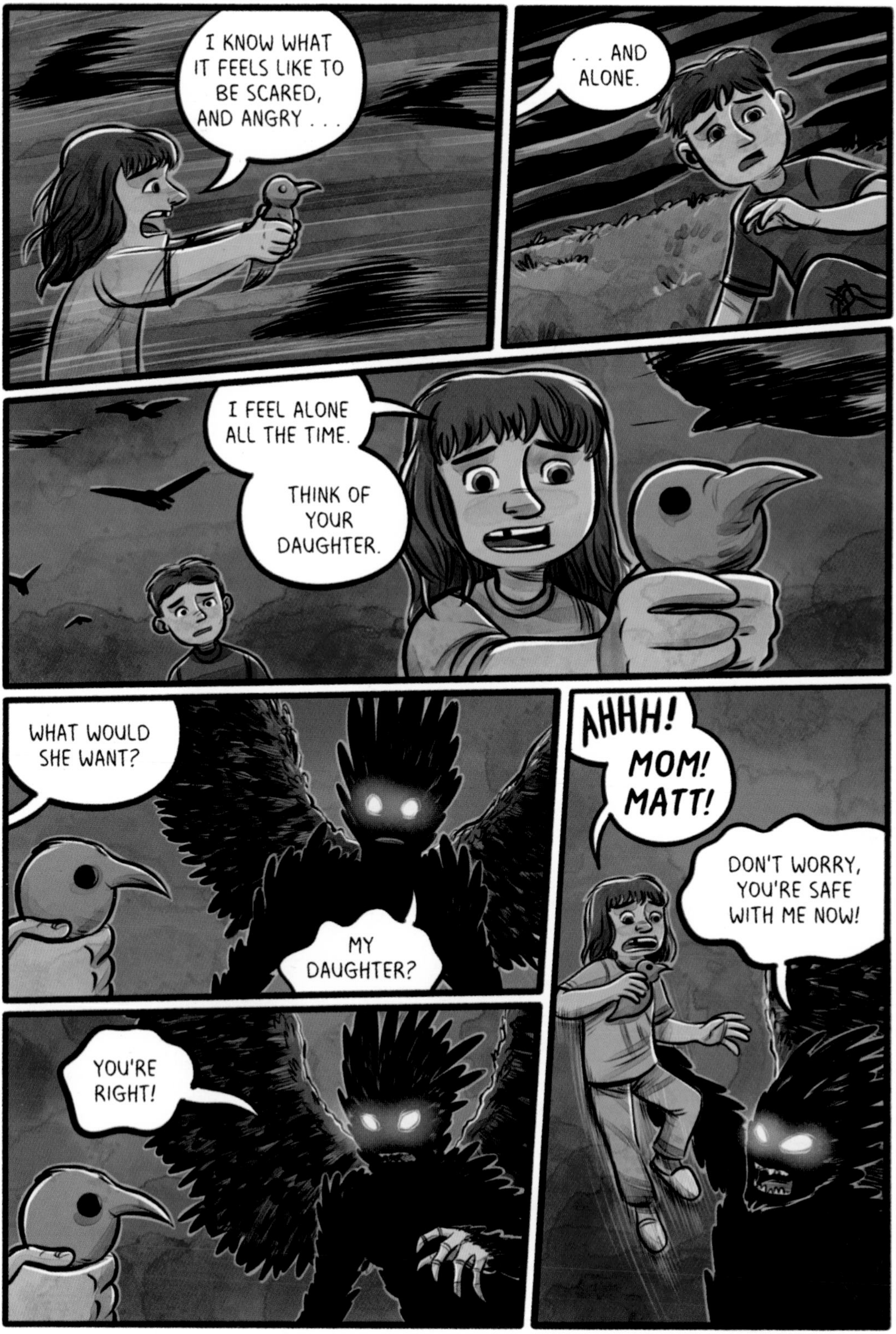
I KNOW WHAT IT FEELS LIKE TO BE SCARED, AND ANGRY . . .
. . . AND ALONE.
I FEEL ALONE ALL THE TIME.
THINK OF YOUR DAUGHTER.
WHAT WOULD SHE WANT?
MY DAUGHTER?
YOU'RE RIGHT!
AHHH!
MOM! MATT!
DON'T WORRY, YOU'RE SAFE WITH ME NOW!

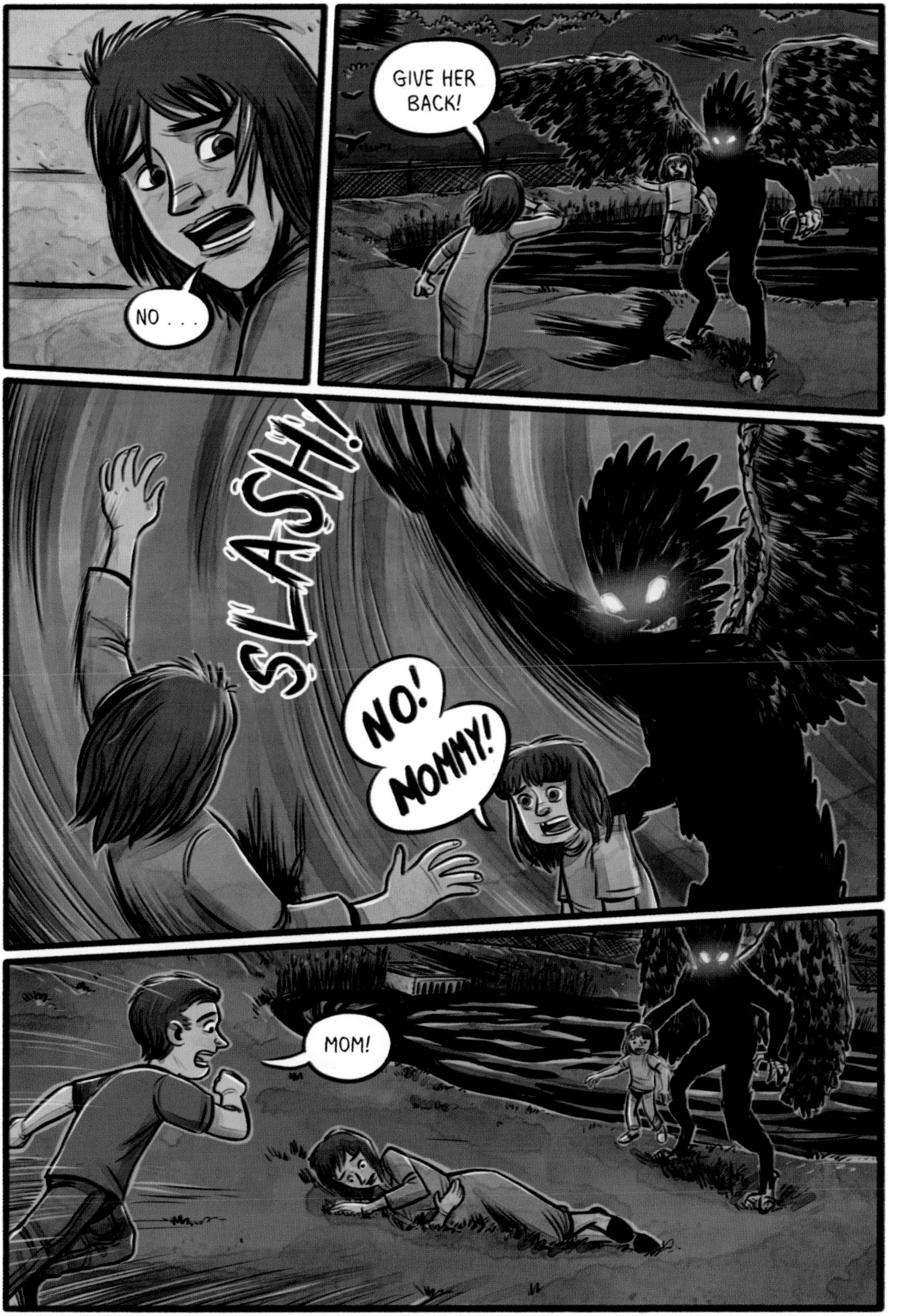
NO . . .
GIVE HER BACK!
SLASH!
NO! MOMMY!
MOM!

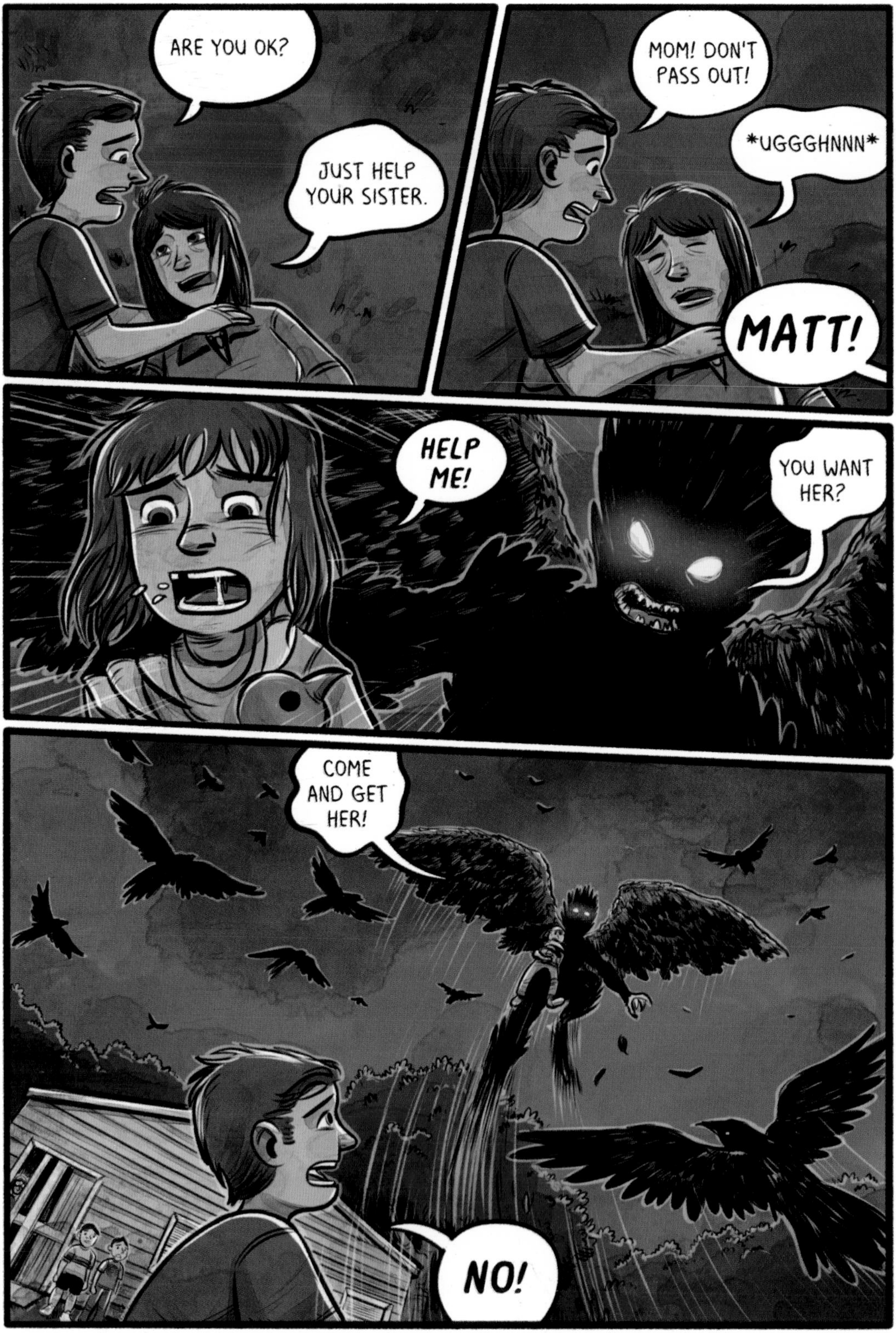
ARE YOU OK?
JUST HELP YOUR SISTER.
MOM! DON'T PASS OUT!
UGGGHNNN
MATT!
HELP ME!
YOU WANT HER?
COME AND GET HER!
NO!

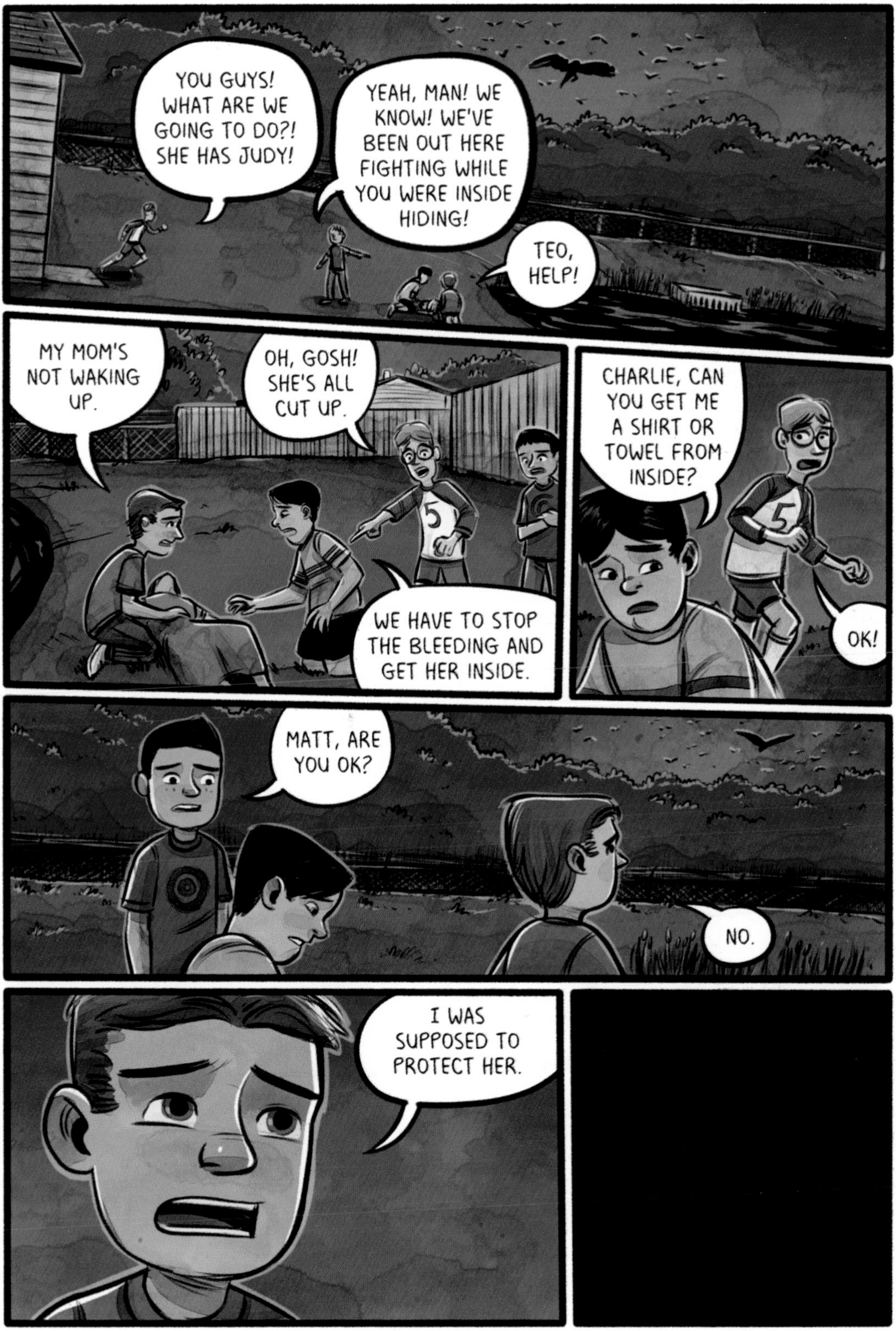

YOU GUYS! WHAT ARE WE GOING TO DO?! SHE HAS JUDY!
YEAH, MAN! WE KNOW! WE'VE BEEN OUT HERE FIGHTING WHILE YOU WERE INSIDE HIDING!
TEO, HELP!
MY MOM'S NOT WAKING UP.
OH, GOSH! SHE'S ALL CUT UP.
WE HAVE TO STOP THE BLEEDING AND GET HER INSIDE.
CHARLIE, CAN YOU GET ME A SHIRT OR TOWEL FROM INSIDE?
OK!
MATT, ARE YOU OK?
NO.
I WAS SUPPOSED TO PROTECT HER.

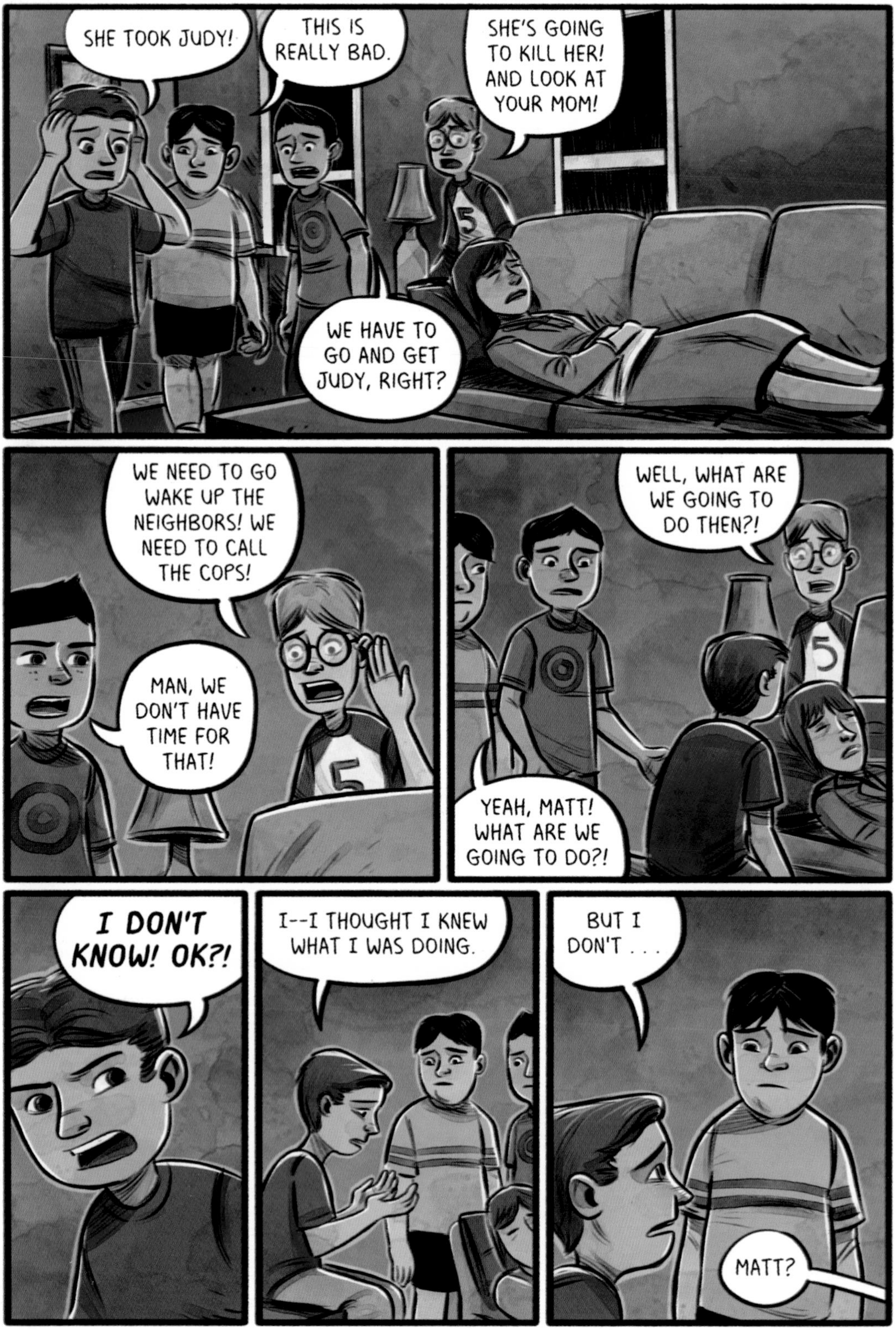

SHE TOOK JUDY!
THIS IS REALLY BAD.
SHE'S GOING TO KILL HER! AND LOOK AT YOUR MOM!
WE HAVE TO GO AND GET JUDY, RIGHT?
WE NEED TO GO WAKE UP THE NEIGHBORS! WE NEED TO CALL THE COPS!
MAN, WE DON'T HAVE TIME FOR THAT!
WELL, WHAT ARE WE GOING TO DO THEN?!
YEAH, MATT! WHAT ARE WE GOING TO DO?!
I DON'T KNOW! OK?!
I--I THOUGHT I KNEW WHAT I WAS DOING.
BUT I DON'T . . .
MATT?

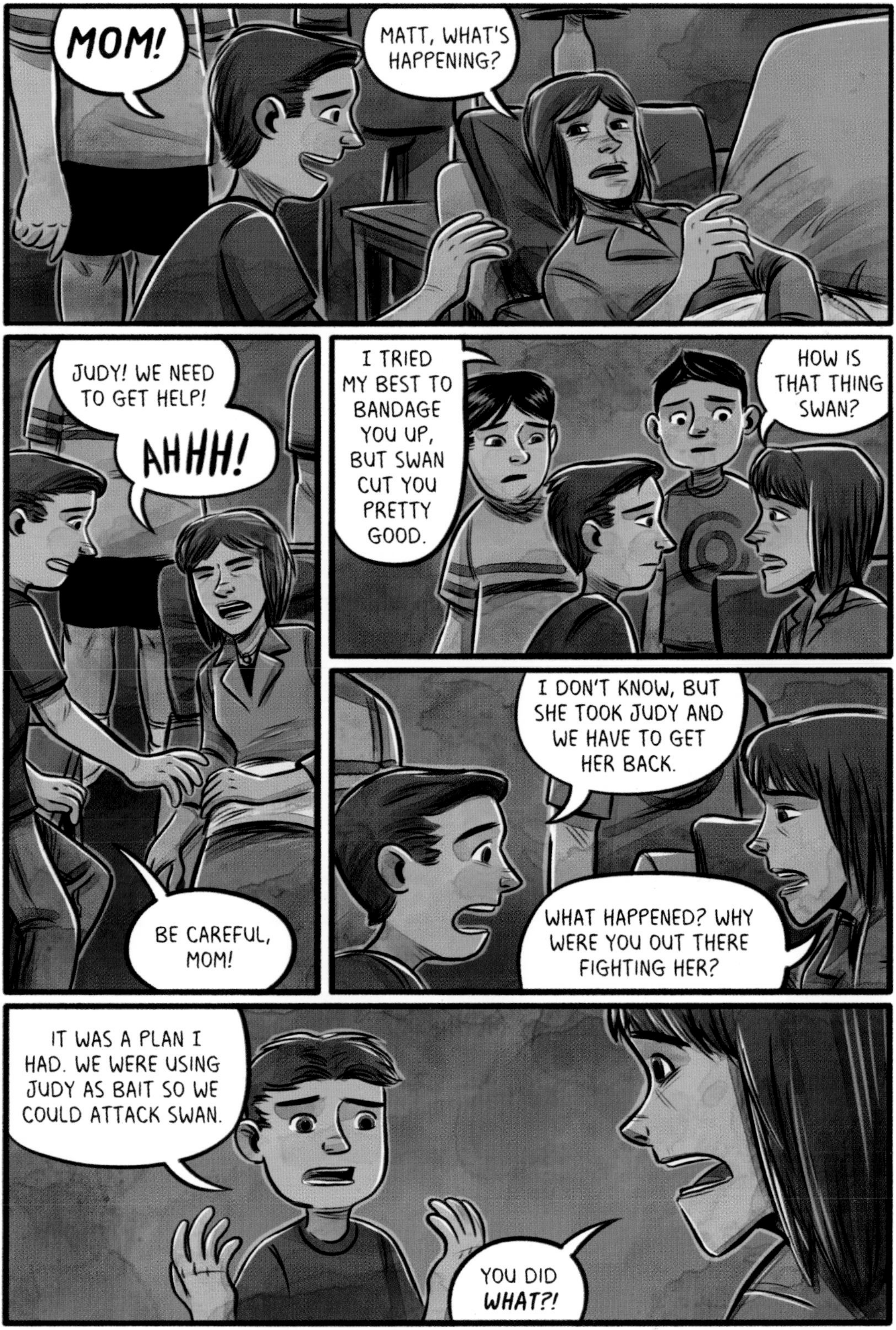
MOM!
MATT, WHAT'S HAPPENING?
JUDY! WE NEED TO GET HELP!
AHHH!
BE CAREFUL, MOM!
I TRIED MY BEST TO BANDAGE YOU UP, BUT SWAN CUT YOU PRETTY GOOD.
HOW IS THAT THING SWAN?
I DON'T KNOW, BUT SHE TOOK JUDY AND WE HAVE TO GET HER BACK.
WHAT HAPPENED? WHY WERE YOU OUT THERE FIGHTING HER?
IT WAS A PLAN I HAD. WE WERE USING JUDY AS BAIT SO WE COULD ATTACK SWAN.
YOU DID **WHAT?!**

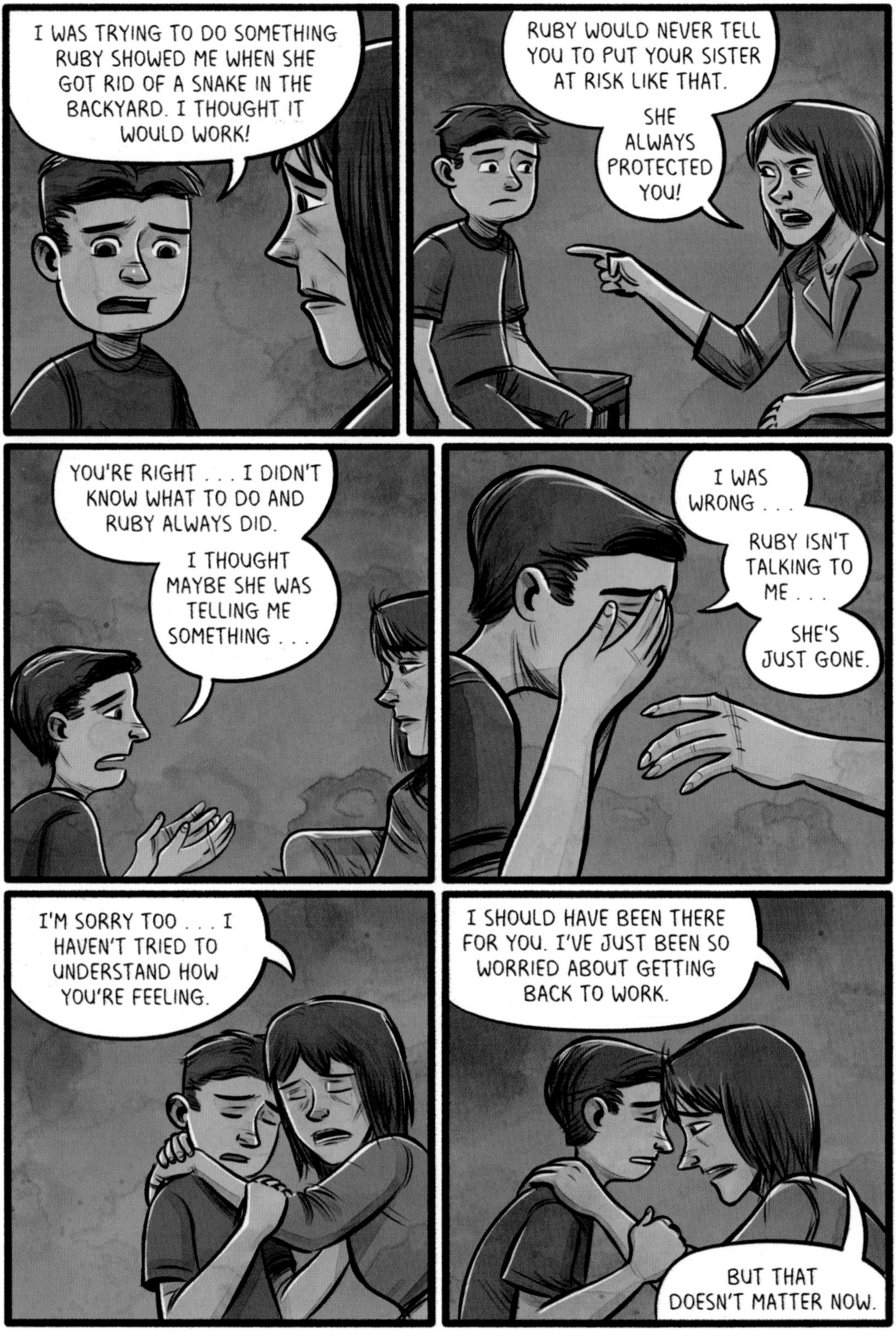
I WAS TRYING TO DO SOMETHING RUBY SHOWED ME WHEN SHE GOT RID OF A SNAKE IN THE BACKYARD. I THOUGHT IT WOULD WORK!
RUBY WOULD NEVER TELL YOU TO PUT YOUR SISTER AT RISK LIKE THAT.
SHE ALWAYS PROTECTED YOU!
YOU'RE RIGHT . . . I DIDN'T KNOW WHAT TO DO AND RUBY ALWAYS DID.
I THOUGHT MAYBE SHE WAS TELLING ME SOMETHING . . .
I WAS WRONG . . .
RUBY ISN'T TALKING TO ME . . .
SHE'S JUST GONE.
I'M SORRY TOO . . . I HAVEN'T TRIED TO UNDERSTAND HOW YOU'RE FEELING.
I SHOULD HAVE BEEN THERE FOR YOU. I'VE JUST BEEN SO WORRIED ABOUT GETTING BACK TO WORK.
BUT THAT DOESN'T MATTER NOW.

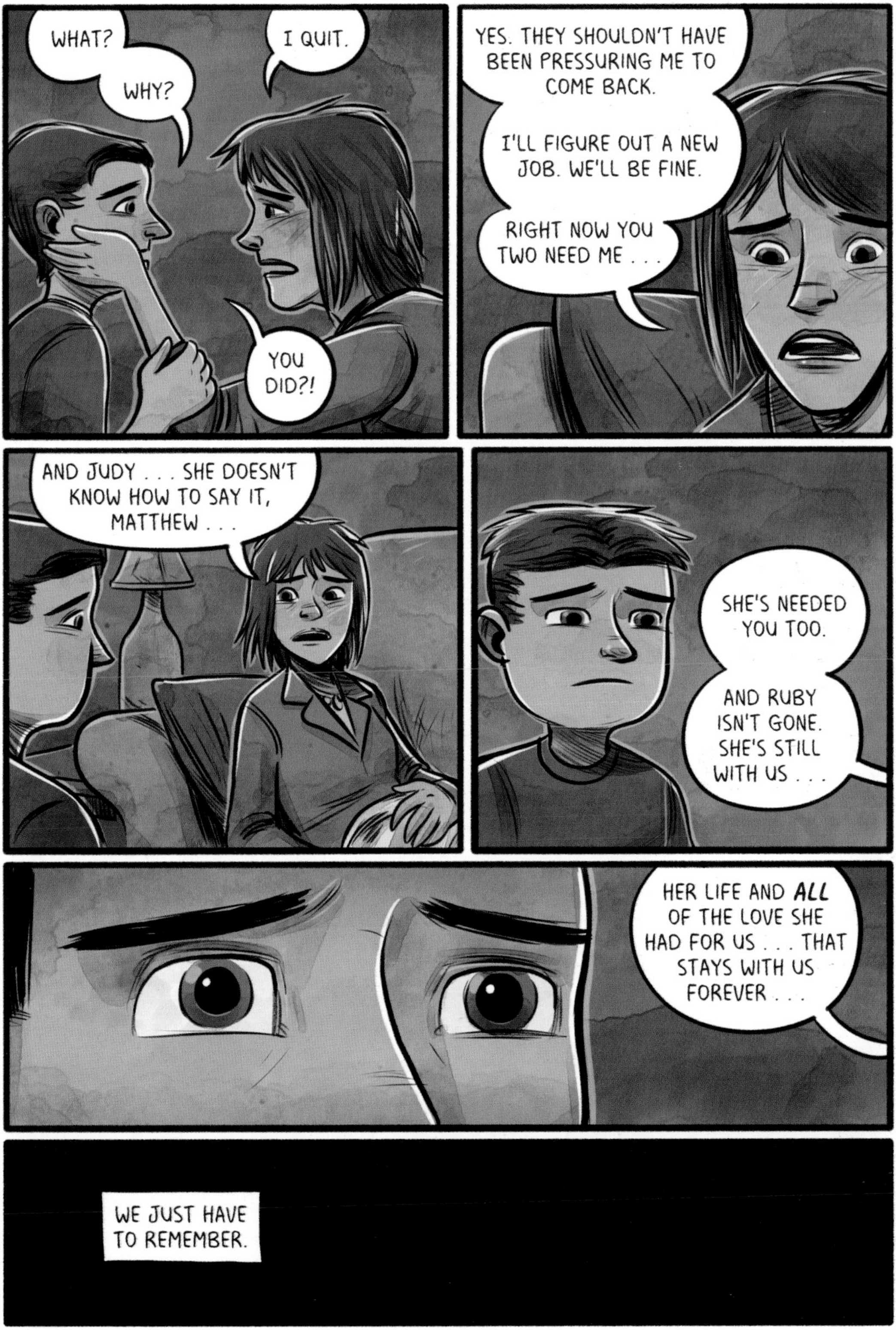
WHAT?
WHY?
I QUIT.
YOU DID?!
YES. THEY SHOULDN'T HAVE BEEN PRESSURING ME TO COME BACK.
I'LL FIGURE OUT A NEW JOB. WE'LL BE FINE.
RIGHT NOW YOU TWO NEED ME . . .
AND JUDY . . . SHE DOESN'T KNOW HOW TO SAY IT, MATTHEW . . .
SHE'S NEEDED YOU TOO.
AND RUBY ISN'T GONE. SHE'S STILL WITH US . . .
HER LIFE AND ***ALL*** OF THE LOVE SHE HAD FOR US . . . THAT STAYS WITH US FOREVER . . .
WE JUST HAVE TO REMEMBER.

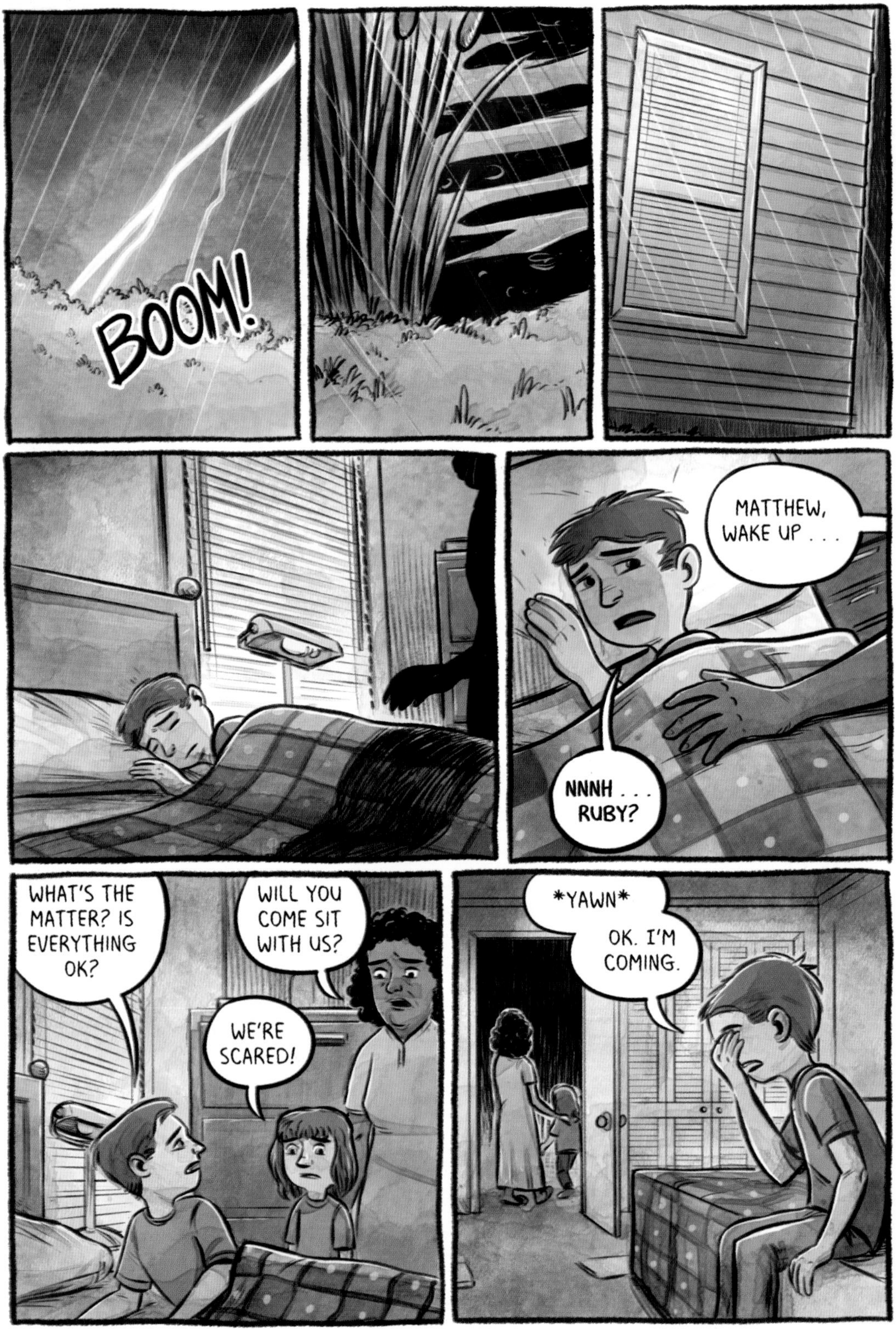
BOOM!
MATTHEW, WAKE UP . . .
NNNH . . . RUBY?
WHAT'S THE MATTER? IS EVERYTHING OK?
WILL YOU COME SIT WITH US?
WE'RE SCARED!
YAWN
OK. I'M COMING.

WHEN IS MOM COMING HOME?

DON'T KNOW. IT WAS A BUSY NIGHT AT THE RESTAURANT.

BOOM!

OH GOODNESS . . . HOW FAR AWAY DO YOU THINK THAT ONE WAS?

FIVE MILES . . . I COUNTED THE SECONDS.

IT SOUNDS CLOSER NOW.

HOW DO YOU KNOW?

YOU COUNT THE SECONDS FROM WHEN YOU SEE THE LIGHTNING STRIKE. EACH SECOND IS A MILE.

IS THAT TRUE?

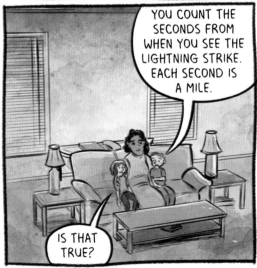

BOOM!

OH NO. THAT ONE WAS FOUR SECONDS.

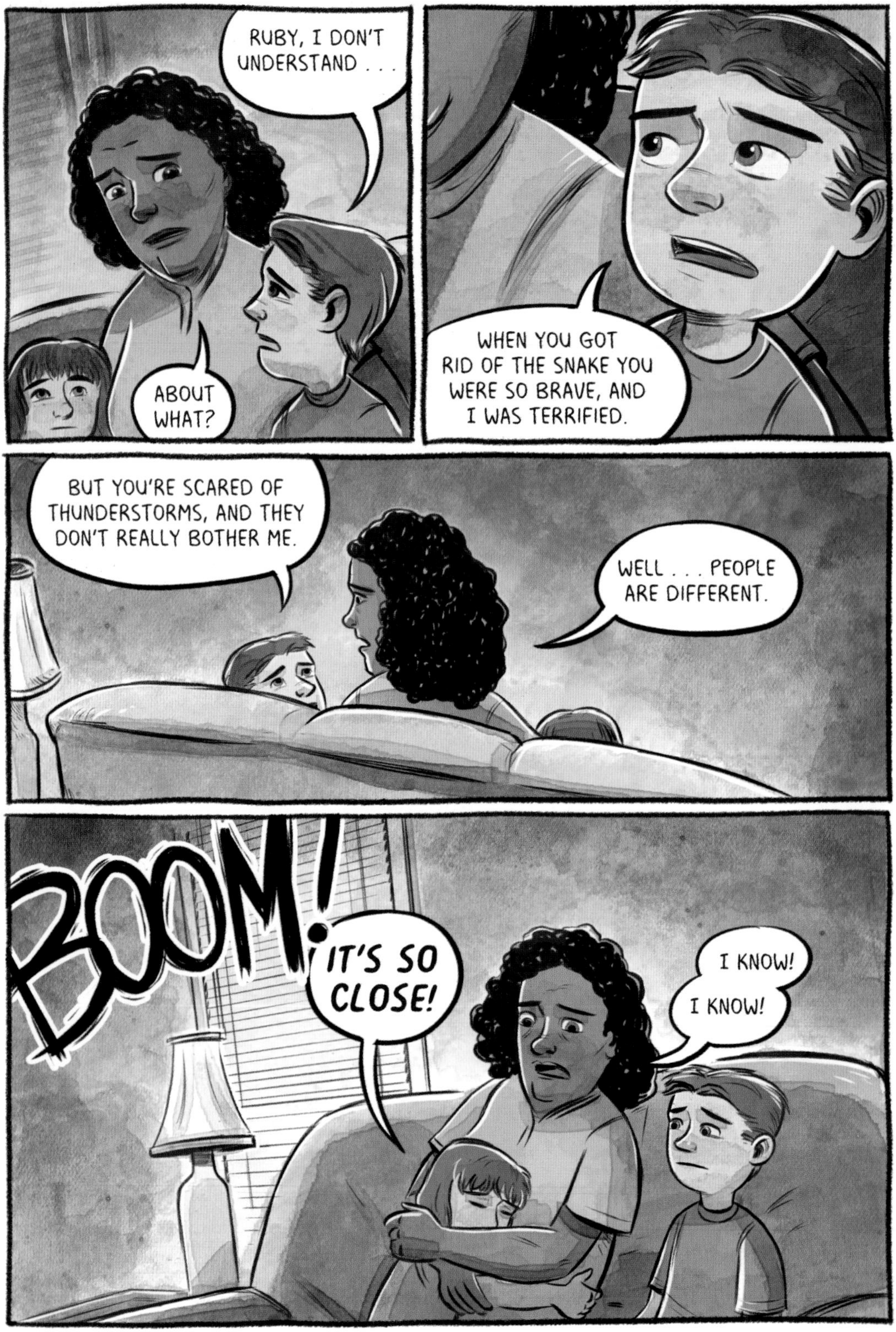

RUBY, I DON'T UNDERSTAND . . .
ABOUT WHAT?
WHEN YOU GOT RID OF THE SNAKE YOU WERE SO BRAVE, AND I WAS TERRIFIED.
BUT YOU'RE SCARED OF THUNDERSTORMS, AND THEY DON'T REALLY BOTHER ME.
WELL . . . PEOPLE ARE DIFFERENT.
BOOM!
IT'S SO CLOSE!
I KNOW!
I KNOW!

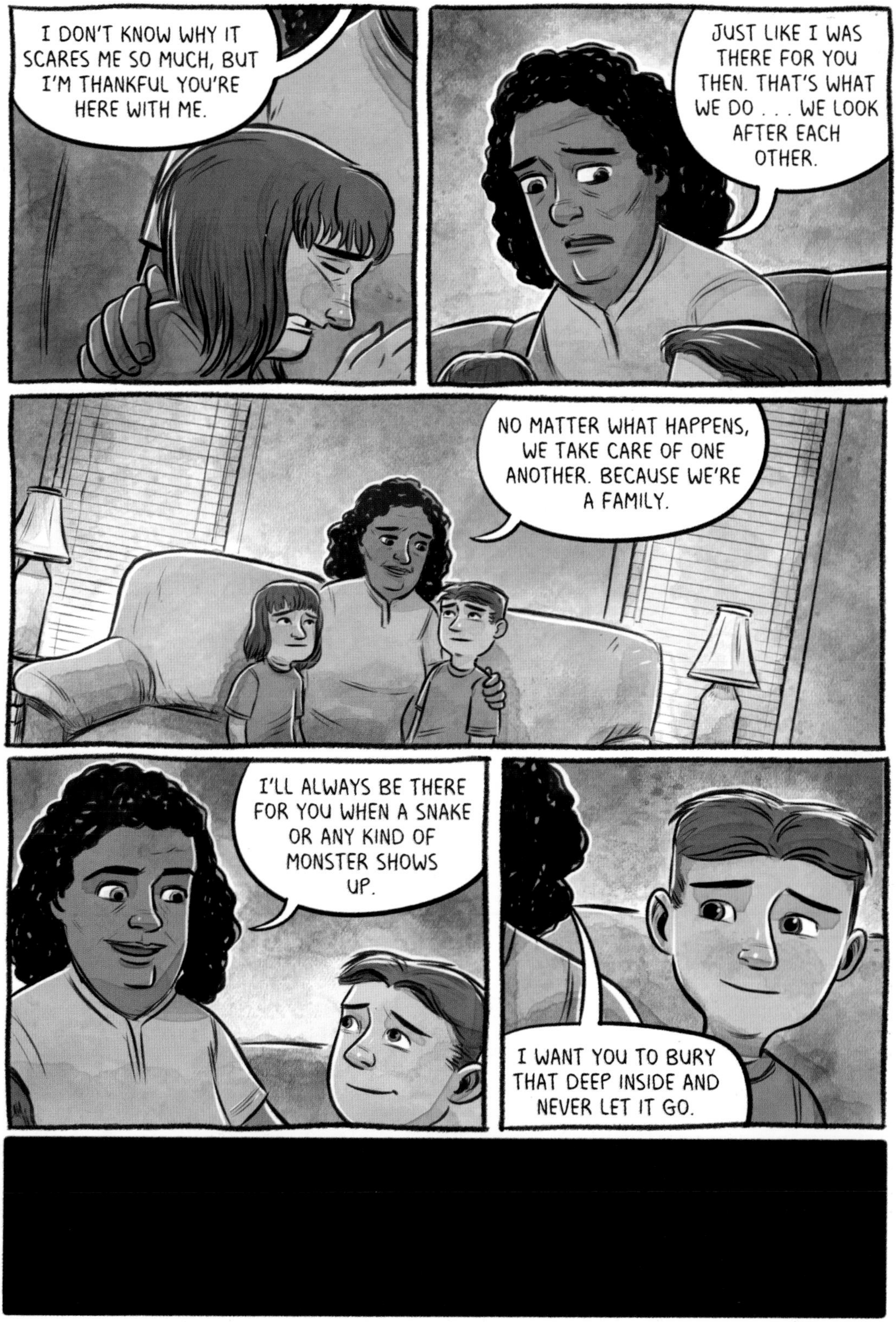
I DON'T KNOW WHY IT SCARES ME SO MUCH, BUT I'M THANKFUL YOU'RE HERE WITH ME.
JUST LIKE I WAS THERE FOR YOU THEN. THAT'S WHAT WE DO . . . WE LOOK AFTER EACH OTHER.
NO MATTER WHAT HAPPENS, WE TAKE CARE OF ONE ANOTHER. BECAUSE WE'RE A FAMILY.
I'LL ALWAYS BE THERE FOR YOU WHEN A SNAKE OR ANY KIND OF MONSTER SHOWS UP.
I WANT YOU TO BURY THAT DEEP INSIDE AND NEVER LET IT GO.

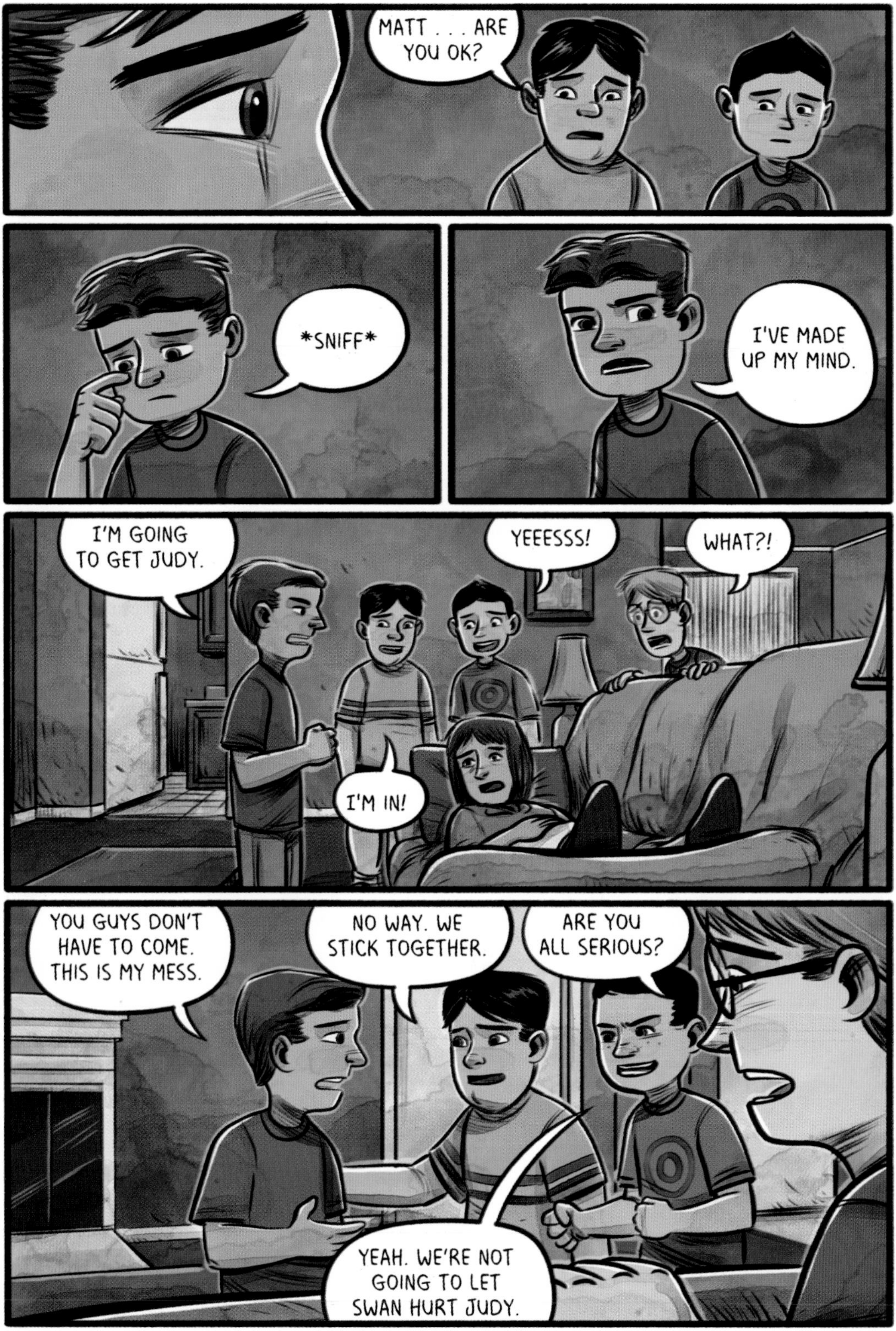
MATT . . . ARE YOU OK?
SNIFF
I'VE MADE UP MY MIND.
I'M GOING TO GET JUDY.
YEEESSS!
WHAT?!
I'M IN!
YOU GUYS DON'T HAVE TO COME. THIS IS MY MESS.
NO WAY. WE STICK TOGETHER.
ARE YOU ALL SERIOUS?
YEAH. WE'RE NOT GOING TO LET SWAN HURT JUDY.

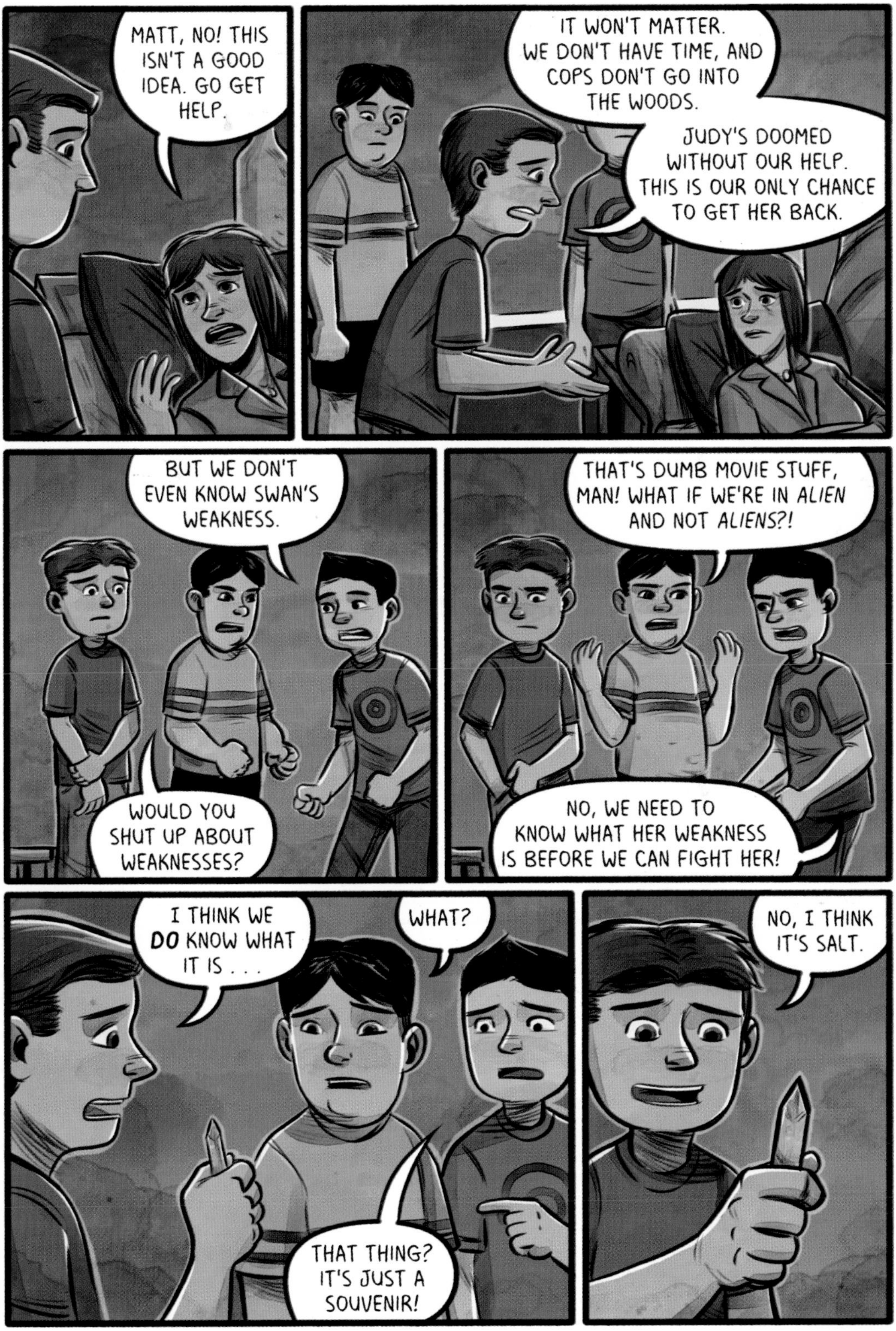
MATT, NO! THIS ISN'T A GOOD IDEA. GO GET HELP.
IT WON'T MATTER. WE DON'T HAVE TIME, AND COPS DON'T GO INTO THE WOODS.
JUDY'S DOOMED WITHOUT OUR HELP. THIS IS OUR ONLY CHANCE TO GET HER BACK.
BUT WE DON'T EVEN KNOW SWAN'S WEAKNESS.
WOULD YOU SHUT UP ABOUT WEAKNESSES?
THAT'S DUMB MOVIE STUFF, MAN! WHAT IF WE'RE IN *ALIEN* AND NOT *ALIENS*?!
NO, WE NEED TO KNOW WHAT HER WEAKNESS IS BEFORE WE CAN FIGHT HER!
I THINK WE **DO** KNOW WHAT IT IS . . .
WHAT?
THAT THING? IT'S JUST A SOUVENIR!
NO, I THINK IT'S SALT.

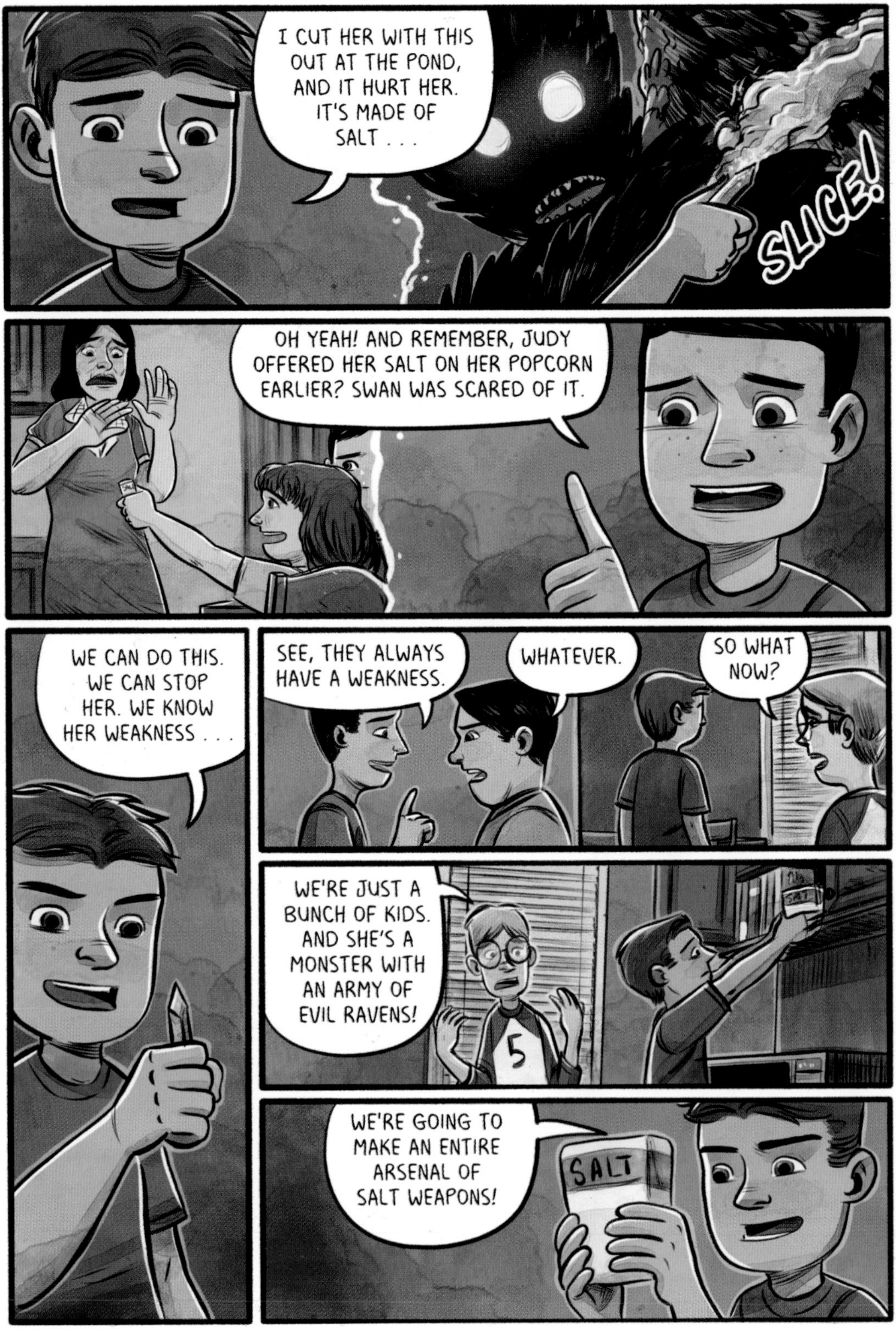
I CUT HER WITH THIS OUT AT THE POND, AND IT HURT HER. IT'S MADE OF SALT . . .
SLICE!
OH YEAH! AND REMEMBER, JUDY OFFERED HER SALT ON HER POPCORN EARLIER? SWAN WAS SCARED OF IT.
WE CAN DO THIS. WE CAN STOP HER. WE KNOW HER WEAKNESS . . .
SEE, THEY ALWAYS HAVE A WEAKNESS.
WHATEVER.
SO WHAT NOW?
WE'RE JUST A BUNCH OF KIDS. AND SHE'S A MONSTER WITH AN ARMY OF EVIL RAVENS!
SALT
5
WE'RE GOING TO MAKE AN ENTIRE ARSENAL OF SALT WEAPONS!
SALT

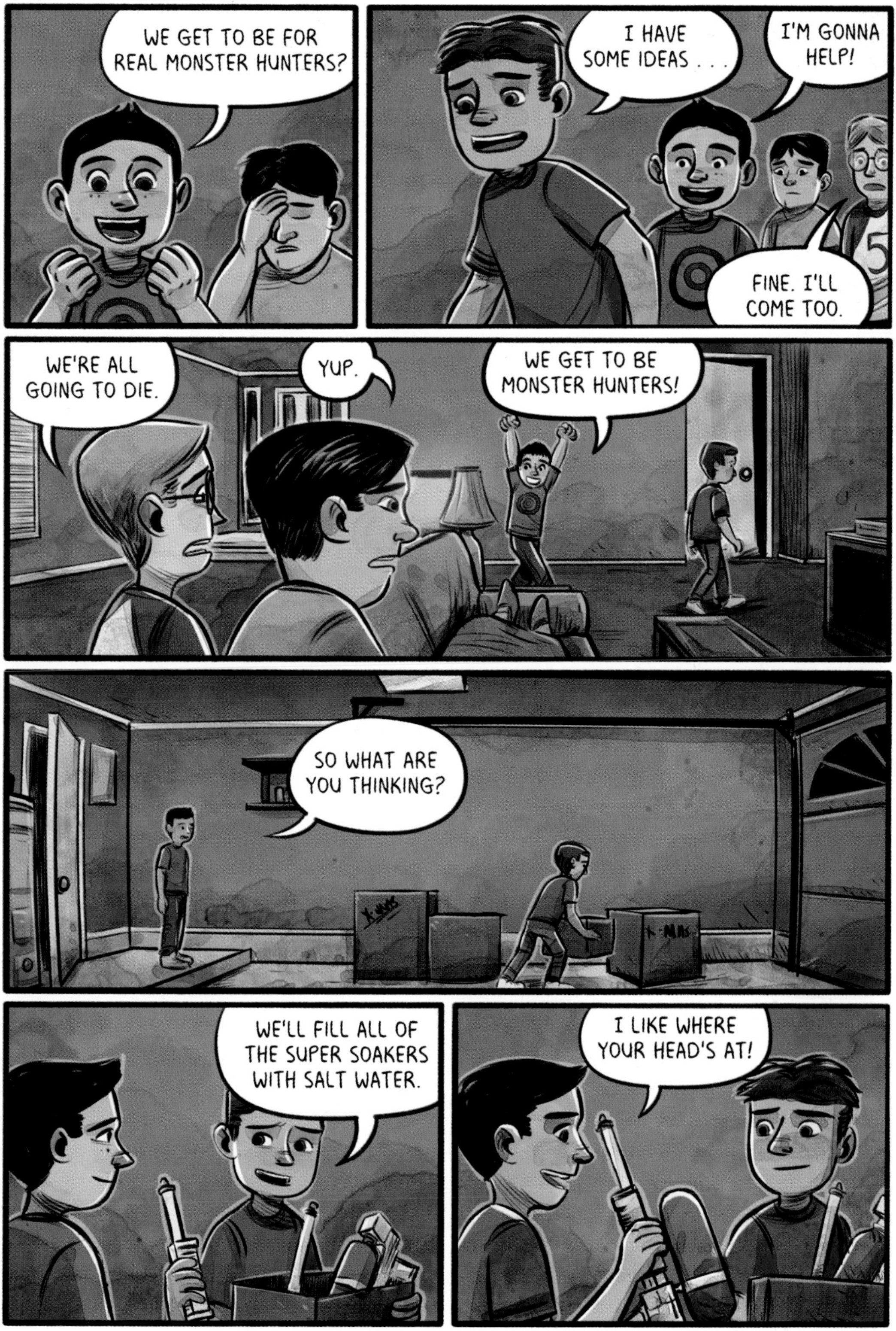
WE GET TO BE FOR REAL MONSTER HUNTERS?
I HAVE SOME IDEAS . . .
I'M GONNA HELP!
FINE. I'LL COME TOO.
WE'RE ALL GOING TO DIE.
YUP.
WE GET TO BE MONSTER HUNTERS!
SO WHAT ARE YOU THINKING?
WE'LL FILL ALL OF THE SUPER SOAKERS WITH SALT WATER.
I LIKE WHERE YOUR HEAD'S AT!

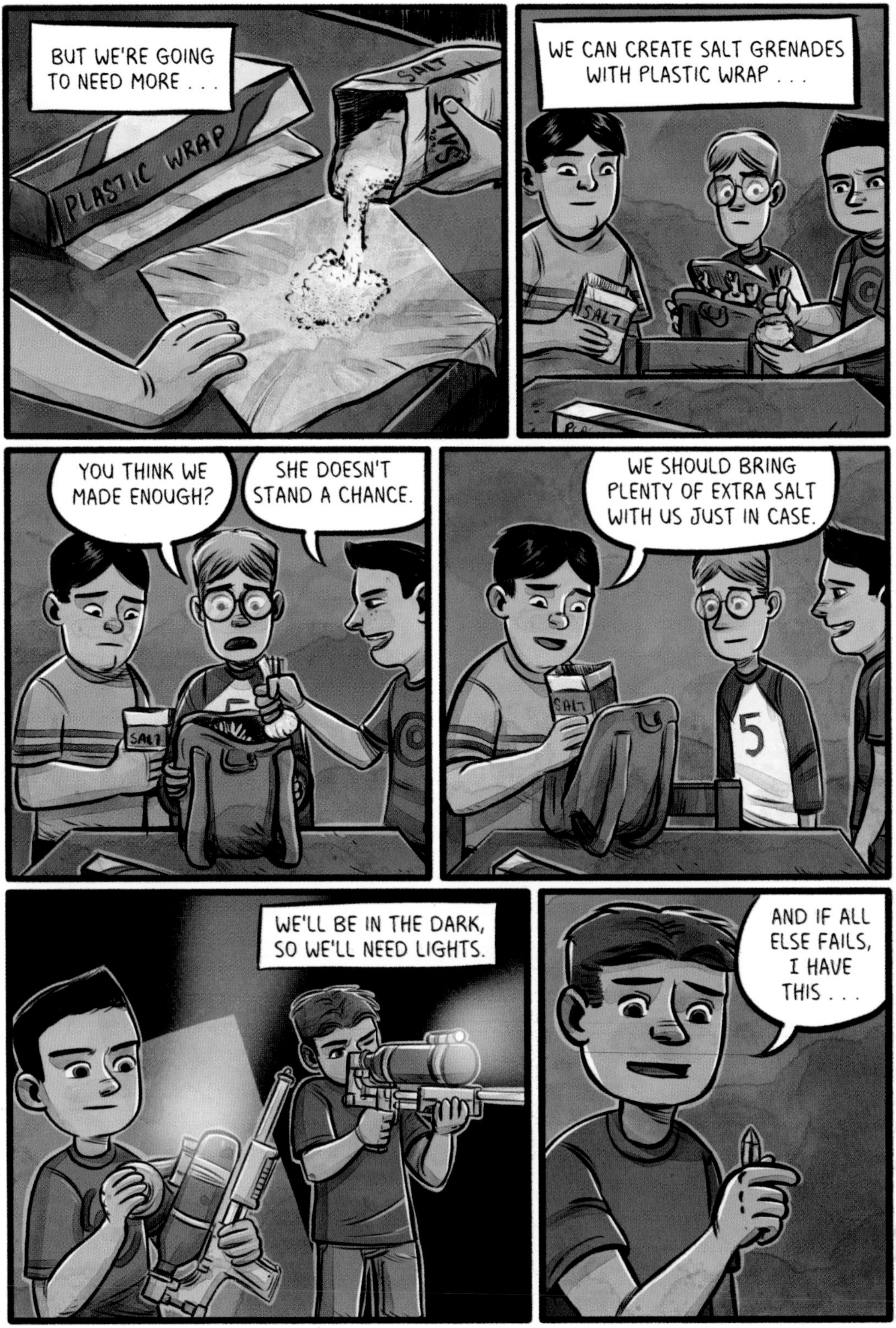
BUT WE'RE GOING TO NEED MORE . . .
PLASTIC WRAP
SALT
WE CAN CREATE SALT GRENADES WITH PLASTIC WRAP . . .
SALT
YOU THINK WE MADE ENOUGH?
SHE DOESN'T STAND A CHANCE.
SALT
WE SHOULD BRING PLENTY OF EXTRA SALT WITH US JUST IN CASE.
SALT
5
WE'LL BE IN THE DARK, SO WE'LL NEED LIGHTS.
AND IF ALL ELSE FAILS, I HAVE THIS . . .

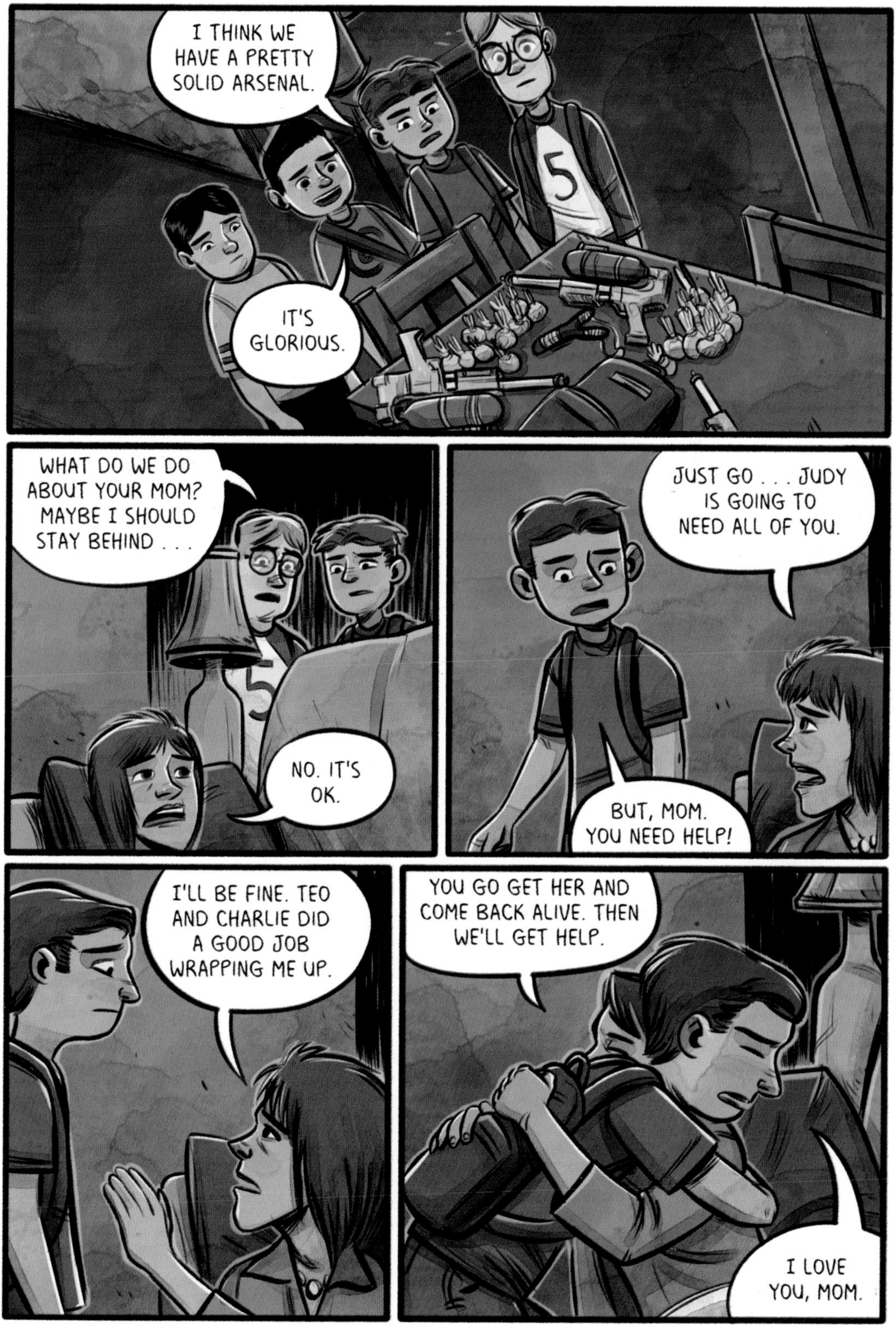
I THINK WE HAVE A PRETTY SOLID ARSENAL.
IT'S GLORIOUS.
WHAT DO WE DO ABOUT YOUR MOM? MAYBE I SHOULD STAY BEHIND . . .
NO. IT'S OK.
JUST GO . . . JUDY IS GOING TO NEED ALL OF YOU.
BUT, MOM. YOU NEED HELP!
I'LL BE FINE. TEO AND CHARLIE DID A GOOD JOB WRAPPING ME UP.
YOU GO GET HER AND COME BACK ALIVE. THEN WE'LL GET HELP.
I LOVE YOU, MOM.

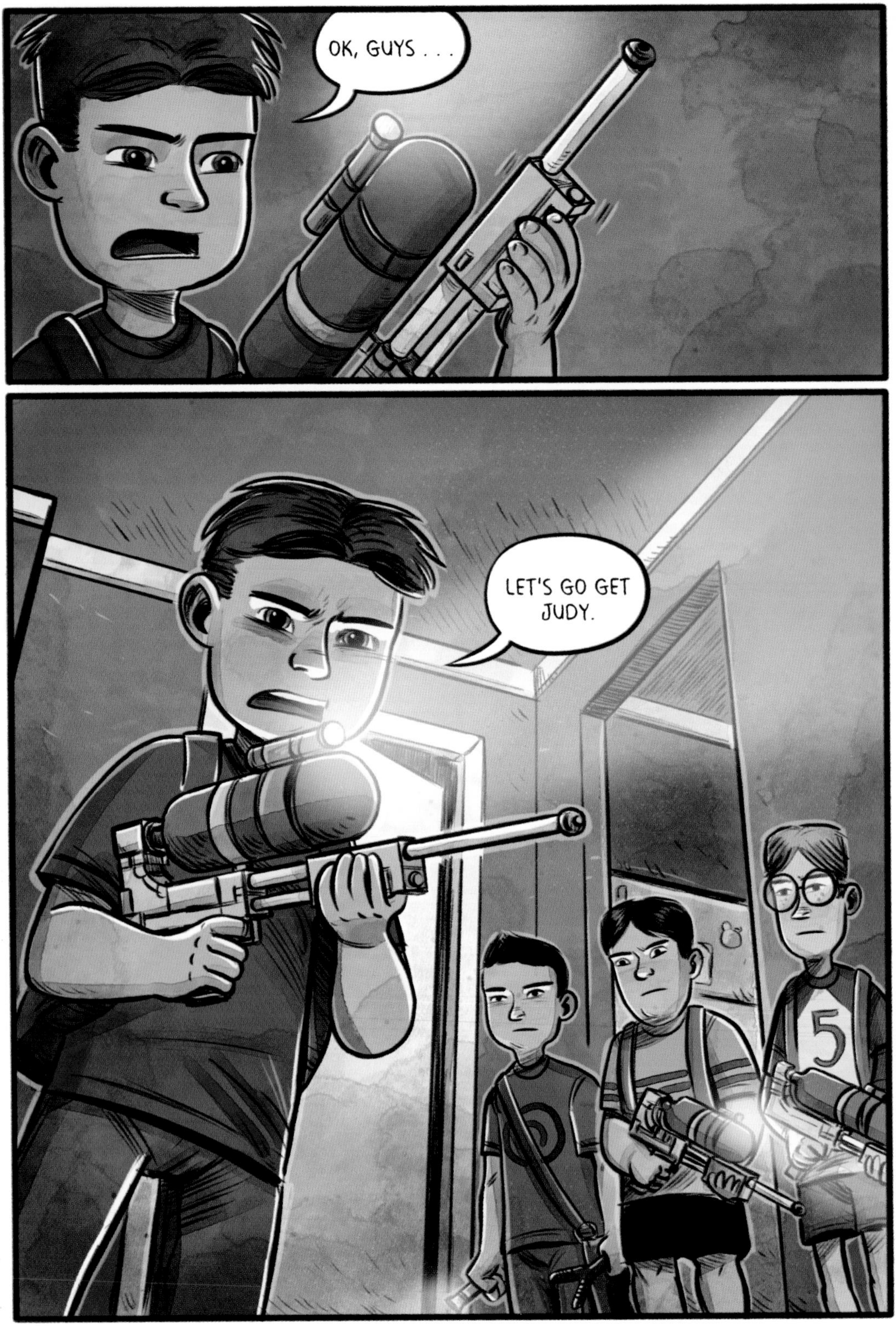
OK, GUYS . . .
LET'S GO GET JUDY.

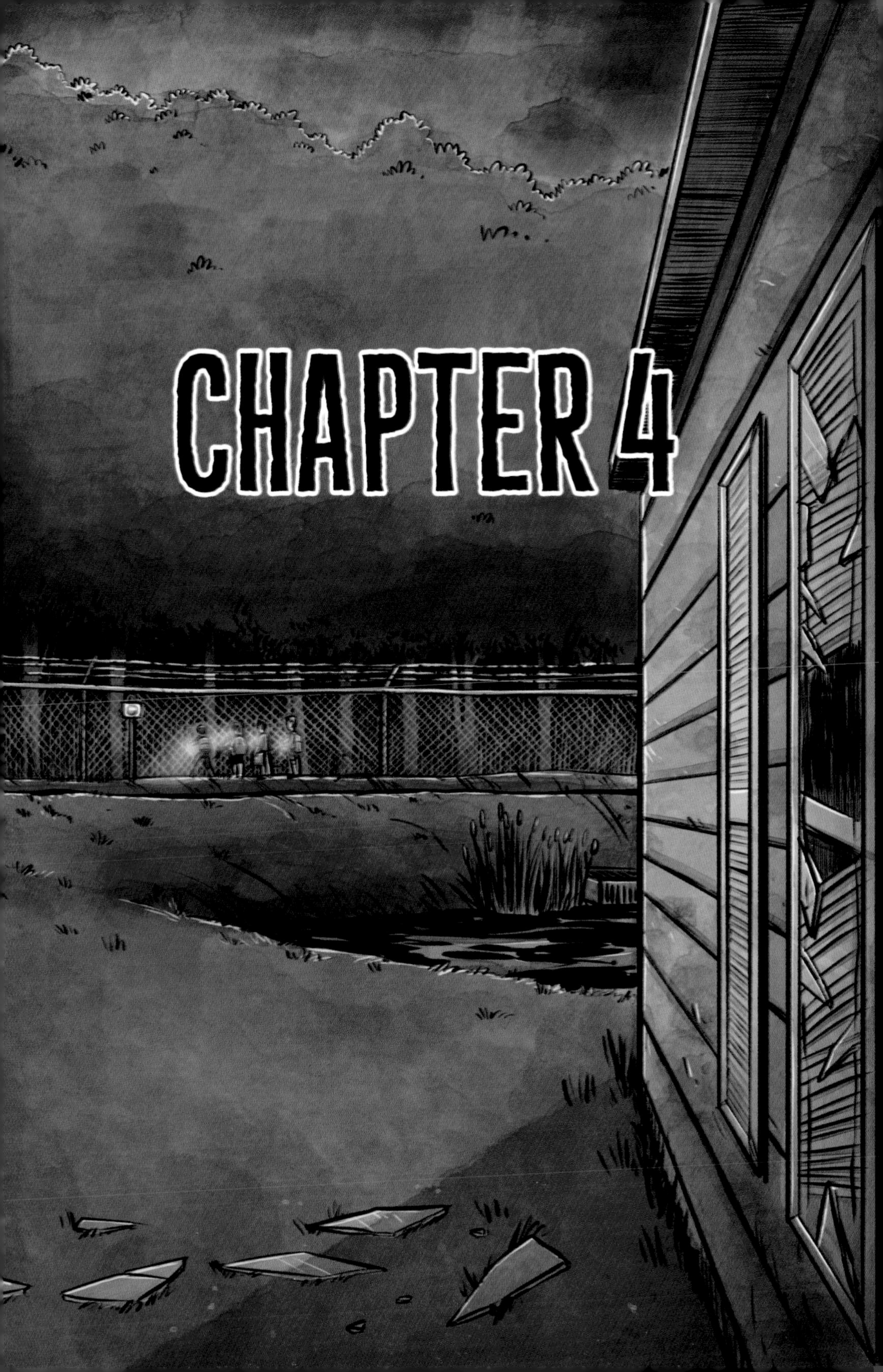
CHAPTER 4

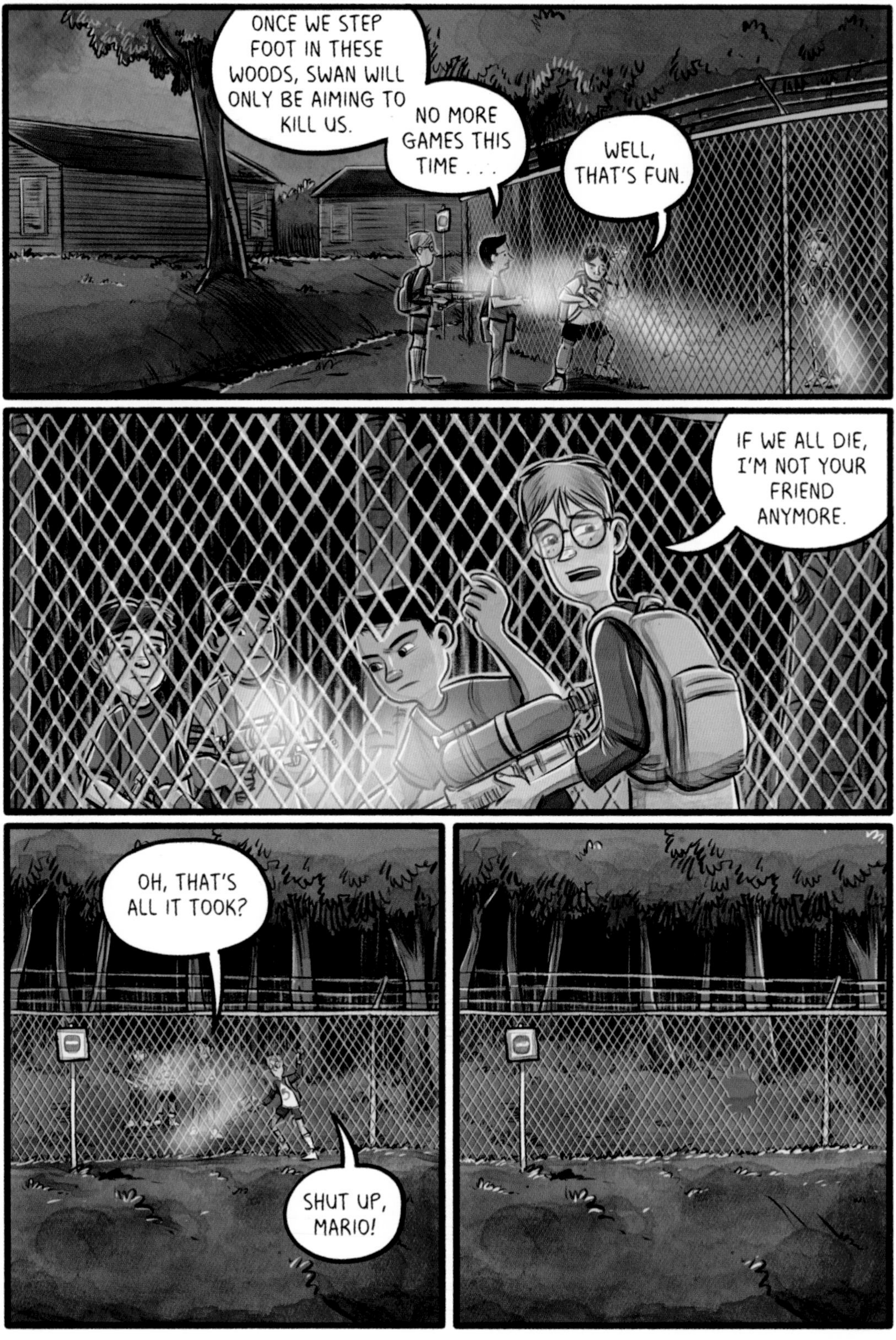
ONCE WE STEP FOOT IN THESE WOODS, SWAN WILL ONLY BE AIMING TO KILL US.
NO MORE GAMES THIS TIME . . .
WELL, THAT'S FUN.
IF WE ALL DIE, I'M NOT YOUR FRIEND ANYMORE.
OH, THAT'S ALL IT TOOK?
SHUT UP, MARIO!

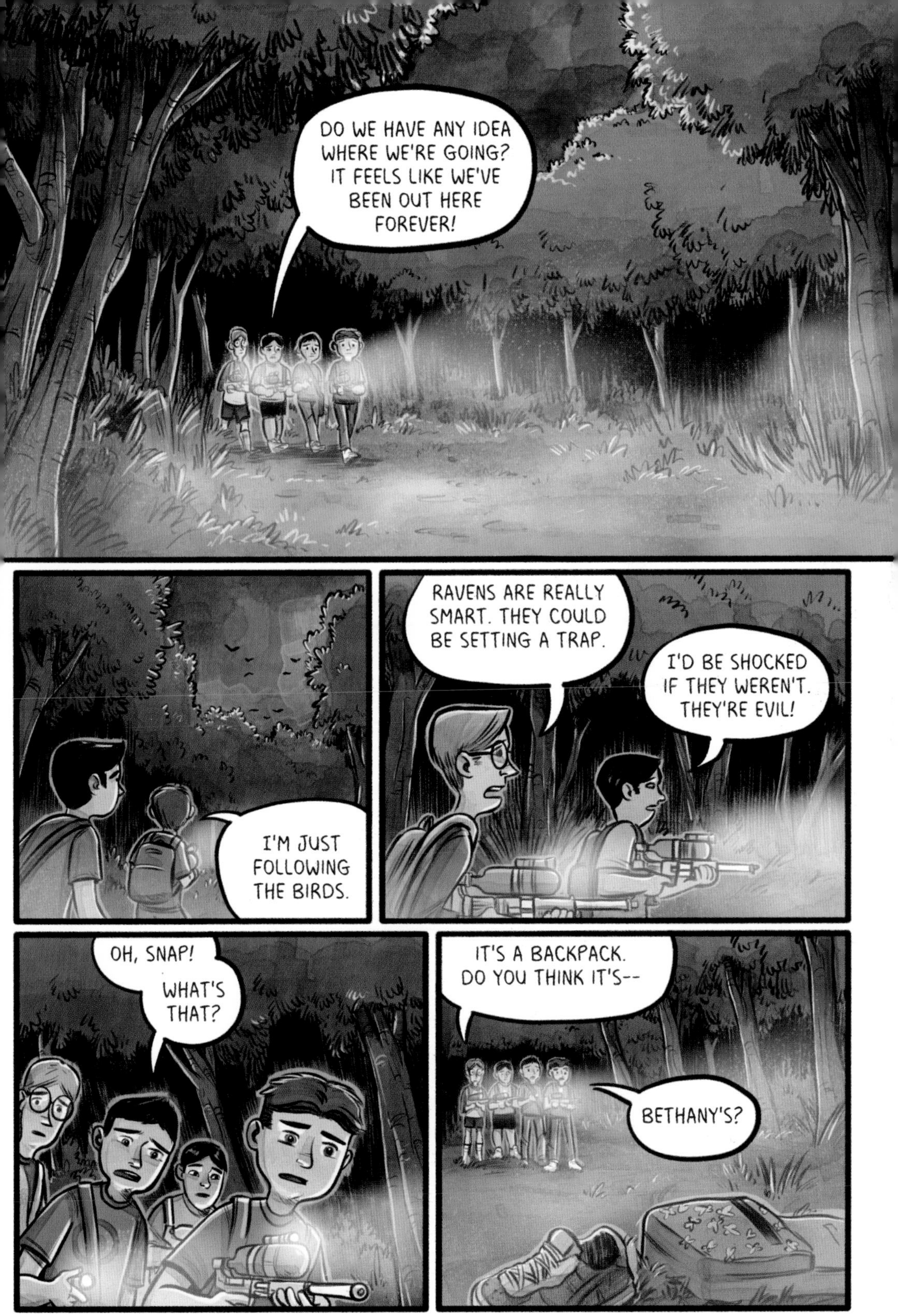
DO WE HAVE ANY IDEA WHERE WE'RE GOING? IT FEELS LIKE WE'VE BEEN OUT HERE FOREVER!
I'M JUST FOLLOWING THE BIRDS.
RAVENS ARE REALLY SMART. THEY COULD BE SETTING A TRAP.
I'D BE SHOCKED IF THEY WEREN'T. THEY'RE EVIL!
OH, SNAP!
WHAT'S THAT?
IT'S A BACKPACK. DO YOU THINK IT'S--
BETHANY'S?

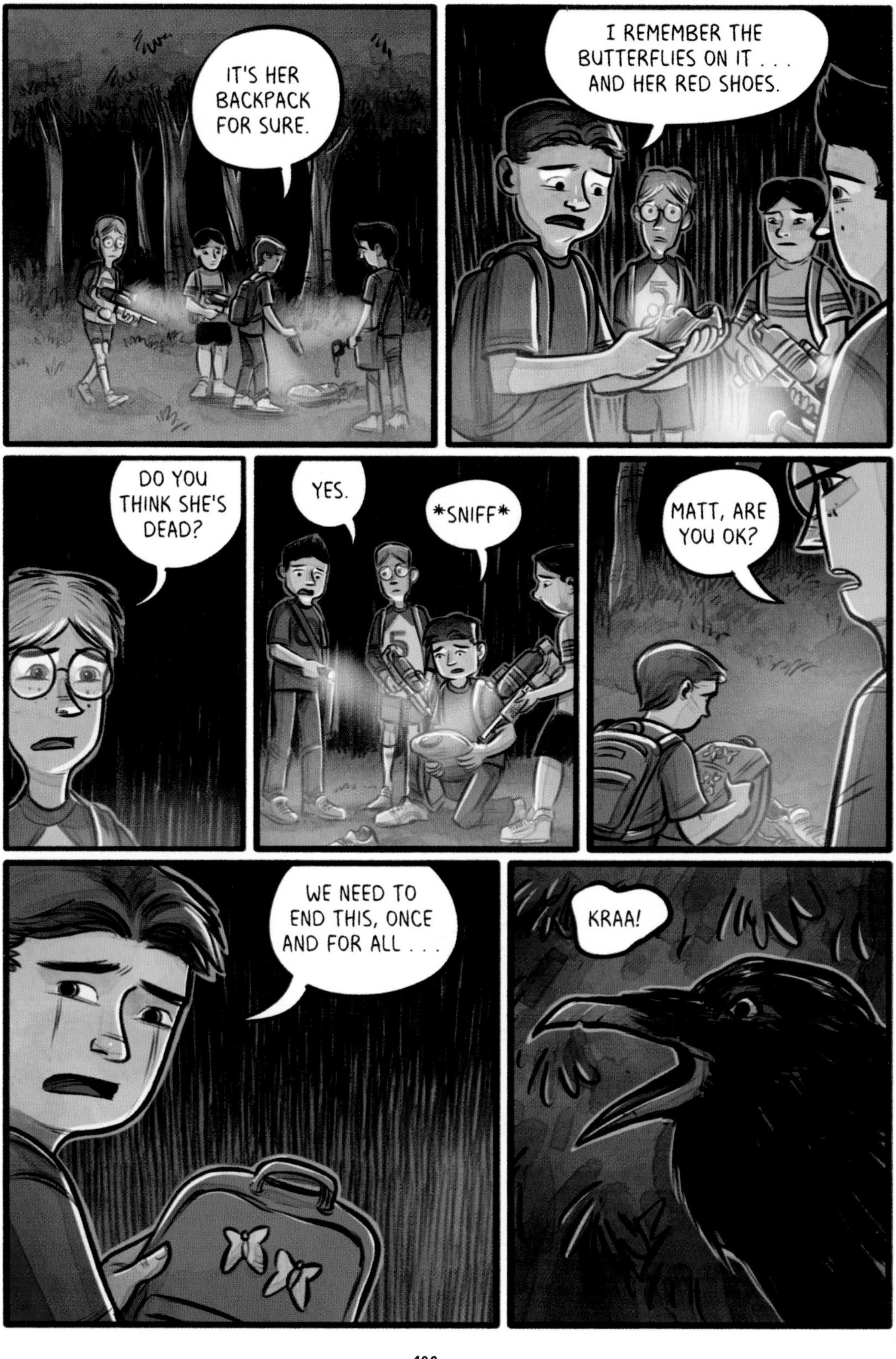
IT'S HER BACKPACK FOR SURE.
I REMEMBER THE BUTTERFLIES ON IT . . . AND HER RED SHOES.
DO YOU THINK SHE'S DEAD?
YES.
SNIFF
MATT, ARE YOU OK?
WE NEED TO END THIS, ONCE AND FOR ALL . . .
KRAA!

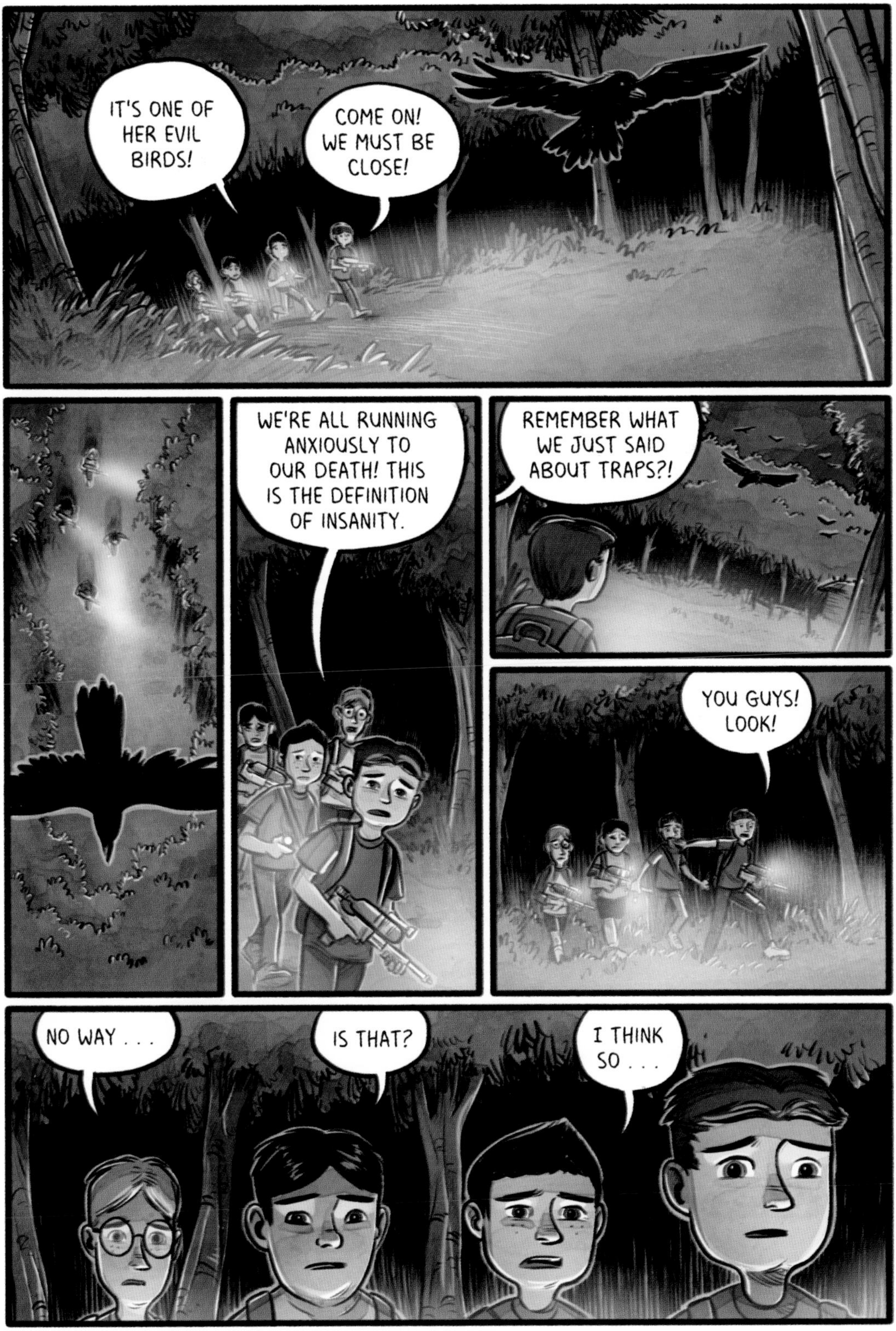
IT'S ONE OF HER EVIL BIRDS!
COME ON! WE MUST BE CLOSE!
WE'RE ALL RUNNING ANXIOUSLY TO OUR DEATH! THIS IS THE DEFINITION OF INSANITY.
REMEMBER WHAT WE JUST SAID ABOUT TRAPS?!
YOU GUYS! LOOK!
NO WAY . . .
IS THAT?
I THINK SO . . .

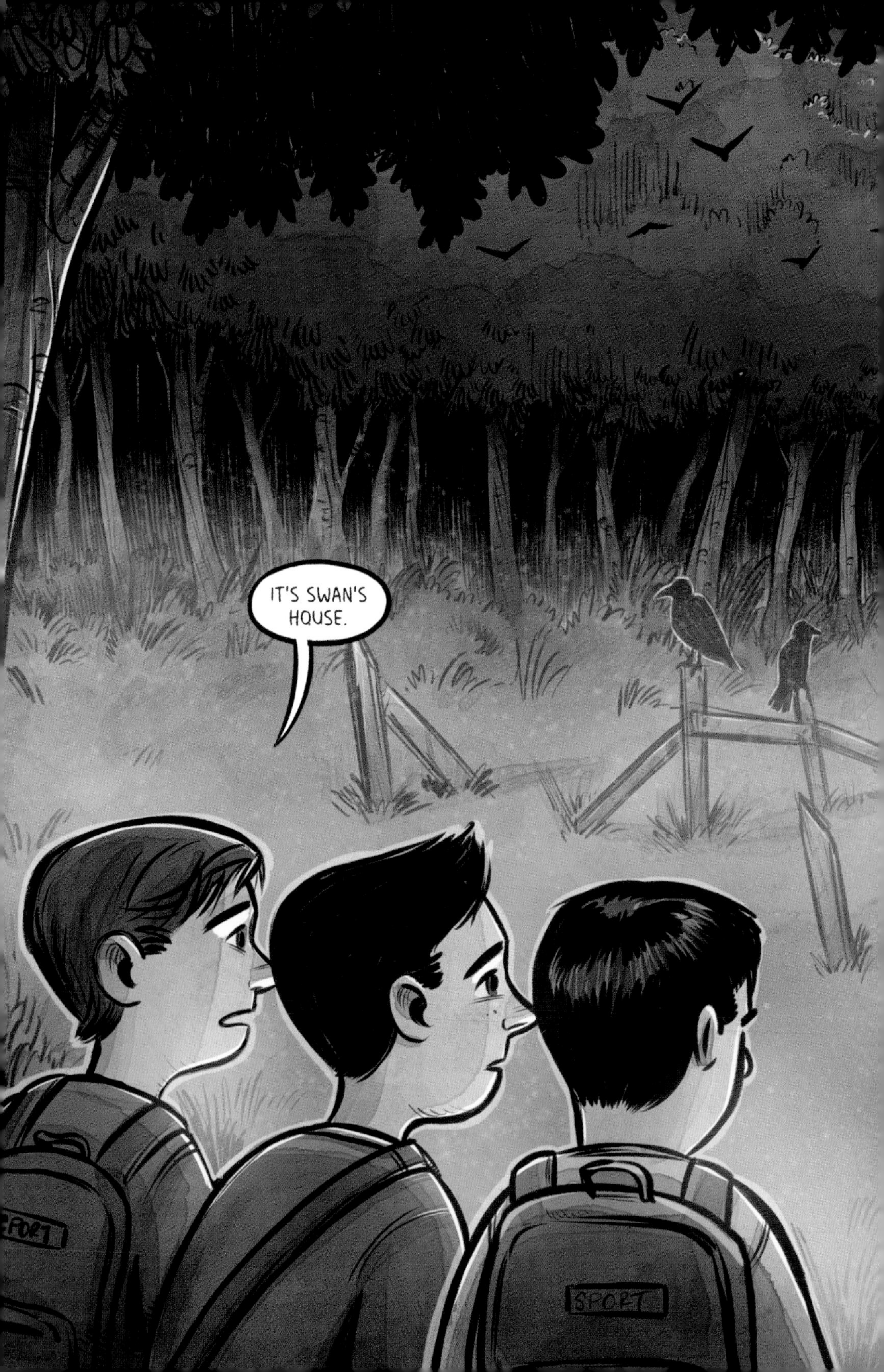
IT'S SWAN'S HOUSE.
SPORT
SPORT

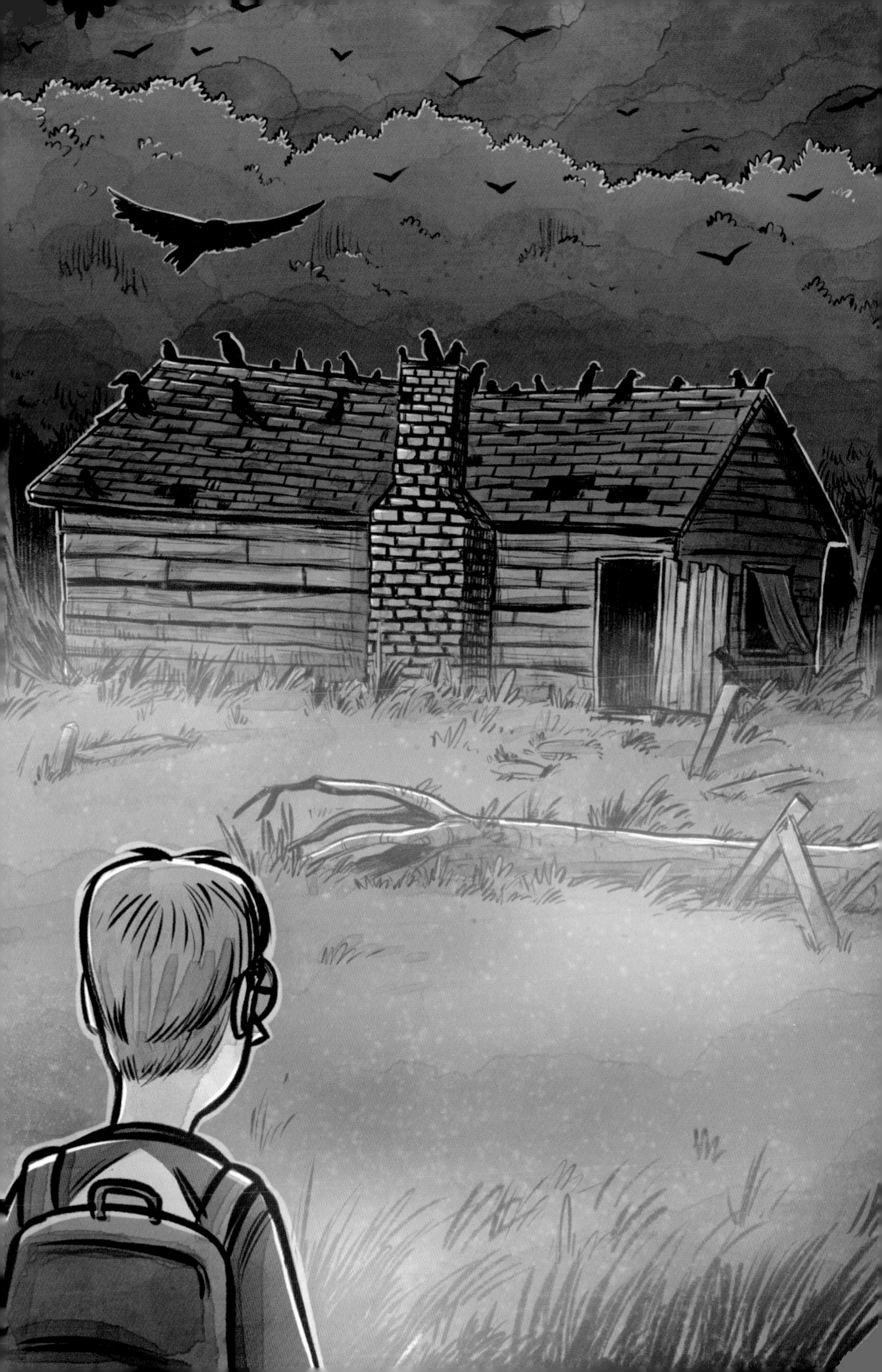

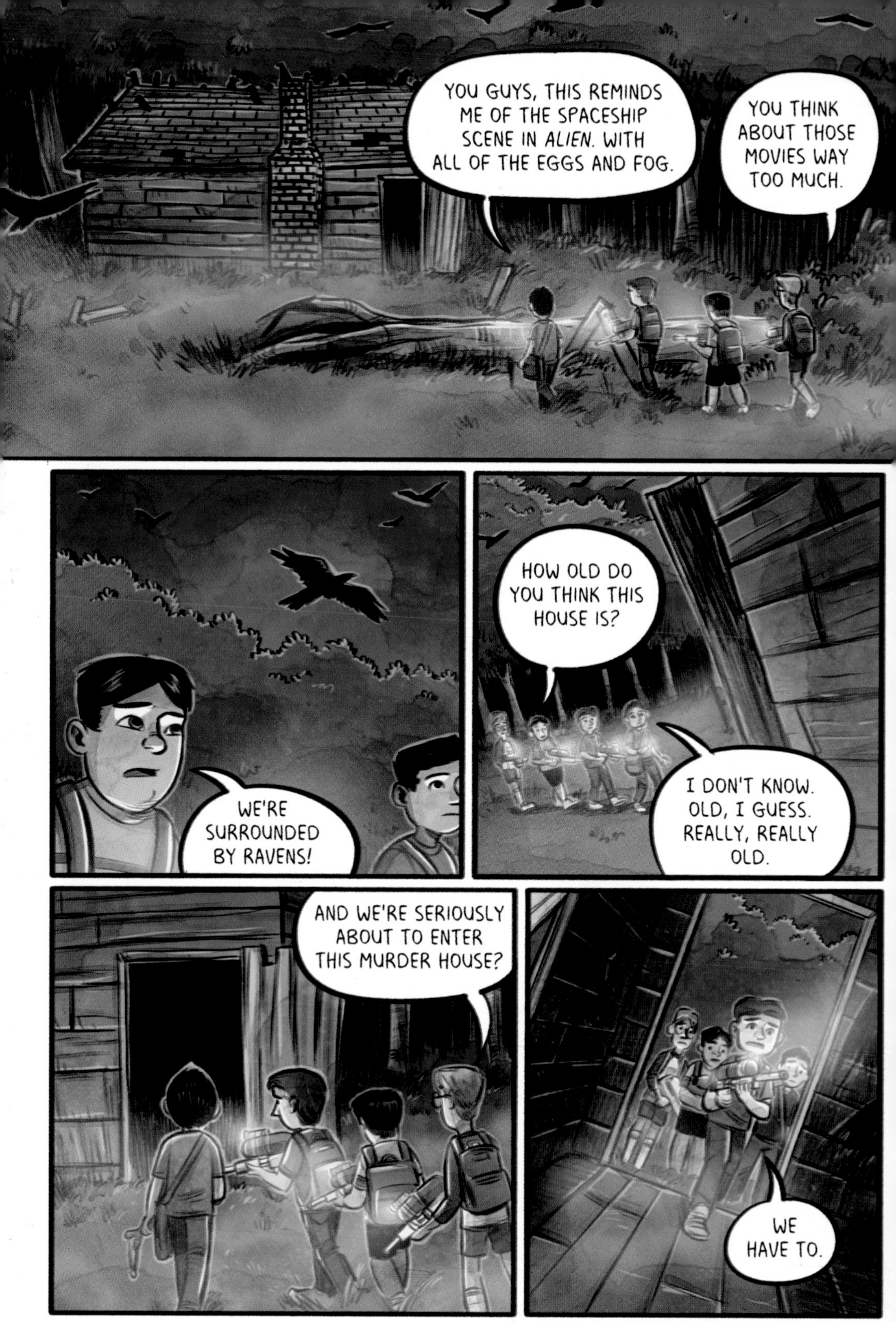
YOU GUYS, THIS REMINDS ME OF THE SPACESHIP SCENE IN *ALIEN*. WITH ALL OF THE EGGS AND FOG.
YOU THINK ABOUT THOSE MOVIES WAY TOO MUCH.
WE'RE SURROUNDED BY RAVENS!
HOW OLD DO YOU THINK THIS HOUSE IS?
I DON'T KNOW. OLD, I GUESS. REALLY, REALLY OLD.
AND WE'RE SERIOUSLY ABOUT TO ENTER THIS MURDER HOUSE?
WE HAVE TO.

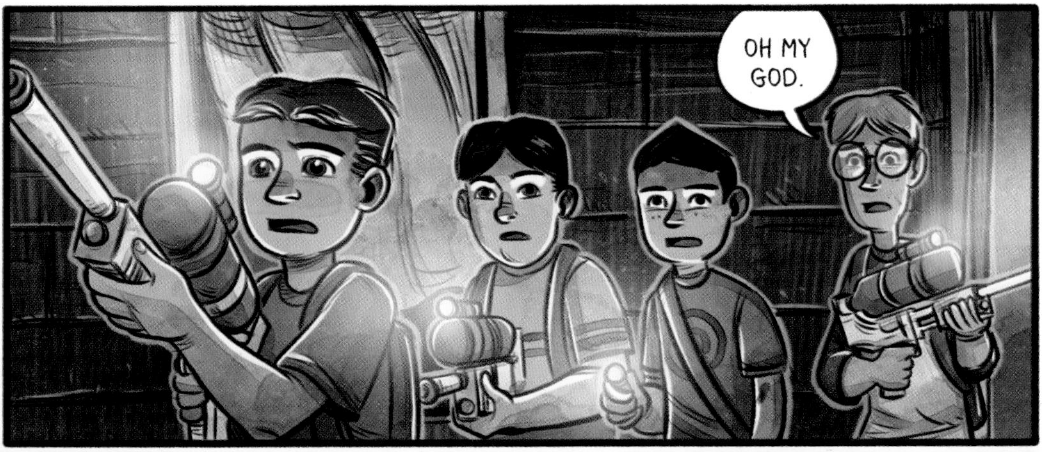
OH MY GOD.

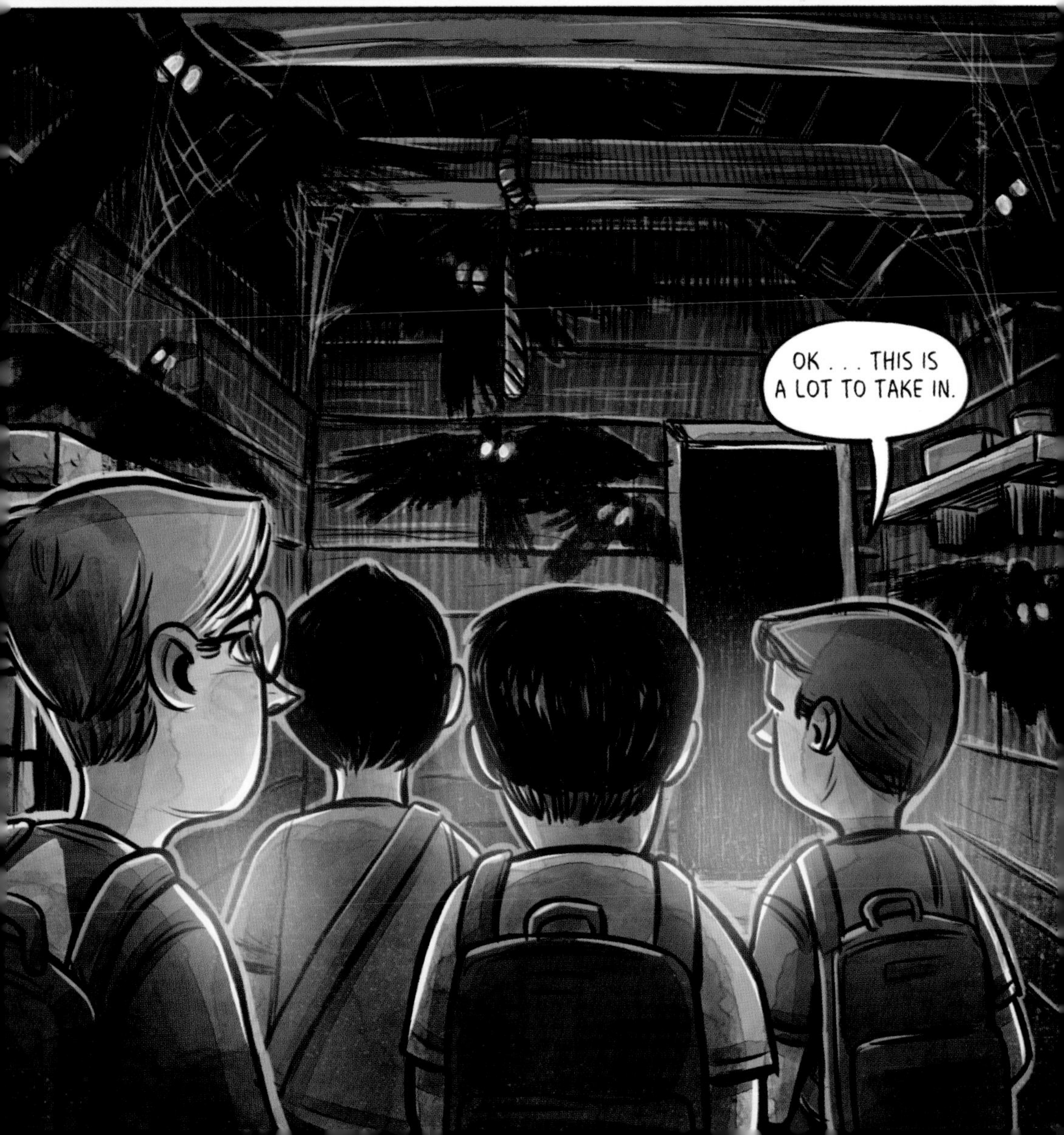
OK . . . THIS IS A LOT TO TAKE IN.

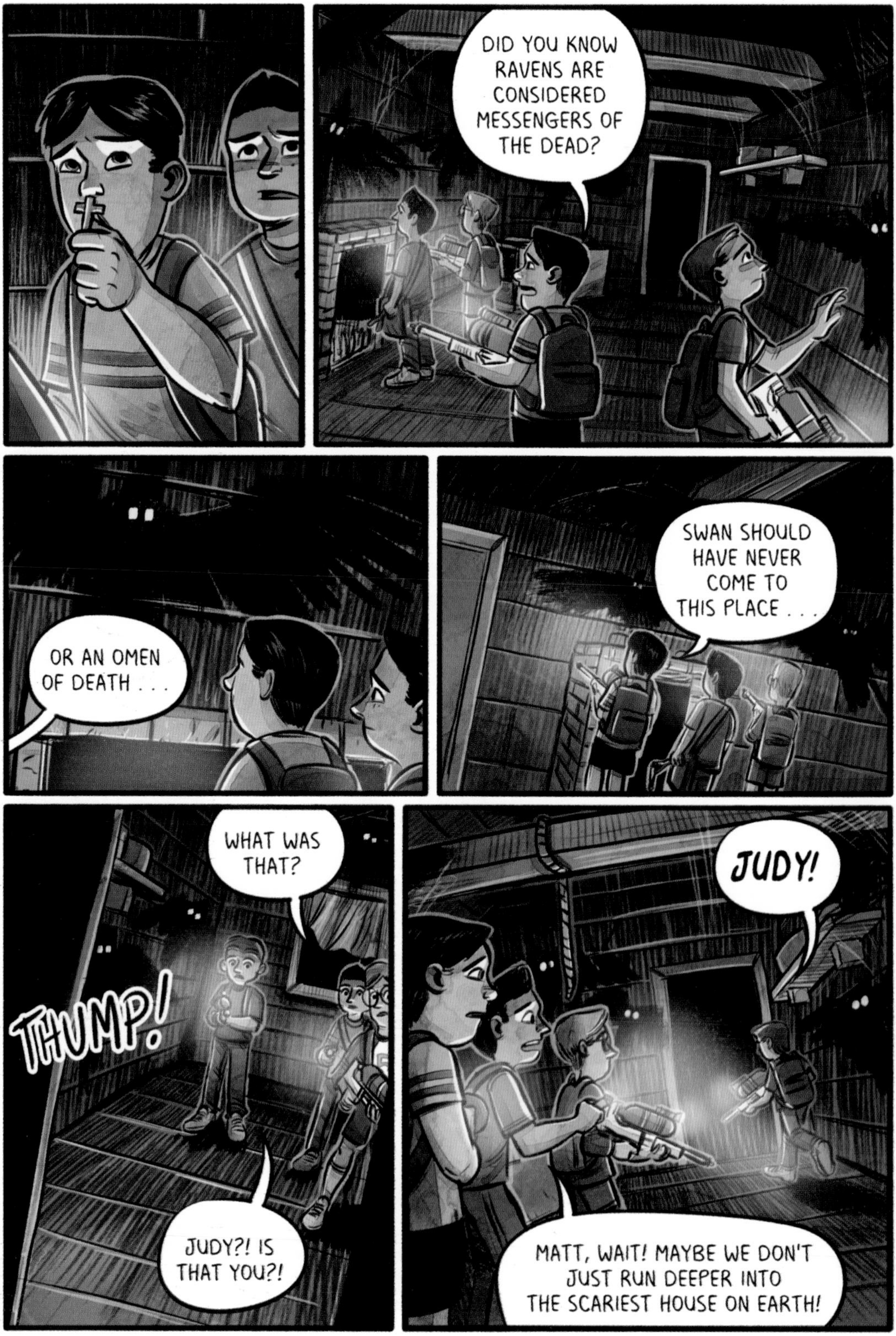
DID YOU KNOW RAVENS ARE CONSIDERED MESSENGERS OF THE DEAD?
OR AN OMEN OF DEATH . . .
SWAN SHOULD HAVE NEVER COME TO THIS PLACE . . .
THUMP!
WHAT WAS THAT?
JUDY?! IS THAT YOU?!
JUDY!
MATT, WAIT! MAYBE WE DON'T JUST RUN DEEPER INTO THE SCARIEST HOUSE ON EARTH!

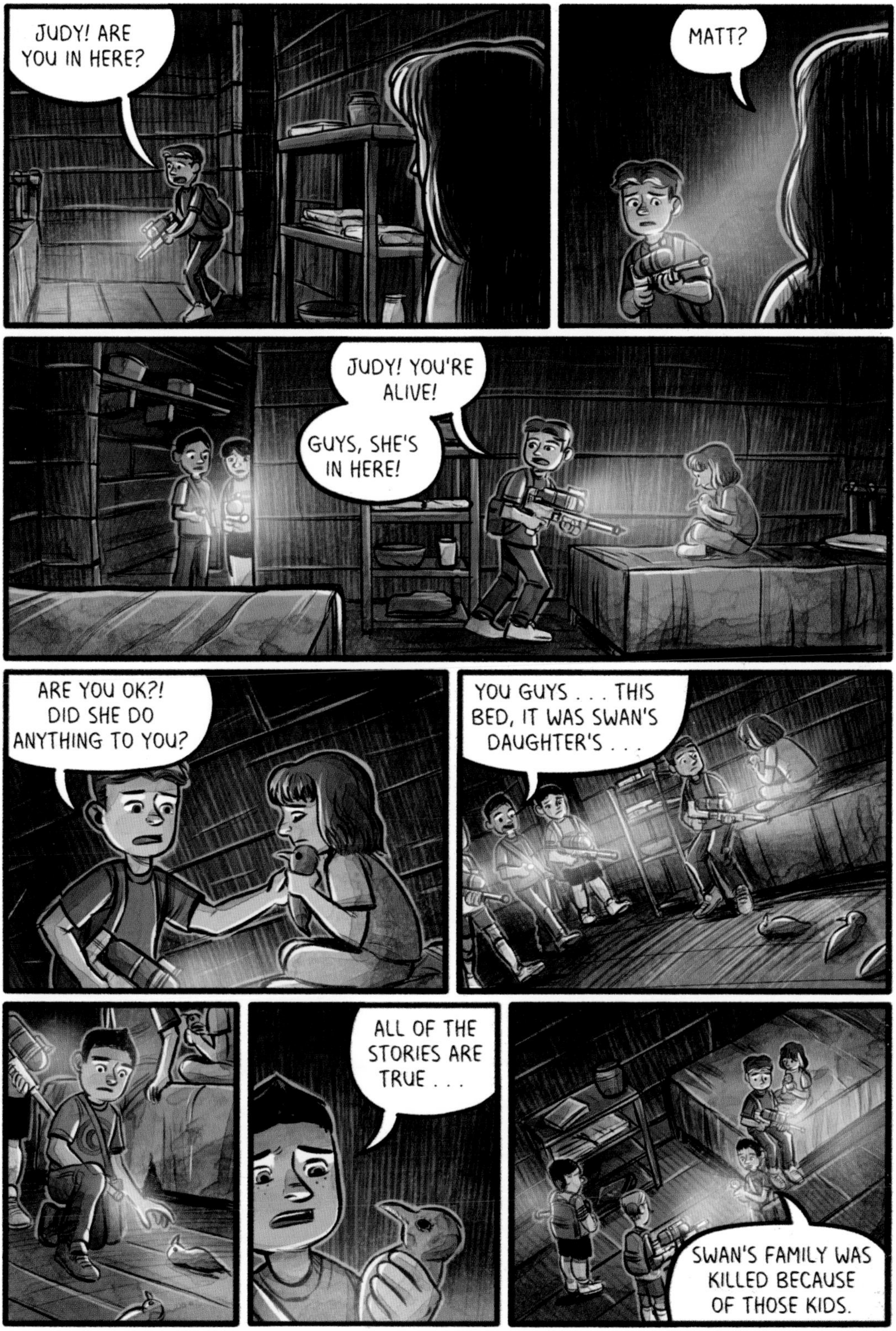
JUDY! ARE YOU IN HERE?
MATT?
JUDY! YOU'RE ALIVE!
GUYS, SHE'S IN HERE!
ARE YOU OK?! DID SHE DO ANYTHING TO YOU?
YOU GUYS . . . THIS BED, IT WAS SWAN'S DAUGHTER'S . . .
ALL OF THE STORIES ARE TRUE . . .
SWAN'S FAMILY WAS KILLED BECAUSE OF THOSE KIDS.

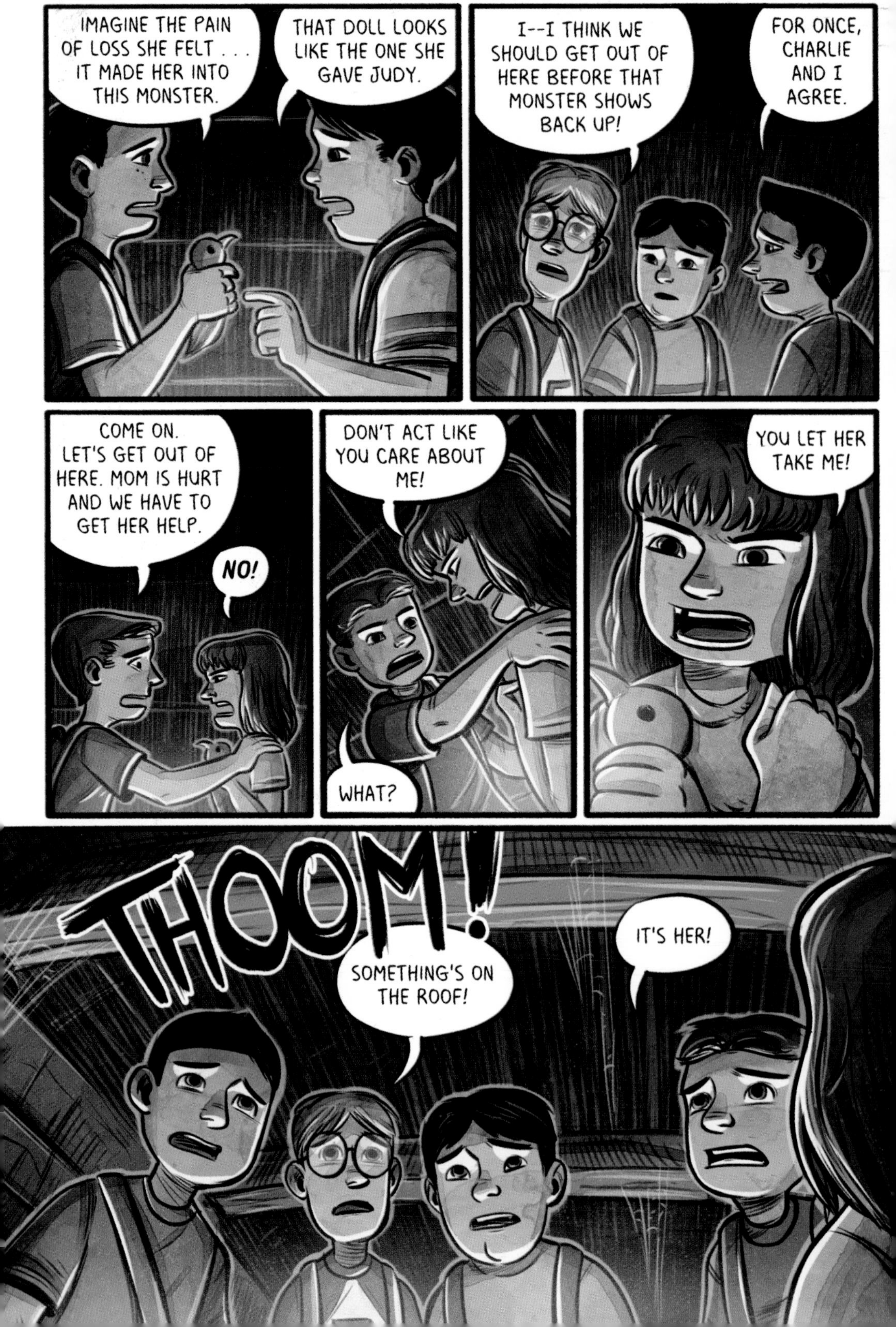
IMAGINE THE PAIN OF LOSS SHE FELT . . . IT MADE HER INTO THIS MONSTER.
THAT DOLL LOOKS LIKE THE ONE SHE GAVE JUDY.
I--I THINK WE SHOULD GET OUT OF HERE BEFORE THAT MONSTER SHOWS BACK UP!
FOR ONCE, CHARLIE AND I AGREE.
COME ON. LET'S GET OUT OF HERE. MOM IS HURT AND WE HAVE TO GET HER HELP.
NO!
DON'T ACT LIKE YOU CARE ABOUT ME!
WHAT?
YOU LET HER TAKE ME!
THOOM!
SOMETHING'S ON THE ROOF!
IT'S HER!

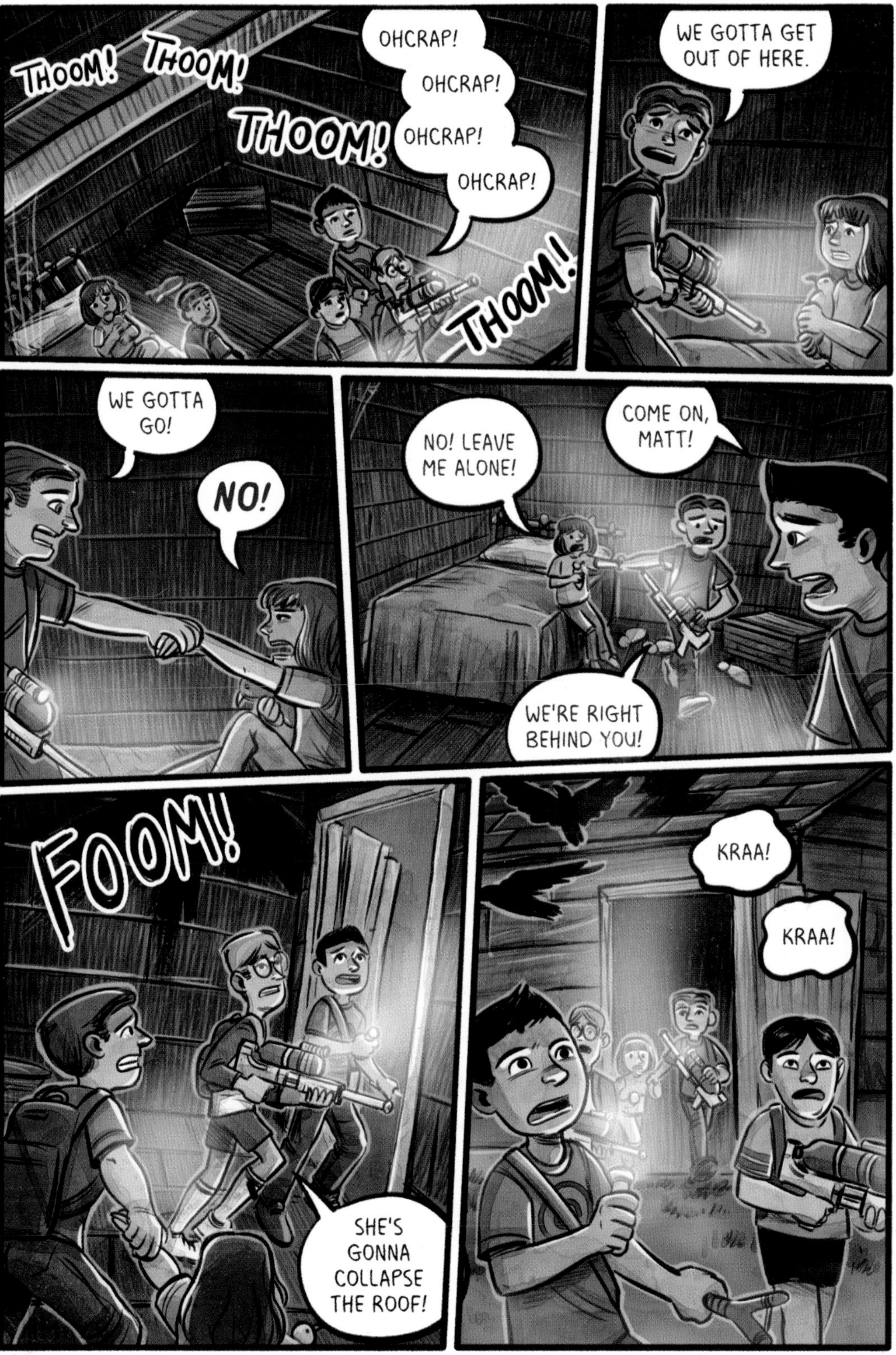
THOOM! THOOM!
THOOM!
OHCRAP!
OHCRAP!
OHCRAP!
OHCRAP!
THOOM!
WE GOTTA GET OUT OF HERE.
WE GOTTA GO!
NO!
NO! LEAVE ME ALONE!
COME ON, MATT!
WE'RE RIGHT BEHIND YOU!
FOOM!
SHE'S GONNA COLLAPSE THE ROOF!
KRAA!
KRAA!

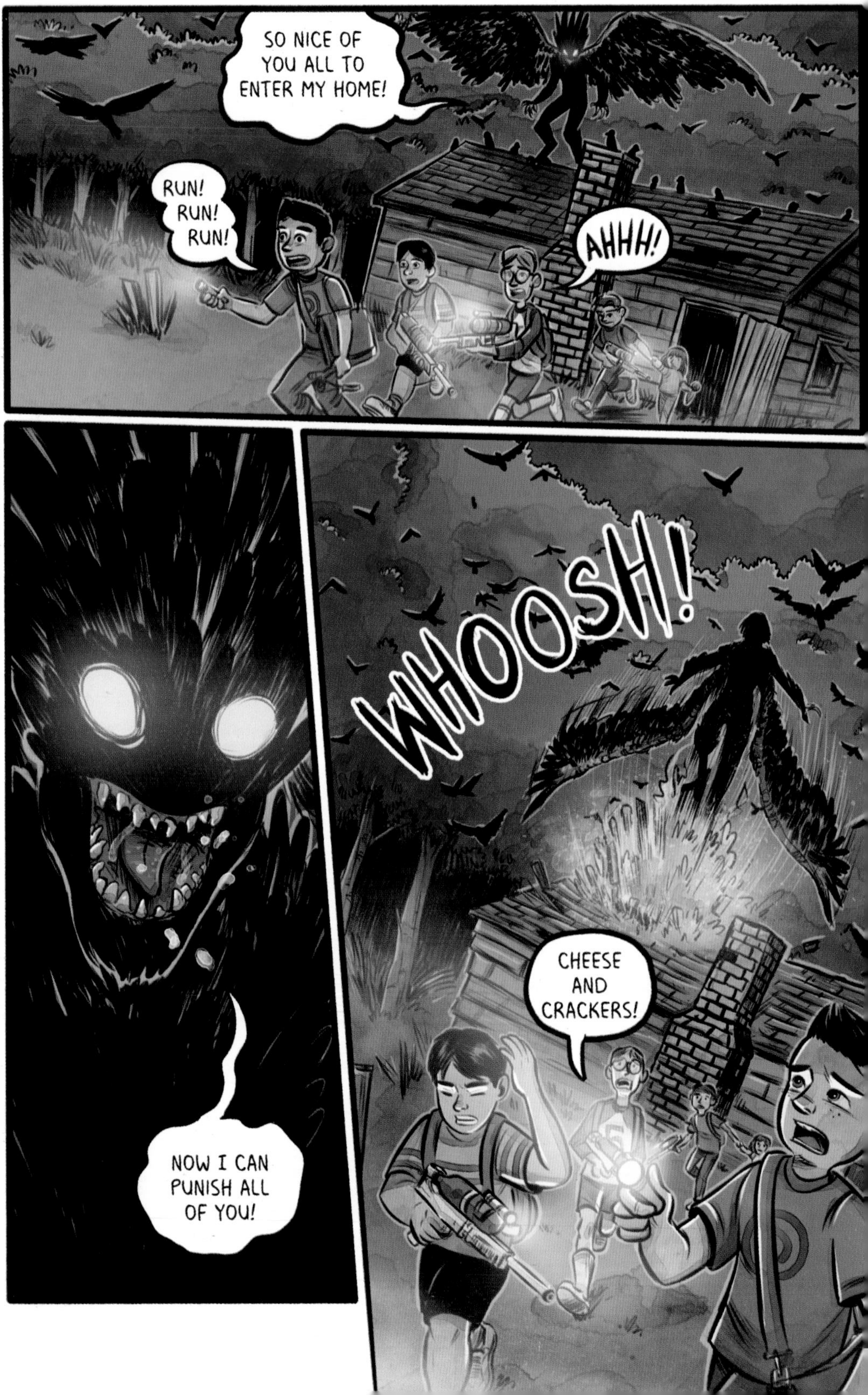
SO NICE OF YOU ALL TO ENTER MY HOME!
RUN! RUN! RUN!
AHHH!
NOW I CAN PUNISH ALL OF YOU!
WHOOSH!
CHEESE AND CRACKERS!

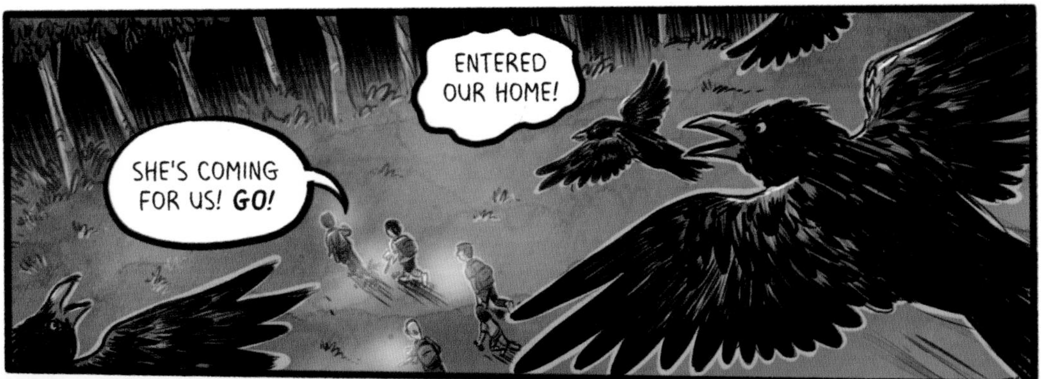
ENTERED OUR HOME!
SHE'S COMING FOR US! **GO!**

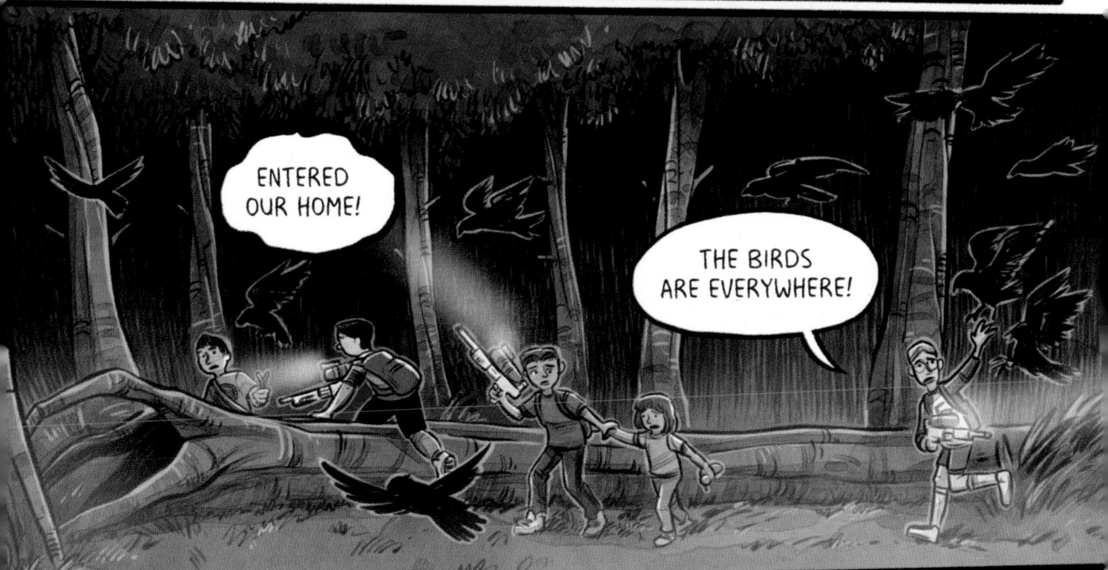
ENTERED OUR HOME!
THE BIRDS ARE EVERYWHERE!

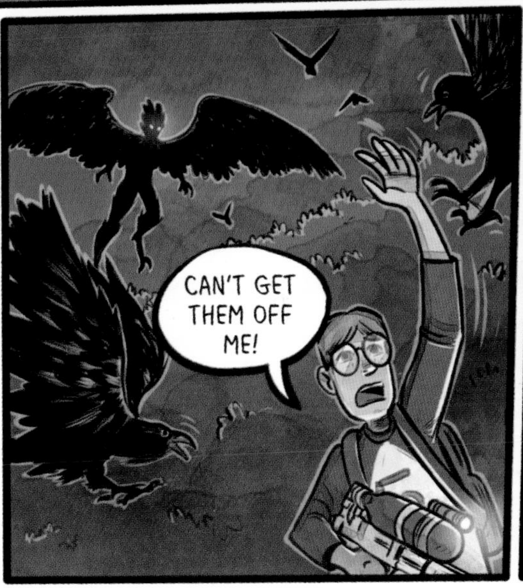
CAN'T GET THEM OFF ME!

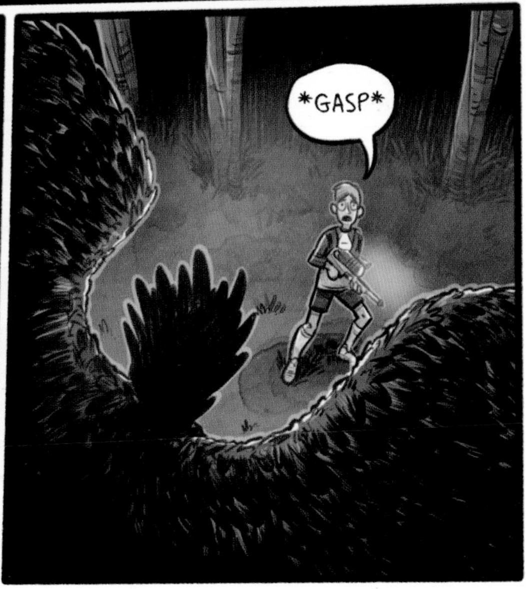
GASP

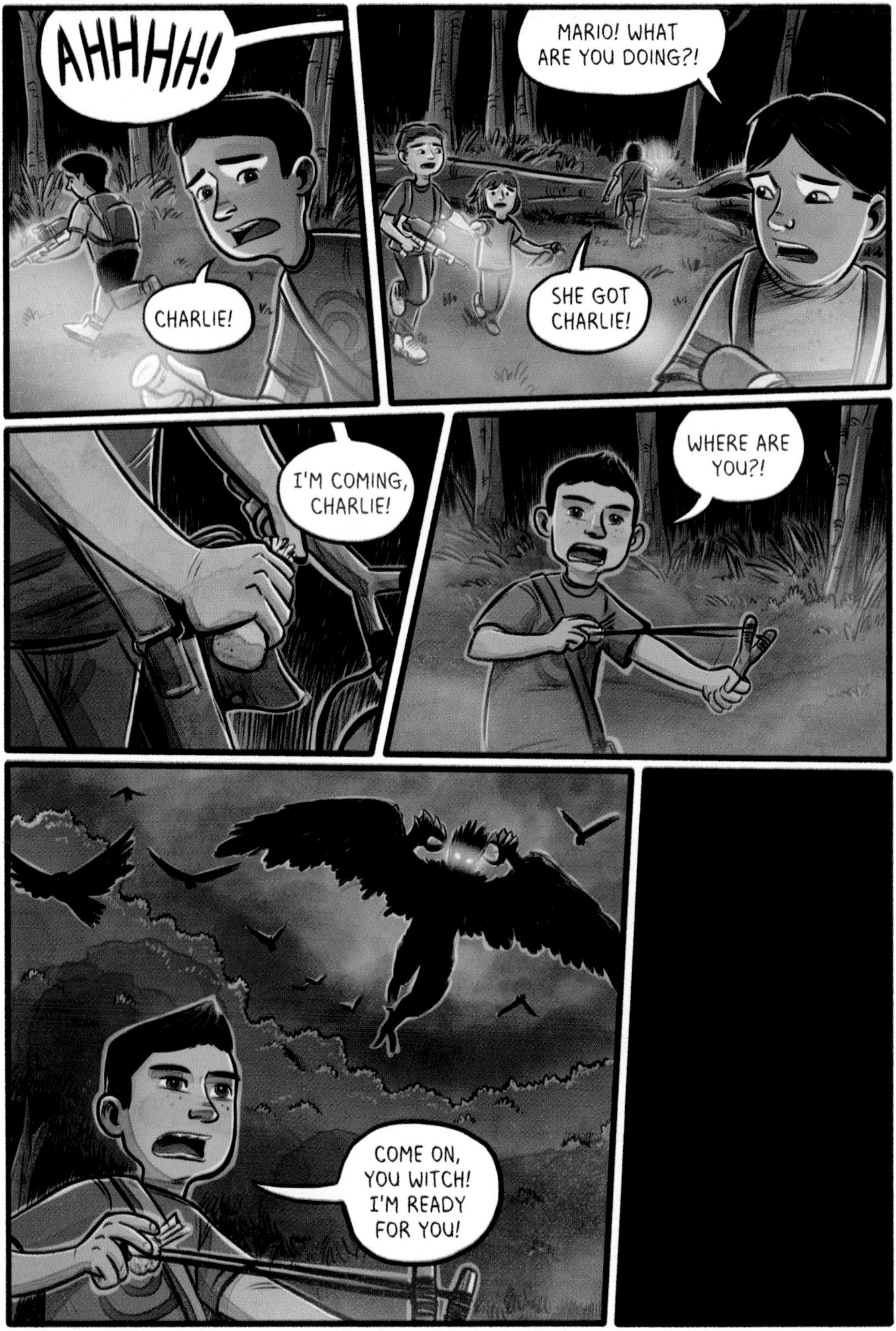
AHHHH!
CHARLIE!
MARIO! WHAT ARE YOU DOING?!
SHE GOT CHARLIE!
I'M COMING, CHARLIE!
WHERE ARE YOU?!
COME ON, YOU WITCH! I'M READY FOR YOU!

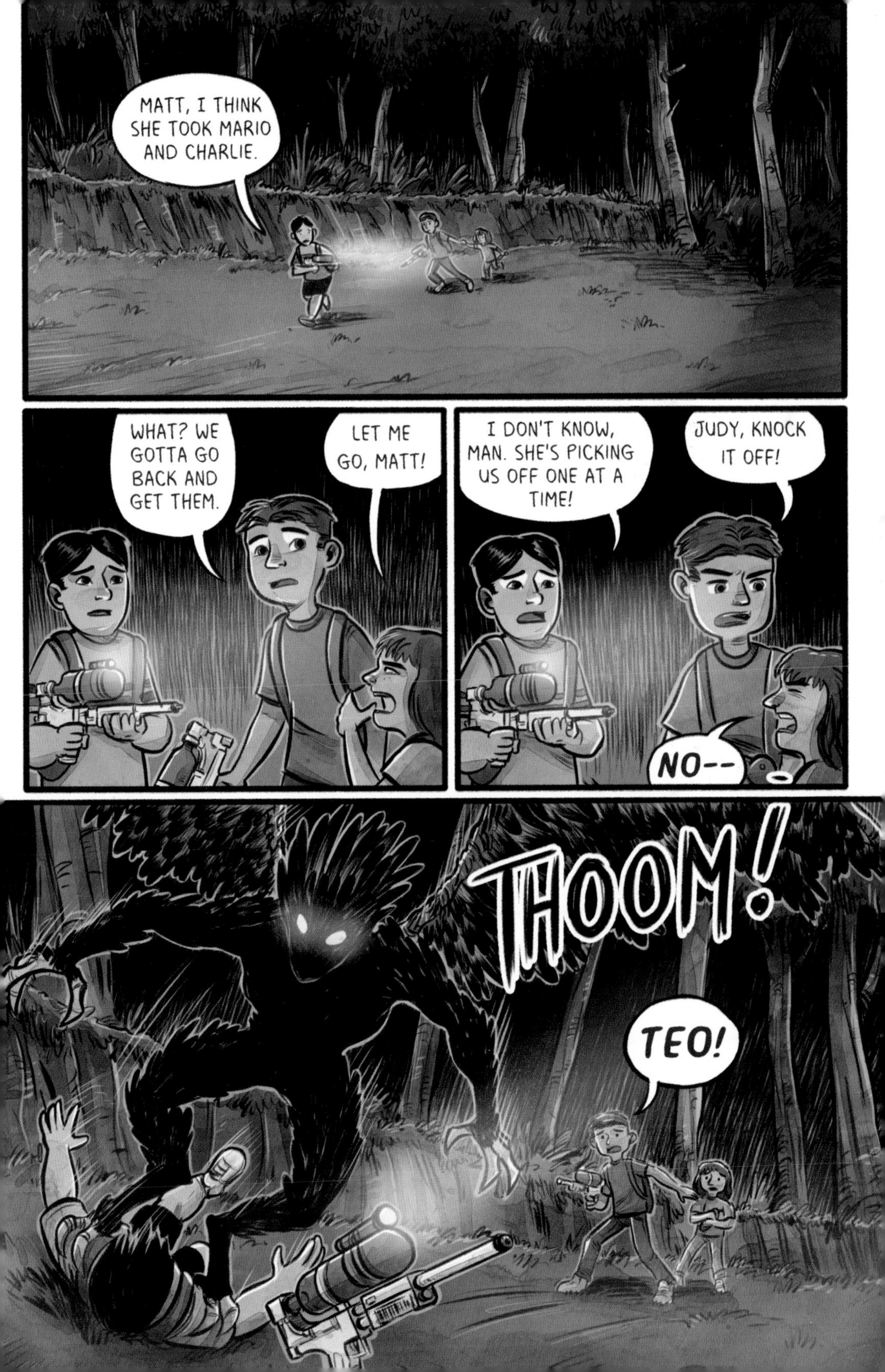
MATT, I THINK SHE TOOK MARIO AND CHARLIE.
WHAT? WE GOTTA GO BACK AND GET THEM.
LET ME GO, MATT!
I DON'T KNOW, MAN. SHE'S PICKING US OFF ONE AT A TIME!
JUDY, KNOCK IT OFF!
NO--
THOOM!
TEO!

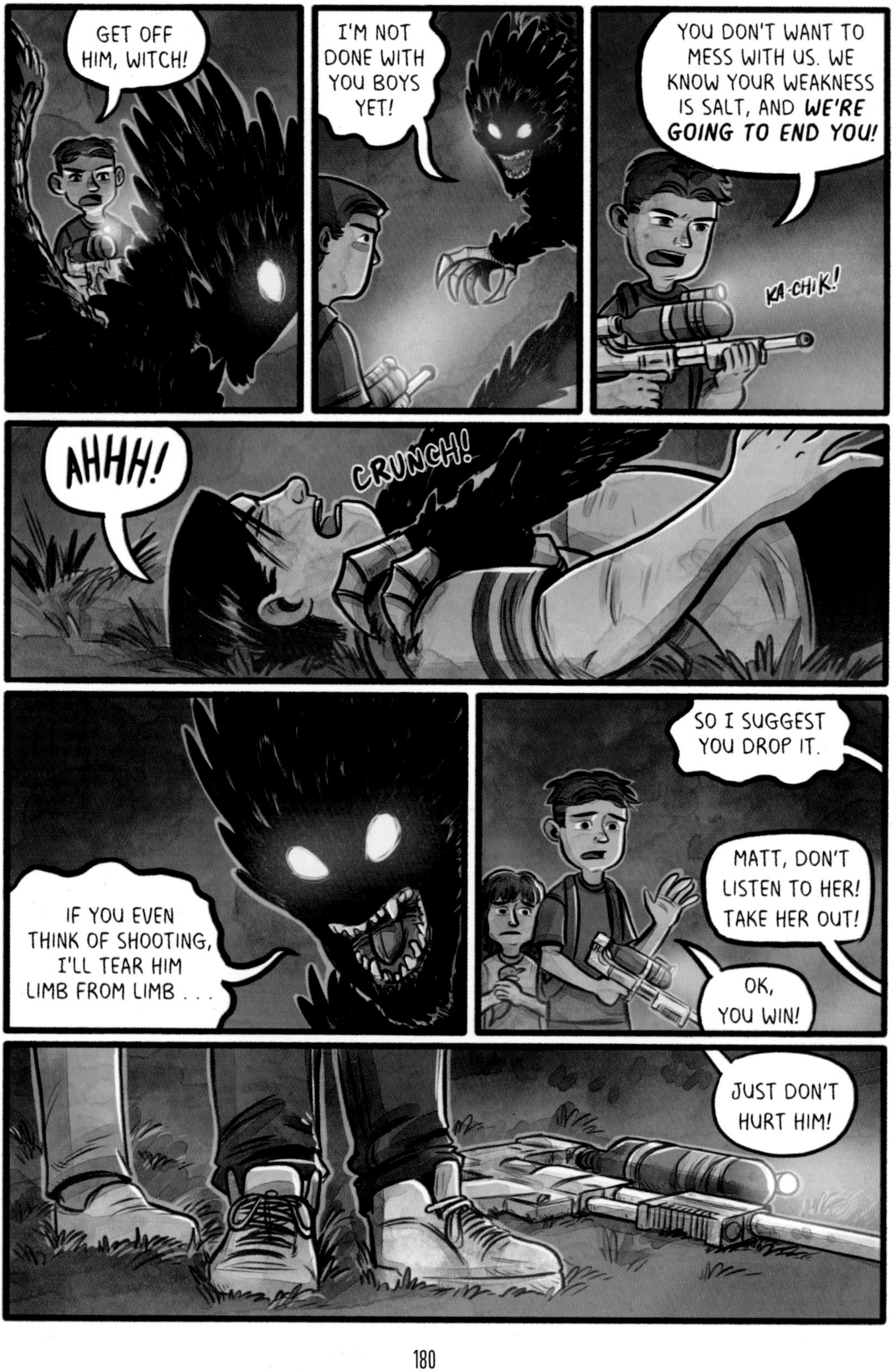
GET OFF HIM, WITCH!
I'M NOT DONE WITH YOU BOYS YET!
YOU DON'T WANT TO MESS WITH US. WE KNOW YOUR WEAKNESS IS SALT, AND **WE'RE GOING TO END YOU!**
KA-CHIK!
AHHH!
CRUNCH!
IF YOU EVEN THINK OF SHOOTING, I'LL TEAR HIM LIMB FROM LIMB . . .
SO I SUGGEST YOU DROP IT.
MATT, DON'T LISTEN TO HER! TAKE HER OUT!
OK, YOU WIN!
JUST DON'T HURT HIM!

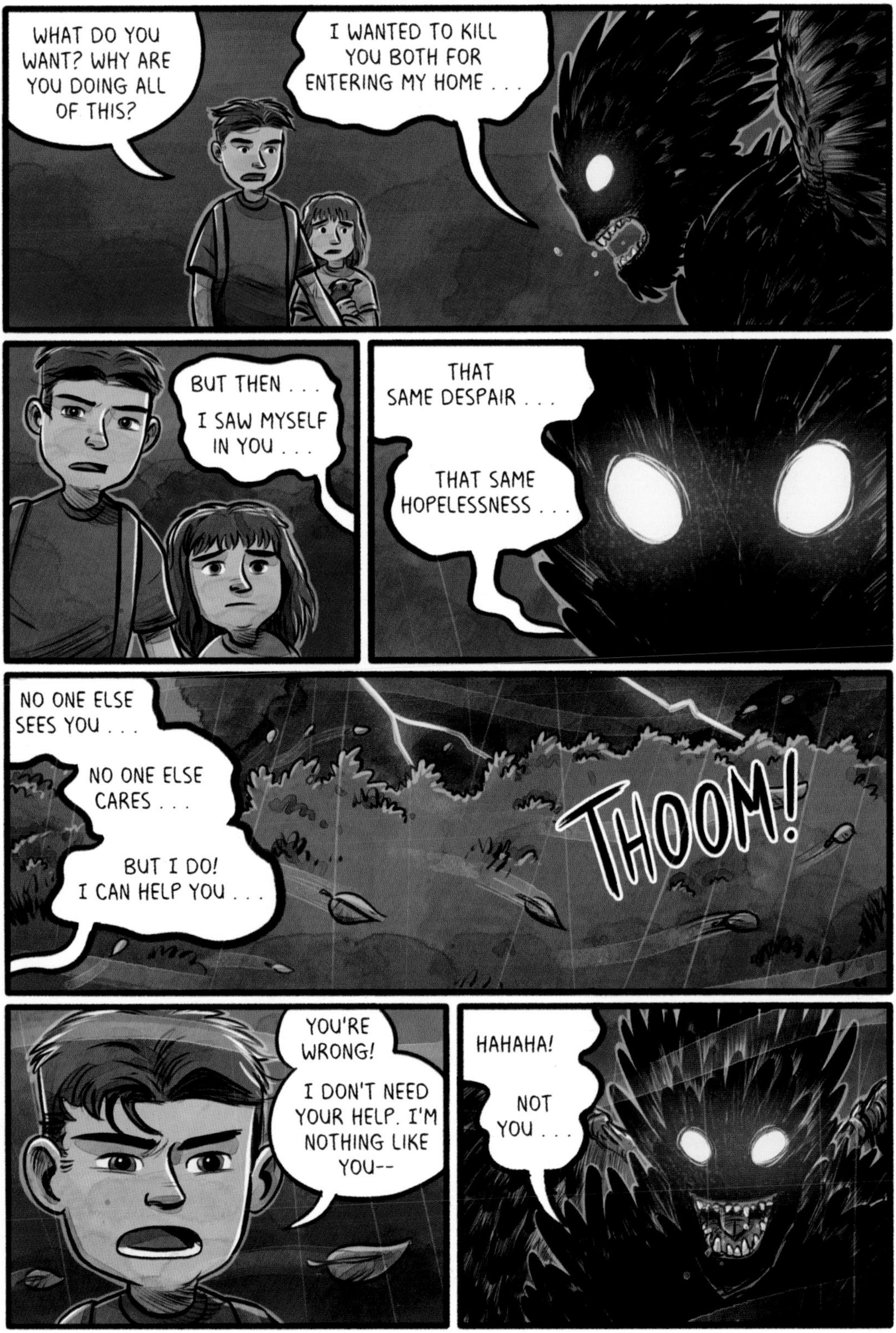
WHAT DO YOU WANT? WHY ARE YOU DOING ALL OF THIS?
I WANTED TO KILL YOU BOTH FOR ENTERING MY HOME . . .
BUT THEN . . .
I SAW MYSELF IN YOU . . .
THAT SAME DESPAIR . . .
THAT SAME HOPELESSNESS . . .
NO ONE ELSE SEES YOU . . .
NO ONE ELSE CARES . . .
BUT I DO! I CAN HELP YOU . . .
THOOM!
YOU'RE WRONG!
I DON'T NEED YOUR HELP. I'M NOTHING LIKE YOU--
HAHAHA!
NOT YOU . . .

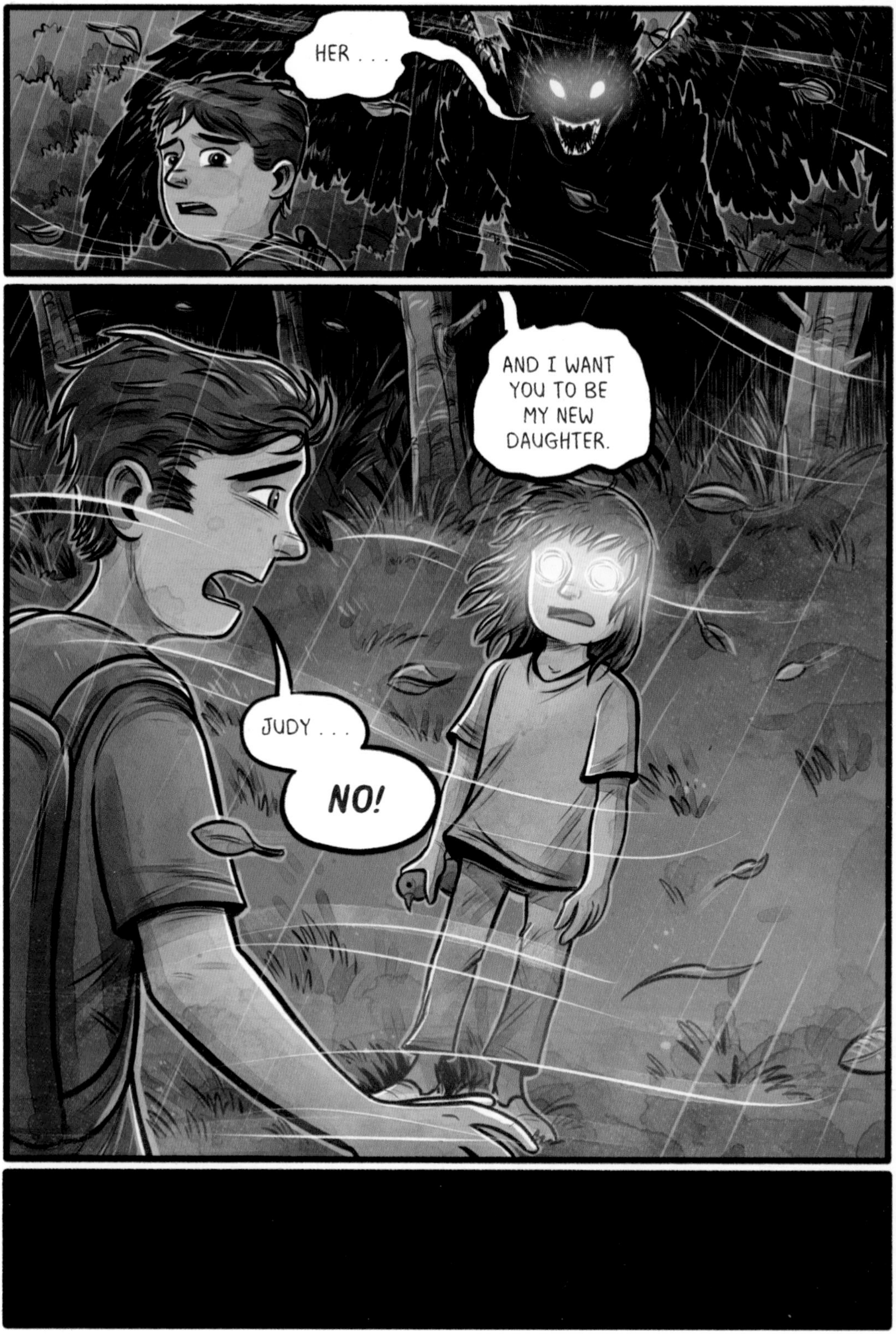
HER . . .
AND I WANT YOU TO BE MY NEW DAUGHTER.
JUDY . . .
NO!

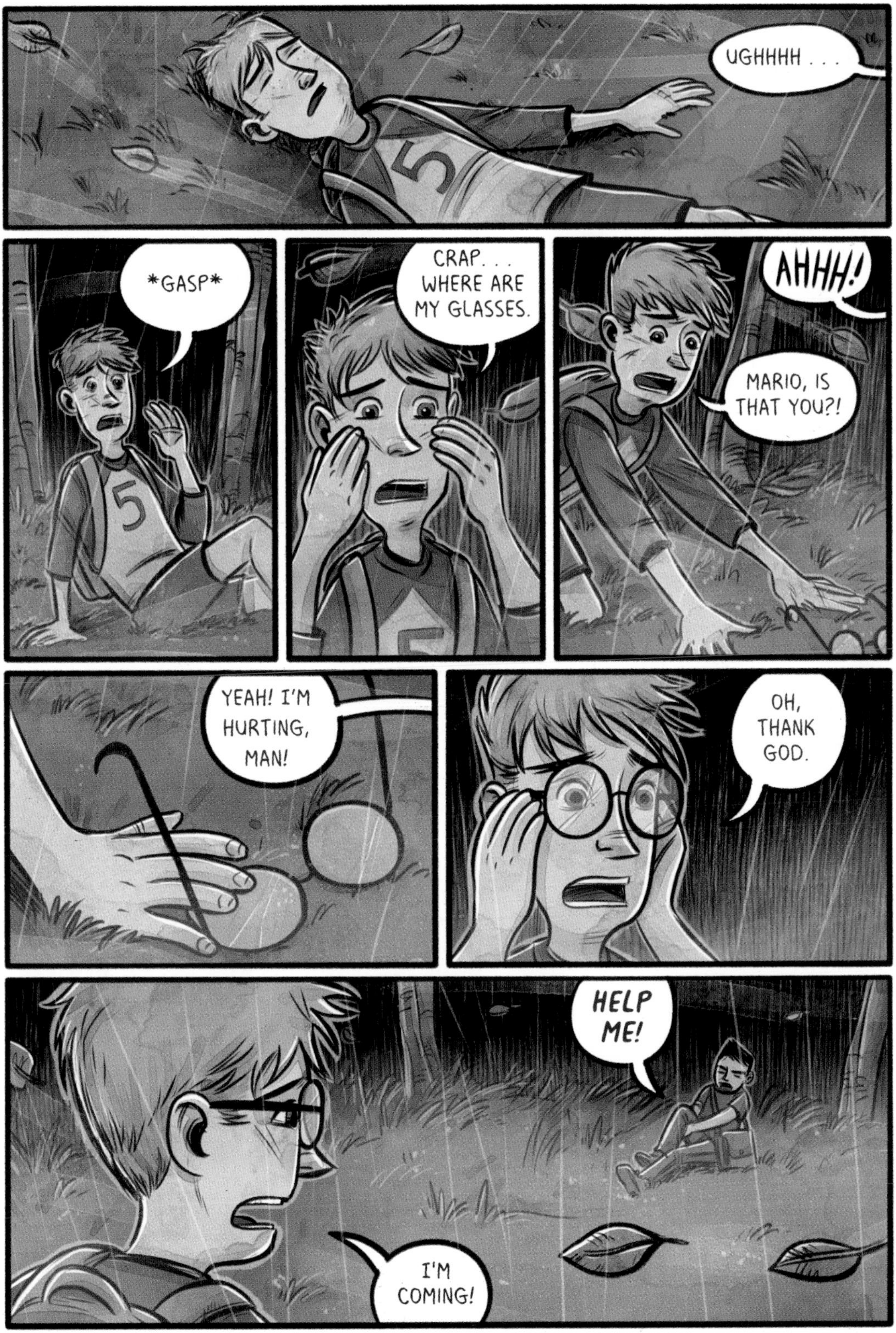
UGHHHH . . .
GASP
CRAP. . . WHERE ARE MY GLASSES.
AHHH!
MARIO, IS THAT YOU?!
YEAH! I'M HURTING, MAN!
OH, THANK GOD.
HELP ME!
I'M COMING!

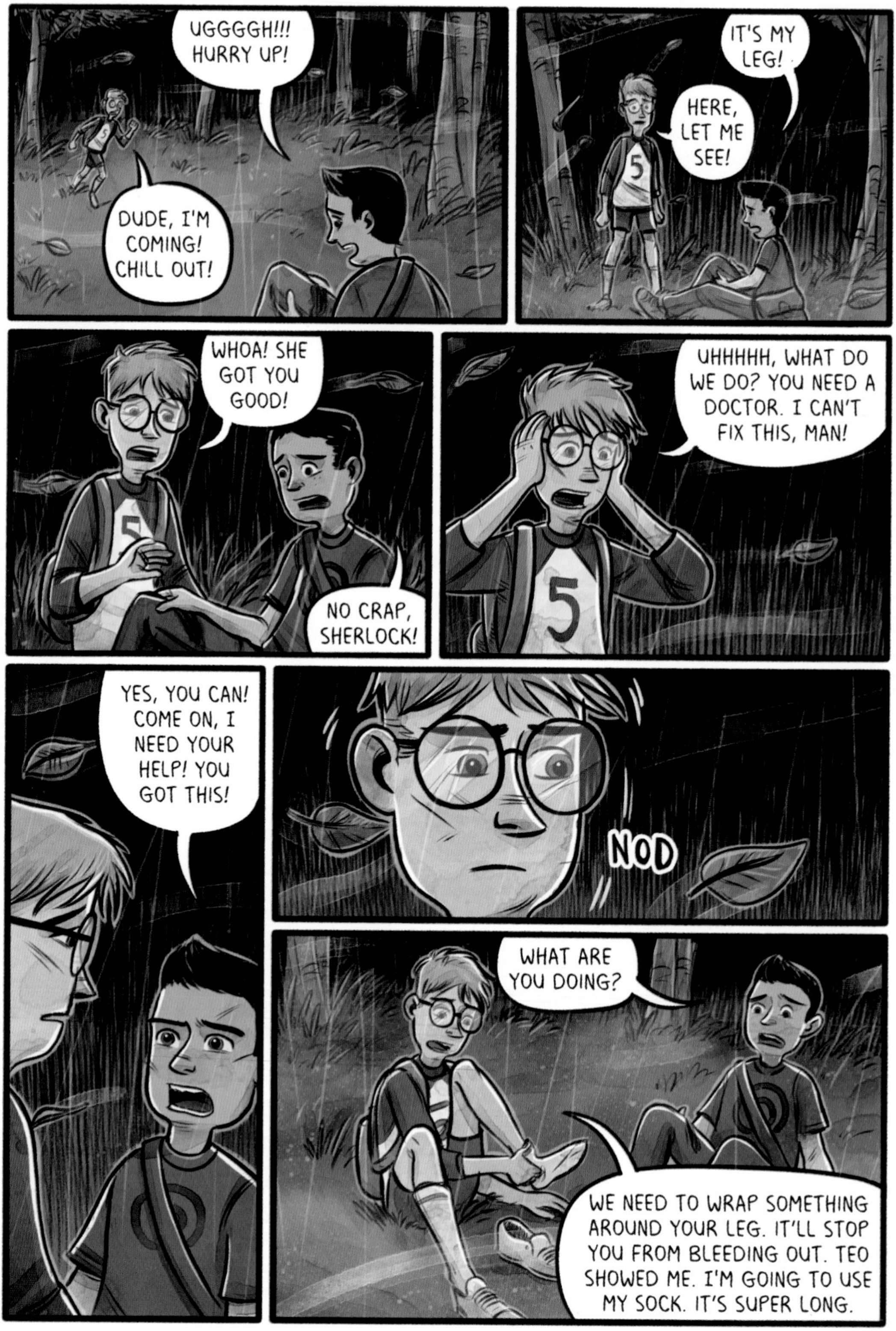
UGGGGH!!! HURRY UP!
DUDE, I'M COMING! CHILL OUT!
IT'S MY LEG!
HERE, LET ME SEE!
WHOA! SHE GOT YOU GOOD!
NO CRAP, SHERLOCK!
UHHHHH, WHAT DO WE DO? YOU NEED A DOCTOR. I CAN'T FIX THIS, MAN!
YES, YOU CAN! COME ON, I NEED YOUR HELP! YOU GOT THIS!
NOD
WHAT ARE YOU DOING?
WE NEED TO WRAP SOMETHING AROUND YOUR LEG. IT'LL STOP YOU FROM BLEEDING OUT. TEO SHOWED ME. I'M GOING TO USE MY SOCK. IT'S SUPER LONG.

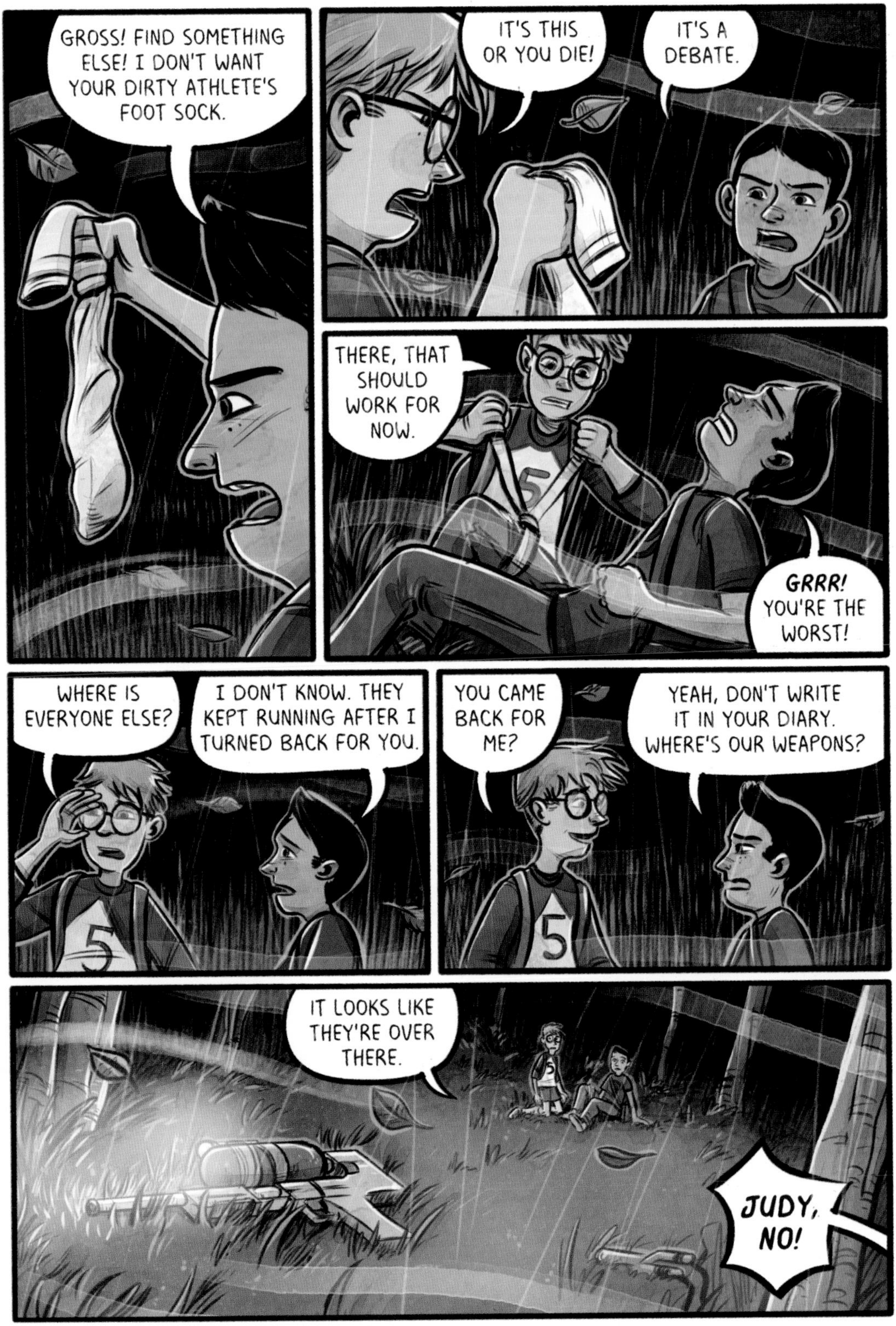
GROSS! FIND SOMETHING ELSE! I DON'T WANT YOUR DIRTY ATHLETE'S FOOT SOCK.
IT'S THIS OR YOU DIE!
IT'S A DEBATE.
THERE, THAT SHOULD WORK FOR NOW.
GRRR! YOU'RE THE WORST!
WHERE IS EVERYONE ELSE?
I DON'T KNOW. THEY KEPT RUNNING AFTER I TURNED BACK FOR YOU.
YOU CAME BACK FOR ME?
YEAH, DON'T WRITE IT IN YOUR DIARY. WHERE'S OUR WEAPONS?
IT LOOKS LIKE THEY'RE OVER THERE.
JUDY, NO!

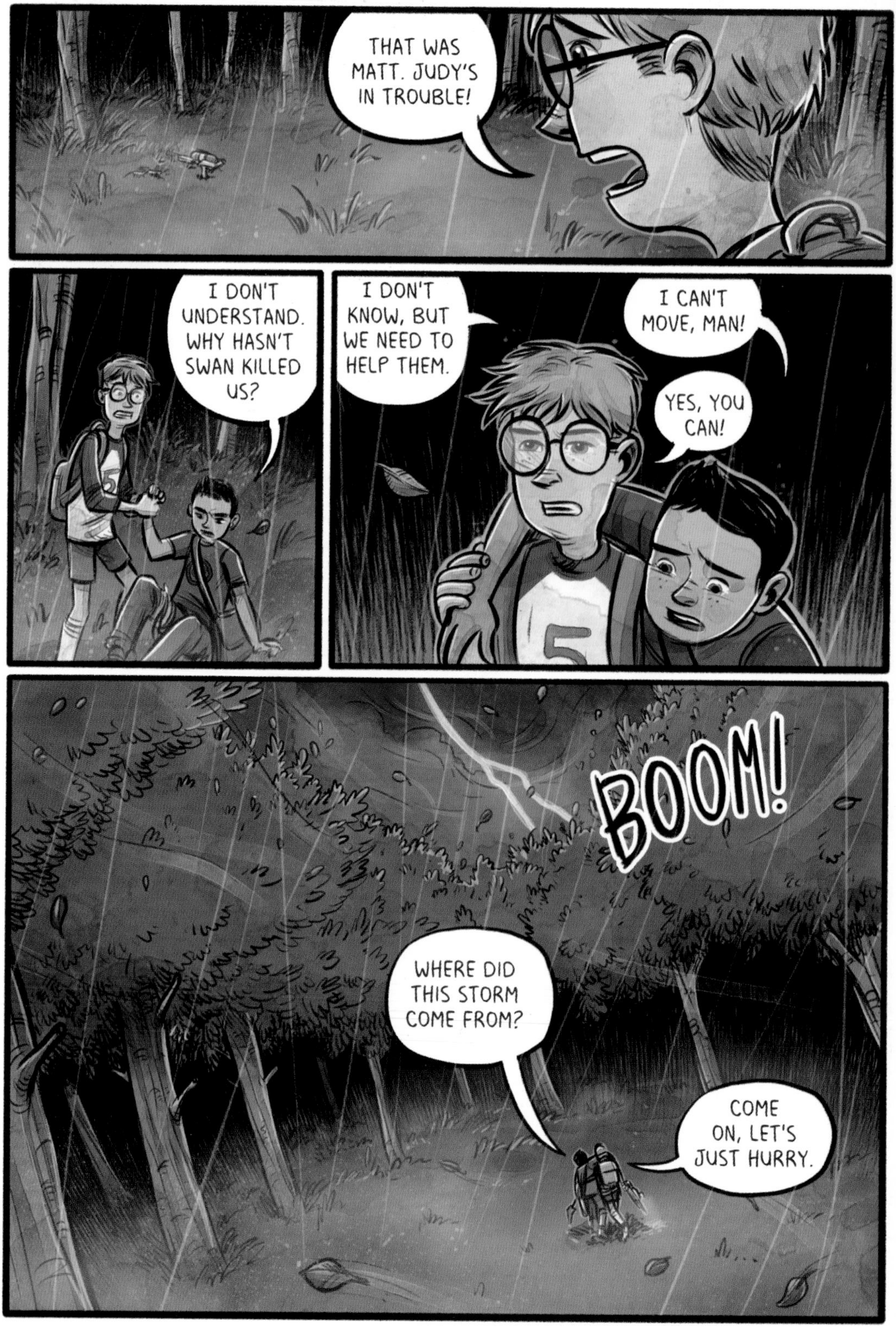
THAT WAS MATT. JUDY'S IN TROUBLE!
I DON'T UNDERSTAND. WHY HASN'T SWAN KILLED US?
I DON'T KNOW, BUT WE NEED TO HELP THEM.
I CAN'T MOVE, MAN!
YES, YOU CAN!
BOOM!
WHERE DID THIS STORM COME FROM?
COME ON, LET'S JUST HURRY.

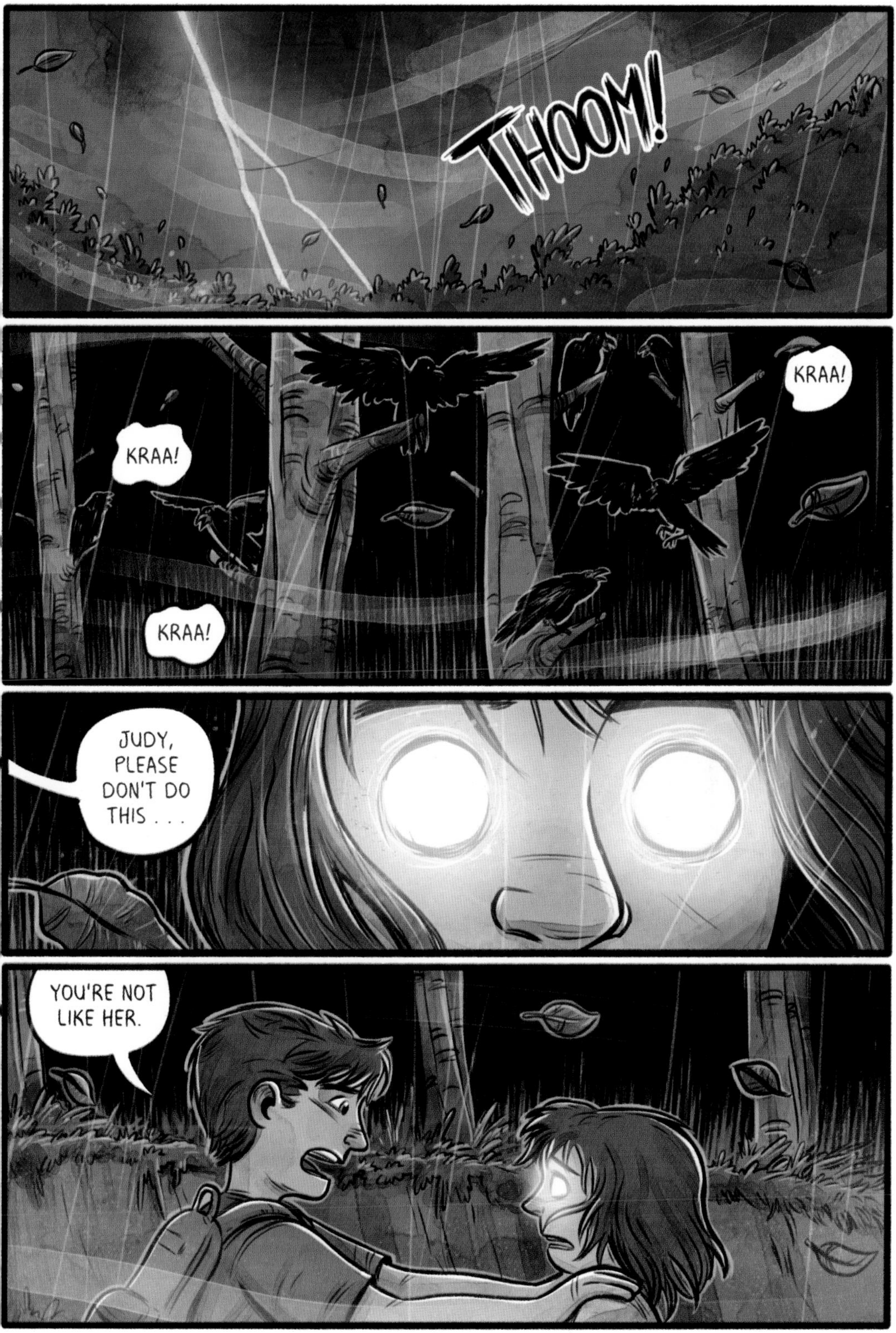
THOOM!
KRAA!
KRAA!
KRAA!
JUDY, PLEASE DON'T DO THIS . . .
YOU'RE NOT LIKE HER.

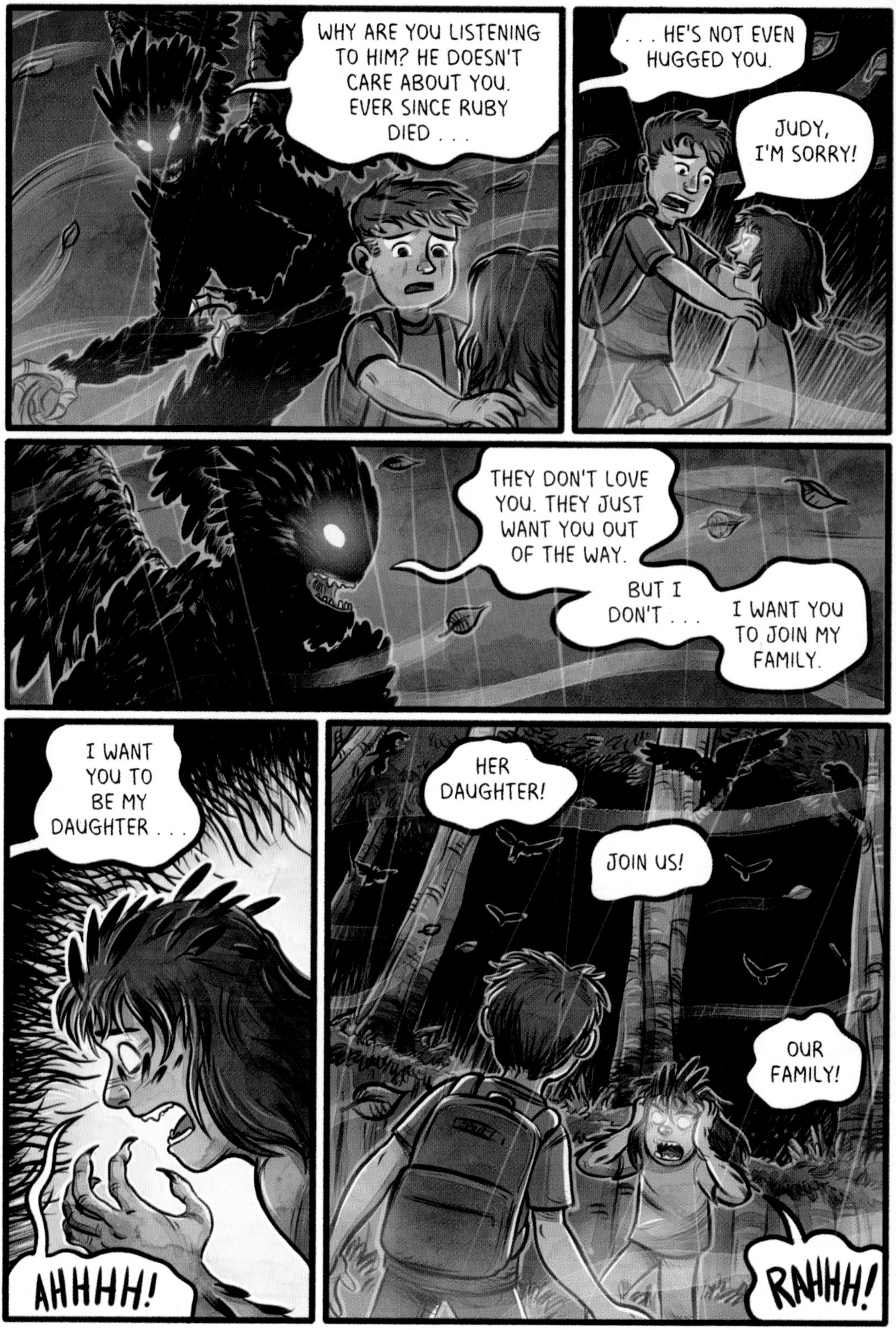

WHY ARE YOU LISTENING TO HIM? HE DOESN'T CARE ABOUT YOU. EVER SINCE RUBY DIED . . .
. . . HE'S NOT EVEN HUGGED YOU.
JUDY, I'M SORRY!
THEY DON'T LOVE YOU. THEY JUST WANT YOU OUT OF THE WAY.
BUT I DON'T . . .
I WANT YOU TO JOIN MY FAMILY.
I WANT YOU TO BE MY DAUGHTER . . .
AHHHH!
HER DAUGHTER!
JOIN US!
OUR FAMILY!
RAHHH!

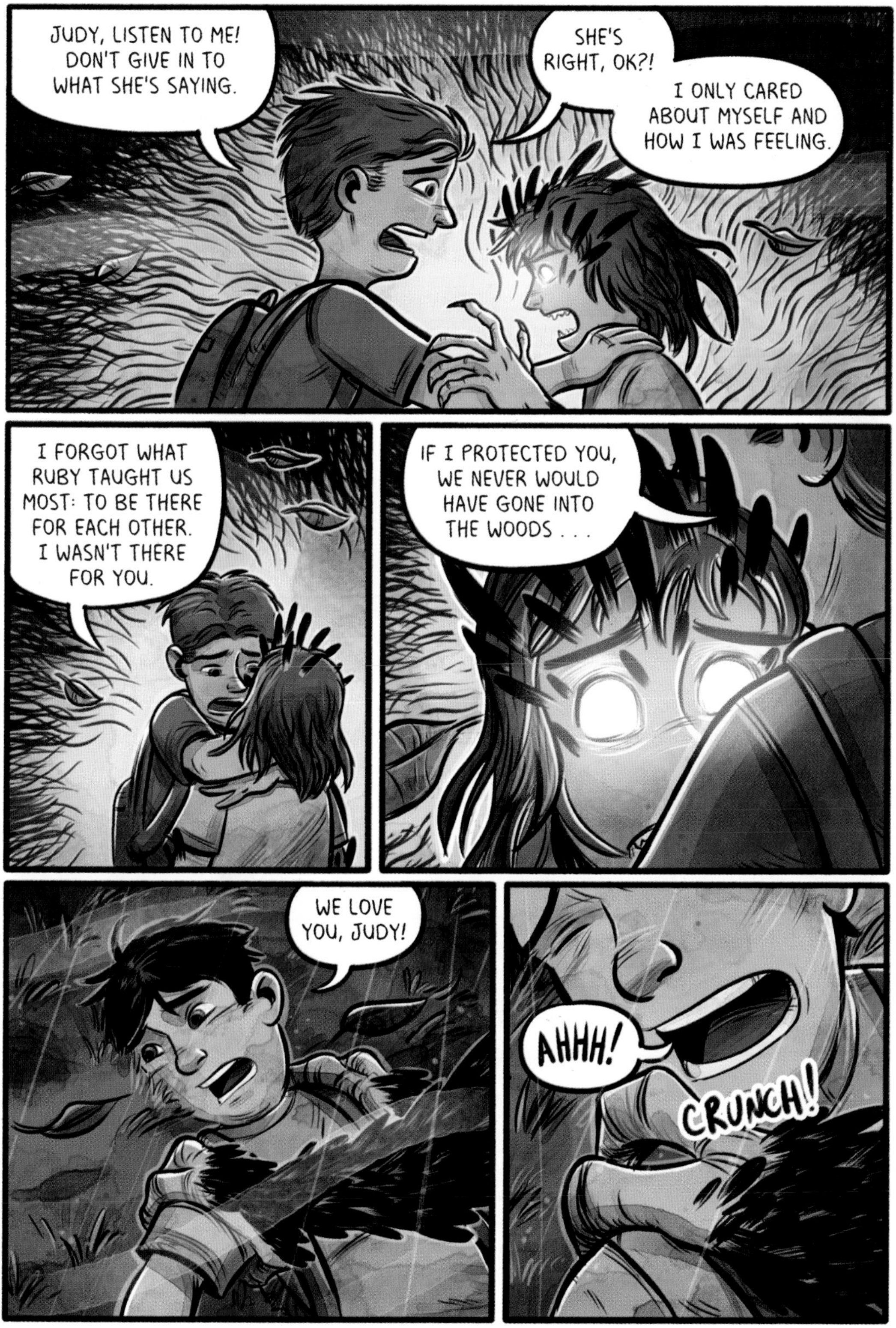
JUDY, LISTEN TO ME! DON'T GIVE IN TO WHAT SHE'S SAYING.
SHE'S RIGHT, OK?!
I ONLY CARED ABOUT MYSELF AND HOW I WAS FEELING.
I FORGOT WHAT RUBY TAUGHT US MOST: TO BE THERE FOR EACH OTHER. I WASN'T THERE FOR YOU.
IF I PROTECTED YOU, WE NEVER WOULD HAVE GONE INTO THE WOODS . . .
WE LOVE YOU, JUDY!
AHHH!
CRUNCH!

GIVE IN TO YOUR CHANGE, JUDY.

FORGET WHO THEY ARE . . .

THEY DON'T CARE ABOUT YOU, AND WHEN YOU'RE LIKE ME YOU CAN PUNISH THEM TOO . . .

THAT'S WHY I'VE KEPT THEM ALIVE . . .

THEY'LL BE YOUR FIRST HUNT!

I SHOULD HAVE BEEN THERE FOR YOU. REMEMBER WHEN WE USED TO SIT TOGETHER WITH RUBY DURING THUNDERSTORMS AND IT MADE YOU FEEL BETTER?

I'M SITTING WITH YOU NOW. REMEMBER WHAT RUBY TAUGHT US . . . *I LOVE YOU!*

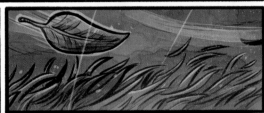

MATT . . .

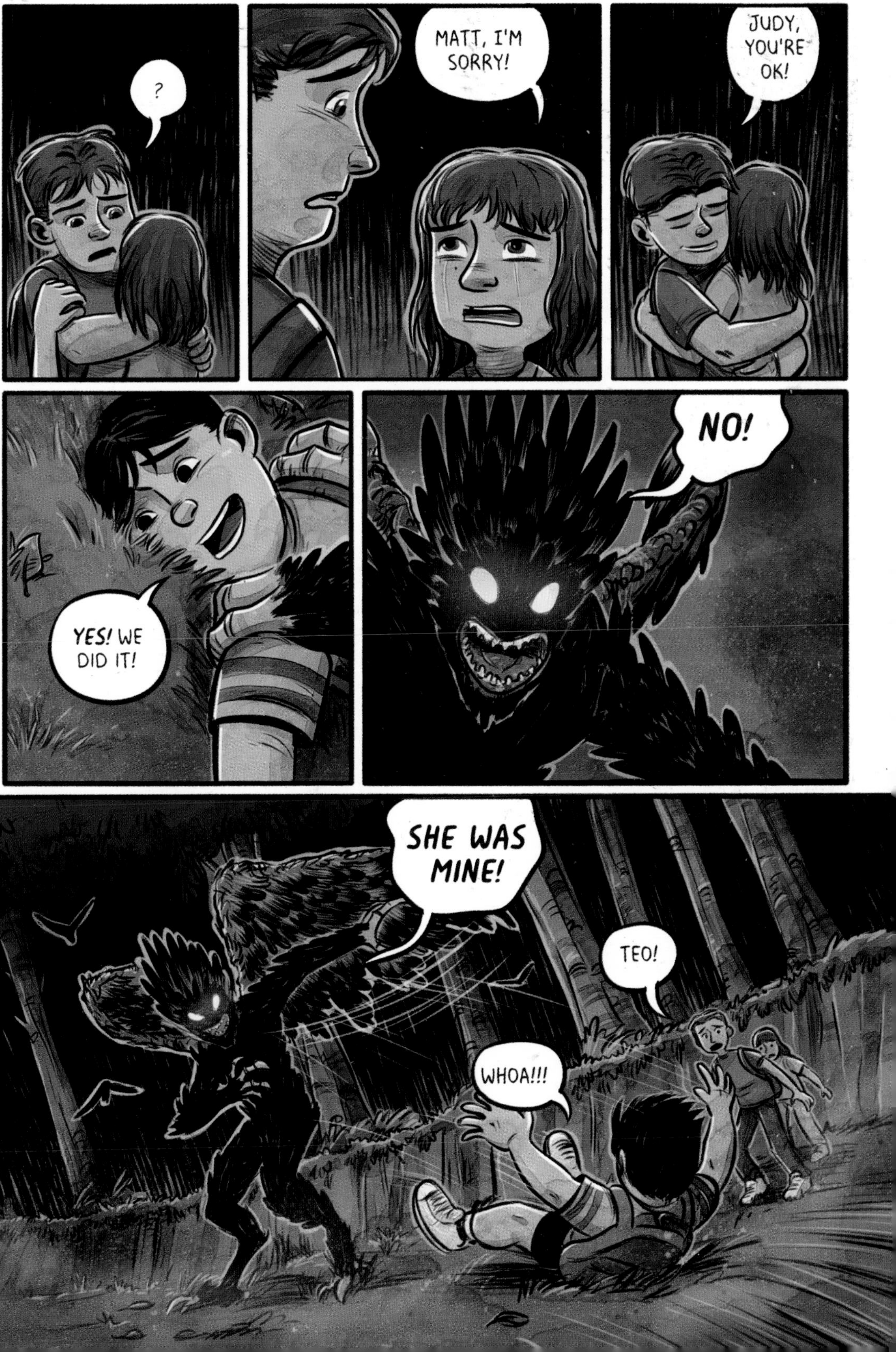
?
MATT, I'M SORRY!
JUDY, YOU'RE OK!
YES! WE DID IT!
NO!
SHE WAS MINE!
TEO!
WHOA!!!

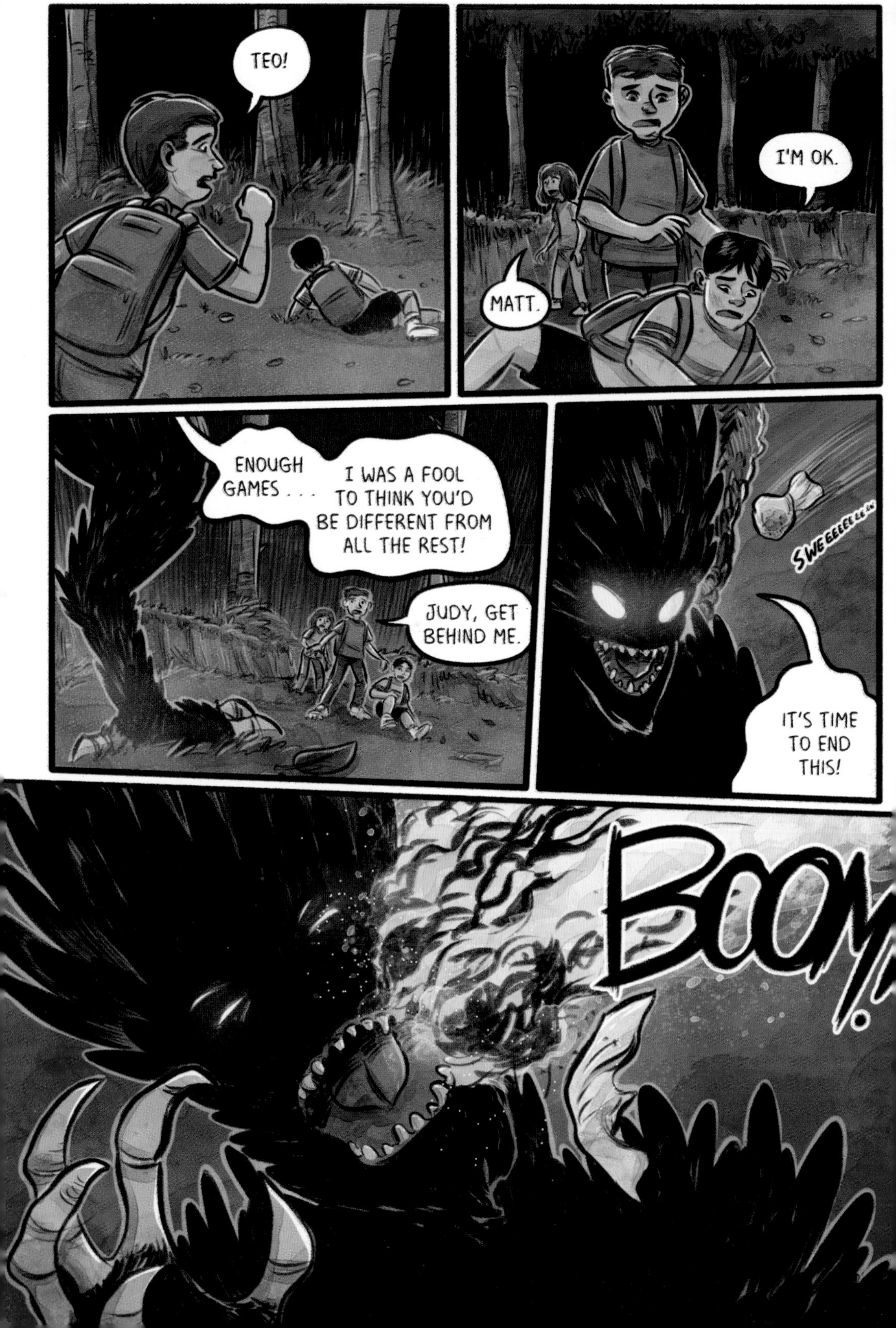
TEO!
I'M OK.
MATT.
ENOUGH GAMES . . .
I WAS A FOOL TO THINK YOU'D BE DIFFERENT FROM ALL THE REST!
JUDY, GET BEHIND ME.
SWEEEEEEE
IT'S TIME TO END THIS!
BOOM!

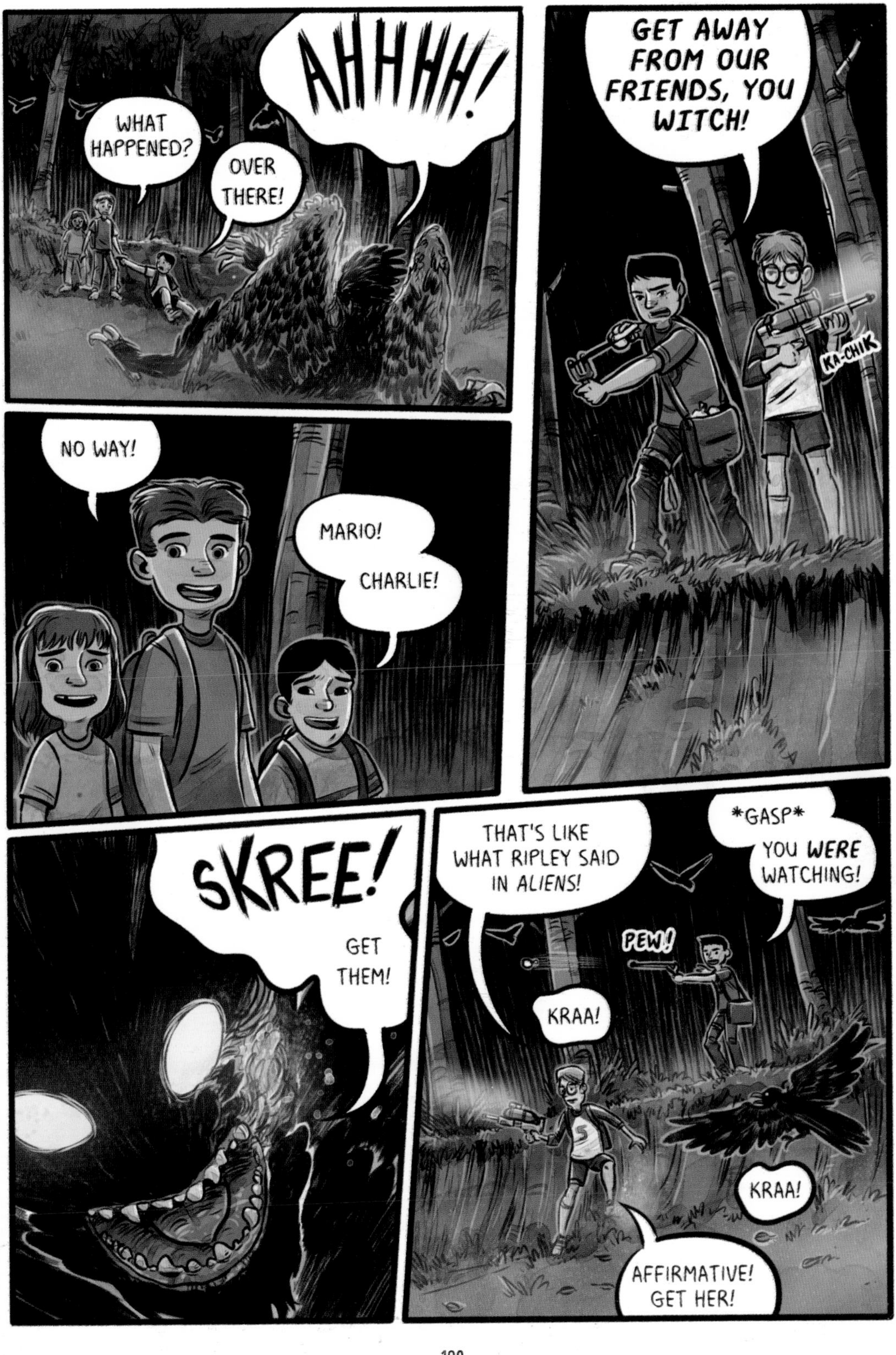
WHAT HAPPENED?
OVER THERE!
AHHHH!
GET AWAY FROM OUR FRIENDS, YOU WITCH!
KA-CHIK
NO WAY!
MARIO!
CHARLIE!
SKREE!
GET THEM!
THAT'S LIKE WHAT RIPLEY SAID IN ALIENS!
GASP
YOU WERE WATCHING!
PEW!
KRAA!
KRAA!
AFFIRMATIVE! GET HER!

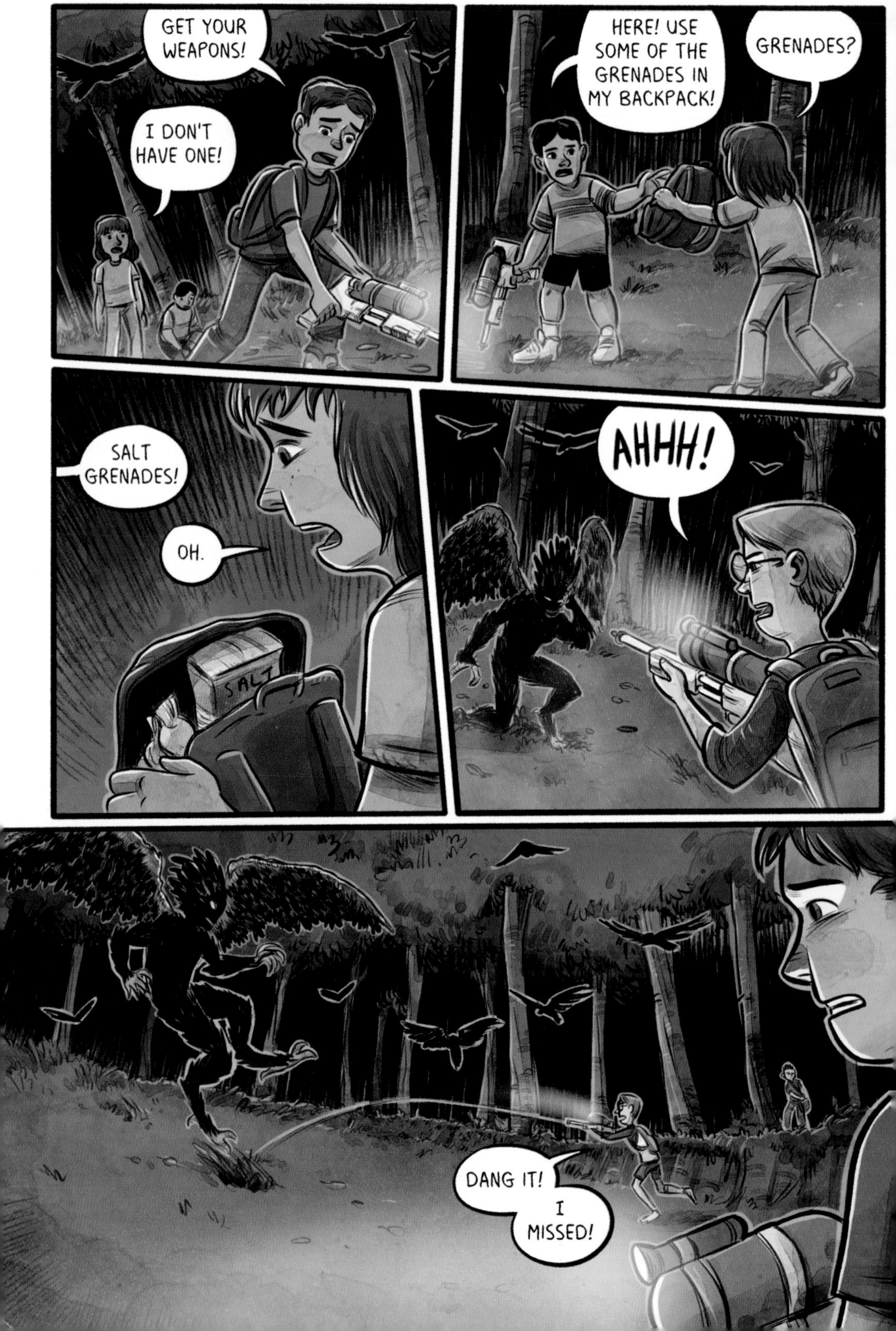
GET YOUR WEAPONS!
I DON'T HAVE ONE!
HERE! USE SOME OF THE GRENADES IN MY BACKPACK!
GRENADES?
SALT GRENADES!
OH.
SALT
AHHH!
DANG IT!
I MISSED!

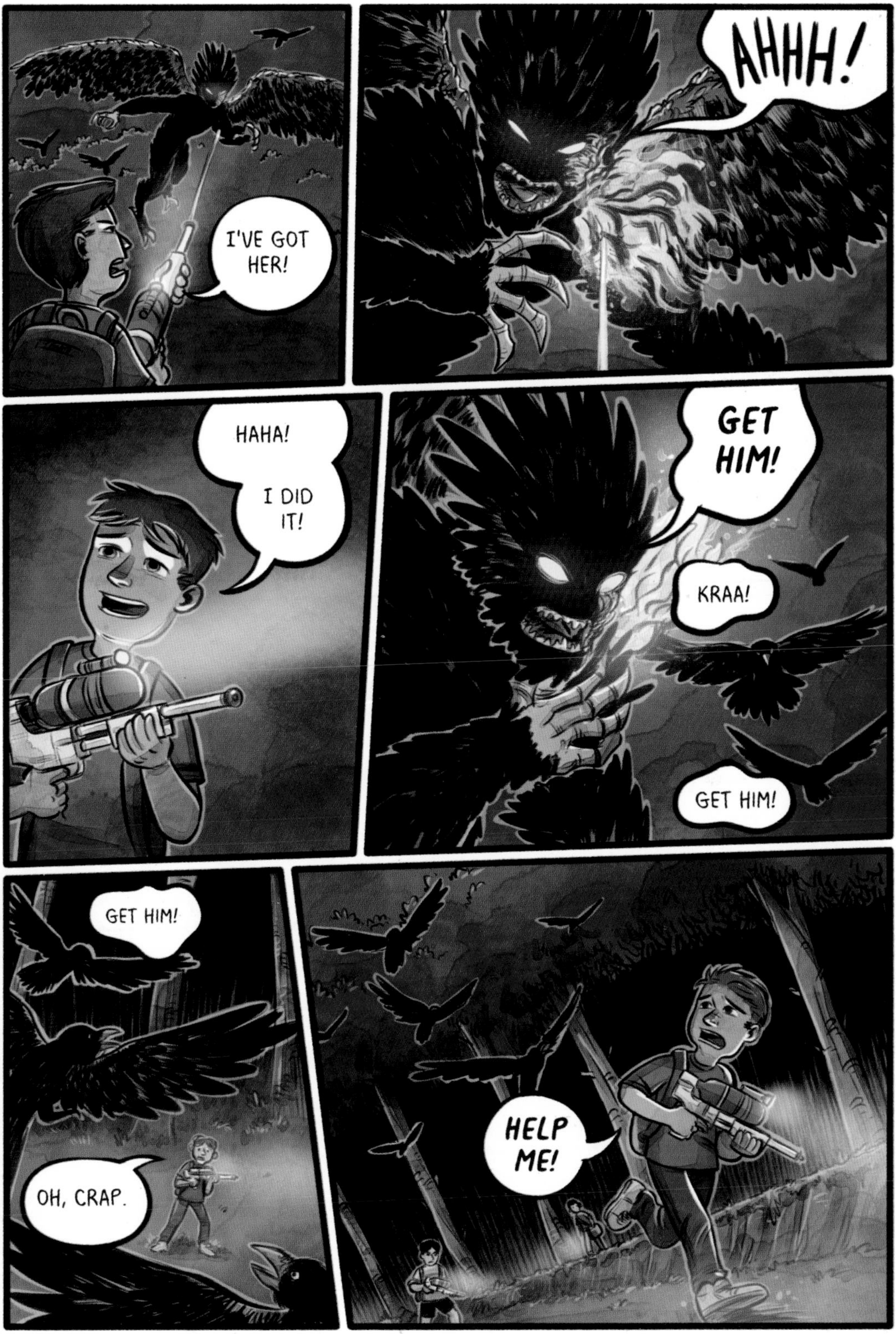
I'VE GOT HER!
AHHH!
HAHA!
I DID IT!
GET HIM!
KRAA!
GET HIM!
GET HIM!
OH, CRAP.
HELP ME!

I'M COMING, MATT!

OK, MARIO. YOU'VE GOT HER IN YOUR SIGHTS . . .

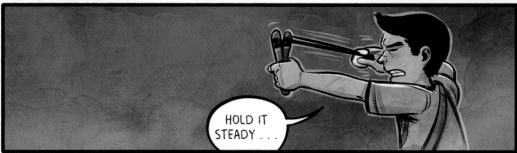

HOLD IT STEADY . . .

SLING!

AND RELEASE!

AGGHHH!

HA! SUCK IT, BEAST!

OH, CRAP!

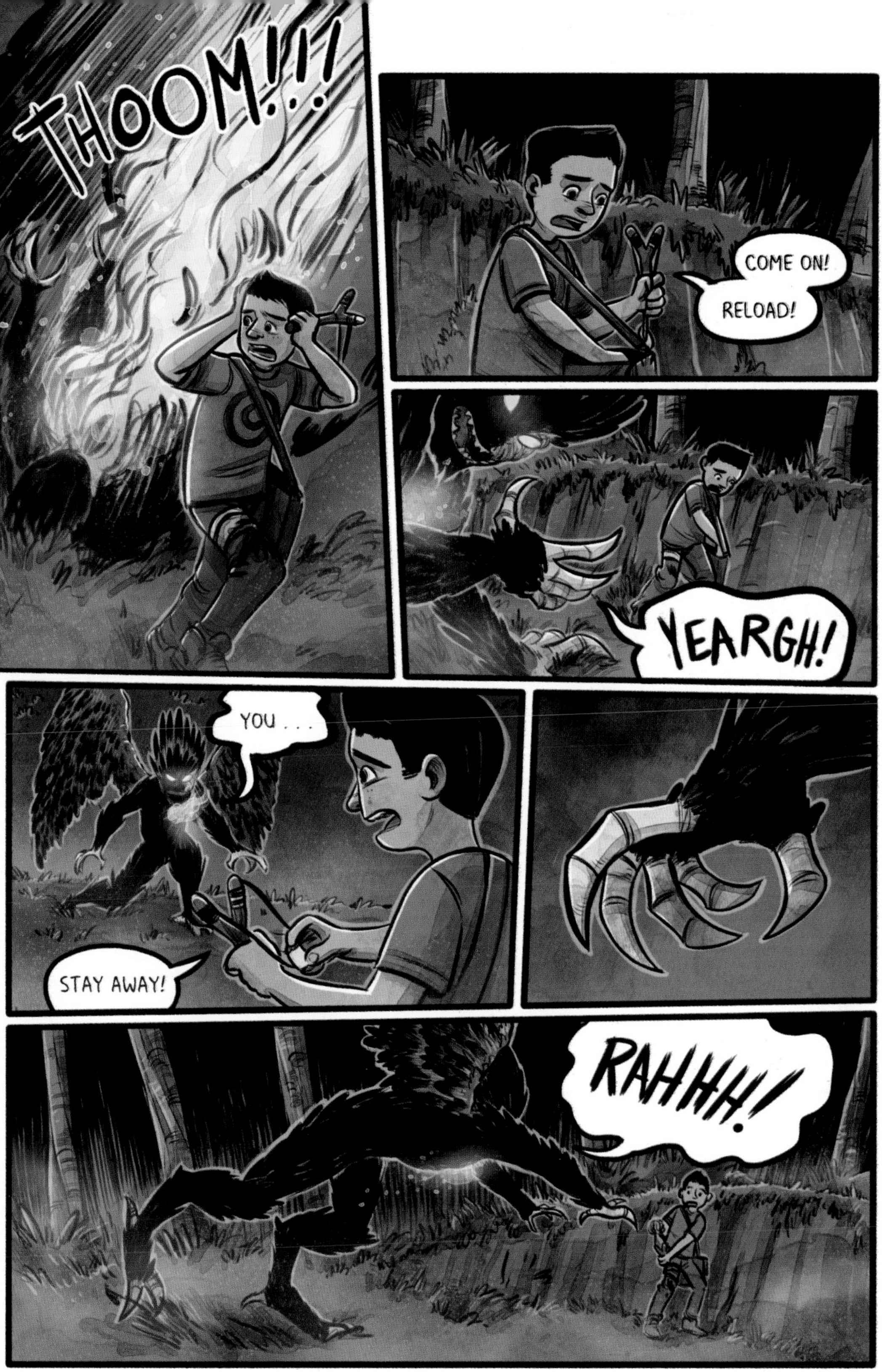
THOOM!!!
COME ON!
RELOAD!
YEARGH!
YOU . . .
STAY AWAY!
RAHHH!

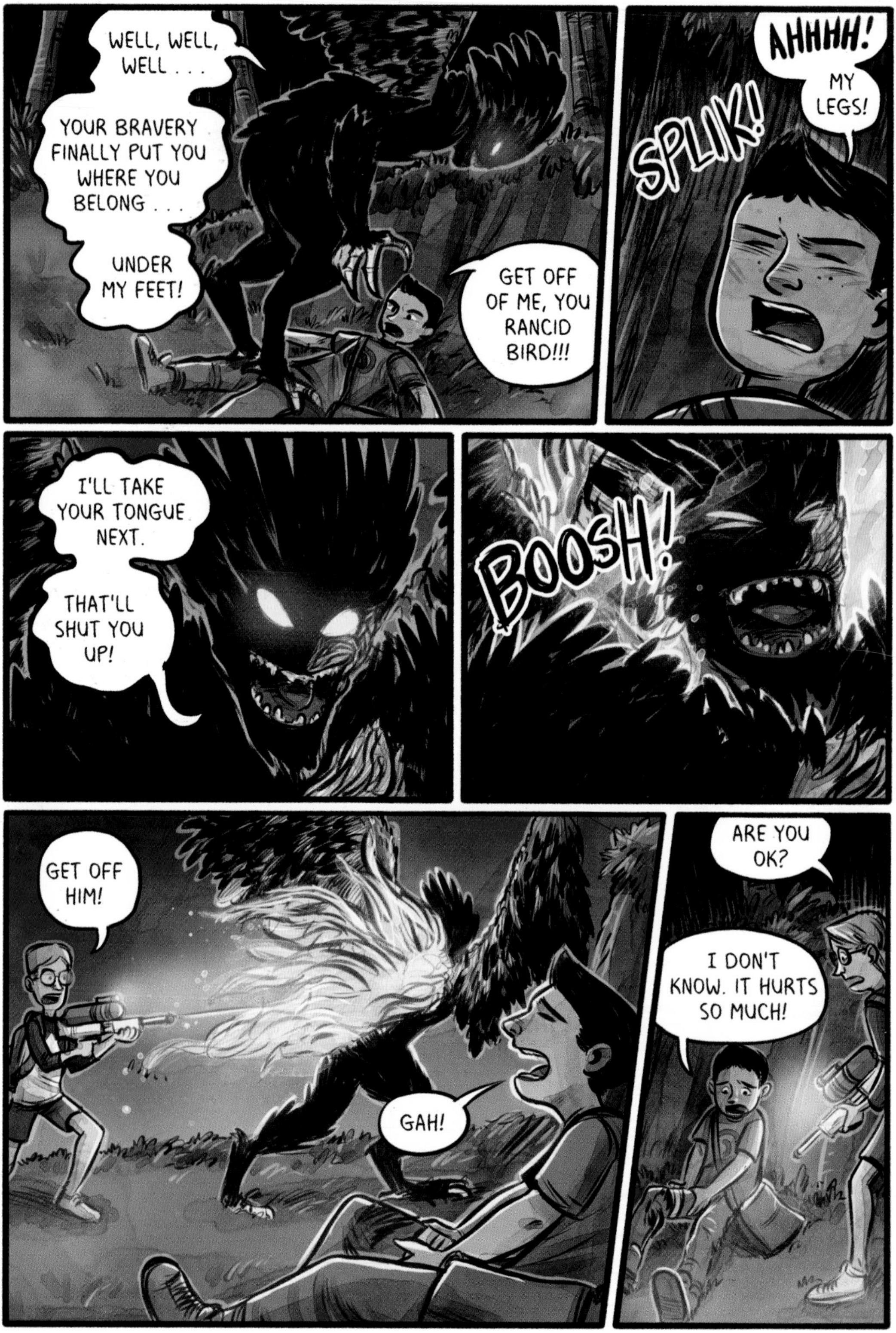
WELL, WELL, WELL . . .
YOUR BRAVERY FINALLY PUT YOU WHERE YOU BELONG . . .
UNDER MY FEET!
GET OFF OF ME, YOU RANCID BIRD!!!
SPLIK!
AHHHH!
MY LEGS!
I'LL TAKE YOUR TONGUE NEXT.
THAT'LL SHUT YOU UP!
BOOSH!
GET OFF HIM!
GAH!
ARE YOU OK?
I DON'T KNOW. IT HURTS SO MUCH!

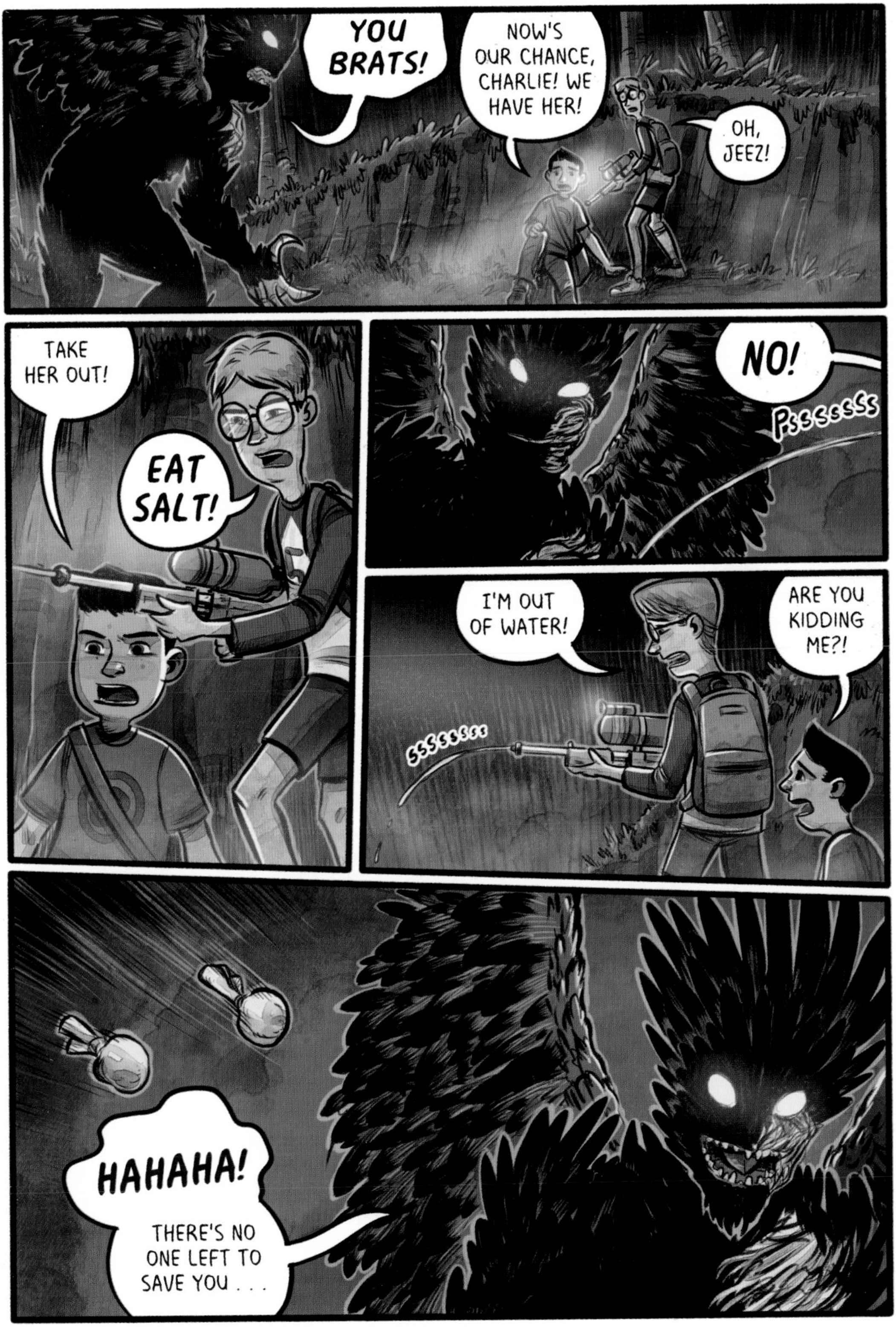
YOU BRATS!
NOW'S OUR CHANCE, CHARLIE! WE HAVE HER!
OH, JEEZ!
TAKE HER OUT!
EAT SALT!
NO!
PSSSSSSS
I'M OUT OF WATER!
ARE YOU KIDDING ME?!
SSSSSSSS
HAHAHA!
THERE'S NO ONE LEFT TO SAVE YOU . . .

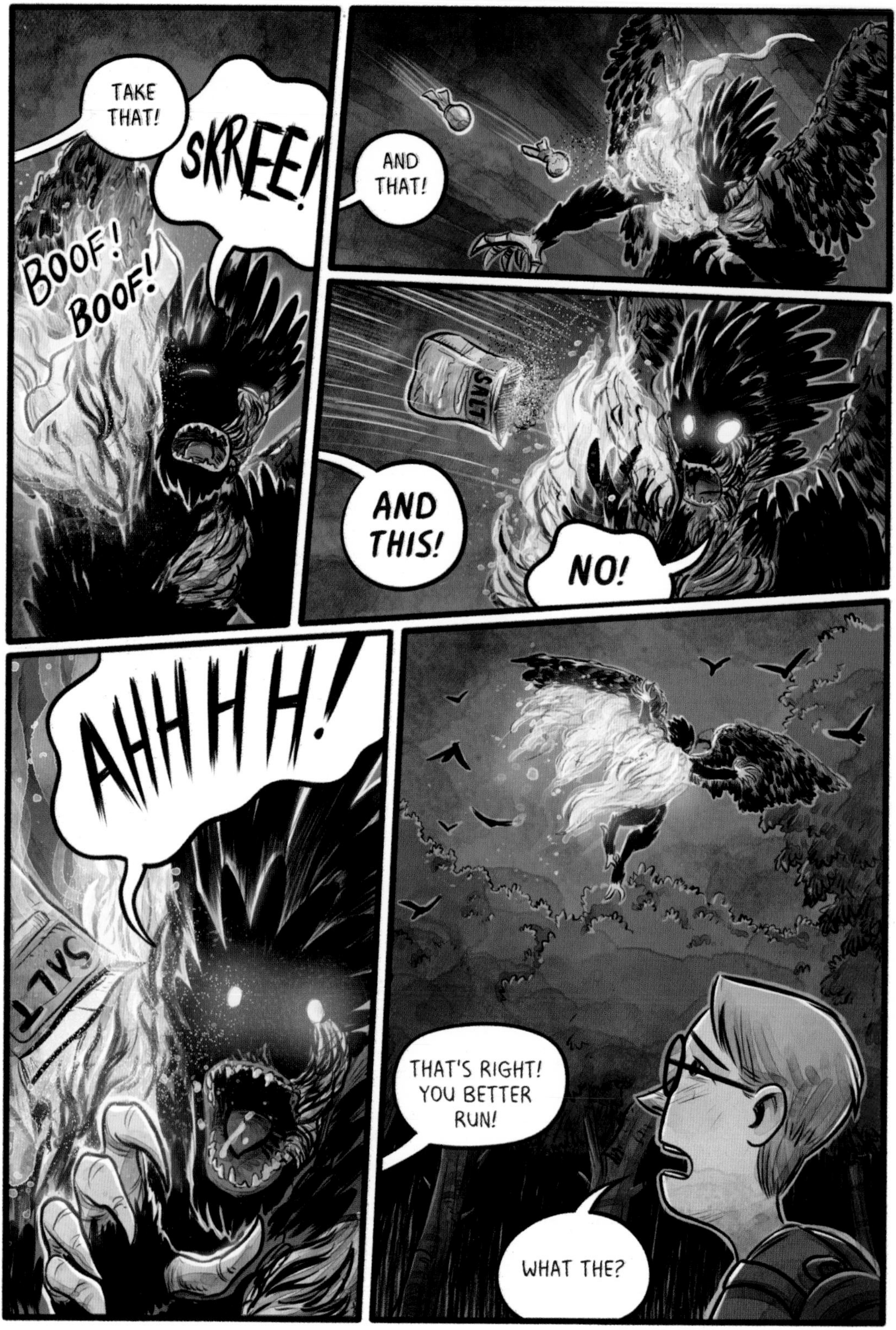
TAKE THAT!
SKREE!
BOOF! BOOF!
AND THAT!
SALT
AND THIS!
NO!
AHHHH!
SALT
THAT'S RIGHT! YOU BETTER RUN!
WHAT THE?

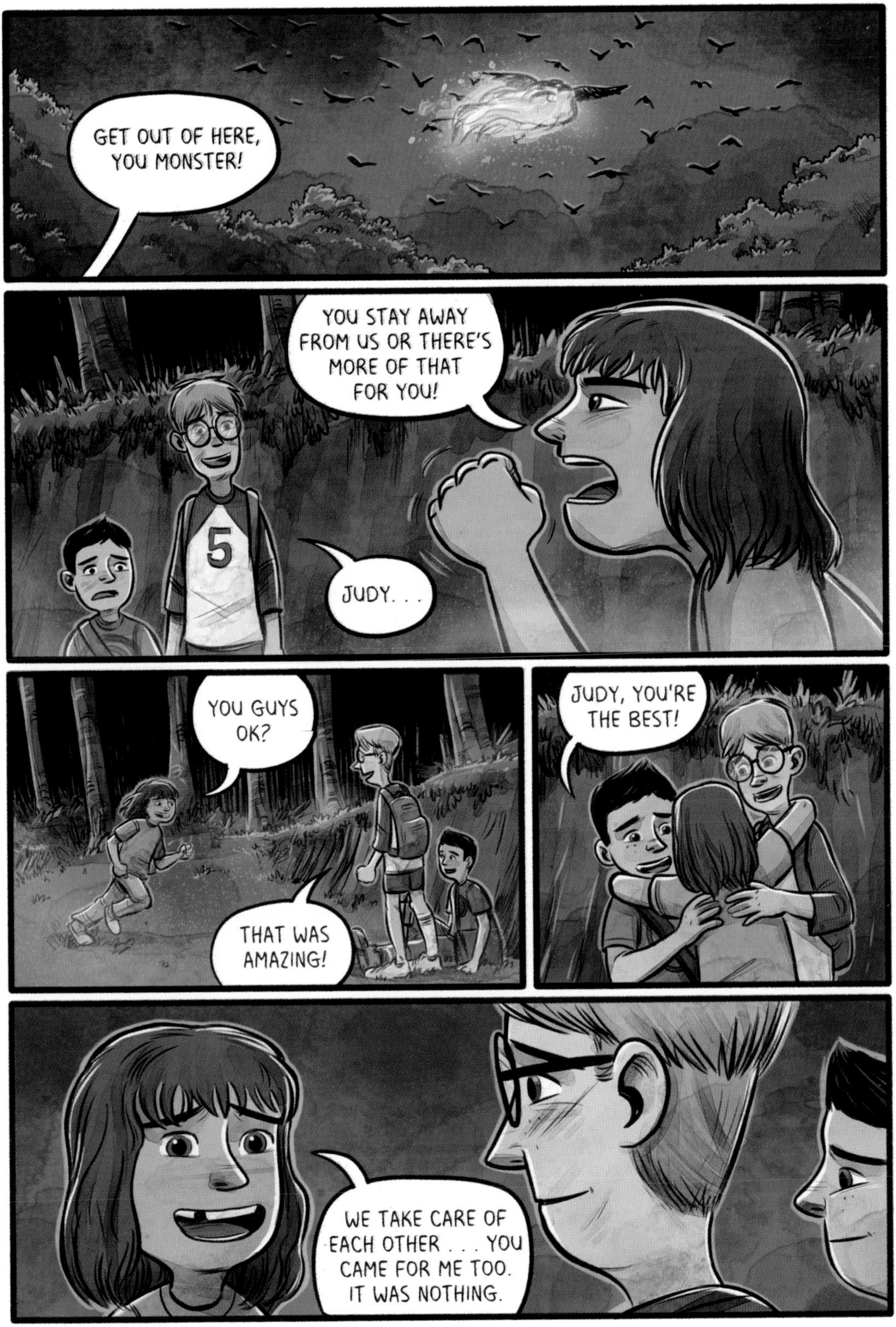
GET OUT OF HERE, YOU MONSTER!
YOU STAY AWAY FROM US OR THERE'S MORE OF THAT FOR YOU!
JUDY. . .
YOU GUYS OK?
THAT WAS AMAZING!
JUDY, YOU'RE THE BEST!
WE TAKE CARE OF EACH OTHER . . . YOU CAME FOR ME TOO. IT WAS NOTHING.

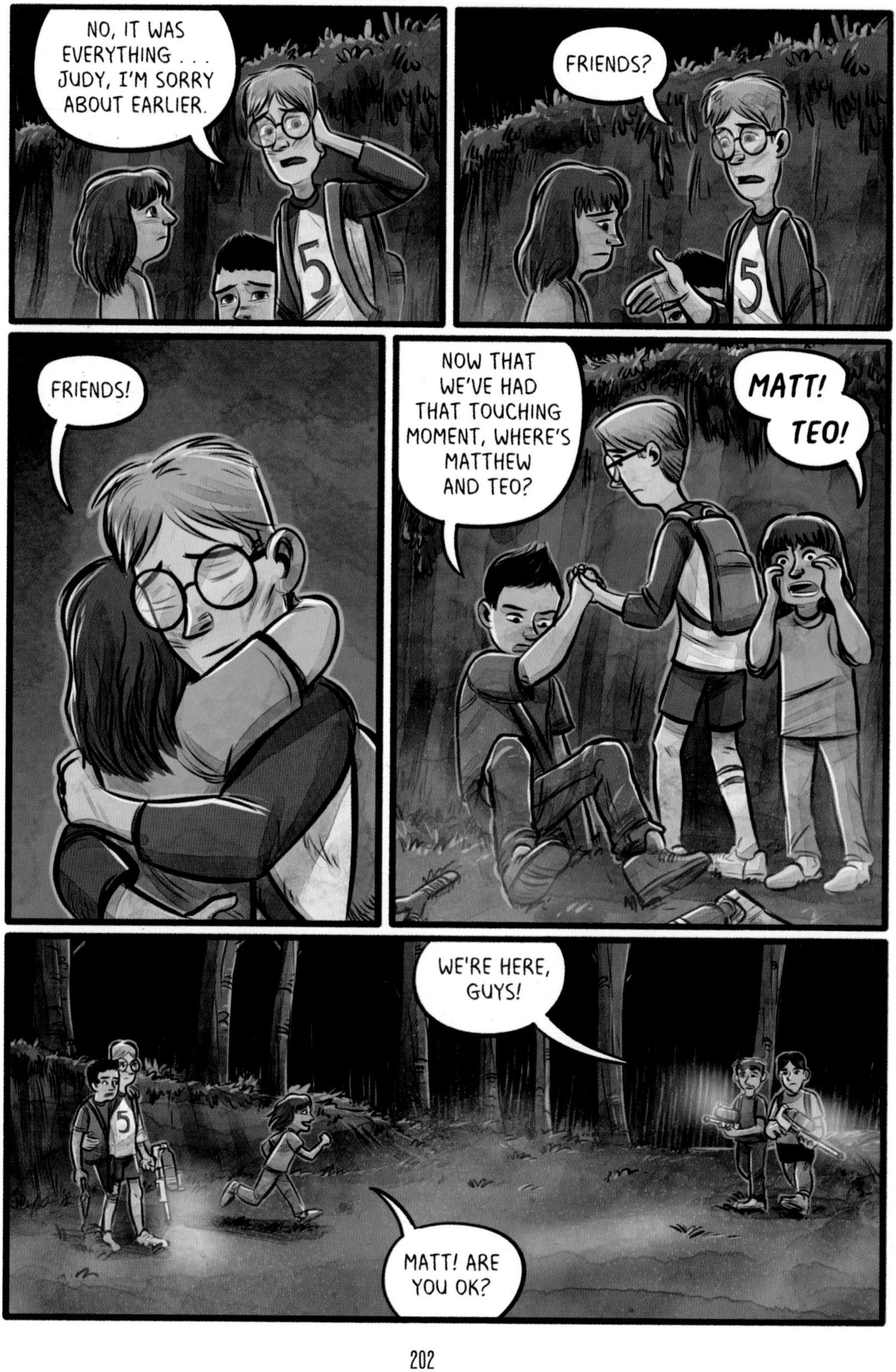

NO, IT WAS EVERYTHING . . . JUDY, I'M SORRY ABOUT EARLIER.
FRIENDS?
FRIENDS!
NOW THAT WE'VE HAD THAT TOUCHING MOMENT, WHERE'S MATTHEW AND TEO?
MATT!
TEO!
WE'RE HERE, GUYS!
MATT! ARE YOU OK?

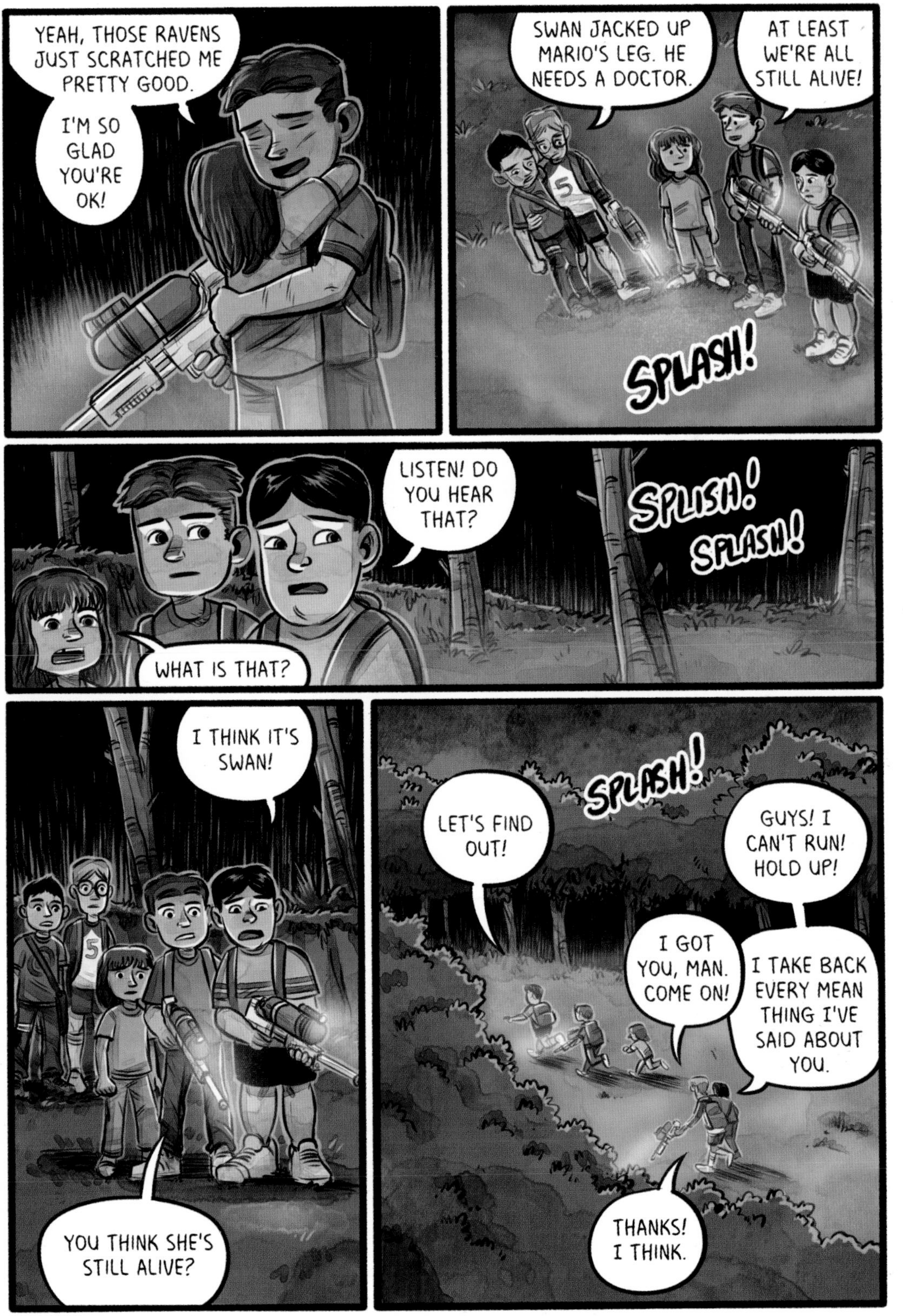
YEAH, THOSE RAVENS JUST SCRATCHED ME PRETTY GOOD.
I'M SO GLAD YOU'RE OK!
SWAN JACKED UP MARIO'S LEG. HE NEEDS A DOCTOR.
AT LEAST WE'RE ALL STILL ALIVE!
SPLASH!
LISTEN! DO YOU HEAR THAT?
SPLISH!
SPLASH!
WHAT IS THAT?
I THINK IT'S SWAN!
YOU THINK SHE'S STILL ALIVE?
SPLASH!
LET'S FIND OUT!
GUYS! I CAN'T RUN! HOLD UP!
I GOT YOU, MAN. COME ON!
I TAKE BACK EVERY MEAN THING I'VE SAID ABOUT YOU.
THANKS! I THINK.

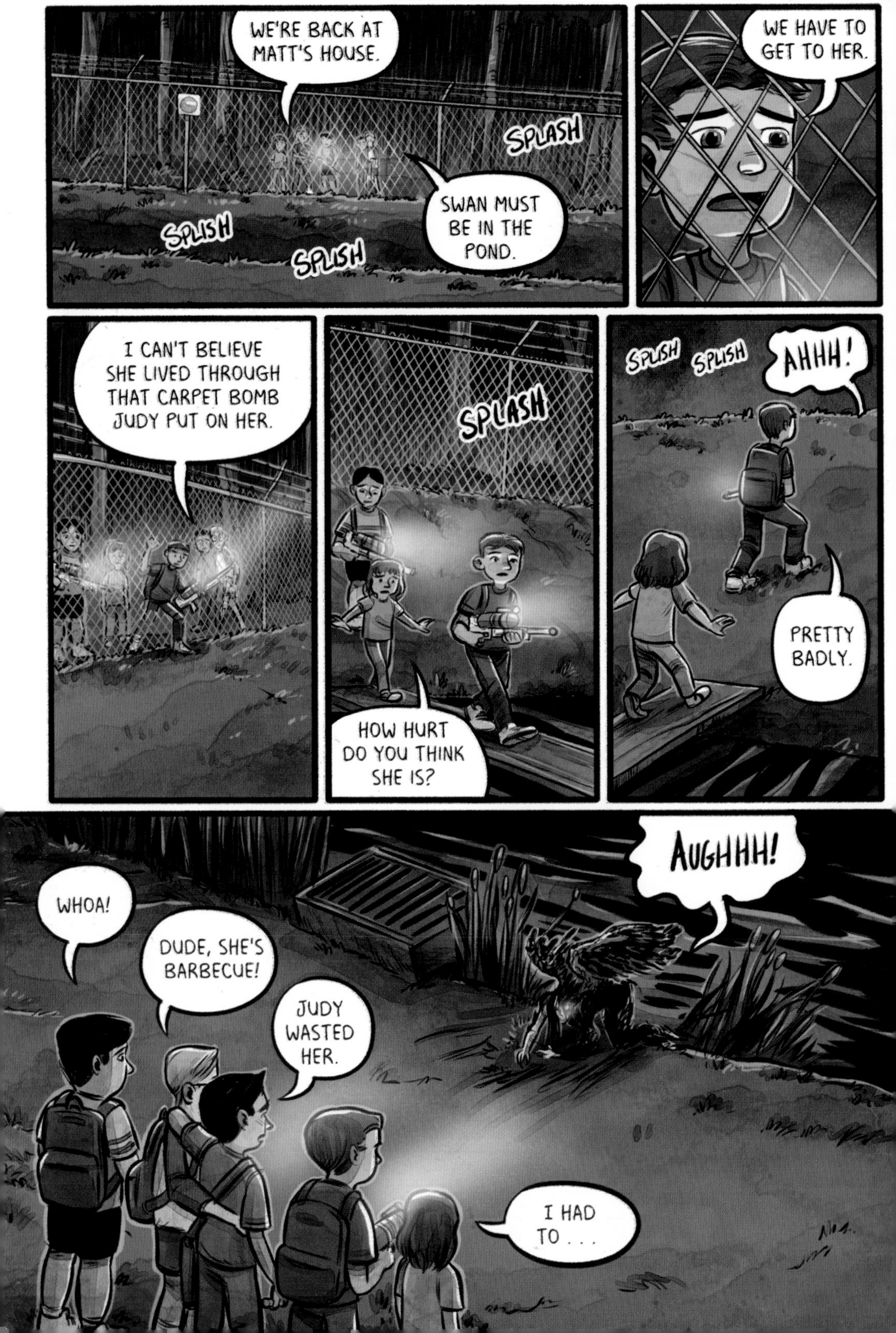
WE'RE BACK AT MATT'S HOUSE.
SPLASH
SPLISH
SPLISH
SWAN MUST BE IN THE POND.
WE HAVE TO GET TO HER.
I CAN'T BELIEVE SHE LIVED THROUGH THAT CARPET BOMB JUDY PUT ON HER.
SPLASH
HOW HURT DO YOU THINK SHE IS?
SPLISH
SPLISH
AHHH!
PRETTY BADLY.
AUGHHH!
WHOA!
DUDE, SHE'S BARBECUE!
JUDY WASTED HER.
I HAD TO . . .

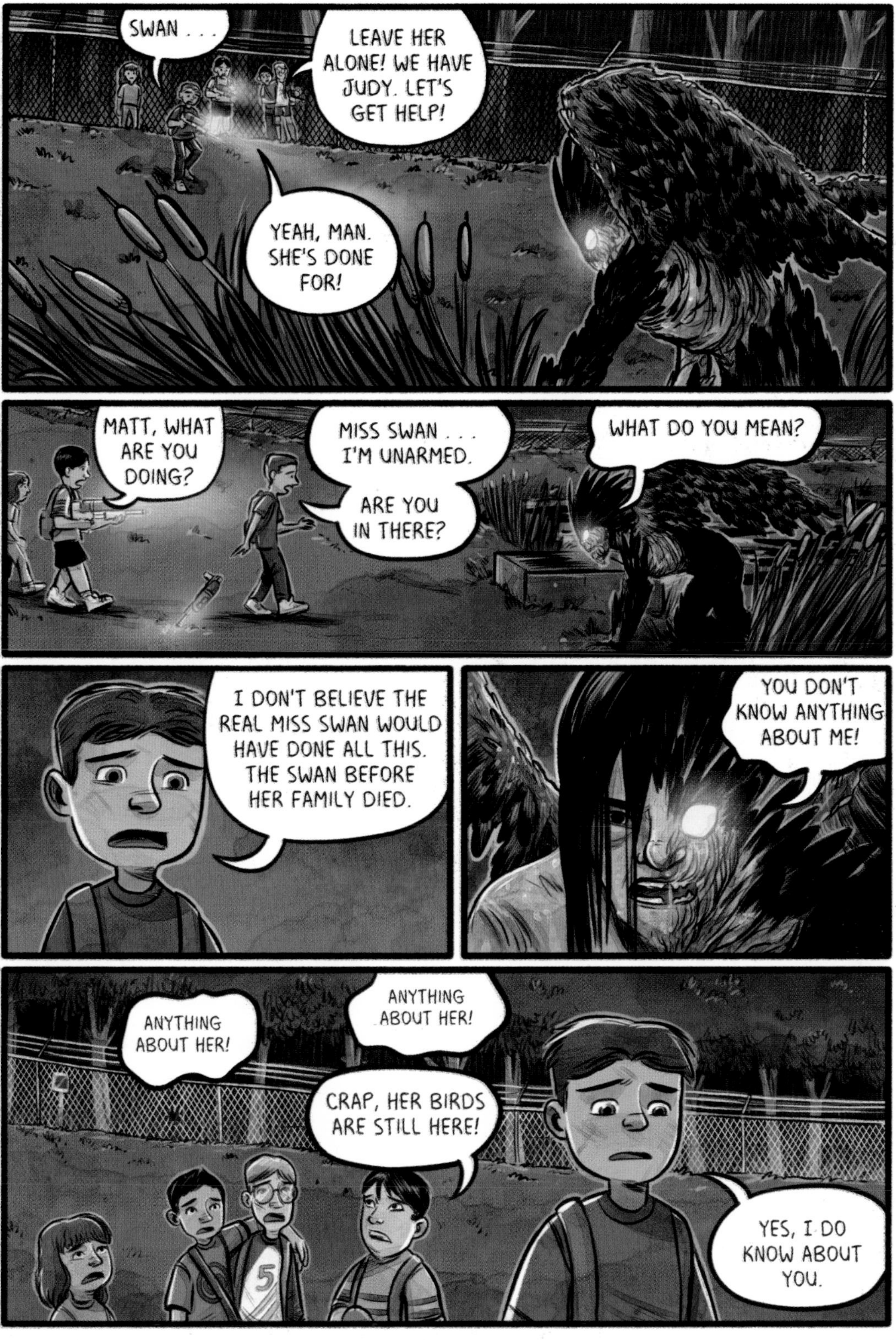
SWAN . . .
LEAVE HER ALONE! WE HAVE JUDY. LET'S GET HELP!
YEAH, MAN. SHE'S DONE FOR!
MATT, WHAT ARE YOU DOING?
MISS SWAN . . . I'M UNARMED.
ARE YOU IN THERE?
WHAT DO YOU MEAN?
I DON'T BELIEVE THE REAL MISS SWAN WOULD HAVE DONE ALL THIS. THE SWAN BEFORE HER FAMILY DIED.
YOU DON'T KNOW ANYTHING ABOUT ME!
ANYTHING ABOUT HER!
ANYTHING ABOUT HER!
CRAP, HER BIRDS ARE STILL HERE!
YES, I DO KNOW ABOUT YOU.

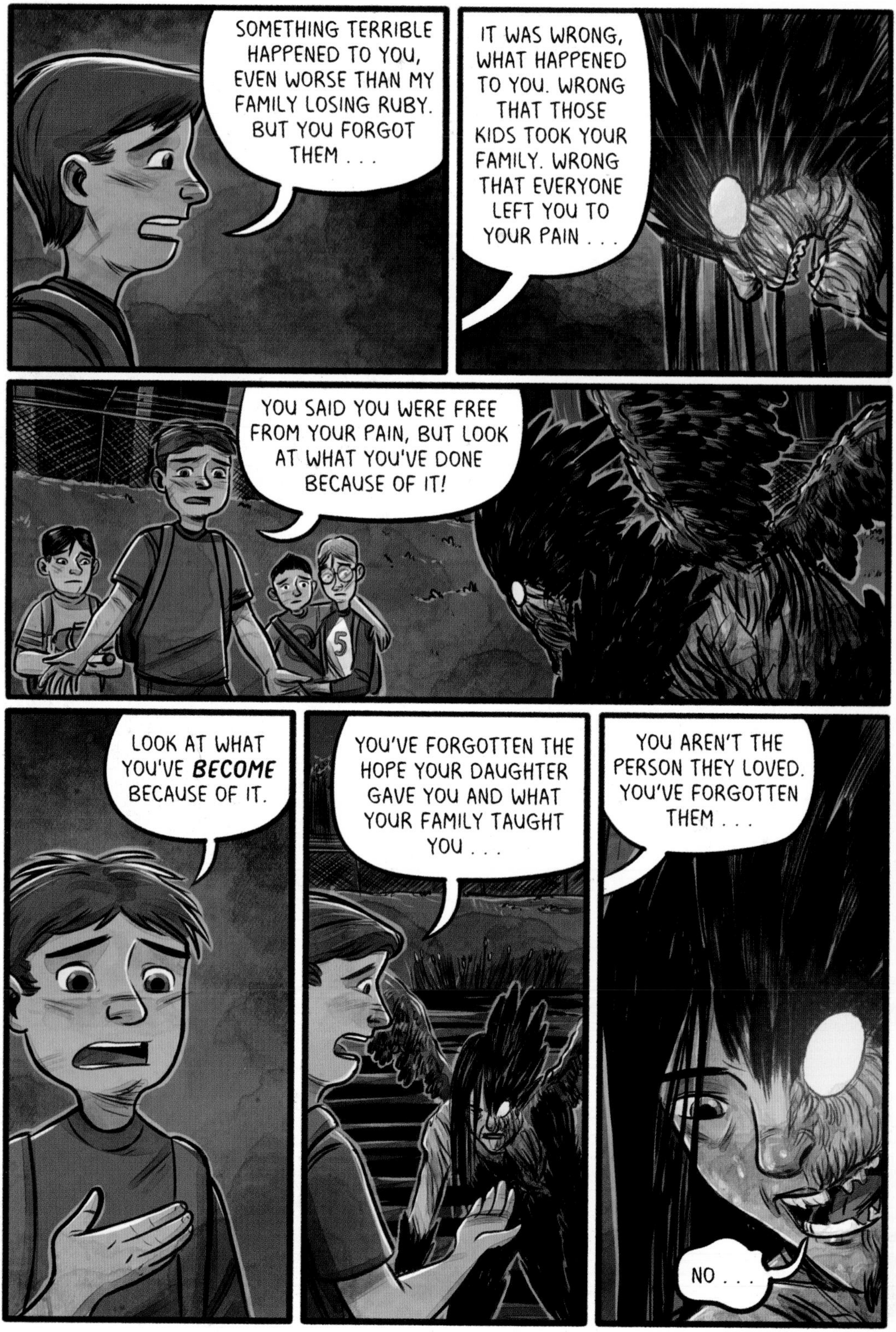
SOMETHING TERRIBLE HAPPENED TO YOU, EVEN WORSE THAN MY FAMILY LOSING RUBY. BUT YOU FORGOT THEM . . .
IT WAS WRONG, WHAT HAPPENED TO YOU. WRONG THAT THOSE KIDS TOOK YOUR FAMILY. WRONG THAT EVERYONE LEFT YOU TO YOUR PAIN . . .
YOU SAID YOU WERE FREE FROM YOUR PAIN, BUT LOOK AT WHAT YOU'VE DONE BECAUSE OF IT!
LOOK AT WHAT YOU'VE ***BECOME*** BECAUSE OF IT.
YOU'VE FORGOTTEN THE HOPE YOUR DAUGHTER GAVE YOU AND WHAT YOUR FAMILY TAUGHT YOU . . .
YOU AREN'T THE PERSON THEY LOVED. YOU'VE FORGOTTEN THEM . . .
NO . . .

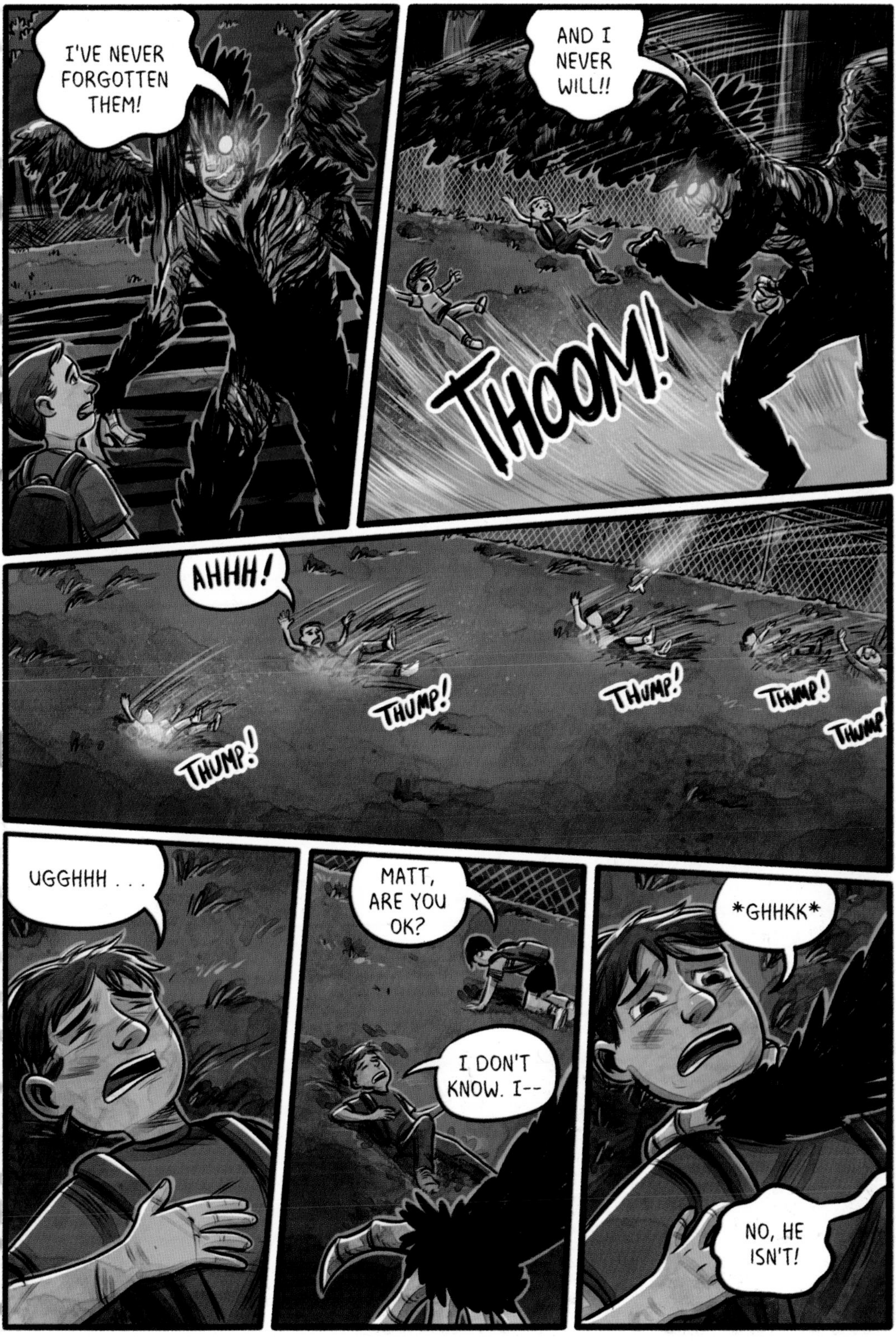
I'VE NEVER FORGOTTEN THEM!
AND I NEVER WILL!!
THOOM!
AHHH!
THUMP!
THUMP!
THUMP!
THUMP!
THUMP!
UGGHHH . . .
MATT, ARE YOU OK?
I DON'T KNOW. I--
GHHKK
NO, HE ISN'T!

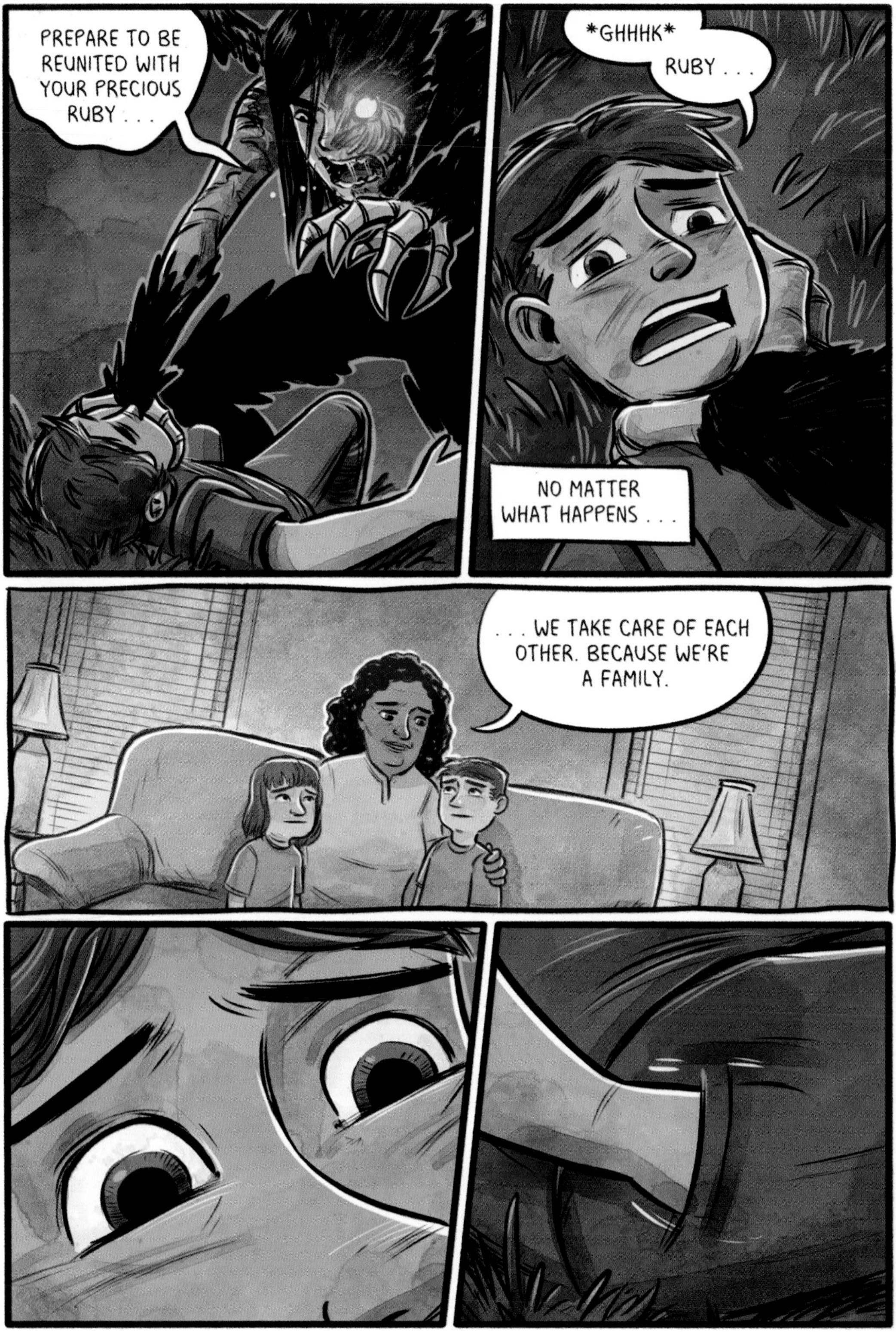
PREPARE TO BE REUNITED WITH YOUR PRECIOUS RUBY . . .
GHHHK
RUBY . . .
NO MATTER WHAT HAPPENS . . .
. . . WE TAKE CARE OF EACH OTHER. BECAUSE WE'RE A FAMILY.

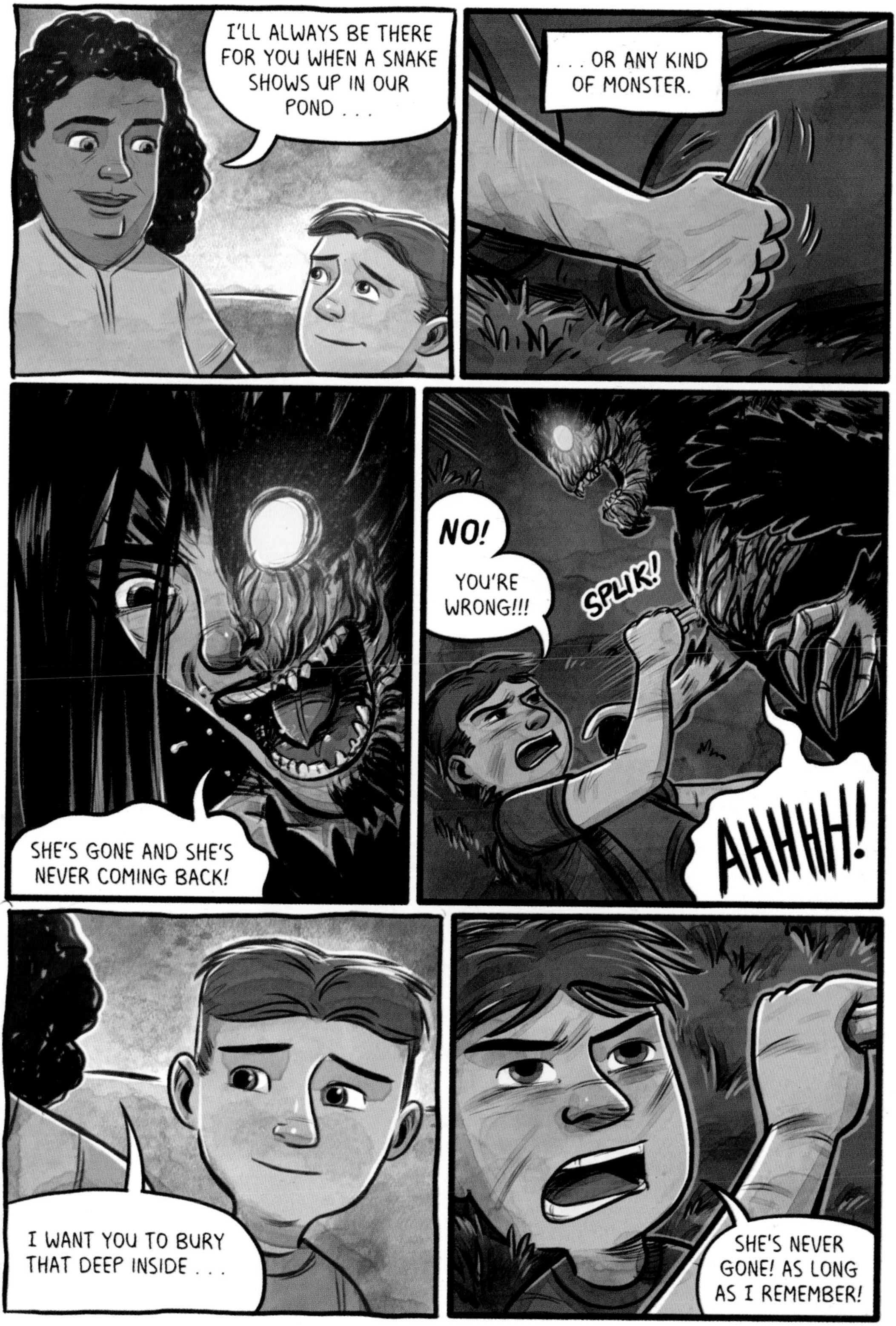

I'LL ALWAYS BE THERE FOR YOU WHEN A SNAKE SHOWS UP IN OUR POND . . .
. . . OR ANY KIND OF MONSTER.
SHE'S GONE AND SHE'S NEVER COMING BACK!
NO!
YOU'RE WRONG!!!
SPLIK!
AHHHH!
I WANT YOU TO BURY THAT DEEP INSIDE . . .
SHE'S NEVER GONE! AS LONG AS I REMEMBER!

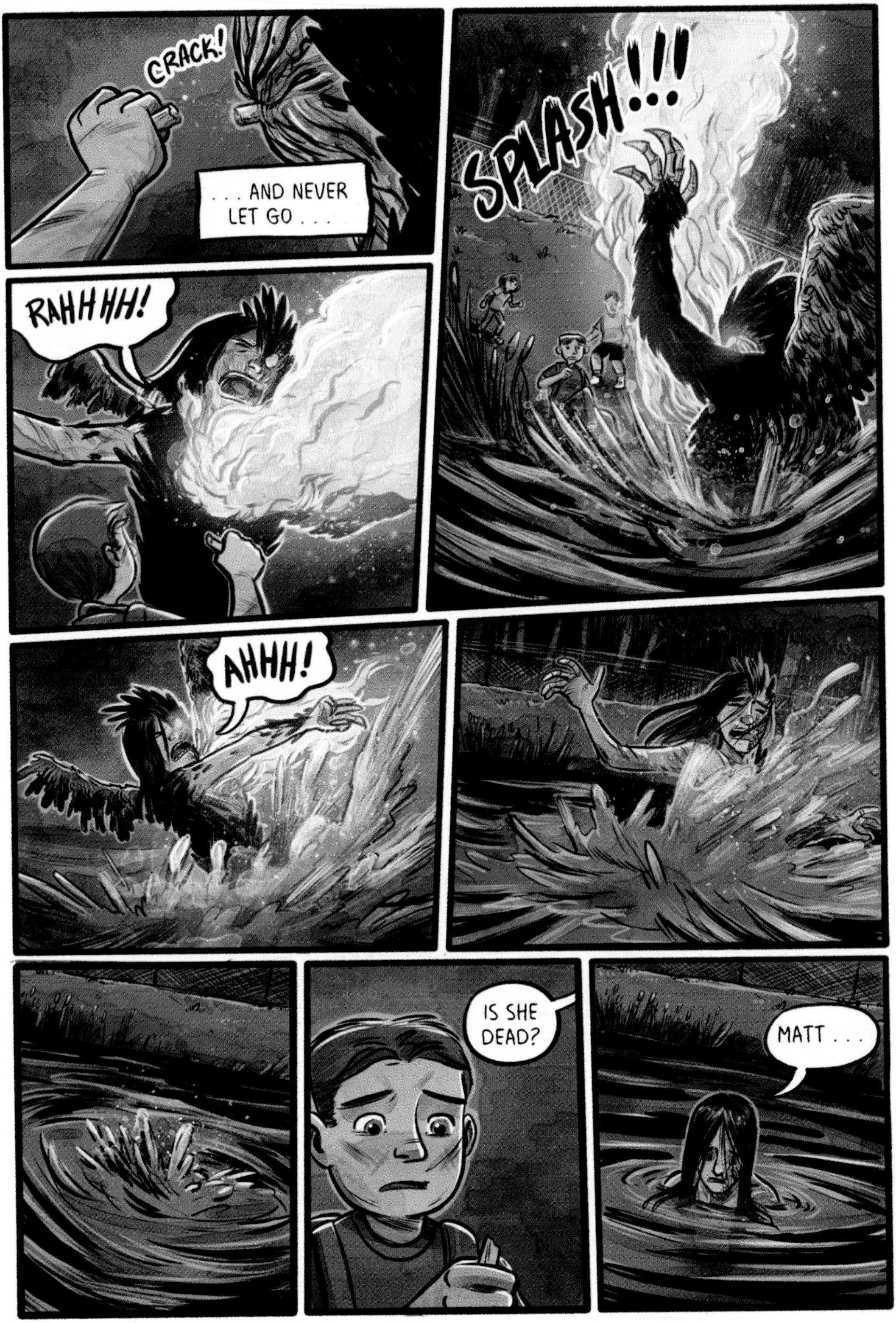
CRACK!
. . . AND NEVER LET GO . . .
SPLASH!!!
RAHHHH!
AHHH!
IS SHE DEAD?
MATT . . .

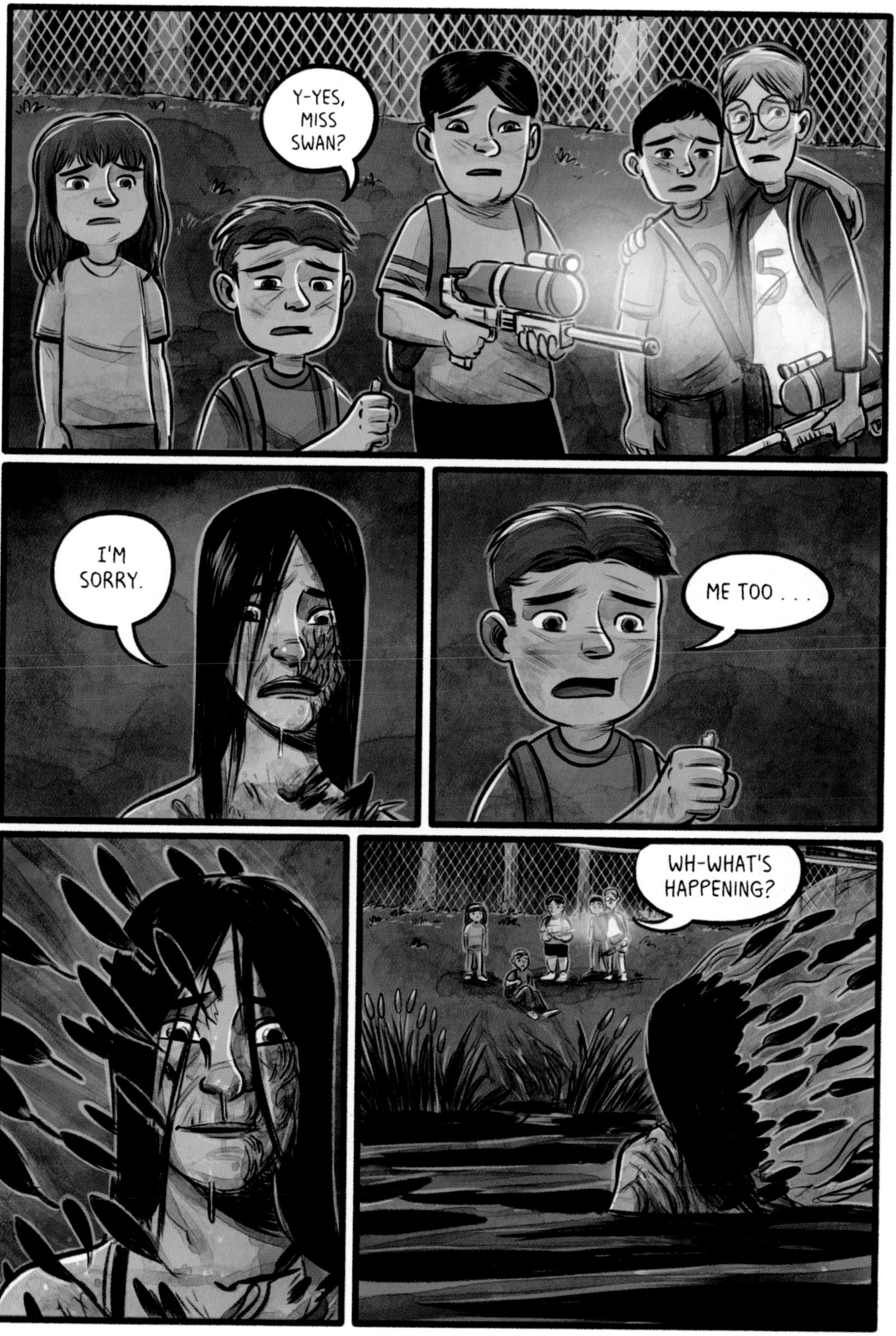
Y-YES, MISS SWAN?
I'M SORRY.
ME TOO . . .
WH-WHAT'S HAPPENING?

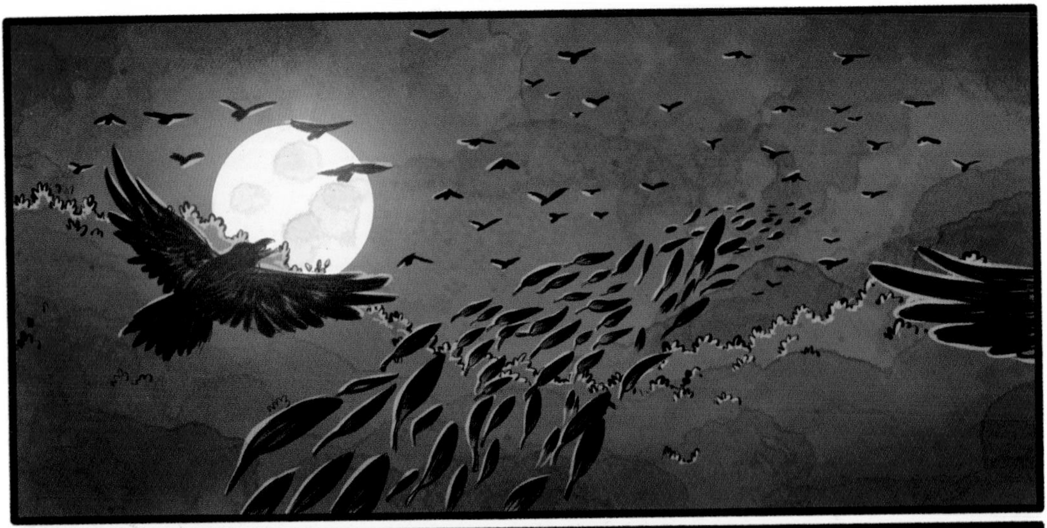

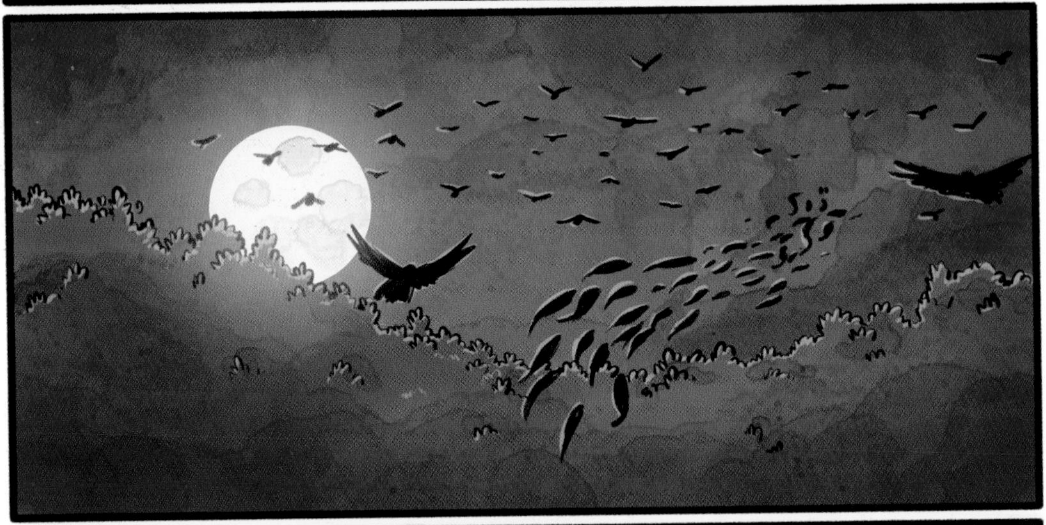

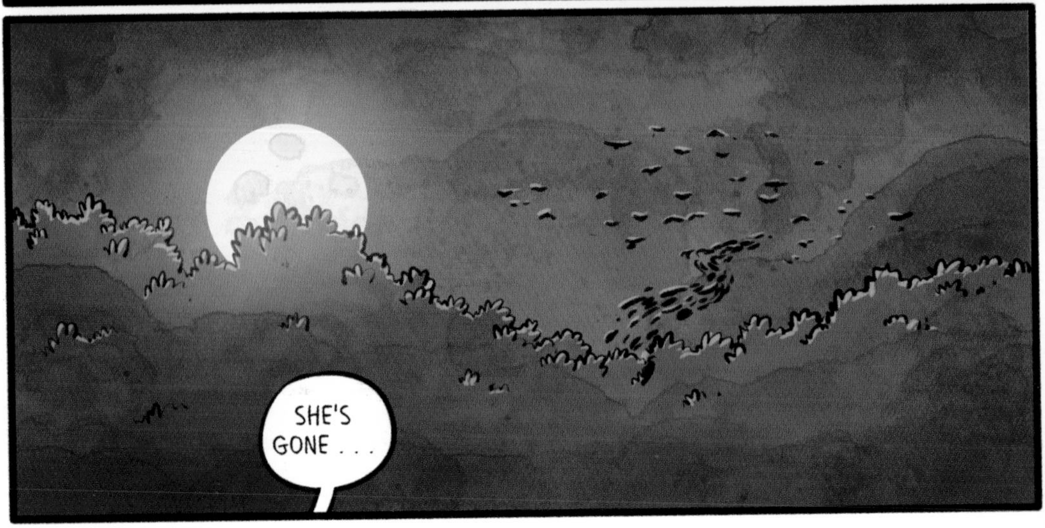
SHE'S GONE . . .

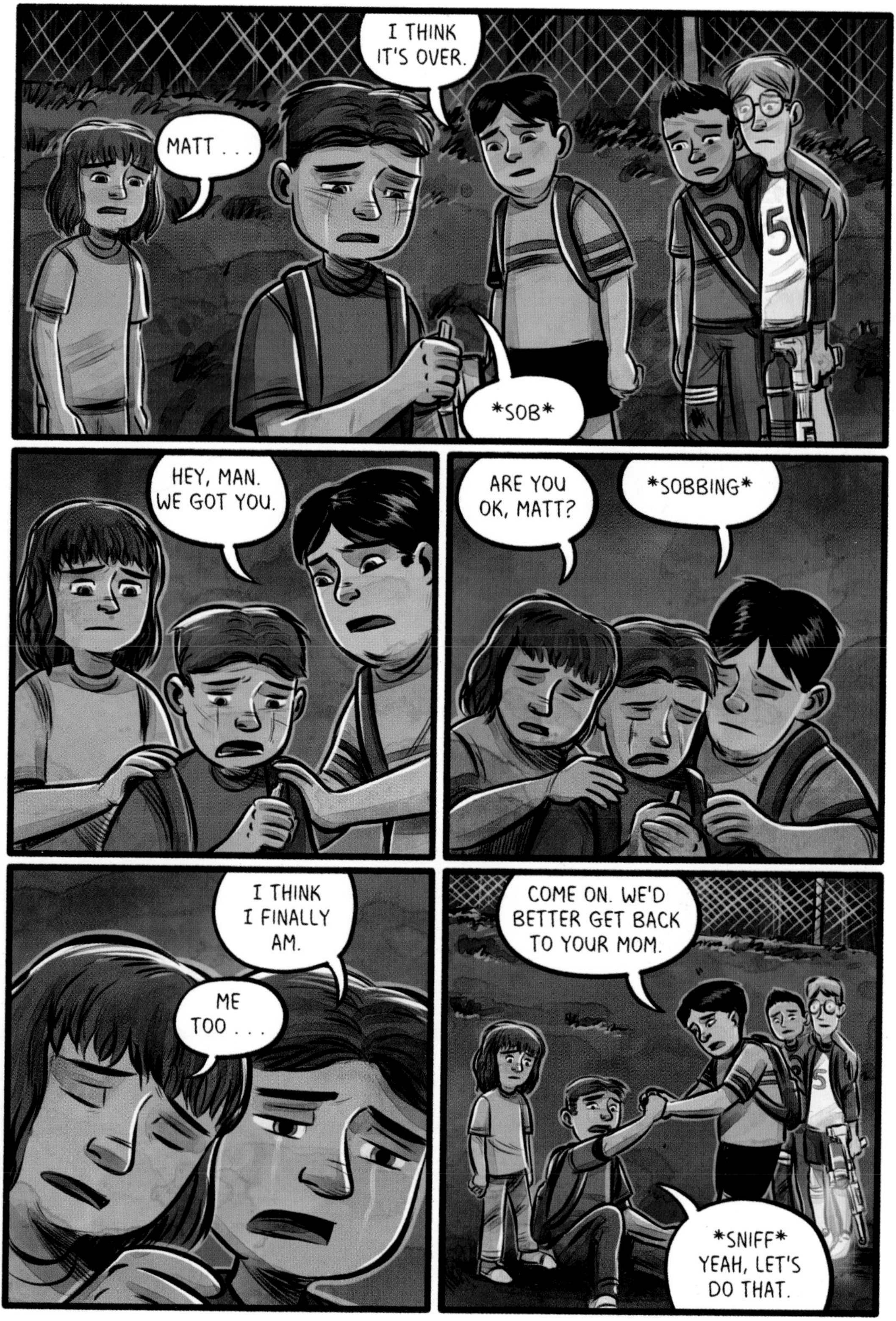
MATT . . .
I THINK IT'S OVER.
SOB
HEY, MAN. WE GOT YOU.
ARE YOU OK, MATT?
SOBBING
I THINK I FINALLY AM.
ME TOO . . .
COME ON. WE'D BETTER GET BACK TO YOUR MOM.
SNIFF YEAH, LET'S DO THAT.

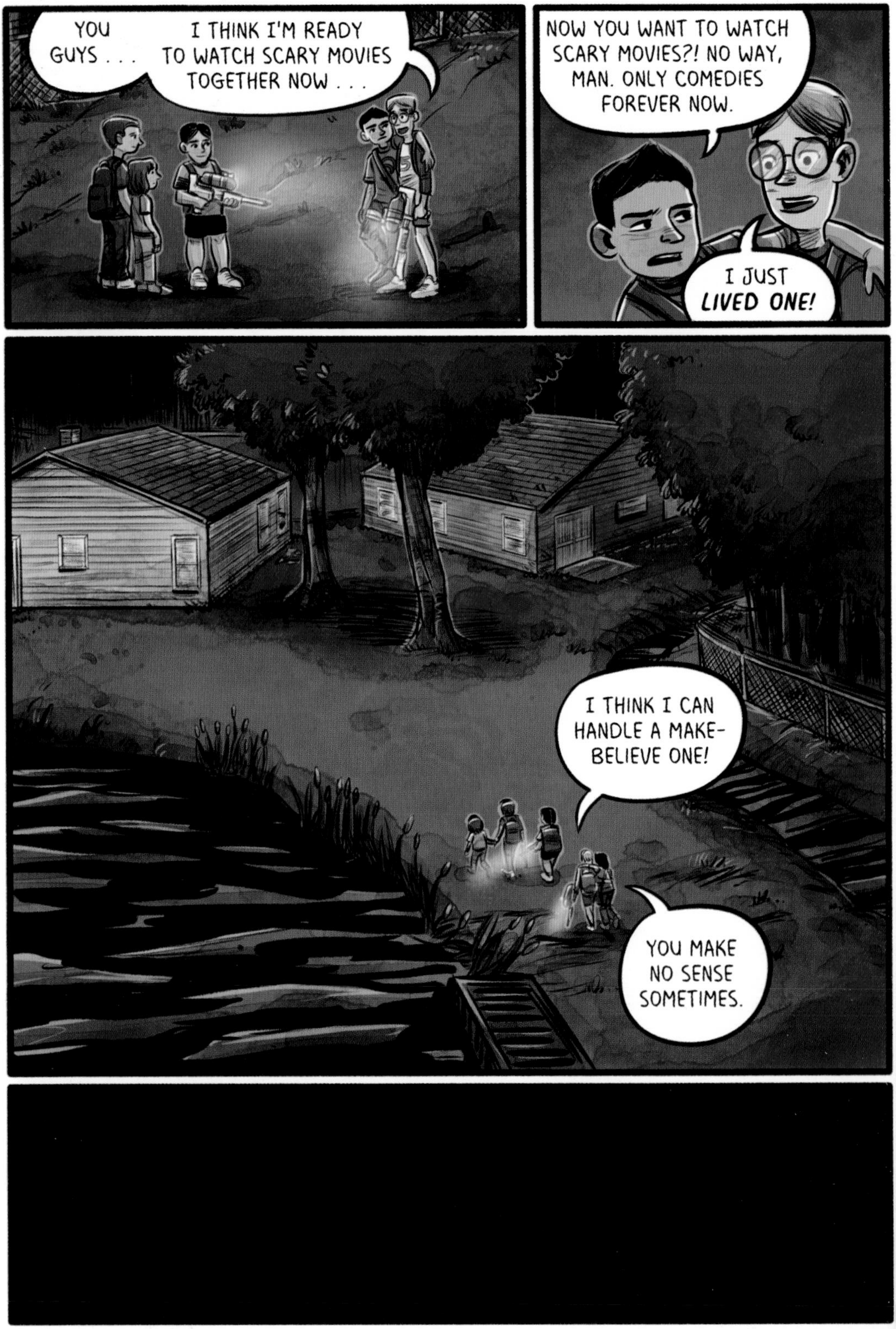
YOU GUYS . . .
I THINK I'M READY TO WATCH SCARY MOVIES TOGETHER NOW . . .
NOW YOU WANT TO WATCH SCARY MOVIES?! NO WAY, MAN. ONLY COMEDIES FOREVER NOW.
I JUST **LIVED ONE!**
I THINK I CAN HANDLE A MAKE-BELIEVE ONE!
YOU MAKE NO SENSE SOMETIMES.

EPILOGUE

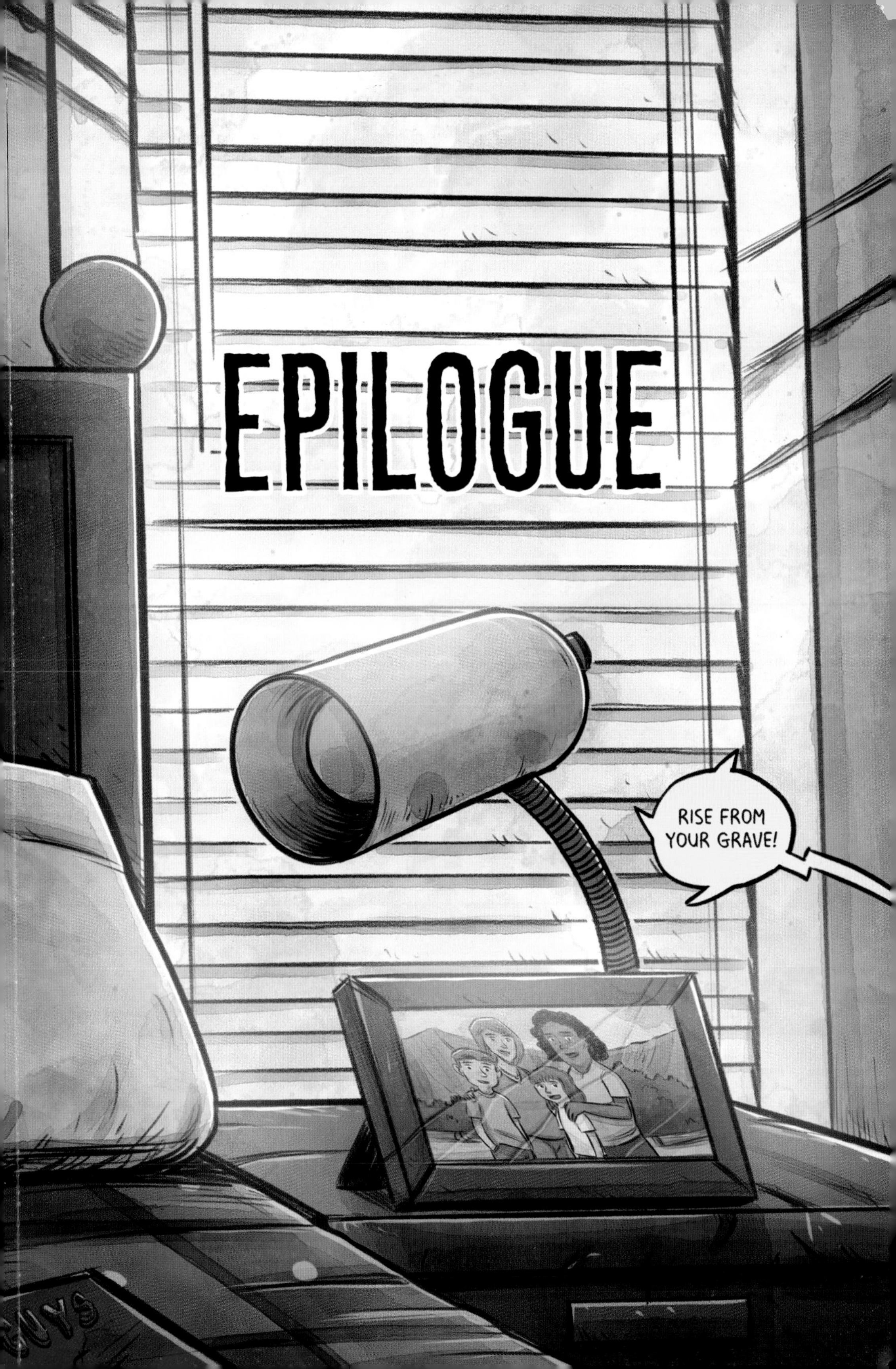
RISE FROM YOUR GRAVE!

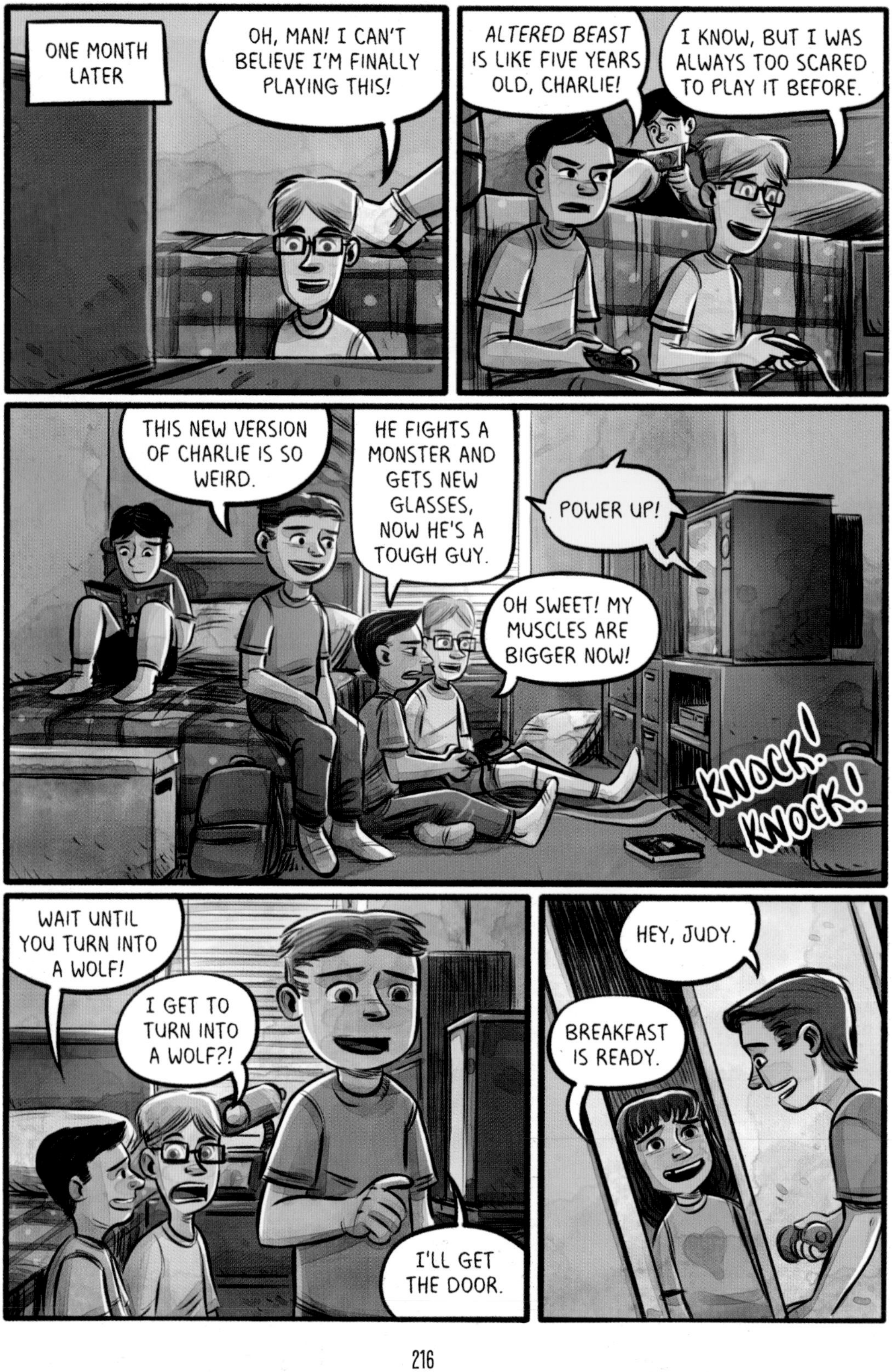
ONE MONTH LATER
OH, MAN! I CAN'T BELIEVE I'M FINALLY PLAYING THIS!
ALTERED BEAST IS LIKE FIVE YEARS OLD, CHARLIE!
I KNOW, BUT I WAS ALWAYS TOO SCARED TO PLAY IT BEFORE.
THIS NEW VERSION OF CHARLIE IS SO WEIRD.
HE FIGHTS A MONSTER AND GETS NEW GLASSES, NOW HE'S A TOUGH GUY.
POWER UP!
OH SWEET! MY MUSCLES ARE BIGGER NOW!
KNOCK! KNOCK!
WAIT UNTIL YOU TURN INTO A WOLF!
I GET TO TURN INTO A WOLF?!
I'LL GET THE DOOR.
HEY, JUDY.
BREAKFAST IS READY.

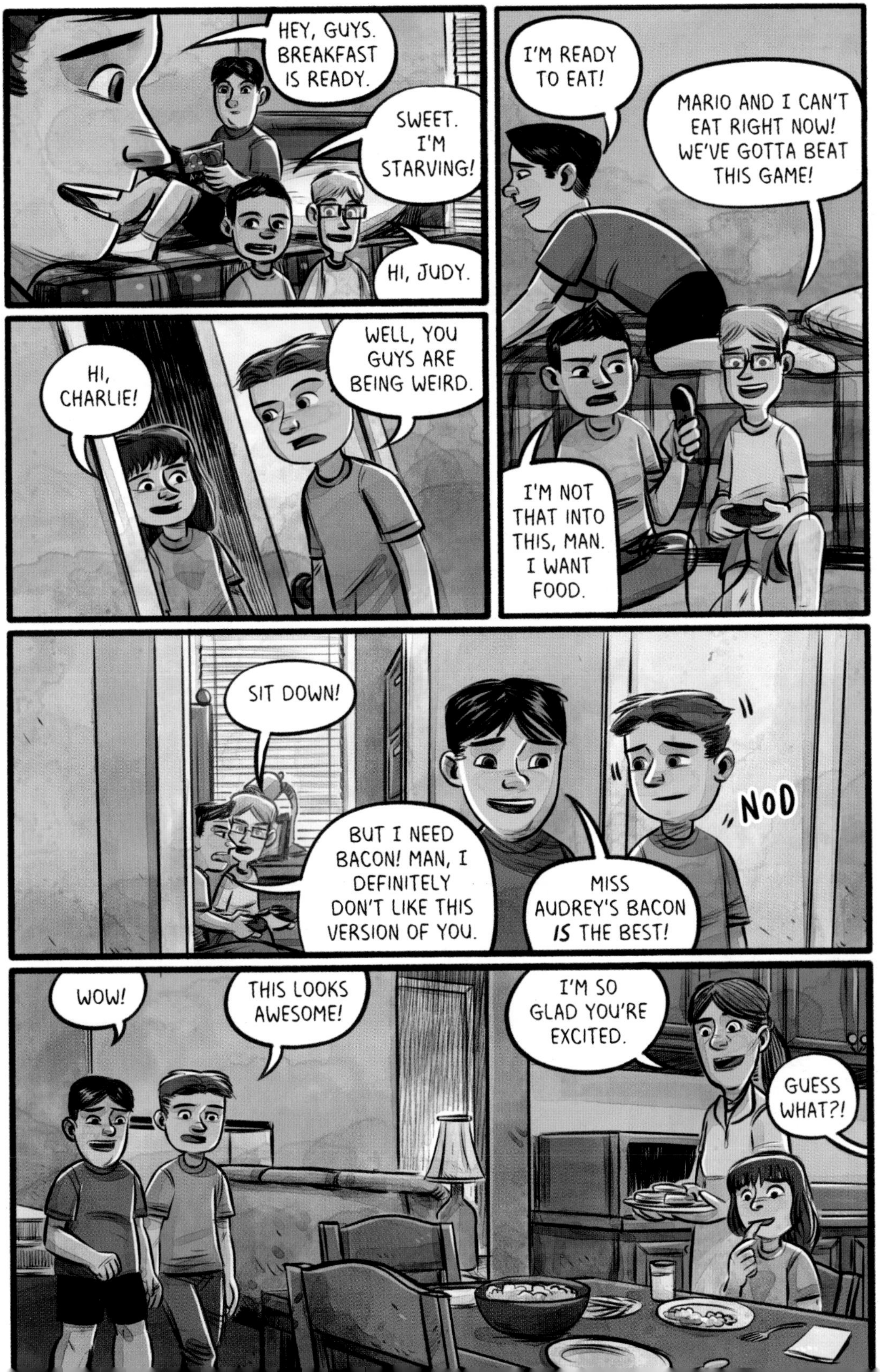
HEY, GUYS. BREAKFAST IS READY.
SWEET. I'M STARVING!
HI, JUDY.
I'M READY TO EAT!
MARIO AND I CAN'T EAT RIGHT NOW! WE'VE GOTTA BEAT THIS GAME!
HI, CHARLIE!
WELL, YOU GUYS ARE BEING WEIRD.
I'M NOT THAT INTO THIS, MAN. I WANT FOOD.
SIT DOWN!
BUT I NEED BACON! MAN, I DEFINITELY DON'T LIKE THIS VERSION OF YOU.
MISS AUDREY'S BACON *IS* THE BEST!
NOD
WOW!
THIS LOOKS AWESOME!
I'M SO GLAD YOU'RE EXCITED.
GUESS WHAT?!

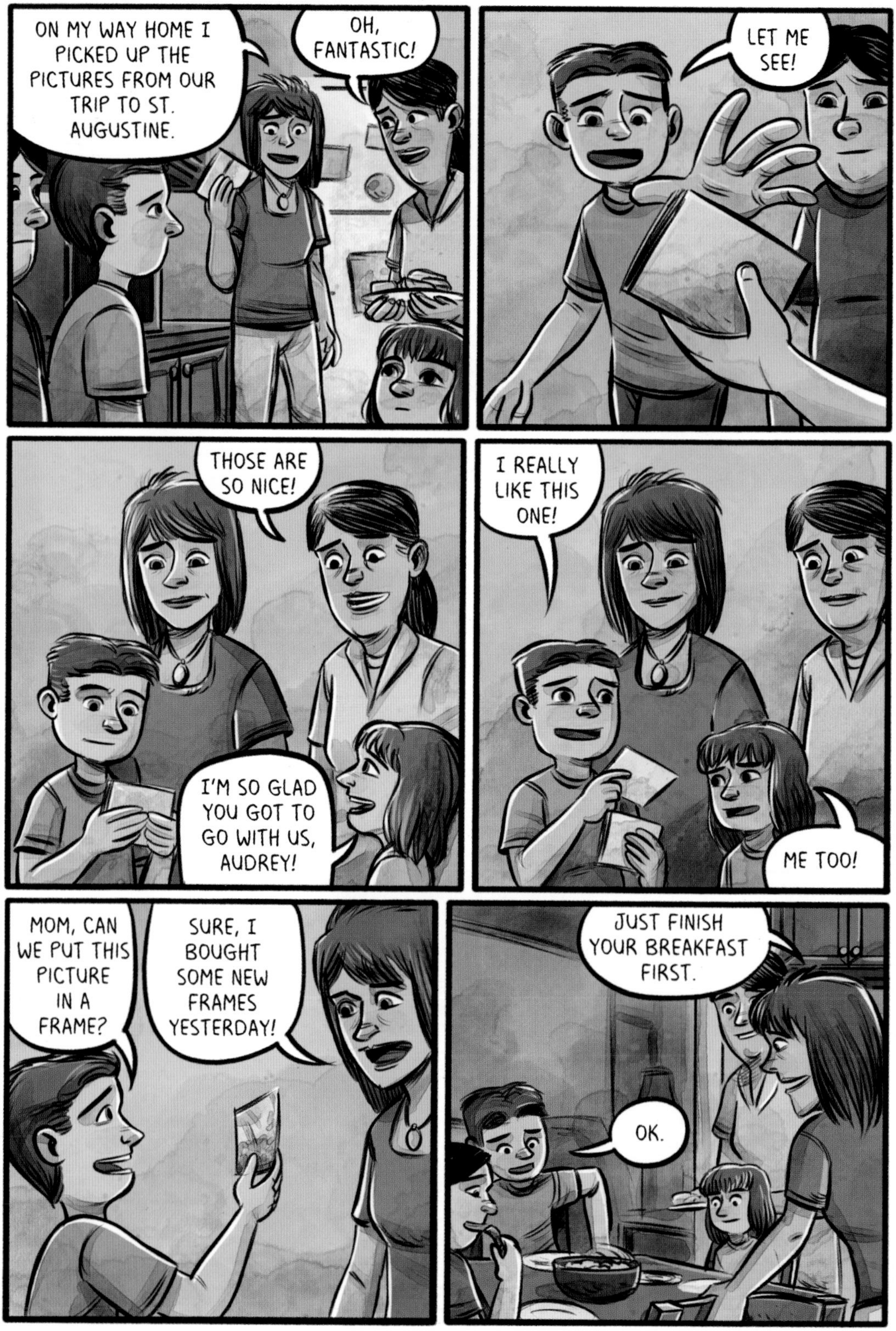
ON MY WAY HOME I PICKED UP THE PICTURES FROM OUR TRIP TO ST. AUGUSTINE.
OH, FANTASTIC!
LET ME SEE!
THOSE ARE SO NICE!
I'M SO GLAD YOU GOT TO GO WITH US, AUDREY!
I REALLY LIKE THIS ONE!
ME TOO!
MOM, CAN WE PUT THIS PICTURE IN A FRAME?
SURE, I BOUGHT SOME NEW FRAMES YESTERDAY!
JUST FINISH YOUR BREAKFAST FIRST.
OK.

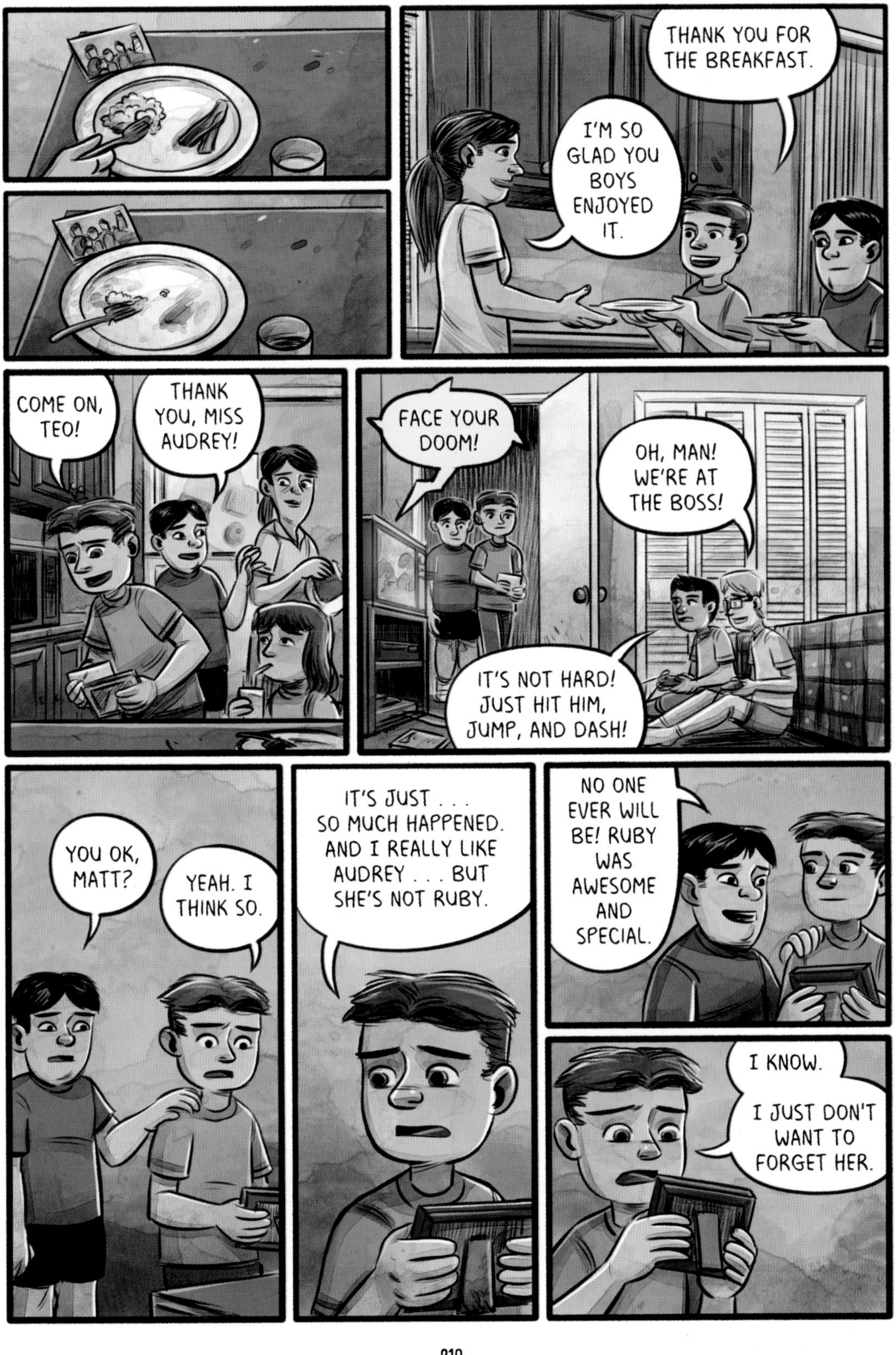
THANK YOU FOR THE BREAKFAST.
I'M SO GLAD YOU BOYS ENJOYED IT.
COME ON, TEO!
THANK YOU, MISS AUDREY!
FACE YOUR DOOM!
OH, MAN! WE'RE AT THE BOSS!
IT'S NOT HARD! JUST HIT HIM, JUMP, AND DASH!
YOU OK, MATT?
YEAH. I THINK SO.
IT'S JUST . . . SO MUCH HAPPENED. AND I REALLY LIKE AUDREY . . . BUT SHE'S NOT RUBY.
NO ONE EVER WILL BE! RUBY WAS AWESOME AND SPECIAL.
I KNOW.
I JUST DON'T WANT TO FORGET HER.

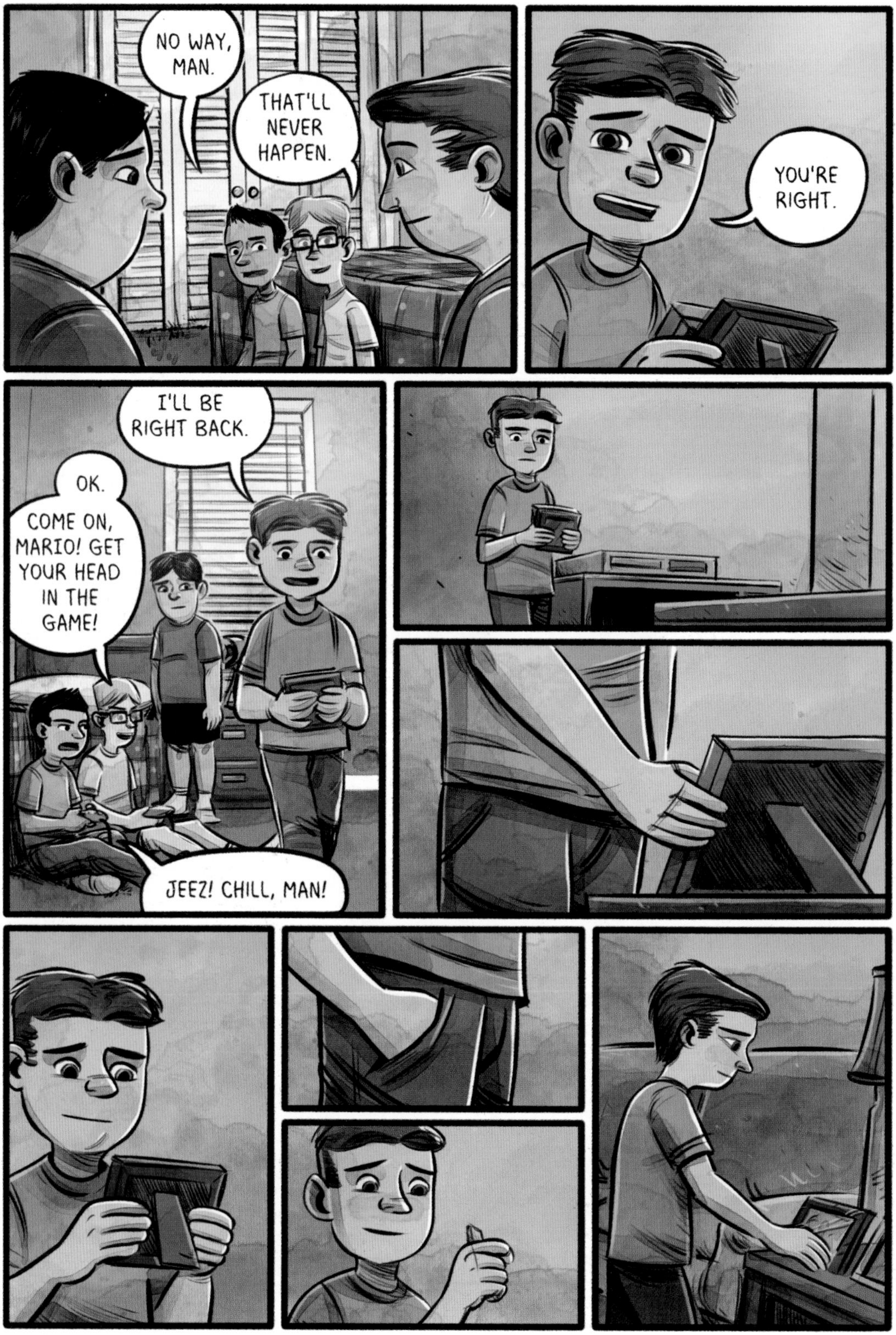
NO WAY, MAN.
THAT'LL NEVER HAPPEN.
YOU'RE RIGHT.
I'LL BE RIGHT BACK.
OK.
COME ON, MARIO! GET YOUR HEAD IN THE GAME!
JEEZ! CHILL, MAN!

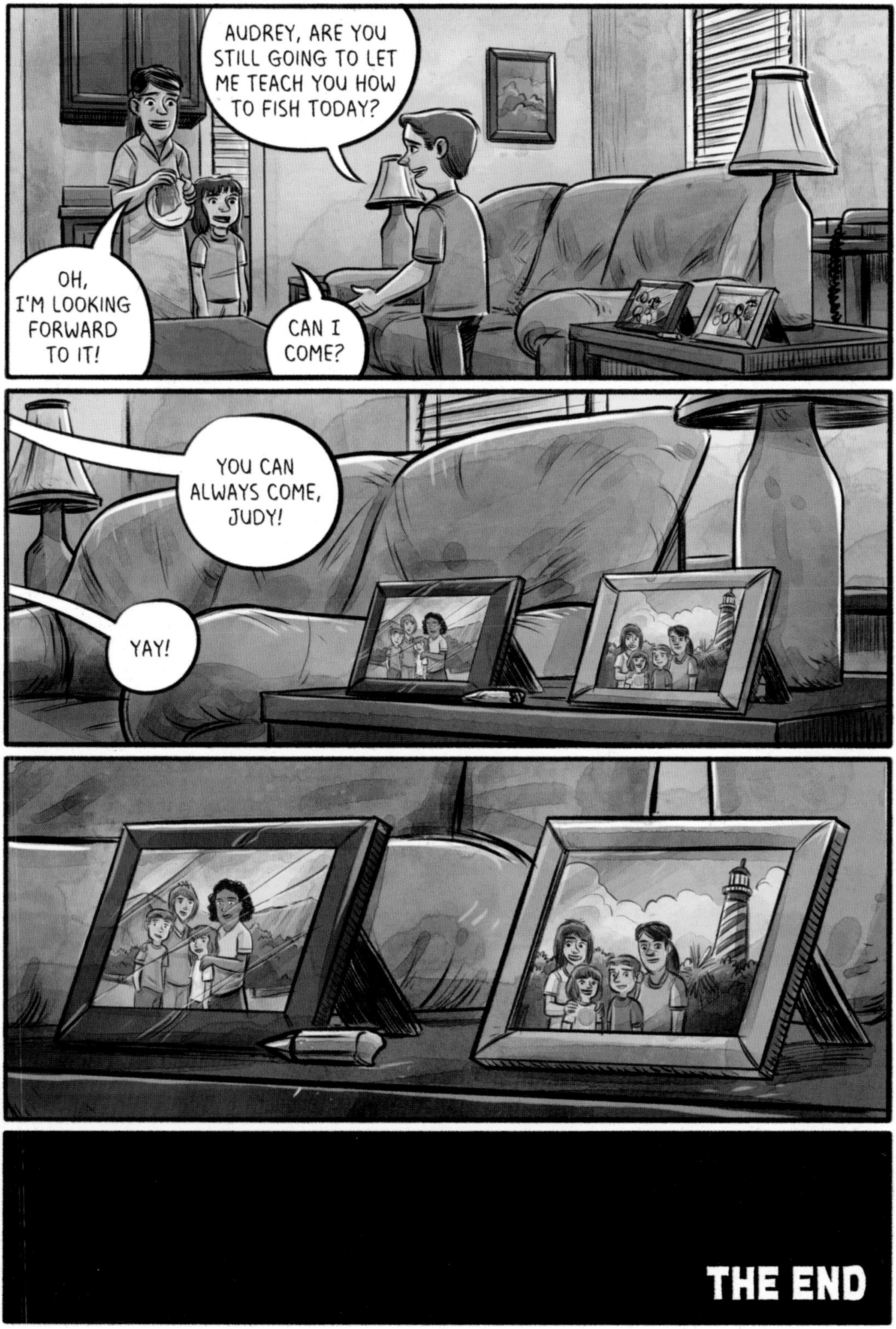
AUDREY, ARE YOU STILL GOING TO LET ME TEACH YOU HOW TO FISH TODAY?
OH, I'M LOOKING FORWARD TO IT!
CAN I COME?
YOU CAN ALWAYS COME, JUDY!
YAY!
THE END

Color flatting assistance by Viviane
Regina, Story Regina, Kev Brett,
Savana Byrne, Renea Fractor, and
Journey Regina

SPECIAL THANKS TO:

My awesome wife, Viviane, and kids, Story, Journey, and Shepherd, for their support and understanding as I've chased this crazy dream of making comics. My mom, Renea Fractor, for believing in my dreams as a little kid and jumping in to help me realize them as an adult.

My amazing agent, Elena Giovinazzo, and everyone at Pippin Properties. Chris Hernandez at Razorbill for helping me turn this idea into a book I'm really proud of. Jessica Jenkins for her art direction and that awesome logo design!

Josh Ulrich, Stephen McCranie, Kazu Kibuishi, Mike Maihack, Jason Brubaker, Brian Russell, and Wes Molebash for being great friends and cartoonists who supported this project from the beginning. Matt Nelson for pushing me to make custom brushes.

The real-life Ruby for being amazing to us kids—we miss you. Jennifer Blackmar for being a great sister, even when my friends slept over. Chris, Jei, and Michael, who made childhood a lot of fun. To all of my family and friends, who constantly support me with their love and kindness.

To Christ, who is always with us, even when things are hard.